JUGGERNAUT

JUGGERNAUT

STEN OMNIBUS 2

Chris Bunch *and* Allan Cole

This omnibus edition includes
Sten 4: Fleet of the Damned
Sten 5: Revenge of the Damned
Sten 6: The Return of the Emperor

www.orbitbooks.net

ORBIT

First published in Great Britain in 2012 by Orbit

Copyright © 2012 by Allan Cole and Christopher Bunch

Sten 4: Fleet of the Damned
First published in 2000 by Orbit
Copyright © 1982 by Allan Cole and Christopher Bunch

Sten 5: Revenge of the Damned
First published in 2001 by Orbit
Copyright © 1989 by Allan Cole and Christopher Bunch

Sten 6: The Return of the Emperor
First published in 2001 by Orbit
Copyright © 1991 by Allan Cole and Christopher Bunch

The moral right of the authors has been asserted.

A CIP catalogue record for this book
is available from the British Library.

ISBN 978-0-356-50161-1

Typeset in Sabon by Palimpsest Book Production Limited, Falkirk, Stirlingshire

Printed and bound by
CPI Group (UK) Ltd, Croydon, CR0 4YY

Papers used by Orbit are from well-managed forests
and other responsible sources.

MIX
Paper from
responsible sources
FSC® C104740
www.fsc.org

Orbit
An imprint of
Little, Brown Book Group
100 Victoria Embankment
London EC4Y 0DY

An Hachette UK Company
www.hachette.co.uk

www.orbitbooks.net

Contents

STEN 4:
FLEET OF
THE DAMNED

To
Owen Lock
Shelly Shapiro
and
Russ Galen

Indictable Co-Conspirators

Note

The titles of Books 1, 2, 3, and 4 are derived from 17th-century A.D. Earth and were a series of commands used to bring oceanic warships of the British Navy into battle. Book 5's title was a semi-formal command to ship's gunners.

—AC and CRB

BOOK ONE

LINE OF BATTLE

Chapter One

The Tahn battle cruiser arced past the dying sun. The final course was set, and in a few hours the ship would settle on the gray-white surface of Fundy – the major planetary body in the Erebus System.

Erebus would seem to be the last place that any being would want to go. Its sun was so near extinction that it cast only a feeble pale yellow light to its few heavily cratered satellites. The minerals left on those barren bodies would barely have supported a single miner. Erebus was a place to give one dreams of death.

Lady Atago listened impatiently to the radio chatter between her crew and the main port com center on Fundy. The voices on the other end seemed lazy, uncaring, without discipline – a marked contrast to the crisp string of words coming from her own crew. It grated her Tahn sensibilities.

The situation on Fundy had been neglected too long.

Lady Atago was a tall woman, towering over many of her officers. At casual glance some might think that she was exotically beautiful – long, flowing dark hair, wide black eyes, and sensuous lips. Her body was slender, but there was a hint of lushness to it. At the moment it was particularly well set off in her dress uniform: a dark green cloak, red tunic, and green form-fitting trousers.

At second glance all thoughts of beauty would vanish as a chill crept up the spine. This was Tahn royalty. A nod of her head could determine any one of many fates – all of them unpleasant.

As her ship punched into landing orbit, she glanced over at her captain, who was monitoring the actions of the crew.

'Soon, my lady.'

'I'll require one squad,' she said.

Her head turned away, dismissing the captain. Lady Atago was thinking of those undisciplined fools awaiting her on Fundy.

The big ship settled to the ice about half a kilometer from the port center. The engines cut off, and the ship was instantly enveloped in gray as sleet slanted in from a stiff wind.

Most of the surface of Fundy was ice and black rock. It was an unlikely place for any enterprise, much less the purpose it was being put to by its present occupants.

The Tahn were preparing for war against the Emperor, and the Erebus System was the cornerstone of their plan. In great secrecy, Erebus had been converted into a system-wide warship factory.

So distant and so undesirable was Erebus that there was little likelihood that the Eternal Emperor would discover their full-out effort to arm themselves until it was too late. Thousands of ships were being built, or converted, or refitted.

When Lady Atago's battle cruiser entered the system, she could partially see those efforts. Small, powerful tugs were towing hundreds of kilometer-long strings of the shells that would be turned into fighting ships and then transported to ground for final refitting. Huge factories had been hastily constructed on each of the planets, and the night skies had an eerie glow from the furnaces.

The Tahn had drafted every available laborer down to the barely skilled. The poor quality of their work force was one of the several reasons the Tahn had chosen to concentrate so much of their manufacturing on planets rather than in space. Deep space required highly trained workers, and that was something that the massive arming had stretched to the near impossible. Also, deep-space factories required an enormous investment, and the Tahn could already hear the coins clicking out of their treasury vaults.

They wanted as many ships as possible, as cheaply as possible. Any malfunctions, no matter how life-threatening, would be the problem of the individual crews.

The Tahn were a warrior race with stamped steel spears.

Lady Atago paused at the foot of the ramp, surrounded by a heavily armed squad of her best troops. This was her personal bodyguard, chosen not only for military skills and absolute loyalty but for size as well. Each member of the squad dwarfed even Lady Atago. The troops shuffled in the sudden, intense cold, but Atago just stood there, not even bothering to pull her thermo cloak about her.

She looked in disgust at the distant port center. Why had they landed her so far away? The incompetent fools. Still, it didn't surprise her.

Lady Atago began walking determinedly through the snow; the squad followed her, their harness creaking and their boots crunching through the icy surface. Big gravsleds groaned past, hauling parts and supplies. On some of them, men and women clung to the sides, catching tenuous rides back and forth from their shifts at the factories that ringed the port with smoke and towering flames.

The Lady Atago turned her head neither left nor right to observe the strange scene. She just stalked on until they reached the center.

A sentry barked from a guard booth just outside the main door. She ignored him, brushing past as her squad snapped up their weapons to end any further inquiry. Their boot-heels clicked loudly as they marched down the long hallway leading to the admin center.

As they turned a corner, a squat man came half running toward them, hastily arranging his tunic. Lady Atago stopped when she saw that he was wearing the uniform of an admiral. The man's face was sweating and flushed as he reached them.

'Lady Atago,' he blurted. 'I'm so sorry. I didn't realize you were arriving so soon, and—'

'Admiral Dien?' she said, stopping him in midgobble.

'Yes, my lady?'

'I will require your office,' she said, and she walked on, Dien stumbling after her.

The Lady Atago sat in silence as she scanned the computer records. Two of her squad stood at the door, weapons ready. The others had placed themselves strategically about the overlush offices of the admiral.

When she had first entered the office she had given it one quick glance. A slight curl of a lip showed what she thought of it: very un-Tahn-like.

As she scrolled through records, Dien muttered on in an endless stream of half explanations.

'There . . . there . . . you can see. The storm. We lost production for a day.

'And that item! We had to blast new landing strips to handle the freighters. The pressure was enormous, my lady. The sky was black with them. And we had insufficient facil—'

He stopped abruptly as she palmed a switch and the computer screen went blank. She stared at it for a long, long time. Finally, she rose to her feet and turned to face the man.

'Admiral Dien,' she intoned. 'In the name of Lord Fehrle and the Tahn High Council, I relieve you of your command.'

A painter or a physicist would have been in awe at the shade of white the man's face became. As she started out of the room, one of her squad members came forward.

'Wait, my lady. Please,' Dien implored.

She half turned back, one perfect eyebrow lifting slightly. 'Yes?'

'Would you at least allow me . . . Uh, may I keep my sidearm?'

She thought for a moment. 'Honor?'

'Yes, my lady. Honor.'

There was another long wait. Then, finally, she replied. 'No. I think not.'

The Lady Atago exited, the door closing quietly behind her.

Chapter Two

Sten and Lisa Haines squirmed through the mass confusion of the spaceport. As the main port for Prime World, Soward had always suffered from overcrowding. But this was clotting ridiculous – it was arm to tendril to antenna in beings.

The two became increasingly bewildered and unsettled as they pushed their way to the rented gravcar.

'What the hell is going on?' Sten asked, not really expecting a reply.

'I don't know,' Lisa said, 'but I think I'm already losing my tan, and if we don't get out of here, I'm gonna be sick.'

'Give me a break,' Sten said. 'Homicide detectives don't get sick. It's part of the job requirement.'

'Watch me,' Lisa said.

Sten grabbed her by the arm and steered the police captain around a staggering hulk of a young soldier.

'I don't think I've seen so many uniforms,' he said, 'since basic training.'

They slid into the gravcar, and Sten checked with local traffic control for clearance. They were told there would be a minimum forty-minute wait. An hour and a half later – after repeated delays blamed on military traffic – they were finally able to lift away.

Things weren't much better as they cut through the city en route to Lisa's place. Fowler was in nearly three-dimensional gridlock. The two hardly spoke at all until they finally cleared the outskirts and headed for the enormous forest where Lisa had her houseboat moored.

'Was it always like this?' Lisa asked. 'Or did I just get used to it?'

Commander Sten, formerly of the Eternal Emperor's Household Guard, didn't bother answering. The uniforms plus the host of military vehicles and convoys they had spotted made it all pretty obvious.

It almost seemed as if Prime World were bracing for an invasion. That was an impossibility, Sten was sure. But the Emperor sure as clot was mobilizing for a major military undertaking. And, Sten knew, anything that involved shooting was almost certainly going to require that he once again risk his young ass.

'I don't think I even want to know – yet,' he said. 'Besides, we got a few days leave left. Let's enjoy them.'

Lisa snuggled up to him and began softly stroking the inside of his thigh.

By the time they reached Lisa's houseboat, the almost heady peacefulness they'd found on their long leaves from their respective jobs had returned.

The 'boat' swung lazily on its mooring lines high above the broad expanse of pristine forest. The forest was one of the many protected wilderness areas the Emperor had set aside on Prime World. However, since the headquarters planet of his enormous empire was overcrowded and rents and land prices were astronomical, people were forced to become fairly creative about finding living space.

Lisa's salary as a cop was hardly overwhelming. So she and a great many other people had taken advantage of a loophole in the Emperor's Wilderness Act. One couldn't build *in* the forest, but the law didn't say anything about *over* the forest.

So her landlord had leased the unsettleable land and then provided large McLean-powered houseboats to anyone would could pay the freight. It was a squeeze, but Lisa made sure she could afford it.

They tied up to the side and walked across the deck to the door. Lisa pressed her thumb against the fingerprint lock, and the door slid open. Before they entered she carefully checked the interior – a cop habit she would never lose. It was one of many things she shared in common with Sten. After his years of Mantis service, it was impossible for him to enter a room without making sure that things were reasonably as they should be.

A few minutes later, they were sprawled on a couch, the windows opened wide to clear out the musty air.

Sten sipped at his beer, half hoping it would wash away the slight feeling of sadness growing in his belly. He had been in love before, had known his share of women. But he had never been alone with a lady for this long a time, with no other requirement than to enjoy.

Lisa squeezed his hand. 'Too bad it's almost over,' she said softly.

Sten turned to her.

'Well, it ain't over yet,' he said. He pulled her into his arms.

Sten and Lisa had performed admirably, everyone agreed, in thwarting the high-level conspiracy against the Emperor. Things hadn't worked out even close to perfection, of course, but one can't have everything.

Regardless, they had both been promoted and awarded leaves of several months. Thanks to Sten's old Mantis chum, Ida, there was more than enough money to enjoy the leave in style.

So the two had bought tickets to a distant world that consisted mostly of vast ocean and thousands of idyllic islands. They had charted an amphib and had spent week after blissful week hopping from island to island or just mooring out in the gentle seas, soaking up the sun and each other.

During those months they had purposefully avoided all news of or contact with the outside. There were scorched nerves to soothe and futures to be vaguely considered.

Sten wasn't too sure how much he was looking forward to his own immediate future. The Emperor had not only promoted him but had heavily advised that he switch services from the army to the Imperial Navy. Advice from the Commander And Chief Of All He Surveys, Sten knew, was the same thing as an order.

So it was with a mixture of dread and some excitement that Sten contemplated what would come next. Entering the navy, even as a commander, meant that he would have to start all over again. That meant flight school. Sten wondered if he could get his old job back if he washed out. Clot, he'd even be willing to go back to being a nice, dumb, not-a-care-in-the-world private.

Right. And if you believe that, my boy, there's some prime swamp land available at a dead bargain price on a Tahn prison planet.

Sten came slowly awake. He felt to one side and noted Lisa's absence. She was across the large main room of the houseboat, shuffling through her computer files for mail and phone calls.

'Bill,' she muttered. 'Bill, bill, bill, letter, bill, police union dues, letter . . . Clot! Knock it off, you guys. I've been on vacation.'

'Anything for me?' Sten asked lazily. Since he had no home address – nor had he since he was seventeen – he had left word for everything to be forwarded to Lisa's place.

'Yeah. About fifty bleeping phone calls. All from the same guy.'

Sten sat up, a nasty feeling growing slowly from his stomach to his throat.

'Who?'

'A Captain Hanks.'

Sten walked over to her and bent over her shoulder, tapping the keys to bring up the file. There they were, all right: call after call from a Captain Hanks. And Lisa hadn't been exaggerating by much – there were nearly fifty of them.

Sten tapped the key that gave him Hanks's recorded message. He was a shrill, whiny man whose voice went from basic urgency to ten-alarm emergency. But the gist of it was that Sten was wanted immediately, if not sooner. As soon as he returned he was to consider any remainder of his leave canceled. He was to report to Imperial Flight Training.

'Drakh,' Sten said.

He walked away from the computer and stared out the open window at the green waving forest, his brain churning. He felt Lisa gentle up behind him, her arms coming softly around his waist.

'I feel like crying,' she said. 'Funny. I don't think I ever have.'

'It's easy,' Sten said. 'You just squint up your eyes and think about almost anything at all.'

Sten did not report immediately as ordered. He and Lisa had a lot of good-byes to say.

Chapter Three

The Eternal Emperor had definite ideas about a picnic.

A soft rain of five or ten minutes that ended just before the guests arrived added a sweetness to the air.

Said rain had been ordered and delivered.

He thought that a breeze with just a bit of an invigorating chill in it whetted appetites. As the day progressed, the breeze should become balmy, so the picnickers could loll under the shade trees to escape the warming sun.

Said gentle, shifting winds had also been ordered.

Last of all, the Eternal Emperor thought a barbecue the best form of all picnics, with each dish personally prepared by the host.

The Eternal Emperor scanned the vast picnic grounds of Arundel with growing disappointment as he added a final dash of this and splurt of that to his famous barbecue sauce. Meanwhile, all over the picnic grounds, fifty waldo cooks manning as many outdoor kitchen fires exactly copied his every dash and splurt.

Hundreds of years before, the Emperor's semi-annual barbecue had begun as a nonofficial event. He started it because he loved to cook, and to love to cook is to watch others enjoy what you have lovingly prepared. At first, only close friends were invited: perhaps 200 or so – a number he could easily handle with a few helpers. In fact, the Emperor believed there were many dishes that reached near perfection when prepared in quantities of this size: his barbecue sauce, for instance.

It was a simple event he could comfortably fit on a small shaded area of the fifty-five-kilometer grounds of his palace.

Then he had become aware of growing jealousy among the members of his court. Beings were irked because they felt they were not part of a nonexistent inner circle. His solution was to add to the guest list – which created a spreading circle of jealousy as far out as the most distant systems of his empire. The list grew to vast proportions.

Now, a minimum of 8,000 could be expected. There was no way the Emperor could personally prepare food in those proportions. The clotting thing was getting out of hand. It was in danger of becoming an official event – the likes of an Empire Day.

He had been tempted to end the whole thing. But the barbecue was one of the few social occasions he really enjoyed. The Eternal Emperor did not consider himself a good mixer.

The solution to the cooking was simple: he had a host of portable outdoor kitchens built and the waldo cooks to tend them. Every motion he made, they duplicated, down to the smallest molecule of spice dusted from his hands. The solution to the now-official social nature of the event, however, proved impossible. So the Eternal Emperor decided to take advantage of it.

He invited only the key people in his empire to Prime World, and he used any potential jealousy of the uninvited to his advantage. As he once told Mahoney, 'It's a helluva way to flush 'em out of the bush.'

The Emperor sniffed his simmering sauce: Mmmm . . . Perfect. It was a concoction whose beginnings were so foul-looking and smelling that Marr and Senn, his Imperial caterers, refused to attend. They took a holiday in some distant place every time he threw a barbecue.

The original creation was born in a ten-gallon pot. He always made it many days in advance. He said it was to give it time to breathe. Marr and Senn substituted 'breed,' but the Emperor ignored that. The ten gallons of base sauce was used sort of like soughdough starter – all he had to do was to keep adding as many ingredients as there were beings to eat it.

He dipped a crust of hard bread into the sauce and nibbled. It was getting better. He looked around the picnic area again. All the fires were ready. The meat was stacked in coolers, ready for the spits. The side dishes were bubbling or chilling, and the beer was standing in barrels, ready to be tapped.

Where were the guests? He was beginning to realize that either some of the beings he had invited were terribly late or they had no intention of coming at all. Already, retainers were putting tarps on tables that would obviously not be used.

Clot them! What's a picnic without a few ants? He refused to have his good time spoiled. The sauce, he told himself. Concentrate on the sauce.

The secret to the sauce was the scrap meat. It had taken the Emperor years to convince his butchers what he meant by scrap. He did not want slices off the finest fillet. He needed garbage beef, so close to spoiling that the fat was turning yellow and rancid. The fact that he rubbed it well with garlic, rosemary, and salt and pepper did not lessen the smell. 'If you're feeling squeamish,' he always told Mahoney, 'sniff the garlic on your hands.'

A few more gravcars slid in. Guests hurried out, blinking at the smoke rising from the fires. The Emperor noticed that they were gathering in tiny groups and talking quickly in low voices. There were many glances in his direction. The gossip was so thick, he could smell it over the sauce.

The sauce meat was placed in ugly piles on racks that had been stanchioned over smoky fires – at this stage the recipe wanted little heat, but a great deal of smoke from hardwood chips. The Emperor liked hickory when he could get it. He constantly flipped the piles of meat so that the smoke flavor would penetrate. In this case, the chemistry of the near-spoiled scraps aided him: they were drying and porous and sucking at the air.

Then he – and his echoing waldoes – dumped the meat into the pot, filled it with water, and set it simmering with cloves of garlic and the following spices: three or more bay leaves, a cupped palm and a half of oregano, and a cupped palm of savory to counteract the bitterness of the oregano.

Then the sauce had to simmer a minimum of two hours, sometimes three, depending upon the amount of fat in the meat – the more fat, the longer the simmer. The picnic grounds smelled like a planet with an atmosphere composed mostly of sulfur.

The Emperor saw Tanz Sullamora arrive with an enormous retinue that easily took over two or three tables. Sullamora would be a booster. The merchant prince was not a man whose company the Emperor particularly enjoyed. He didn't like the fawning clot, but he needed him. The man's industrial influence was huge, and he had also had close connections with the Tahn, prior to the current difficulties. The Emperor hoped that when the current difficulties were settled, those connections could be re-established.

The Eternal Emperor had experienced many difficulties in his life – not to mention in his reign – but the Tahn had to be high up there on the lost sleep list.

They were an impossible people from a warrior culture that had been steadily encroaching on his empire. A thousand or two years ago he could have easily solved the problem by launching his fleets in one massive raid. But over time the politics of his commercial empire had made this an impossibility, unless he were provoked – and the provocation would have to be costly. The Eternal Emperor could not strike the first blow.

A few months earlier he'd had the opportunity to begin building a diplomatic solution to his difficulties. But the opportunity had been lost through betrayal and blood.

Who was that young clot who had saved the Emperor's royal ass? Stregg? No, Sten. Yeah. Sten. The Eternal Emperor prided himself on remembering names and faces. He kept them logged by the hundreds of thousands in his mind. Stregg, he remembered, was a vicious drink that Sten had introduced him to. It was a good thing to remember the young man by.

While he was waiting for the meat to simmer to completion, he could drink many shots of Stregg and prepare the next part of the sauce at his leisure.

There were many possibilities, but the Emperor liked using ten or more large onions, garlic cloves – always use too much garlic – chili peppers, green peppers, more oregano and savory, and Worcestershire sauce. He had once tried to explain to Mahoney how Worcestershire was made, but the big Irishman had gagged when told that the process started with well-rotted anchovies.

He sautéed all that in clarified butter. Then he dumped the mixture into another pot and set it to bubbling with a dozen quartered tomatoes, a cup of tomato paste, four green peppers, and a two-fingered pinch of dry mustard.

A healthy glug or three of very dry red wine went into the pot. Then he added the finishing touch. He stirred in the smoky starter sauce that he had prepared in advance, raised the heat, and simmered ten minutes. The sauce was done.

He drank some more Stregg.

Two of his cooks speared an enormous side of beef on a spit and set it rotating over the fire. Meanwhile, a pig's carcass was being quartered and set turning. It was time to start the barbecue.

By now, the Emperor realized that all the guests who were coming were there. A quick glance at the tables showed that a full two-thirds of his invitation list were busy elsewhere.

The Emperor decided to check the list later. He would remember the names.

He got out his brush and started sopping the roasting meat with sauce. The fire flared with the rich drippings. A smoky perfume filled the air all over the picnic grounds as the waldo cooks followed his motions. Usually, this was the time when the Emperor would settle back for a lazy basting: a beer for him, a brush of sauce for the meat.

It was also a time when he pretended great indifference to the rapturous faces of his guests. His mood blackened as he saw the sea of faces tight and worried.

What were the Tahn doing, anyway? Intelligence was zilch. Mercury Corps had never been the same since he had promoted Mahoney.

'Clotting Mahoney,' he said aloud. 'Where the hell is he when I need him?'

The voice came from just behind him. 'Fetching you a beer, Your Highness.'

It was Major General Ian Mahoney, commanding general, First Guards Division. He clutched two mugs overflowing with foam.

'What the clot are you doing here? You weren't invited.'

'Arranged some leave, sir. Perks of being your own CG. Thought you wouldn't mind.'

'Hell, no. If you're gonna sneak up on a man, I always say, do it with beer.'

Chapter Four

Mahoney wiped the last of the sauce off his plate with the thick stub of garlic bread, bit into the bread, and sighed. He took a deep honk of beer and then squeegeed the plate with the rest of the bread. He popped it down and settled back.

The Eternal Emperor, who'd barely touched his own plate, was watching him with great interest.

'Well?' he said.

'Heaven,' Mahoney said. He took another sip of beer. 'Excuse me. Heaven, sir.'

The Emperor took a small bite from his own plate, frowning. 'Maybe a bit too much cumin this time.'

Mahoney gave a deep belch. He looked at the Emperor inquiringly, and the man passed his nearly full plate over to Mahoney, who shoveled in a mouthful of satisfying proportions.

'No. Not too much cumin,' the Emperor said. He leaned his chair back to catch the last warm light of the sun. The Eternal Emperor appeared to be a man much younger than Mahoney. Midthirties, perhaps. Heavily muscled – like an ancient decathlon champion. He let the sun soak in, waiting to hear Mahoney's *real* purpose.

Finally, Mahoney took one more swig of beer, wiped his lips, straightened his tunic, and sat up in near attention in his seat.

'Your Majesty,' he said, 'I respectfully request permission to deploy the First Guards in the Fringe Worlds.'

'Really,' the Eternal Emperor said. 'The Fringe Worlds? I suppose you're worrying about the Tahn.'

Mahoney just looked at his boss. By now, he occasionally knew when he was being toyed with.

'Yes, sir. The Tahn.'

The Eternal Emperor could not help sweeping the picnic grounds with his eyes. The few guests who had bothered to show had left early, and the waiter bots were already cleaning up. In half an hour the area would be pristine – all broad lawns and rare azaleas.

The Eternal Emperor pointed to one of the flowering bushes.

'You know how many years I worked on those, Mahoney?'

'No, sir.'

'Too many. The things love dry climates. Aussie deserts, that kind of drakh.'

'Aussie, Your Majesty?'

'Never mind. Point is, I hate clotting flowers. Can't eat the SOBs. What's the damned use of them? I say.'

'Exactly, sir. What's the use of them?'

The Eternal Emperor plucked a flower from a nearby bush and began stripping it, petal by petal.

'What do you think they're up to? The Tahn, I mean.'

'With all due respect, Your Majesty, I think they're getting ready to kick our rosy red behinds.'

'No drakh. What the clot you think I've been doing?'

The Emperor pulled the handle of a keg and sudsed more beer

into his glass. He started to drink, then set the glass down. He thought for a while, making endless concentric rings that cut in on each other again and again.

'The trouble, Mahoney,' he finally said, 'is that I got a clot more to move than the Tanh. Just to hold what I have, I have to double my fleet. For a counterattack, I need another third. For a full assault, twice more.

'A thousand years ago or so, I swore I'd never come to this. Silliness. Too big. Too much to protect.

'My, God, do you know how long it takes to bid out a simple ship contract nowadays?'

Mahoney, wisely, didn't answer.

'I tried to make up for it,' the Emperor continued, 'by creating the best intelligence corps that ever . . . well, that was ever.

'And what the hell do I get? I get drakh.'

'Yes, sir,' Mahoney said.

'Oh, do I hear a scent of admonishment in that, General? Criticism for your promotion?'

'And transfer, sir.'

'And transfer,' the Emperor said. 'Under normal circumstances I would have said that I need a little disapproval in my life. Disapproval, properly put, keeps an Eternal Emperor on his toes.

'That's the theory, anyway. Can't really say. Don't have any other bosses of my type to rely on.'

Mahoney had found the proper moment. 'Who *can* you rely on, sir?'

There was silence. The Emperor watched the plates being swabbed, the forks being scrubbed, and the tables being put away. Besides the workers, the Emperor and Mahoney were the only two left. Mahoney finally tired of waiting on the Emperor's next move.

'About my request, sir. First Guards, Fringe Worlds?'

'I need to know more,' the Emperor said. 'I need to know enough to buy a great deal of time.'

'Then it's the First Guards, sir?'

The Emperor pushed his glass aside.

'No. Request refused, General.'

Mahoney almost bit his tongue through, trying to keep back his logical response. Silence, again, was the wiser course.

'Find out for me, Mahoney, before you tell me I've missed a bet,' the Eternal Emperor said.

Mahoney did not ask how.

The Emperor rose, leaving his nearly full glass.

'I guess the barbecue's over,' he said.

'I suppose so, sir.'

'Funny. All those no-shows. I imagine most of my alleged allies are thinking deeply about what kind of a deal to make with the Tahn. In case I lose.'

The Eternal Emperor was wrong about that. The time for *thinking* was long past.

Chapter Five

Phase one of Imperial Flight Training was on the vacation world of Salishan. Sten and his fellow pilots-to-be motlied together at a reception center, broken down into thirty-being companies, and were told to stand by for shipment to the base itself.

The trainees ranged from fresh-out-of-basic men and women, to graduates of one or another of the civilian-run preparatory schools that fed into the navy, to a scattering of already serving officers and enlisted people. Mostly they were military virgins, Sten noted by the absence of decorations, the untailored newly issued semi-dress uniforms, and the overly stiff bearing that the conditioning process had ground into them.

But Sten could have been blind and known that his classmates were fresh meat.

As they waited for the gravsled, there was excited speculation – because they were on a rec-world, this should be easy duty. They should be able to get passes into paradise on a regular basis. Even the base itself would be palatial.

Sten kept a straight face and looked away.

He caught an amused flash from another trainee on the other side of the throng. That man, too, knew better.

Sten eyed the man. He looked like every commando officer's image of the perfect soldier: tall, rangy, battlescarred. His uniform was the splotched brown of a Guards unit, and he wore three rows of decorations and a Planetary Assault Badge. He was a hard man who had seen his war. But he sure as hell was not the idea most people had of a pilot. Sten wondered what strings the man had pulled to get into training.

A gravsled grounded, and a dignified-looking chief got out, holding a clipboard.

'All right,' the chief said. 'If you people will form a line, we'll check you off and take you out to join the rest of the class.'

Five minutes later, after the sled had lifted and cleared the beautiful city, the chief's next command was phrased differently. 'You candidates knock off the chatter! This isn't a sewing circle!'

A basic rule of the military: Your superior's politeness is directly proportional to the proximity and number of potentially shocked civilians.

Sten, who had been through, he sometimes thought, almost all of the Empire's military schools from basic, Mantis, environmental, medical, weapons, et cetera ad ennui, also wasn't surprised that the landscape below them had become pine barrens.

In Eden, the military will build its base next to the sewage dump.

He was slightly surprised that the base, at least from the air, didn't look that bad. Most of it looked to be a standard naval base, with hangars, repair facilities, and various landing fields and hardstands.

To one side of the base was an array of three-story red brick buildings surrounded by gardens: base headquarters.

His second surprise came as the gravsled grounded in front of those buildings.

Sten, at that moment, remembered another basic law of military schooling and swore at himself. All military courses start by grinding the student into the muck and then reforming that being into the desired mold.

The instructors would illustrate this by instantly zapping some poor standout slob on arrival.

And Sten was a potential standout.

Hastily, he unbuttoned his tunic and unpinned his ribbon bar. The decorations were all real, even though a good percentage of them had been awarded for some highly classified Mantis operations, and the citation itself was a tissue. But there were too many of them for any young commander to deserve.

The ribbon bar was jammed into a pocket just as the canopy of the gravsled banged open and a rage-faced master's mate started howling orders.

'*Out, out, out!* What are you slime doing just sitting there! I want to see nothing but asses and elbows!'

New blood grabbed duffel bags and dived over the sides of the sled, and the mate kept screaming.

'You! Yes, you! You, too, come to think! Hit that ground! Do push-ups! Do many, many push-ups!'

Oh, Lord, Sten thought as he scrambled out. I'm back in basic training. Even the clottin' words are the same. This master's mate could be, except for sex, the duplicate of . . . what was her name? Yes. Carruthers.

'I want three ranks yesterday, people! Tall donks on my left, midgets over there.'

Not for the first time, Sten was grateful that he was slight, but not so small as to qualify for the feather merchant squad.

Eventually the master's mate got tired of screaming and physical training. Sten thought he was doing all right – in the chaos, he had only had to turn out some fifty knee bends. There were too many other and more obvious victims for the mate to pick on.

'Class . . . ten-hup! Right hace! For'd harch.'

Sten was grateful that at least all of them had been subjected to the barracks-bashing conditioning. He decided that he would not like to see what happened if one of the trainees went out of step.

They were marched into the central quadrangle, brought to a halt in front of a reviewing stand, and turned to face it.

On cue, a tall, thin man came out of one building and paced briskly to the stand. He looked typecast for what he was: a one-star admiral and the school commandant. No doubt a longtime pilot who'd flown every ship the Empire fielded in every circumstance known. Unfortunately, his voice didn't match the part. It would have been more suited to an operatic tenor.

Sten waited until the commandant introduced himself – Admiral Navarre – and then put most of his mind on other topics.

This was The Speech, given to every student at every military course by every commandant, and said the same things:

Welcome. This will be an intense period of training. You may not like how we do things, but we have learned what works. Those of you who learn to adjust to the system will have no troubles, the others . . . We have strict discipline here, but if any of you feels treated unfairly, my office is always open.

Ratcheta, ratcheta, ratcheta.

Phase One of flight training was Selection. The object of this phase was to determine absolutely that every candidate was *in fact* qualified to fly.

It was already famous throughout the Imperial military as a washout special.

Admiral Navarre informed them that, due to the unfortunate political situation, Phase One would be accelerated. Clotting wonderful, Sten thought.

Each student was told to remove his or her rank tabs. From that moment on, they would be referred to only as 'candidate.'

Ho, ho. Sten had a fairly good idea of some of the other titles: clot, drakh, bastard, and many, many other terms expressly forbidden under Imperial regulations.

That was about all that was worthy of note.

The main part of Sten's mind was reminding him that he was now a candidate. Not a hot-rod commander, not the ex-head of the Emperor's Gurkha bodyguards, not a Mantis covert specialist.

In fact, not even an officer.

Think recruit, young Sten. Maybe you can make it that way.

Sten was sort of neutral about becoming a pilot. He was here only because of personal and private suggestions from the Emperor himself. The Emperor had told him that the next stage in Sten's career should be a transfer to the navy – accomplished – and flight school.

Wash out of flight school, however, and Sten would probably be ordered into the logistics section of the navy.

He wondered for the hundredth time how hard it would be, if he *did* fail, to get back to the army and Mantis Section.

Somewhere during Sten's ponderings Navarre had finished, walked off, and the mate had the trainees doubling around the buildings, their duffels left stacked in front of the reviewing stand.

Now we meet the killers, Sten thought, or whatever flight school calls their drill sergeants, and they shall illustrate to us how worthless we are and how they're going to destroy us for even breathing hard.

That was, more or less, how the scenario went – with some considerable surprises.

The class was stopped in the middle of a huge square that was ankle-deep sand. The mate dropped them once more into push-up position, then disappeared. Minutes passed. A couple of the candidates collapsed into the sand. They would pay.

For Sten, the front-leaning rest position was no more than an annoyance.

A man ambled toward them, not at all the kind of sadist that Sten was expecting. Drill instructors always looked to be better soldiers than any of their student swine could dream of becoming. This man was heavily overweight and wore a rank-tabless, somewhat soiled flight coverall. One of the pockets was torn. The man walked up and down the line of prone candidates. He *tsk*ed once when another student went flat, wheezing.

'Good day, beings.' The man's voice was a husky drawl. 'My name is Ferrari. You will call me Mr Ferrari or sir, or you shall surely perish.

'I am your chief instructor pilot.

'During this period, I shall do my best to convince you that becoming a pilot is the least desirable, most miserable manner a being could spend its existence.

'Like our honorable commandant, my door, too, is always open.

'But only for one purpose.

'For you to resign.

'During the long reaches of the days and nights that will follow, I sincerely want each and every one of you to consider just how easy it would be for this torment to stop.

'One visit to my office, or even a word to any of the other IPs, and you can be on your way to what I am sure would be a far superior assignment.

'By the way: we instructors here in Phase One personally feel that Sheol itself would be more favorable.

'Those of you from different cultures who don't know what Sheol is can ask a fellow student. But I am quite sure our program will also explain.

'Those of you who are still on your hands may stand. Those of you who collapsed should begin crawling. I would like you, while still on your stomachs, to crawl on line to the edge of this exercise yard.

'Crawl twice around it, please.

'This is not an exercise in sadism, by the way. I seem to have dropped a quarter-credit piece sometime today, and would be infinitely grateful if one of you would recover it.'

Sten, seeing the weak-armed slither past him, hoped that none of them would get cute, take a coin from his or her own pocket, and give it to Ferrari in hopes that the long crawl would be ended. Ferrari would certainly examine the coin, declare with sorrow that there must be some mistake since the date proved the coin not his, and pull that candidate's toenails.

Ferrari stepped to one side.

Now comes the hands-on thug.

This man also wore a blank flight suit, but one that was tailored and razor-creased. A long scar seamed his face, and the man limped slightly. His voice had the attractive rasp of a wood file on metal.

'My name is Mason.

'I can't use words like Mr Ferrari does, so I'll keep it short.

'I've looked at all of your files.

'Drakh. All of you.

'There is not one of you qualified to fly a combat car.

'If we screw up, and let any one of you onto a flight deck, you will end up killing someone.'

He tapped the scar.

'That's how I got this. They let somebody – somebody just like one of you clowns – into my tacflight.

'Midair collision.

'Eighteen dead.

'My job now is easy. All I have to do is keep one of you from killing anyone but himself.

'Maybe you've heard something like this from another instructor, and think I'm just talking.

'Wrong, clots.

'I personally hate each and every one of you.'

He looked up and down the formation. Sten chilled a little. He had, indeed, heard variations on that speech from DIs.

But Sten had the feeling that Mason really *meant* it.

'I've got one peculiarity,' Mason added. 'I'm going to make sure that every one of you washes out, like I said.

'But every selection course, there's one person that, for some reason, I hate more than most of you trash.

'And I pick him out early.

'And he never makes it.'

Again, Mason looked up and down the class.

Sten knew, moments before the snake's head stopped, whom he would be looking at.

Clot, clot, clot, Sten thought, while remaining as petrified as any chicken caught by the glare of the snake.

Chapter Six

By the time Ferrari and Mason had finished the torment they called 'muscle toning,' it was later afternoon. The master's mate – and Sten would never learn his name – took over the formation, doubled the trainees back to the barracks they were assigned to, and dismissed them.

The exhausted candidates timidly entered the brick building through double glass doors, knowing that inside would be another werewolf masquerading as an IP.

They also expected that the barracks, no matter how good-looking on the outside, would be polished plas floors, echoing squad bays, and clanging elderly lockers, just like in basic training.

They were very wrong.

Drawn up inside the foyer, which resembled the lobby of an exclusive small hotel, were about fifty middle-aged beings. They looked and were dressed like the retainers Sten had known at the Imperial palace.

One of them stepped forward.

'I would imagine you young people might like a chance to relax in the recreation room before we show you to your quarters. We hope you find the facilities adequate.'

He waved them through sliding doors into a large wood-paneled room twenty-five meters on a side. At one end was a large stone fireplace. Along the walls were drink and food dispensers and, between them, computer terminals and game machines. Above them hung abstract paintings.

In the room were games tables and luxurious easy chairs and sofas.

Sten's alertness went to condition red! He saw one candidate gape an expression accentuated by the double rings of white fur around his eyes. The candidate scrubbed a small black hand over his gray-furred chest in excitement.

'Beer! They have a beer machine!' He started forward.

'Maybe you don't want to be doing that.'

Sten, also about to say something, saw that the caution came from that scarred infantry sergeant.

'Why not?'

'Oh, maybe because they told us they were gonna be testing us for physical dexterity and like that, and a hang-over doesn't speed up your reaction time.

'Or maybe they're watching that machine, and anybody who uses it gets down-carded for lack of moral fiber.'

'That doesn't make sense.' That came from a very small, very exquisite woman. 'Every pilot *I've* ever known swills alk like it was mother's milk.'

'No drakh,' the sergeant agreed. 'But that's *after* they get their wings. And maybe Selection is what makes 'em drink that way.'

Maybe the sergeant was right, or maybe he was just paranoiac. But regardless, the beer machine sat unused throughout Selection.

Sten's quarters were also quite interesting. They consisted of two rooms – a combined bedroom/study decorated in soothing colors, and a 'fresher that included not only the usual facilities, but an elaborate Jacuzzi.

Sten had the idea that Ferrari's muscle toning would continue throughout Selection.

Unpacking took only moments – Sten, as a professional, had learned to travel light. The only extraneous gear he had in his duffel was the fiches he'd collected over the years, now micro/ microfiched, and his miniholoprocessor that, in off-duty hours, he used to recreate working miniatures of industrial plants.

Sten had gotten the idea that he would have little time to play with the holoprocessor, but decided to hook it up regardless.

The manufacturers were lying, he decided after a few moments. Their universal power connection wasn't that universal, at least not universal enough to include the powerplate hookups that his room had.

Sten went out into the corridor, intending to see if his cross-hall neighbor had a diploid plug that would work, and also to check the terrain.

He tapped at the door, a tentative tap meant to tell whoever was inside that this was not an IP, so he/she didn't have to conceal whatever he/she might have been doing.

A sultry voice came through the annunciator, a voice as soothing as any emergency surgery nurse could have.

Sten told the box what he wanted.

'Orbit a beat, brother, and I'll be with you.'

Then the door opened, and Sten dropped into horror.

Sten was not a lot of things:

He certainly wasn't ethnocentric. The factory hellworld he'd been raised in had given him no sense of innate culture.

He was not xenophobic. Mantis training and combat missions on a thousand worlds with a thousand different life forms had kept that from happening.

He also was not what his contemporaries called a shapist. He did not care what a fellow being looked or smelled like.

He thought.

However, when a door is opened and someone is confronted by a two-meter-tall hairy spider, all bets are off.

Sten was – later – a little proud that his only reaction was his jaw elevatoring down past his belt line.

'Oh dear,' the spider observed. 'I'm most sorry to have surprised you.'

Sten really felt like drakh.

The situation called for some sort of apology. But even his century had not yet developed a satisfactory social grace for a terminal embarrassment. Sten was very pleased that the spider understood.

'Can I help you with something?'

'Uh . . . yeah,' Sten improvised. 'Wanted to see if you knew what time we mess.'

'About one hour,' the spider said after curling up one leg that, incongruously, had an expensive wrist-timer on it.

'Oh, hell. I'm sorry. My name's Sten.'

And he stuck out a hand.

The spider eyed Sten's hand, then his face, then extended a second leg, a pedipalp, laying its slightly clawed tip in Sten's palm.

The leg was warm, and the hair was like silk. Sten felt the horror seep away.

'I am Sh'aarl't. Would you care to come in?'

Sten entered – not only for politeness but because he was curious as to what sort of quarters the Empire provided for arachnids.

There was no bed, but instead, near the high ceiling, a barred rack. The desk took up that unoccupied space, since the desk chair was actually a large round settee.

'What do you think – so far?'

'I think,' the lovely voice said, 'that I should have my carapace examined for cracks for ever wanting to be a pilot.'

'If you figure out why, let me know.'

The social lubricant was starting to flow, although Sten still had to repress a shudder as Sh'aarl't waved a leg toward the settee. He sat.

'I involved myself in this madness because my family has a history of spinning the highest webs our world has. If you don't mind a personal question, why are you here?'

Sten knew that if he told Sh'aarl't that the Eternal Emperor himself had punted him into this mess, he'd be ascribed either a total liar or someone with too much clout to be friendly with.

'It seemed like a good idea at the time.'

'Perhaps I might ask – what is your real rank?'

'Commander.'

Sh'aarl't exuded air from her lungs. Of course she was female – even huge Araneida seem to follow the biological traditions. 'Should I stand at attention? I am but a lowly spaceman second.'

Sten found himself able to laugh. 'Actually, I'd like to see it. How does somebody with eight legs stand at attention?'

Sh'aarl't side-jumped to the center of the room, and Sten tried not to jump vertically. Attention, for a spider, was with the lower leg segments vertical, the upper ones at a perfect forty-five-degree angle toward the body.

'At full attention,' Sh'aarl't went on, 'I also extend my fangs in a most martial attitude. Would you like to see them?'

'Uh . . . not right now.'

Sh'aarl't relaxed and clapped a pedipalp against her carapace. Sten surmised, correctly, that this signified amusement.

'I guess you had no trouble with the push-ups today.'

Again the clap.

'How serious do you think these beings are?' Sh'aarl't asked, changing the subject.

'I dunno about Ferrari,' Sten said. 'But that Mason scares the clot out of me.'

'I also. But perhaps if some of us hang on and survive until others are washed out . . . Certainly they *can't* throw everyone away – given what the Tahn are preparing. Am I right?'

Sten realized that she was desperately looking for reassurance, and so modified his answer from 'I think these people can do anything they want' to, 'Nope. There's got to be a couple of survivors. Speaking of which – why don't we go downstairs. See if this—' Sten almost said spiderweb '—tender trap they've put us in also feeds the fatted lamb.'

'Excellent idea, Commander.'

'Wrong. Candidate. Or Sten. Or you clot.'

Again the clap.

'Then shall we descend for dining, Sten? Arm in arm in arm in arm . . .'

Laughing, the two went out of the room, looking for food.

Later that night, there was a finger tap at Sten's door.

Outside was one of the barracks staffers. If the staff members all looked, to Sten, like palace retainers, this man would be the perfect butler.

After apologies for disturbing Sten, the man introduced himself as Pelham. He would be Sten's valet until Sten completed Phase One.

'Complete or get flunked, you mean.'

'Oh, no, sir.' Pelham appeared shocked. 'I took the liberty, sir, of looking at your file. And I must say . . . perhaps this is speaking out of school . . . my fellow staff members and myself have a pool on which of the candidates is most likely to graduate. I assure you, sir, that I am not being sycophantic when I say that I put my credits down on you with complete confidence.'

Sten stepped back from the doorway and allowed the man to enter.

'Sycophantic, huh?' Sten vaguely knew what the word meant. He went back to his desk, sat, and put his feet up, watching Pelham sort through the hanging uniforms.

'Mr Sten, I notice your decorations aren't on your uniform.'

'Yeah. They're in the pocket.'

'Oh. I assume you'll want—'

'I will want them put in the bottom of the drawer and ignored, Pelham.'

Pelham looked at him most curiously. 'As you desire. But these uniforms are desperately in need of a spot of refurbishment.'

'Yeah. They've been at the bottom of a duffel bag for a couple of months.'

Pelham collected an armload of uniforms and started for the door. 'Will there be anything else required? You know that I'm on call twenty-four hours.'

'Not right now, Pelham. Wait a moment. I have a question.'

'If I may help?'

'If I asked you who Rykor was, what'd be your reaction?'

Pelham was very damned good – the only response to Sten's mention of the walruslike being who happened to be the Empire's most talented psychologist was a rapidly hidden eye flicker.

'None, sir. Would you explain?'

'I'll try it another way. What would you say if I suggested that you, and all the other people in this barracks, all of you who're so helpful and such great servants, were actually part of Selection?'

'Of course we are, sir. We realize that the candidates desperately need study time and relaxation time, and we try to help by taking care of the minor—'

'Not what I meant, Pelham. One more time. What would be your reaction if I said I thought that all of you are trained psychs, and this whole barracks, relaxed and gentle, is a good way to get us off guard and find out what we're really like?'

'You are joking, sir.'

'Am I?'

'If you are not, I must say I am very honored. To think that *I* have the talents to be a doctor.' Pelham chuckled. 'No, sir. I am just what I appear.'

'You did answer my question. Thank you, Pelham. Good night.'

'Good night, sir.'

Dr. W. Grenville Pelham, holder of seven degrees in various areas of psychology, applied psychology, human stress analysis, and military psychology, closed the door and padded down the hall. Some meters away from Sten's room, he allowed himself the luxury of low laughter.

Chapter Seven

The first weeks of Selection were quite simple – the IPs bashed the trainees' brains out in the morning, at noon, and in the evening. There were also unexpected alerts in the middle of the night, although the callouts were always handled by the staff. The IPs never entered the barracks.

In between the physical and mental harassment, the tests went on. To a large extent, they duplicated the basic exams – reflex testing, intelligence quotient testing, and so forth. The testing standards, however, were far higher than when a being entered the military. Also, the tests were readministered severally and at unexpected times.

Sten was not impressed.

He had the idea that this duplication wouldn't have happened before the Emergency began. There must have been better, if slower, ways to test for the same abilities.

Sten was starting to develop an active hatred for the Tahn.

Sten's belief that the testing was catch-as-catch-can turned from theory into certainty the day he was shuttled into a tiny room that had nothing more in it than a large chair and a livie helmet. His instructions were to seat himself, put the helmet on, and wait for further developments.

Sten had been through this, way back before basic training.

The idea was that, through the livie helmet, he would experience certain events. His reactions would be monitored by psychologists, and from this re-experiencing and reacting, his personality could be profiled.

When Sten had gone through the experience before, the livie tape had been that of some not very bright but very heroic guardsman who got himself slaughtered trying to kill a tank. It had made Sten nearly throw up and had, by his reaction, disqualified him for normal infantry, but made him an ideal candidate for the essentially lone-wolf Mantis Section.

Before he sat down, he went behind the chair and checked the tape in the feed. Various codes appeared, then the title: SHAVALA, GUARDSMAN JAIME, COMBAT/DEATH, ASSAULT ON DEMETER.

Possibly there could be some kind of validity for that choice – for prospective infantry types. But for pilots?

Sten examined the helmet and found the input line. A little subversion was called for.

He curled his right fingers, and the surgically sheathed knife in his arm dropped into his hand. The double-edged dagger was one of Sten's best-kept secrets. He had constructed it himself from an impossibly rare crystal. It had a skeleton grip, and its blade was only 2.5 mm thick, tapering to less than fifteen molecules wide. In other words, it could cut through practically anything. But in this case cutting wasn't what Sten was interested in.

He used the knife's needle point to rearrange a few tiny wires inside the sheath of the helmet input line. Then he replaced the knife and, as ordered, sat down and put the helmet on.

Let's see. The tape has just begun. I should express bewilderment. Fear. Excitement. Doubt as to my ability. Shock on landing. Determination to accomplish the mission.

Sten's Mantis schooling had included indoctrination on the various ways to fool *any* sort of mental testing machine, from the completely unreliable polygraph through the most sophisticated brainchecks of Imperial Intelligence. The key, of course, was to truly believe that what you were thinking or saying was the truth.

This training worked. Coupled with a conditioned, near-eidetic memory, it made Sten mental test-proof.

Let's see now . . . Shavala should have seen that clotting tank show up . . . Horror . . . seen his combat teammates slaughtered . . . Anger . . . seen the tank rumble on . . . More determination . . . doodle around the tank getting various pieces shot off . . . Pain and still more determination . . . hell, the clot should be dead by now. Shock and such.

Sten pulled a corner of the helmet away from his ear and heard the tape behind him click to a halt.

More shock. Pride at being part of this Imperial stupidity.

Sten decided that was enough input, took the helmet off, and stood. He set an expression of sickness and firmness on his face and went out of the room, artistically stumbling just beyond the door.

Sten gasped to the hilltop, then checked his compass and watch. He decided he could take four minutes to recover.

The exercise was a modified version of that military favorite, the Long Run or March. But, typical of Selection, it had a twist.

Candidates were given a map, a compass, and a rendezvous point that they were supposed to reach at a certain time. Once that point was reached, however, there was no guarantee that the exercise was over. Generally the candidate was merely given, by an IP, another RP and sent on his or her way.

The exercise didn't have much to do with pilot training, but it had a lot to do with tenacity and determination. Plus, Sten grudged, it probably showed which beings had learned that their brains were fools, telling the body to quit when the body's resources had barely begun to work.

Again, it was simple for Sten – Mantis teams ran these exercises as recreation.

But it did trim the candidates. Already ten of the thirty-plus candidates in Sten's group had withered and vanished.

Sten, flat on the ground, feet elevated, and in no-mind, heard footsteps.

He returned to reality to see the small woman who on their first day had made the cogent observation about pilots trot smoothly toward him.

Instead of going flat and shutting the systems down, she dropped her pack, went flat, and began doing exercises.

Sten was curious – this was an interesting way to con the mind into going one step farther. He waited until she finished, which added an extra minute to his time.

The downhill side of this part of the course was rocky. Sten and the female candidate – Victoria – were able to talk as they went.

Data exchange: She was a lieutenant in the navy. She was trained as a dancer and gymnast. Successful, Sten guessed, since she'd performed on Prime World. Sten even thought he'd heard of a couple of the companies she'd been with.

So why the service?

A military family. But also, dancing was work. She said being a professional dancer was like being a fish in sand.

Sten found the breath to laugh at the line.

Plus, Victoria went on, she had always been interested in mathematics.

Sten shuddered. While he was competent at mathematics – any officer had to be – equations were hardly something he joyously spent off-duty time splashing around in.

Sten's internal timer went off – it was a break for him. Victoria kept on moving at her inexorable pace.

Sten watched her disappear in the distance and felt very good.

If there was anyone who was guaranteed to get through this guano called Selection and become a pilot, it had to be Victoria.

Sten ducked as the wall of water came green over the boat's bows and smashed against the bridge windows.

The boat swayed, and Sten's stomach did handstands. Shut up, body. This is an illusion. Shut up, head, the answer came back. I am going to be sick. The hell with you.

Sten, puking to the side, had to fight to follow the instructions whispered at him.

'This is a twenty-meter boat. It is used to procure fish commercially. You are the captain.

'This boat has been returning to harbor, running just ahead of a storm.

'The storm has caught your boat.

'Somewhere ahead of you is the harbor. You must enter that harbor safely to complete the exercise.

'Your radar will show you the harbor mouth. But it is a failure-prone installation.

'You also know that the entrance to this harbor crosses what is called a bar – a shallowing of depth. During storm times, this bar can prevent any ship entering the harbor.

'Good luck.'

Sten had become experienced enough with the testing to instantly look at his radar screen. Ah-hah. There . . . somewhat to the right . . . so I must direct this craft . . . and, just as implicitly promised, the radar set hazed green.

Sten evaluated the situation – the illusion he was experiencing through the helmet. Unlike the Shavala-experience, in these tests any action Sten took would be 'real.' If, for instance, he steered the ship onto the rocks, he would experience a wreck and, probably, since Selection people were sadistic, slow drowning.

Simple solution. Easy, Sten thought.

All I have to do is hit the antigrav, and this boat will—

Wrong. There were only three controls in front of Sten: a large, spoked steering wheel and two handles.

This was a two-dimensional boat.

There were gauges, which Sten ignored. They were probably intended to show engine performance, and Sten, having no idea what kind of power train he was using, figured they were, at least at the moment, irrelevant.

Another wave came in, and the ship pitched sideways. Sten, looking at his choices, threw the right handle all the way forward, the left handle all the way back, and turned the wheel hard to the right.

The pitching subsided.

Sten equalized the two handles – I must have two engines, I guess – and held the wheel at midpoint.

Ahead of him the storm cleared, and Sten could see high rocks with surf booming over them. There was a slight break to the left – the harbor entrance.

Sten steered for it.

The rocks grew closer, and crosscurrents tried to spin Sten's boat.

Sten sawed at throttles and wheel.

Very good. He was lined up.

The rain stopped, and Sten saw, bare meters in front of him, the glisten of earth as a wave washed back. Clotting bastards – that's what a bar was!

He reversed engines.

A series of waves swept his boat over the stern. Sten ignored them.

He got the idea.

When a wave hits the bar, the water gets deep. All I need to do is wait for a big wave, checking through the rear bridge windows, and then go to full power. Use the wave's force to get into the harbor.

It worked like a shot. The huge wave Sten chose heaved the boat clear, into the harbor mouth.

Sten, triumphant, forgot to allow for side currents, and his boat smashed into the causeway rocks.

Just as anticipated, not only did his boat sink, Sten had the personal experience of drowning.

Slowly.

GRADE: PASSING.

By now, Sten had learned the names of his fellow candidates.

The hard sergeant, who Sten had figured would be thrown out immediately, had managed to survive. Survive, hell – so far he and

Victoria had interchanged positions as Number One and Number Two in the class standings. A specialist in ancient history would not have been surprised, knowing the man's name – William Bishop the Forty-third.

Sten, not knowing, was astonished, as were the other candidates, who had dubbed the sergeant 'Grunt,' a nickname he accepted cheerfully.

The furry would-be beer aficionado, whose name was Lotor, was a valued asset. He was the class clown.

Since normal military relief valves such as drunkenness, passes, and such were forbidden, the candidates tended to get very crazy in the barracks. Lotor had started the watersack war.

Sten had been the first victim.

There had been an innocent knock on his door at midnight. He'd opened the door to get a plas container of water in the face.

Sten, once he'd figured out who the culprit was, had retaliated by sealing Lotor in his shower with the drain plugged. He'd relented before the water level hit the ceiling.

Lotor, after drying his fur, had escalated. He had decided that Sten had allies, Sh'aarl't being one. So he'd tucked the floor fire hose under Sh'aarl't's door and turned it on.

Sh'aarl't, awakened when her room got half-full, had sensibly opened the door and gone back to sleep.

Lotor had not considered that making a spider an enemy was a bad thing to do.

The next night, Sh'aarl't had spun her web out from her window up a floor to Lotor's room and gently replaced his pillow with a water bag.

Lotor, again looking for a new target, went after Grunt. He tied an explosive charge to a huge water bag, rolled it down the corridor, knocked on Bishop's door, and then scurried.

Grunt opened his door just as the water bag blew.

His revenge required filling Lotor's room with a huge weather balloon filled with water. Bishop, being the combat type he was, didn't bother to figure out whether Lotor was present when he set the trap.

It took most of the barracks staff to free Lotor.

At that point, through mutual exhaustion and because no one could come up with a more clever escalation, the watersack war ended.

The only good effect it produced was the linking of Lotor, Bishop, Sten, and Sh'aarl't into a vague team.

*

The team adopted Victoria as their mascot. She wasn't sure why but was grateful for the company. The four never explained, but it was just what Sten had felt on the map exercise: One of them had to make it. And Victoria was the most likely candidate.

The five had discussed their options – which all agreed were slim – and also what those IPs really would turn out to be if they were required to wear uniforms instead of the blank coveralls.

Victoria had the best slander on Ferrari. She said the sloppy man must have been a Warrant-1, who probably blackmailed his commanding officer while stealing every piece of Imperial property that wasn't bonded in place.

They had laughed, shared a cup of the guaranteed-no-side-effects herbal tea, and headed for their rooms and the omnipresent studying.

At least most of them did.

Possibly the herbal tea had no *reported* effects.

Sten and Victoria bade Sh'aarl't good night at her door. Sten meant to walk Victoria to her room but found himself asking her into his own room.

Victoria accepted.

Inside, Sten gloried and disrobed Victoria pressured the bed and plumped the pillows. She touched a finger to her flight suit zip, and the coverall dropped away from her tiny, absolutely perfect body.

Sten had fantasized about making love to a ballerina – specifically Victoria. He hadn't suggested it because he had the rough idea that if he suggested and she accepted, his capabilities would be exactly as impotent as Mason daily suggested.

Tension and all that.

Sten may have been accurate about his own potential. But he had no idea how creative an ex-professional dancer could be.

The next day both Victoria and Sten tested very, very low on the various challenges.

They'd had less than an hour's sleep.

Chapter Eight

Selection moved on from written or livie tests to live problems, giving Ferrari and Mason a chance for real hands-on harassment.

Sten had the idea that the particular situation he was facing would be a real piece, since Ferrari was beaming and even Mason had allowed his slash of a mouth to creep up on one side.

'This is what we call a Groupstacle,' Ferrari explained genially. Group. Obstacle.

The group was Bishop, Victoria, Lotor, Sten, and six others.

The obstacle was:

'We're standing here,' Ferrari said, 'in the control room of a destroyer. Flower class, in case you're curious. It looks terrible, does it not?'

He waited for the chorus of agreement from the candidates.

'The reason it looks so bad is because it has crash-landed on a certain planetoid. This planetoid has acceptable atmosphere and water. But there is nothing to eat and very little which can be made into shelter.'

Ferrari smiled.

'Any of you who are eco-trained, do not bother to explain how illogical this planetoid must be. I do not set up these problems, I merely administer them.

'At any rate, you see this control room we are standing in? Yes. Terribly ruined by the crash. You see this open hatchway, exiting onto the planetoid, which is quite colorfully provided.

'Personally, I must say that I do not believe that trees can ever be purple. But I wander. Mr. Mason, would you care to continue?'

'Thank you, sir.

'I'll cut it short. You losers have crashed. The only way you're gonna live is by getting your survival kits out. The kits are down this passageway. You got two problems – the passageway is blocked.'

No kidding, Sten thought, staring down the corridor. He admired how carefully the problem had been set up. As they entered the huge chamber, it did look as if half of a ship was crashed into a jungle, crumpled and battered.

The inside of the ship was, with some exceptions – and Sten was noting those exceptions carefully – exactly like the flight deck and nearby passageways of a destroyer.

Sten wondered why, before the IPs had led the group into the chamber, Mason had taken Bishop aside and told him something – something very important from the way that Grunt had reacted.

Mason continued. 'Second problem is that the power plant is in a self-destruct mode. You've got twenty minutes until this ship blows higher'n Haman.

'If you don't get to your supplies, you fail the problem. All of you.

'If you're still working on the problem when the twenty minutes run out, you fail the problem. All of you.'

'Thank you, Mr. Mason.'

'Yessir.'

'The problem begins . . . now!'

There was a stammer of ideas.

Victoria had cut in – clot everything. What did they have to take out?

Grunt had said that was stupid – first they needed some kind of plan.

Lotor said that if they didn't know how deep the drakh was, how could any plan be possible?

The situation was simple. The corridor to the survival kits was blocked by assorted ship rubble that could be easily cleared. But x-ed across the corridor were two enormous steel beams, impossible to move without assistance.

Two candidates proved that, straining their backs trying to wedge the beams free.

Lotor was standing beside a much smaller beam in the corridor ahead of the blockage.

'This,' he said, 'might make a lever. If we had a fulcrum.'

'Come on, Lotor,' Grunt put in. 'We don't have any clottin' fulcrum.'

'Hell we don't,' Victoria said. 'Couple of you clowns grab that big chart chest up on the flight deck.'

'Never work,' Bishop said.

Sten eyed him. What the hell was the matter with Grunt? Normally he was the first to go for new ideas. While two men shoved the map chest down toward the block, Sten did his own recon around the 'ship.'

By the time he came back to the corridor, the map chest sat close to the blocking beams. The small beam went under one, and everybody leaned.

The first beam lifted, swiveled, and crashed sideways. The team gave a minor cheer and moved their lever forward.

'This is not going to work,' Bishop said.

Another candidate stepped back. 'You're probably right.'

He spotted a red-painted panel in the metal corridor, clearly marked ENVIRONMENT CONTROL INSPECTION POINT. *Do not enter without class 11 Clearance. Do not enter unless ship is deactivated.*

The candidate shoved the panel open. A ductway led along the corridor's path.

'Okay. This is it,' the candidate announced.

'Didn't you read the panel?' Sten asked.

'So? This ship's about as deactivated as possible.'

'You're right,' Bishop agreed.

Again, Sten wondered.

The candidate forced himself into the ductway. The panel clicked closed behind him. After five seconds, they heard a howl of pain.

The demons who set up the Selection tests had provided for that. In that ductway should have been superheated steam. But this was a dummy, so all the candidate got was a mild blast of hot water – enough for first-degree burns – and then the ductway opened and dumped him out on the other side of the set, where Ferrari told him he was dead and disqualified from the test.

After the 'death' of the candidate, the team redoubled efforts to lever the second beam free.

Sten did his basic physics, said 'no way,' and looked for another solution. He went through the ship and then outside, looking for anything that could become a tool.

He found it.

By the time he'd dragged the forty meters of control cable that must have exploded from the ship's skin into the jungle back into the corridor, the others were panting in defeat.

There was seven minutes remaining.

Sten did not bother explaining. He ran the 2-cm cable down to the beam, looped it, and wrapped a series of half hitches around it. Then he dragged the cable back up to a solid port frame that had pulled away from the ship's walls, and back toward the beam.

Bishop stopped him. 'What the clot are you doing?'

'I'm sending kisses to the clotting Emperor,' Sten grunted. 'Gimme a hand.'

'Come on, Sten! You're wasting time.'

'One time. Listen up, Grunt. We're gonna block and tackle this cable and yank that beam out.'

'Sten, I'm not sure that is going to work. Why don't we talk about it?'

'Because we got five minutes.'

'Right! We don't want to do anything wrong, do we?'

And Sten got it.

'Nope.'

His hand knifed out, palm up. Sten's hands could kill, maim, or coldcock any being known to the Imperial martial arts.

The knife hand sliced against Bishop's neck, just below his ear. Bishop dropped like a sack of sand.

'Shaddup,' Sten commanded against the shout of surprise. 'Get this clottin' cable back around and then we have to pull like hell. Bishop was a sabotage factor. I saw Mason give him orders. Come on, people. We got to get out of this place!'

The block-and-tackled pulley yanked the beam free, and the team had its supplies out of the storage room and were clear of the 'ship' a good minute before time ran out.

Bishop, after recovering consciousness, told Sten he was right – Mason had told him to be a saboteur.

Ferrari grudged that they were one of the few teams to successfully complete the test in five years.

GRADE: OUTSTANDING.

Chapter Nine

Sten was having problems.

It wasn't that he was quite a mathematical idiot – no one in the Imperial Forces above spear-carrier second class was – but he did not have the instinctive understanding of numbers that he did, for example, of objects. Nor could he, in the navigational basic courses Phase One shoved at them, translate numbers into the reality of ships or planets.

And so he got coaching.

From Victoria, there was no problem, since everyone knew that she was the only guaranteed graduate. But Bishop?

Math geniuses are supposed to be short and skinny, talk in high voices, and have surgically corrected optics.

So much for stereotypes, Sten thought glumly as Bishop's thick fingers tabbed at computer keys, touched numbers on the screen, and, with the precision and patience of a pedant, tried to help Sten realize that pure numbers more exactly described a universe than even a picture or words, no matter how poetically or OEDly chosen.

Sten looked at the screen again and found no translation.

'Clottin' hell,' Bishop grunted to Victoria. 'Get the fire ax. *Something's* got to get through to him.'

Victoria found the solution.

It took less than one evening to crosspatch Sten's miniholo-processor into the computer. When he input numbers, the holo-processor produced a tiny three-dimensional star-map.

Eventually, after many many problems, Sten glimmered toward an understanding.

His grade:

MATHEMATICAL PERCEPTIONS: NEED IMPROVEMENT.

*

For some unknown reason, almost every school Sten had been punted into tested for gravitation sensitivity.

Sten could understand why it would be necessary to know how many gees someone could withstand or how many times one could alter the direction of a field before the subject threw up – but once that was found out, why was retesting necessary?

Sten knew that he personally could function as a soldier, without benefit of a gravsuit, at up to 3.6 E-gravs. He could work, seated, under a continuous 11.6 E-gravs. He would black out under a brief force of 76.1 E-gravs or a nearly instantaneous shock of 103 E-gravs.

All this was in his medfiche.

So why retest?

Sten decided that it was just part of the applied sadism that every school he had attended, back to the factory world of Vulcan, had put him through.

But of all the test methods he hated, a centrifuge was the worst. His brain knew that there was no way his body could tell it was being spun in a circle to produce gravitic acceleration. But his body said 'bet me' and heaved.

Of course Phase One used a centrifuge.

Sten curled a lip at the stainless steel machinery craning above him in the huge room.

'You look worried, Candidate Sten.' It was Mason.

Sten hit the exaggerated position that the IPs called attention. 'Nossir. Not worried, sir.'

'Are you scared, Candidate?'

Great roaring clichés. Sten wished that Alex was with him. He knew the chubby heavy-worlder would have found a response – probably smacking Mason.

Sten remembered, however, that Kilgour had already gone through flight school. Since Sten hadn't heard anything, he assumed that Alex had graduated – without killing Mason.

Sten decided that Kilgour must have been sent to another Phase One than this one, made a noncommittal reply to Mason, and clambered up the steps into one of the centrifuge's capsules.

Later that night, Sten's stomach had reseated itself enough to feel mild hunger.

He left his room, still feeling most tottery, and went for the rec room. One of the food machines would, no doubt, have something resembling thin gruel.

Sh'aarl't, Bishop, and Lotor sat at one of the game tables in complete silence. Sten took his full cup from the slot and sat down beside them. Lotor gave him the news.

'They washed Victoria today.'

Sten jumped, and the soup splashed, unheeded, in his lap.

Bishop answered the unasked question. 'She failed the gee-test.'

'No way,' Sten said. 'She was a clotting gymnast. A dancer.'

'Evidently,' Sh'aarl't said, 'vertigo is not uncommon – even in athletes.'

'How many gees?'

'Twelve point something,' Bishop said.

'Clot,' Sten swore. Even mild combat maneuvers in a ship with the McLean generators shut down could pull more than that.

He realized that all of them spoke of Victoria in the past tense. Phase One may have been sadistic in some ways, but when a candidate was disqualified, he was immediately removed. Sten was a little surprised that the three had any idea at all on what had flunked the woman.

He also realized that with Victoria, their talisman for possible graduation to the next phase, gone, none of them felt any hope of making it.

Chapter Ten

The bulletin display in the barracks' lobby was known, not inappropriately, as 'The Tablet of Doom.' Sten read the latest directive as it flashed for his attention: 1600 hours, this day, all candidates were directed to assemble in the central quadrangle. He wondered what new form of mass torment the IPs had devised. There were, after all, only a few days left in Phase One, and there were still survivors in the program, including Sh'aarl't, Bishop, and Lotor.

Then he caught the kicker.

DRESS UNIFORM.

Sten was in a world of trouble. He had been quite correct hiding his ribbons upon entering the school. He noticed that those with more decorations or rank than the IPs felt appropriate seemed to get far more than their share of attention and harassment. Thus far, in spite of Mason's evident personal hatred, Sten had managed to run somewhat silent and somewhat deep.

Oh, well. All good things seize their bearings eventually.

'My, don't we look pretty, Candidate,' Mason crooned. 'All those ribbons and bows.'

Sten had considered not putting the medals on. But he knew that under the current circumstances it was an offense of basic regulations for a soldier not to wear the decorations to which he was entitled. It would be just like the IPs to look up everyone's record jacket, then check chests or sashes for exactitude and use any difference to bust another candidate out.

Sten yessired Mason while marveling at Chief Instructor Pilot Ferrari. So much for the theory that fat slobs only get promoted to warrant officer. That might be his current serving rank, but Ferrari was now wearing the stars of a fleet admiral, with decorations banked almost to his epaulettes.

Sten noticed, in spite of his awe, that there appeared to be a soup stain just above Ferrari's belt line.

'If I'd known you had all those hero buttons, Candidate,' Mason went on, 'I would have given you more attention. But we still have time.'

Fine. Sten was doomed. He wondered how Mason would nuke him.

Minutes later, he found out.

Ferrari had called the class to attention and congratulated them. The formal testing was complete. Any of them still standing was successful. All that remained was the final test.

'Do not bother,' Ferrari said, 'going through your notes and memories in preparation. The end test we are quite proud of, not the least because it has everything yet nothing to do with what has gone before. You have twenty-four hours to consider what such an examination might be. We find that suspense is good for the soul. The test, by the way, will be administered singly. Each instructor pilot will choose candidates, and it is his responsibility at that point.'

And now Sten knew how Mason was going to get him.

Chapter Eleven

The aircraft – at least Sten guessed it was an aircraft – was the most clotting impossible collection of scrap metal he had ever seen. It consisted of a flat metal platform about two meters in diameter, with two seats, two sets of what Sten thought to be controls, and a windscreen. The platform sat atop two metal skids. Behind it was some sort of power plant and then a long spidered-metal girder that ended in a side-facing fan blade. Above the platform was another fan, horizontal to the ground, with twin blades each about six meters long. The device sat in the middle of a wide, completely flat landing ground. Two hundred meters in front of the aircraft, a series of pylons sprouted.

Sten and Mason were the only two beings on the landing field. Sten turned a blank but – he hoped – enthusiastic face toward Mason.

'We got a theory here in flight school,' Mason said. 'We know there are natural pilots – none of you clowns qualify, of course – and also a lot of people have flown a lot of things.

'No sense testing someone for basic ability if we put them on their favorite toy, is there? So what we came up with is something that, as far as we know, *nobody* has flown for a thousand years or so. This pile of drakh was called a helicopter. Since it killed a whole group of pilots in its day, when antigrav came around they couldn't scrap-heap these guys fast enough.

'You're gonna fly it, Candidate. Or else you're gonna look for a new job category. I hear they're recruiting planetary meteorologists for the Pioneer Sectors.'

'Yes, sir.'

'Not that we're unfair. We're gonna give you some help. First you get two facts: Fact number one is that this helicopter, unlike anything else I've ever heard of, really doesn't want to fly at all. It won't lift without bitching, it glides like a rock, and it lands about the same if you don't know what you're doing. Fact number two is it's easy to fly if you're the kind of person who can pat his head and rub his stomach at the same time.'

Sten wondered if Mason was making his notion of a joke. Impossible – the man was humorless.

'Next, you and me are gonna strap in, and I'm gonna show you how the controls work. Then you'll take over, and follow my instructions. I'll start simple.'

Right, simple. Ostensibly, the few controls were easy. The stick in front controlled the angle of the individual fan blades – the airfoil surface – as they rotated. This stick could be moved to any side and, Mason explained, could make the helicopter maneuver. A second lever, to the side, moved up and down, and, with a twist grip, rotated to give engine speed and, therefore, rotor speed. Two rudder pedals controlled the tiny fan at the ship's rear, which kept the helicopter from following the natural torque reaction of the blades and spinning wildly.

The first test was to hover the ship.

Mason lifted it, lowered it, then lifted it again. It seemed easy.

'All you got to do is keep it a meter off the ground.'

He told Sten to take the controls.

The helicopter then developed a different personality and, in spite of Sten's sawing, dipped, bounced the front end of the skids on the field, then, following Sten's over-controlling, reared back . . . then forward . . . and Mason had to grab the controls.

'You want to try it again?'

Sten nodded.

He did better – but not much. Power . . . keep that collective in place . . . real gentle with that stick.

Sten didn't prang it this time, but the required meter altitude varied up to about three.

Sten's flight suit was soaked with sweat.

Again.

The variable came down to plus or minus a meter.

Mason was looking at Sten. 'All right. Next we're going to move forward.'

Mason moved the helicopter forward about fifty meters, turned, and flew back, then repeated the whole maneuver.

'I want you to hold two meters altitude and just fly down there in a straight line. I'll tell you when to stop.'

The helicopter porpoised off. He scraped his skids twice, and his flight toward those distant pylons was a side-winder's path. Mason took over and put Sten through the same routine three more times. Sten had no idea if he was about to be trained as a pilot or a weatherman.

The next stage took the helicopter all the way down to the pylons and S-curved through them. The first time Sten tried it, he discovered he had straight and level flight somehow memorized – the helicopter clipped every single pole as it went down the course. By the fourth try, Sten managed to hit no more than four or five of them.

Mason was looking at him. Then Mason signaled – he had it.

Sten sat back and, per orders, put his hands in his lap.

Mason landed the ship back where it had started, shut down, and unbuckled. Sten followed, stepping off the platform and ducking under the rotors as they slowed.

Mason was standing, stone-faced, about thirty meters away from the helicopter. 'That's all, Candidate. Report to your quarters. You'll be informed as to your status.'

Sten saluted. Clot. So much for the Emperor's ideas about Sten.

'Candidate!'

Sten stopped and turned.

'Did you ever fly one of these things before?'

And Sten, through his honest denial, felt a small glint of hope.

Chapter Twelve

A day later, Sten's name, as well as Bishop's, Sh'aarl't's, and Lotor's, went on the list: *Phase One. Accepted. Assigned to Imperial Flight Training, Phase Two.*

In Phase Two, they would learn how to fly.

There should have been some kind of party. But everyone was

too tired to get bashed. Of the 500 candidates, fewer than forty had been selected.

According to the clichés, graduation should have been announced by the IPs lugging in cases of alk and welcoming the candidates to the thin, whatever-colored line. Instead, Sh'aarl't, Sten, and Bishop split a flask of herbal tea while they packed. All they wanted was away.

Waiting near the sleds that would take the candidates to their ships were Ferrari and Mason.

Again according to cliché, there should now have been understanding on one hand and acceptance on the other. But Mason's expression was exactly that of the first day – he looked as if he was sorry that any of them had made it. And he turned an even harder stare on Sten.

Sten returned it.

Clot forgiveness and understanding – he wanted to meet Mason in an alley behind a hangar sometime and give him a scar to match the first one. Preferably across the throat . . .

Chapter Thirteen

The label 'the Fringe Worlds' suggests some sort of geographical or political cohesiveness to the spattered cluster that occupied space between the Empire and the Tahn System. There was almost none.

The cluster had been slowly settled by Imperial pioneers. They were not the radicals or the adventurers who had explored, for instance, the Lupus Cluster. They were people wanting things to be a little more simple and peaceful. A large percentage of them were retired military or civil servants starting a second, or even third, career. Others wanted a chance to establish themselves in comfort as small manufacturers or business people.

But if there were no hero pioneers, there also were none of the villains that pioneering creates. Not, at least, until the expansion from the Tahn empire brought new, and somewhat different, immigrants.

What government there was in the Fringe Worlds mirrored the settlers themselves. Whether confined to a single world or including a half dozen or so systems, it was generally some species of parliamentarianism, ranging from mildly liberal to mildly authoritarian. Since prospective tyrants went elsewhere, what armed forces existed were somewhere between customs police and coastal guards. The only unifying political force the cluster had was an economic summit that met to iron out modern problems every five years or so. It was a backwater cluster, content to remain as it was.

Until the Tahn.

The Tahn who immigrated into the Fringe Worlds were financially backed by their leaders, as the Tahn birth rate and political ambitions clamored for Lebensraum. These were true pioneers, looking for more. Since their culture encouraged communal economics, they naturally had an advantage over the ex-Imperialists. And so the situation escalated into violence – riots and pogroms.

The Imperial settlers were there first, so they had a chance to modify the government. Tahn were not permitted extensive freeholds. They were excluded from voting. They were physically ghettoized into enclaves either rural or urban.

The Tahn settlers' resentment was fed by the Tahn Empire itself, which wanted the cluster added to its holdings.

The revolutionary movement was not only popular but well backed by the Tahn. And the Empire had done little to solve the problem. After all, backwater areas with minor problems – riots, no matter how bloody, are not as bad as active genocide – get minor attention.

The Imperial garrisons assigned to the Tahn worlds were fat and lazy. Instead of being peacekeepers, the officers and men tended to agree with the settlers. The Tahn, after all, *were* different – which meant 'not as good as.'

There had been a brief time, not long before, when the confrontation between the Empire itself and the Tahn might have been prevented. Some of the more farsighted Tahn revolutionaries had recognized that if the confrontation occurred, they were liable to be crushed in the middle. Very secretly they had sent the head of the organization to Prime World. Godfrey Alain had been murdered in a plot that was aimed against the Emperor himself. Final negotiations between the Empire and the peace faction of the Tahn Council had also ended in blood.

The war drums were not even slightly muted, especially on the Fringe Worlds.

But no one in the cluster seemed to know how close Empirewide war was.

Chapter Fourteen

The dusty gravcar sputtered feebly over a country lane. It was an elderly design: long, boxy, with an extended rear cargo area. And the way it was balking, it was plain that it had been under constant and varied lease since it had left the factory.

The salesman hunched over the controls seemed as weathered and as old as the vehicle. He was a large man with a broad, friendly face and bulky shoulders that strained at his years-out-of-date coveralls. The man hummed peacefully to himself in an off-key voice timed to the sputtering McLean drive engine. As he drove in apparent complete ease and relaxation, his eyes swiveled like a predator's, drinking in every detail of the landscape.

This was poor land, pocked with rocks and wind-bowed clumps of trees. It seemed to be one dry gale away from becoming a permanent dust bowl.

During the course of the day, the salesman had skimmed past a half a dozen sharecropper farms tended by a few hollow-eyed Tahn immigrants. He had hesitated at each place, noted the extreme poverty, and gone on. None of them were places where a normal being would have even asked for a friendly glass of water. Not because of the hostility – which was real and more than apparent – but because if it had been given, it might have been the last few ounces of water left on the farm.

In the distance he spotted a sudden shot of green. He shifted course and soon came upon a large farm. The earth seemed comparatively rich – not loam, but not rock either – and was heavily diked with irrigation ditches. In the middle of the spread were big shambling buildings surrounding a small artesian pond. This would be the source of wealth. Several people were working the field with rusted, creaking machinery.

Still humming, the man eased the gravsled to a stop next to a cattle guard. He pretended not to notice the instant freezing of the people in the field. He casually got out under their burning stares, stepped over behind a bush, and relieved his bladder. Then he struck a smoke, gazed lazily about, and walked over to the fence railing. He peered with mild interest at the men and women in the field – one pro judging the work of others. He gave a loud snort. If he had had a mustache, the honk would have blown it up to his bushy eyebrows. The snort seemed to be both a nervous habit and a comment on the state of things.

'Nice place,' he finally said. His voice hit that perfect raised pitch that a farmer uses to communicate to a companion many rows away.

The group drew back slightly as a middle-aged Tahn, nearly the salesman's size, strode forward. The salesman smiled broadly at him, pointedly ignoring the others who were picking up weapons and spreading slowly out to the side.

'Wouldn't think you could grow kale crops in these parts,' the salesman said as the Tahn drew closer. He looked more closely at the fields. ''Course they do look a little yellow-eyed and peaked.'

The man stopped in front of him, just on the other side of the fence. Meanwhile, his sons and daughters had half ringed the salesman in. He heard the snicks of safeties switching off.

'Next town's about forty klicks down the road,' the farmer said. It was an invitation to get the clot back in the gravcar and get out.

The elderly salesman snorted again. 'Yeah. I noted that on the comp-map. Didn't seem like much of a town.'

'It ain't,' the Tahn said. 'Next Imperial place gotta be two, maybe two and a half days go.'

The salesman laughed. 'Spotted me, huh? What the hell, I ain't ashamed. Besides, being a farmer is the only citizenship I claim.'

The man stared at him. 'If you're a farmer,' he said, 'what you doin' off your spread?'

'Gave it up after eighty years,' the salesman said. 'You might say I'm retired. Except that wouldn't be right. Actually, I'm on my second career.'

The farmer's eyes shifted, checking the positions of his brood. He inspected the horizon for any possible Imperial reinforcements. 'That so?'

Death was whispering in the salesman's ear.

'Yeah,' he said, unconcerned. 'That's so. Sell fertilizer gizmos now. My own design. Maybe you'd be interested in one.'

He pulled out a much-used kerchief and honked into it. Then he looked at the kale fields again. He noted some blackened areas in the distance; this was just one of many Tahn farms, he understood, that had been hit by roving gangs of Imperial settlers.

'Wouldn't help with the withering, but one of my fellas sure as hell would take the yellow out.'

'Mister,' the farmer said, 'you're either a damn fool, or—'

The salesman laughed. 'At my age,' he said, 'I've gotten used to a lot worse things than being called a fool.'

'Listen, old man,' the farmer said. 'You're Imperial. Don't you know better than to come near a Tahn place?'

The salesman snorted. 'Pish, man. You're talkin' politics. Never gave a damn about politics. Only thing I got in common with politicians is what I sell. Matter of fact, fertilizer's a lot more useful. And my stuff don't stick to your boots, either.'

He turned to the cargo compartment of his gravsled. Instantly weapons came up. The salesman just pulled several small bottles out of a carton. He held one out for the farmer, his face total innocence.

'My calling card,' he said.

Cautiously, the Tahn farmer reached over the fence and took one of the bottles. He looked at the printing on the side. The salesman figured that the time was ripe for introductions.

'Ian Mahoney,' he said. 'Fine cider and fertilizer . . . Go ahead. Try it. Whipped that batch up myself. A little raw, but it'll do the job.'

The farmer opened the bottle and sniffed. The sweet smell of apples drifted out. And underlying it, there was the sharp odor of alcohol.

'It's nothing serious,' Mahoney said. 'Maybe seventy-five proof or so. Take a shot.'

The farmer sipped, then sucked in his breath. It was good stuff all right. Without hesitation, he chugged down the rest of the bottle.

'That's damn fine cider,' he said.

Mahoney snorted. 'You oughta see my fertilizer. Nothing clotting organic in it. All pure, sweet-smelling chemicals. Great for the plants, and you don't have to worry about the kids getting ringworm – long as you keep 'em away from your cattle.'

The farmer laughed. Mahoney noted the weapons being lowered. Then, with some relief, he saw the Tahn wave his hulking children over to him in a friendly gesture.

'Say, mister,' the farmer said. 'You got any more of that cider?'
'Sure thing.'

And with a honk of his nose, a grin, and a scratch of his behind, Major General Ian Mahoney, commander of the Imperial First Guards Division, reached into the back of his gravcar to buy the boys a drink.

Chapter Fifteen

It was a country inn – large, gleaming white, with exposed stained beams of expensive wood. The gravcars lined up outside were all reasonably new and worth many, many credits. For kilometers around, the farmland was sleek and water-proud. The name of the place was the Imperial Arms Inn.

Bloody figures, Mahoney thought as he reached for the door.

He heard voices shouting from within in heated debate.

'Clottin' low-life Tahn. Up to me, police'd clear out every one of them.'

'Clot the police. We gotta take care of our own business. A being oughta kill his own snakes. I say we all get together one night and—'

Mahoney was spotted instantly as he walked inside. A church-hall hush fell over the room. Mahoney automatically honked into his handkerchief – cursing mentally to himself that he had ever dreamed up that touch – and strolled over to the bar.

He eased his bulk into a stool. 'Shot and a beer, friend,' he told the bartender.

All around him, every person was listening intently to each word he said. The bartender filled up a mug and placed it before him. A second later, a shot glass chinked beside it.

'Traveling through?' the bartender asked, sounding way too casual.

'Sure am,' Mahoney said. 'But real slowly, today. Hell of a hang-over.'

He took a sip of his beer and chased it with the full shot. The bartender refilled it.

'Party too hard, huh?'

Mahoney groaned. 'You don't know the half of it,' he said. 'I happened by the McGregor place, yesterday. You know the spread – maybe thirty klicks out?'

The bartender nodded, as did the rest of the room. Everyone knew the McGregors.

'They just married off their last kid,' Mahoney said. That was far from news to the crowd in the inn. 'I showed up just at reception time. Hit it right off with those nice people. They made me stay and filled me right up with all I could eat and drink.' He snorted through his increasingly reddening nose. ''Course, they didn't have to twist my arm much.'

Mahoney felt the room relax. A moment later it was all a-babble again. The bartender even bought him the next shot. Mahoney sipped at it and peered about the bar, just one friendly face looking for another.

A well-dressed, overstuffed man strolled over to him, carrying his drink. He sat down beside Mahoney.

'You look like you might be in sales,' the man said.

Mahoney laughed. 'Hell, does it change a fellow that quick? Farmed two-thirds of my life. Now I'm into sales. Sorta.'

'What do you mean by sorta?'

Mahoney instantly warmed to the man. He began dragging out circulars and brochures.

'Fertilizer plants is my game,' he said. 'Look at these boys. Small, cheap, and you get an output for anything from a kitchen garden to a big sucker of a farm.'

The man seemed genuinely interested. 'Say, maybe we could use something like that.'

Mahoney peered at him through his old man's bushy eyebrows. 'No offense, but you don't seem the farmin' type.'

'No offense taken,' the man said. 'I'm into hardware. Got thirty-two stores and growing.'

'Say, you *are* a find. Let me tell you about these little guys.' And Mahoney went into what he called his dancing-bear act. It took many drinks and the good part of an hour. Other men joined the conversation. And soon Mahoney was handing out bottles of his 'calling card.'

By now his mission had taken him to eleven or more Fringe World planets in nearly that many systems. He had his cover story fine-tuned. Now he was winding up on the Empire's capital world for the Fringe System: Cavite.

Mahoney was passing himself off as an elderly farmer who had spent most of his life tending a large, rich spread on one of the key Imperial agricultural systems. He was also a habitual tinkerer, constantly inventing little devices to solve problems that irritated him.

Fertilizer was one of his big bugaboos. Mahoney could go on for hours about the rotten quality and expense of the average fertilizer – and he frequently did, to the dismay of casual dinner guests. Anyway, Mahoney the farmer had invented the dandy little fertilizer plant, then put his own money up to found a small company.

Presently, he was acting as his own advance man, touring agricultural areas to brag about his wares. The fact that he wasn't asking for any money out front but was merely asking people if one of his salesmen could visit in a month or so eased the suspicions of even the overly hostile settlers of the Fringe Worlds.

Mahoney also thought his homemade cider was a nice touch, as was his old man's chatter, with his knowledge of farming trivia and the ability to bore just about anyone. His only regret was the snort he had adopted to go with the act. Now he couldn't stop, and he was wondering if he would ever be able to cure himself of the self-made habit. He was also bemoaning the fact that his constant snorting was turning his nose bright red.

'Sounds great to me,' the hardware man said. 'Government give you any trouble in the licensing?'

Mahoney snorted a particularly snotty blast. 'Licenses? Government? What kind of fool you think I am? Clot, dealt with the damned government all my life. Do everything they can to wreck a farm, if you let them.'

There were angry mutters of agreement from the gathered farmers.

'Besides, I only got maybe thirty years or more in me. Time I got through those licensing butt bungs, I'd be long dead.'

The logic was ancient and irrefutable.

'What about shipping? They givin' you any trouble about that?'

'Well, I ain't shippin' just yet. Right now, I'm gettin' to know people, show off my plants. Why? You think I'll have any trouble in these parts?'

The hardware man exploded. 'Clottin' right! I got orders stacked all over the place. Cash orders. And with all this business of the Tahn going on, I'm about ready to go broke.'

He went into a long litany of complaints, which were added to and spiced up by comments from a slowly growing crowd with Mahoney at its center.

They told him about the sneaky, lazy Tahn, about the attacks on their property and their counterattacks. They told him about an economy that was almost paralyzed, and about incompetent cops and worse than incompetent Imperial garrison troops.

They went on about their suspicions: mysterious lights over Tahn enclaves, probable stockpiling of weapons, and professional Tahn troops slipping in to reinforce their filthy brethren.

The Imperial settlers, of course, were blameless. They had tried so hard to bear up under the burden. Everyone in the bar had made a personal sacrifice, hadn't he? Why, they had even dipped deep into their bank accounts to buy weapons to protect their farms and Imperial property.

Through it all, Mahoney allowed his face to become grimmer and grimmer in agreement. He rarely interrupted, except to snort or to buy another round of drinks.

By the time the night was over, he could have filled an entire fiche with his report.

He was also beginning to realize that the situation with the Mercury Corps was even worse than he had told the Emperor. The intelligence he was getting was at complete odds with what the Emperor had been hearing. In the Fringe Worlds, the corps had been pierced, corrupted, and broken.

It was enough to swear a good Irishman off drink.

Chapter Sixteen

'. . . so then we told this Imperial piece of drakh to put his back taxes where the star don't shine and get the clot out of our county.'

The big Tahn woman howled with laughter at Mahoney's story and pounded him on the back.

'Only way to deal with them,' she said. She gave a huge beery belch and peered out into the night. 'Turn here.'

Mahoney did as directed, and soon he was topping a rise. Just before them was the glow of the Tahn communal farm that his companion was headwoman of. Mahoney had met her at a local watering hole. Frehda was a big middle-aged woman who had spent most of her years managing the fortunes of a large Tahn enclave. Over vast quantities of beer, chased by a dozen bottles of his cider, they had become fast friends.

Mahoney had readily accepted her invitation to spend a few days at her enclave 'to see how we do things in these parts.' She assured him it would be an education. Mahoney had other reasons to believe her; little prickles of rumor and bar talk had led him in this direction.

Even at night the enclave was impressive. As they approached, Mahoney could see many large steel barracks surrounded by what seemed to be a fairly sophisticated security system and nasty razor-wire fencing. As he approached the gated main entrance, the figures of two heavily armed Tahn farmers loomed out.

Frehda shouted a few friendly obscenities at them by way of greeting.

'Who's the fella, boss?' one of them wanted to know.

'Salesman pal,' Frehda said. 'Good man. Drink anybody 'cept maybe me under the table.'

There were chuckles at this. Mahoney gathered that alcohol consumption was just one of many things Frehda was noted for. He had secretly used up nearly half of his ready supply of sobriety pills during the evening to keep even vaguely straight.

'I'll put him up at my place,' Frehda went on. 'Maybe one of you can give him a look-see around in the ayem.'

'Anything in particular you wanna see, mister?' one of the Tahn asked. Mahoney caught an undertone of suspicion. Frehda might be the boss lady, but she was way too drunk for someone to take her at her word on a stranger.

'Got any pigs?' he asked.

''Course we got pigs. What do you think we are, share-croppers?'

Mahoney snorted. 'No,' he said. 'Just that I got a soft spot for pigs. Been studying all my life. I could write volumes on pigs.'

'He can talk them, too,' Frehda said. 'Just about wore my ear out till I got him drunk enough to go on to somethin' else.'

The two Tahn guards relaxed. They chuckled among themselves and waved the gravcar through.

*

Mahoney came awake to blinding sunlight piercing the barred windows of his room, and loud, barked shouts. His head was thumping from last night's excess – he hadn't been able to get away from bending elbows with Frehda for hours.

There were more shouts. They had a peculiar quality to them. Like commands? Giving an automatic snort that burned his delicate nose membranes, Mahoney got out of his cot and started dressing. Let us see, Ian, what we can see.

Mahoney blinked out of Frehda's portion of the barracks. And the first thing he noted surprised even him.

Several men were putting twenty or more teenage Tahn through what seemed to be a very militarylike obstacle course. Ho, ho, Mahoney, me lad. Ho, clotting ho. He wandered over by one of the men and watched the kids go at it. Whenever any of them slowed or got tangled in an obstacle, there were immediate shouts of derision from the adults.

'Whatcha got here, friend?'

The man looked at him. 'Oh, you the salesman guy staying with Frehda, right?'

Mahoney snorted an affirmative.

'To answer your question, mister, we're just givin' the kids a little physical training. Whittle off some of the baby fat.'

Riiight, Mahoney thought.

'Good idea,' Mahoney said. 'Kids these days are lazy little devils. Gotta keep the boot up.'

He looked over at a coiled barbed-wire fence that a large farm boy was vaulting over.

'What's that contraption?' he asked.

'Oh, that's a hedgehog. About the same size as all the fencing around here.'

Mahoney had to grab himself by the throat to keep from reacting in some obvious way. So, you call it a hedgehog, do you, mate? Mahoney *knew* that the man standing next to him was no poor Tahn farmhand. He was a professional soldier sent out by the Tahn military to train young meat for the slaughter to come.

'Must be hell on the britches,' Mahoney joked, rubbing an imaginary sore spot on his behind.

The man thought this was pretty funny. 'Least you can sew up pants,' he said.

Mahoney spent the next two days lazily touring the farm – which was well off even by Imperial settler standards – making casual talk and casual friends and wolfing down the enormous meals the communal farm kitchen shoveled out.

Except for that first obvious soldier he had met and possibly one or two others, everyone seemed to be exactly as he appeared. What he had here were several hundred hardworking Tahn farmers who had gotten tired of the poverty imposed on them by the Imperial majority. So they had pooled their talent and funds to make a life of it.

From some of the stories he heard over the table, their success had not set well with the local gentry and rich Imperial farmers. There had been many attacks, some of them quite nasty.

Mahoney could understand why the farmers had fallen so easily for the infiltrating soldier boys. Now they could protect themselves. Also, from their comments, Mahoney realized that they saw this as only a temporary solution. Sooner or later, unless events intervened, the commune would fall. Mahoney got the idea that the Tahn soldiers were promising an eventual rescue by their empire system. Tahn warships would someday come screaming in over the horizon, and the settlers would all rise up in support of their genetic friends of the cradle.

Mahoney knew from experience that in reality all those kids and their fathers and mothers would be used as a bloody shield for the pros.

Hadn't he done it himself back in his Mantis Section days?

The farmers had given him free rein. He was allowed to go anywhere he wanted – except one place. Every time he had come near it, he had been edged away. About half a klick from the pig creches was a large, fairly modern – for the Fringe Worlds – grain silo. It was prefab, but still, it was an expensive thing to import and then to build.

At first Mahoney expressed interest in it, just to keep up his role. Actually he didn't give a clot.

'Oh, that,' his guide had said. 'Just a silo. You seen better. Always clottin' up on us one way or the other. You ain't interested in that. Now, let me show you the incubators.

'Bet you never seen so many chicks crackin' shells in your life.'

This was not a chick ranch. The birds were used only for local consumption. Therefore, the incubator was far from a machine to delight a tired old farmer's eyes.

So, what was with the silo? Mahoney casually brought it up. And each time he was guided away. Ian, he told himself, it's time you risked your sweet Irish ass.

*

He slipped out the last night of his stay, ghosting across the farm past the obstacle run and then the grunts of the pigs. It was easy. He picked up one of the soldiers snoring away in his hidey-hole on the path to the silo. Rotten discipline.

He circled the position, and soon he was inside the silo. A primitive sniffer was the only security, and he quickly bypassed it before he entered.

The silo was suspiciously empty. There were only a few tons of grain. Considering the bulging storage areas spotted about the farm, the space was much needed.

A Mantis rookie could have found the arms cache in a few minutes. Mahoney caught it almost as soon as he peeped his flash-beam around the inside of the structure.

In one corner was a large, busted-down bailer. One doesn't bail grain, and this was hardly the place to put a temporary mechanic's shop. The bailer was a rust bucket, except for the joint of one leg, which was shiny with lubricant. Mahoney gave a couple of test twists and pulls and then had to jump back as a section of the floor hissed aside.

Beneath the bailer was a room nearly the size of the silo floor. Carefully stacked in sealed crates were every kind of weapon that a soldier could need. About half of them were things that no farmer with the kind of training Mahoney guessed these people were getting could use. This stuff was for pros.

He caught the slight sound of a small rodent just behind him and to his left. Rodent? In a modern silo?

Mahoney back-flipped to his right as a hammer blow just grazed the side of his head. He half rolled to his left, then rolled to the right, hearing the chunk of something terribly heavy and sharp smash down.

As he came to his feet, he could sense a large blackness rushing at him. He fingertipped out a tiny bester stun grenade, hurled it, and then dropped to the floor, burying his head in his arms. His shoulders tensed for the blow, and then there was an almost X-ray flash through his hands.

It took Mahoney many shaky seconds to come up again. He woozily tried to figure out what had happened.

The bester grenade produced a time blast that erased very recent memory and time to come for some hours. As near as Mahoney could figure, he was missing only a few seconds.

He peeped his beam to the dark shape slumped near him. Oh, yes. It was the soldier who had been sleeping on duty. There must be some other alarm system besides the one he had dismantled.

Mahoney found it and disarmed it. He dragged his peacefully snoring opponent out and tucked him back into his bushes where he belonged. Then he rearmed both systems and slid back to his room.

He made loud, cheery good-byes to his new Tahn friends the next day, passing out presents, jokes, and kisses where kisses belonged.

Mahoney gave the snoozing sentry a few extra bottles of cider, and the man beamed broadly at him, clapped him on the back, and told him to be sure to stop by if he was ever in the area again.

The invitation was sincere.

Chapter Seventeen

'I could tell you how to solve your Tahn problem,' the farmer said, 'and we don't need the damned government to do it!'

The farmer was a short man with an expansive waistline and soft hands. His spread was many times larger than the Tahn communal farm Mahoney had recently visited, and from what Ian could gather, the Imperial settler spent his days tapping in figures on his computer or huddled with his bankers.

Mahoney beetled his brows in deep interest. He was seated at the dinner table with the man, his tubby pink-cheeked wife, and their large brood of obnoxious children. One of the snotty so-and-sos was trying to get his attention, tapping his sleeve with a spoon dripping with gravy.

'A moment, son,' Mahoney soothed, 'while I hear what your father has to say.' Little clot, he thought, I'll wring your bloody neck if you touch me with that thing again.

'Go on,' he told the farmer. 'This is a subject that concerns all of us.'

'Clottin' right,' the farmer said. 'The Tahn are lower than drakh and bleeding us all.'

'Please, dear,' his wife admonished. 'The children.' She turned to Mahoney. 'I hope you'll forgive my husband's language.'

Mahoney gave an understanding smile. 'I've heard worse.'

The woman giggled back. 'So have I. Still . . . If you had to *live* with these Tahn, you'd understand why my husband becomes so heated. They really are—' She leaned closer to Mahoney to make her point. '*Different*, you know.'

'I can imagine,' Mahoney said. He settled back with their good after-dinner port to listen to the farmer expand on his subject. It was enough to chill the blood of a tyrant.

Mahoney was absolutely sure what was going to be in his report to the Eternal Emperor. But he had decidedly mixed feelings about it. Like, who were the heroes and who were the villains?

'Yes, please,' he said. 'Another splash of port would go down just fine.'

Chapter Eighteen

Imperial Flight School, Stage or Phase Two, began in deep space. Sten and the others in his class, now referred to as 'mister,' regardless of sex or whether they were even human, started with pressurized spitkits – space taxis.

Learn . . . learn in your guts . . . which direction to apply force. Understand when to brake. Learn how to calculate a basic orbit from point A to (radar-seen) point B. Then do it again.

Once they were competent, the next step put them in actual ships. More time passed as they learned, still in space, the use of the secondary – Yukawa – drive.

As they grew proficient, the navigational bashing intensified. A ship under AM2 drive, of course, could hardly find its 'course' under any but mathematical conditions.

Sten, in spite of his worries about calculating, was getting by.

He still needed occasional offshift coaching from Bishop, but things were coming more easily.

One thing that helped, Sten thought, was that he was hardly a raw recruit. During his time in Mantis, he had gone through a great deal of real combat, from mass landings to solo insertions to ship-to-ship combat. There was a large mental file based on personal experience backlog that made it easier for Sten to translate raw numbers into a clotting great asteroid that he would rather not intersect orbits with.

On the other hand, Sten's experience also made it hard for him to keep his mouth shut on occasion.

Phase Two of flight training differed from Phase One in that the IPs seemed as if they wanted all the students to graduate. But it was far from being perfect.

Too much of the tactics was theoretical, taught by IPs who had never flown combat in their lives or who were reservists called back as part of mobilization.

A lot of what was taught, Sten knew from experience, was a great way to suicide. He wondered about the teachings he didn't have a reference point on – were they equally fallacious?

It was a great subject for BS. But only Bishop and he could really debate the point; with the others it quickly became a great excuse to slander whichever IP was on the 'Most Hated' list for the week.

Training progressed. All the students were rated as at least acceptable in deep space.

Then the hard part started: landings, takeoffs, maneuvers on worlds with various atmospheres, weather, and gravitation. Thus far training had washed out only a dozen cadets and killed just three.

But then it got dangerous.

Lotor had one bad habit – and it killed him.

A somewhat talented pilot, he stood above midpoint in the class standings. His failing, Sten learned later, was not uncommon.

Lotor felt that a flight was over and done with when he had his ship within close proximity of its landing situation. Sh'aarl't had told him repeatedly the old cliché that no flight is complete until one is sitting at the bar on one's second round.

Lotor's oversight couldn't be considered very dangerous in a time when antigravity exisited. He probably could have flown privately or even commercially through several lifetimes without problems.

The Empire trained for emergencies, however.

Situation: A combat team was to be inserted on a near-vacuum world. The ground was silicate dust pooled as much as twenty meters deep. Sharp boulders knifed out of the dust bowls.

Requirement: The combat team had to be inserted without discovery; a landing on Yukawa drive would stir up enough dust to produce a huge cloud that would hang for hours and surely give the team away. Also, the ship had to be landed in such a manner as to leave no lasting imprint in the dust.

Solution: Hang the ship vertically about fifty meters above the surface. Cut Yukawa drive and back down on the McLean generators. Hold centimeters above the surface long enough for the mythical combat team to unload, then take off.

The IP gave the situation to Lotor, who analyzed it and found the correct solution.

The two of them were in a Connors-class delta-winged light assault ship. Flight training not only taught emergency situations but, very correctly, sometimes used unsuitable ships. Sten agreed with that – he'd spent enough time in combat to know that when one desperately needed a wrench, sometimes a pair of pliers would have to make do.

But the wide wings were the final nail.

Lotor nosed up and reduced Yukawa drive. The ship dropped a meter or so, and he caught it on the McLean generators. He slowly reduced power, and the ship smoothed toward the dust below.

The trap of an antigravity screen, of course, is that 'down' is toward the generator and bears no relationship to where 'real' vertical should be.

The ship was three meters high and, to Lotor's senses, descending quite vertically. Close enough, he must have decided, and he slid the generator pots to zero.

The ship dropped a meter, and one wing hit a protruding boulder. The ship toppled.

According to the remote flight recorder, at that moment the IP hit the McLean controls at the same instant that Lotor figured out that something was very wrong.

Lotor kicked in the Yukawa drive. By the time he had power, the ship had already fallen to near horizontal. The blast of power, coupled with the McLean push, pinwheeled the ship.

Cycloning dust hid most of the end. All that the cameras recorded was a possible red blast that would have been produced as the cabin opened like a tin and the ship's atmosphere exploded.

It took most of the planet day for the dust to subside. Rescue crews felt their way in, looking for the bodies. Neither the corpse of Lotor nor the IP was ever recovered.

Sten, Sh'aarl't, and Bishop held their own wake and attempted to sample all the beers that Lotor had not gotten around to trying before his death.

Chapter Nineteen

Others in the class were killed, some stupidly, some unavoidably. The survivors learned what Sten already knew: No amount of mourning would revive them. Life – and flight school – goes on.

The barracks at Imperial Flight Training were not as luxurious as the psychologically booby-trapped ones in Phase One. But passes were available, and the pressure was lightened enough for cadets to have some time for consciousness alteration – and for talk.

A favorite topic was What Happens Next. Sten's classmates were fascinated with the topic. Each individual was assuming, of course, that he would successfully get his pilot's wings.

They were especially interested in What Happens Next for Sten. Most of the cadets were either new to the service or rankers – they would be commissioned, on graduation, as either warrant officers or lieutenants. Sten was one of the few who was not only already an officer but a medium-high-ranking one. The topic then became what would the navy do with an ex-army type with rank.

'Our Sten is in trouble,' Sh'aarl't opined. 'A commander should command at least a destroyer. But a destroyer skipper must be a highly skilled flier. Not a chance for our Sten.'

Sten, instead of replying, took one of Sh'aarl't's fangs in hand and used it as a pry top for his next beer.

'It's ambition,' Bishop put in. 'Captain Sten heard somewhere that admirals get better jobs on retirement than busted-up crunchies, which was all the future he could see. So he switched.

'Too bad, Commander. I can see you now. You'll be the only flight-qualified base nursery officer in the Empire.'

Sten blew foam. 'Keep talking, you two. I always believe junior officers should have a chance to speak for themselves.

'Just remember . . . on graduation day, I want to see those salutes snap! With all eight legs!'

Sten discovered he had an ability he did not even know existed, although he had come to realize that Ida, the Mantis Section's pilot, must have had a great deal of it. The ability might be described as as mechanical spatial awareness. The same unconscious perceptions that kept Sten from banging into tables as he walked extended to the ships he was learning to fly. Somehow he 'felt' where the ship's nose was, and how far to either side the airfoils, if any, extended.

Sten never scraped the sides of an entry port on launch or landing. But there was the day that he learned his new ability had definite limits.

The class had just begun flying heavy assault transports, the huge assemblages that carried the cone-and-capsule launchers used in a planetary attack. Aesthetically, the transport looked like a merchantman with terminal bloats. Sten hated the brute. The situation wasn't improved by the fact that the control room of the ship was buried in the transport's midsection. But Sten hid his dislike and wallowed the barge around obediently.

At the end of the day the students were ordered to dock their ships. The maneuver was very simple: lift the ship on antigrav, reverse the Yukawa drive, and move the transport into its equally monstrous hangar. There were more than adequate rear-vision screens, and a robot followme sat on tracks to mark the center of the hangar.

But somehow Sten lost his bearings – and the Empire lost a hangar.

Very slowly and majestically the transport ground into one hangar wall. Equally majestically, the hangar roof crumpled on top of the ship.

There was no damage to the heavily armored transport. But Sten had to sit for six hours while they cleared the rubble off the ship, listening to a long dissertation from the instructor pilot about his flying abilities. And his fellow trainees made sure it was a very long time before Sten was allowed to forget.

Chapter Twenty

Sten loved the brutal little tacships. He was in the distinct minority.

The tacships, which varied from single- to twenty-man crews were multiple-mission craft, used for short-range scouting, lightning single-strike attacks, ground strikes, and, in the event of a major action, as the fleet's first wave of skirmishers – much the same missions that Sten the soldier was most comfortable with.

That did not logically justify liking them. They were over-powered, highly maneuverable – to the point of being skittish – weapons platforms.

A ship may be designed with many things in mind, but eventually compromises must be made. Since no compromises were made for speed/maneuvering/hitting, that also meant that comfort and armor were nonexistent in a tacship.

Sten loved bringing a ship in-atmosphere, hands and feet dancing on the control as he went from AM2 to Yukawa, bringing the ship out of its howling dive close enough to the surface to experience ground-rush, nap-of-the-earth flying under electronic horizons. He loved being able to hang in space and slowly maneuver in on a hulking battleship without being observed, to touch the LAUNCH button and see the battlewagon 'explode' on his screen as the simulator recorded and translated the mock attack into 'experience.' He delighted in being able to tuck a tacship into almost any shelter, hiding from a flight of searching destroyers.

His classmates thought that while all this was fun, it was also a way to guarantee a very short, if possibly glorious, military career.

'Whyinhell do you think I got into flight school anyway?' Bishop told Sten. 'About the third landing I made with the Guard I figured out those bastards were trying to kill me. And I mean the ones on *my* side. You're a slow study, Commander. No wonder they made you a clottin' officer.'

Sten, however, may have loved the tacships too well. A few weeks before graduation, he was interviewed by the school's commandant and half a dozen of the senior instructors. Halfway through the interview, Sten got the idea that they were interested in Sten becoming an instructor.

Sten turned green. He wanted a rear echelon job like he wanted a genital transplant. And being an IP was too damned dangerous, between the reservists, the archaic, and the inexperienced. But it did not appear as if Sten would be consulted.

For once Sh'aarl't and Bishop honestly commiserated with Sten instead of harassing him. Being an IP was a fate – not worse than death but pretty similar.

Sten's fears were correct. He had been selected to remain at Flight Training School as an instructor. Orders had even been cut at naval personnel.

But somehow those orders were canceled before they reached Sten. Other, quite specific orders were dictated – from, as the covering fax to the school's commandant said, 'highest levels.'

The commandant protested – until someone advised him that those 'highest levels' were on Prime World itself!

The biggest difference between the army and the navy, Sten thought, was that the navy was a lot more polite.

Army orders bluntly grabbed a crunchie and told him where to be and what to do and when to do it. Or else.

Naval orders, on the other hand . . .

You, Commander Sten, are requested and ordered, at the pleasure of the Eternal Emperor, to take charge of Tac-Div Y47L, now being commissioned at the Imperial Port of Soward.

You are further requested and ordered to proceed with TacDiv Y47L for duties which shall be assigned to you in and around the Caltor System.

You will report to and serve under Fleet Admiral X. R. van Doorman, 23rd Fleet.

More detailed instructions will be provided you at a later date.

Saved. Saved by the God of Many Names.

Sten paused only long enough to find out that the Caltor System was part of the Fringe Worlds, which would put him very close to the Tahn and where the action would start, before he whooped in joy and went looking for his friends.

He was going to kiss Sh'aarl't.

Hell, he felt good enough to kiss Bishop.

Graduation from Phase Two was very different from the last day in Selection.

The graduates threw the chief IP into the school's fountain. When the school commandant protested mildly, they threw him in as well.

The two elderly officers sat in the armpit-deep purple-dyed water and watched the cavorting around them. Finally the commandant turned to his chief.

'You would think, after all these years, that they could find *something* more original to do than just pitch us here again.'

The chief IP was busily wringing out his hat and didn't answer.

Sh'aarl't, Bishop, and Sten bade leaky farewells, vowing to write, to get together once a year, and all the rest of the bushwa service people promise and never do.

Sh'aarl't was still awaiting orders. Bishop's orders were exactly what he wanted – pushing a large, unarmed transport around the sky from one unknown and therefore peaceful system to another.

Sten wondered if he would ever see either of them again.

Chapter Twenty-One

There was no pomp and there was carefully no ceremony when Lady Atago transferred her command from the battleship *Forez* to the infinitely smaller *Zhenya*.

Admiral Deska had spent a good portion of his military career studying his superior. She despised the frills and displays of military recognition. All that she required was that one do exactly as she indicated without hesitation. She became very thoughtful about any icing upon that requirement.

Despite their size, the *Zhenya* and her sisterships were a major tech miracle for the Tahn. The design and development of the ships would have cost even the Imperial naval R&D staff a good percentage of its budget.

The *Zhenya* was intended for mine warfare of the most sophisticated kind, a type of combat that the Imperial Navy had given little attention.

It had been a very long time since the Empire had fought a war with an equal. Even the brutal Mueller Wars were, ultimately, a limited uprising. Mines were used in positional warfare to deny passage to the enemy or to provide stationary security for one's own positions. They could also be laid to interdict the enemy's own ship lanes. Mines simply hadn't seemed relevant to the navy strategists.

The other reason for the navy's lack of interest in mine warfare was its unromantic nature. A mine was a heavy clunk of metal that just sat there until something made it go bang, generally long after the minelayer had departed. Mine experts didn't wear long white scarves or get many hero medals, even though mines, in space, on land, or in water, were one of the most deadly and cost - efficient ways of destroying the enemy.

The Tahn were less interested in glamour than in any and every method of winning a war. The *Zhenya* was one of the keys to their future.

Sophisticated space mines, of a kind never seen before, could be laid with impossible speed by the *Zhenya*. Each mine was basically an atomic torpedo that was immediately alerted to any ship in its vicinity. A 'friendly' ship would be transmitting on its Identification – Friend or Foe com line, and the mine would read the code and ignore that ship. An enemy ship or one not transmitting the current code to the mine would find a very different reaction. The mine – and any other mines within range – would activate and home on the enemy ship. With thousands of mines in any one field, even the most heavily armed Imperial battleship would be doomed.

The Tahn had also solved another problem. Space warfare, even one with established battle lines, was very mobile and its conditions changed rapidly. Retreating or attacking through one's own minefield could be lethal, even if the mine had identified the oncoming ship as friendly. It still was a large chunk of debris to encounter at speed. And if battle conditions changed, the minefield might

have to be abandoned – it took a lot of time and caution to sweep
a field and then re-lay it.

The *Zhenya* could retrieve and redeploy mines almost as fast as
it could lay them. It was an interesting way to be able to create,
define, or modify the field that the enemy would be forced to fight
on – in theory.

The *Zhenya*-class ships had yet to be proved. In the Tahn's haste
to add the ships to their combat fleets, there had been many failures
– all ending with the deaths of the entire crew.

Deska was confident that all the problems with the *Zhenya* and
her sister ships had been solved, but not so confident that he felt
safe risking the Lady Atago's life. He explained this to her, and she
listened with seeming interest. She thought for a moment.

'Assemble the crew,' she said finally.

Although it was a small crew, gathered together they filled the
Zhenya's mess hall. The Lady Atago waited quietly until everyone
was available and then began to speak.

'Our task today,' she said, 'is to prove the worth of the *Zhenya*.
On our success, much is dependent. You understand this, do you not?'

No one said a word. The audience barely breathed. But there
was a stiffening of attention.

'Previous trials have ended in disappointment,' she continued.
'This is why I am with you today. If you die, I die. It is therefore
required that every one of you perform his individual task to his
supreme abilities.'

She swept the room with her never changing eyes of absolute zero.

'It goes without saying,' she hammered home, 'that if there is a
failure today, it would be best for any of you not to be among the
few survivors.'

She dropped her eyes and flicked at a crumb left on the otherwise
spotless mess table in front of her. The crew was dismissed.

The drone tacship drove toward the *Zhenya* at full power. Between
the robot and the minelayer hung a cluster of the newly developed
mines. Lady Atago stood behind the mine control screen, watching
closely.

'Report.'

'All mines report incoming ship as friendly.'

'Change the recognition code.'

Sweat beaded one tech's forehead. It was at this point that the
accidents had occurred. All too often, when the IFF code was
changed, the mine either refused to attack a no-longer-friendly

– according to the recognition code – ship or launched on every ship within range, including the minelayer.

This time the control board barely had time to report the change in status and register that the mine was reporting an enemy ship before six mine-missiles launched.

The drone tacship fired back with antiship missiles. Two of the mines were exploded.

The third mine hit the robot and tore out its hull. Less than a second later, a score more were hunting the debris. The rest made note of the kill and returned to station.

'Did the mines show any response to the drone's electronic countermeasures?' Atago asked.

The tech consulted a nearby screen. 'Negative. All transmissions from the enemy were ignored once it had been identified.'

The Lady Atago turned her attention from the screen to Admiral Deska. She allowed one perfect eyebrow to raise a millimeter.

'You may inform the council, Admiral,' she said, 'that we will begin full production.'

A half hour later the flagship was once again the *Forez*.

Lady Atago went quietly back to her maps and battle plans.

Chapter Twenty-Two

Sten landed on Cavite, central world of the Caltor System, as a commander without a fleet.

Among the other shortcomings of the tacships was that their tiny supply holds limited their range. Their delicate engines also required far more frequent maintenance intervals than did most Imperial craft. So the four tacships that were to be Sten's command had been berthed in a freighter and now were somewhere between Soward and Cavite.

Sten made the long haul from Prime to Cavite as a liner passenger.

He spent the voyage going through pictures, sketches, abstracts, and envelope projections, as besotted with his new assignment as any first lover.

Part of the time he devoted to a quick but thorough study of what was going to be his base planet. Cavite was about two-thirds the size of Prime World and sparsely settled. There was little industry on Cavite – mostly it was an agriculture-based economy, with a little fishing and lumbering. The climate was also similar to Prime – fairly temperate, with a tendency to snow a bit more than on Prime.

The rest of the time Sten pored over details involving his ships. It did not matter that at present his command consisted only of four brand-new Bulkeley-class vessels and himself. He was to man his ship on arrival on Cavite.

Under separate covers, a fax had gone to Admiral van Doorman, requesting full cooperation.

Sten had arrived on Soward just before his four ships were 'launched.' There wasn't a great deal of ceremony – the hull builder had signed the ships over to a secondary yard, a transporter gantry had picked up the ships, complete less armament, electronics, controls, and crew compartment, and had lugged them across the huge plant.

Incomplete as they were, Sten was in love the first time he had seen the sleek alloy needles sitting on their chocks. To him, the entry in the new *Jane's* update fiche was poetry:

6406.795 TACTICAL ASSAULT CRAFT

Construction of a new class of tactical ship by the Empire has been rumored, but as this cannot be confirmed at present, this entry must be considered tentative. Intelligence suggests that these ships are designed to replace and upgrade several current classes now considered obsolescent.

It has been suggested that these ships will bear the generic class of BULKELEY. Development of this class is considered to be under construction, with no information as to the number of ships contracted for, commissioning dates, or deployment dates. To repeat: All information must be considered quite tentative.

Sten figured that the editor of *Jane's* was practicing the age-old CYA, since the rest of the data was entirely too clotting accurate for his comfort:

CHARACTERISTICS:
TYPE: Fleet patrol craft
LENGTH: 90 meters est. (actually 97 meters)
D: Approx. 1400 fl.
CREW: Unknown
ARMAMENT: Unknown, but theorized to be far heavier than any other ships in this category.

The rest of the entry was a long string of unknowns. Sten could have filled in the details.

Each ship carried a crew of twelve: three officers – CO, weapons/XO, engineering – and nine enlisted men.

And they *were* heavily armed.

For close-in fighting, there were two chainguns. Medium-range combat would be handled by eight launchers firing Goblin VI missiles, now upgraded with better 'brains' and a 10-kt capacity. There were three Goblins for each launcher.

For defense there was a limited countermissile capability – five Fox-class missiles – but a very elaborate electronic countermeasure suite.

Bulkeley ships were intended either to sneak in unnoticed or to cut and run if hit. But the Bulkeley class craft were designed as ship killers.

Main armament was the Kali – a heavy, 60-megaton missile that was almost twenty meters long. Packed inside the missile's bulbous skin was a computer nearly as smart as a ship's and an exotic ECM setup. The missile was launched in a tube that extended down the ship's axis. Three backup missiles were racked around the launch tube.

Crew space, given all this artillery and the monstrous engines, was laughable. The captain's cabin was about the size of a wall closet, with pull-down desk and bunk. It was the most private compartment on the ship, actually having a draw curtain to separate the CO from the rest of the men. The other two officers bunked together, in a cabin exactly the size of the captain's. The crew bunks were ranked on either side of the ship's largest compartment, which doubled as rec room, mess hall, and kitchen.

The only cat that could have been swung inside the ship would have been a Manx – a Manx kitten.

Big deal. If Sten had wanted luxury, he would have opted for Bishop's plan and flown BUCs.

Chapter Twenty-Three

Standard operating procedure: When an officer arrives at his new duty station, he reports to his new commanding officer.

In the Guard this had meant that one was to show up at the unit's orderly room in semi-dress uniform. Officer and his new fearless leader would size each other up; the newcomer would be given his new responsibilities and whatever trick tips the old man chose to pass on and set in motion.

The navy, Sten had learned, was slightly more formal.

The 'invitation' to meet Admiral van Doorman had been hand delivered. And was printed. On real paper. That, Sten figured, meant full-dress uniform. Whites. Gloves. Clot, even a haircut.

By scurrying and bribing, Sten had gotten the batman assigned to his temporary bachelor officer's quarters to electrostat-press his uniform and borrow or steal a pair of white gloves from someone. The haircut was easy, since Sten kept his hair about two centimeters from shaven.

The card requested the pleasure of his company at 1400 hours. Sten gave himself an extra hour for the civilian grav-car to wind through the packed streets of Cavite City. Even then, he arrived at the main entrance to the naval base with only twenty minutes to spare.

His mouth dropped when the sentry at the gate checked only Sten's ID, then in a bored manner waved the gravcar forward.

Nice, Sten thought. Here we are on the edge of everything, and the taxi drivers can go anywhere they want. Great security.

He paid the driver at dockside, got out, and then goggled.

The flagship of 23rd Fleet was the Imperial Cruiser *Swampscott*. Sten had looked the ship up and found out that it had been built nearly seventy-five years previously; it was periodically upgraded instead of being scrapped. The description gave no inkling of just how awesome the *Swampscott* had become – awesome in the sense of atrocious.

The cruiser evidently had been built to the then limits of hull design, power, and armament. Upgrading had started by cutting the ship in half and adding another 500 meters to the midsection. The next stage had added bulges to the hull.

After that, the redesigners must have been desperate to meet the additions, since the *Swampscott* could now be described as a chubby cruiser that had run, very hard, into a solid object without destruction.

As a grand finale, there were twin structures atop the hull, structures that would be familiar to any Chinese Emperor of the T'ang Dynasty of ancient Earth.

Since the *Swampscott* had never fought a war, these excrescences did not matter. The ship, polished until it glowed, was used for ceremonial show-the-flag visits. It would settle down in-atmosphere in as stately a manner as any dowager queen going down steps in a ball gown. If a planetary assault had ever been required, the *Swampscott* would either have spun out of control or wallowed uncontrollably. In a wind tunnel, a model of the *Swampscott* might have been described as having all the aerodynamics of a chandelier.

Sten recovered, checked the time, and hurried into the lift tube.

Exiting, he saw not one but four full-dress sentries and one very bored, but very full-dressed, officer of the deck.

He saluted the nonexistent and unseen 'colors' – toward the stern – and the OOD, then gave the lieutenant a copy of the invitation and his ID card.

'Oh, Lord,' the lieutenant said. 'Commander, you made a real mistake.'

'Oh?'

'Yessir. Admiral van Doorman's headquarters are downtown.'

Downtown? What was that navalese for? 'Isn't this the flagship?'

'Yessir. But Admiral van Doorman prefers the Carlton Hotel. He says it gives him more room to think.'

Sten and the lieutenant looked at each other.

'Sir, you're going to be very late. Let me get a gravsled out. Admiral van Doorman's most insistent about punctuality.'

This was a great way to start a new assignment, Sten thought.

Admiral van Doorman may have insisted on punctuality, but it applied only to his subordinates.

Sten had arrived at the hotel in a sweaty panic, nearly twenty minutes late. He had been escorted to the lower of van Doorman's three hotel suites, reported to the snotty flag secretary at the desk, and been told to sit down.

And he waited.

He was not bored, however. Awful amazement would have been a better description of Sten's emotional state as he eavesdropped on the various conversations as officers came and went in the huge antechamber:

'Of course I'll try to explain to the admiral that anodizing takes a great deal of work to remove. But you know how he loves the shine of brass,' a fat staff officer said to a worried ship captain.

'Fine. We have a deal. You give me J'rak for the boxing, and I'll let you have my drum and bugle team.' The conversation was between two commanders.

'I do not care about that exercise, Lieutenant. You've already exceeded your training missile allocation for this quarter.'

'But sir, half my crew's brand-new, and I—'

'Lieutenant, I learned to follow orders. Isn't it time you learn the same?'

Real amazement came as two people spilled out of a lift tube. They were just beautiful.

The ship captain was young, dashing, tall, handsome, and blond-haired. His undress whites gloved his statuesque body and molded his muscles.

His companion, equally blond, wore game shorts.

They were laughing, enjoying the free life.

Sten hated their guts on sight.

Chattering away, the two sauntered past Sten, down a corridor. The woman suddenly made some excuse, stopped, put her foot upon a chair arm, and adjusted the fastener on her sports shoe. And her eyes very calmly itemized Sten. Then she laughed, took her companion's arm, and disappeared. She had a figure that made it nearly impossible not to stare after. So Sten stared.

'That's definitely off limits, Commander,' the flag secretary said.

Not that he cared, but Sten raised a questioning eyebrow.

'The lady is the admiral's daughter.'

Sten wanted to say something sarcastic, but he was saved by the buzzing of the annunciator. He was escorted into the admiral's office.

The term 'office' was a considerable understatement. The only chambers that Sten had seen more palatial were some of the ceremonial rooms in the Imperial palace. Always the cynic, he wondered if the suite had been furnished with van Doorman's private funds or if he had fiddled something.

Fleet Admiral Xavier Rijn van Doorman was equally spectacular. This was a man whose very presence, from his white coiffed mane to his unwavering eyes to his firm chin to his impressive chest, shouted command leadership. This was a leader men would follow into the very gates of hell. After ten minutes of conversation, Sten had a fairly decent idea that was where most of them would end up.

It could have been said about van Doorman, as it had been about another officer centuries earlier, that he never allowed an original thought to ruin his day.

But still, he was the very image of a leader: fit to address any parliament, soothe any worried politician, address any banquet, or show any banner – and totally incompetent to command a fleet that Sten knew might be only days from being the first line of defense in a war.

Van Doorman was a very polite man, and very skilled in the minefields of social inquisition. He must have scanned Sten's fiche before Sten had entered the room. Certainly he was most curious about Sten's previous assignment – at the Imperial palace itself, as CO of the Emperor's Gurkha bodyguard.

Van Doorman was proud that he had managed to attend several Empire Days and had once been presented to the Emperor himself as part of a mass awards ceremony.

'I'm sure, Commander,' van Doorman said, 'that you'll be able to bring us up to speed on the new social niceties. The Fringe Worlds are somewhat behind the times.'

'Sir, I'll try . . . but I didn't spend much time at ceremonial functions.'

'Ah, well. I'm sure my wife and daughter will help you realize you know more than you think.'

Clotting great. I am going to have to be polite to the whole family.i

'You'll find that duty out here is most interesting, Commander. Because of the climate, and the fact that all of us are so desperately far from home, we make allowances in the duty schedule.'

'Sir?'

'You will find that most of your duties can be accomplished in the first watches. Since I don't want my officers finding this station boring – and boredom does create work for idle hands – I make sure that qualified officers are available for those necessary diplomatic functions.'

'I'm not sure I understand.'

'Oh, there are balls . . . appearances on some of the minor worlds . . . we have our own sports teams that compete most successfully against the best our settlers can field. I also believe that all duty makes Jack a very dull officer. I approve of my officers taking long leaves – some of the native creatures are excellent for the hunt. We provide local support for anyone interested in these pursuits.'

'Uh . . . sir, since I've got brand-new ships, where am I going to find the time for those kinds of things?'

'I've received a request to provide as complete cooperation as possible to you. That goes without saying. I'll ensure that you have a few competent chiefs who'll keep everything Bristol fashion.'

Sten, at this point, should have expressed gratitude and agreement. But as always, his mouth followed its own discipline.

'Thank you, sir. But I'll still have to pass. I'm afraid I'll be too busy with the boats.'

Seeing van Doorman's expression ice up, Sten cursed himself.

Van Doorman picked up a fiche and dropped it into a viewer. 'Yes. The boats. I'll be quite frank, Commander. I have always been opposed to the theory of tactical ships.'

'Sir?'

'For a number of reasons. First, they are very costly to run. Second, it requires a very skilled officer and crew to operate them. These two conditions mean that men who should be serving on larger ships volunteer for these speedcraft. This is unfair to commanders of possibly less romantic craft, because men who should become mates and chiefs remain as ordinaries. It is also unfair to these volunteers, since they will not receive proper attention or promotion. Also, there is the issue of safety. There is no way I can be convinced that service on one of your, umm, mosquito boats could be as safe as a tour on the *Swampscott*.'

'I didn't know we joined the service to be safe and comfortable, sir.' Sten was angry.

And so, even though it showed only as a slight reddening around his distinguished temples, was van Doorman. 'We differ, Commander.' He stood. 'Thank you for taking the time to see me, Commander Sten. I've found this conversation most interesting.'

Interesting? Conversation? Sten got up and came to attention. 'A question, sir?'

'Certainly, young man.' Van Doorman's tone was solid ice.

'How will I go about crewing my ships, sir? I assume you have some SOP I should follow?'

'Thank you. All too many of you younger men lack an understanding of the social lubrication.

'You'll be permitted to advertise your needs in the fleet bulletin. Any officer or enlisted man who chooses to volunteer will be permitted – after concurrence from his division head and commanding officer, of course.'

Clot. Clot. Clot.

Sten saluted, did a perfect about-face, and went out.

Van Doorman's last, when translated, meant that Sten could recruit his little heart out. But what officer in his right mind would allow a competent underling to volunteer for the boats?

Sten knew he'd get the unfit, the troublemakers, and the square pegs. He desperately hoped that the 23rd Fleet had a whole lot of them.

Chapter Twenty-Four

Space is not black. Nor can spaceships creep along. Nevertheless, that was what Commander Lavonne visualized his ship, the Imperial Destroyer *San Jacinto*, doing as it moved into the Erebus System.

He was a spy, slithering slowly through the night.

The DesRon commander had detailed the *San Jacinto* for this mission. The navy prided itself on never volunteering for, but never rejecting, a mission, no matter how absurd or suicidal.

Officially, the assignment was not that out of the ordinary. Imperial destroyers were designed for scouting capabilities.

But only under wartime conditions. And not when, according to every bit of club poop that Lavonne had heard, every single specially designed spy ship that had entered the Tahn sectors disappeared tracelessly.

Orders, however, are orders.

Lavonne had spent some time planning his tactics before he plotted a course. This included shutting down every possible machine that could possibly be picked up by an enemy sensor – from air conditioning to the caffmachines in the mess. He theorized that the spy ships had been discovered because their course had originated from Imperial or Fringe worlds. So he'd selected a course that first sent the *San Jacinto* toward an arm of the Tahn Empire. The course then moved from the second point of origin farther into solidly Tahn-controlled clusters. His third course sent the destroyer back 'out,' closing with the Erebus System he had been directed to recon.

On a galactic and null-time scope, the *San Jacinto*'s course could be plotted as a hesitation forward.

For short periods of time the ship would enter AM2 drive. Then it would drop out and hold in place. During that holding, every normal sensor, plus the specially installed systems provided, was used to see if the *San Jacinto* might have been detected.

Lavonne knew that Imperial sensors were superior to anything the Tahn had. Since no Tahn ship had been detected by his screens, he felt he was still hidden in the shadows.

The *San Jacinto* hesitated toward the dying sun of Erebus.

And he found what he was looking for.

Input flooded. The system was a huge building yard and harbor. There were more Tahn ships in this one sector than intelligence estimates provided for the entire Tahn Empire.

Lavonne, at this point, should have closed down the sensors and scooted. He had far more data than any other infiltrating Imperial ship had gotten. Possibly, if he had fled, his ship could have survived.

Instead, Lavonne, hypnotized by what he was seeing, crept onward. After all, Imperial forces had a secret – AM2, the single power source for stardrive, provided only by the Empire, was modified before being sold to other systems. On the *San Jacinto*'s screens, Lavonne knew, any Tahn ship's drive would show purple.

Lavonne did not know that certain Tahn ships had their drive baffled. The power loss was more than compensated for by their indetectability.

So when the screens went red and every alarm went off, the *San Jacinto* was far too close.

Lavonne slammed into the control room as the GQ siren howled and read the situation instantly: To their 'right' flank, a minefield had been detected; ahead lay the central Erebus worlds; and coming in from the 'left,' at full drive, was a Tahn battleship, schooled by cruisers and destroyers.

At full power, Lavonne spun the *San Jacinto* into a new orbit. Their only chance was flight – and Lavonne's canniness. The emergency escape pattern led not out of the Erebus System toward the Fringe Worlds but rather toward the center of the Tahn Empire. Once he lost his pursuers, he could reset his course toward home.

Lavonne had a few minutes of hope – a new Imperial destroyer such as the *San Jacinto* should be able to outdistance any battleship or cruiser. The worst that Lavonne should face would be the Tahn destroyers.

Those few minutes ended as an analyst reported in properly flat tones that the battleship was outdistancing its own escorts and closing on the *San Jacinto*. Within five hours and some minutes, he continued, the battleship, of a previously unknown type, would be within combat range of the *San Jacinto*.

The battleship was the *Forez*. Admiral Deska paced the control room as his huge ship closed on the destroyer. He, too, was computing a time sequence.

Could the *Forez* come within range of the Imperial destroyer before it could conceivably escape?

If the Imperial spy ship survived, all of the elaborate Tahn plans, from improved ship design to construction to obvious strategy, would be blown.

He considered the ticking clock. There would be no problems. The Imperial ship was doomed.

At four hours and forty minutes, Commander Lavonne realized the inevitable.

There was one possible chance.

Lavonne ordered the ship out of AM2 drive, hoping that the Tahn battleship would sweep past. Their response was instantaneous.

Very well, then. Lavonne sent his ship directly at the *Forez*.

Sometimes the lapdog can take on the mastiff.

Lavonne ordered flares and secondary armaments fired at will. He hoped that the explosions, and whatever clutter his ECM apparatus could provide, might be some kind of smoke screen.

Lavonne knew that the *San Jacinto* was doomed. All he could hope was that his ship might inflict some damage on the huge Tahn battlewagon now filling the missile station's sights.

He was only light-seconds from coming into range when the *Forez* launched its main battery.

Six Tahn missiles intersected with the *San Jacinto*'s orbit as Lavonne's finger hovered over the red firing key.

And there was nothing remaining of the *San Jacinto* except a widening sextuplicate bubble of gas and radioactivity.

BOOK TWO

LET ALL DRAW

Chapter Twenty-Five

Throughout their history, the Tahn were always a bloody accident waiting to happen to anyone unfortunate enough to pass their way. It was a civilization born in disaster and nurtured by many battles.

Even the Eternal Emperor could barely remember the feud that had started it all. The origins of the Tahn lay in a huge civil war occurring in a cluster far from their present homelands. Two mighty forces lined up on opposing sides and went at it for a century and a half. The cluster in question was so peripheral to the Emperor that it was more than convenient for him to ignore the whole thing and let them settle it themselves.

Eventually, the people who were to become the Tahn suffered a final crushing defeat. The winners gave the survivors two choices: genocide or mass migration. The Tahn chose flight, an episode in their history that they never forgot. Cowardice, then, became their race's original sin. It was the first and last time the Tahn ever chose life over even certain death.

Almost the entire first wave of the massive migration was composed of warriors and their families. This made the Tahn a group of people unwelcome in any settled society they approached. No one was foolish enough to invite them to share his hearth. This was another factor in the Tahn racial memory. They considered themselves permanent outcasts, and from then on they would treat any stranger in kind.

The area they finally settled was one of the most unwanted sectors of the Empire. The Tahn put down roots in a desolate pocket surrounded by slightly richer neighbors and began to create their single-purpose society. Since it was military-based, it was no wonder that it was so sharply stratified: from the peasant class to the ruling military council was as distant as the farthest sun.

The greatest weakness of the Tahn, however, became their greatest strength. They prospered and expanded. Their neighbors became edgy as the Tahn neared the various borders. Most of them tried to negotiate. In each case, the Tahn used negotiation only as a tool to gain time. Then they would attack with no warning. They would throw their entire effort into the fray, ignoring casualties that would have given pause to almost any other being.

The Tahn fought continually for over three hundred years. In the end they had eliminated their neighbors and carved out an empire. It was no matter that they had lost nearly eighty percent of their population in doing so. They had rebuilt before, and they could do it again.

The Eternal Emperor was now facing a revitalized Tahn Empire many many times its original size. The explosive growth had created a host of problems for the Tahn: there were more dissidents than ever before, and frequent and bloody ousters from the Tahn High Council were increasingly common.

Unwittingly, the Emperor had solved this for them. The Tahn were once again united in purpose and in their bitter world view.

Chapter Twenty-Six

A few weeks later, Sten was no longer a commander without a fleet. His four Imperial tacships, the *Claggett, Gamble, Kelly*, and *Richards*, had been off-loaded and lifted into temporary fitting-out slips in the huge Cavite naval yard.

But he remained a commander without a crew. The aftermath of the interview with Admiral van Doorman had produced exactly what Sten anticipated – zero qualified volunteers showed up.

But the 23rd Fleet *did* have its share of malcontents and such.

After twenty interviews, Sten thought of the punch line from a long-forgotten joke of Alex's: 'Great Empire, not *that* shaggy.'

If Sten had been put in command of a destroyer, he might have been able to fit those applicant-losers into ship's divisions without problems. But not with four twelveman ships plus a skeleton maintenance staff.

Time was running short. On three occasions he'd had a 'friendly' visit from one of van Doorman's aides.

The man had sympathized with Sten over his problems and had promised he would do everything possible to keep things from van Doorman's attention – just a favor from one officer to another. Sten surmised that the aide couldn't get his gravcar back to van Doorman quickly enough to report how deep in drakh this young misfit was.

Or maybe Sten was getting paranoid. It was quite conceivable – all his time was spent on the tacships. When he remembered to eat, he opened a pack of something or other, heated it, and ate absentmindedly, his mind and fingers tracing circuitry, hydraulics, and plumbing across the ships' blueprint fiches.

This particular day he had climbed out of the greasy boiler suit he had been living in, pulled on a semidress uniform, and set out to do war with the 23rd Fleet's logistics division.

Every military has a table of organizations and equipment giving exactly how many people of what rank are authorized in each command and what items of equipment, from battleships to forks, are also allowable. The organization with too many or too much can get gigged just as badly as one that's short of gear.

Sten had found out that the 23rd Log authorized one day's basic load for ammunition and missiles – that being the amount of firepower a ship, in combat, would use up at maximum. Resupply in time of war for Sten's tacships would mean breaking off their patrol routine and returning to Cavite's enormous supply dumps.

Sten had tried to reason with the officer, starting with the logical point that the aborting of patrols when the weapons ran dry was hardly efficient and ending with the possibly illogical point that maybe, in time of war, those supply dumps might just get themselves bombed flat.

The officer didn't want to hear about patrol problems, shook his head in irritation at the mere mention of possible hostilities, and laughed aloud at the idea that Cavite couldn't destroy any attacker long before it had time to launch.

It was shaping up to be one of those days.

Sten set his sled down outside the security fence surrounding the fitting-out slips and absently returned the sentry's salute at the gate.

'Afternoon, Commander.' The sentry liked Sten. He and his fellow guards had a private pool as to when van Doorman would relieve the commander and send him back to Prime for reassignment. It would be a pity, but on the other hand, the sentry's guess was only a couple of days away, and drink money was far more important than the fate of any officer.

'Afternoon.'

'Sir, your weapons officer is already onboard.'

Sten was in motion. 'Troop, I want the guard out. Now.'

'But—'

'Move, boy. I don't *have* a weapons officer!'

The guard thumbed the silent alarm, and within moments there were five sentries around Sten, nervously fingering their loaded willyguns.

Sten took out the miniwillygun he always carried in the small of his back and started for the *Claggett*, the only ship with an entry port yawning.

A saboteur? Spy? Or just a nosy Parker? It didn't matter. Sten put his six men on either side of the port and went silently up the ladder.

He stopped, listening, just at the mouth of the ship's tiny lock. There were clatters, thumps, and mutters sounding from forward. Sten was about to wave the guards up after him when the mutter became distinguishable:

'C'mon, y' wee clottin' beastie. Dinnae be tellin't me Ah cannae launch twa a' once.'

Sten stuck his head out the port. 'Sorry, gentlemen. I screwed up. I guess I do have a weapons officer. I'll file a correction with the OOD.'

The puzzled sentries saluted, shrugged, and walked away.

Sten went forward.

'Mr Kilgour!' he snapped at the hatch into the control room, and had the pleasure of seeing a head bang in surprise into a computer screen. 'Don't you know how to report properly?'

Warrant Officer Alex Kilgour looked aggrieved, rubbing his forehead. 'Lad, Ah figured y'd be off playin't polo wi y'r admiral.'

Alex Kilgour was a stocky heavy-worlder from the planet of Edinburgh. He'd been Sten's team sergeant in Mantis Section, and then Sten had gotten him reassigned to the palace when Sten commanded the guard. Kilgour had made the mistake of falling in love and applying for a marriage certificate, and the Emperor had shipped him off to flight school months ahead of Sten, also commissioning him in warrant ranks.

Sten had no idea how or why Kilgour was on Cavite – but he was very clotting glad to see him, regardless.

'It wasn't much of a task t' be assigned to y'r squadron, young Sten,' Kilgour explained over two mugs of caff in the closet that passed for the *Claggett's* wardroom.

'First, Ah kept tabs, knowin't y'd be runnin' into braw problems y' c'd no handle. Then a word here, a charmin't smile there, an' whiff, Kilgour's on his way. But enow a' young love. Clottin' brief me, Commander. Where's th' bonny crew?'

Sten ran through the problems. Alex heard him out, then patted Sten's shoulder in sympathy, driving the deck plates down a few centimeters.

'Noo y' can relax, wi Kilgour here. Y'r problem, son, is y' dinnae be lookin't for volunteers in the right places.'

'Like hell! I've been recruiting everyplace but the cemeteries.'

'It'll no get s' bad we'll hae to assign the livin't dead, Commander. You hae nae worries now. Just trust me.'

Chapter Twenty-Seven

'Dinnae they be a fine bunch,' Kilgour said proudly.

Sten looked askance at the thirty-odd beings glowering at him, then behind him at the firmly sealed portals of the prison. 'How many murderers?'

'Nae one. Twa manslaughters wa' the best Ah could do. Th' rest—'

Sten cut Kilgour off. He would have time later to agonize over the fiches. Suddenly the prisoners in front of him appeared as – at least potentially – shining examples of sailorly virtue. The problem was that Sten, never adept at inspiring speeches, was trying to figure out what to say to these beings to convince them that they did not want to remain in the 23rd Fleet's safe, sane stockade.

Alex leaned closer to him to whisper. 'Ah could warm 'em up, if ya like, lad. Tell 'em a joke or three.'

'No jokes,' Sten said firmly.

Alex's response was immediate gloom.

'No even the one about the spotted snakes? Tha's perfect for a braw crew such as this.'

'You will *especially* avoid the one about the spotted snakes. Kilgour, there are laws about cruel and unusual punishment. And if you even dream spotted snakes, I'll have you keelhauled.'

Still glaring, Sten turned his attention to the task at hand. The glare must have had a great deal of heat behind it, because the men instantly stopped their shuffling and shifting.

Oh, well. At least he had their attention. Now all he had to do was some fancy convincing. Basic speechmaking – always talk to a crowd as if it were one person and choose one being in that crowd to address directly.

Sten picked out one man who looked a little less dirty, battered, and shifty than the others and walked up to him.

'My name's Sten. I'm commissioning four tacships. And I need a crew.'

'Y' comin' here, you're scrapin' the bottom,' another prisoner said. 'Sir.'

The prisoner spat on the ground. Sten stared at him. The man's eyes turned away. 'Sir,' he grunted reluctantly.

'No offense, sir.' That was the prisoner whom Sten had picked as the centerpiece. 'But what's in it for us?'

'You're out. Your records'll get reviewed. I can wipe your charge sheets if I want. If you work out.'

'What 'bout rank?' yet another prisoner asked.

'You qualify for a stripe, you'll get it.'

'What'll we be doing?'

'Running patrols. Out there.'

'Toward the Tahn?'

'As close as we can get.'

'Sounds like a clottin' great way to get dead.'

'It is that,' Sten agreed. 'Plus the quarters'll make your cells here look like mansions, the food would gag a garbage worm, and my officers'll be all over you like a dirty shipsuit. Oh, yeah. You'll be lucky to get liberty once a cycle. And if you do, it'll probably be on some planetoid where the biggest thing going is watching metal oxidize.'

'Doesn't sound like there's much in it.'

'Sure doesn't, sir.' This was a fourth prisoner. 'Can I ask you something? Personal?'

'GA.'

'Why are *you* doin' it? Tacship people are all volunteers. You lookin' for some kind of medal?'

'Clot medals,' Sten said honestly. Then he thought about what he was going to say. 'You could probably get my ass in a sling if you told anybody this – but I think that we're getting real close to a clottin' war.'

'With the Tahn.' Sten's target nodded.

'Uh huh. And I'd a lot rather be out there moving around when it happens than sitting on my butt here on Cavite. Or, come to think about it, sitting here in this pen.'

'I still think any of us'd be clottin' fools to volunteer.'

'Just what I'm looking for. Clotting fool volunteers. I'll be in the head screw's – sorry, warden's – office until 1600 if any of you feel foolish.'

To his astonishment, Sten got seventeen volunteers. He never realized that the final convincement was his slip of the tongue – only somebody who had been a jailbird or on the wrong side of the law would call the warden a screw.

Chapter Twenty-Eight

'How many generations has your family been warriors. Lieutenant Sekka?' Sten asked with some incredulity.

'For at least two hundred,' the man across from him said. 'But that was after the Sonko clan emigrated from Earth. Before that, we Mandingos, at least according to legend, had been fighting men for another hundred generations. That's not to say that all of us have been just warriors. We have been military scholars, diplomats, politicians . . . there was even one of us who was an actor. We do not often discuss him, even though he was reputedly excellent.' Sekka laughed. His baritone chortle was just as pleasing to the ear as the man's perfect voice.

Sten looked again at Sekka's fiche. It looked very good – there were just enough reprimands and cautions from superior officers to match the letters of merit and decorations.

'You like taking chances, don't you?'

'Not at all,' Sekka said. 'Any course of action should be calculated, and if the potential for disaster is less than that for success, the choice is obvious.'

Sten put the fiche back in its envelope and shoved a hand across the tiny folding desk. 'Lieutenant, welcome the hell aboard. You'll skipper the *Kelly*. Second ship on the left.'

Sekka came to attention, almost cracking his skull on the overhead. 'Thank you, sir. Two questions. Who are my other officers?'

'None, yet. You're the first one I've signed up.'

'Mmm. Crew?'

'You have four yardbirds and one eager innocent. Assign them as you wish.'

'Yessir.'

'Lieutenant Sekka? I have a question. How'd you hear about this posting?'

Sekka lifted an eyebrow. 'Why from the admiral's note in the current fleet proceedings, sir.'

Sten covered. 'Right. Not thinking. Thank you, Lieutenant. That's all. On your way out, would you ask Mr Kilgour if he would report to me at his convenience?'

'Kilgour. You didn't.'

'Ah did.'

'How?'

'The typsettin' plant o' th' shitepokes who run tha' lyin' publication hae na in th' way ae security.'

'So you blueboxed into it, and phonied the admiral's own column?'

'Is tha' nae aye harsh way t' put it?'

Alex, ever since his scam back on Hawkthorne and later with the prisoners, fancied himself quite the recruiter.

Sten changed the subject. 'Is there any way he could trace who did it?'

'Trace me, lad? Th' man wha' solved a conspiracy again' our own Emperor?'

Sten put his head in his hands. 'Mr. Kilgour. I know the navy is dry. But would there, by some odd chance . . .'

'By an odd chance, there is. Ah'll fetch the flask.'

Chapter Twenty-Nine

Alex liked some rain, like the nearly constant gray drizzle of his home world. But the tropical buckets that came down on Cavite tried his patience sorely. He counted unmarked alcoves down the narrow alleyway, found the correct one, and tapped on the barred door. From the inside his tapping probably sounded like a sledgehammer warming up.

'What is the word?' a synth-voice whispered.

'It's aye wet oot here, an Ah am lackit th' patience,' Alex complained. Not particularly angry, he stepped back and rammed a metal-shod boot-heel into the door.

The door split in half, and Alex pulled the two halves out of his way and entered.

He had time to notice that the inside of the brothel was quite nice, if one fancied red velvet and dark paintings, before the first guard came down the corridor at him. Alex batted him into the wall with one of the door halves. His mate came dashing toward Alex, was picked up, and went back up the corridor, in the air, somewhat faster than he had come down.

'Ah'm looki't for a Mister Willie Sutton,' he announced.

'Do you have a warrant?' the synth-voice asked.

'No.'

'Are you armed?'

'What kind of ae clot y' thinkit Ah am? A course.'

'Please keep your hands in plain sight. There are sensors covering you. Any electronic emission which is detected will be responded to. You will be constantly in the field of fire from automatically triggered weapons. Any hostile act will be responded to before you could complete such an action.'

Alex sort of wanted to test his reflexes against the robot guns, but he was trying to be peaceful.

'You will continue down to the end of the corridor, past the entrance to the establishment proper. At the end of the corridor, you will find stairs. Continue up them, and then down the hall to the second door. Enter that room and wait, while we determine whether a Willie Sutton is known to anyone on the premises.'

Alex followed instructions. As he walked past, he looked into the whorehouse's reception area, fell in love twice, smiled politely at those two women, but continued on.

Kilgour was on duty.

The room was more red velvet and more elderly paintings, dimly lit by glass-beaded lamps. The furniture was unusual, consisting of three or four wide, heavily braced hassocks. Kilgour stood with his back close to one wall and waited.

The door on the other side of the room opened.

'Would my thoughts be correct in assuming you are interested in applying for work as my bodyguard?'

'Willie Sutton' waddled into the room. It was a spindar, a large – two meters, choose any direction – scaled creature that looked like an oversize scaly pangolin with extra arms. Since spindars' own names were not pronounceable by the *Homo sapien* tongue, they generally took on a human name, a name prominent in whatever field the spindar chose to excel in.

Kilgour had no idea who Willie Sutton had been, but he was fairly sure that the human had not been a philanthropist.

'Warrant Officer Alex Kilgour,' he identified himself, not answering the question.

'You, then, are a deserter, as I am?'

'Na, Chief Sutton. But Ah hae consider't it.'

'You are not from the military police. Certainly not, from your grimace. How might my establishment and myself be of service to you? I am assuming, for the sake of argument, that you mean me no harm.'

'We want you to come back.'

The spindar chuffed and sat back on its tail. 'To the fleet? Hardly likely. During the years I served, I experienced enough courts-martial to find the experience irritatingly redundant.'

Sutton was telling the truth. There probably had been no supply specialist in the Imperial Navy who had been tried so many times, almost always on the same offense: misappropriation of imperial supplies and equipment.

There also probably had been no supply specialist who had been promoted back up from the ranks so many times, again almost always for the same accomplishment: Due to the outstanding performance and support of (insert rank at time) Sutton, (insert unit or ship name) accomplished its mission well within the assigned limits in an exemplary fashion.

'We need a thief,' Kilgour said.

The spindar chuffed twice more. Alex explained the problems that he and Sten faced.

The spindar, thinking, extruded claws from a forearm and raked part of the carpet beside him into shreds. Alex noted that the carpet was torn up in other parts of the room.

'What about the present charges that, shall we say, made it desirable for me to absent myself from my last duty station?'

Kilgour took two fiches from inside his shirt and handed them to Sutton. 'Tha first's y'r real service record. Tha original. Consider tha a present.'

The spindar scratched himself.

'Tha second's a new record, which, dinnae wish t' be't braggin't, Ah helped create. Couldnae be cleaner. You report back, and Ah'll hae tha in th' records in minutes.'

'An entirely fresh beginning,' the spindar marveled.

'M'boss say't there's a slight condition. If y' thinkit y' could be worryin't th' same scam on us, bad things c'd happen. About those, Ah'll say nae more.'

'The mechanics of pandering and prostitution,' the spindar said, almost to himself, 'have become most predictable. You humans have such a limited sexual imagination. Return to duty.' He chuffed. 'What a peculiar proposition.' Chuff. 'Tell your commander I shall provide an answer by this hour tomorrow.'

Chapter Thirty

Sten lolled back in his chair. His feet were stretched out lazily, crossed at the ankles, measuring the width of his desk. Inside he was tense, coiled, waiting for the hammer to fall. Outside he was doing his best to appear to be the cool, uninvolved navy commanding officer.

Personally, Sten thought he probably looked like a damned fool. All he needed right now was a knock of urgency on his door to spoil the entire persona.

The door *was* knocked upon. The raps were urgent; equally urgently, the door slammed open. Sten nearly compacted his knees getting his feet off the desk. Wildly, he thought for an instant which face he should present – bored CO indifference or calm CO concern. There was no stopaction camera there, or time to show the twists in his face as Alex and the spindar, Sutton, burst in.

'What seems to be the—' Sten started.

'Sir!' Sutton blurted. 'We've been taken!'

Sten reflexively glanced about. Was the *Gamble* being boarded? Was Cavite being invaded? The admiral's daughter violated? Taken? By whom? Sten skipped the why and where and assumed the now.

Mostly, what Sten was really worrying about was how he was going to untangle his feet and leap into position. Alex saved his behind by sort of explaining.

'Wha' Mr Sutton, here, is sayin't, Commander, is we been busted. I dinnae care t' guess wha for, but we been pushin't the motive a wee bit a' late.'

Sten buried a laugh. He had a pretty good idea what was going on. But Alex had been running on his luck a great deal. It was time for Sten to run it back. He placed a look of great concern on his face. He almost *harummphed*. With as much dignity as could be mustered in a three by two-meter space, Sten rose to his feet.

'What, gentlemen, could possibly be the problem?' His voice was very casual and cool.

'We're trying to tell you, sir,' Sutton said. 'We're being invaded by the cops!'

Sten allowed himself to be drawn out the door.

At dockside, drawn up before the *Gamble*, was a phalanx of Black Marias with five police gravsleds per side and two cops per vehicle.

'I told you, sir,' Sutton said. 'We've been taken.' He turned to Alex with accusation in his eyes and an angry quiver in his voice. 'You turned me in.'

'You? Who th' clottin' hell are you? Dinnae hae reference of grandeur, lad. They're bleedin' bustin' us all!' Alex gave Sten a glance. 'I dinnae suppose we hae good graces here. But, if w' do, Ah'd be serious usin' them now, Sten!'

Sten maintained his superiority of silence. Oddly enough, it did seem to have an effect on the two beings next to him. There was an agonizing moment, then a hiss from the lead sled in the column. The driver's door opened, and an enormous member of the Cavite police force unreeled himself out. There was another moment for brushing of tunic and flicking at stray hairs. Then measured boot-heels advanced toward Sten. There was an official piece of paper held in his thrust-out hand.

'A warrant, Ah'll ween,' Alex whispered.

Sten was silent.

The cop marched up to Sten, tossed him a smart salute, and handed him the document. Alex peered over at it, his face breaking into amazement.

'You dinnae?' he said.

'I did,' Sten said. 'Thank you, Constable Foss,' he said formally.

'With pleasure, sir,' Foss said. 'Now, begging your pardon, sir, but we're all on Ten-Seven. Can you process twenty recruits in less than an hour? Or should some of us come back?'

Alex finally came through. 'Twenty of you, aye? Come in, come in, said the cider to the fly.'

Moments later, he and Sutton were lining up the cops.

'So, thae be what it's come to, then?' he whispered to Sten. 'Recruitin' clottin' fuzz.'

Sten gave Alex his best and most practiced CO look. 'Ain't war hell?'

*

First Lieutenant Ned Estill was a miracle captured in amber. He looked sharp! Sounded sharp! Was sharp! And his resume was as crisp and clean as his dress whites. He snapped Sten a knife-edged salute, heels clicking like a shot.

'If that will be all, *sir*!'

Sten had rarely been confronted with such perfection. Estill was the kind of officer who made even a commander feel the grime around his collar. The comparison was especially pertinent because Sten and Alex were dressed in filthy engineer's coveralls. Estill's interview had been impromptu – an interruption of a greasegun's-eye tour of the ship. Sten had as much difficulty in dismissing the man as he and Alex had in quizzing him. How do you deal with a naval recruiting poster?

'We'll be gettin' back to you, Lieutenant,' Alex said, solving Sten's immediate gape. Sten almost had to physically hold up his jaw as Estill wheeled 180 perfect degrees and clicked – not walked – down the gangway.

Sten sagged back against the hull in relief.

'Who sent him?' Sten wanted to know. 'He's gotta be a spy, or something. Nobody, but nobody that good would ever volunteer for our dinky little boats.'

'He nae be a spy,' Alex said, 'alto' he be a van Doorman lad his whole career. The wee spindar checked him out.'

'Okay,' Sten said, 'but look at his record. Honors, awards, medals, prized exploration assignments. Personal commendations from every superior officer.'

'All peacetime, lad,' Alex reminded. 'Also, nae *one* good word from his ultimate superior – van Doorman himself.'

'Estill's too good,' Sten said. 'I don't trust him.'

'We got crew enough for the four ships,' Alex said, 'but we're still lackin' two captains.'

Sten mulled that over for a bit, wondering if Lieutenant Estill was an answer to his prayers or the seeding bed for future nightmares. Besides, did Estill have . . .

'Luck, Ah wonder if the lad has luck?' Alex said, completing Sten's thought. 'How desperate are we?'

'If I could put a good first mate with him . . .' Sten mused.

There was a thrumming of engines overhead, and a loud voice crackled through a hailer across the docks. 'Hey, you swabbies get off your butts and give a lady a hand!'

Sten and Alex looked up to see a rust bucket of a towship hovering overhead. The tow pilot already had one ship dangling from its cradle and was moving into position over the *Gamble*. Long, slender robo arms snaked out and started unfastening the dock lines.

'What in the clot do you think you're doing?' Sten yelled up.

The woman's voice crackled out again. 'What's it look like? Moving your ship to the engine test stands. You are on the schedule, aren't you? Or doesn't your captain keep the ranks informed of what's going on?'

'You can't move two ships at once!' Sten shouted back.

'Wanna clottin' bet? Hell, on a good day I can pull three. Now, get cracking with that line, mister!'

A bit bemused, the two men did what the woman said. And then they watched in awe as she maneuvered *Gamble* into a sling below the first ship in a few seconds flat. The tow engines roared to full power, and she started away.

'That lass is *some* pilot, young Sten,' Alex said. 'Ah've rarely seen the likes of her.'

But Sten was paying him no mind; he was already running along the docks after the tow as it wound its way toward the test stands. By the time he reached the yard, the pilot was already transferring the *Gamble* over into the work berth.

'Hey, I'm comin' aboard!' Sten yelled, and without waiting for permission he swarmed up the netting to the towship.

A little later, he found himself squeezed into the tiny pilot's cabin. In person, the woman was even more stunning than her obvious flying talents. She was slender and tall, with enormous dark eyes and long black hair tucked into her pilot's cap. She was looking Sten over, speculatively and a bit amused.

'If this is your way of asking a lady out for a beer,' she said, 'I admire the clot out of your gall. I get off in two hours.'

'That isn't what I had in mind,' Sten said.

'Oh, yeah? Say, what kind of a sailor are you, anyway?'

'A *commander* type sailor,' Sten said dryly.

The woman gave him a startled look, then groaned. 'Oh, no. Me and my big ensign yap. Well, guess there goes my job. Ah, what the clot! I was lookin' for one when I found this gig.'

'In that case,' Sten said, 'report to me tomorrow at 0800 hours. I got an opening for first mate.'

'You gotta be kidding.' The woman was in shock.

'Negative. Interested?'

'Just like that, huh? First mate?'

'Yep. Just like that. Except from now on you gotta call me "sir"!'

She chewed that over, then nodded. 'I guess I could get used to that.'

'Sir,' Sten reminded.

'Sir,' she said.

'By the way, what's your name?'

'Luz, Luz Tapia. Oh, clot, I mean Luz Tapia, sir.'

With one shot, Sten had solved the problem of the *Richards* and his doubts about Estill.

Only the problem of a skipper for the *Claggett* remained. But so far the last hurdle seemed insurmountable. Alex and Sten gloomed over the few remaining names on their list.

'What a sorry lot,' Alex said. 'Ah wouldnae make ae of these clots cap'n ae a gravsled.'

Sten had to agree. To make matters worse, he was quickly running out of time. And van Doorman hadn't been making things easy for him. His aides had been swamping Sten with regular calls asking for status reports and issuing thinly veiled threats.

For one of the few times in his life, Sten found himself stumped.

There was a loud scratching at the door.

'In!' Sten shouted.

There was a pause, and then the scratching came again, louder than before.

Sten jumped to his feet. 'Who the clottin hell . . .' He slapped at the button, and the door hissed open. Sheer horror looked him in the face. Sten whooped with delight.

'What the clot are you doing here?' he yelled.

'Heard you were looking for a captain,' the horror replied.

And Sten fell into Sh'aarl't's arms and arms and arms.

Chapter Thirty-One

Even as he walked under the baroque gates into the officer's club grounds, Sten began calling himself several kinds of a dumb clot.

Across the vast pampered garden – which Sten was sure was tended by poor swabbies pressed into service by their superiors – he could see the palatial and sprawling building that housed the club.

Even by Prime World standards it would be considered posh. The building was many-columned and pure white. It was lit by constantly playing lights. The central structure had a copper-yellow dome that looked suspiciously as if it had been gold-leafed. Sten gritted his teeth as he thought how many ships could have been outfitted at the obvious cost.

He could hear the sounds of his partying brother and sister officers. Somehow the laughter seemed a little too loud, the howls of enjoyment a little too shrill.

Sten almost turned back. Then he thought, To hell with it. He had come here to celebrate with a by-God decent meal and a few too many drinks. He walked on, determined to have a good time. Besides, everybody on van Doorman's staff couldn't be clots, could they? There were sure to be a few interesting beings, right?

Just to his left was a large tree, cloaked in darkness. As he passed it, a figure came out of the shadows toward him. Sten pivoted, his knife sliding into his palm. The figure seemed to lunge for him, and just as Sten was about to strike, he smelled a strange mixture of strong alcohol and heady perfume. Instead of striking, he caught – and his arms were suddenly filled with surprising softness.

The young woman bleared up at him and then gave a slightly twisted grin of faint recognition. 'Oh, s'it's you,' she giggled. 'Come to give me a cuddle, huh?'

It was Brijit van Doorman. The admiral's daughter. And she was quite drunk.

Sten desperately tried to push her upright and away – doing his best, but failing, to keep from touching places he ought not to touch. Visions of firing squads danced in his head.

'Was'a matter?' Brijit protested. 'Din't ya ever see a girl get a tiddle little, I mean a little tiddly, before?'

'Please, Ms van Doorman . . .' Sten fumbled.

She collapsed against him; as Sten clutched at her, she slid out of his arms as if she were greased and tumbled to the lawn. She was suddenly stricken by a mixture of laughter and hiccups.

'Had a *hic* con – con – contest. Drinking con – *hic* – test. I won.'

'So I see,' Sten said.

'He didn't like it.'

'Who's he?' Sten asked.

Brijit became very formal. '*He* is my fiancé. Old whatisbod.

Rey. Right, Rey Hall – uh, Halldor. My true true true love.'

The firing squad disappeared from Sten's mind to be replaced by a small figure being keelhauled. The figure looked very much like Sten.

'Why don't I go get Rey?' Sten said.

'No, no, no. He's with Daddy. Daddy doesn't like me to drink either.'

This was all just as clotting wonderful as it could get. At least that was what Sten thought until Brijit started to cry. Not nice, soft little ladylike sobs either, but a loud bawl. Sten saw several people peering curiously out the window.

'Let me take you home,' Sten said.

She stopped crying immediately. She gave him a little conspiratorial look. 'Right. Home. Then nobody will ever know.'

'Absolutely,' Sten said. 'No one will know. Okay, up we go, now.'

It took him a good five minutes to get her to her feet. But that didn't do much good, as she kept sagging toward the ground each time. Finally, Sten picked her up and carried back along the path and through the gates to his gravcar.

He had barely cleared the ground when she lapsed into total unconsciousness. Sten was about ready to explode. Of all the clotting little . . . Ah, what the hell. He'd find the way. He punched her name into the gravcar's directory, found her address, and set the autopilot.

As they swept through the city, he took a good look at her. Except for a slight flush in her features and a bruised look about her mouth, no one could tell she had a load on.

What the hey, so she got a load on? Sten imagined that it wasn't very pleasant being related to van Doorman. So she wanted to kick her heels up a little? She had a right to, didn't she?

Asleep, Brijit seemed very peaceful, little-girl-innocent and . . . and . . . Get a hold of yourself, Sten. So she's a knockout. She's also the admiral's daughter, remember? Do not think those thoughts. Do not think them at all.

Brijit never woke up when they reached her house, and Sten had to carry her in and tuck her into bed. He palmed a switch to turn off the lights, sighed, and let himself out.

He found a furious blond man waiting for him at his gravsled. The man was in uniform and wore the insignia of a commander. The last time Sten had seen him had been outside van Doorman's office – he'd been wearing shorts and accompanying Brijit. It did not require much of Sten's deductive powers to figure out who the man was.

'So, there you are, you clot! I'll teach you to—'

The man swung at Sten, starting at his knees and coming straight up. Sten stepped back lightly, and the man almost fell from the force of the swing.

'You must be Rey Halldor,' Sten said. 'Brijit's fiancé.'

'You're clotting right I am,' Halldor said, swinging again.

Sten ducked, holding out both hands, trying to make peace. 'Listen, Halldor. I didn't have anything to do with it. She got drunk. I found her. I took her home. Period. That's it. Nothing else happened.'

Halldor charged, windmilling. Sten tried to dance aside, but one of the blows caught his ear. It hurt like hell.

'Okay, you clot,' Sten said.

One arm stiffened. A hand connected, and the man found himself lying on his back, looking foolishly up at Sten.

'You . . . you hit me,' said an astonished Halldor.

'You're clottin' right I hit you, Commander,' Sten said. 'And if you get up, that's not all I'll do.'

'I want your name. Now, you clot.'

'The clot you are speaking to is Commander Sten, at your service.'

'This isn't the end of it,' Halldor said.

'Right.'

Sten vaulted into his gravcar. He almost broke the control panel punching in the code that would take him home.

I just love how you meet people, young Sten. Isn't it just wonderful how you got all the rough edges polished off on Prime World?

Chapter Thirty-Two

'Hey, Chief. I think I got something,' Foss said.

Warrant Officer Kilgour, in spite of his years with the less-than-militarily-correct Mantis teams, was offended. 'The term is Commander or Sten, son. And that is not the way to report.'

Sten, amused, didn't bother to wait for Foss to rejargon. He was instantly across the *Gamble*'s command deck – easily done, since it measured four meters on a side – and was staring at the screen.

'Well,' he said, waiting for the ship's computer to give him a better analysis than a blip, sector, and proximity, 'we have something. I guess it ain't birds.'

Foss flushed.

Sten's flotilla was on its third week of shakedown. It had not been a thrill a minute.

Combine hardened felons with a naval background with policemen with no military background with eager volunteers with fairly virginal officers, then add to that four state-of-the-art patrolcraft. State of the art is correctly redefined by any engineer or technician with field service as: It will promise you everything and deliver you very little. Under stress or when you really need it, it will break. The Bulkeley-class tacships fulfilled these requirements very exactly.

Sten and Alex had managed twenty hours of sleep each since the *Gamble*, *Claggett*, *Kelly*, and *Richards* had launched from Cavite Base. The launch, intended to be a smooth soaring out of atmosphere, had been a limp toward space. The AM2 drive on Sh'aarl't's ship, the *Claggett*, had refused to kick in on command, and the formation had crawled into a holding orbit on Yukawa drive. It took hours of circuit running before they discovered that someone at the builder's yard had left his lunchtime tabloid – headline: 'Emperor to Finally Wed? Escorts Beauty from Nirvana to Ball' – between two filter screens.

Sten's comment about birds was not a joke – the ship's screens had identified one of Cavite's moons as aquatic waterfowls, and the identification had been confirmed by the ship's *Jane's*. Still worse, the suggested response from the weapons computer had been bows and arrows. Of course, the professionally paranoid recruits from Cavite's police department saw signs of sabotage and Tahn sympathies among the builders. Sten knew better – over the years he'd learned that the more sophisticated a computer was, the more likely it was to independently develop what in humans would be called a sense of black humor. Foss had managed to find the glitch and recircuit it within a day.

Eric Foss was a rare find. If he hadn't been the initial source of recruitment from the police, Sten and Alex might have passed him over. He was a large, red-faced young man just barely old enough to join the military, much less the police. He'd spent his few short months on the Cavite force as a traffic officer.

Despite his bulk, the young man was so quiet, so calm, that he almost seemed asleep. But his test scores on communications of all kinds were awesome and not to be believed. Sten had personally tested him again – and the scores had improved. If Sten had been a superstitious man, he might have thought Foss a sensitive. But instead, he put him in charge of flotilla communications.

Shakedown had continued, always interesting in a morbid sort of way. The fire-system nozzles had been misaligned and filled the weapons compartments with foams; fuel-feed passages were warped; the galley stoves took a Ph.D. to understand, and the refreshers were worse.

On the other hand, all of the ships had power beyond the manufacturer's specs; target acquisition was superfast, and the missile-firing tests went flawlessly.

Unexpectedly, the crewmen and women managed to meld fairly painlessly. The only incident had been one of the ex-cons pulling a knife on an ex-policeman in an argument over the last piece of soyasteak. But the ex-cop had broken the man's arm in six places, snapped the knife in two, and told the officer of the watch that the other poor fellow must have tripped over something.

Even the command ranks were working into shape. Sh'aarl't, on the *Claggett*, was just as good as Sten had anticipated. Lamine Sekka, on the *Kelly*, was awesome, and Sten understood how the man's family had survived all those generations as warriors. Lieutenant Estill, backed by Ensign Tapia on the *Richards*, was coming along. He still had a tendency to follow slavishly on its anticipation every order, but Sten had hopes.

At least no one had fed himself into the power chamber, and no one had rammed anything. Both Sten and Alex, maintaining their public air of 'not quite right, guys, try it again,' were pleased.

But sleep was becoming an increasingly attractive future.

Seven more ship-days, Sten had promised himself. Then we are going to practice landing and concealment on the prettiest and most deserted world we can find and practice deep Zen breathing.

At that point, the contact alarm went off. The screen changed from a blip to a blur of words:

OBJECT IDENTIFIED AS NON-NATURAL. OBJECT IDENTIFIED AS AM2-POWERED SPACECRAFT. OBJECT ON PROJECTED ORBIT . . . (NONCOLLISION) . . . NO *JANE'S* ENTRY CONGRUENT WITH SHIP PROFILE . . . SHIP OUTPUTTING ON NO RECEIVABLE WAVELENGTH . . . SHIP *TENTATIVE* . . . *TENTATIVE* . . . OPERATING UNDER SILENT RUNNING CONDITIONS . . .

The words became an outline of the oncoming ship. Sten and Alex eyed the screen.

'Ugly clot, wha'e'er she be,' Alex said.

'Almost as ugly as the *Cienfuegos*,' Sten said, referring to a spy ship, camouflaged as a mining explorer, on which they had almost managed to get themselves killed during their Mantis days.

Alex got it. 'Wee Foss, gie her a buzz on the distress freak.'

Before Foss could key the frequency, the screen changed again: ANALYSIS COMPLETE OF DRIVE EMISSION – DRIVE CODING SUGGESTS SHIP FROM TAHN WORLDS.

Sten keyed the mike. 'Unknown ship . . . unknown ship . . . this is the Imperial Tactical Ship *Gamble*. You are operating in a closed sector. I repeat, you are operating in a closed sector. Prepare for inspection.'

Without waiting for a response, he reached over Foss's shoulder and keyed the com to the 'talk between ships' circuit. '*Clagett, Kelly, Richards*, this is *Gamble*. All ships, general quarters. All weapons systems on full readiness. All ships slave-link to my flight pattern. All commanders stand by for independent action. This may not be a drill. If fired on, return fire. I say again, this may not be a drill. *Gamble* out.'

A speaker bleated. 'Imperial Ship *Gamble*, this is the *Baka*. Do not understand your last, over.'

There was another frequency change. '*Baka*, this is *Gamble*. I say again my last. Stand by for boarding and inspection.'

'This is *Baka*. We wish to protest. We are a civilian exploration ship under correct charter. If there has been any error in our course, we will accept escort out of the restricted sector. We do not wish to be boarded.'

'This is *Gamble*. We are warping parallel orbit. You will be boarded within . . . eight E-minutes. Any attempt to evade boarding or resistance will be met with the appropriate countermeasures. This is *Gamble*. Out.'

Sten turned to Alex. 'Mr. Kilgour. You . . . me . . . sidearms. Four men with willyguns. Move!'

Sten's crew may not have been fully trained as sailors, but they were fairly skilled at breaking and entering. Breaking was not necessary – the *Baka* had its lock extended and ready. The entrance slid open. Two men were on either side of the tube, willyguns held – not quite – leveled. The other two flanked Sten and Alex. They started down the tube, and their stomachs jumped a little as they crossed from their own artificial gravity field to that of the *Baka*.

The *Baka*'s inner port opened.

Sten expected to be met with fuming and shouts. Instead there was quiet outrage.

The ship's CO introduced himself as Captain Deska. He was a man of control – but a man who was most angry. 'Captain . . . Sten, this is totally unwarranted. I shall lodge a protest with my government immediately.'

'On what grounds?' Sten asked mildly.

'We have been hijacked merely because we are Tahn. This is rank discrimination – my company has nothing to do with politics.'

My company? A ship's captain working for someone would hardly have said 'my.' Sten decided that this Deska wasn't terribly good at fraud. 'You are in a forbidden sector,' he said.

'You are incorrect. We have the correct clearances and permission. In my cabin.'

Sten smiled politely. He would be most interested in inspecting said clearances.

Deska led the way to his cabin. The ship corridors, unlike those of a normal exploration ship, were immaculate and freshly anodized. The crew members were also unusual – not the bearded loners and technicians that normally made up a long-cruise explorer but clean-shaven, cropped-haired, and wearing identical coveralls.

It did not take Sten long to peruse the clearances. He snapped the fiche off and stood up from the small console in Deska's Spartan quarters.

'You see,' Deska said. 'That permission was personally requested and cleared by your own Tanz Sullamora. If you have not heard of the man—'

'I know who he is. One of our Imperial biggies,' Sten said. 'As a matter of fact, I know him personally.'

Was there a slight flicker from Deska?

'Excellent,' Deska said heartily.

'Interesting ship you have here,' Sten went on. 'Very clean.'

'There is no excuse for lack of cleanliness.'

'That's my theory, too. Of course, I'm not a civilian . . .' Sten changed the subject. 'Your crew's sharper than mine. You run a taut ship, Captain.'

'Thank you, Commander.'

'I don't think you want to feel too grateful. This ship, under my authority as an officer of the Empire, is under custody. Any attempt at resistance or disregard of my orders will be countered, if necessary, by force of arms. You are instructed and ordered to proceed, under my command, to the nearest Imperial base, in this case Cavite, at which time you are entitled to all protection and recourse available under Imperial law.'

'But why?'

Sten touched buttons on two small cased pouches on his belt. 'Do you really want to know, Captain Deska?'

'I do.'

'Fine. By the way, I just shut off my recorder and turned on a block. I assume you have this room monitored. Nothing else we say will be picked up, I can guarantee you.

'Captain, you are busted because I think you're a spy ship. No, Captain. You asked me, and I'm gonna tell you. Every one of your men looks like an officer – and you do, too. Tahn officers. If I were a sneaky type, I'd guess that you are some kind of high-level commander. And you came out here, with a pretty good forgery to cover yourself, to check out the approaches to Cavite. Just in case the balloon goes up. Am I wrong, Captain?'

'This is an outrage!'

'Sure is. But you're still busted. And by the way, even if you manage to convince Cavite you are innocent, innocent, innocent, all the hot poop your scanners have been picking up will be wiped before we release you.'

Admiral Deska, second-in-command of Lady Atago's combined fleet, just looked at Sten. 'You are very, very wrong, Commander. And I shall remember you for a very, very long time.'

Chapter Thirty-Three

'You did what?' Sten blurted. He did not even notice that he had forgotten to say 'sir.' Not that van Doorman needed an excuse to get angry.

'I did not ask you for a comment, Commander. I merely took the courtesy of informing you as to my decision. Since you are slightly deaf, I shall repeat it:

'After considerable investigation by my staff, supervised by myself, we have determined that the boarding of the Tahn Scientific Ship *Baka* was in error. Admittedly, they had accidentally entered a proscribed area of space, but their commanding officer, a Captain Deska, told me that their charts were out of date and in error.'

'Sir, did you personally examine those charts?'

'Commander, be silent! Captain Deska is a gentleman. I saw no reason to question his word.'

Sten, heels locked, stared glumly down at van Doorman's desk.

'I also personally commend an apology to his superiors and to his company headquarters on Heath, which is the capital of the Tahn System.'

Sten, once again, did not know when to keep his mouth shut. 'Sir. One question. Did you at least have techs wipe the ship's recorder systems?'

'I did not. How could he have navigated home if I did?'

'Thank you, sir.'

'One further point. You should consider yourself lucky.'

'Sir?'

'Since it would prove an embarrassment to the officers and men of the 23rd Fleet if Imperial headquarters were to hear of this debacle, of course there is no way that I can place the correct letter of reprimand in your personal fiche.'

Translation: van Doorman hadn't reported the incident to Prime World.

'I shall tell you something else, young man. When you were first assigned to my command, I had my doubts.

'The navy is a proud and noble service. A service composed of gentlebeings. You, on the other hand, were formed by the army. Necessary types, certainly. But hardly correct from the navy point of view.

'I hoped that you would change your ways from the examples you would see around you, here on Cavite. I was most incorrect. You not only have isolated yourself from your peers, but have chosen to associate with, and I am not exaggerating, scum from the lowest circles of our society.

'So be it. You came from the gutter . . . and choose to swim in it. At my first opportunity, the first time you make the most minor error, I shall break you, Commander Sten. I shall dissolve your entire unit, have you court-martialed, and, I most earnestly hope, send you to a penal planet in irons. That is all!'

Sten saluted, pivoted, and marched out of van Doorman's office, out of the hotel, and deep into the grounds – where, behind a tree, he laughed himself back into sanity. Admiral van Doorman probably believed he had stuck Sten's guts on a pole and waved them high overhead. He really should have taken lessons from the most polite Mantis instructor.

Scum Sten headed back for his ships. Not only did he want a drink, he wanted to find out – Alex would know – what the clot 'irons' were.

Chapter Thirty-Four

'Boss, you look like you could use a drink.'

'Many,' the Emperor said. 'Drag up a pew and a bottle, Mahoney.'

Building drinks was simple – it consisted of grabbing a bottle of what the Emperor called scotch from the old roll-top desk and half filling two glasses.

'What,' Mahoney asked after slugging down his drink and getting a refill, 'is burning Sullamora's tubes? He's stomping around the anteroom like you just nationalized his mother.'

'Clot,' the Emperor swore. 'I told him I know he's innocent six times already. Of course the *Baka*'s papers were forged. I went and told him very clear, I went and shouted in his ear.'

Mahoney just gave him a puzzled look.

The Emperor sighed. 'Never mind. I guess when you leave I'll have to pat his poo-poo again.'

'Speaking of that, sir.'

'Yeah. I know.'

The matter at hand was the boarding and subsequent release of the *Baka*. van Doorman may not have filed a report, but one of

Mahoney's agents, put in place in the days when Mahoney had run Imperial Intelligence – Mercury Corps – had.

'First thing we've got to do, sir, is bust that clotting van Doorman down to brig rat third class.'

'I've never been able to figure out if beings become soldiers because they're simple, or whether wearing a uniform makes them that way,' the Emperor said. He paused and drank. 'van Doorman has got six – count them, six – of my idiot members of parliament who think he's the most brilliant swabbie since Nelson.'

'You're just going to leave him running amok with the 23rd Fleet?'

'Of course not. I am going to amass, most carefully, a very large stone bucket. At the appropriate time, I'll run some of my pet politicos out to the Fringe Worlds on a fact-finding mission. They'll come back and tell me how terrible things are. After that, I'll be reluctantly forced to give van Doorman another star and put him in charge of iceberg watching somewhere.'

'Sir, I don't think we have that kind of time. Both my agent and Sten agree that every swinging Richard on the *Baka* was a Tahn officer. They are getting ready to hit us.'

'Forget Doormat for a minute, refill my goddamned glass, and tell me what you want to do. And no, I am not going to authorize a preemptive first strike on Heath.'

'That,' General Mahoney said, following orders, '*was* going to be one of my options.'

'Remember, Ian. I don't start wars. I just finish them.'

Mahoney held up a hand. He had heard time and again the Emperor's belief that no one wins in a war and that the more wars that are fought, the weaker the structure of the society fighting them becomes. 'What about this one, sir? What about—'

'You tried that one before, General. And I am *still* not going to redeploy your First Guards on the Fringe Worlds. We are, right now, about one millimeter from going to war with the Tahn. I am doing everything I goddamned know to keep that from happening. I plonk your thugs out there, and that would be it.'

Mahoney framed his sentence very carefully. The Emperor may have considered Mahoney a confidant and even maybe a friend – but he still was the Eternal Emperor, and one step over the line could put General Mahoney out there looking for icebergs with van Doorman. 'No offense, sir. But supposing you can't stop the Tahn? Meaning no disrespect.'

The Emperor growled, started to snap, and decided to finish his drink instead. He got up and stared out the window at the palace gardens below. 'There is that,' he said finally. 'Maybe I'm getting too set in my ways.'

'Then I can—'

'Negative, General. No Guards.' The Emperor considered for another moment. 'How long has it been since the First Guards went through jungle refresher training?'

'Six months, sir.'

'Way too long. I'm ashamed of you, Mahoney, for letting your unit get fat and sloppy.'

Mahoney didn't even bother to protest – the Emperor had his scheming look about him.

'Seems to me I own some kind of armpit swamp out in that part of the universe. Used to be a staging base back in the Mueller Wars.'

Mahoney crossed to one of the Emperor's computer terminals and searched. 'Yessir. Isby XIII. Unoccupied now except by what the fiche says are some real nasty primordials and a caretaker staff on the main base. And you're right. It's very close to the Fringe Worlds. It'd take me . . . maybe a week to transship from there.'

'Would you stop worrying about the Fringe Worlds? The solution with those gentle and lovable Tahn will be diplomatic. The only reason I'm punting you out there is to see whether mosquitoes like Mick blood.' Then the Emperor turned serious. 'Christ, Mahoney. That's the best I can think of. Right now, I'm starting to run out of Emperor moves.'

And Major General Ian Mahoney wondered if maybe he'd better make sure his own life insurance policy was current.

Chapter Thirty-Five

The twenty-seven members of the Tahn Council sat in various attitudes of attention as Lady Atago detailed the progress on Erebus. Even on screen her chilly efficiency cut across the light-years separating her from the Tahn home world of Heath. If there was any deference in her manner to her superiors, it was only to her mentor, Lord Fehrle, the most powerful member of the council.

'. . . And so, my lords and ladies,' she was saying, 'in summation, the fleet is at sixty percent strength; fuel and other supplies, forty-three percent; weapons and ammunition, seventy-one percent.'

Fehrle raised a finger for attention. 'One question, my lady,' he said. 'Some of the members have expressed concern about crewing. What is the status, if you please?'

'It displeases me to say, my lord,' Atago said, 'that I can only give you an estimate. To be frank, training has not yet come up to Tahn standards.'

'An estimate will do,' Fehrle said.

'In that case, I would say we have enough manpower to place a skeleton crew aboard all currently operational ships. There would be gaps in key positions, of course, but I believe these deficiences could be overcome.'

'I have a question, if you please, my lady.' This was from Colonel Pastour, the newest member of the council. Fehrle buried a groan of impatience and shot a glance at Lord Wichman, who just gave a slight shake of his head.

'Yes, my lord?'

'How long before we can be at full strength?'

'Two years, minimum,' Lady Atago said without hesitation.

'In that case,' Pastour continued, 'perhaps the other members would benefit from your counsel. Do you advise us to proceed with the action under discussion?'

'It is not my place to say, my lord.'

'Come, come. You must at least have an opinion.'

Lady Atago's glare bored through him. Good, Fehrle thought. She's not going to be caught out by Pastour's seemingly innocent question.

'I'm sorry, my lord. I do not. My duty is to follow your orders, not to second-guess the thinking of the council.'

But Pastour would not give up so easily. 'Very admirable, my lady. However, as the fleet commander, you must have some estimate of our chances for success if we act immediately.'

'Adequate, my lord.'

'Only adequate?'

'Isn't adequate enough for any Tahn, my lord?'

Pastour flushed, and there were murmur of agreement from around the table. Fehrle decided to break in. Although the old colonel made him uneasy in his wavering, it was not good to threaten the unanimity of the council.

'I think that will be all for now, my lady,' he said. 'Now, if you will excuse us, we will be back to you within the hour with our decision.'

'Thank you, my lord.'

Fehrle palmed a button, and the screen image of Lady Atago vanished.

'I must say, my lord,' Wichman said, 'that I'm sure that I echo the sentiments of the other members of the council by expressing my pleasure in your choice of Lady Atago to command the fleet.'

There were more murmur of agreement, except from Pastour, who had recovered and merely gave a chuckle.

'Right you are,' he said. 'Except if I were you, Lord Fehrle, I'd keep a weather eye on that woman. She's just a bit too good for comfort.'

Fehrle ignored him. Pastour sometimes had a way of saying the oddest things. And at the moment, Fehrle was questioning his own decision to raise the man to the council. Well, no use worrying about that now. The fact was that Pastour was one of the key industrialists in the Tahn Empire. He also had the uncanny ability to raise large guard units – all of which he financed from his own pocket – where seemingly there had been few warm bodies available.

Also, Lord Wichman's supreme militancy – even for a Tahn – served as a counterbalance to Pastour. Wichman was one of Fehrle's master strokes. He was a man who had risen through the ranks of the military and could boast nearly every award for heroism that the Tahn Empire had to offer. More importantly, he had a way with the masses, and in his role as minister of the people, he seemed to be able to get any kind of sacrifice necessary from the working class. How he got that cooperation, no one cared to know.

In another time, the Tahn Council would have been most closely compared to a politburo system of government. Each member represented key areas of society. The various viewpoints were discussed and whenever possible added to the political stewpot. All decisions were unanimous and final. There was never a vote, never any public dissension. Each matter was thoroughly discussed in private, compromises made whenever necessary, and the plan agreed upon. A meeting of the council itself was a mere formality for the record.

And so it was with no trepidation at all that Fehrle addressed his fellow lords and ladies.

'Then, I assume we are all agreed,' he said. 'We proceed with the attack on the Emperor as planned?'

There were nods all around – except one.

'I'm not sure,' Pastour said. 'I still wonder if maybe we ought to wait until we are at full readiness. In two years, we'll have the Empire in the palm of our hand.'

There was an instant hush in the room. Everyone looked at Fehrle to see how he would react.

Fehrle did his best to keep the impatience out of his voice. 'This has all been discussed before, my lord,' he said. 'The longer we wait, the longer the Emperor has to build more ships. We cannot win a manufacturing war with the Eternal Emperor. You of all people should know that.'

'Yes, yes. But what if this operation doesn't succeed? We are risking our entire fleet! Where will we be if we lose that? Back under the Emperor's thumb, that's where, I tell you!'

Wichman instantly shot to his feet, his eyes bulging and his face scarlet with anger. 'I will not stay in the same room with a coward!' he shouted.

The room erupted as Wichman began to stalk out. Fehrle slammed his hand down on the table. Wichman froze in midstep. Silence reigned again in the room.

'My lords! My ladies! Do you forget where you are?'

Fehrle glared around at each member. They all squirmed in their seats uncomfortably. Then he turned to Pastour and gave him a frosty smile.

'I'm sure the good colonel misspoke. We all know from his reputation that he is no coward.' He glanced over at Wichman. 'Don't you agree, my lord?'

Wichman's shoulders slumped, and he walked silently back to his seat. 'I apologize for my rudeness,' he said to Pastour.

'And I for mine. You must forgive me. I have a great deal more to learn about the workings of the council.'

The tension crept away, and Lord Fehrle brought the meeting back to order.

'It's settled, then. We attack immediately!'

Everyone shouted in agreement. Pastour's voice was the loudest of all.

Chapter Thirty-Six

'Mr Kilgour,' Foss said, wistfully looking at the display in front of him, 'can I ask you something?'

'GA, lad.' Kilgour checked the time. There was an hour and a half to go before the shift changed – and a little inconsequential conversation might help kill the boredom.

'Look at all those fat freighters down there. When you were young, did you ever want to be a pirate?'

Kilgour chuckled. 'Lad, Ah hae input f' ye. When Ah was wee, Ah *was* a pirate. Come frae a long line a' rogues, Ah do.'

Foss glanced at Kilgour. He was still not sure when his XO was extending his mandible. He turned back to the screen.

Sten's four ships had been assigned escort duty. Even though the increasing tension with the Tahn had reduced merchant traffic through the Fringe Worlds, there were still certain shipments that had to be routed through the area. The ships were now dispatched in convoys and given integral escort. In addition, during passage near the Tahn sector, Imperial ships were attached for support. Hanging 'below' Sten's ships were five tubby merchants from Tanz Sullamora's fleet, one container link with four tugs, two hastily armed auxiliary cruisers, and one archaic destroyer, the *Neosho*, from van Doorman's fleet.

Sten couldn't figure out van Doorman's thinking – if, indeed, the admiral was ever guilty of that. He seemed more interested in keeping his ships on the ground than in space. Possibly, Sten hazarded, the admiral was worried that he would forget them if they weren't in plain sight. Van Doorman was, even though the term's origins were long-lost, a perfect bean counter.

This didn't apply to Sten's tiny flotilla. Van Doorman proved true to his word. He wanted Sten's butt on toast. He evidently thought the best way to crucify Sten was to keep him busy. The *Claggett, Gamble, Kelly*, and *Richards* were used as everything from dispatch runners to chartmakers to the present duty – high escort on this merchant run. Sten didn't think much of van Doorman's plot – if Sten had wanted to ruin someone's career, he would have kept the person underfoot at all times. Sten was also not upset that his ships were kept on the run – he was still shaking his somewhat motley crew down.

The only problem was the wear and tear factor on the delicate engines. If it weren't for Sutton's brilliance in conniving far more parts and even spare engines than authorized, all four tacships would have been redlined by now.

And so the four ships dozed on high escort. The skipper of the *Neosho* had cheerfully agreed with Sten's plan to keep his flotilla above the convoy proper, enabling the Bulkeley-class's superior electronics to umbrella the convoy. He had promptly stuck the *Neosho* at proud point and, as far as Sten could tell from intership transmissions, was spending most of his time on the lead merchantman.

Sten was slightly envious – rumor had it that Sullamora's ships were most plush, and their crews didn't believe in Spartan thinking – but not very.

Sten kept his crews on minimal watch – with one exception. The electronics suite was fully manned and watching. There had been entirely too many nonreports from ships passing through this sector. There were many possible explanations: Merchant ships were notoriously sloppy for transmitting sector-exit reports; accidents did happen; pirates; or Question Mark.

Pirates made no sense. In spite of the livie fantasies, it was impossible for a private individual, given the Imperial control of AM2, to operate a raider for very long. It was the Question Mark that intrigued Sten and Alex.

Four days into the assignment, their question was answered.

General quarters clanged Sten from his cubicle, where he was filling out another of van Doorman's interminable status reports, to the command deck.

The convoy was below and ahead of his ships – Sten noticed that, as always, one freighter was lagging to the rear of the formation. But on the monitor three unknown ships were coming in from 'low rear.' Sten checked the prediction screen. Their path would intersect that rear freighter in minutes.

Electronics does not necessarily simplify command: Sten, nearly simultaneously, ordered all weapons systems on the *Gamble* to standby; alerted his other three ships; cut to the supposedly open command link between ComEscort and ComConvoy, though he got no answer; braced himself and cut onto the assigned transmission band to all convoy ships; and turned away from the convoy screen.

'Below' him was instant chaos. The *Neosho* and the Commander/ Escort's lead merchantman continued, unhearing – Sten guessed it must be a helluva party. Two freighters immediately took evasive action and almost collided. A third freighter sought an orbit directly away from the convoy. The container link began lumping like a giant inchworm, as if all of the tug skippers had suddenly decided to go their own way. The lagging merchantman suddenly and uselessly went to full power, and the two auxiliary cruisers began bleating questions.

Sten was too busy to worry about them.

'All tacships, this is *Gamble*. Switch to independent command. Acquire targets. Please monitor my attempts to communicate with unknown ships. Permission to fire at commander's discretion, over.'

He made another switch to the sector's emergency band, which, in theory, every ship should be monitoring.

'Unknown ships . . . this is the Imperial Ship *Gamble*. Identify yourselves . . . alter trajectory . . . or prepare to be attacked.'

The com screen stayed blank. Kilgour pointed at another screen, which showed violet haze from all three ships.

'First th' wee *Baka* . . . noo thae' clowns. Ah thinkit tha Tahn be playin't games.'

Another screen had a computer projection of the three incoming raiders.

'Spitkits,' Kilgour murmured. 'Ah'll hazard tha' raiders be converted patrolcraft. Raiders wi' enough to blast a civilian an' a prize crew for boardin'.'

Foss, at the control board, eyed Kilgour. Maybe the man from Edinburgh *had* been a pirate.

'Tacships,' Sten ordered, 'engage and destroy incoming ships!'

Kilgour had the *Gamble* on an intersection orbit, coming 'down' on the incoming ships. Evidently they were intent on the merchantman. 'Weapons selection, sir?'

'We won't waste a Kali. Give me firing prox on a Goblin.'

Kilgour had the control helmet on. 'And six . . . and five . . . and four . . . and three . . . and one. Goblin on th' way, mate.'

The first raider never knew what happened. It simply vanished. The second and third split formation – one ship 180-ing on a return orbit at full power. Sten checked an indicator – the raider's top speed was less than two-thirds of that of any of the tacships.

The third ship, perhaps with a brighter skipper, tried another tactic. It launched two ship-to-ship missiles and, also at full power, tried an evasion orbit, one that would lead it within a few light-seconds of the lagging merchantman. Perhaps the raider thought he could lose himself in the clutter around the freighter.

'*Clagget . . . Kelly . . . Richards*,' Sten ordered. 'You want to nail the one that's homeward bound for me? I'll take the sneaky guy.'

'Roger, *Gamble*,' came the cultured voice of Sekka. 'But you do appear to be allowing yourself all the fun.'

'Negative, *Kelly*. While you're at it, maybe you could snag me a prisoner or two? And maybe try to get a back projection on where these guys came from?'

'We'll try. *Kelly* out.'

While Sten was talking, Alex had already deployed three Fox countermissiles and produced two satisfactory explosions from the raider's own launch.

'Closing . . . closing . . . closing . . .' came the monotone from Foss.

'Unknown ship, this is the Imperial Ship *Gamble*. Cut power immediately!'

Nothing showed onscreen.

'Puir lad,' Alex observed. 'Puir stupid clot. Wha' he should'a don wha launch on yon freighter an' hopit we're soft-hearted enough to look for survivors . . . Goblin launched. Ah'll try t' takit just the wee idiot's drive tubes . . . closin't . . . hit . . . ah well.' The raider became another expanding ball of gas.

'*Gamble*, this is *Claggett*. Raider exploded. No survivors observed.'

'All tacships, this is *Gamble*. Resume previous orbit.'

'*Gamble*, this is *Neosho*. What is going on, over?' The query was rather plaintive.

Foss correctly left the transmission unanswered while Sten and Kilgour figured out a response that wouldn't get them court-martialed when they returned to Cavite.

Chapter Thirty-Seven

Sten cleared off the small surface that served as his desk, turned on the pinlight/magnifiers, and eased his chair closer. He had determined that this was going to be a perfect evening – one of the rare nights he had absolutely alone to pursue his hobby.

He had given the crews of his ships twelve-hour passes, leaving him relatively free of responsibility. He poured himself a tumbler of Stregg, swirled the crystal liquid around in the glass, and sipped. The fire lit down to his toes.

He sighed in anticipated pleasure, then lifted out the tiny black case and snapped it open. It contained a dozen or more tiny cards, each jammed with computer equations. Sten's passion was holographic models of ancient factories and scenes. One card, for instance, contained in its microcircuits a complete early-twentieth-century Earth lumber mill, with working saws and gears and belts. Every machine in the mill was controlled by a miniature worker, who went about his individual tasks – as best as Sten could research them – exactly as he had many centuries ago. Sten had completed the mill during his last assignment on Prime World.

He had started his latest model during flight school. It was one of his more difficult moving holographic displays. He slid the card into its slot and palmed the computer on. Small figures working in a sprawling field leapt out onto the desk. What Sten was recreating was an ancient British hops field. From his research he knew that hops – used in the beer-brewing process – were grown on towering tripod poles. When harvest time came each year, men and women were recruited from all over the country. The plants were so tall, with the fruited vines at the very top, that the workers strode through the fields on stilts to pick them.

Thus far, Sten's display consisted of the fields of hops, most of the workers, and the ox-drawn carts used to haul out the harvest. Months of work lay ahead of him before he could complete the rest of the sprawling farm. He tickled a few keys on his computer to call up an incomplete ox cart. Then he got out his light pen to start sketching in a few more details.

There was a tentative scratching at his cabin door. Sten felt the anger rise. For clot's sake, he had given strict orders to be left alone. Ah, well. 'In!' he called.

The door hissed open, revealing a badly frightened sentry. 'Begging your pardon, sir, but . . .' The man started stumbling over his words. 'But . . . uh, there's a lady.'

'I don't care if it's the Queen of – oh, never mind. Who is it?'

'I think it's the admiral's daughter, sir.'

Clot! That was just what he needed. A drunk for company. 'Tell her I'm not here.'

The sentry started to back out, hesitated, and then pushed something forward. It was a single rose and a small gift-wrapped package.

'She said to give you this, sir,' the sentry plunged on. 'Said it was to say she was sorry. Uh . . . uh . . . I think she'd know I was lying, sir, if I told her what you said.'

Sten took pity on the man, accepted the gifts, and waved him out. 'I'll be with her in a minute.'

He placed the rose to one side, took a hefty snort of his Stregg for courage, and slit open the package. There was a small computer card inside – identical to the ones he used in holography. What in the world . . . He slid it into one of the drives. A three-dimensional model of a tower jumped out on his desk. It was a perfect replica of one of the barns used by the ancient hop farmers! How had she known?

No matter how one looked at it, this was one hell of a way to apologize.

They had a midnight picnic-style dinner at one of the most fashionable restaurants on Cavite. Brijit van Doorman insisted on buying.

Sten almost hadn't recognized the woman when he had met her on deck. The last time he had seen her, she had been beautiful but drunk, with a spoiled pout on her lips. This time there was no pout, just large anxious eyes and a nervous little smile.

'I almost hoped you weren't here,' she said in a soft voice. 'I'm not very good at saying sorry – especially in person.'

'I'd say you're very good at it,' Sten said.

'Oh, you mean the little barn.' She dismissed the gift with a wave. 'That was easy. I just asked your friend, Alex. We've spoken on and off for days.'

So that was why the tubby heavy-worlder had gone out this evening, with mysterious chuckles at no apparent jokes and pokes into the ribs of the others.

'I assume he also said I'd be onboard tonight.'

Brijit laughed. 'Is that such a betrayal?' she asked.

Sten looked at the long, flowing hair and the equally flowing body. 'No. I don't think so.'

Somehow, the stroll back to her gravcar led to a lingering talk that neither seemed to want to cut off with a thank you and good-bye. Which led to the dinner invitation. Which took them to the restaurant that Sten was sure even Marr and Senn would envy back on Prime World.

It was an exotic outdoor café perched on the end of a private landing strip. The center was a beer garden, where the patrons could gather and drink and converse as the late-night picnic baskets were packed with their orders. Surrounding the beer garden were many small opaque bubblecraft. Each craft was large enough to comfortably fit the basket and two people.

Sten was not surprised that Brijit had made reservations. They waited about an hour in the quiet garden, talking, sipping at their drinks, and watching the bubbles silently drift off into the night to swirl around and around the restaurant in darting orbits, like so many fireflies.

Sten told her about himself as best he could, skipping with hidden embarrassment over his Mantis Section years. Strange that he should feel that way. The lies were so drilled in and part of him that normally they seemed almost real. Perhaps his discomfort was just a product of the warm night and the chilled wine.

Brijit chattered on about herself and her navy-brat upbringing, which had involved jumping from system to system as her father rose through the ranks. Although unstated, Sten got the idea that she was uncomfortable about the pomp that van Doorman liked to dress his command with. Uncomfortable, but guilty about her discomfort.

Eventually they were summoned to their own private bubblecraft. They boarded, the gull-wing port closed softly in on them, and they lifted away.

There must have been more than a hundred items in the basket, all bite-sized, with no flavor exactly the same as the last.

Brijit told Sten the rest of her story over brandy. Of course, there had been a lover.

'I think he was about the handsomest man I've ever met,' she said. 'Don't get me wrong. He wasn't the big-muscles type. Kind of slight. Wiry slight. And dark.' She paused. 'He was a Tahn.'

It all came together then for Sten. The admiral's daughter and her Tahn lover. Sten could imagine how van Doorman would handle a situation like that. It would be very painful for both parties. It would also be something van Doorman would never let his daughter forget.

'I only have one question,' Sten said.

'Oh, you mean Rey?'

'Yeah, Rey. I understand you two are engaged.'

'Rey thinks we're engaged. Father *knows* we're engaged. But as far as I'm concerned—' She broke off, staring down at the lights of Cavite.

'Yes?'

Brijit laughed. 'I think Rey is a clot!'

'So, what do you plan on doing?'

Brijit leaned back on the soft couch that spanned one side of the bubble. 'Oh, I don't know. Play the game, I guess. Until something better comes along.'

Sten had heard tones of something like this before. 'Aren't white knights a little out of fashion?'

Brijit came up from the couch and snuggled herself under one of his arms. She peered up at him with a mock batting of large liquid eyes. 'Oh, sir,' she said softly, lifting up her lips. 'I don't believe in white knights at all.'

A moment later they were kissing, and Brijit was falling back on the couch. Her dress slid up, revealing smooth ivory flesh covered only by a wisp of silk between her thighs that was held in place by a slender gold chain about her waist.

Sten brushed his lips across the softness of her belly. Then he unclasped the chain.

Chapter Thirty-Eight

'This is Imperial Tacship *Gamble*. Request landing clearance.'

There was no visual onscreen, but Sten could feel the controller down on the planetoid below goggle.

'This is Romney. Say again your last.'

'This is the *Gamble*,' Sten repeated patiently. 'I want to land on your crooked little world.'

'Stand by.'

There was a very long silence.

'Ah think, young Sten, y're givin't these smugglers more slack'n's warrantable.'

'Maybe.'

At last the transmitter crackled. 'Imperial ship . . . this is Jon Wild. I understand you want *landing instructions*.'

'Correct.'

'Since when does the Empire knock on doors like ours?'

Kilgour relaxed. 'You were right, lad. Now we're gettin't some-wheres.'

'This is the *Gamble*. When we want to trade.'

'Trade? There's just one ship up there.'

'Correct, Sr. Wild.'

'Clear to land. Follow the GCA beam down. I wish I could make some kind of threat if you're lying to me. However . . . this conversation is being recorded, I know, and I have a right to counsel, legal advice, and such . . .' The voice turned mildly plaintive.

'It would be interesting if you're telling the truth,' Wild continued. 'A vehicle shall be waiting to transport you to my quarters. Romney. Out.'

*

Jon Wild was a piece of work – as was his planetoid. Romney was a planetoid hanging just outside anyone's known jurisdiction. It had been domed generations earlier as a transmission relay point. But technology had made the relay station obsolete, and it was abandoned.

It had taken Sten some time to find Romney. Actually, the whole idea had been Kilgour's.

'Lad, wid'y vet m'thinkin't,' he had begun. 'When y' hae ae dictatorship ae th' Tahn, y' hae violators, human nature bein't wha' it is. Correct?'

'We saw enough of that when we were on Heath,' Sten agreed.

'Glad y' concur. If y' hae pimps ae thieves an tha', dinnae it be possible t' hae smugglers?'

Sten got it instantly and put Kilgour in motion. The tacships had gone out beyond the Fringe sectors and hung in space, silently monitoring single-ship movements. None of these reports had gone to 23rd Fleet Intelligence – Sten knew that there would be an immediate order to investigate. Eventually there had been enough data to run progs. Yes, there were smugglers, moving in and out of the Tahn worlds. Yes, they did have a base – actually, less a base than a transfer point for goods coming from Imperial worlds intended for import to the Tahn.

But there are smugglers and smugglers. Sten had swooped on a number of ships heading for Romney, checked cargoes, and interrogated crews. Satisfied, he had marooned, on a conveniently outlying planet sans communications, the smugglers and survival supplies.

He had enough to discuss the state of the galaxy with whoever led or spoke for the smugglers. Evidently that person was Jon Wild. Sten had conjured many pictures of what a master smuggler might look like, from a grossly over-dressed and overfed sybarite to a slender fop. He did not expect a man who looked as if he would be most satisfied working in Imperial Long-dead Statistics.

Nor had he expected that Wild's headquarters would resemble a dispatch center. From appearances, the smuggler chief would have been a most satisfactory number two for Tanz Sullamora's trading empire.

Wild had offered alk to Sten and Alex and seemed unsurprised when it was refused. He sipped what Sten surmised to be water, taking his time in his evaluation.

'You wish to trade,' he finally said. 'For what?'

'You saw my ship.'

'Indeed. It appeared most efficient.'

'Efficient, but not very comfortable.'

'Doesn't Admiral van Doorman supply you properly?' Wild asked with buried amusement. Sten did not bother answering.

'What gives you the impression,' Wild continued, 'that I might be of help?'

Sten wasn't interested in fencing. He handed over the manifest fiches from the smuggling ships he had seized. Wild put them into a viewer, then took his time responding.

'Let us assume that I had something to do with these shipments,' Wild said. 'And let us further assume that in some manner I could provide equivalent resupply for your ships, Commander. Briefly – how much of a rake-off are you looking for?'

Kilgour bristled. Sten put a hand on his arm.

'Wrong, Wild. I don't give a damn about your smuggling.'

'Uh oh.'

'My turn now. I've seized your cargoes just to make sure you weren't moving arms or AM2 into the Tahn worlds. You aren't.'

Wild seemed honestly shocked. 'One thing I am most proud of, commander. I have no truck with war or its trappings. But if I can manage to provide, for people who have the means to pay for it, some small items that make life more convenient, without forcing my customers through the absurdity of customs and thou-shalt-nots . . . I will pursue the matter.'

'Thank you, Sr. Wild. We'll be equally frank with you.'

Sten and Alex's plot was fairly simple. They had monitored the smugglers' movements long enough to show that the same ships were coming in and out. Therefore, these smugglers had orbits plotted that did not intersect the intense Tahn patrols. Since they were not trading in guns or fuel, Sten wasn't bothered – obviously the Tahn would be forced to pay with hard credits, credits that would not be spent on their own worlds. Slight though it probably was, this might marginally unsettle the Tahn currency base.

Sten's proposal was most simple – he would like any military information that Wild's men and women came up with. In exchange, so long as they held to the no-war-stuff policy, he would leave them completely alone.

Wild shook his head and poured himself another glass of water. 'I don't like it,' he said.

'Why not?'

'Nobody's that honest.'

Sten grinned. 'I said we'd like to trade for good things, Sr. Wild. I didn't say that we'd strike an honest bargain.'

Wild relaxed in relief. 'I, of course, will have to discuss this with my captains.'

'Best y' be doin't it w' subtlety, Wild,' Kilgour said. 'If y' leak to the Tahn, an' we get ambushed . . .'

'You may assume subtlety, Warrant Officer,' Wild said. 'I have been smuggling for half a century, and, thus far, no one has gotten closer to my operation than you two.' He stood. 'I do not foresee any difficulties from my officers,' he finished. 'Now, would you care to examine my orbit plots so we may determine the most logical meeting places?'

Chapter Thirty-Nine

'Ah think we're a wee bit lost, young Sten.'

'This is clottin' ridiculous. We both aced navigation school. How can we be lost three klicks outside the base? Lemme look at the map again.'

Sten and Alex pored over the map of Cavite City one more time. The other members of the *Claggett*'s crew hovered nearby, trying not to laugh too obviously at their superiors.

'Okay, one more time,' Sten said. 'South on Imperial Boulevard.'

'We done tha'.'

'Left at Dessler.'

'Check.'

'Then right at Garret.'

'We bloody done tha' too.'

'Now we should see a skoshie little alleyway about half-way down Garret. The alley cuts straight through to Burns Avenue. That's the theory, anyway.'

'Tha be'it a rotten theory. Tha's nae such street!'

The problem they were having was that Cavite's street system was as much of a warren as ancient Tokyo. To compound their difficulties, half the street signs had been obliterated or ripped out by roving street gangs.

Their journey had started out innocently enough. Sten had decided to reward his people for all their hard work by treating them all to a big bash of a dinner. He had told them to pick out any place at all, and hang the expense. He was mildly surprised when the vote came in. Almost every crew member had elected to chow down at a Tahn restaurant. In particular, they picked the Rain Forest. It was an out-of-the-way little spot that boasted the spiciest Tahn food in the city.

Sten had no objection, but he was curious. 'Why Tahn food? What's wrong with the native stuff?'

He was greeted with a chorus of 'bleahs,' which he took to mean that the best of the native fare boarded on bland greasy. So, the Rain Forest restaurant it was. Sten and his crew had some last-minute refitting to do aboard the *Gamble*, so the plan was for the others to go ahead, to be met at the restaurant later.

Sten was shocked when they reached the center of the city. Imperial started out as a broad, clean street that wound past high-class shops, hotels, and gleaming business offices. Then it became what could best be described as a war zone. The street itself was pitted with gaping holes.

Half the shops were either boarded up or burned out. The hulks of abandoned vehicles lined either side of the street. The few people they saw – except for the seven-man squads of cops in full riot gear – were furtive things that scurried into dark corners when they spotted the *Gamble*'s crew.

'What the clot's going on here?' Sten wanted to know.

Foss, who had been out on the streets of Cavite a great deal more, explained. When the Tahn had started beating their war drums, it had made the locals as nervous as hell. First a few, then a flood began fleeing, leaving their businesses and homes abandoned. Unemployment had become fierce, which had led to a booming membership in street gangs. The Tahn section of the city, moreover, had become an embattled slum ghetto, at the mercy of Tahn-bashing gangs.

'You mean that's where this restaurant is? Smack dab in the middle of a riot area?'

'Something like that, sir.'

'Clotting wonderful. Next time we eat bland and greasy.'

But there was nothing else to do but press on, following the map that the security guard at the base gate had said was AM2 bulletproof. Sten was now thinking fondly of what strings he could pull to bust that clotting guard down to spaceman second.

Sten shoved the map back at Alex. 'We must have taken a wrong turn,' he said. 'There's only one thing we can do. Go all the way back to Dessler and start again.'

Everyone groaned.

'They'll have eaten all the food by the time we get there,' Foss said. Then he remembered himself. 'Begging your pardon, sir.'

'What other choice do we have?'

'Ah could alw'ys tell tha spotted snake story,' Kilgour offered. 'Just ta keep our spirits up, like.'

Before Sten could strangle Alex, a joygirl came around the corner. She was dressed in one of the dirtiest, most revealing costumes Sten had ever seen. Also, unlike the other people they had seen so far that night, she didn't seem to have a drop of fear in her blood. Her walk was cool and casual. She was also wearing, Sten noted, an enormous pistol around her waist.

'Uh, excuse me, miss?'

The joygirl looked Sten up and down. Then she glanced over at the other crew members. 'You gotta be kidding,' she said. 'I'm not taking *all* you swabbies on. I'd be out of work for a week.'

'No, no,' Sten said. 'You got me wrong. I just need a little help.'

'I'll bet you do.'

Sten finally got her attention by waving a handful of credits at her. He explained the problem. The lady shook her head in disgust at their stupidity and pointed at a sagging gate half-hidden by a rusted-out gravsled.

'Right through there,' she said. 'Then it's left, left, and then it'll fall on your thick skulls.'

Two minutes later they were hoisting foaming mugs at the Rain Forest, doing their best to catch up with their shipmates.

The restaurant was aptly named. Hidden under its small dome *was* a forest. Tables were scattered among trees and beside gentle waterfalls. There was a soft breeze coming from somewhere. Colorful birds and huge insects with lacy wings flitted over the diners. The owner was one Sr. Tige, an elderly, gentle Tahn who seemed honestly to enjoy watching the delight on his patrons' faces when they dug into his food.

The menu was as exotic as the atmosphere, with more than thirty items offered. The food ranged from mild-hot to burn-your-scalp-off and was meant to be washed down with big mugs of a delicate Tahn beer. Most of the dishes were served family style in huge crockery bowls.

Sten groaned, patted the small swell at his belt, and leaned back into his seat.

'One more bite,' he said, 'and I turn into a hot-air vehicle.'

'What's the matter. Commander? Out of training?' Luz grinned at him and began spooning out another mound on her plate.

'Where do you put it?' Sten wasn't joking. He couldn't believe the enormous quantities of food she had piled into that slender figure.

'Would you believe a wooden leg, sir?'

Luz was in civvies tonight, and she was wearing a halter top that just covered her small, shapely breasts and the shortest pair of pure white shorts this side of Prime World. Her legs were long and tawny and smooth. Sten glanced down at her legs – he couldn't help but admire them – and shook his head.

'No. Wood I *definitely* don't believe!'

Then he caught himself and flushed. Watch it, Sten, he thought. You can't be doing what you'd love to be doing! Luz saw the blush and smiled. She knew what he was thinking. She gave his hand a gentle pat and then politely turned away and began chattering nonsense to Sekka. Sten realized that in some odd way he had just been rescued. He loved her for it.

There was a crashing sound and loud shouts. Startled, Sten looked up to see a terrified young couple quivering just inside the door. The man's face was bloodied, and the woman's clothing had been ripped. The man was Tahn. There was a splintering of plas as a heavy weight struck a door.

People outside were shouting. 'Throw him out . . . clottin' Tahn fooling with our women . . .'

Sr. Tige pointed to a back door, and the couple started running for it. But just then the main door crashed open, and four bully boys burst in. They spotted the couple, howled in glee, and rushed toward them. Sr. Tige put up an arm to stop them, but one man smashed him to the floor. The others, led by a hulking thug swinging an equally large club, advanced on the pair.

'First you, you piece of filth,' he said to the young Tahn. 'Then your slut.'

'You're disturbin' our meal, lad,' came a soft Scot voice.

The bully boys turned to see Alex and Sten standing just behind them.

'After you pay the damages,' Sten said, 'you can go.'

The man with the club gave a booming laugh. 'More Tahn lovers,' he said.

Across the room, Sten saw his crew members coming to their feet, but he waved them back.

'I think he's trying to insult us,' Sten said to Alex.

'Aye. He wa' brung up bloody rude, this lad.'

Without warning, the big man swung the club at Alex with all his strength. Alex didn't even bother ducking or stepping aside. He caught the club in midswing and plucked it away as if from a child. The force of the swing, however, carried the big man toward Alex. The heavy-worlder grabbed an elbow, spun him around, and booted him toward the door. The kick lifted the man from the floor, and he crashed headfirst into a wall. He slumped to the ground.

Enraged, the other three charged. Sten slipped under a knife thrust and left that man howling on the floor with a broken wrist; he struck out with three fingers at another, catching him in the throat. At the last split instant he pulled the punch just enough to avoid crushing the larnyx. He spun on one heel to deal with the other man. But that was unnecessary. Alex had the man suspended from the floor by his belt buckle and was talking soothingly.

'Now, Ah know ye be'it all drunked up, lad. So we will nae hold it again' ye. Hand over the credits and you can go, peaceful like.'

The man was too frightened to respond. Alex was getting impatient, so he upended him, gave him a shake, and credits crashed out to the ground. Then, quite casually, he lofted the man out the door. He and Sten frisked the others, relieved them of their money, and booted them out.

Sten walked over to Sr. Tigc, who was comforting the couple. He handed the credits to the old Tahn.

'If this isn't enough, sir,' he said, 'my crew and I would be glad to take up a collection to make up the difference.'

'Many, many thanks, young man,' he said. 'But you must leave, quickly. Before they come back with others.'

Sten shrugged. 'So. I think we've got more than enough forces to handle them and their crowd.'

The old man shook his head. 'No. No. You don't know how it is here . . .'

From outside there was an angry rumbling sound. Sten rushed over to the door. Now he knew what the old Tahn was talking about.

In the short time that had elapsed, a mob of over a hundred Imperial settlers had gathered outside. They were screaming for blood. Down the street Sten could see many more pouring around the corner. The oddest part of the whole scene was the big Black Maria just on the outskirts of the growing crowd. There were a half a dozen cops standing there, jeering and egging the mob on.

Sten felt a tug at his shoulder.

'I know how to deal with this,' the old man told him.

A switch to one side of the main door brought thick steel grating crashing down to lock into drilled holes in the floor. Around the dome there was the sound of more clanging steel as grating slid in to close up the windows.

'Out. Out, please,' the man said. 'We will be safe here. But if you stay, you will be arrested.'

Numbly, Sten found himself creeping out the back door with his crew.

'You know, lad,' Alex said in a low voice. 'Ah'm not too sure we chos'it the correct side.'

Sten had not one word of reply.

Chapter Forty

The next few weeks for Sten and the others were paradoxical. They *knew* that the war was moments away. Each report from Wild's smugglers verified their feelings – Tahn ships were being commissioned and assigned to battlefleets daily. The civilians on Heath had already become accustomed to regulated hours and ration chips.

Cavite was the exact opposite. It seemed to Sten that Admiral van Doorman, his officers, and his men retreated further and further into a fantasy world. To the officers, van Doorman's parties became steadily more lavish. To Sten's enlisted men, the other sailors of the fleet grew more and more sloppy and less concerned.

But the times, even in retrospect, appeared golden.

Perhaps, for Sten, an element was his love affair with Brijit. But that was only one element.

Perhaps the link-up with Wild was another part of it. The smuggler was very conscious of his end of the bargain. Sten decided that he and the others were eating better than when he had been assigned to the Emperor's own court. In fact, he was, for the first time in his life, wondering if maybe he was getting fat.

Another factor might have been that there were *none* of the troubles that Sten and Alex had expected from their pickup crew. Even Lieutenant Estill seemed to be fitting in perfectly. What few problems came up were handled quickly by a fat lip applied sensitively by Mr Kilgour, who had taken on the personal role of flotilla master-at-arms.

But the real reason was that the four tacships, and the people who volunteered for them, were doing exactly as they wanted and as they were supposed to – without anyone shooting at them.

Sten kept his ships off Cavite as much as possible. Even for a major teardown his ground crews would be sardined into the ship they would be tearing down and taken to a completely deserted beach world. Major inspections were regarded as nightmares, and no one in Cavite's yard could understand why the engine and hull specialists were coming back with tans and happy smiles.

Sten was an instinctual flier – but the sensation that had struck him was that of speed, of flying low-level with some relatable objects veering up and past him. Now, on those long slow watches, he found another joy.

The tacships spent long shifts just observing, hanging above a planetary system's ecliptic, possibly correcting starcharts, possibly monitoring Tahn ship movements, possibly evaluating those worlds as Tahn outposts. Sten should have been bored.

He never was. Alex had modified one of the *Gamble*'s Goblin missiles, removing the warhead and replacing it with extra fuel cells.

It was Sten's joy, offwatch, to put on a spare control helmet and float 'his' Goblin out into deep space. He knew that the perceptions of a star being 'above' or a planet 'below' him were the false analogues provided by computer. He also knew that his feelings of heat from a nearby sun, or cold from an ice planet, were completely subjective. But he still reveled in them. To him, this was the ultimate form of the human dream of flight. It was even better, because he knew that if anything happened, he was really safely on board the *Gamble*.

The shifts and days drifted past. Sten frequently had to check patrol time by the ship's log. If the supplies would have held out, Sten thought he might have remained in space forever, beyond human reach or response.

It was after such a fugue that Sten encountered the *Forez* for the first time, and Admiral Deska for the second.

The *Kelly* and the *Gamble* had been attempting to plot a meteor stream's track. Lieutenant Sekka had insisted that the meteors came from a single exploded planet. Sten had argued that merely because the boulders were somewhat oversize didn't necessarily indicate anything. But, in amusement, he had authorized a backplot on those rocks.

Every alarm siren in the universe brought the fun and games to an end. Alex and Sten, on the *Gamble*'s command deck, and Lieutenant Sekka, on the *Kelly*, stared at the screen.

'Wha' we hae here,' Kilgour finally said, 'is the biggest clottin' battlewagon Ah hae ever seen. Imperial or Tahn. An' tha's nae entry in *Jane*'s f'r it.'

'Stand by, emergency power,' Sten said. He checked their position. They were supposedly in a neutral sector, although Sten had a fair idea that if the Tahn were feeling feisty, that wouldn't help.

There was a com blast that sent the readings into the red. 'Foreign ship. Identify or be blasted.'

'Impolite clots,' Kilgour muttered.

Sten went to the closed circuit to Sekka. '*Kelly*, if the shooting starts, get out of it.'

'But—'

'Orders.'

He changed channels.

'Imperial Tacship *Gamble* receiving.'

The screen cleared. It took Sten a moment to recognize the Tahn officer, in full-dress uniform, standing behind the communications specialist. But he did.

'Captain Deska. You've gotten a promotion.'

Deska, too, was puzzled – and then he remembered. He did not seem pleased at the memory. He covered nicely. 'Imperial ship . . . we are not receiving your transmissions. This is the Tahn Battleship *Forez*. You have intruded into a Tahn sector. Stand by to be boarded. You are subject to internment.'

'I wish,' Sten said to Alex, 'we had Ida with us.'

Alex grinned. Their gypsy pilot in Mantis Section had once hoisted her skirts, with nothing underneath, after hearing a similar command.

Sten, not being good at repartee, shut down communication. '*Kelly*. Return to Cavite at full power. Full report. Keep it under seal for forty-eight E-hours or until my return, whichever comes first.'

'I did not accept command in order to – yessir.'

That got one worry out of the way – the *Kelly* was several light-minutes behind Sten's ship, and Sten figured there was no way that Sekka could get caught.

He thought for a moment. 'Mr Kilgour.'

'Sir.'

'I would like a collision course set for this *Forez*.'

'Sir.'

'Three-quarters power.'

Someone on the *Forez* must have computed Sten's trajectory. The emergency circuit yammered at him. Sten ignored it.

'Lad, thae hae a great ploy. But hae y' consider't we may be ae war already? Tha' Tahn'd know afore we did.'

Sten, as a matter of fact, had not. It was a little late to add that into the equation, however.

'New orbit . . . get me a light-minute away from that clot . . . on count . . . three . . . two . . . now!'

An observer with systemwide vision would have seen the *Gamble* veer.

'Tahn ship appears to have weapons systems tracking,' Foss said.

'Far clottin' out. Foss, I want that random orbit of yours . . . on count . . . two . . . one . . . now!'

Foss had come up with a random-choice attack pattern that Sten had used to train the Fox antimissile crews. Foss swore it was impossible for anyone, even linked to a supercomputer, to track a missile using such an orbit.

There were two considerations: The *Gamble*, no matter how agile, could not compare to a missile. Also, its effects on the crew, despite the McLean generators, were unsettling.

Sten took it as long as he could. Then he had a slight inspiration. 'New trajectory . . . stand by . . . I want a boarding trajectory!'

'Sir.'

'Goddammit, you heard me!'

'Boarding trajectory. Aye, sir.'

The two ships bore toward each other again.

'Mr Kilgour, what honors do you render a Tahn ship?'

'Clot if Ah know't, Skipper. Stab 'em in tha' back ae tha' be a Campbell?'

Sten swore to himself. It would have been a great jape. He had never worried about the *Forez*. At least not that much. First, he thought that if war had been declared – or had even begun sans declaration – Admiral Deska would have ground Sten's nose in it. Second, he assumed that the *Forez's* missiles were probably larger than the *Gamble* herself. And third, tacships do not attack, let alone reattack, battleships.

The *Forez* and the *Gamble* passed each other barely three light-seconds apart. It was not close enough, in spite of Kilgour's claims, to chip the anti-pickup anodizing on the *Gamble's* hull.

A ship in space, with its McLean generators on, had no true up or down, so the *Forez's* response to the close pass would have been known only to the officers and men on its bridge and navcenter. But Sten, watching in a rear screen, was most pleased to see the huge Tahn battleship end-over-end-over-end three times before it recovered.

'Emergency power, Mr. Kilgour,' he said, and was unashamed of a bit of smugness.

'Lad,' Alex managed. 'Y're thinki't y're entirely too cute t' be one ae us humans.'

Chapter Forty-One

Sten, heels locked and fingers correctly curled at the seams of his uniform, wondered which of his multifarious sins van Doorman had discovered. For some reason, however, van Doorman seemed almost cheerful. Sten guessed that it was caused by the maze of painters and carpenters he had threaded his way through entering the admiral's suite at the Carlton Hotel.

'Commander, I realize that ceremony evidently means little to you. But are you aware that Empire Day is less than seventy-two hours from now?'

Sten was. Empire Day was a personal creation of the Eternal Emperor. Once every E-year, all Imperial Forces not engaged in combat threw an open house. It was a combination of public relations and a way of showing the lethality of the usually sheathed Imperial saber. 'I am, sir.'

'And I am mildly surprised. I wanted to issue instructions for the proper display of your ships and men.'

'Display, sir?'

'Of course,' van Doorman said, a trace irritably. 'The entire 23rd Fleet will be open to visitors, as usual.'

'Uh . . . I'm sorry, sir. We can't do it.'

Van Doorman scowled, then brightened. Perhaps this might be the excuse he needed to gulag Sten. 'That was not a request, Commander. You may take it as a direct order.'

'Sir, that's an order I can't obey.' Sten sort of wanted to see how purple his admiral would get before he explained but thought better of it. 'Sir, according to Imperial Order R-278-XN-FICHE: BULKELEY, all of my ships are under a security edict. From Prime World, sir. There's a copy in your operations files, sir.' Sten was making up the order number – but such an order *did* exist.

Van Doorman sat back in his chair after probably rejecting several comebacks. 'So you and your crew of thugs will just frowst about on Empire Day. Most convenient.'

And then Sten had his idea, inspired by the thought of Empire Day – and the Emperor, who loved a double-blind plan. 'Nossir. We'd rather not, sir, unless that's your orders.'

Before van Doorman could answer, Sten went on. 'Actually, Admiral, I had planned to set an appointment with your flag secretary today, to offer a suggestion.'

Van Doorman waited.

'Sir, while we can't allow anyone close to our ships, there's no reason that they can't be seen. Everyone on Cavite's seen us take off and land.'

'You have an idea,' van Doorman said.

'Yessir. Is there any reason that we could not do a flyby? Perhaps after you deliver the opening remarks?'

'Hmm,' van Doorman mused. 'I *have* watched your operations. Quite spectacular – although as I have said before, I see little combat value in your craft. But they are very, very showy.'

'Yessir. And my officers are very experienced in in-atmosphere aerobatics.'

Van Doorman actually smiled. 'Perhaps, Commander, I have

been judging you too harshly. I felt that you really did not have the interests of our navy at heart. I could have been mistaken.'

'Thank you, sir. But I'm not quite finished.'

'Go ahead.'

'If you would be willing to issue authorization, we could provide quite a fireworks display as part of the flyby.'

'Fireworks aren't exactly part of our ordnance.'

'I know that, sir. But we could draw blanks for the chainguns and remove the warheads on some of the obsolete missiles we have in storage.'

'You are thinking. That would be very exciting. And it would enable us to get rid of some of those clunkers, before we get gigged for having them at the next IG.'

Sten realized that van Doorman was making a joke. He laughed.

'Very well. Very well indeed. I'll issue the authorization today. Commander, I think you and I are starting to think in the same lines.'

God help me if we are, Sten thought. 'One more thing, sir.'

'Another idea?'

'Nossir. A question. You said the *entire* fleet will be on display?'

'Outside of two picket boats – that is my custom.'

Sten saluted and left.

The war council consisted of Sten, Alex, Sh'aarl't, Estill, Sekka, and Sutton and was held in one of the flotilla's engine yards.

'This is to be regarded as information-only, people,' Sten started. He relayed what had happened at the meeting with van Doorman. The other officers took a minute to absorb things, then put on their what-a-dumb-clottin'-idea-but-you're-the-skipper expressions.

'Maybe there's madness to my method. I got to thinking that if I were a Tahn, and I wanted a time to start things off with a bang, I could do a helluva lot worse than pick Empire Day.

'Every clotting ship our wonderful admiral has is gonna be sitting on line. Security will be two tacships and shore patrolmen on foot.'

'Tha's noo bad thinkin',' Alex said. 'Th' Tahn dinna appear to me t'be't standin't on ceremony like declarations of war or like that.'

'And if they hit us,' Sh'aarl't added, 'I'd just as soon not be sitting on the ground waiting.'

'Maybe I'm slow, Commander,' Estill said. 'But say you're right. And we're airborne when – and if – they come in. But with, pardon me, clotting fireworks?'

Alex looked at the lieutenant with admiration. It may have been the first time he had used the word 'clot' since being commissioned. Being in the mosquito fleet was proving salutory for Estill's character.

'Exactly, Lieutenant,' Sten said. 'We're going to have great fireworks. Goblin fireworks, Fox fireworks, and Kali fireworks. Van Doorman's given us permission to loot his armory – and we're going to take advantage.'

Tapia laughed. 'What happens if you're wrong – and ol' Doormat calls for his fireworks?'

'It'd be a clottin' major display, and we'll *all* be looking for new jobs. Vote?'

Van Doorman would probably have relieved Sten on the spot just for running his flotilla with even a breath of democracy.

Kilgour, of course, was all for it. As was Tapia. Sekka and Sh'aarl't gave it a moment of thought, then concurred. Estill smiled. 'Paranoiacs together,' he said, and raised his hand.

'Fine. Get work crews together, Mr Sutton, and some gravsleds.'

'Yes, sir. By the way, would you have any objections if some of my boys happen to be terrible at mathematics and acquire some *extra* weaponry?'

'Mr Sutton, I myself could never count above ten without taking my boots off. Now, move 'em out.'

Chapter Forty-Two

Sr. Ecu floated just above the sand, which had been sifted to a prism white – a white even purer than the minuscule sensors that whiskered from his wings. He settled closer to the garden floor, shuddered in disgust, and gave a faint flap to a winglet. A puff of dust rose from the sand, and he was in position again.

Lord Fehrle had kept him waiting for nearly two hours. The

impatience he felt now had little to do with the length of the waiting. Sr. Ecu was a member of a race that treasured the subtle stretchings of time. But not now, and not in this environment.

He supposed that he had been ushered into the sand garden because the Lord Fehrle wanted to impress him with his sense of art and understanding. Besides patience, the Manabi were noted for their sensitivity to visual stimulation.

The sand garden was a perfect bowl with a radius of about a half a kilometer. In this area were laid exactly ten stones, ranging in size from five meters down to a third of a meter. Each stone was of a different color: earth colors varying from deep black to a tinge of orange. They had all been mathematically placed the proper distance apart. It was the coldest work of art that Sr. Ecu had seen in his hundred-plus years. During the two hours of waiting he had considered what may have been in Lord Fehrle's mind when he created it.

The thinking was not comfortable. If one stone had been ever so slightly out of place or if a patch of sand had not been as perfect as the rest, he would have felt much better. He had tried to change the shape of it all with his own presence.

Sr. Ecu's body was black with a hint of red just under the wing tips. His tail snaked out three meters, narrowing to a point that had once held a sting in his race's ancestral past. He had tried moving himself around from point to point, hovering for long minutes as he tried physically to break up the cold perfection that was the garden. Somehow he kept finding himself back in the same place. If nothing more, his physical presence in the perfect spot added to the psychological ugliness of the place.

Even for a Tahn, on a scale of one to ten, Lord Fehrle rated below zero as a diplomat. This was an estimation that Sr. Ecu could make with authority. His own race was noted for its diplomatic bearing – which was the reason Fehrle had requested his presence.

In any other circumstances Sr. Ecu would have left in a diplomatic huff after the first half hour. Anger at insult can be a valuable tool in intrasystem relations. But not in *these* circumstances. He was not sure that the Manabi could preserve their traditional neutrality, much less a future, if the Tahn and the Empire continued on their collision course.

So he would wait and talk and see in this obscenity of a garden that perfectly illustrated the Tahn mind.

It was another half hour before Lord Fehrle appeared. He was polite but abrupt, acting as if *he* had been kept waiting instead of the Manabi. Fehrle had sketched in the current status of relations between the Empire and the Tahn. All of this, except for smaller details, the Manabi knew. He dared Fehrle's impatience by saying so.

'This is a textbook summation of the situation, my lord,' he said. 'Most admirable. Almost elegant in its sparseness. But I fail to see my role.'

'To be frank,' Fehrle said, 'we intend to launch a full-out attack.'

All three of Sr. Ecu's stomachs lurched. Their linings had been sorely tested in the past, to the point where he had been sure he would never be able to digest his favorite microorganisms again. This, however, was true disaster.

'I beg you to reconsider, my lord,' he said. 'Are your positions really so far apart? Is it *really* too late to talk? In my experience . . .'

'That's why I asked you here,' Fehrle said. 'There is a way out. A way to avoid total war.'

Sr. Ecu knew the man was lying through his gleaming teeth. However, he could hardly say so. 'I'm delighted to hear that,' he said. 'I suppose you have some new demands. Compromises, perhaps? Areas of concern to be traded for firm agreements?'

Fehrle snorted. 'Not at all,' he said. 'We will settle for nothing less than total capitulation.'

'If I may say so, that is not a very good way to resume negotiations, my lord,' Sr. Ecu murmured.

'But that is where I intend to begin, just the same,' Fehrle said. 'I have a fiche outlining our position. It will be delivered to you before you leave for Prime World.'

'And how much time shall I tell the Emperor's emissaries they have to respond?'

'Seventy-two E-hours,' Lord Fehrle said flatly, almost in a monotone.

'But, my lord, that's impossible. It would take a miracle for me to even *reach* Prime World in that time, much less to set up the proper channels.'

'It's seventy-two hours just the same.'

'You must listen to reason, my lord!'

'Then you refuse?'

Now Sr Ecu understood. Fehrle wanted a refusal. Later he could say that he had done his best to avert full war but that the Manabi would not undertake the mission. He had to admire the plan, as in a way he admired how perfectly ugly the man's garden was.

Because there was no way in his race's coda that Sr. Ecu could undertake the mission.

'Yes, my lord. I'm afraid I must refuse.'

'Very well, then.'

Lord Fehrle turned without another word and stalked off across the white sand. Sr. Ecu rippled his wings and in a moment was soaring away, his own self-esteem and his race's neutrality shattered.

Chapter Forty-Three

The weather report for Empire Day was disappointing: overcast with occasional rain, heavy at times. Rotten weather for a holiday – but it would save the lives of several thousands of beings on Cavite and, perhaps, be responsible for Sten's survival on that day.

Sten had restricted his crews to the flotilla area twenty-four hours beforehand. There had been grumbles – Empire Day for the 23rd Fleet was not only show-and-tell day but a rationale for some serious partying. Not that there was much time for bitching – they were too busy loading and resupplying the ships. And quickly the crew members, seeing live missiles and ammunition being not only loaded but racked and mounted, figured that something very much out of the ordinary was going on.

The ships were ready to launch at 1900 hours. Sten was amused to see that the final load actually was fireworks, acquired by Sutton from some of his black-market contacts. Sten put everyone under light hypno sleep and tried for a little rest himself – without result.

Wearing a slicker against the occasional spatters of rain, he spent the middle hours of the night pacing around his ships and wondering why he had ever wanted to be the man in charge of anything.

He roused his people at 0100.

The *Kelly, Claggett, Gamble,* and *Richards* lifted near-silently on Yukawa drive at 0230. Dawn would be at 0445. Admiral van Doorman would open the ceremonies at 0800.

The Tahn, too, had their timetable. It was based around that of the 23rd Fleet.

A month earlier, a Tahn working inside fleet headquarters had copied the Empire Day schedule fiche, and it had been immediately relayed offworld. The fiche occupied a small screen on one side of the *Forez*'s bridge. Neither Lady Atago nor Admiral Deska needed to consult it.

Nearby hung a second, newly completed battleship – the *Kiso* – of the same class as the *Forez*. The Tahn battlefleet waited just on the edge of Cavite's stellar system. Nearly numberless cruisers, destroyers, attack ships, and troopships filled out the fleet.

Other battlefleets, equally massive, had been assigned other targets in the Fringe Worlds. Lady Atago was to destroy the 23rd Fleet and its base on Cavite.

On the tick, Atago ordered the attack.

Remote sensors scattered offworld were destroyed, jammed, or given false data to transmit. To make sure there was no alert, at 0500 five squads of commando Tahn, some of whom had been trained on Frehda's farm, hit the 23rd Fleet's SigInt center. Other Tahn, correctly uniformed as Imperial sailors, took over the center.

At 0730, the main elements of Atago's battlefleet were just out-atmosphere. The two picket boats, their crew members hung over and their screens focused, against orders, on the display field below, barely had time to see the incoming Tahn destroyers before they were destroyed.

On the field, Admiral van Doorman, flanked by Brijit and his wife, checked the time – ten minutes – and then started up the steps of the reviewing stand.

Staff officers and civilian dignitaries were already waiting.

In the ionosphere, the Tahn assault ship opened its bays, and small attack craft spewed downward.

Sten's problem, after lift, was where to hide. If he was correct and Cavite was about to be hit, it would be hit hard. He had full confidence in his tacships – but not in an orbital situation where he might be facing a battleship or six.

Nor was the cloud cover the answer, as any ship attacking from offworld would be using electronics. The clouds wouldn't even show up on most shipscreens.

Sten's best solution was to take his flotilla out over the ocean, some twenty kilometers away from Cavite, and hold at fifty meters over the sea. He figured that he would probably be buried in ground clutter and very hard to pick up.

Foss was the first to pick up the attacking ships.

'All ships,' Sten ordered. 'Independent attacks. Conserve munitions and watch your tails. We're at war!'

Kilgour had the *Gamble* at full power, headed back for Cavite.

The first V-wing of Tahn launched air-to-ground metal-seeking missiles at 1000 meters, pulled momentarily level, and scattered frag bombs down the length of the field.

The parade ground became a hell of explosions.

Van Doorman had time enough to see the missiles, gape once, and throw himself on top of his wife and daughter before all thought vanished and sanity became trying to hold on to the pitching ground under him.

The Tahn ships lifted, banked, and came back on a strafing pass. Most of the dignitaries and staff officers not killed by the bombs were shattered with chaingun bursts.

Van Doorman lifted his head and saw, through blood, the ships coming back in. That was all he remembered.

He didn't see the *Richards* and *Claggett* come in on the flank, their own chainguns raving, or the thinly armored Tahn ships cartwheel into the field, their pinwheeling wreckage doing as much damage to the 23rd Fleet's ships as the missiles had.

Seeing the *Richards* and *Claggett* pull ahead of him, Sten changed his mind and his tactics. He ordered the *Kelly* into wingman's slot and climbed for space.

The Tahn assault ship was not expecting any response from the maelstrom below and was an easy target. The *Gamble*'s weapons systems clicked through Kali choice to Goblin, and Kilgour fired.

The hull of the ship gaped, and red flame seared out.

In the *Kelly*, Sekka had taken away his weapons officer's control helmet – *he* was the warrior of generations. The chant he was muttering went back 2,000 years as his sights crossed and settled on the huge bulk of the *Forez*. Without orders, he launched the Kali.

Even under full AM2 power, the *Kelly* jolted as the huge missile chuffed out the center launch tube, and its own AM2 drive launched it.

For Sekka, there was nothing but the growing bulk of the Tahn battleship in his eyes as he became the Kali.

The missile was well named. It struck the *Forez* on a weapons deck. Two-hundred-fifty Tahn crewmen died in the initial explosion, and more were killed in the blast of secondary explosions.

Sekka allowed himself a tight smile as he pulled off the helmet, seeing, onscreen, four attacking Tahn destroyers. That was nothing. And if they killed him, what was death to a Mandingo warrior?

It was possible that the two Tahn cruisers did not ever expect attack from a ship as small as the *Gamble*. Certainly they seemed to take no significant evasive action and launched only a handful of countermissiles before Kilgour had Goblins at full power, targets locked.

Sten knew that the Goblins could injure a cruiser, but he did not expect the nearly simultaneous explosions; seeing the screen begin flashing NO TARGET UNDER ACQUISITION, Alex lifted his weapons helmet.

'Lad, wha's th' matter wi' their blawdy cruisers?'

Sten, seeing a pack of destroyers coming in, too late to save their charges, was busy with evasive action.

Lady Atago, on the bridge of the *Forez*, braced herself as the battleship shuddered under another explosion. Part of her brain was pleased – in spite of catastrophe, the men and women she had trained were responding efficiently and without panic.

'Your orders?'

Atago considered the choices. There was only one. 'Admiral Deska, cancel the landing on Cavite. We cannot proceed with only one capital ship. The other landings on the secondary systems may proceed. You and I shall transfer our flags to the *Kiso*. Order the *Forez* to proceed to a forward repair base.'

'Your orders, milady.'

Sten saw the Tahn fleet begin its withdrawal as he and his ships returned to base.

It wasn't much of a victory. Below on Cavite, the 23rd Fleet, the only Imperial forces in the Fringe Worlds, was almost completely destroyed.

The Tahn war had just begun.

BOOK THREE

ON THE WIND

Chapter Forty-Four

The attack on the Caltor System and Cavite was not the actual beginning of the war. That had occurred one E-hour earlier in an attack against Prime World and the Emperor himself.

Nearly simultaneously, thousands of Tahn ships savaged the Empire. Missions varied from invasion to base reduction to fleet battles. At the end of the initial phase, the Tahn estimated their success at better than eighty-five percent. It was one of the blackest days in the Empire's history.

The attack coordination had been exceedingly complex, since the Tahn wanted to reap the maximum benefits possible from Empire Day. Technically the minute of vengeance – what more prosaic cultures might call D-day – was at the same tick of the ammonium maser clock that each fleet commander had on his or her bridge.

Actually, of course, there were adjustments, since each of the Imperial worlds used its own time zoning. There also were readjustments to keep the attacks within a close enough time frame to prevent the Empire from coming to full alert.

Almost more important to the Tahn was a 'moral' readjustment. Somehow the Tahn felt it perfectly legitimate to begin a war without the usual roundelay of escalating diplomatic threats but dishonorable to not strike at – their phrase – the throat of the tiger.

Prime World.

The Eternal Emperor.

The choice of Empire day to begin the war was made for several reasons. The Tahn correctly assumed the Imperial military would be collected and relaxed; there would be, if the attacks were successful, an inevitable lowering of Imperial morale; and, finally, because this was the one day of the year when everyone knew where the Emperor was – at home, expecting visitors.

Home was a oversize duplicate of the Earth castle Arundel, with a six- by two-kilometer bailey in front, surrounded by fifty-five kilometers of parkland. Housed in the bailey's V-banked walls were the most important elements of the Empire's administration. The castle itself contained not only the Emperor, his bodyguards, and considerable staff but the command and control center for the entire Empire. Most of the necessary technology was buried far under Arundel, along with enough air/water/food to withstand a century-long siege.

The visitors the Emperor was expecting were his subjects. Once a year the normally closed-off castle was opened up for a super-spectacle of bands, military displays, and games. To be invited or somehow to wangle a ticket to Empire Day at the palace was an indication of signal achievement or purchase.

It had taken four years for the Tahn to prepare for their attack on Arundel. The only possible assault that could be made was a surgical strike – there was no way that the Tahn could slip a fleet or even a squadron of destroyers through the Empire's offworld security patrols.

Except for Empire Day, the airspace over Arundel was sealed. All aerial traffic on Prime World was monitored, and any deviation from the flight pattern put the palace's AA sections on alert. An intrusion into the palace's airspace was electronically challenged once and then attacked. It was equally impossible to approach the palace on the ground – the only connection between Arundel and the nearest city, Fowler, was by high-speed pneumosubway.

Except for Empire Day . . .

On Empire Day huge troop-carrying gravlighters were used to move tourists from Fowler to the palace. The security precautions were minimal – all passengers were, of course, vetted and searched. The lighters themselves were given a fixed flight pattern and time, in addition to being equipped with an IFF – Identification – Friend or Foe – box linked to the palace's aerial security section.

These precautions were ludicrously easy to subvert.

Oddly enough, the Tahn may have felt it dishonorable not to attack the Emperor – but, on the other hand, they preferred to do the dirty work through a cut-out. 'Honor' in a militaristic society is most often Rabelaisian: 'Do what thou wilt shalt be the whole of the law.'

Three highly committed Tahn immigrants – revolutionaries from the late Godfrey Alain's Fringe World movement – had been chosen and moved into position by Tahn intelligence two years previously. One was instructed to find a minor job at Fowler's port, Soward. A second found employment as a barkeep. The third was hired as a gardener by the occupants of one of the luxurious estates that ringed the Imperial grounds. He was an excellent gardener – the merchant prince who employed him swore he had never had a harder or more conscientious worker.

The method of attack would be by missile, a rather specially designed missile. The Tahn surmised correctly that Arundel was faced with nuclear shielding, so a conventional nuke within practical limits would not provide complete destruction. The final missile looked most odd. It was approximately ten meters long and was configured to provide a very specific sensor profile, a profile closely matching that of a much larger Guard gravlighter.

Inside it were two nuclear devices. Tahn science had figured out how to utilize the ancient shaped-charge effect – the Munro effect – with atomics. For shrouding and cone they used imperium, the shielding normally used to handle Anti-Matter Two, the Empire's primary power source. Behind the first device was the guidance mechanism, and back of that was the second device. The missile's nose was sharply pointed, less for aerodynamics than for blast effect.

Besides the guidance system, the missile also contained a duplicate of the IFF box that would be used by the gravlighters on Empire Day.

The missile had been smuggled, in three sections, onto Prime World some months previously, transported to a leased warehouse, assembled, and set in its launch rack by a team of Tahn scientists.

The three Tahn from the Fringe Worlds were never told the location of the missile; they were merely instructed to be in certain locations with certain equipment at a certain time.

Two days before Empire Day, the Tahn who was a ramp rat at Soward installed a small timer-equipped device in a specified gravlighter's McLean generator.

One day before Empire Day, the controller for the three men boarded an offworld flight and disappeared.

At 1100 on Empire Day, the three men were in place.

The gardener sat ready behind the controls of one of his employer's gravsleds. No one in the mansion would notice – two canisters of a binary blood gas had seen to that.

The other two were atop a building in Soward, near the launch site, one watching a timer, the other counting gravlighters as they lifted off toward Arundel.

Number seven was 'theirs.'

On the field, the pilot of the sabotaged gravlighter applied power. The lighter raised, belched smoke, and clanked down. The field's dispatcher swore and ordered a standby unit up to cross-load the passengers.

On the building, the timer touched zero, and the first man fingered a switch on his control box. At the warehouse, explosive charges blew a ragged hole in the roof. McLean-assist takeoff units lifted the missile into the air, then dropped away as the Yukawa drive cut in and the missile smashed forward at full power.

Kilometers away, the third man also went into action. At the commanded time, he lifted the gravsled straight up. His mouth was very dry as he hoped that the palace's aerial sensors would be a little slow.

His own control panel beeped at him – the missile was within range. He focused the riflelike device toward Arundel, dim in the morning haze, and touched a switch. A low-power laser illuminated Arundel's gateway. A second beep informed him that the missile had acquired the target.

For the three Tahn, their mission was accomplished. Now their orders were to evade capture and make their way to a given rendezvous point outside Soward. Of course, Tahn intelligence had no intention either of making a pickup or of leaving a trail. Both the launch and the aiming control boxes contained secondary timers and explosive charges. Seconds after the missile signaled, they went off.

No one saw the explosion that vaporized the Tahn as they scurried toward a ladder, but a watch officer at Arundel saw the gravsled ball into flame and pinwheel down. His hand was halfway to an alert button when the automatic sensors correctly interpreted that the gravlighter headed for the palace was moving at a speed far beyond reason and screamed warning.

The Eternal Emperor was in his apartments alternately cursing to the head of his Gurkha bodyguards about the necessity to wear full-dress uniform and pinning on various decorations. Captain Chittahang Limbu was half listening and smiling agreeably. Limbu was still somewhat in awe of his current position. Formerly a Subadar major, he had been promoted to Sten's old job as head of the Emperor's bodyguard. This was the highest position a Gurkha had ever held in Imperial history.

He was fondly remembering the celebration his home village had thrown for him on his last leave, when the overhead alarm bansheed its warning.

The Emperor jumped, sticking himself with a medal pin. Limbu was a stocky brown blur, slapping a switch on the panel at his waist and then manhandling the Emperor forward, toward a suddenly gaping hole in the wall.

Whatever was happening, his orders were clear and in no way allowed for the Gurkhas' love of combat.

The missile's impact point was almost perfect. The thin nose squashed as designed, allowing the missile to hang in place for a microsecond. The first nuke blew, and its directional blast tore through the shielding. The missile continued to crumple, and then the second bomb exploded.

And Arundel, heart of the Empire, vanished into the center of a newborn sun.

Chapter Forty-Five

Sten itemized chaos as he slowly steered his combat car over the rubble that had been Cavite City's main street. This was not the first city or world that he had been on when the talking stopped and the shooting started. But this appeared to be the first time he had been in on the ground floor of an Empirewide war.

Experience is valuable, he reminded himself, which avoided his worry about Brijit.

Sten had brought his miraculously undamaged ships down onto Cavite Base at nightfall. Sometimes dishonesty pays – he had located his supply base in a disused warehouse in the test yards. As a result, the weaponry and supplies that Sutton had acquired had not been touched by the Tahn attack.

He ordered his boats to resupply and return to low orbit

immediately. He would try to find out from fleet headquarters how bad things really were.

Cavite Base was a boil and confusion of smoke and flame.

Sten commandeered a combat car and headed for the Carlton Hotel. If it still stood, he assumed that what remained of van Doorman's command staff would be there.

Cavite City hadn't suffered major damage, Sten estimated. Imperial Boulevard – the central street – had absorbed some incendiary and AP bombs or rockets, but most of the buildings still stood. There weren't any civilians on the night-hung streets other than rescue workers and firefighting teams. Contrary to legend, disaster generally made people pull together or retreat into their homes – rioting in the streets had always been a myth.

Sten veered the combat car aside as a gravsled, hastily painted with red crosses on the landing pads, whistled past. In the distance, he could hear the sounds of combat. That was the storming of the Sigint center – since the Tahn had not been able to land, those revolutionaries who had occupied the center had died to the last man.

Sten did not know, or much care, what the shooting signified – the situation was bad enough right now for him. He grounded the combat car outside the Carlton and started for the entrance.

Security, he noted wryly, had improved – three sets of SP men checked him before he hit the main doors. But some things did not change. The two dress-uniformed patrolmen still snapped their willyguns to salute as he came up the steps. Sten wondered if either of them realized that their uniforms were now spattered with muck, blood, and what appeared to be vomit.

If Cavite City was chaos, Admiral van Doorman's headquarters was worse. Sten desperately needed to know how bad the damage was and what his orders should be. He started at the fleet operations office. It was dark and deserted. Only the computer terminals flashed and analyzed the disaster of the day. A passing tech told him that all operations personnel appeared to have died in the attack.

Fine. He would try fleet intelligence.

Sten should have known what was going on when he saw that the door to the intelligence center yawned wide, with no sentries.

Inside, he found madness – quite literally.

Ship Captain Ladislaw sat behind a terminal, programming and reprogramming. He greeted Sten happily and then showed him what dispositions would be made on the morrow, moving the gradated dots that were the ships of the 23rd Fleet across the starchart covering one wall.

The Tahn would be repelled handily, he said. Sten knew that most of the ships he was chessboarding around were broken and smoking on the landing field at the base.

He smiled, agreed with Ladislaw, then stepped behind him, one-handed a sopor injection from his belt medpak, and shot it into the base of the ship captain's spine. Ladislaw folded instantly across his printout of impossibilities, and Sten headed for van Doorman's office.

Admiral Xavier Rijn van Doorman was quite calm and quite collected. His command center was an oasis of peace.

Sten saw Brijit peering in from the half-open door that led to van Doorman's quarters and thanked Someone that she was still alive.

Van Doorman was studying the status board over his desk. Sten glanced at it and winced – the situation was even worse than he had anticipated. For all intents and purposes, the 23rd Fleet had ceased to exist.

At dawn that morning, the 23rd Fleet strength consisted of one heavy cruiser, the *Swampscott*, two light cruisers, some thirteen destroyers, fifty-six assorted obsolete patrolcraft, minelayer/sweepers, Sten's tacdiv, one hospital ship, and the usual gaggle of supply and maintenance craft.

The status readout showed one light cruiser destroyed, and one heavily damaged. Six destroyers were out of action, as were about half of the light combat ships and support elements.

The oddness was that the *Swampscott* was untouched. It had survived because of Sten's attack on the *Forez*. The *Swampscott* had been one of Atago's self-assigned targets.

Sten's orders were simple – to keep his tacships in space. Van Doorman would provide any support necessary until the situation straightened itself out. Sten was given complete freedom of command. Any assistance Intelligence or Operations could provide was his for the asking – one madman, and corpses.

Just wonderful, Sten thought.

Yessir, Admiral.

His snappy salute was returned with equal fervor. He saw the blankness in van Doorman's eyes and wondered.

In the corridor, Brijit was in his arms and explaining. Her mother had died in the attack. There was nothing left. Nothing at all.

Probably Sten should have stayed with her that night. But the coldness that was Sten's sheath, the coldness that had come from the death of his parents years before on Vulcan, the coldness that had seen too many drinking friends die, stopped him. Instead there was a hug, and he was hurrying toward the com center. He wanted the *Gamble* in for a pickup.

As the *Gamble* flared in, settling in the middle of the boulevard outside the Carlton, Sten found time to be amazed at van Doorman's ability to control himself.

That was another cipher. But one to watch very carefully, Sten thought, as the *Gamble's* port yawned and he ran toward it.

He had already forgotten van Doorman, Brijit, and the likelihood that he and his people would die in the Caltor System.

His mind was hearing only 'independent command . . .'

Chapter Forty-Six

The eternal emperor spotted something and waddled, bulky in his radiation suit, through the nuclear ruin that had been one of his rose gardens. Behind him, willyguns ready, moved two suited Gurkhas – Captain Limbu and a naik. Above and to their rear floated a combat car, guns sweeping the grounds.

Limbu had been successful in shoving the Emperor into the McLean-controlled slide tube that led 2,000 meters into the underground sanctuary and control center under the castle, then had dived after him. Radiation-proof air locks had slammed closed as they fell.

Very few others aboveground had lived – there were only a handful of Gurkhas, less than one platoon of the newly reformed Praetorian guard, and fewer than a dozen members of the Imperial household staff. Arundel and its immediate grounds were leveled. The outer layer of the bailey walls had been peeled, but there had been little damage to the administrative offices inside them.

The only structure still standing inside the palace grounds was the Imperial Parliament building, some ten kilometers from ground zero. This was ironic, because its survival was owed to the fact that the Emperor, not wishing to look at his politicians' headquarters, had built a kilometer-high mountain between the palace and the Parliament building, a mountain that successfully diverted the blast from the twinned bombs.

Civilian casualties on the planet were very slight, most of the destruction having been restricted to the Emperor's own fifty-five-kilometer palace grounds.

The Emperor bent, awkwardly picked something up from the ground, and held it out for the Gurkhas' admiration. Somehow, one solitary rose had been burnt to instant ash yet had held together. The Gurkhas looked at the rose, faces expressionless through their face shields, then spun, hearing the whine of a McLean generator. Their guns were up aiming.

'No!' the Emperor exclaimed, and the guns were lowered.

Floating toward the Emperor was a teardrop. Through its transparent nose, the Emperor recognized the black and tinted-red body of a Manabi. Given the circumstances, it could only be Sr. Ecu.

The teardrop hovered a diplomatic three meters away.

'You live.' The observation was made calmly.

'I live,' the Emperor agreed.

'My sorrows. Arundel was very beautiful.'

'Palaces are easy to rebuild,' the Emperor said flatly.

The teardrop shifted slightly in a breeze.

'Are you speaking for the Tahn?' the Emperor asked.

'That would have been their desire. I declined. They wished me to deliver an ultimatum – but without allowing me sufficient time to travel from Heath to Prime.'

'That sounds like their style.'

'I now speak both for the Manabi. And for myself.'

Most interesting, the Emperor thought. The Manabi almost never spoke as a single culture. 'May I ask some questions first?'

'You may ask. I may decline to answer.'

'Of course.'

Ecu shifted his suit so that he appeared to be looking at the Gurkhas.

'Never mind,' the Emperor assured him. 'They won't talk any more than you will.'

That was most true – neither a Gurkha nor a Manabi would release any information unless specifically ordered. And both races were impervious to torture, drugs, or psychological interrogation.

'I have just arrived on Prime. What are your estimates of the situation?'

'Lousy,' the Emperor said frankly. 'I've lost at least half a dozen fleet elements; forty systems, minimum, have either fallen to the Tahn or are going to; my Guard divisions are being decimated; and it's going to get a lot worse.'

Ecu considered. 'And your allies?'

'They are,' the Emperor said dryly, 'still conferring about the situation. My estimates are that less than half of my supposed friends will declare war on the Tahn. The rest'll wait to see how things shake out.'

'What are your ultimate predictions?'

The Emperor considered the ashen rose for long moments. 'That question I shall not answer.'

'I see. I now speak,' Ecu said formally, 'for my grandsires, my fellows, and for those generations yet to be conceived and hatched.'

The Emperor blinked. Ecu was indeed speaking for the entire Manabi.

'We are not a warlike species. However, in this struggle, we declare our support for the forces of the Empire. We shall strive to maintain an appearance of neutrality, but you shall be permitted access to any information we have gathered or shall gather.'

The Emperor almost smiled. This was the only good news in an otherwise tragic universe.

'Why?' he asked. 'It looks like the Tahn will win.'

'Impossible,' Ecu said flatly. 'May we speak under the rose?'

'I already said—'

'I repeat my request.'

The Emperor nodded. A metalloid rod slid from Sr Ecu's suit – the Emperor again motioned down the Gurkhas' weapons – and touched the Emperor's helmet.

'I think,' Ecu's voice echoed, 'that even your most faithful should not hear the following.

'Would you agree that the Tahn believe that Anti-Matter Two is duplicatable or that, given a Tahn victory, they could learn the location of its source?'

Again there was long silence. Where and how AM2 had come into being was the most closely held secret of the Empire, since only AM2 held the Empire together, no matter how tenuously.

'That may be what they're thinking,' the Emperor finally admitted.

'They are wrong. Do not bother responding. We believe that the only – and I mean only – source of AM2 is yourself. We have no knowledge or intelligence how this occurs, but this is our synthesis.

'For this reason, we predict there can only be two results from this war: either you shall be victorious, or the Tahn shall win. And their victory will mean the total destruction of what low level of civilization exists.'

The probe collapsed, and its tip brushed the edge of the rose.

Dry, powdery ash dusted the Emperor's gauntlet.

Chapter Forty-Seven

'How completely are you willing to interpret Admiral van Doorman's orders, Commander?'

Sten waited for Sutton to elaborate. The four tacship skippers, plus Sutton and Kilgour, were attempting to plot their tactics for the weeks to come, although none of them believed the Tahn had any intentions of letting the ruins of the 23rd Fleet survive that long.

They were gathered in the crammed supply warehouse that Sutton had cozened for storing the division's supplies.

'I am . . . humph . . . growing most fond of these ships of ours,' the spindar continued. 'They remind me all too much of my species' own offspring. Even after they are no longer biologically connected to the pouch, they must remain within close range of it, or perish.'

Sten caught the analogy. His tacships, due to their cramped quarters and limited ammunition/food/air supplies, were most short-ranged.

'The Tahn'll be hitting Cavite again,' Sh'aarl't said. 'Maybe just carpet bombing, maybe invasion. I'd rather not have our supplies just sitting here waiting.'

'Not to mention,' Sekka added, looking around at the mad assemblage of explosives, munitions, rations, and spare parts, 'what would happen if one mite of a bomb happened to come through the roof.'

'Quite exactly my point,' the spindar chuffed. 'Cavite Base is not my idea of a burrow/haven.'

'First problem,' Sten said. 'No way will van Doorman approve us moving the boats, the supplies, and your support people offworld.'

'Do you plan on telling him?'

'I don't think he'd even notice,' Estill put in.

'Agreed. Second problem – how can we move all this drakh? We don't have enough cargo area as it is on the boats.'

'I foresaw our dilemma,' Sutton said. 'It would seem that there is a certain civilian who owes me a favor. A very enormous favor.'

'Of course he has a ship.'

'Of course.'

'How,' Sh'aarl't asked skeptically, 'has he been able to keep it from being requisitioned?'

'The ship in question is, harrumph, used to transport waste.'

'A garbage scow?'

'Somewhat worse than that. Human waste.'

Sten whistled tunelessly. 'The swabbies are gonna love it when they find out they're traveling via crapper.'

'Tha'll dinna mind, Skipper,' Kilgour said. 'Considerin't tha believ't tha're in't already.'

'Very funny, Mr Kilgour. I'll let you pass the word down.'

'No problem, lad. One wee point. Does any hae an idea where we'll be hiein' twa?'

'Poor being,' Sh'aarl't sympathized, patting Alex on the shoulder with a pedipalp. The heavy-worlder was so used to her by now that he didn't even flinch. 'Where else would we go but among common thieves?'

'Ah'll be cursit! Y'r right, Sh'aarl't. M' mind's gon't.'

'Romney!' Sten exclaimed.

'Exactly,' Sh'aarl't said. 'If anybody's able to stay invisible to the Tahn, it'll be the smugglers.'

'Wild must've zigged when zaggin' wae th' answer,' Alex said soberly.

Sten didn't answer. He was bringing the *Gamble* closer to Romney's shattered dome. The other three ships and the transporter waited a planetary diameter out.

'Negative ElInt, sir,' Foss reported.

If the Tahn were waiting in ambush, Foss's instruments would have picked something up. Sten reduced Yukawa drive power, and the *Gamble* dropped slowly through the tear in the dome.

Romney was a graveyard.

Sten counted six – no, seven – smashed ships around the landing field. Where Wild's headquarters had been was only a crater. The other buildings – com, living quarters, hangars, and the enormous storage warehouses – were blasted ruins.

'Bring the other ships in,' he ordered. 'I want them dispersed around the field. I want all hands suited up and in front of that first hangar in one hour.'

'Gather around, people,' Sten said.

The formation broke and formed a ragged semicircle around their CO.

'Foss . . . Kilgour. What'd you find?'

'It looks,' the electronics tech said cautiously, 'like Wild and his smugglers did get hit by surprise.'

'An' by th' Tahn,' Alex added. 'W' found' it three unblown't project'les.'

'Bodies?'

'Na, there'd be th' weirdness. Noo a one. An th' warehouses be't emptied flat.'

'Couldn't the Tahn have landed and looted the place?'

'Wi'oot takin't Wild's weaponry wi' 'em?' Kilgour pointed to where a seemingly untouched SA missile battery sat abandoned. Sten nodded. Foss's electronics analysis and Kilgour's Mantis-trained estimate agreed with his own.

'Fine. Troops, this is going to be our home away from home. Mr Sutton, I want that transport unloaded ASAP. All hands. Second, full power back to Cavite. You'll have the *Richards* for escort. I want you to scrounge all the bubbleshelters you can find. Foss, let Mr Sutton know what you'll need to set up a detection station from Cavite, and how much of Wild's electronics you can salvage.

'Here's the plan, friends. This is still going to be our forward base. We'll move bubbles *inside* the hangars and warehouses. We'll move some of those smaller buildings around, wreck 'em up a bit, and use them for overhead cover. Even if the Tahn decide to recheck Romney, they're still going to find a dead world.'

Assuming, Sten continued mentally as he dismissed his unit, they go by visuals and self-confidence only. If they put sniffers or heat sensors inside the dome – that'll be all she scrolled.

But it was still better odds than they had on Cavite.

Chapter Forty-Eight

The biggest question the beings of the 23rd Fleet kept asking themselves was why the Tahn hadn't hit Cavite again.

The damage done by Sten's tacships – the destruction of two cruisers and assorted in-atmosphere ships, plus the damage to the *Forez* and an assault ship – was hardly enough to discourage the Tahn. Probably only complete obliteration of Lady Atago's entire fleet would have done that.

Certainly the 23rd was no longer a threat. With the exception of Sten's tacdivision, van Doorman's shattered force was mainly impotent.

The same question was being asked by Atago's crew members as well.

The outsystem landings had been very successful. Atago and Admiral Deska had been restructuring their invasion plans for Cavite when orders arrived. Lady Atago was to report to the Tahn Council at once for further instructions. Her fleet was ordered to consolidate existing gains but to make no major attacks on Imperial forces.

Admiral Deska spent the time waiting for Atago's return driving the repair crews working on the *Forez* even harder and staring at a wallscreen that showed the extent of the Tahn victories – at least, those either the Empire or the Tahn had chosen to report.

On the screen Deska had assigned orange to the Tahn galaxies, blue to the Empire, and red for the Tahn conquests. On a time-sweep, it was most impressive, as the Tahn spread red tentacles out and out, sweeping deeply into Imperial space. Only a handful of systems still showed cerulean, and those at the base of Deska's screen – worlds yet to be attacked.

The blue glimmer that represented the Caltor System was

shameful to Deska. He had failed. And the Tahn did not welcome failure of any sort.

A cursory examination of their language was adequate proof, as well as being an illustration of the problems that any non-militaristic culture faced in trying to deal with the Tahn. Since the Tahn 'race' or 'culture' was an assemblage of various warrior societies, their language was equally an assemblage of soldierly jargon and buzzwords. Still worse – the first Tahn Council had decided that their race needed a properly martial manner of communication. So skilled linguists had created what was known as a semivance tongue, in which the same word had multiple definitions. In this manner, an emotional connation was automatically given.

Three examples:

The verb *akomita* meant both 'to surrender' and 'to cease to exist'; the verb *meltah* was both 'to destroy' and 'to succeed'; the verb *verlach* was defined as 'to conquer' and 'to shame.'

There was an excellent chance, Admiral Deska knew, that Lady Atago, in spite of Lord Fehrle's protection, might be ordered to expiate the disgrace of her fleet with ritual suicide. He doubted, given her rank, that any worse penalty could be assessed. In that event, Deska knew, he would share her fate.

He forced himself into a fourth-level dhyana state, no-mind, no-fear, no-doubt, as he waited for the battle cruiser that bore either Lady Atago or his new fleet commander to couple locks with the *Kiso*.

The lock irised, and Lady Atago boarded the *Kiso*. Deska allowed himself a moment of hope. He enlarged the monitor pickup until Atago's face filled his screen. Of course there was no expression on her classic mask features. Deska snapped the monitor off. In her own time, Atago would tell him.

And in her own time, Atago did.

Indeed, the Tahn Council was not pleased with the failure. Other admirals who had failed to fully complete their instructions had already been cashiered, demoted, or removed. Atago, Deska surmised, had also been scheduled for relief. But the continued existence of the Imperial presence on the Caltor worlds suggested an alternative plan. Deska was surprised that the plan came not from Lord Fehrle, Atago's protector, but from Lord Pastour.

'This is not as we expected,' the industrialist had said, though Lady Atago did not report the conversation to Admiral Deska, 'but there may be harvest buds in this weed.'

'Continue.'

'I would think,' Pastour went on, staring at the wallscreen that was a larger and more up-to-date version of what Deska had projected for himself, 'that this Caltor System shines as much for the Emperor as for us.'

'Probably,' Lord Fehrle agreed.

'We agree that one of the biggest factors for our eventual success is that the Emperor makes his assessments as much through emotion as logic?'

'You are rechewing old meat. Of course.'

'Bear with me. Not being a senior member of the council, not as skilled as yet in decision making of this scope, sometimes I must reason aloud.

'So we have agreed on one fact. Now, fact B is that the Emperor might be seeking some kind of success to convince those beings who have not yet cast in with us to remain faithful.'

'We shall accept that as a fact,' Lord Wichman said.

'Given these two facts, I would suggest that we allow at least three – no, correction, four – reliable intelligence sources to leak to the Empire that the reason for the failure in the Caltor System was due to inept command and the use of second-line forces.'

'Ah.' Wichman nodded.

'Yes. Perhaps we might convince the Emperor to commit more forces than this shabbiness of a fleet that we have already demolished. Once these reinforcements are landed – we close the net.'

'There is soundness to your idea,' Lord Fehrle said. 'Another fact. We know that the—' he touched a memcode button '—23rd Fleet is poorly led and has filed specious intelligence in the past. So of course we must make no changes in our own forces that might cause this van Doorman to sound an alarm. The plan is excellent. I admire Lord Pastour for his battle cunning.'

His eyes swept the other twenty-seven members. There was no need for a vote.

'I will make one addition,' Lord Wichman added. 'Might we not be advised to reinforce Lady Atago with one of our reserve landing fleets? Thus the Imperial forces shall not simply be defeated, but completely annihilated.' He glanced across the chamber for Lord Fehrle's approval.

'So ordered. And sealed,' Fehrle said. He turned to the screen showing Lady Atago. 'That is all, Lady Atago. A full operations order shall be couriered to you when you return to your fleet.'

Her screen blanked. Fehrle stared at the smooth grayness. And you had better have the luck of battles with you this time, he thought. Because if you fail once more, there shall be no way I can protect you.

Orders went out before Atago's battle cruiser could take off from Heath – three full Tahn landing forces, with supply, support, and attack craft, would be committed to her fleet, and the intelligence plants would be made at once.

None of this was necessary. The Eternal Emperor had already ordered Major General Ian Mahoney and his First Guards to establish a forward operating base on the world of Cavite.

Chapter Forty-Nine

The only hope of survival that Sten and his four tacships had was never to be where or when they were anticipated. Even a Tahn corvette, forewarned, had more than enough armament to obliterate any of the Bulkeley-class ships. Sten's constant counsel was for them to think like a minnow in a school of sharks.

The next stage after finding a semi-hidden base of operations was to pick a target that the ships could hit and get out of with some expectation of survival.

The three systems nearest to Caltor swarmed with Tahn ships, all on constant alert and looking for glory. What Sten's people had to do was to hit where they weren't expected – and to hit where the maximum damage could be done.

That meant the Tahn supply route.

Of course the Tahn would have their supply lines more heavily guarded near the Caltor System. But what about farther out, closer to their own systems? It seemed unlikely that the Tahn would waste fuel, ships, or men, since the only Imperial forces within reach were the remnants of van Doorman's fleet. And they must think that the tacships that had worked over the Cavite landing force were far too short-ranged to reach deep into their own empire.

Indeed, the tacships *were* short-ranged – in terms of rations and armament, not fuel. Each of them had onboard enough AM2 to fuel their drives for half a year.

Sten hoped the Tahn were as logical as he was.

And so the four tacships became parasites. A survey ship whose drive mechanisms had been destroyed in the Tahn's first attack was borrowed, lifted off Cavite by the tacships – Tapia's tug experience was most valuable – and packed with supplies on Romney. Then, with Sten's own boats still linked to the survey ship, they took off.

Their initial course took them far to one side of the worlds now occupied by the Tahn. Somewhere between nowhere and lost, they reset their course toward the heart of the Tahn worlds.

They advanced very slowly, their sensors reaching out, hour after hour, keeping watch-on, watch-off. They knew – semi-knew/hoped like hell – that any Tahn ship could be picked up by them before they showed up on the Tahn screens. They were not searching blindly. Sten had assumed that at least one supply route would lead from Heath, the Tahn capital world, toward the newly occupied systems near Cavite. He projected that route as a line, and other, unknown routes coming toward those worlds.

Two weeks out, they made their final resupply from the survey ship, stuck it into a tight orbit around an uninhabited world, and crept on. By then, the small, overworked air recyclers in the tacships were groaning for relief, leaving the ships and crew smelling like very used socks. Sten wondered why none of the war livies ever pointed out that soldiers stink: stink from fear, stink from fatigue, stink from uncleanliness.

And then dual alarms shrilled. The four ships went to general quarters and waited for orders.

Four transports lined across one of Sten's screens. Their drives were, of course, unshielded, so the purple flare from the ships told Sten instantly that they were Tahn. But more interesting were a series of tiny flickers from another screen.

'Shall we take them?' Sh'aarl't asked from the *Claggett*.

'Negative. Stand by.'

Sten, Kilgour, and Foss studied those flickers.

'Too wee t' be't ships,' Alex said.

'Navaids,' Foss suggested.

'Not this far out,' Sten said. 'Are they broadcasting?'

Foss checked his board. 'Negative, sir. We're picking up some kind of low-power static. Maybe activating receivers on standby?'

'Some kind of transponder? Or a superantenna?'

'Bloomin' unlikely,' Kilgour said.

Sten wanted a closer look. He slid behind Kilgour's weapon's console and put on a control helmet. 'I want a Fox launch. Keep the warhead on safe.'

Kilgour reached over his shoulder and tapped a key.

Sten, 'seeing' space through the countermissile's radar, moved it toward the light flicker, keeping the missile barely above minimum speed. The flickers grew, and his perspective changed as his 'vision' went to radar. He perceived dozens of the objects, now solid blips. Sten reversed the missile and applied power until he was no longer approaching the objects, then re-reversed and waited for some kind of analysis from his ship, which now seemed to be far behind him, even though he still sat motionlessly at the console.

'There's no interconnection between them,' Foss said. 'Physical or electronic. At least not in its present state.'

'What it looks like,' Sten said slowly, 'is a minefield.'

'Y're bonkers, lad. E'en th' Tahn whidna put out mines in th' void on th' zip chance some wee unfortunate'd wander into it.'

'Do mines have to be passive?'

'Mmm. Strong point.'

Sten lifted the helmet off and turned to the other two on the command deck. Foss was thinking, tapping his fingernails against his teeth.

'Maybe that static is from their receivers. You know, it wouldn't be too hard to set up. Sure. You could build it on a breadboard.'

Electronics jargon hadn't changed all that much over the centuries . . . and still managed to leave Sten and Kilgour blank.

'I meant, sir, it'd be easy to jury-rig. You put a missile out there, with a receiver-transmitter. Your own ships have some kind of IFF, so the missile knows not to go after them. Anybody else comes within range, the missile activates and goes after them. If you wanted to get tricky, you could even program your missiles to move around or sweep themselves if you wanted to. Probably the circuit'd look something like this . . .' Foss blanked a screen and picked up a light pen.

'Later wi' the schematics, lad,' Kilgour said. 'The question is, What are we going to do about them?'

'Maybe they're not set to go after something as small as a tacship,' Sten said.

'Will y' b' willin't t' bet on that?'

'My momma didn't raise no fools.'

'Which means we cannae go down agin' th' convoys like a sheep ae th' fold, then.'

'Not necessarily. And maybe we don't even need to. Mr. Kilgour, have the mate break out three shipsuits.'

'A lad could get killed doin't this,' Kilgour growled. The three men hung inches away from one of the Tahn mines.

Once Sten, Foss, and Kilgour had exited the *Gamble*, turning the deck over to Engineer Hawkins, they had used an unarmed Goblin and its AM2 drive to bring them closer to the mine. Sten was fairly sure the small Goblin wouldn't present enough mass to activate the mine. Fairly sure, he reminded himself, could get one fairly dead.

Half a kilometer away from one of the mines, Sten parked the Goblin, and the three used their suit drives to close in.

The mine was about five meters long and cylindrical, with drivetubes at one end. It was nested inside its launch/monitor/control, a doughnut-holed ring with a diameter of about six meters.

The three orbited the mine until they were sure they saw no obvious booby traps, then moved in toward what they hoped was an inspection panel. Foss unclipped a stud drive from his suit's belt.

'Okay to try it, sir?'

'Why not?'

Sten opened his mike to the *Gamble* and started a running description of what was happening. If Foss erred and the mine went off, the next team to try it – if there was a next team – wouldn't make the same mistake.

Foss touched the drive to a stud and applied power.

'We're pulling the first stud, lower left side, now . . . it looks standard. Any resistance? The first stud is out. Second stud, upper right. It's free. Third stud, lower left, also out. All studs removed. The panel is free. We are moving it out two centimeters. There are no connections between the panel and the mine.'

All three men peered through the narrow access port while Foss probed the interior with his helmet spot.

'What do we have?'

'Sloppy work, sir.'

'Foss, you aren't grading an electronics class!'

'Sorry, sir. If we're right . . . the way they've got the plates rigged . . . yeah. Pretty simple.'

'This is Sten. Going off for a moment. Clear.' Sten shut down the tight beam to the *Gamble* and motioned the other two away from the mine. 'Can we disarm these brutes, Foss?'

'Easy. Cut any of three boards I spotted out, and all these'll be good for is ornamental wastebaskets.'

'So all we have to figure is what kind of range the mines have, defuse enough so we've got operating room, and we're back in business.'

Kilgour clonked a heavy arm three times on Sten's helmet. The clonks, evidently intended as sympathetic pats on the head, sent them pirouetting in circles. They ended staring upside down at each other.

'Puir lad,' Alex sympathized. 'It's aye the pressure cooker a' command. T' be't so young an' so brainburned.'

'You have a better idea?'

'Ah do. An *evil* plan. Worthy ae a Campbell. Best ae all, it means we dinnae e'en hae t' be around t' be causin't braw death an' destruction.'

'GA.'

'If y' buy't, can Ah tell the lads ae th' wee spotted snakes?'

'Not even if your plot'll win the war single-handed. Come on, Kilgour. Stop being cute and talk to us.'

Kilgour did.

The Tahn convoy was made up of eight troop transports, each carrying an elite battalion landing force, intended to augment the Tahn Council's planned trap in the Caltor System, plus three armament ships and a single escort. The escort was a small patrol craft intended to be more a guide than protection.

Their course led them within light-seconds of a certain minefield. The convoy commander, a recently recalled reservist, was very uncomfortable.

As a merchant service captain, he had become convinced years ago that machinery was out to get him. The bigger the machine, the more homicidal its intentions. He tried to keep machines with explosives inside them well clear of his nightmares.

That tiny superstitious part of him was not surprised when a lookout reported activity in the minefield. And then the reports cascaded in – the mines had activated themselves and were closing in.

Convinced that his Identification – Friend or Foe box was dysfunctional, the convoy commander ordered his ship to be closed up with another.

The move had no effect.

He screamed for condition red on the all-ships channel. Crews raced for action quarters stations, and collision panels closed on the transports.

The missiles hammered toward the convoy, their speed increasing by the second.

Fifteen of them impacted on the eleven transports. The mine-missiles were designed to be able to sardine-can a warship, and so the thin-skinned transports simply became flame, then gas, and then nothing except expanding energy.

What Sten's crew had done, working under the diabolism of Kilgour and Foss, was not simply to defuse the mines. Instead, Foss had analyzed what the IFF broadcast from the Tahn ships would be, then reprogrammed the mines to use that as a firing and homing signal.

The convoy had vanished, except for the tiny patrolcraft. Sten had not needed to be so cautious; the mines were, indeed, set to ignore small craft.

Six missiles had been launched that did not find their targets in time. They orbited aimlessly, without instructions.

The captain of the patrolcraft would have been best advised to put on full power and get out to report. Instead, he opened fire on one of the missiles – which activated a secondary program: if fired on by any ship of any size, seek out that target.

There was a final explosion – and the beginnings of a mystery. How could a convoy entirely vanish in a perfectly secure and guarded sector?

Sailors do not like mysteries but love to talk about them. Very shortly, the word was out – the Fringe Worlds were jinxed. Better not ship out with that destination, friend.

The convoy disappearance also forced the Tahn to divert badly needed escorts from the forward areas both for escort duty and to hunt for what the council theorized was some kind of Q-ship, an Imperial raider masquerading as a Tahn vessel.

Sten countermined four more fields before he ordered the tacships back to Romney.

They had begun to fight back.

Chapter Fifty

'Commander Sten,' Admiral van Doorman said, turning away from the screen that showed Sten's after-action report, 'my congratulations.'

'Thank you, sir.'

'You know,' van Doorman said, as he stood and paced toward one of the screened windows in his command suite, 'I am afraid that it's just too easy in this navy to adopt a particular mind-set. One becomes set in his ways. You decide that there is only one group of standards. You think that the smaller the ship, the less capable it is. You think that a show of force is all that's needed to maintain Imperial security. You think – hell, you think all manner of things. And then one day you find that you are wrong.'

That, Sten thought, was a fairly honest and accurate summation and indictment of the admiral. Maybe add in a love for bumf and spit and polish, and a streak of stubborn stupidity. Now will this make van Doorman do something sensible, like resign, or maybe take poison like the Tahn do when they custer the works? Ha. Ha.

'I have decided to award you the Distinguished Service Order, and authorize you to award four Imperial Medals to any members of your division whose actions you deem outstanding.'

'Thank you, sir.' Sten would rather have had two spare engines for his tacships and a full resupply of missiles.

'I would like you and whichever four you choose back at this headquarters by 1400 hours. Dress uniform.'

'Yessir. May I ask why?'

'For the award ceremony. I'll arrange to have full livie coverage. And a conference afterward for the media.'

'Sir . . . I, uh, don't think that's a good idea.'

'Don't be modest, Commander! You have won a victory. And right now Cavite – not just Cavite but the entire Empire – needs some good news.'

'I am not being modest, sir. Sir . . . there are four more booby-trapped minefields out there. If we put the word out on what happened . . . sir, that'd foul up the whole operation.'

Van Doorman actually considered what Sten had said. He reseated himself at his desk and rubbed his chin in thought. 'Would it be possible that a, shall we say, different explanation of the action be provided?' Translation: Can we lie?

'Possibly, sir. But . . . won't the livie people want to talk to my crew? I don't think they could carry it off. They aren't trained in disinformation.'

Kilgour would slaughter Sten if he knew he had said that – Alex was one of the best liars in the line of duty whom Sten had ever met.

'It would be chancy,' van Doorman agreed. 'Perhaps you're right. I'll postpone the media conference for the moment.' He changed the subject. 'Commander, one further thing. I don't wish to change your orders – you're doing admirably as an independent. But I'd like you to consider a more immediate focus for your future actions.'

'Such as?'

'Whenever possible, I would appreciate your division hitting the closer Tahn-occupied systems.'

'That could be difficult, sir. Their cover is pretty tight.'

'This is most important.'

'A question, sir. Why the change?'

'I am preparing to mount an operation within the next few weeks that will need full fleet support. Unfortunately, I can't be more specific at present – we're operating under total security.'

So much for van Doorman's brief flash of reality. Sten could have mentioned that he probably had a higher security clearance than anyone in the 23rd Fleet, including its admiral. Or that it was clottin' hard to support an attack – a retreat? – if one didn't know what was going on. Or that total security for the clotpoles on van Doorman's staff probably meant that it was all over the officer's club by now.

'Yessir,' Sten said. 'My staff and I will prepare some possible scenarios for you.'

'Excellent, Commander. And again, my congratulations.'

Sten highballed the admiral and left. He was wondering if van Doorman was contagious. Scenario? And staff? That would consist of four officers, one warrant officer, and a spindar plotting over a bottle. He started looking for Brijit.

Sten hoped to find her in some romantic setting – perhaps in a flowered glen out of sight and sound of the war. He also hoped that Brijit would have recovered from her mother's death enough to have a bit of lust in her heart.

He found her ninety feet underground, wearing a blood-spattered set of coveralls and maneuvering a gurney past a rockchewer.

Someone on van Doorman's staff had an element of brains and cunning. The Empire Day attack had packed Cavite's hospitals solidly, and this unknown planner evidently knew enough about the Tahn method of waging war to realize that putting the ancient red cross on a hospital roof provided an excellent aiming point. So the base hospital had gone underground into solid rock. It was also directly under the building that had been, years before, the Tahn consulate for the Fringe Worlds.

Sten helped Brijit slip the casualty into an IC machine, then asked when she got offshift. Brijit smiled tiredly and told him tomorrow. Sten would be long offworld by then. So much for romance.

Brijit managed another smile, one with some empathy. She had a fairly good idea what Sten had in mind. Instead, she took him to the crowded staff mess hall and fed him a perfectly vile cup of caff.

She had volunteered for the hospital the day after her mother's funeral. The pre-war world of whites, boredom, and garden parties was burnt away.

Sten was most impressed and was about to say something, when he started really listening to Brijit's exhausted chatter.

It was Dr Morrison this and Dr Morrison that, and how hard Dr Morrison was working, and how many lives had been saved. Brijit, Sten gathered, was Dr Morrison's main OR nurse. And he realized that even if he were in that flowered glade with Brijit, all that would happen was that she would possibly ask him to make a garland for Dr Morrison.

Oh, well. Sten couldn't honestly evaluate himself as being anyone's ideal main squeeze, even ignoring the fact that a tacship commander's life span is measured in mayflies.

Brijit's features suddenly softened and then brightened. Sten remembered that she had looked that way at him not too long ago.

'There she is now! Dr Morrison! Over here.'

Commander Ellen Morrison, Imperial Medical Corps, was, Sten had to admit, almost as beautiful as Brijit. She greeted Sten coolly, as if he were a prospective patient, and sat down. Brijit, almost reflexively, took Morrison's hand.

Sten talked for a few more minutes about inconsequentialities, finished his caff, made his excuses, and left.

War changes everything it touches. Sometimes even for the better.

A few days later, van Doorman got his famous victory, courtesy of the Imperial Tacship *Richards*, Lieutenant Estill, and Ensign Tapia. Or at least everyone except Tapia thought he did.

They were a week out of Cavite when they got their target. It was one of the monstrous Tahn assault ships that were the launch base for the in-atmosphere attack craft. The ship, according to the *Jane's* fiche, would be lightly armored and, if hit before the bulkheads that subdivided the hangar deck could be closed, should become an instantly satisfactory torch.

The problem was that the ship was escorted by one cruiser and half a dozen destroyers, and no one on the *Richards* was in a particularly suicidal mood that watch.

Tapia let Estill run up and knock down half a dozen attacks on the computer before she made her suggestion. Even though it was extremely irregular, Estill was learning from his time in the tacdiv. He turned the deck over to her and announced that if her idea worked, he would 'fly' the Kali on the attack.

At full power the *Richards* sped ahead of the Tahn ships, made a slight correction in course, and then went 'dead' in space, directly intersecting what Tapia calculated the Tahn ships' course to be. She shut down all power, including the McLean artificial-gravity generator. Then anything that wasn't armament was pitched out a port – chairs, rations, metalloid foil configured to provide excellent radar reflection, and even the two spare shipsuits.

Then they waited. With even the recirculators off, the air got thick very quickly.

Their passive detectors picked up the Tahn sensing beams.

They continued to wait.

A single Tahn destroyer flashed out from the pack and figure-eighted, its computer obviously analyzing just what was dead ahead.

'This'll be interesting,' Tapia whispered unnecessarily to Estill.

Interesting was one way to put it. If their camouflage as a wreck didn't work, they would be staring at that destroyer on an attack run. Tapia didn't know if either their reflexes or the *Richards'* power would get them away in time.

The *Richards'* passive screens went dead, and Tapia started breathing again. If the ruse had failed, the screens would have told her that a ranging computer was on the tacship. 'Any time you're ready, Lieutenant.'

Estill nodded. Tapia fed power to his board. Estill put out a narrow ranging beam to the Tahn assault ship. Closing . . . closing . . . in range.

Tapia slammed her power board on . . . buzzed the engineer, who did the same . . . and the *Richards* came alive. Two seconds later, Estill launched his Kali.

Alarms blared on the Tahn ships. The destroyers went into an attack pattern, and the cruiser full-powered to protect her charge. The assault ship went to an emergency evasive pattern.

Tapia was too busy to see what was going on. She had full power on the *Richards*, an eccentric evasion orbit fed in, and was now interested in survival.

The Kali was only a few seconds from strike when the Tahn assault ship fired its forward bank of antimissiles.

They should have been useless.

Standard doctrine for any weapons officer using the control helmet on a missile was to stay with the bird through contact. But somehow to Estill this meant a kind of death. At the last moment he hit the firing contact and jerked the helmet away.

The explosion blanked the rear screens of the *Richards*.

'We got it!' Estill shouted. The helmet went back on, and he launched a flight of Goblins to track to their rear.

Tapia read a proximity indicator – there were Tahn missiles coming at them. Closing . . . negative. The *Richards* was outrunning them.

Tapia had only a moment to check the main screen for a blink. And that blink showed her the same number of Tahn blips as had been there ten minutes before.

No one believed her – except the Tahn. The Kali had indeed detonated on an antimissile. Four main frames of the assault craft were warped, but the forward Tahn repair yards would have the assault ship back in commission within days.

Tapia tried – but no one wanted to hear the truth.

Lieutenant Ned Estill was an instant hero. Van Doorman awarded him the Galactic Cross, even though technically the medal could be given only on direct Imperial authority. The livie people went berserk – Lieutenant Estill could not have been more of a hero if they had been able to custom design one. His face and deeds were blazoned Empirewide within hours.

Tapia privately reported to Sten what she thought had actually happened. Sten considered, then told her to forget it. He didn't give a damn about medals, the Empire could do with a few hero types, and Estill honestly believed that he had destroyed the assault ship.

He did order, though, that all officers and weapons specialists renew their capabilities in a simulator. Once was an error. If Estill made the same mistake again, he could end up very dead.

And Sten couldn't afford to lose the *Richards*.

Lieutenant Lamine Sekka still seethed. The conversation with Sten had started in acrimony and gotten intense from there. What made it worse was that the original idea had been Sekka's.

Sten had attempted to follow van Doorman's vague instructions to harry the nearby worlds as much as possible. Harrying required intelligence. Specific – such as which worlds were occupied by what forces in which conditions.

The tacdiv spent too many hours as spy ships before anyone could start determining targets.

Sekka had found one of the juiciest.

A distinguishing feature of one planet was a river many thousands of kilometers long. Above its mouth, which looked more like an estuary, was a huge alluvial plain. It was a perfect infantry staging base for the Tahn. They had put an estimated two divisions of troops on the floodplain, using it as a temporary base until the landing in the Caltor System.

Sekka had even been able to determine where the divisions' headquarters were most likely sited.

Sten was congratulatory. 'Now. Go kill them, Lieutenant.'

'Sir?'

Sten was very tired and a little snappish. 'I said – take ship. Put armament on ship. Destroy Tahn.'

'I am not a child, Commander!'

Sten took a deep breath. 'Sorry, Lamine. But what's the problem? You found yourself a cluster of bad people. Take care of them.'

'Maybe I'm not sure what – exactly – you want me to do.'

'Let's see.' Sten ran through his arsenal mentally. 'Here's what I'd suggest. First yank your Goblin launchers. Put eight more chainguns in their slots. Get rid of all but two of the Fox counter-missiles. You'll need extra canisters of projectiles.

'Take the Kali out. There's a busted-up close-support ship over in the boneyard. It should still have a belt-fed Y-launcher. Turn that around and mount it nose first down the Kali tube.

'You'll want to use two-, maybe three-kt mini-nukes. When you come in, I'd suggest you put the launcher on a five-second interval.'

'Is there anything else, Commander?' Sekka's voice was shaking.

'If I knew where we could get some nice, persistent penetrating nerve gas . . . but I don't. I guess that's all.' Sten was deliberately not noticing Sekka's reactions, hoping he would not be required to respond. He was wrong.

Sekka was on his feet. 'Commander, I am not a murderer!'

Sten, too, was up. 'Lieutenant Sekka, I want you at attention. I want your ears open and your mouth shut.

'Yes. You are a murderer. Your job is to kill enemy soldiers and sailors – any way you can. That means strangling them at birth if somebody would invent a time machine! Who the hell do you think operates those ships you've been shooting at? Robots?'

'That's different.'

'I said shut up, Lieutenant! The hell it is! What did you expect me to tell you to do? Wait until those troops load into their tin cans and then hit them? Would that make things more legitimate? Or maybe wait until they land here on Cavite?

'Maybe your family has been living on legend too many generations, Lieutenant Sekka. You had best realize that if it wasn't for war, every *warrior* would be tossed in the lethal chambers for premeditated homicide.

'That's all. You have your orders. I want you offplanet in forty E-hours. Dismissed!'

'May I say something, sir?'

'You may not! I said dismissed!'

Sekka brought up a perfect salute, pivoted, and went out. Sten slid back down into his chair. He heard a low chuckle from the other entrance to *Gamble*'s mess hall.

Alex walked in and found another chair.

'I'm not running a combat unit,' Sten groaned. 'This is a clottin' divinity school!'

'Puir tyke,' Alex sympathized. 'Next he'll be thinkin't tha be rules a' war. P'raps it'd cheer y' lad, if Ah told th' story ae th' spotted snakes again.'

Sten grinned. 'I'd keelhaul you, Alex. If I had a keel. Come on. Let's go put our Rover Scouts to bed.'

Sekka had followed orders and lifted off. His insertion plan had worked perfectly – and its perfection tasted like ashes. He had brought the *Kelly* in-atmosphere at night and under cover of a storm, far below the horizon, at sea. He had submarined his tacship into the river's mouth and then carefully navigated upriver until his ship sat on the bottom, directly next to the Tahn base. The Tahn did not bother to run any sea or river patrols on the world, which was in a highly primitive stage of evolution.

His crew members were as grim and quiet as he was.

Sekka had decided that what he had been ordered to do was wrong – but he would do it as perfectly as he knew how. Remembering his own days in training, he decided that the most vulnerable time any army has is about an hour after dawn. Even if the unit practices dawn and dusk stand-tos, an hour later everyone is busy with personal cleanup, breakfast, and evading whatever noncoms are looking for drakh details.

At the time click he brought the *Kelly* out of the water and, at full Yukawa drive, on a zigzag pattern crossing directly over the headquarters areas. He had the ship set for contour flying at four meters.

When he crossed the perimeter, he ordered the crew members manning the additional chainguns to open fire. He personally triggered the Y-launcher and saw the small nuclear bombs arc thousands of feet into the air before they started their descent. By the time they hit and exploded, he would be many kilometers away.

Sekka had all rear screens turned off. He was a murderer. Possibly Commander Sten was right and *all* warriors were murderers. But he did not need to be a witness.

The attack, by one small ship, lasted for twenty minutes. At its end, when the *Kelly* climbed for space and went to AM2 drive, one divisional headquarters was completely destroyed and the second had taken forty percent casualties. Of the 25,000-plus Tahn soldiers, nearly 11,000 were dead or critically wounded. Both divisions had ceased to exist as combat formations.

Lieutenant Lamine Sekka refused a proffered medal, requested a three-day pass, and stayed catatonic on drugs and alcohol for the full three days.

Then he treated his hangover, shaved, showered, and went back to duty.

Sh'aarl't had found herself a great target. The problem was that no one could figure out how to destroy it without getting blown out of the sky in the process.

It was a Tahn armaments dump. The Tahn had found a wide cliff-ringed valley. They had studded the rim of the valley with anti-aircraft missiles and lasers and maintained overhead patrols as well as an armed satellite in a synchronous orbit just out-atmosphere. To make the situation worse, the world – Oragent – was under almost complete and constant cloud cover.

Sh'aarl't had tracked Tahn resupply ships to the world and figured out their approximate landing point. There had been more than enough traffic to arouse her interest. She assumed some kind of supply dump, since very few of the ships landing or taking off from Oragent were combat craft.

To narrow the field further, she stalked a single unescorted ship, bounced it, and launched a single missile, carefully steered to just remove the ship's power train. Then she had planned to dissect the ship with Fox missiles until she found out what it was carrying.

The missile exploded – and the Tahn ship was obliterated.

'We may theorize,' Sh'aarl't told her weapons officer, 'that barge wasn't carrying rations.'

'Dunno, ma'am. The Tahn like their food spicy.'

'Bad joke, mister. Since you're being bright today, how are we going to snoop and poop into that arms depot?'

It was a good question. Finding out what was under those clouds by manned recon could well have been fatal. Any other intelligence gathering would have to be done without alerting the Tahn.

Sh'aarl't put the *Claggett* down on one of Oragent's moons and thought about the problem.

Step one was to set up a stabilized camera with a very long lens. Infrared techniques and computer enhancement helped a little. She now could see the vaguely circular area that was the depot. She chanced a few laser-ranging shots and got enough input to suggest that the depot was in a valley. A series of infrared exposures, taken over time, also showed blotches of heat emanation from one area of the valley floor – what probably was the landing field – and occasional spatters from the cliff walls. AA lasers, most likely.

At that point, she returned to Romney and consulted with Sten and Kilgour.

It was pretty easy to determine what *couldn't* be done. Dumping a missile straight down at the dump wasn't very likely to be successful. Even a MIR Ved Kali – and nobody was sure that the missile could be so modified – wouldn't get past the satellite, let alone the ring of AA batteries.

Possibly a specialized Wild Weasel ship might be able to suppress the target acquisition systems long enough for a raid – but Wild Weasels were just one of the many craft the 23rd Fleet was fresh out of.

'The problem is,' Sh'aarl't said, 'there's no way in.'

'Correction, lass,' Alex said. 'Tha's noo high-tech way in. An' Ah'll wager th' Tahn are thinkit th' same ae you.'

Sten got Alex's hint. 'Maybe,' he said doubtfully. 'But first I don't think Doorknob's gonna loan us any of his marines for a landing force. And even if he does, you want to bet they're any more ept than the rest of his people?'

'Ah was noo thinki't aboot borrowin't misery when there's need for but twa of us.'

'Us,' Sh'aarl't snorted. 'Who is us?'

'Why, me an' Fearless Commander Sten, ae course.'

'I'll assume you aren't trying another bad joke.'

'Nope. Ah'm bein't dead straight.'

'That's drakh, Mr Kilgour,' Sh'aarl't said. 'You two aren't super-commandos. I don't know what you did before, Kilgour, but our death-defying leader was just a straight old Guards officer. Remember?'

Yes. Well, that was the cover that both Sten and Alex had on their service record to hide their years in Mantis.

'Y're noo hesitatin', are y'? Worri't aboot keepin't up wi' an old clot like me, Commander? Or p'raps y're feelin't soft. Ah hae noticed your wee paunch a' late.'

To Sh'aarl't, this was rank insubordination. She waited for the thunder. Instead, Sten looked injured.

'I am not getting fat, Kilgour.'

'Ah, you're right, lad. It's naught but the hangin' ae y'r coverall.'

'You two are serious!'

'Maybe it's the only way to do it,' Sten said.

'You know that Imperial regulations has an article saying that an officer has the duty to relieve his commander in, and I quote, "instances of incapacitating injury, failure to perform the ordered mission, or" – my emphasis – "mental injury,' end quote?'

'In this fleet ae th' damn't, lost, crazy, an' brainburnt, Lieutenant, who'd be th' judge?'

'All right. One more try. There's no way that two swabbies can take out an entire arms depot. That only happens in the livies.'

Sten and Alex looked at each other. A clotting arms depot? Hell, there were several system governments that had found Sudden Change thrust upon them courtesy of a couple of Mantis operatives.

'I assume that you've got a plot more than just going in cuttin' and thrusting?' Sten asked.

'Ah dinnae hae a plot a' yet,' Alex admitted. 'But som'at'll come to mind.'

'Dinnae fash, Mr Kilgour. A thought has occurred to me.'

'Thinkit, noo. We're in th' crapper for sure.'

'On your way out, would you ask Foss to haul his butt in here?'

Sh'aarl't looked at them analytically. She was not stupid. 'Very interesting,' she observed. 'Either both of you have gone bonkers – or somebody's lying to me.'

'Pardon?'

'I remember somebody told me once that when somebody gets scooped up by the Imperial sneakies, their service record gets phonied up. Any comments?'

'Great story, Sh'aarl't. We'll have to talk about it sometime. Well, Mr Kilgour? Time's a-wastin".'

The implementation of Sten's plan would be low-tech, but the method of attack was exceedingly technical. Or possibly anti-technical.

Sten would not have known what a petard was if one had been set off in his air lock – but he, along with Hamlet, hoped that it would indeed be great sport to hoist the Tahn by their own.

The possible solution lay in the sophistication of current fire-control and anti-aircraft systems.

The days of brave, keen-sighted gunners crouched behind their weaponry and opening up on overhead aircraft were long gone. A missile launch site or laser blast would be remoted to a central, fixed operation fire-control center. This center – Sten theorized it would be located in the valley's center – would have a current sitrep on aerial traffic, fed in by radar, the orbital satellite, and other air- or ground-based sensors.

If the controlled airspace was intruded on, the fire-control system would evaluate the threat, bring the anti-aircraft complex to alert if necessary, allocate targets to the various weapons, and open fire.

The individual weapons might or might not have the capability of local control in the event of the center's destruction. But the maximum crew the individual guns would have could be a gunner or two, certainly a couple of service techs, and possibly a few guards for ground security.

Since the weapons would be remotely aimed and fired, positioning them required a bit more work than just exact geographic siting. It was also necessary to program each gun with a no-fire zone, so that regardless of what an attacking aircraft might be doing, it would be impossible for any gun to fire, for instance, across the valley if another weapon was in its line of fire. Also, since the guns over-looked a highly explosive ammo dump, under no circumstances would it be possible for any weapon to fire down into the valley.

Sten proposed to alter those circumstances.

Blueboxing a local fire-control system was, Foss said, as easy as going to sleep listening to one of Kilgour's stories. The problem would be hooking it up.

Fortunately, not all of the Tahn ships shot down on Cavite on Empire Day had been completely destroyed. Sten and Foss grubbed through the wreckage, carefully examining all possible connections the Tahn used. They also examined the abandoned weaponry – Sten assumed it would have come from Tahn sources – on Romney.

Fortunately, there were no more than a dozen options. Foss also assumed that there would be a certain number of similarities between Imperial weapons controls and those of the Tahn.

The final device, dubbed by Foss a 'fiendish thingie,' consisted of one control box, anodized the same color as the electronic boxes found in the wreckage, dangling cables, and a separate power source. They fit into two backpacks and weighed about twenty-five kilos each.

Sutton managed to find in some storehouse two sets of the phototropic Mantis-issue camouflage uniforms that semifit Alex and Sten. A combat car was given a radar-absorbing anodizing and fitted with a sensor-reflecting overhead cover. Neither of them would work perfectly, but Sten was working from Alex's original supposition – that the Tahn wouldn't be looking that hard in his direction. He hoped.

Sh'aarl't insisted that the *Claggett* make the insertion – she had found the target, and even if she wasn't going to mount the attack, it was still her eggsac. Sten couldn't tell whether her ruffed hair meant that she was angry, convinced that her CO was mad, or worried.

She brought the *Claggett* in-atmosphere on the far side of the satellite, then contour flew until the tacship's sensors began picking up the signals from the Tahn depot. Again, she assumed the superiority of the Imperial sensors.

Sten and Alex unloaded and broke the combat car out of the slung cargo capsule below the *Claggett*. Their pickup point would be the same, two planetary days away.

Sh'aarl't waved a mournful mandible, the lock hissed closed, and the *Claggett* hissed away.

Sten and Alex boarded the car and, very slowly, floated, barely a meter above the ground, in the general direction of the arms depot. Their course was not plotted as a direct line but zigged toward the valley. If the unknown object that was their combat car was picked up by the Tahn, possibly a route that didn't point directly at the valley could be disarming.

Both men were lightly armed – if the drakh came down, their only plan would be to throw down a base of fire and then go to ground.

They had miniwillyguns and four bester grenades. Sten and Alex both carried kukris – the curved fighting knife they had learned to use and admire while serving with the Gurkhas – and Sten had his own tiny knife buried in the sheath under the skin of his forearm.

Sten landed the combat car when they were about ten kilometers away from the valley and waited for darkness. Through the twilight, he could see the mountain ring surrounding the valley. The view through binocs suggested that the valley might be an old volcanic crater. Certainly the mountain walls around it were very steeply sloped. That was all to the good – maybe no one would expect visitors from that direction.

At full dark, Sten crept the car forward, grounding it finally at the base of the walls. They pulled on hoods fitted with light-enhancing goggles, shouldered their packs, and started up.

The climb was a hard scramble, but they didn't need to rope up. The biggest problem was the loose shale underfoot. A slip not only would send them broadsliding back down but probably would set off alarm devices. Their preplotted course led them up toward one of the laser blasts near the canyon mouth.

It seemed as if Kilgour's tactical thinking was correct – no one would be looking for some stupid foot soldiers to try an insertion.

The first alarm was wholly primitive – a simple beam break set about a meter above the ground. Whatever smaller creatures inhabited the world could pass under the beam and not disturb any guard's somnolence.

Sten and Alex became smaller creatures and did the same.

The second line of defense might have taken a bit longer to circumvent, consisting of a series of small hemispherical sensors intended, most likely, to pick up an intruder of a certain physical type – it could be preset to go off when it picked up something moving of a certain size, a certain body temperature, or even by light ground disturbances set off by body weight. Kilgour was ready to subvert that sensor with a standard-issue Mantis bluebox, the

so-called Invisible Thug transmitter. That proved to be unnecessary
– the system wasn't even turned on. But just to make sure it wouldn't
be turned on after they passed, Sten slid his knife out of his arm,
slit the sensor's metalloid housing open, and stirred its electronic
guts vigorously.

So far, the mission was very standard – a recruit halfway through
basic Guard training could have infiltrated the site.

Next should have been a contact alarm set of wires. It was, and
was carefully stepped through by the two men.

They shut the power down on their see-in-the-dark hoods, lay
on their stomachs inside that wire, and started looking for the
sentry. Ahead of them was the cliff rim, and bulking above it the
laser gun, and beside it two mobile vans that would house the crew.

Sten scanned the area with his binocs set for light amplification,
passive mode. If someone else was using a scope, the binocs would
pick it up first. Negative. He switched to active mode.

He found the guard. He was sitting on the steps of one of the
vans, his projectile gun leaning against the van walls. His attention
seemed to be focused on the ground between his boots.

Sten could imagine Alex mentally purring 'No puhroblem.' They
turned their hoods back on and slid forward the laser.

Kilgour found the fire-control center input leads to the laser and,
after making sure they weren't alarm-rigged, disconnected them.
They sorted through the octopus of leads on their own bluebox.
Luck was in session – one of Foss's leads fit perfectly.

The new lead was fed down the gun and under its base plate.
Bluebox and backup power sources were then bonded to the base
plate. Alex loosened the lock on the bluebox's one external readout,
and it glowed dimly. If everyone was right, they were go, and the
petard was hissing.

Sten and Alex became part of the night again and slithered
downslope to the combat car. Sten knew this would not work –
nothing that sneaky ever performed vaguely up to expectations.

The next stage, after and if they were picked up by the *Claggett*,
might be interesting.

The *Claggett's* command deck was armpit to elbow, since both
Sten and Alex had insisted on witnessing the results, if any, of their
great ploy.

Sh'aarl't had brought her tacship in-atmosphere at a distance
carefully calculated to be just within the range of the Tahn satellite's sensors, then dived for the ground.

That, they hoped, would put the anti-aircraft systems on full alert.

Then Sh'aarl't launched two remote pilot vehicles that had been modified to give sensor returns matching the tacship. Sh'aarl't and her weapons officer each wore control helmets – Sh'aarl't's looked more like a figure-eight safety mask that sat just above her eyes – and sent the RPVs streaking for the valley.

Four kilometers distance . . . Sh'aarl't murmured, 'They have us,' . . . three kilometers . . . and the fire-control system ordered all tracking weapons to open fire.

One of those tracking weapons, of course, was the laser that Sten and Alex had boogered. It swung, not away from the valley but toward its center. Its bell depressed, unnoticed, toward the valley's floor. The RPVs were two kilometers away from the valley when the cliff walls exploded into flame and violet light, as did a seventy-five-meter-high by 200-kilometer-square stack of ship-to-ship missile containers. The fireball rolled across the flatland, and two other dumps went up.

The fire-control system wasn't concerned with what was happening inside the valley. It continued firing. One RPV was hit by two laser blasts and three missiles. It vanished, and Sh'aarl't, back in the *Claggett*, swore and pulled her control helmet off.

An analysis computer – part of the fire-control system's backup – realized that one laser gun was dysfunctional and cut it out of circuit. That triggered the bluebox's own power source and activated a second program. On quickfire, the laser pulsed light beams back and forth across the valley.

Alarms in the gun's mobile vans clanged up and down. The techs darted out and saw that their gun was systematically destroying what it had been intended to protect.

They ran toward the override controls just as the second RPV, almost inside the valley's mouth, veered in flames into a cliff wall, and the entire arms depot blew.

Sh'aarl't had the *Claggett* screaming for space, one set of eyes scanning screens for any Tahn interceptions but most of her attention focused on the screen that showed a boil of flame and smoke on the horizon, blasting almost to the fringes of the atmosphere.

Sten and Alex looked at each other.

'It worked,' Sten said in some surprise.

'Aye. When dinnae a ploy ae mine *ever* misfire?'

'Of *yours*?'

'Ah, leave us no be't choosy. A plan ae *ours*.'

'Well,' Sten said resignedly. 'I guess I should be glad he's giving me some of the credit.'

Chapter Fifty-One

Fleet Admiral Xavier Rijn van Doorman's battle plan was ready to implement. He'd dubbed it 'Operation Riposte.' Sten might have named it 'Lastgasp,' but he guessed it wasn't apropos to disillusion one's heroes before they trundled into the valley of death.

Not that van Doorman had been particularly optimistic when the briefing began.

There had been eight beings in the room: van Doorman; Sten's instant enemy, Commander Rey Halldor; four captains; two lieutenants; and Sten. The captains were destroyer skippers; the two lieutenants helmed minesweepers.

Van Doorman had introduced everyone, then said that his initial appreciation was not to go beyond the briefing room under any circumstances. Probably quite correctly, since what he said was completely depressing. Most accurate, but still depressing.

The Tahn, he had begun, must be only days away from mounting a second invasion attempt on Cavite. If such an assault was made, van Doorman admitted frankly that the 23rd Fleet would be unable to stop it.

But it was intolerable to just sit and wait to be hit.

Van Doorman's strategy was not unlike Sten's operations – he wanted to hit the Tahn now and get them off guard. It was possible that what was left of the 23rd Fleet might be able to keep the Tahn off guard until the Empire could support Cavite, and then drive the Tahn off the Fringe Worlds.

From the intelligence operations Sten had seen, the Empire might be a long time in doing that.

But at least van Doorman had a plan, Sten had to admit. It was not, surprisingly, all that bad – at least in the briefing.

'I propose,' van Doorman began, 'to detach four of my destroyers to be the main striking element of what I have named Task Force Halldor.' He nodded at the commander beside him. 'Commander Halldor will be in direct charge of the combat maneuvering. Commander Sten and his tactical division have determined that the Tahn are moving planetary assault forces to the following systems.' A wallscreen lit up, showing the immediate space around Cavite. Four systems gleamed. 'The Tahn are taking no chances – they're moving their troop and assault ships in system, using the system ecliptics for screens, and moving close to the planets themselves, thereby utilizing them for cover. While they are providing heavy escort for these convoys, Commander Sten reports escort elements are very light between the convoys and the planets themselves. Gentlebeings, that gave me the plan.'

The plan was for the task force to lurk just out-atmosphere of one of the planets that lay on the Tahn convoy route. There should be enough screen clutter to prevent the task force from being detected by the oncoming Tahn escorts.

'This will be,' van Doorman went on, 'the attack configuration to be used.'

Another screen lit.

The two minesweepers would be in front of the destroyers, which would be spaced out in finger-four formation. This, van Doorman admitted, was not the ideal attack configuration. But with only six destroyers still intact, and having committed four of them to the task force, he was very unwilling to lose any of them to a Tahn minefield.

Sten's tacships would provide flank security for the destroyers. Van Doorman hoped that the task force could get inside the escort screen before they were discovered.

'If we are lucky,' he said, 'such will be the case. In that event, Commander Sten, you are additionally tasked with giving the alert when the Tahn ships *do* attack.'

At least, Sten thought, he hadn't been ordered to stop the Tahn. A Tahn destroyer could obliterate a tacship with its secondary armament and without thinking. Heavier ships . . . Sten decided he didn't want to compute that event.

The destroyers were ordered to go for the transports and to avoid battle with combat ships.

'Get in among 'em,' van Doorman said, a note of excitement oozing into his orders. 'Like a xypaca in the poultry.'

The destroyers were to make two passes through the convoy,

then retreat. Sten's tacships were then to take advantage of any targets of opportunity before withdrawing. Sten was instructed to plot the retreating destroyers' courses and avoid them in his own retreat – the mine-sweepers would be laying eggs in that pattern.

'Finally,' van Doorman said, 'I shall be waiting one AU beyond the area of engagement with the *Swampscott* to provide cover. I would prefer to accompany the attack. But the *Swampscott*—' He stopped. Sten finished mentally: Couldn't get out of its own way; had never been in a fleet engagement; had spiders in the missile launch tubes; would conceivably blow up if full battle power was applied. At least no one could say van Doorman lacked courage.

Van Doorman finished his briefing and passed out fiches of the operations order. Then, very emotionally, he drew himself to attention and saluted his officers.

'Good hunting,' he said. 'And may you return with your prey.'

Prey. Sten had the same pronunciation if not the same spelling.

He stopped Halldor in the corridor. 'When you attack,' he started diplomatically, 'what plots will you be using?'

'I'll provide your division with my intentions,' Halldor said, most coolly.

Great, Sten thought. Brijit's in the arms of Morrison, both of us are losers, and you can't let it go. 'That wasn't going to be my question,' he went on. 'Since my boats'll be out there on the flanks, and I guess you'll be launching missiles in all directions, I wanted to make sure none of my people get in the way of a big bang.'

Halldor thought. 'You could put your IFFs on when we go in . . . and I'll have your pattern programmed into the missiles.'

'Won't work, Commander. We're squashable enough when the big boys play. Holding a flare in the air won't make us any more invisible. Maybe you could feed a size filter into them. So they won't want to play tag with us teenies.'

Halldor looked Sten up and down. 'You're very cautious, aren't you, Commander?'

Prod, prod, Commander. How would you like a prod in the eye? Sten just smiled. 'Not cautious, Commander Halldor. Cowardly.'

He saluted Halldor and went back to brief his people.

The battle off the planet of Badung might possibly have gone into Imperial history and fleet instructional fiches as a classic mosquito action.

That wasn't what happened.

Napoleon supposedly said, when one of his generals was up for a marshal's baton, after listening to a reel of the man's victories, 'The hell with his qualifications! Is he lucky?'

And whatever van Doorman's other attributes were, being lucky was not among them.

The battle began perfectly. The task force was able to position itself close to Badung without discovery.

A Tahn convoy did appear – five fat and happy transports escorted by six destroyers, a cruiser, and assorted light patrolcraft.

Halldor ordered the attack.

And things went wrong.

Halldor's own destroyer was hit by something – a mine, space junk, never determined – in the weapons space and holed. He remoted command to a second destroyer while his own ship limped toward the cover of the *Swampscott*. The other three destroyers continued the attack.

Sten winced, staring at the main screen on the *Gamble*. He didn't need to look at the battle computer to see what had happened and what was – or in this case was not – going to happen.

The three destroyers launched their shipkillers at extreme range. The reasons were many – with the exception of Sten's people, none of the 23rd Fleet's weaponeers had seen much combat. In peacetime they would perhaps be permitted to live-fire one missile per year, and despite manufacturer's claims, simulators do not properly simulate.

Another reason might have been the rumors about the Tahn's own anti-ship missiles. Supposedly they had heavier warheads, superior guidance, and speed greater than that of most commissioned warships. None of those stories were true, although the Tahn shipkillers were very, very fast. The Tahn ships were lethal simply because their men and women had been thoroughly trained for years before the war started.

A third reason was the rapidly spreading rumor that there was something very wrong with the Imperial missiles. They did not go where directed, they did not compute as programmed, and they did not explode when or where they should. That rumor was absolutely true.

The three Imperial destroyers therefore swept only half-way through the Tahn convoy before reversing their action. Seconds later another destroyer was hit and destroyed. The after-action report claimed that the destroyer had been hit by an anti-ship missile launched by the cruiser. Sten, however, from a position of vantage, had seen the flare of a short-range missile from one of the transports. Evidently the Imperial cruiser's ECM crew wasn't paying attention or wasn't fast enough to acquire the target.

Two down.

The remaining two destroyers went to full power, retreating. As they fled toward the barely comforting umbrella that the *Swampscott* would provide, they launched three missiles each – untargeted as far as the computers on Sten's tacships could determine.

Later, they claimed hits. According to their reports, one Tahn destroyer was obliterated, the cruiser took a major hit, two transports were destroyed, and another Tahn destroyer was lightly hit. Five hits for six launches.

Unfortunately, all claims were wrong.

None of the Imperial officers or sailors reporting hits were lying – they saw missile explosions on their screens, near or fairly near the blips of Tahn ships, and assumed the best. That has always been the case in battle – people see what they want to believe.

There was only one hit.

Possibly Halldor had failed to relay the orders to put a size screen on the missiles, although he claimed otherwise. Or possibly the missile itself lost the program.

But that single missile hit perfectly, directly amidships on the *Kelly*.

Lieutenant Lamine Sekka, warrior of 200 generations, died with all his crew before his spear had been more than bloodied, along with two officers and nine sailors.

A quarter of Sten's command was gone in that one blinding flash.

Chapter Fifty-Two

The return to Cavite was a glum limp. Not only had the task force gone zero-zero, Sten knew, but his crews were still in shock. Tacship service was not unlike the Mantis teams – normally they took very light casualties, being specialists in getting out of the way of the heavy artillery. But inevitably the numbers caught up, and when they did, very few friends would make it to the wake.

The task force limped home because, moments after the surviving ships rendezvoused with the *Swampscott* and the withdrawal started, *Swampy* had blown out one of her aged drivetubes. The tacships and the destroyers ended up escorting the cruiser back to Cavite.

To their surprise, Cavite was a boil of spacecraft. Huge ships – transports, assault landing craft, combat fleets – filled the skies and packed the fleet's landing grounds. Two battleships hung on the outer reaches of the atmosphere.

For a moment Sten thought that the Tahn had pulled an end run and landed on Cavite while the Imperial forces were stalking the convoy. And then his computer growled at him and began IDing the ships.

There was a full Imperial fleet plus landing and support ships for an entire Guards division.

Sten and Alex exchanged glances. They didn't say anything – Foss and his ears were on the command deck. But the thought was mutual – perhaps they weren't all doomed. Maybe this war was not going as badly as they thought. With these reinforcements, they might be able at least to hold the Tahn.

The icing on the cake was finding out that the unit was the First Guards, perhaps the best of the Imperial elite, headed by General Mahoney, Sten and Alex's old boss in Mantis.

They landed and ordered Sutton and the ground crews to get the three boats fueled, supplied, and armed for immediate takeoff. Kilgour made a slight change. Ground crews always felt as much a part of their assigned craft as any combat crew person. And Alex knew that the support teams of the *Kelly* would not only be mourning but endlessly wondering if something they had done quickly or maybe not exactly could have contributed to the ship's destruction. The *Kelly's* ground crews were taken off duty and given six hours liberty.

Liberty in shattered Cavite City wasn't much. Large portions of the city, still occupied by Tahn settlers, were off limits and most chancy to enter with anything other than an armored gravsled. Half of the stores owned by Imperial immigrants were shuttered or burnt out, and their proprietors had fled.

Passage price on any of the merchant ships that were daring

enough to make the passage to Cavite and skillful enough to evade the Tahn patrols was simply set – How much do you own in liquid assets? Only the quite rich need apply for a corner space in a stinking cargo hold.

Sten filed his immediate after-action report. Then he and Kilgour freshened up, put on their least tired sets of coveralls, and started looking for Guards headquarters.

They found General Mahoney in a cacophony of underlings. Division headquarters was set up in a collection of armored carriers half a kilometer from the landing field. Sten wondered why Mahoney wasn't working out of his command assault ship.

Mahoney spotted them standing outside his personal carrier. Four gestures in sign language: Stand by. Ten minutes. I'm in the drakh.

It took twenty minutes before the last officer had his orders and was scurrying away. And then Mahoney brought them up to speed.

There may have been icing, but there wasn't any cake, the general informed them rather grimly.

'Quite a fleet,' he said, indicating a monitor screen. 'Admire it real fast, gentlemen. Because it's only going to be around for another fourteen hours or so. I don't know what they nomenclature this kind of operation in Staff College, but I'd call it Dump and Depart.'

'An' there's a reason?' Alex asked. 'Or is the wee navy afeard a' gettin' their tunics messed?'

'Clot yes, there's a reason,' Mahoney said. 'And if I didn't have a staff conference in . . . twenty minutes, I'd pull up a bottle and give you all the gory details. But I'll give you an overall.

'First of all, the Empire's up against it. Bad. I assume you two thugs have accessed van Doorman's 'Eyes-only' sitreps from Prime?'

They had – Sten through a computer tap and Alex by making friends with a semi-lovely cipher clerk on the *Swampscott*. The reports were uniformly disastrous.

'The real status is even worse,' Mahoney said. 'This big chubby fleet that's all around us? Maybe it'd give you a start if somebody said it's the only still-intact strike force for a quarter of this galaxy?'

Sten blinked.

Mahoney smiled grimly. 'The Tahn, and all their new allies who're scrambling aboard, haven't missed much. Two things you might find interesting – so far we haven't been able to mount one single offensive. Not against Tahn systems, not even to recover any of the systems we've lost. The fleet gave my transports cover – and as soon as we're off-loaded, they're going to load up every dependent and any Imperial settler whose got brains enough to evacuate. Then everything except a few of the assault ships and patrol boats haul ass for safety.'

Sten grimaced.

'There aren't a whole clottin' lot of other options,' Mahoney said. 'The Empire can't take the chance of losing this fleet.'

'It's none of my business, sir. But why're you here? Seems to me,' Sten said, 'like all that's going to happen is the First Guards'll go down the sewer pipe with the rest of us.'

'Your CO's a cheery sort,' Mahoney commented.

'Aye, sir. He's thinkit tha's a sewer pipe to go doon.'

'Okay. This – like the rest of the drakh I've said – is classified. We're supposed to hold Cavite. Sooner or later what goes around'll come around. And the Empire will need a springboard to strike back from.'

'What brainburn came up with *that*?'

'Your ex-boss,' Mahoney said.

Sten backwatered – even though this was most informal, he didn't think it quite bright to be insulting the Eternal Emperor. 'Sorry, sir. But I still don't think it's going to work.'

Even though there was no one else in the carrier, Mahoney lowered his voice. 'I don't either, Commander. I think the Emperor still thinks that he's got time to play with. Because sooner or later, we're going to win. He's putting his chips on sooner.'

'Personal question, sir. What's your opinion?'

'I think that you and I and the Guards and van Doorman's fleet are going to end up providing some top-quality martyrs for Imperial recruiting,' Mahoney said frankly. 'Oh, well,' he finished. 'I guess things aren't going to get much worse.'

Mahoney was wrong.

Three hours later, even before the fleet had finished off-loading Mahoney's supplies, two Tahn destroyers hit Cavite Base. Missiles killed one of them, and the second was battered into retreat by one of the battlewagons.

But the fleet admiral had absolute orders. If the Tahn made *any* attack, he was to abort and withdraw at once, regardless of mission status on Cavite.

Ports hissed shut, and the Imperial fleet whined into the air and vanished into AM2 drive, leaving the skies of Cavite as bare as they had been before – leaving more than 7,000 Imperial civilians abandoned.

Two days after that, Tahn bombs thundered down on Cavite. The invasion bombardment had begun.

Chapter Fifty-Three

The first attack was successful. Too successful.

Forty non-nuclear bombs had been skip-launched by Tahn ships, darting into the upper reaches of Cavite's ionosphere and then away. All of them had similar targets – Imperial communication and/or computer centers. Thirty-one of them hit on target, or close enough to cause significant damage. Six more sent the com centers offline for at least an hour. Two were destroyed by a very alert Guards surface-to-air missile team, and the last was blown out of the sky by a patrol boat.

Of course the bombs had to have been guided. Mahoney and his superskilled Guard technicians had less than three hours to make their analysis.

Could the bombs have been remote-flown by operators in the Tahn ships? Highly unlikely, because not only were the fixed centers of the 23rd Fleet hit—including two strikes on the critical Sigint center – but three of Mahoney's semi-mobile sites were hit as well. It would be almost impossible for any human operator to have reflexes fast enough to spot the antenna array and significantly divert a downward-plunging bomb quickly enough to make a hit.

Also, none of Mahoney's ECM experts had picked up any transmission on any band aimed at the bombs.

Van Doorman, whose electronics ability stopped just short of understanding how electrical current in a cable can alternate and still work, had his own theory: the Tahn had developed a secret weapon.

Unsurprisingly, all estimates from fleet technicians echoed his theory. They knew on which side their circuit boards were buttered.

Mahoney listened to the admiral's theory politely, made

noncommital noises, and got off the com. He already had his own ideas – and teams – in motion.

Any military is a juggernaut in more ways than the amount of force it can exert. It also tends to stick with any plan that has worked once or twice until it is proved that the enemy is on to it. That translates to friendly casualties, sometimes appallingly high, and sometimes even then the lesson is not learned.

For instance, during one of Earth's periodic wars, Earth Date A.D. 1914–1918, the military situation stalemated itself into trench warfare, with both sides fighting from fixed positions dug into the earth. The commander on one side, a certain Haig, ordered his troops to attack front-ally and in parade-ground lines. Sixty thousand men were killed on his side in the first day alone.

After that, anyone not entirely gormless would have either relieved himself for terminal stupidity or else found a different set of tactics. But with only a few exceptions, that same battle plan was used until the war ground to an exhausted halt – each time with a casualty rate almost as catastrophic.

The Tahn were guilty of this mental laziness as well. Their system of using an agent in place to laser-guide either a bomb or a missile had worked extraordinarily well previously on a hundred or more worlds. There was no need to come up with a different method for the initial bombardment of Cavite that would precede the invasion. Especially when there were Tahn agents in place and many trained and eager members of the various Tahn revolutionary organizations available, despite the losses taken after the failure of Empire Day.

Habit was certainly part of Lady Atago and Admiral Deska's decision to use aimed bombs. A second factor may have been their quite justified contempt for the Imperial forces. But there was a vast difference between the sloths and recruits of the 23rd Fleet and the hard men of the First Guards. The Empire might not have fought a major war for many years – but the First Guards were very experienced as the Empire's fire brigade. Most of the men of the Guard were careerists, and almost half of them had more than twenty years of combat experience, off and on.

Among their specialties were city fighting and security sweeps. There were more than fifty bomb controllers in place around Cavite City, hidden in attics or unused buildings or operating from long-set-up mole holes in offices or apartments.

Two battalions of Guards were deployed. They worked in five-person teams, five-finger machines. The first man knocked or rang on the door, standing to its side. Two more crouched, weapons ready to either side. The last two were back and to either side to provide covering fire or to keep anyone from sniping out a window. Any resistance, or refusal to answer, and the door came down. Any supposition that General Mahoney had a tendency to disregard civil liberties when it was expedient was most correct. Besides, any investigating commission would be set up only if they held Cavite, and only after the war was won.

Direction-finder gravsleds swept down the streets and over the buildings themselves.

Before the next wave of Tahn tacships came in for the launch, forty-seven guidance sites had been found; either the sites were eliminated along with their operators, or the Tahn fled, leaving their gear behind. The dozen or so left were IDed and removed after they attempted to illuminate the bomb targets.

The bombs scattered across the city. Harmlessly, if looked at from the military sense – only three significant targets were damaged. But they shattered Cavite City. There were 6,000 civilian casualties. The military defines its terms most selfishly.

The Tahn, however, did not escape unscathed. Sten's three tacships and a flight of patrolcraft were waiting on an anticipated orbit pattern. Twelve Tahn tacships were destroyed. The Tahn, expecting that their attacks would disrupt Cavite's air defenses, had sent in second- and third-class ships.

Three more waves came in, again at the Tahn-dictated interval of three hours. All three attacks were decimated. All three bombing missions went wild. And more citizens, both Imperial and Tahn, died.

Then Lady Atago changed her tactics.

So did Sten.

> *'She's gane till her father's garden,*
> *And pu'd an apple, red and green;*
> *Twas a' to wyle him, sweet Sir Hugh,*
> *And to entice him in.'*

Alex stopped muttering and looked at Foss. 'What're y' gawkin't a', swab?'

'Didn't know you spoke any foreign languages, sir.'

'Dinna be makin't fun ae th' way Ah speak. Ah hae yet t' makit up thae fitness report.'

'So? "There'll be no promotion/This side of the ocean/So cheer up my lads/Clot 'em all,"' Foss also quoted. 'Sir.'

The person to be wiled was of course not Sir Hugh, but the Tahn commander. And Sten was not planning to use an apple, either green or red. Instead, hung under each of the three tacships was a long, streamlined pod. It contained a full, destroyer-intended ECM suite, far more powerful if not as sophisticated as the countermeasure equipment on the Bulkeley-class tacships. Signals were fed from the pods and the tacships own electronics down a half-kilometer-long cable to strange and wonderfully configured polyhedrons below. The tacships hung about 200 meters above the main landing field.

'D' y' really thinkit this'll go?' Alex asked.

'Why wouldn't it?' Sten said.

'Ah. Try a differen' way. Supposin't it works aye too well?'

'We go boom.'

'Ah no mind bein't expendable – but thae's no joy in bein't expungeable.'

Sten had figured that when the operator-guided bombing missions failed, the next approach would be more conventional.

It was. Four Tahn destroyers multiple-fired operator-guided missiles from in-atmosphere, 1000 meters above the ground and about 400 kilometers away from Cavite City.

'I have a launch . . . I have multiples . . .' Foss suddenly announced in a monotone, his eyes pinned to a screen.

Equal reports chattered in from the *Claggett* and the *Richards*.

'All ships . . . stand by,' Sten ordered. 'On my order, activate . . . now!'

Foss touched a switch, and the electronic countermeasure pod hummed into life.

The Tahn operators were navigating their missiles with both radar and visual sensing fed into their control helmets. The visual range was extraordinarily easy to jam. Without excitement, the Tahn controllers put full attention on their radar guidance.

Their sensors punched through the clutter that was Cavite looking for their targets: large metallic objects. This strike was after what was left of the 23rd Fleet and the few ships Mahoney had remaining.

The skilled Tahn controllers found targets . . . their weapons computers kept all missiles from homing on a single ship . . . and the targets grew in the operators' radar eyes.

Narrow beams kept any of them from seeing those stationary ships move.

'Half speed,' Sten ordered.

The tacships climbed.

'Do you have them?'

'Uhh . . . that's an affirmative. All missiles homing as projected.'

'Full power . . . now! Drive power . . . now!'

The tacships bolted into space.

The missiles were very close to the Imperial ships – or so the operators thought. What they were closing on were the radar-spoofing polyhedrons instead of the 23rd's grounded ships. Almost all of the missiles had their own automatic homing mechanisms active and, therefore, tried to follow the ships.

Stabilizing guidance systems tumbled, and the missiles spun out of control. A few, still under operator control, lost their targets and kept on keeping on while the controllers tried to figure out what had happened. A warship cannot vanish tracelessly.

Six of the missiles managed to track the false targets for a few moments until their fuel ran out and the missiles self-destructed.

A few AUs out, Sten ordered power cut, counted noses, and realized that they had gotten away with it. But that, he knew, would be a one-time-only gimmick.

He wondered what would happen next.

Chapter Fifty-Four

Time became a blur for Sten and his crews. Their clocks and calendars were events half-remembered in mumbled exhaustion: That was the day we ran that recon patrol. No. We were escorting the sweepers then. Remember, that's when the *Sampson* blew up? You're full of drakh. We were out on a doggo ambush then.

No one knew for sure. Any of them would have traded their chances on an afterlife for two shifts of uninterrupted sleep, a meal that wasn't gobbled cold from a pak, or – don't even whisper it – a bath.

The ships stank almost as much as the sailors did, smelling of fear, fuel fumes, ozone, sweat, and overheated insulation. They were also starting to wear out. The Kali launcher on the *Richards* was kaput. That did not matter too much – there were only three of the giant missiles left. Both chainguns on the *Claggett* were capable of only intermittent fire, and its tell-me-thrice battle computer had lost a lobe. Sten's own ship, the *Gamble*, had only six Goblin launchers that still tracked.

All of the Yukawa drive units needed teardown – they were many, many hours outside the regulated service intervals. The AM2 drives still functioned, unsurprisingly since they had approximately as many moving parts as a brick. But the navcomputers were all causing problems – projected courses had to be run four times and averaged. When there was time, at least.

And the Tahn forces kept getting stronger and bolder. Sten almost hoped for the day of invasion to come.

In the meantime, there were the missions. Escort X ships . . . patrol Y sector . . . escort Guard Unit Z and provide cover until its forward firebase is secure . . .

Routine missions.

It was on one such 'routine' mission that they encountered the ghost ship.

A stationary sensor had reported an inbound transport following a highly abnormal course. The transport did not respond to any communication attempts, nor did its IFF give the correct automatic responses for the assigned time period. Both radar and a flash visual identified the ship, however, as a standard-design Imperial fleet tender.

Sten assumed some sort of Tahn trap.

He positioned the *Gamble* and the *Claggett* at an intersection point on the transport's orbit and waited. The *Richards* was grounded, partially torn-down on Romney. Sutton and his crew were sure that this time they had figured out what was wrong with the Yukawa drives and promised a quick fix.

The transport broke the detector screens a few hours later. The two tacships waited. Sten expected that a couple of Tahn destroyers would be lurking somewhere behind the tender. But there was nothing. The *Gamble's Jane's* fiche identified the transport as an Atrek-class tender, the IFT Galkin.

Sten chanced challenging the transport. The automatic IFF response was weeks out of date. Foss could not get any sort of response other than that, nor was the transport broadcasting on any wavelength that could be received by the *Gamble*.

Sten launched his eye-modified Goblin to have a closer look. Possibly the transport was a dummy.

There was no response.

Sten matched orbits with the transport, put a recorder on, and circumnavigated the ship. Both locks and all cargo ports were sealed. There was no sign that any of the lifeships had been launched. Finally Sten brought the Goblin in until one fin touched the outer lock door. If the transport was a booby trap, that should set it off.

The detectors still reported no other ships onscreen. Still, Sten had a crawling feeling that the *Galkin* might be the bait for a nasty Tahn surprise.

He opened the tight beam to the *Claggett* to discuss the situation with Sh'aarl't. She was in complete agreement with him. It smelled very much like a trap. There was only one way to find out. Someone had to board the ship.

'Sh'aarl't . . . Kilgour and I are boarding. I want you about a light-second off, on the transport's back orbit.'

Sh'aarl't came back at him instantly. 'That doesn't sound too wise to me, Sten,' she said. 'If we are jumped, the *Claggett* would be outgunned by almost anything the Tahn threw at us – practically down to a lifeboat.'

She had a strong point. Sh'aarl't and her weapons officer, Ensign Dejean, would check things out. The *Gamble* would play rear guard. Kilgour moved the ship into position and they both watched the screen as the *Claggett's* AM2 drive flared. A few moments later, the *Claggett* was docking with the *Galkin*.

Even at close range, there was nothing strange noted visually by either Sh'aarl't or Dejean. Their suit sensors also showed nothing beyond the normal. Sh'aarl't keyed her mike. 'We're boarding.'

Sten buried the instinct to say something stupid, like 'be careful.' Instead, he bent his head closer to the monitor, listening to the crackle of the two voices.

Dejean, expecting a bolt of lightning to leap from the ship to his suit glove, touched the outer lock control. It obediently irised open. Sh'aarl't and Dejean hesitated, then entered. Sh'aarl't's perceptions swung as the *Galkin*'s McLean gravity generators provided a new 'down' for them. Their boots touched the inside of the lock – again there was no sudden explosion.

'My suit shows normal atmosphere,' Dejean reported. 'But I have no intention of trusting it.'

They kept their suit faceplates sealed. Sh'aarl't touched the inner lock control. It, too, opened.

She increased transmitter output power enough to punch through the ship's atmosphere and outer hull. They rhinoceros-waddled in their armored combat suits into the *Galkin*.

They found nothing. The ship, from machinery spaces to the engine room, was completely deserted. None of the lifeships had been launched. All spacesuits, from survival type to the small, two-person work capsules, were racked.

Both beings found it more comforting to continue the search with weapons ready. Sh'aarl't turned on a recorder at her waist and fed the information back to the *Gamble*.

They checked the crew quarters. Not only were they deserted, the lockers that should have held the crew's personal effects were empty.

Dejean checked the ship's stores. They were bare, as if the *Galkin* had never been supplied before it took off.

Sh'aarl't ignored the crawl of fear down her back spine and went to the control room. She found the ship's log and ran it back. The Imperial Fleet Tender *Galkin*, Captain Ali Remo in command, had taken off from the planet of Mehr some six cycles previously. Complement forty-two officers, 453 enlisted. Captain Remo carefully noted they were six officers, thirty-four men under authorized complement.

The *Galkin* had been ordered to reinforce the 23rd Fleet on Cavite.

She key jumped to the log's last entry:

IMPERIAL DATE . . . SHIP DATE 22, THIRD WATCH. OFFICER OF THE WATCH: LT. MURIEL ERNDS, SECOND OFFICER ENSIGN GORSHA, ENGINE ROOM CHIEF ARTIFICER MILLIKEN. COURSE AS SET, NO UNPLOTTED OBJECTS DETECTED. 2240 SHIPS HOURS GENERAL QUARTERS DRILL ORDERED PER CAPTAIN'S INSTRUCTIONS. TIME TO FULL READINESS 7 MINUTES, 23 SECONDS. STAND DOWN FROM DRILL ORDERED, 2256 SHIPS HOURS. 2300 STANDARD REPORT INPUT

. . . and the log automatically recorded the readout monitoring the *Galkin*'s condition.

Sten paced the control room of the *Gamble*, listening intently to everything Sh'aarl't said.

'It all looks perfectly normal,' she reported. 'Except for the fact that sometime after 2300 hours, every man, woman, and being on the *Galkin* decided to vanish.'

Sten looked at Alex. The stocky Edinburghian looked very unhappy.

'Ah noo believe he ghosts,' he said, 'but—'

'Wait a minute! I think we got something!' Sh'aarl't's voice crackled excitedly over the monitor.

Sten waited much longer than a minute. He became impatient. 'Report, Sh'aarl't! What *have* you got?'

'Well, according to the log—'

There was an eerie silence as her voice stopped in mid-sentence. It was if the *Gamble*'s com system had gone dead. Before Sten could say a word, Foss sat bolt up in his chair.

'Skipper! I don't understand it! They're gone!'

Sten rushed to his side and looked at the screen. The large blips that had represented the *Claggett* and the *Galkin* had disappeared.

'It's gotta be some kind of malfunction with the system,' Sten said, knowing even as he said it that it wasn't so.

'Not a chance, sir,' Foss said, his voice cracking.

It wasn't necessary to give any orders – within bare moments, the *Gamble* was at battle stations, the drive at instant readiness. Foss ran every test and every electronic search pattern in the book, plus a few more he had invented.

Once again: nothing.

There was nothing on the radar, nothing on the intermediate or deep sensors, and no directional pickup on any broadcast frequency, including emergency. At one light-second, the two docked ships should have been on visual. But the screens were blank.

'Quarter power,' Sten ordered. 'Bring us up over that ship real slow.'

All inputs remained negative.

'Back-plot the orbit. Mr. Kilgour, I want a figure-eight search pattern. Half speed.'

'Aye, sir.'

They searched in a gradually widening moving globe pattern for three full E-days. But the *Claggett*, Sh'aarl't, her two officers, and nine enlisted had vanished along with the *Galkin*.

There was no explanation. And there never would be one.

Chapter Fifty-Five

Three hours out of Romney, the com began yammering onscreen, the message sent en clair:

ALL SHIPS . . . ALL SHIPS . . . CAVITE UNDER ATTACK. INVASION BY TAHN UNDER WAY. ALL SHIPS RETURN TO HOME BASE. ATTACK, REPEAT ATTACK.

Foss already had the fiche in the navcomputer.

'On command,' Sten said. 'Commit.'

'Attack repeat attack,' Alex snorted. 'Tha' dinnae be a command! Thae's an invite t' Culloden.'

Kilgour was right. No *Claggett* . . . no *Kelly* . . . Sten assumed the *Richards* was getting slapped back together on Romney. Sten had no intentions of plummeting his very thin-skinned tacship – or, come to think about it, his own rather thin-skinned body – into the middle of a fleet melee.

He turned the intercom on and read the broadcast from Cavite to his crew without allowing any emotion to enter his voice. Then he said equally flatly, 'If anyone's got an idea on what we do when we hit Cavite, input, please.'

Alex reached across and kept his finger on the intercom button. 'A wee modification as wha' our commander's sayin'. Ideas tha' dinnae win ae of us medals what be posthumous. Mr Kilgour's mum dinnae be boastin' as her lad comes home ae a box.'

There weren't any ideas.

'Great,' Sten muttered. 'We're about as thick in the tactics department as van Doorman.'

'Dinnae fash. We'll do flash fakin't it.'

*

Lady Atago and Admiral Deska had made very sure that there was
no possibility of the invasion failing a second time. More than 500
ships swarmed the Caltor System. The Imperial 23rd Fleet wasn't
outmanned so much as buried.

Mahoney had stationed Guard detachments on every world and
moonlet of the system. Each detachment was given as sophisticated
a sensing system as possible. That was not much, even though every
detector that could be found had been stripped out of downed or
civilian ships, and emplaced. The strike-back weaponry was equally
juryrigged.

Everything from missiles to private yachts to out-atmosphere
runabouts to obsolete ships had been hung in space and linked to
the improvised guidance systems. Even Ensign Tapia's tug had been
roboticized, its control room a deserted spaghetti of wiring.

Most of these improvised missiles were either destroyed long
before they found a target or went wonky and missed completely.

But some of them got through.

'Go for the transports,' Mahoney had told his guardsmen. They
tried. Troopships were ripped open, sardine-spilling Tahn soldiers
into space or sending them pinwheeling and igniting like meteorites
into atmosphere.

But the Tahn were too strong.

Mahoney watched from his new headquarters, burrowed a
hundred meters into a hillock near Cavite Field as, one by one, his
com teams lost contact with the off-Cavite detachments. Mahoney's
face was quite impassive.

A tech glared down at her general from a com set on one of the
balconies above the central floor. Solid imperium, she thought in
fury. The clot doesn't even care.

In actuality, Mahoney *was* trying to analyze what he felt. Not
one report, he thought with approval, of any of my people breaking.
What about you, Ian? You've taken . . . let's see, about twenty-five
percent casualties. What does that feel like? Not too bad, he thought.
No worse, say, than getting your right arm amputated without
anaesthetic. Don't feel sorry for yourself, General. If you do something dumb like crying or swearing, your whole division could break.

What arrogance, he marveled. And what would it matter if they
did? This is the last time around, isn't it? There isn't going to be
enough left of the First Guard to compose a suicide note.

Like you told Sten, he thought. All we're doing is building martyrs
for the cause. And enough of that, Ian. You have work to do.

Mahoney pointed to an operator and was instantly linked to all surviving detachment commanders. 'They're still coming in, people. Get your reserves out of their holes and ready to go.'

The ground around Mahoney shuddered suddenly, and the lights flashed twice before finding a functioning emergency circuit.

The Tahn were hitting Cavite itself.

The lead elements of Tahn ships were unmanned strafers. As ordered, the naval and Guard anti-aircraft teams held their fire. Ammunition and missile reserves were almost nonexistent. Wait, they had been told, for the real targets: manned ships. That was expected to be the second wave.

But Atago's tactics were different.

The second element was made up of twenty small assault transports. The transports broke up, and from each ship, six troop capsules dropped toward the city below. In each capsule was a team of Tahn commandos.

Unlike the larger Imperial troop capsule that used wings and tear-away chutes for braking, these capsules were fitted only with retrorockets, set to fire when the capsule was pointed downward and very close to the ground.

Some of them never corrected, and the rockets sent the capsules pinwheeling before they crashed at full speed. Even the ones that functioned correctly only slowed the capsules down to approximately 50 kph. The internal shock bracing was supposed to provide the rest of the cushioning – of a sort. Thirty percent of the commandos were able to stumble out of their wrecked capsules, form up, and head for their assigned objectives.

That was quite satisfactory – Lady Atago had anticipated and allowed for an eighty percent loss on landing. The Tahn cynicism had gone still further – *none* of the assigned objectives were expected to be taken. This had not been told to the commandos at their briefing. Nor was their real mission revealed – to pinprick the Imperial defenders, to distract them from the main force landings.

One team of commandos did reach its objective – the Carlton Hotel that Atago had theorized might still be used by the 23rd Fleet headquarters. But it had been abandoned weeks ago – van Doorman had returned to the *Swampscott*, which was sitting in the deep revetment near Cavite Field. And the commandos were distracting, but only to the Guard teams who had been ordered to maintain street patrols. The Tahn commandos failed, but in failing they caused casualties and ammunition expenditures. The Empire could afford neither.

The third wave was the heaviest. Four battleships, including the now-repaired *Forez*, Atago and Deska's flagship; twenty cruisers; and a horde of destroyers raved fire at the planet. In the center of the formation were seventy-five fat-bellied assault transports.

Previously hidden Imperial missile launchers rose from bare ground, out of buildings and sheds, and even, in the case of one particular inspired team, from an abandoned double-decked transport gravsled. It was almost impossible to miss.

But it was equally impossible to hit all of the Tahn ships. Sixty-three of the transports grounded in a ring some 400 kilometers outside Cavite City, and their sides clamshelled and Tahn assault troops stormed out.

Lady Atago allowed herself a smile of satisfaction. To her, all that remained was mopping up.

Chapter Fifty-Six

The *Gamble* hung in space, hopefully hidden from the Tahn forces landing on Cavite by one of the world's moons. Sten's entire crew, less Foss, who was minding the sensors, was crammed onto the tiny mess deck reviewing the options.

The problem was that neither Sten nor Kilgour could figure out an attack plan against the Tahn that did not include their own destruction. As Alex pointed out, 'As far ae Ah can ken, th' job description dinnae ken kazikami, or wha'e'er th' word is.'

Sten might have accepted the military necessity of a suicide mission, given a strategic target that might stop the Tahn. But every idea that was suggested and run up on the battle computer showed that the *Gamble* had a ninety-nine-point-more-nine's chance of never getting through the Tahn outer destroyer screen; setting up and making an attack run on one of the Tahn heavies looked to be impossible.

'What about slingshotting?' Contreras, ex-cop, now the *Gamble*'s bosun's mate, asked. 'Full power around this moon, then around Cavite and hit 'em when we come back through.'

'Won't work,' Sten said. 'The Tahn'll pick us up the minute we come out from shadow. That'll give them more than enough time to set up a prog and nail us on the way in.'

Contreras tugged at her ear and sank back into thought.

'We can't just sit here, sir.' McCoy said. An ex-jailbird, he was now master's mate, engine room.

'Do we have any idea what's left of our fleet?'

'We're still picking up broadcasts that Foss says are from the *Swampscott*. And there seem to be a couple destroyers still in the air.'

'Maybe we do wait,' McCoy tried. 'Sooner or later, somebody down on Cavite's gonna try one. We hit the Tahn from the other side when they do.'

Sten gnawed a fingernail. 'Crappy plan,' he said finally. 'Anybody got a better one?'

There were negative head shakes all around.

'Okay, McCoy. We'll give it a shot. Everybody not on watch get their heads down.'

Hypno-conditioning let any of them go instantly to sleep and return to full alertness at command. But the ship's detector alarms went off before any of them had made it to their bunks.

Sten sprinted to the command deck. Foss indicated one screen with a solitary blip to one side.

'That's the *Richards*, sir. Correct IFF response. And that . . .'

Sten didn't need an explanation – the second screen showed another, larger indication. Tahn, of course. Probably a heavy destroyer.

Foss touched keys and moved the two images onto the larger center screen. 'It's closing on the *Richards*.'

Sten had the mike open and broadcast power at full, breaking com silence. The Tahn ship would certainly pick up his broadcast, but he might be able to save the *Richards* now and worry about his own skin later.

'*Richards . . . Richards . . .* this is *Gamble*. Bogey on intersection orbit. Closing on you. Bogey location—'

The *Richards* cut in. '*Gamble* . . . we have him. I shackle . . . X-ray delta . . . Two. Unshackle. Over.'

Lieutenant Estill – Sten noted that his voice stayed quite calm – was using a simple voice code. X-ray: main engine. Delta: damaged. Two: fifty-percent power loss.

'This is *Gamble*. Heading yours, over.'

Sten hit the GQ alarm. 'I want an interception course, Mr Foss. Engines!'

'Ready, sir.'

'Primary drive full emergency. Secondary drive full standby.'

'Sir.'

'All weapons stations report launch readiness.'

'All live stations ready, sir.'

'Mr. Foss. What do we have?'

There was now a third blip on the main screen. A red line threaded from the third blip – Sten's ship – toward the Tahn destroyer and the *Gamble*. Suddenly the dot on the screen that was the *Richards* shimmered, coming out of AM2 drive.

'*Gamble* . . . this is *Richards*. Status now I shackle X-Ray delta four. I say again four, over.'

Main drive out completely.

'AM2 drives *can't* break down,' Foss said.

'Th' hell they can't,' Alex said. 'Tha's one that did. Now shut up and mind your screens.'

'This is *Gamble*. I shackle Yankee alfa one break Mike tango echo, over.'

Yankee: secondary – Yukawa drive. Alfa: engage. One: full power. Mike: maneuver. Tango: toward. Echo: enemy.

'This is *Richards*. I shackle. Yankee also delta. Three.'

Sutton hadn't been able to repair the *Richards*, or his repairs hadn't worked for long.

There were three points of view: To the Tahn destroyer, the *Richards* appeared to come to a halt as the destroyer closed. To Sten, both ships moved across his main screen. A stationary observer, hanging in space, would not have mental reactions fast enough to perceive any of the three ships as they went past at many times light-speed.

Foss superimposed two time ticks on the main screen. The left was the estimated number of seconds before the Tahn ship would come within launch range of the *Richards*. The right showed time before Sten could attack the destroyer. The seven-second differential could doom the *Richards*.

'Kali. Stand by.'

'Ah'm ready.'

'Foss. Distress flares ready to launch.'

'Distress . . . yessir. Ready.'

'Flares . . . fire! Kali! Launch!'

The huge missile slid out of the *Gamble*'s nose just as two distress flares bloomed, radiating through broadcast, radar, and visual wavelengths.

One second later the Tahn ship launched two anti-ship missiles at the *Richards*.

'Alex . . . don't worry about what I'm doing. Get that destroyer.'

'Lad, Ah'm in a world ah m' own. Dinna fash.'

'Distress signals again . . . launch!'

Sten was hoping that the flares would shake up the Tahn. Maybe the destroyer's weaponeers would divert their missiles toward the *Gamble*. They didn't. The *Richards* was far too sitting a quacker to ignore.

But the failure wasn't complete. Possibly the controllers' attention was broken for a critical quarter second. Because the first missile missed the *Richards* completely – not too hard, since the tacship wasn't that much bigger than the missile was. The second missile went off close enough to the *Richards* to blank its blip on Sten's screen.

Clear screen – and the *Richards* was still there!

'Ah now th' worm'll turn,' Kilgour murmured – and triggered the Kali.

Sixty megatons blew the Tahn ship in two. One-third of the destroyer – its midsection – ceased to exist except as raw energy. Some of the stern, pouring sparks and a flash of flame, pinwheeled on. The remnants of the bow started on a tangented orbit toward Sten.

'*Richards* . . . *Richards*. . . this is *Gamble*. Over.'

Dead air.

'This is *Gamble*. Are you receiving me?'

Foss saw an ancillary meter flicker. 'Sir . . . there's a 'cast from a suit radio on the *Richards*. Stand by.' He added another frequency.

'. . . this is the *Richards*. I say again, this is the *Richards*.' It was Tapia's voice.

'This is the *Gamble*. The destroyer's killed. Give status, over.'

'*Richards*. Seven dead. Three wounded. XO in command.'

'This is *Gamble*. We're matching orbit. Stand by for pickup.'

'Negative on that,' Tapia said. 'The main lock's crushed. We can't reach the emergency. And our secondary drive is going any second now. Stand clear, *Gamble*.' Tapia's voice was a monotone.

'*Richards* . . . this is *Gamble*. Are survivors in suits?'

'That's affirmative.'

'Can you reach the Kali inspection hatch?'

With the *Richards*'s Kali launcher down, the tacship's centerline launch tube was empty.

'We can. Can you open the outer hatch? We have no weapons.'

'The can opener is on the way, over.' Sten closed the com. 'Alex?'

Alex diverted control to a Fox countermissile and launched. The small missile sped far beyond the *Richards* at full launch speed before Alex could cut its power and bring it looping back toward them.

'We'll try quarter speed,' he said – and sent the Fox into the *Richards*. Even with the warhead on safe, the Fox still ripped nearly a meter off the tacship's nose.

'Ah would'a made a braw surgeon,' he said proudly.

Sten reopened the com. 'Come on out.'

Five suited figures oozed out of the launcher and drifted through space. It took only seconds for Sten to maneuver the *Gamble* alongside. McCoy was already suited and out of the lock. A magnetic line lassoed the survivors of the *Richards*.

Sten sent the *Gamble* away from the *Richards*.

How long it was and how far away they were when the *Richards*'s Yukawa units blew varied in the later telling, depending on the audience's credulity and how many alks the teller was into the evening.

The five survivors were pulled onboard and treated. Sten personally unsuited Ensign Tapia and half carried her to his own bunk. He was being solicitous, he told himself, because she was a very capable officer and a friend as well. Not even his conscious mind believed that rationalization. But again, there wasn't time.

He had to return to Cavite. Without his main armament, there was little good he could do in space.

So all he had to do was slip through the Tahn net off Cavite, maneuver through the attacking forces, find a safe landing at Cavite Base, and then scuttle for a bomb shelter.

No problem, he desperately hoped. We're a lucky ship.

The *Gamble*'s luck ran out eight miles high above Cavite. A six-ship flight of interceptors jumped the *Gamble*. Sten tried to climb for space – but the battle computer showed three destroyers that could intercept.

The interceptors had speed and maneuverability on the *Gamble*. Sten sent his ship at speed toward the ground, zigging in a random pattern.

Kilgour sent three Fox countermissiles to the rear. Two

interceptors sharded, and then the rest of the flight was in range. Sten saw the tiny silver flickers of light under the interceptors' main airfoils.

'I have seven . . . no . . . eight observed launches,' Foss said, his voice starting to crack. 'Intercept time . . .'

And three of the missiles hit the *Gamble*. Sten heard the hammer blows, saw flame flare from the control panel, noted the mist-hung mountains below filling the frozen main screen, and felt the manual controls go dead.

The Tahn interceptor flight commander pulled out of his dive and half rolled. He watched the smoke-pluming Imperial tacship vanish into the mist, then ordered his squadron to return to the mother ship.

It had been a very good day for him. Five . . . no, this would be the sixth Imperial his flight had downed. He determined to order an issue of spirits as a reward.

BOOK FOUR

TAKE EVERY MAN

HIS BIRD

Chapter Fifty-Seven

The Eternal Emperor considered what would adequately describe his current mood. Angry – no. Far beyond that. Enraged. Not that – he wasn't showing any emotion. At least so he hoped. Standard Galactica wasn't helping much. He ran through some of the more exotic languages learned from equally unusual beings.

Yes. The Matan word 'k'loor' applied, which could be loosely translated as a state compounded equally of worry, unhappiness, hatred, and anger; a state whose existence, though, allowed extreme clarity of thought and an ability to instantly reach and act on a conclusion.

Self-description didn't, however, improve the Imperial mood.

A lot of his ire was self-directed. He had miscalculated serially on when the Tahn would be ready to fight, the state of his own armed forces, and how weasely some of his most trusted allies would prove.

Add to that the fact that he was pacing back and forth outside a sports palace, in front of a stern-faced and geriatic guard armed with a huge, studded club that he had trouble lifting. Time was wasting.

Once again, the delay was his own fault.

The Eternal Emperor had set himself up with many fall-back positions. Even if, for instance, the entire command center under Arundel had been destroyed, duplicate centers existed on a dozen worlds. There were also three secret centers known only to the Emperor.

He had allowed for other secondary centers, personnel, and instructions for the other elements of his administration. He had missed only one.

Perhaps hopefully, perhaps cynically, he had established no secondary hall for his Parliament. Possibly he had hoped that if the building were destroyed, it would contain the legislators whose presence he found mostly abhorrent. But the building on the other side of the mountain was intact, if somewhat radioactive. And only a handful of parliamentarians had been in it when the Tahn missile struck.

Until the building was decontaminated, one of Prime World's sports centers had been commandeered.

That did not explain the Emperor's wait outside its doors. But that, too, was of his own making.

The Eternal Emperor felt that his people should get some flash and filigree with their government. So he had stolen a ceremony from one or another ancient Earth government.

In theory he was allowed to attend Parliament only at the indulgence of the majority. That meant that ceremonial guards would bar his entrance, he would insist on his right to enter as Emperor, and he would be refused. He would then insist on his right to enter with force of arms. Again he would be refused. Only on the third, humbly worded polite request would he be allowed in. All of the above drakh was done with flowery speech and equally absurd pirouettings.

The Emperor had been proud of this. He thought ceremony an idle tide of pomp and avoided it as much as possible. Entering Parliament was necessary only a couple of times a year for carefully choreographed occasions. The real work of governing was done at the palace, in committee meetings or by carefully negotiated edict.

But now, when he was forced by emergency to address Parliament, he was faced with this – this foofaraw of his own invention.

He looked behind him at Captain Limbu and his second Gurkha bodyguard, daring them to show a slight glint of humor. The Emperor was well aware that the Nepalese found almost everything funny, especially if it involved a superior and embarrassment. Their faces were mahogany. The Emperor grunted and turned back to the front. Probably, he thought, just before the doors swung open and the ancient guard saluted with the mace, almost dropping it in the process, probably they were angry because they had been forced to disarm.

Again he was wrong. The Gurkhas merely had excellent poker faces. And the loss of their normal willyguns, grenades, and the kukri knife wasn't important – both men had tiny miniwillyguns in their tunics, guns that Imperial Intelligence guaranteed would pass through any inspection other than a complete shakedown.

The Emperor waited outside the semicircle of seats while the prime minister ceremoniously welcomed him, assured him of the undying support of his subjects, and then invited him to enlighten them with his wisdom.

Undying support, the Emperor thought as he walked down the aisle. Less than half of the legislators were present. Entire galaxies that had been loud in their pre-war support had now declared their neutrality and withdrawn from the government or announced for the Tahn.

The Emperor wore a plain white uniform with the five stars and a wreath on each epaulette that designated him commander in chief/naval forces. He could have worn a thousand different uniforms of the various Imperial forces he was CIC of but chose, again, simplicity.

There was a single decoration on his left chest – the emblem of a qualified ship's engineer. Of all the awards that had been made, this, he once told Mahoney, was the one he was proudest of. It was, he continued, the only one that he had earned instead of being bribed with.

The Emperor spoke, looking straight at the audience – not at the Parliament but at the red light on the livie camera mounted above and beyond the legislators. That was the real audience. His speech would be transmitted within minutes Empirewide, sim-translated into half a million different languages.

'One cycle ago,' he began without preamble, 'our Empire was knifed in the back by those whom we treated honorably as equals. The Tahn struck without cause, without warning, and without mercy. These are beings who worship their own gods with bloody hands – gods of disease, destruction, and chaos.

'I will not lie to you, my fellow citizens. They struck for our vitals. Not without success. They should welcome this brief candle. Because their success will be brief, indeed.

'War is the ultimate evil. But sometimes it must be fought. And even those wars fought for the most selfish of goals are given noble reasons. The most brutal tyrant will find, somewhere, a spark of decency in his heart, a spark that justifies his slaughter.

'But not the Tahn. Some of you may have seen their pirate propaganda 'casts. What do they want?

'They want the overthrow of our Empire.

'They want my destruction.

'But what do they offer? What do they promise?

'According to the Tahn, their victory will allow all beings an equal share in glory. What is this glory they promise? It is not more food. It is not greater security. It is not the knowledge that generations yet unborn will not be subject to the perils of this time. No. None of that is spoken of.

'Just this glory. Sometimes they call it the destiny of civilization. They mean *their* civilization.

'Those worlds and those peoples that have fallen to the Tahn and groan without hope or witness under their lash could tell us what this destiny brings.

'Despair. Degradation. And finally death. Death that is the only boon that the Tahn really grant, because only death will grant freedom from their tyranny.

'I said before that the Tahn have had their victories. I also said that these victories should be savored by them in haste. Because now the tide is on the turn.

'I speak now to those peoples subjugated by the Tahn. Be of good heart. You are not forgotten. The Tahn will be driven out. Peace will return.

'Now I wish to turn my attention to those who have listened to the blandishments of the Tahn, like dogs drawn to the sweetness of putrefaction. Consider the Tahn and their ways. Before this war, any alliances they made were shattered as soon as it became convenient. The only alliance the Tahn recognize is that between master and slave.

'Study their past. And think of an ancient saying: "He who wishes to sup with the Devil should bring a very long spoon."

'Next, I wish to speak directly to the enemy.

'You are very loud in your boasts of your strength. You blazon your winnings. You babble of the closeness of victory.

'Boast as you wish. But you shall find, as you reach out for this final conquest, that it shall recede and recede again from your grasp.

'Your soldiers and sailors will find nothing but death in all its unpleasantries. They will face not just an enemy armed and terrible in his armor in the battle lines, but the deadly anger of those they have outraged in their arrogance. The plight of your noncombatants will be great. They shall never see their young return. And, in time, their own skies will be flames.

'The Empire will return, with fire and sword.

'And finally, I am speaking to the warlords of the Tahn, whose ears are probably sealed in disdain from my words. You sowed this wind. Now you shall reap the whirlwind.

'Those who know me know I do not promise what I cannot

fulfill. Therefore, today, I make but one promise. One generation from now, the word "Tahn" shall be meaningless, except for historians walking the dark corridors of the past.

'You began this war. I shall finish it. The Tahn, with all your might and circumstance, shall lie forgotten in the dust!'

The Eternal Emperor pivoted and stalked from the podium.

He knew it was a good speech when he had written it.

He had upgraded it – the entire legislature was up and applauding. They'd clottin' better, he thought. And then he noticed that even the livie techs, the most jaded of observers, were shouting, their recorders abandoned.

Now all the Eternal Emperor had to do was find a way to keep his promise.

Chapter Fifty-Eight

The *Gamble's* damage-control computer found a semi-damaged redundant circuit, and Sten felt the ship's controls come vaguely back to life.

The tacship was less than 1,500 meters above the ground, ground quite invisible through the hanging fog that the ship was plummeting through. Sten's hands blurred over the control board. Nose thrusters – full emergency. Main Yukawa drive – full emergency.

Various blaring alarms and flashing indicators suggested to Sten that the controls' life span would be mayfly brief. He had time to kick the McLean generators to full power before the *Gamble's* board went dead again. The problem to be pondered was: If the *Gamble's* plummet was halted before it crashed, the ship would blast straight back up, into the probably waiting sights of the Tahn interceptors. If not, the possibilities were various in their unpleasantries. Sten slammed the impact lock on his control chair's safety harness and braced.

The *Gamble* was almost vertical when it struck.

Ship luck had returned for one final moment. Given the probabilities of hitting a mountainous crag, a glacier, or a scree field, the *Gamble* slid, tail first, into a high-piled snowfield. The snow compressed and melted, braking the *Gamble's* speed.

Another panel clanged into red life. DRIVE TUBES BLOCKING was the central catastrophe. Sten's hand was poised over the emergency power cutoff breaker when the ship's computer decided that it might be dying but preferred something less Wagnerian than what would happen, and beat Sten to it.

All power cut, and the *Gamble* shuddered to a halt.

There was very complete silence, except for the dim hissing as the hot shipskin was cooled by the melting snow around it.

In blackness, Sten fumbled toward a cupboard and found a batterypak light. Pearly light illuminated the battered control deck.

'All compartments – report.' That was another virtue of a ship as small as the *Gamble* – Sten's shout could be heard in most compartments and was quickly passed to even the stern drive station. Sten unsnapped his harness and started to his feet. Suddenly there was a rumble, and Sten staggered. The rumble grew louder, and then the *Gamble* shuddered and pitched a few more degrees to the side.

There was alarm from crew members, then silence again.

'What the hell was that?' Sten asked.

'Ah dinnae ken,' Alex said. 'Prog some'at nae good, though.'

Sten waited for something else to happen.

It did not. The *Gamble* was evidently in its final resting place. Sten took stock.

Things were not good. One of the wounded sailors from the *Richards* had been killed in the crash. Of Sten's own crew, McCoy, the engine master's mate, had been electrocuted when one of his engine monitor boards shortcircuited. Two other sailors were dead, and Sten had two sailors with major injuries. Everyone else had bangs, bruises, or minor breaks.

The ship was dead. The only transceivers functional were the shipsuits and the tiny individual rescue units, and Sten was not about to use them. First of all, he assumed that whatever was left of the Imperial Forces would be somewhat busy at the moment, and he also would rather not have any Tahn units homing on any broadcast.

They would have to rescue themselves.

Sten told Kilgour to break out the emergency gear while he and Tapia, who was now semi-functional, attempted to figure out how much rescuing they would need.

It looked to be considerable. The main lock was crushed history. Sten managed to muscle the emergency lock open slightly, then swore as icy water jetted into the ship.

They weren't trapped, at least. They could put on spacesuits, put the casualties in bubblepaks, and get out of the *Gamble*. Which would leave them in very cold water – not a problem in spacesuits – but the water must be refreezing rapidly.

'So we swim out,' Sten said.

'Looks like it, sir.'

'And we better full-drive it. I don't think any of us except for Kilgour can bash through an ice cube.'

Sten and Tapia found Kilgour in a bashing mood. He had just finished going through the ship's emergency supplies. For some reason, sailors never believe they may actually have to abandon ship. And so their emergency kits tend to be maintained perfunctorily and sometimes raided for necessities. The sailors of the *Gamble* were no different.

'We'll worry about that when we get to the surface,' Sten said, 'Move them out.'

With everyone in the shipsuits and the casualties bubble-pakked, the emergency port was opened fully. Water flooded the compartment. Sten and the others had death grips on anything sturdy. The current boiled around them, and then the water rose over the sailors' heads into the next level.

Kilgour was the first to exit the ship. He held one of the two cutting torches from the *Gamble*'s tiny machine shop. He set it at full power, aimed it up, and cut in his suit's rockets. He started slowly upward through the solidifying sludge of the rapidly freezing lake around the *Gamble*. A line was snap-linked from his suit to the other crew members.

Sten was the last man out. He hung in the black water outside the port for a moment. This was the end of his first command. At least, he told himself, we went out fighting, didn't we, lady?

Then the line went taut, and Sten started upward. There was something wrong with his suit's cycler. His vision was a bit blurred. That was the explanation. No rational being becomes sentimental over inanimate metal, of course. Definitely something had gone wonky with the environmental controls.

Kilgour's suit rockets, intended for use offworld, gave him just enough power to overcome the spacesuit's neutral buoyancy and drift him toward the surface.

'Be a mo,' his voice suddenly crackled in Sten's headphones.

'The situation's clottin' strange. Ah seem't to've hit air. But . . . Skipper, Ah'd like a wee consultation.'

Sten unclipped from the line and put more power on his suit rockets. He broke through a few centimeters of ice, surfaced beside Alex, and shone his suit light around.

The scene *was* strange. They floated in a small, rapidly freezing lake created from the water melted by the *Gamble*'s drive and skin heat. Next to them was the battered nose of the *Gamble*, protruding about half a meter above the ice scum.

That alone was not too strange – but just a couple of meters overhead arced a low, icy ceiling.

'This makes no sense at all,' Sten thought out loud.

Tapia surfaced beside him. 'Maybe it does,' she said. 'Do you know anything about snow, sir?'

That wasn't one of Sten's specialities – most of his experience with the stuff came from the snowscape mural that his mother had hocked six months of her life for, back on Vulcan. There had been a couple of Mantis assignments on frozen worlds, but the weather had been just another obstacle, not worth analyzing.

'Not a clottin' lot,' he admitted. 'As far as I'm concerned, it's just retarded rain.'

'That rumble we heard? Maybe that was an avalanche.'

'So now we're *really* buried?'

'Looks like it.'

Tapia was exactly right. What had happened was that the *Gamble* had buried itself in the deep, perpetual snowfield. Its nose was within a few meters of the surface. But 500 meters above the valley, the ship's driveshock had weakened a snowy cornice. It broke free, and a thousand cubic meters of snow and rock avalanched down and across the valley.

The wreckage of the *Gamble* was buried more than forty meters below the snowfield. When they had opened the emergency port, the water pouring into the ship had lowered the level of the minilake around the *Gamble*. The ice that had formed at the base of the snow slide now formed the roof of the dome above them.

'Th' problem then,' Alex said, 'is how we melt on up. Th' suits dinnae hae power enow to gie us airborne. An' tha' snow up there dinnae be load-bearin'.'

There was a solution – one that had all the neatness of a melee.

They paddled clumsily, towing the bubblepaks toward the edges of the under-snow lake. Paddling became crawling atop the ice, breaking through, crawling on again, until eventually the surface was solid enough to hold them.

From there, all they had to do was tunnel.

Being in spacesuits, they fortunately didn't have to worry about smothering. Kilgour half forced, half melted his way, curving upward. 'Y' dinnae ken Ah wae a miner in m' youth,' he said, burning a particularly artistic hairpin bend in the snow.

'Are you sure we're headed up?' Sten asked.

'It dinnae matter, lad. Ae we're goin't up, we'll hit air an' be safe. Ae we're goin't doon, we'll hit sheol an' be warm an' in our rightful place.'

Sten scraped snow from where it was icing up on one of his suit's expansion sleeves and didn't answer. Then he noticed something. There was light. Not just light from their suit beams or Kilgour's cutting torch but a sourceless glow all around them.

Seconds later, they broke free onto the surface of Cavite.

Sten unsealed his faceplate. The air tasted strange. Then he realized that he had not breathed unfiltered, unrecycled air for . . . he realized he couldn't remember.

Helluva way to fight a war, he thought.

And speaking of war, the next step would be finding their way down out of the mountains. And the question was. Would their suit power last long enough for them to hit the warm flatlands? An unpowered suit was as useless as the *Gamble*, ruined in the ice below them.

One catastrophe at a time, he told himself. Probably his sailors, who had less than no experience at ground combat, would get jumped and massacred by a Tahn patrol first.

It would be warm, at least. Sten turned back to his people and started organizing them for the long march.

Chapter Fifty-Nine

On the third day after the Cavite landings began, Lady Atago transferred her flag from the *Forez* to a mobile command post on the planet itself. Her headquarters were in a monstrous armored combat command vehicle – dubbed Chilo class by Imperial Intelligence. The huge – almost fifty meters wide by 150 meters long – segmented ACCV traveled on forty triad-mounted three-meter-high rolligons, cleated low-pressure pillow wheels that gave the vehicle amphibious capabilities as well. Any obstacle the rolligons couldn't pad their way over caused the triad mount to rotate, bringing another wheel into use atop that obstacle. Also, the ACCV was segmented and could twist both vertically and laterally.

It rumbled forward, escorted by a full squadron of tanks and armored ground-to-air missile launchers only a few kilometers behind the fighting lines.

The few Imperial ships still airworthy would never be able to penetrate the AA umbrella – but Atago chose to take no chances. The site she had chosen for her next CP location had several advantages – it was very close to the most promising salient that had been punched through the Tahn lines, there were open areas for ship landings nearby, and there was no need for elaborate camouflage.

The camouflage would be provided by a very large building. It had formerly been a university library in one of Cavite City's satellite towns. And under the new Tahn rule, neither repositories of Imperial propaganda nor education would be necessary.

Six McLean-powered gravsleds were positioned just under the building's eaves, and then the ACCV reversed into the building. Three floors crunched and fell around the vehicle's mushroom dome, but the building held. From the air, Atago's command post was invisible. She was sure that her support ECM units would successfully spoof Imperial detectors.

Also, the tacship division that had plagued the Tahn had been destroyed. Lady Atago was mildly sorry that the division commander, Sten, had not been captured. A show trial could have been arranged, with a suitable punishment broadcast over Imperial com channels. That might have served to discourage some of the more aggressive officers still resisting the Tahn.

But still, Lady Atago was not particularly pleased with the course of the invasion.

The Tahn did have the main Imperial fighting units sealed in the perimeter around Cavite City and were slowly closing the noose. The perimeter had shrunk to less than 200 square kilometers. There were scattered Imperial forces still resisting elsewhere on Cavite, but their destruction would be accomplished within a few days.

The Imperial area now enclosed just Cavite City – and Tahn penetration patrols were already reaching the outskirts of the city – the naval base, and the heights beyond it. Tahn subaqua units had already interdicted any possible retreat by sea.

But the cost was Pyrrhic.

Three complete Tahn landing forces – about the equivalent of four Imperial Guard divisions – had been landed, together with their support units.

They had been decimated. No, Lady Atago corrected herself. The casualties were far greater than one in ten. The spearhead force had driven hard toward Cavite City – and had smashed into the Guard defenses. Four assaults had been mounted and then shattered. In such an event, the Empire would have pulled the unit from combat and held it in reserve until reinforcements had brought it back to combat readiness.

The Tahn were more pragmatic. Their units, once committed to battle, were never withdrawn until they were victorious. Otherwise, they continued in the front lines until taking at least seventy percent casualties. The few survivors would be used to reinforce other formations; the unit itself was retired and completely reformed from scratch.

That had been the fate of the spearhead landing force.

The second landing force had been ordered to attack through the survivors. They, too, had been destroyed.

The Tahn had fought too many battles against the unprepared or the unskilled.

The First Guards Division were neither. They fortified every advantageous position. When they were hit, they held until the last minute. Then they fell back – into previously prepared locations. The Tahn, thinking they had won the objective, set about consolidating. And then the Guard assault elements counterattacked.

At the very least, they caused another ten percent casualties. But mostly they retook the position. It was expensive for the Guards, of course. But far more expensive for the Tahn.

Still worse were the battles in towns. The Guard had every position defended, with supporting cross fire.

Battle into one house – and the Guard would retreat. The house would be taken under cross fire from two other linking positions.

There was never a moment when a Tahn commander could say that his position was secure.

Night was the worst time.

Ian Mahoney had trained his troops to double-think. They held and fought every position that the Tahn wanted. But they never considered a fixed position vital. At night, they sent company-size patrols beyond the front, patrols that hit every target of opportunity.

Night attacks by the Tahn were a perplexity. Recon patrols would report that the Imperial lines were lightly held. An attack would be made – and be destroyed.

Contrary to conventional military thought, the First Guards held their lines very lightly. There was no attempt to completely garrison the front. Tahn patrols could probe and reprobe, finding nothing. Once the Tahn soldiers had broken through, they would be hit from all sides by carefully husbanded reserves, striking from hidden strongpoints.

But the Tahn, by sheer strength of numbers, were winning.

Lady Atago was very sure of that – so sure that, sitting in the privacy of her compartment, she was planning the surrender of the Guards.

A livie team had already been requested from Heath and was standing by. She had full-dress uniforms ready for herself and for the Tahn guard of honor that would escort her.

Admiral van Doorman – if he was still alive – would not be worthy to grant the surrender. But this Mahoney might.

Yes, she decided. It would be a very picturesque ceremony – perfect propaganda for the Tahn war machine. The surrender would be made on the main field at Cavite Base. The livie crews would show the wrecks and damage of that field.

Drawn up would be the ragged remnants of the Imperial Forces. On cue, General Mahoney would advance to meet Lady Atago.

Did he possess a sword? It did not matter, Lady Atago decided. He would have some sort of sidearm. Lady Atago would accept the sidearm and promise graceful treatment to those surrendered soldiers.

Of course that would not be granted – Lady Atago knew that none of those soldiers would appreciate such treatment. Death could be the only award for anyone who was unfortunate enough not to die in battle. But they would be killed in an honorable manner. By the sword.

That also would be recorded by the livie crews. Perhaps, after the Tahn victory over the Empire, those records would be beneficial to future soldiers of the Tahn.

Lady Atago's future was fully planned.

And after the fall of Cavite, she would attack the heart of the Empire itself.

Her mentor, Lord Fehrle, would be pleased.

Or possibly not, she thought, smiling slightly. She had not been impressed with Fehrle of late. Perhaps he would not be the man who would lead the Tahn to final victory.

Perhaps someone else might be more qualified. Someone who had herself seen the heart of combat.

Lady Atago allowed herself to chuckle. The future at that moment seemed very bright and very bloody to her . . .

Chapter Sixty

Sailors and airmen have at least one commonality: they think that somewhere in their Universal Rights they're guaranteed No Walking. Sten's people bitched thoroughly enough for a full company of grunts on being told they were going to Hike Out.

The bitching lasted only about seven kilometers. By then no one had enough stamina left for anything beyond lifting foot from snow, pushing leg forward, putting foot down, lifting other foot from snow . . . and, every half an hour, relieving one of the sailors carrying the bubblepak stretchers.

The spacesuits were even more useless than Sten had originally estimated. Never intended for use on a planetary surface, their pseudo-musculature compensated for less than half of the suit's weight. So walking was a herculean chore.

Sten wished they had powered bunnysuits. Or fur coats. If you are wishing, he thought, why not a new tacship?

If the suits had been less heavy or the weight could have been compensated for with McLean generators, they could have floated over the drifts. Or else improvised snowshoes from tree branches. Instead, they waded doggedly onward.

As night dropped down, Sten looked for a bivvy site. At the edge of the valley they were following, there was a huge tree with snow banked up to its lower limbs. Sten remembered a bit of trivia from a Mantis survival course and ordered his people to burrow toward the tree's trunk. The snow had not completely filled the area around the trunk, and there was a small, circular cave. By rolling about, they compressed the snow, enlarging the cave.

Kilgour checked the wounded. Sten was most grateful for Mantis cross-training, since his TO didn't include a medic. Alex was most competent – Mantis emergency med school would have qualified him as a civilian surgeon very easily. Not that there was much that could be done – their medpak was limited. Kilgour changed burn and stasis dressings and narcoed the injured. One of the wounded would die during the next few hours.

They settled in for the night. None of the sailors believed Tapia or Sten when they were told that they wouldn't need the suit heaters at all, until they saw the exhaled heat from their bodies melt the snow around them to water, which quickly became ice. The temperature in the cave made the space almost livable. Sten widened the hole around the tree's trunk for an air passage.

And so the night crawled into day. The mortally wounded soldier had died during the night. They found a rocky cleft, interred the corpse in its bubblepak, and used three willygun rounds to seal the crevice. Then they started out again.

The next day was a constant trade. Walking with faceplate shut made one warm – warm, and rapidly drained the suit's air supply. If the faceplate was opened and atmosphere breathed, the suit's heater went full on, depleting the powerpak and increasing the chance of facial frostbite.

The skies cleared about noon, and Cavite's sun blazed down. That made matters worse – Contreras went temporarily snowblind; she had to close her faceplate and set it for full polarization. And the snow melted.

There was also the increased chance of being spotted by a Tahn ship, although Sten couldn't figure why any Tahn would bother to patrol this white wasteland.

The second night was a repetition of the first, except with less shelter. Alex used the last of the cutter's power to burn a trench in the snow that would at least get them out of the direct blast of the wind.

That night passed hazily. One sailor was constantly on watch. At first light, they swallowed the last of their suits' liquid rations and moved out again.

Sten was somewhat disgusted at himself. He was starting to wheeze a little around the edges. Feeling exhaustion after only two days on the march? That would have been enough to get him returned to unit immediately back in the Mantis Section days. Sten was starting to understand why so many navy types were lardbutted.

Kilgour didn't make it any easier. His home world of Edinburgh was three-gee, and Cavite was E-normal. And somehow, even though he resembled an anthropomorphized beer keg, he had managed to keep in condition. He tanked through the snow as if it weren't there, as if he weren't wearing a shipsuit, and as if he weren't laden down with the front end of a bubblepak and carrying a medpak and two weapons.

Also, he kept making jokes – or trying to. Sten had to threaten him with close arrest to keep him from telling the awesomely imbecilic spotted snake story – Sten had heard it once back during Mantis training – three times too many. Kilgour had other stories that were almost as bad.

'Ha' Ah gie y' aboot in' time Ah were tourin't th' estate,' he began cheerily to Ensign Tapia.

'What's an estate?' she growled as she almost fell face first into a drift.

'Ah, wee Sten, pardon, Commander Sten, hae dinnae spoke th' Ah'm th' rightful Laird Kilgour ae Kilgour?'

'I have no idea what you're talking about.'

'Ah'm tryin't t' tell y' boot th' pig.'

'Pig?'

'Aye. A great mound ae swineflesh, ae were. A' any rate, th' first Ah e'er saw ae tha' pig wae when Ah wa' tourin't th' estate. An'

Ah seeit thae great porker. An' it strikit me, for it hae a wooden leg. Three legs an' aye, a peg.'

'A three-legged pig,' Foss put in suspiciously, having waded up close enough to Tapia to hear the story.

'Aye. A wonderment. So thae's this wee farmer standin't nigh his fence. An' I begin't an say, '"Tha' pig, mister."

'An' he speakit, an say, "Aye, aye. Thae's a pig ae marvel. Three year ago, m' wee lad fall't down. Inta th' pond. Tha' dinnae be anyone around, an' m' heir's a drown't.

'"Doon plung't th' pig, an' pull him out."

'An' Ah'm listen't, an' Ah say't, "Tha's ae marvel. But—"

'An once't 'gain he cuts me off. "Two year gone, m' gran's in th' gravsled, an' the controls go. An' the gravsled lifts an' 'tis headed for yon viaduct."'

'Viaduct?' Tapia asked.

'Noo, tha's a fair question, lass. Ah'll answer in a bit. T' continue. I agree wi' m' wee tenant. "Aye, tha's a pig tha's a wonder. But about—" an' ag'in he chops me.

'"One year past, 'tis a deep winter. Y' c'lect, Laird Kilgour." An Ah says, "Aye, Ah remember."

'An he says, "M' croft catches fire. An' we're all asleep ae' th' dead. But this pig, he storm't ae th' hoose an' wakit us all. Savin't our lives."

'Ae tha' point, Ah hae enough. "Be holdin't tha' speech, man," Ah roars. "Ah 'gree. 'Tis a marvelous hog. Wha' Ah want to know is, *Why th' clottin' wooden leg*!?"

'An th' crofter look't ae me, an' say, "Why, mon, you dinnae eat ae pig like thae all at once!"'

Tapia and Foss, both thinking indictable thoughts about premeditated murder, continued wading through the snow. That was Alex on the march.

But possibly his worst trait was the inveterate cheeriness – the constant chants of 'Only five more klicks, Skipper' grew wearisome. Especially since they were now plowing through snow that was turning to slush.

Slush? Sten looked ahead and realized there weren't any more peaks in front of them. The valley widened out toward foothills. There were now patches of bare rock in the valley center.

They had made it.

Now all Sten had to worry about was getting his non-infantry deckwipes through the Tahn front lines, into Cavite City.

A piece of cake.

Chapter Sixty-One

When the ground stayed flat for seventy-five meters and the temperature went above 15°C, they unpeeled. Kilgour choked politely.

'Th' universe smell't mightily a' feet,' he observed. 'Th' Tahn'll track us by the reek.'

He wasn't exaggerating – they collectively stank like a cesspit. But that lasted only until they ran across the first cattle tank. Kilgour shooed off the three scrawny bovines and charged into the water, tearing off his coveralls as he waded. The others were close behind him.

Sten gave them an hour to scrape off the worst before continuing the march. Now they needed rations and a secure place to plan just how they were going to return to friendly lines.

Navigation was easy – they marched toward the columns of smoke on the horizon that marked the battleground around Cavite City. The land was dry, poor grazing country, spotted here and there with ramshackle farms, most of which were deserted. Sten skirted the few that showed signs of occupation – they didn't look to have enough for their owners let alone be able to resupply Sten.

Then they hit prosperity: green fields and, in the distance, farm buildings. But 2,000 meters from the main building, prosperity showed itself as tragedy. The fields around the farm were deserted.

Sten spread his people out and advanced very cautiously. At 500 meters, he put his sailors into a defensive line in one of the many now-empty irrigation ditches that had made the land arable.

He and Alex went forward.

In the center of the farm was a small artesian pond. Scattered along its banks were fifteen or so bodies. Sten and Alex crouched behind a shed and waited.

A door banged from the main building. Sten thumbed his safety off. The door banged again. And again. It was the wind.

They leapfrogged forward to the first of the bodies. Kilgour sniffed.

'Three. P'raps four days now,' he said. 'Ah wonder if they had a trial first.'

The people had not been killed in combat – each of the men and women had his hands wired behind him or her.

Sten rolled a body over. There was a glint of gold visible around the bloated neck of the corpse. Sten used his gun barrel to pry it free. The glint was a neck emblem.

'They were Tahn,' Sten identified. 'Settlers, by the way they're dressed.'

'Wonder who butchered them?'

Sten shrugged. 'Imperial vigilantes. Tahn troops. Does it matter?'

'M' morbid curiosity, Commander. Let's tumble the house.'

They brought the others into the farmyard. A couple of sailors saw the bodies and threw up. Get used to it, people, Sten thought. From here on out, we won't be fighting a long-distance war.

He, Tapia, and Kilgour went through the main house. It looked as if the building had been picked up, turned upside down, shaken, and then replaced on its foundations. Everything that could be broken was. Anything that could be spoiled was befouled.

'Ah hae a theory. 'Twas no Imperials did this – four days ago, they'd be scuffin' toward Cavite. Tahn soldiers whidny hae taken th' time to be't ae thorough.' As he spoke, he was stuffing unbroken rationpaks into a plas sack. 'My theory,' he went on, 'says tha' these wee folk were tryin't t' walk the fence before th' war. Which dinnae set well wi' other Tahn. When th' Tahn landed, their bro' farmers settled accounts, an—'

Kilgour stopped and picked up a tiny bottle from where it had rolled next to a sideboard. He tossed the bottle to Sten.

Sten read the label: 'Mahoney Cider & Fertilizer Works. Fine Fruit and Poop for 130 Years.'

'We'll be walkin't in th' path ae th' master,' Alex said mock solemnly.

Tapia couldn't understand why, in the middle of this death, her two superiors suddenly started laughing.

From then, they moved only by night.

And they moved very slowly, not only from caution but because of the sailors' inexperience. Sten had a permanent set of toothmarks in his tongue, trying to keep from exploding in anger.

These people were not Mantis. They weren't Guards. Clot, they weren't even infantry recruits. Shut up, Commander, and quit expecting supersoldiers. But at this rate, the war might be over before they reached Cavite City. So? Are you in some special hurry to get back under siege and get killed, Commander? Shut up and keep moving.

On the fourth night, Contreras stumbled onto Frehda's farm – literally, going sprawling across a concertinaed stretch of razor wire. Fortunately, her coveralls kept the wire from inflicting severe cuts. The others unwound her, pulled back to the shelter of a clump of brush, and considered.

Once again Sten and Alex went forward, going through the layers of wire and sensors without being discovered. They lay atop the hill looking down onto the rows of barracks and discussed the matter, using the sign language that Mantis had developed for situations like this. It was a very simple one. Spread hands, for instance, meant 'What is this?'

Mime T – Tahn. Fingers on collar tabs – military? Shake the head. It was obvious – Tahn soldiers would have had far more elaborate security, and probably wouldn't be showing lights.

Sten pointed toward the floodlit barracks and signed a complete question: 'Then what're all those clots with guns and gravsleds doing?' He realized he knew the answer – this was a Tahn revolutionary settlement.

Almost certainly there would be a few Tahn troops down there. He figured that the Tahn would be using those revolutionaries for behind-the-lines security, police duties, and so forth. The 'so forth' probably included dealing with any of the settlers, either Imperial or Tahn, who weren't firmly committed to the cause.

Sten felt that he had a fairly good idea of who had murdered that Tahn family – and also how to get back to Cavite City.

Kilgour had the same plan. By the time Sten looked back at him, Alex had his two hands held, palms together, next to his cheek and his head slumped against them.

Right. Now they needed a sentry.

They found one about seventy-five meters farther along the wire. He was walking his post and staying out of the floodlight glare, his eyes sweeping the darkness behind. They modified their plan slightly.

Kilgour crept forward until he was within four meters of the sentry.

Sten, also snake flat, went around inside of the man, toward the barracks, then crept back. His fingers curled, and the knife slid into his hand.

Breathe . . . breathe . . . eyes down . . . Sten's legs curled under him, and he was up. Three steps, and one hand curled around the sentry's chin, snapping the man's head back and to one side. The knife, held ice pick fashion, went straight down into the subclavian artery. The man was unconscious in two seconds, dead in three and a half.

That gave them their prop for the sleeping sentry trap. It was based on the assumption that in all armies sleeping on guard duty is considered as grave a sin as committing an unnatural act on one's commanding officer.

They dragged the body against a post, pulled its cap over its eyes, and let it relax. Sten and Alex took flanking positions to either side of the body, ten meters away into the darkness, and waited.

Sooner or later, the commander of the guard should check his posts. And sooner or later, he did.

A combat car hummed up from the barracks and wove its way along the perimeter. Sten and Alex were prone, assuming that both occupants would be wearing light-enhancing goggles.

They were – but they were looking for their sentry, not for two thugs in the deep grass.

The guard commander saw his 'sleeping' sentry. Evidently he decided the man needed a lesson, because the car grounded about ten meters away.

Sten slunk toward the combat car.

The Tahn guard officer – one of Frehda's 'advisers' – padded toward his sinning sentry. Next he would bend over the man and bellow. Assuming the sentry survived the initial shock, major punishment would follow. The guard officer looked forward to it – he felt that these Tahn farmers were getting mostly slack, merely because the *real* fighting forces were winning.

He bent – and Alex's hand crashed out of the night in a *teishozuki* palm strike against his forehead. The blow, delivered by a normal man, would have stunned. With the full force of Kilgour's three-gee muscles behind it, the commander's skull crushed as if it had imploded under pressure.

Kilgour removed the weapons belts from the two men and ran toward the combat car.

Sten wiped the blade of his knife on the late driver's tunic and got behind the sled's controls. He pulled the driver's goggles over

his eyes and lifted the car three meters into the air, turned it, and
drove it at full power toward where his sailors waited.

They were mobile again.

Chapter Sixty-Two

The Tahn combat car gave Sten and his deck apes not only mobility
but a cover as well. Sten assumed some logic from the Tahn: all
civilian vehicles would be either grounded or impounded, and all
Imperial gravsleds would be inside the Cavite City perimeter. Ergo,
anything traveling openly must be Tahn.

Sten did cover himself slightly – after he loaded his people, he
found the dustiest road around and made three passes down it
within centimeters of the surface. Then he lifted for Cavite City,
one more harassed combat car driver trying to get his dusty troops
toward the lines.

The only potential problem might be police checkpoints just
behind the lines – but they'd be checking the trip tickets and IDs
of those headed *away* from combat, not toward the sound of guns.

Then they got even luckier. Sten was waved down by a Tahn
road security man as a priority convoy of heavy lifters hurtled
through. The convoy was keeping lousy interval, with hundreds of
meters between its gravsleds. It was simple for Sten to tuck himself
into line near the convoy's end and equally simple to bank down
a side street once they hit the outskirts of the city.

The Imperial perimeter had gotten much smaller. The Tahn,
vastly outnumbering the Empire's forces, were closing the ring. Sten
managed to evade three Tahn street patrols before he decided he'd
pushed their luck far enough.

Two kilometers from the lines, Sten tucked the combat car into
the third story of a shattered building and thought tactically. From
this point, the danger would be steadily greater – the Tahn units

would be looking for penetration patrols in their own lines, and the no-man's-land between the lines would be even more hazardous.

Finally, there could well be the problem of being shot by their own troops – Sten had no idea what passwords or signals were in use.

The answer to their problem was a white-uniformed security patrolman.

White uniforms, Sten mused. In a combat zone?

'W' hae rank an' idle ceremony,' Kilgour observed, lowering his binocs. 'Cannae we be usin't tha?'

'You're just looking for an excuse to gash another screw, Kilgour.'

'True. But dinnae it be braw?'

It was.

Again, Sten and Alex reconned the situation, going from rooftop to rooftop until they had that security patrolman in plain sight. A second patrolman stood on the other side of what had been a city street and now was a less-rubbled section of ruins.

Behind the two military cops were two double chaingun positions. Further to the rear were tanks and missile launchers, positioned around a cluster of tracks. These were obviously command vehicles – they sprouted more antennae than a nest of young brine shrimp. It was the command post of the armored brigade supporting the Tahn landing forces. And it lay directly between Sten and the Imperial lines.

'Shall w' ring ae second goin' ae th' guard?'

They could – and did.

Less experienced – or less cynical – soldiers might have skirted the CP. But to Sten and Alex, this was opportunity.

Intelligence, either personally observed by the two men or taught them in Mantis training: headquarters units had massive security. The security elements may have been selected for their efficiency at first but inevitably would turn into spit-and-polish orderlies. They would be commanded, most likely, by ambitious or well-connected young officers. Their formations would slowly, and almost imperceptibly, transition from combat-based to parade-oriented.

The troopers in such a unit would be promoted and commended for the gloss on their boots and the shine on their buttons. After hours of such blanco drill, such a man had a certain reluctance to wade through the muck just because he had heard a possibly strange sound.

And finally there was the factor of arrogance – who would *dare* attack the powerful?

Sten and Alex proposed to exploit that arrogance.

Tourists goggle when the military changes guards. It's done in front of palaces, with dress uniforms, en masse, at predictable times, and with much clanging of weaponry – preferably chromed and antique. That isn't the way it should work when there may be bad guys around – but tradition is tradition, even if it's only a week or so old.

Sten and his sailors took full advantage of that.

The changing of the Tahn general's guard consisted of several platoons marching in close order up to each guard post, where, amid shouts and clatter, the old guard would be inspected and relieved by the guard commander. On relief, he would clang the butt of his weapons a couple of times and march to the rear of that platoon. The new guard would be positioned, and the platoons would stomp on to the next post.

Naturally, that guard changing was done on the clock, by the clock.

Sten knew that the lowest point in the human soul is four hours after midnight.

And that is when he moved.

Clangs . . . clatters . . . shouted orders . . . and Sten's thirteen people slipped silently past the newly posted and yawning guard, straight toward the heart of Atago's command post.

Marching in plain sight, in formation – Sten desperately hoped that his swabbies were keeping some kind of march step – they went in unchallenged.

Step one – complete. Step two – find a hidey-hole.

Kilgour picked an armoured supply gravsled, grounded about 150 meters from the command tracks. He slipped through the undogged entry hatch, kukri ready. Sten waited outside as backup.

He heard only one dying gurgle before Kilgour's head peered back out. The kukri was unbloodied. Not bad, Sten thought. The lad still has his moves.

He waved the eleven sailors inside. And they waited for dawn.

Sten, Foss, Kilgour, and Tapia kept watch on the track's screens. At this point, the plan deteriorated into opportunity. Sooner or later, sometime around nightfall, Sten thought, there should be some sort of troop movement forward. More chaos. No one would question a group of soldiers moving from a command post toward the front lines. He hoped.

They would move in Tahn uniforms. At first, Sten thought that every man-jill would be so outfitted – one of the barges was full of sealed paks labeled 'Uniforms, Issue, Mk. 113.' But there was further translation: 'Full Dress, Temperate Climate (White).'

Sten thought that if he put his swabbies into those uniforms, they'd probably get out of the CP's lines smoothly – but just might have trouble when they encountered their first Tahn combat troopie.

But there would be another option.

In the early afternoon, Sten thought he'd found it. Combat cars hissed in from the lines, and Tahn officers dismounted.

A command conference, Sten guessed. When this breaks up, we should be able to get up and go.

Then there was a rumble, and a large troop-carrying gravsled hissed toward the command center. A thousand meters above it whined two Tahn battle cruisers.

'Clottin' hell,' Alex observed. He had been watching the screen over Sten's shoulder. 'Th' brass ae surfacin't.'

The gravsled grounded, and a ramp dropped. A line of combat-uniformed Tahn soldiers doubled down it.

'Ah dianne ken th' Tahn be raisin't Goliaths!'

The soldiers *were* very tall. And very broad.

The giants formed two lines on either side of the ramp.

And Sten knew what was going to happen next.

He turned away from the screen and looked at Alex. The heavy-worlder's face was pale.

'W' dinnae hae ae choice, do we, lad?' he whispered.

No, Sten thought. We do not.

He picked up the willygun leaning next to the screen's control panel and checked its sights and load. Then he moved toward the entry port and cautiously eased it open.

Sten was a survivor.

He was also an officer of the Empire.

Situation posited: Formally dressed bodyguards in plain view. Waiting. As are assembled high-ranking officers.

Deduction: Someone of high rank will make an appearance.

Question: Who is that someone?

Answer: Lady Atago. Or Deska.

Question: Is the death of Deska desirable – regardless of sacrifice?

Answer: Probably.

Question: Is the death of Lady Atago desirable?

Answer: Absolutely.

Regardless of the cost, Commander Sten?

Regardless of the cost.

Sten took a hasty sling around his arm, braced against the supply sled's port, and aimed, making sure that the muzzle of his willygun didn't protrude into plain sight.

If Atago came down that ramp, she would die.

And shortly afterward, so would Sten and the sailors he had so carefully tried to keep alive.

Kilgour was moving behind him, shaking people into alertness and whispering.

About 150 meters away, the bodyguards and the Tahn officers snapped to rigid attention.

And Lady Atago started down the ramp.

Aim carefully, Sten, he thought. If it's stupid to die, it's even stupider to get killed after you miss.

The cross hairs of his sight moved across Atago's red cloak and stopped on the center of her green tunic. The Anti-Matter Two round would blow a fist-sized hole in that green.

Sten inhaled, then exhaled half the breath. His finger took up the slack in the trigger.

And then Atago's bodyguards moved, as swiftly and skillfully as a corps de ballet, closing around their charge. All Sten could see was the white of their uniforms instead of green.

He swore, then lifted his eyes.

Atago was still surrounded. And then, still in phalanx, the circle of white giants marched into one of the command tracks, the Tahn officers straggling behind them.

Sten lowered his willygun.

He was breathing as deeply as if he had just run five kilometers or had sex. And the part of his brain that was and always would be a street criminal was reading him the riot act. You. You're disappointed because you're still alive? What the hell is the matter with you? And then that survival brain chortled. Sorry, cheena. I didn't realize you held fire to make sure you wouldn't get blasted. Didn't mean to get critical.

That thought made it worse.

Maybe he had. Maybe he had.

Sten was very quiet and very thoughtful for the remainder of the day.

Kilgour took over. He stripped uniforms off the bodies of the Tahn crewmen he'd killed and ordered five of the sailors to get into them.

Near dusk, the Tahn conference broke up. Lady Atago returned to her gravsled completely shielded by her bodyguards. There was never a minute when Sten could have tried again.

S'be't, as the Jann would have said. Now to worry about the future – and staying alive.

It was very simple, in the whine and hiss of departing officers and scurrying troops, to move straight out from the perimeter, unchallenged, toward the lines.

Kilgour found a shell crater, where they waited until full dark.

He slid up to Sten. 'Lad, dinnae fash. We'll hae a chance again,' he whispered.

Sten grunted.

'A wee thing more, Skipper. Ah dinnae how to say – but Ah been hae'in't troubles wi' m' bowels.'

'So?' Sten managed.

'Those bales ae white uniforms?'

'GA.'

'They nae be white n' more.'

Sten came back to reality and managed a smile.

Now for the last worry – getting killed by their own troops.

If he were commanding a Mantis section, Sten thought, the first time the Imperial troops would realize they had been penetrated was when Sten and his people lined up for morning rations.

But these were sailors.

He found a shelter for his people in some ruins and went forward on his own. Alex lifted a bushy eyebrow, but Sten shook his head.

He moved forward like a weasel from patch to patch of darkness. His fingers found a tripflare, and his body lifted over the wire. A booby mine – avoided.

There – a two-man outpost, both men alert, gun barrels questioning the dark.

He went past them.

Then there was the bunker – the reaction element. No. Too trigger-happy. Sten continued on.

A Guard patrol, coming in from the lines, crept past him. Sten followed them at a discreet distance. One hundred meters farther on, there was a gleam of light as the patrol entered their command post to report.

Sten counted: ten seconds for welcome; ten seconds for the patrol to dump their weapons; another ten as they poured caff.

He went down the bunker steps and slipped sideways through the blackout curtain – a torn blanket – before any of the Imperial guardsmen could react. Then, deliberately casual, he said, 'I'm Commander Sten. Imperial Navy. I've got some people outside the wire to bring in.'

And they were home.

Chapter Sixty-Three

General Mahoney and Admiral van Doorman were glowering at a holographic situation map that filled most of Mahoney's command track when Sten reported in.

'What took you so long?' was Mahoney's sole reaction. Oh, well. Sten hadn't expected exactly the chubby calf treatment – Mahoney's highest compliment when he had been running Mercury Corps had been 'duty performed adequately.'

Then he saw Mahoney hide a grin and felt better.

He scanned the map and felt worse – the Empire was between a rock and a hard place.

Mahoney touched a control, and the overall battlefield vanished, to be replaced with a projection of one segment.

'What's left of your command is holding a section of the line—' Mahoney's pointing finger went through a miniscule half-ruined boulevard. '—just here.' For some reason, Sten thought the area looked familiar.

'Since we have a, uh, certain surplus of ramp rats without any ships to service, your people became infantry. I put your senior warrant – a Mr Sutton, I believe – in charge. He's got your unit, plus I scavenged up another seventy-five clerks, chaplain's assistants, PIO types, and so forth.'

Sten kept his poker face. Great, he thought. Not only do my combat people get destroyed, but all my wrenches are dead, too.

'Oddly enough,' Mahoney continued, 'they've done an exceptional job of holding their positions. For some reason the Tahn have only hit them hard a couple of times.'

'The navy knows how to fight,' van Doorman put in. Mahoney

would not respond to that, especially in front of a lower-ranking officer.

'But since you've decided to rejoin the living,' he continued, 'I'm going to pull your detachment back. I want you to take over this position.'

Again, the table showed another part of Cavite City: a low, bare hillock, not many kilometers from the navy base, surrounded by destroyed housing complexes.

'We thought this was just a park. But one of my G-2 types found out it's an old fort.

'One hundred fifty years ago or thereabouts, whoever was running the 23rd Fleet decided that the base needed additional security. I guess the Imperial appropriations were fat that year. About ten years later the money must've run out, because they abandoned it and let the grass grow. But we think it's still active.'

Mahoney turned to another screen and keyed up a projection. This was a cutaway of the hill itself. There were vertical passages leading to flush-mounted turrets and four horizontal levels below them.

'Typical passive defense,' Mahoney commented. He hit another button and got a vertical schematic of the fort. 'Four AA chain-cannon here . . . here. The turrets are pop-up, and the cannon can be swiveled down to fifteen degrees below horizontal. Each of the main turrets has antipersonnel projectile guns. There are twelve missile silos, but you don't want to get near them. These two little mounts have quad projectile mounts. And that's going to be your new domicile. Any questions?'

'Yessir. First, you said you *think* it's defensible?'

'Hope could be better. As far as the records show, the fort was kept as a reserve strongpoint. So it still should have rations, fuel for the gun mounts, and ammunition. I said don't worry about the missiles – they'll be unstable as all hell by now. If there's no ammunition for the guns in the fort, you're drakh out of luck – all the calibers are as obsolete as the *Swampscott*.'

Van Doorman *harrumphed* but didn't say anything.

'Anything else?'

'Why didn't you move my people out there before?'

'Weel,' Mahoney said, 'there's a slight problem. Seems this fort is about three kilometers inside the Tahn lines. I didn't think your OIC would be a real swiftie at snoop and poop.

'Once you get positioned, give me a full status report. You'll coordinate through this command as to when you begin operations. I'm sure you won't have any trouble finding targets of opportunity.'

'Thank you, sir.' Sten saluted. So whatever remained of his people was going to be used as a fire brigade.

'One thing more, Commander. I'll let you pick a call sign.'

Sten thought a minute.

'Strongpoint Sh'aarl't,' he decided.

'That's all.'

The first order of business, Sten thought, was finding out how badly the Tahn had savaged his crew of innocent technicians.

He expected a disaster.

Sten and Alex flattened as a Tahn rocket screamed in, scattering multiple warheads across what had been a complex of shops. Shock waves hammered at them, and then the ground decided to stabilize for a moment.

Cavite City lay in ruins, ruins sticking up toward the sky like so many hollow, rotten teeth. The streets were almost unusable for ground traffic, blocked by shattered buildings. And in the city there were only two kinds of people – the dead and the moles. The dead had been either left entombed by the blasts that killed them, or hastily cremated when they had fallen. But the city stank of death.

Everything living was underground. Deep trenches had been dug and roofed against overhead blasts. There was no such thing as a civilian anymore – the Imperial settlers and the few Tahn who had decided to stay loyal to the Empire were now indistinguishable from the fighting troops. They served as medics, cooks, and even fought from the same bunkers as the Guardsmen. And they died – the Tahn were very nondiscriminatory about who was and who was not a combatant.

Anyone with no immediate assignment discovered a new fondness for digging. The shelters got deeper and deeper as the siege lengthened.

Sten thought he saw Brijit vanish into an unmarked trench entrance as he and his twelve people worked their way forward, but he wasn't sure. If the trench housed a hospital, it would not have been marked – the eons-old Red Cross provided the Tahn with an excellent aiming point.

The closer they came to the lines, the worse it became. Sten was prepared for his own personal catastrophe.

Instead he got the first pleasant surprise since . . . hell, since

Brijit had gone to bed with him. This war was becoming burdensome, he thought.

Actually, there was a series of pleasant surprises.

Now Sten saw why he had vaguely recognized the area his support people had been assigned to. It was at the slum end of Burns Avenue. Mr Sutton had established his command post in the still fairly undamaged Rain Forest restaurant. Still better was the fact that two of Sr. Tige's sons had stayed with their business/home. The old man had disappeared on the third day after the landing. The sons preferred not to speculate but concentrated on cooking.

Even though the dome was shattered, the birds and insects were either dead or had fled, and the waterfalls were now stagnant green pools, there was still the food. Tige's sons managed to make even the issue rations more than palatable.

Mr Sutton chuffed three times in succession when he saw the thirteen people who had been given up for lost. He went emotionally overboard and patted Alex on the shoulder once – the equivalent, for spindars, of hysterical joy.

And then he reported.

Sten had expected decimation among the motley crew of technicians and chairborne troopers, most of whom were probably slightly unsure of which end of a willygun was hostile and were surely unaware of certain infantry subtleties, like keeping one's head out of the line of fire.

Instead: six dead, fourteen wounded.

'The Tahn mounted – I believe that is the correct phrase – a most determined attack on our second day,' Sutton said. 'Their tactics were most foolish. They sent three waves of soldiers at us. We did not find it necessary to aim carefully. Their casualties were appalling, Commander. Just appalling.

'A day or so later, they attempted us again. Most half-heartedly. Since then, we have seen very little action. They appear to be terrified of us.'

Sten raised an eyebrow – the Tahn were afraid of *nothing*. But there had to be some explanation.

A Guards sergeant commanding an attached support rocket battery provided it. 'Our prog's that the Tahn figured your kiddies'd be a walkover, no offense, sir. They come in dumb, and got dead. Next time, they was just probin'. Then – zipburp. We got curious, so I took out a couple of my people and lifted a prisoner. That's a terrible thing to happen to a Tahn, you maybe know. He says the reason your people didn't get wiped is 'cause everybody figures they're elite. Or decoys.'

'Say what?'

'Put it to you like this, Commander. Your people go out on patrol. Nobody told 'em you're supposed to blackface. Or you ain't supposed to be showin' lights or smoking herb. Th' Tahn thought they were gettin' set up. Progged that your swabs had big backup. Plus, this Tahn told us, they couldn't believe any line animals'd build such clottin' poor positions. Hadda be some kind of trap. Guess they got somebody over there guilty of thinkin', huh?'

Sten laughed. And made a note to give the real skinny to whoever took over his section of the line; he wondered how the man would take the basic instruction – remember, tell your people to act real stupid. But in the meantime, he had to figure out how he was going to move his merry marauders back through the enemy lines to this probably non-existent fort.

Whatever he did, he figured it would get pretty interesting.

Chapter Sixty-Four

As far as Strongpoint Sh'aarl't went, getting there was not half the fun.

It took five full nights for Sten's troopies to reach the long-abandoned fort. It started with the small problem that his sailors thought they were minor heroes instead of lucky sods. They had a group name – Sutton's Sinister Swabbies – which had been created by a livie journalist who had reported on the Battling Bastards of the Bridgehead. That, of course, had made the Empirewide 'casts – there was very little in the way of good news those days.

Alex and Sten privately dubbed their cocky swabs the Clotting Klutzes of Cavite.

Actually, either label would have fit. Through good fortune, they hadn't gotten instantly wiped out. And so they had survived long enough to learn combat tactics instinctually. Proof – they were still mostly alive.

Sten hoped to keep them that way.

He moved his detachment to the friendly point closest to this possibly mythical fort. They were ordered to delouse, drakh, and degrease.

Once again, Sten and Alex went point.

Sten was very tired of being the first man into danger, but he saw no other option. Fortunately, Kilgour felt the same and didn't bother complaining. But both of them would have traded their chances on salvation for eight uninterrupted hours on a feather mattress.

They slid through the Tahn front lines without problems, two floating ghosts. Finding that hilltop of the hidden fort was equally easy. Mahoney had sent an op-aimed missile onto its crest, a missile whose warhead area carried a navbeacon.

There were, according to the fiche, several entryways to the fort. Sten picked the least obvious – a supposedly still-standing power line maintenance shed.

The monitor panel was hinged and counterweighted. It lifted away without complaint. Sten allowed himself to hope that this would be painless.

It wasn't.

He and Alex dropped into the underground passage with a splash. They were in thigh-deep muck. One of the filtering pumps must have stopped operation some years earlier. So had the vector killers.

There were vermin in the tunnel, vermin that thought this was their turf and resented the intruding two-legs. They bit. Sten wished that the livie standard, an area blaster, actually existed. Destroying the multiple-legged waste eaters one at a time with AM2 blasts from their willyguns would have taken an eon. Not to mention that the echoing explosions would have left them quite deaf.

Kilgour had the solution. He pitched bester grenades ahead of him as they waded toward the fort. Time loss wasn't ordinarily lethal, but it was when the air-breathing victims collapsed into water and drowned.

Eventually the tunnel climbed upward, and they waded out of mire. Sten found the master control room and, obeying the TF for the fort, turned the power on.

Lights flickered, and machinery hummed.

That was all Sten needed for the moment – the fort was mannable. The next step was to man it. They returned through the lines and slept through the day.

The second night was spent in a detailed recon of the least perilous route to Strongpoint Sh'aarl't. Sten and Alex broke that route down into 300-meter segments. That was more than enough.

On the third night, they positioned their guides. Sten knew that his befuddled sailors, regardless of their self-opinion, couldn't line-cross without discovery. His idea was to take the sailors he'd walked out of the hills with and use them as route guides. Each guide would be responsible for 300 meters of travel. At the end of his or her route, he or she would pass people on to the next guide.

Almost anyone can learn to traverse – blind and quietly – 300 meters of terrain in one night. Riiiight!

Sten had also loaded the odds on his side. For two nights now Imperial artillery had brought in crashing barrages exactly at midnight along the route to the fort. He figured the Tahn would be chortling at the Empire's predictability and, equally predictably, diving into their shellproofs at midnight.

On the fourth and fifth nights, he moved his sailors forward. The barrages were still mounted but, for those two nights, aimed to either side of the corridor that Sten and his people would move along.

Too elaborate, he'd told himself. Too true, he'd also thought. But you got a better option?

Neither he nor Alex could come up with anything cuter. And so, at midnight of night four, three-person teams moved out beyond the Empire's perimeter, to be met and hand-held onward by guides.

Sten was betting that forty percent of his people would reach the fort before the Tahn discovered them. If twenty percent made it from there and if most of the archaic weapons in the fort worked, he might be able to hold the position. Anything else was pure gravy.

Sten, by 0400 hours of the fifth night, was gloating.

Every single sailor had made it to Strongpoint Sh'aarl't. Sten was starting to believe in them. By silent consent, he and Alex retired their private nickname for the swabbies.

'A'er tha',' as Kilgour pointed out. 'Ee tha' want to christen th'selves th' Kilgour-Killin't Campbells, Ah'll dinnae fash.'

The next task was to find out how much of a white elephant they were fighting from – and how big a fight it would be.

Chapter Sixty-Five

The fort was more of a cement-gray elephant than white, and it wasn't even that much of an elephant. The beings who had mothballed the structure had done a fairly decent job.

Sten found the fort's command center on the second level and sent teams out to investigate the rest of his base.

Foss was staring at the fire and control computer. 'Lord Harry,' he marveled. 'They actually expected people to *shoot* using this beast? Clottin' thing looks like it should have a kick starter.'

He pulled an insulated glove on and touched power switches. According to the specs, the sensor antennae were grid-buried in the fort's armor, so no bedsprings should jump out of the park's grass and give things away.

The air stank of singed insulation – but the computer came to life. Foss unfolded a modern hand-held computer, slid the screen out, and started creating a glossary. The computer worked – but the symbols and readouts were those of a long-forgotten age.

Sten had the environment controls on standby. When they went into action, he would turn them on. But until then, he didn't want vent fans showing above the ground. He and his people would just have to live with the odor. The entire fort smelled musty, like a long-ignored clothes closet.

About half of the visual sensor screens were alive. Sten, once again, didn't use any of the controls that would swivel the pickups.

Okay, he told himself. I can aim at something – I think. Let's see if there's anything working in the bang department.

He went up into the top-level ready rooms. His squad leaders were already assigning troops to them. Sten let them go about their business. He was busy studying the TO boards. Among the missing pieces of data on the fort had been the list of personnel required to man the base. As Sten had suspected, there were supposed to be far more soldiers than he had in his approximately 125-strong detachment.

Sten juggled bodies around. He wouldn't need to worry about the missile crewmen – that helped a lot. Cooks, bakers, and so forth – his people could rustle their own rations. Instead of three shifts, he would run watch on/watch off.

He was still about 400 people short.

Sten continued his inspection, going up the ladders into each of the turrets. Three of the four chaincannon looked as if they would work, and one of the quad projectile mounts would be online.

The maintenance machines had done their work – the cannon gleamed in dust-free, oily darkness. Tapia was studying the guns, trying to figure out exactly how each of them worked. Ideally, they would be automatically loaded, aimed, and fired. But if the command center was hit or the F-and-C computer went down, each turret would have to be capable of independent action.

Tapia was pretty sure that she could test the shell hoists that led from the fourth-level ammo dump up into the turrets without the turrets popping up. Sten told her to run them.

Machinery moaned and hissed. Monitor panels came semi-alive, informed Tapia they did not like the way the machinery was behaving, then shut up as lubricant hissed through long-disused channels and the hoist/loaders showed normal operating conditions.

Tapia glanced around. She and Sten were alone in the turret's command capsule.

'How do I get a clottin' transfer out of this clottin' hen-house outfit?' she asked.

'Problems?'

'Hell, yes. I don't like having to just sit here and wait to get hit. Clottin' better bein' a moving target. And it says real clear on my records that I got claustrophobia. And,' she added, scratching thoughtfully at her neck, 'I think I got fleas, too, off that clottin' bunker I was stuck in.'

Having blown steam, she went back to her on-the-job training. Sten admired the turn of her buttocks under the combat suit, thought a couple of unmilitary thoughts, and continued on his rounds.

Sutton had found the kitchens and brought them to life. He was assisted by two others – the sons of Sr. Tige. The two Tahn explained that they saw no future in sitting around the ruins of the restaurant waiting to get shelled. Besides, none of Sten's troops could cook their way out of a rationpak. Sten should have figured out some way to send them back through the lines.

They were civilians and if captured by the Tahn would be quite legally executed. But then, on the other hand, if Cavite City fell, they would be executed as collaborators, even though everyone on Cavite was supposedly an Imperial citizen. *If* Cavite City fell? Sten wondered if he was getting sick – there was no reason for any sort of optimism. *When* Cavite City fell.

What the clot – the Tiges were probably in no worse shape with him than anywhere else.

Besides, there was business. Sutton ran down the supply station.

The spindar had personally lumbered down the rows of ammunition on the bottom level. The pumps had kept the dump from flooding, and the rack sprays had lubricated the stored rounds at intervals.

Bedding? Mr Sutton lifted a rear leg and scratched the back of his neck. Forget bedding – the dehumidifiers on the third level were wonky. The living spaces themselves were almost uninhabitable.

That wasn't a problem. The troops could doss down in the ready rooms.

Water? Again, no problem. The rain collectors were in perfect condition, as were the purifiers.

Rations?

Sutton was outraged. 'I am preparing a full report, Commander. Cha-chuff. Whoever was the quartermaster was on the dropsy! An out-and-out crook!'

Sten smiled. Sutton was getting moralistic on him.

'Examine this,' Sutton growled, and pointed to a computer screen. 'Imperial regulations specify that each serving trooper is to be afforded a balanced, interesting diet. Am I correct?'

'Imperial regulations specify a lot of things that get conveniently lost in the shuffle.'

Sutton ignored Sten's reference to his past. 'Balanced, interesting, with full provision for nonhumanoid or special diets.'

'GA.'

'Look at what this unspeakable person did! All that we have warehoused here are paked legumes and freeze-dried herbivore flesh! How can I feed my people on things like this? How can the Tiges manage to keep the rations interesting? We might as well hook ourselves up to a mass converter and be done with it!'

'We live on nothing but beans and beef for a few days,' Sten comforted, 'we'll all be our own mass converters.'

'Not humorous.'

'Besides,' Sten continued, 'The Tahn are going to wipe us out before we get bored.'

'Commander, I'm appalled. You have been associating with that Kilgour for entirely too long.'

Sten nodded agreement and went back to the command center. It was time to get in touch with Mahoney and tell him that Strongpoint Sh'aarl't was ready for war.

General Mahoney wanted to make very sure that his new fort would remain undiscovered until exactly the right moment. His com line with Sten was via a ground-cable ULF transmitter. Sten responded with previously coded single-dit signals. Other than that, the fort remained completely passive.

It took Mahoney four days to prepare his major offensive.

A battle can have many objectives – to gain territory, to mask a second attack, etc. Mahoney's attack was designed to kill Tahn soldiers.

He explained his battle plan very carefully to Admiral van Doorman. Once van Doorman understood the plan, he was ecstatic. He was sure that the battle would shatter the Tahn and force them to withdraw from Cavite – or at least to retreat into defensive quarters.

Ian Mahoney wondered how van Doorman had managed to spend so many years in the service and still believe there was a pony in there somewhere.

The most that could happen was that the Tahn juggernaut might be thrown back and stalled for a while. Mahoney saw no other strategy than the one he had begun with – to try to keep fighting until Cavite could be reinforced. This was a possibility that he viewed as increasingly unlikely. But in the meantime, he could make victory increasingly expensive for Lady Atago and the Tahn.

And so, expecting nothing, the Empire attacked.

The Tahn, of course, had air supremacy around the perimeter. Their constantly patrolling tacships made sure that any men or vehicles moving near the lines stood an odds-on chance of being hit.

Farther back, closer to Cavite Base, Mahoney still had enough functioning AA launchers to keep off all but major Tahn air strikes. Under cover of darkness, he moved half of his available launchers

forward and positioned them just inside the perimeter sector near
Strongpoint Sh'aarl't.

Van Doorman had very few warships left besides the carefully
hidden *Swampscott*. But one of them was the destroyer commanded
by Halldor, the *Husha*.

The Tahn normally kept their tacships grounded during darkness,
maintaining air superiority with destroyers equipped with warning
sensors some kilometers beyond the lines. A night sortie by Imperial
ships would bring an instant response, but the Tahn ground-support
craft would not be worn out by constant patrolling.

At sunrise, the Tahn tacships lifted from their forward bases
toward the lines.

At sunrise plus fifteen minutes, the *Husha* bellowed out of its
underground hanger and, at full Yukawa drive, swept toward and
then across the perimeter. Weapons yammering, the *Husha* shattered
the flotilla of Tahn ships patrolling that sector. By the time the
Tahn had cruisers and destroyers over that part of the perimeter,
the *Husha* was already grounded and safe.

Lady Atago and Admiral Deska asked why an Imperial ship
would have made the sweep. The answer was obvious – van
Doorman proposed an attack.

They reinforced their aerial elements and sent them forward over
the lines.

The Tahn ships were easy targets as the Empire's AA tracks
threw off their camouflage and launched.

More Tahn ships, including one cruiser, were killed. The Tahn
infantry was put on full alert.

And the Imperial Forces made their assault.

Atago was surprised – the first wave wasn't made up of Guard
forces. Instead, ragtag soldiers of the naval provisional battalions
went forward.

For the Tahn landing forces, they were easy targets.

The naval battalions held briefly, then reeled back, back beyond
their original positions.

This was the weak point that Atago had been waiting for. This
was a chance to drive a spearhead through the Empire's lines and
possibly take Cavite Base itself.

The time was close to nightfall.

Atago ordered her forces to consolidate their salient. At dawn,
they would attack once more.

Four hours later, both ElInt and SigInt told Atago that Mahoney
was reinforcing the defensive positions with armor. What few assault

tracks were undamaged appeared, indeed, to be moving toward the perimeter.

Very good, Lady Atago thought. Her own heavy equipment outnumbered the Imperial tracks by ten to one. Now was the chance to completely smash the Imperial Forces on Cavite. She stripped her own units bare, sending armor forward, organized by hastily established combat commands.

The plan, she knew, would be that at dawn she would attack. General Mahoney would counterattack with his tanks. And her own mailed fist would rumble forward.

There were three hours until dawn.

Lady Atago slept the sleep of a heroine.

General Ian Mahoney, on the other hand, slurped caff and snarled.

From his side of the lines, things were very different. The attack by the *Husha* had been very deliberate, intended to destroy not only Tahn tacships but their reinforcements. That assault had indeed been made by naval battalions, but battalions commanded by officers from the First Guards, who had carefully choreographed the events. Attack . . . and then fall back beyond the lines.

The Tahn counterattack reached positions predetermined by Mahoney, positions that were actually indefensible.

The backup armor that Mahoney had moved forward was mostly gravsleds equipped with noise simulators. They broadcast using call signs of the Guards armor and on Guards armor wavelengths.

Only sixteen Guard assault tracks were on the front lines. At dawn, they went forward – and were obliterated.

It was a disaster. But none of the Tahn investigated those smoking hulks and found out that they were remote-controlled. Not a single Guardsman died in those tracks.

Atago sent her armor in to attack through the salient.

The com grid hummed, and outside the Imperial perimeter, hydraulics hissed into motion and gun turrets ripped through turf, their cannon seeking and then locking onto their targets.

Strongpoint Sh'aarl't was alive.

Alive and killing.

Chapter Sixty-Six

No one inside the fort was entirely sure that the chaincannon, even though they looked functional, wouldn't blow up when the first round went down the tubes. Sten had ordered the crews out of the turrets and the flash doors sealed before he gave the firing command.

The three cannon roared, sounding like, as Tapia somewhat indelicately put it, 'dragons with diarrhea.' With a rate of fire of 2,000 rounds per minute, the sound was a wall of solid explosions.

The chaincannon had been intended for defense against high-speed aerial attackers. So although the computer may have been primitive by Foss's standards, its ability to acquire the low-speed targets that were the Tahn tanks was infallible.

The shells were supposed to be incendiary, but only about a third of them went off. It didn't matter – the solid sheet of metal simply can-openered the armor.

Sten heard a squeal of 'It works! It works!' – probably from Tapia – as he ordered the gun crews back into the turrets.

Strongpoint Sh'aarl't worked very well indeed.

The first wave of tanks was already rumbling through what had been the Imperial outer perimeter when Mahoney ordered the fort to open up. Meanwhile, three-man Guards teams armed with hunter/killer missiles came out of their spider holes and slaughtered the Tahn tracks within minutes.

Sten had more than enough targets in the three kilometers between the fort and the perimeter.

Lady Atago was holding the bulk of her armor back to reinforce the spearhead. Since the Tahn knew they had air superiority and were out of line-of-sight of the perimeter, they had the tanks stacked up along the approach routes bow to stern.

Sten, or rather, Foss – or rather the fort's computer – let the chaincannon follow those jammed rubbled roads. The computer tabbed sixty tanks hit and destroyed, and then a series of sympathetic explosions sent fireballs boiling down the streets. The computer, a little sulkily, told Foss that it had lost count.

A red light gleamed – the quad projectile turret, Alex in charge, was in action. The Tahn infantry had recovered from the shock of being hit from the rear and were attacking toward the hill. As long as the anti-personnel chaingun kept firing, it would keep the grunts well out of effective range. Nothing hand-held could punch through the fort's armor – or so the archaic specifications promised.

'All turrets. You're on local control. Find your own targets.'

Finally Tapia had some power. She sat in the command capsule on the gunlayer's sight. It looked not unlike a padded bicycle sans wheels, with a hood atop its handlebars. The handlebars, backed by the turret's own computer, were slaved to the cannon.

Four tanks blew apart before the attacking column was able to reverse out of sight behind a building. Out of sight – but not safe. Tapia shouted for the cannon's rate-of-fire control to maximum and chattered a long burst along the ruin's base. The building toppled, crushing the tanks.

Tapia experimented. If she kept firing her gun at maximum rate, the fort would run dry – a gauge showed that the ammo lockers for the gun were already down to eighty percent capacity. She learned how to conserve. Set the cannon's rate of fire to minimum (about 750 rpm) and tap the firing key. Exit one tank.

This was interesting, Tapia thought. She spotted six armored fighting vehicles crossing into the open, spun her sights, but was too late as another turret blew them into scrap metal. Tapia swore and looked around the battlefield again.

The fort was surrounded by the hulks of burning tanks. Smoke plumed up into a solid column around the strongpoint. Tapia switched her sights from optical to infrared and found something interesting.

A track – and it ain't shooting at me. Very interesting. The track was in fact a command track housing the Tahn armored brigade commander. Since the CT had required an elaborate communications setup yet its designers hardly wanted the track to be readily identifiable as the brains behind an attack, the main gun had been replaced by a dummy. Tapia chortled, aimed carefully, and . . .

And the fort shook and her ears clanged in spite of the protective muffs all of the sailors wore.

In the command center, Sten hit a red control, and all of the turrets popped down, leaving nothing but a featureless hilltop for the now-positioned Tahn artillery to shoot at. The environmental system had finished venting the fort and had stored air in backup tanks. If Atago deployed a nuke or chemicals, Sten was ready to switch the fort into its own environment.

Sten doubted that would happen – Lady Atago needed this real estate to attack through. And only in the war livies did soldiers choose to fight in the balky, uncomfortable, and dangerous fighting suits if there was any other option.

'All combat stations. Report.'

'Turret A. All green.'

'Turret C. We're fine. Noiser'n hell, Skipper.' That was Tapia, of course.

'Turret D. They're knocking up some dust. No damage.'

'No puh-roblems from the shotgun squad, boss,' Kilgour reported from the antipersonnel turret.

Sten was starting to be a little impressed with whoever had built this fort, regardless of their obviously moronic inspiration.

A screen lit. It was Mahoney. With the fort in the open, he had reverted to a standard com link with Sten.

'Report!' Mahoney, in midoperation, was all efficiency.

'Strongpoint Sh'aarl't,' Sten said, equally formally, 'at full combat readiness. Expended weaponry filed . . . now! No casualties reported. Awaiting orders.'

Mahoney cracked a smile. 'Adequate, Commander. Stand by. They'll be hitting you full-strength next.'

'Understood. Sh'aarl't. Out.'

The Tahn assault tracks were pulled back out of range of the fort's cannon. Atago tried air strikes.

Sten, not expecting any real results, switched the fire and control computer for aerial targets. Now on fully automatic, the guns elevated, whined, and spat fire.

Tahn tacships were sharded out of the skies. This should not be happening, Sten told himself. I am manning an archaic weapons system. Hasn't technology progressed?

Foss had the explanation. Archaic, was it? The guns were tracking, and the projectiles' proximity fuses were detonating on long-abandoned frequencies. None of the Tahn ships had ECM sets broadcasting on those frequencies.

Sten was starting to feel a certain fondness for his ancient gray elephant.

'Shall we abandon the attack, Lady?'

Atago ran yet another prog on the computer. 'Negative.'

Deska tried not to show surprise. 'The attrition rate from that one fort is unacceptable.'

'This is true. However, consider this. That fort is quite effective. The Imperial Forces are weak. Therefore, if that fort can be destroyed, we should be able to punch completely through their lines. And all that is necessary is to change our tactics. Which I have already done. The first stage shall commence within moments.'

It was fortunate for the Tahn that Lady Atago had tried to prepare for any eventuality when she structured her battle plans. She hit Strongpoint Sh'aarl't with monitors.

Monitors should not have been part of the Tahn fleet for the Cavite operation, since there would be no conceivable use for the single-purpose behemoths.

Monitors were large, bulky warships. They were heavily armored and carried light secondary antimissile armament. Their only weapon was a single monstrous launch tube located along the ship's centerline, much as the Kali launch tubes on the Bulkeley-class tacships were located, but enormously larger. The missile – projectile – fired by the monitors was, in fact, somewhat larger than a tacship.

A monitor was a miniature spacecraft powered by AM2 engines. It was guided by a single operator into its target, and was intended for offplanet warfare, to be used against fortified moonlets or planetoids only.

Tahn intelligence had told Atago that no such space forts existed in the Fringe Worlds. Atago decided, however, to add two to her fleet, just in case. Now those two monitors were deployed against Sten's fort.

One monitor hovered, nose down, just outside Cavite's atmosphere, and fire belched from its nose. The missile flashed downward.

The reason that monitors weren't used against close-range targets became obvious. At full AM2 drive, it is almost impossible for the operator to acquire his target and home the missile in. Automatic homing was also, of course, too slow. The vast stand-off distances of space warfare were vital for success, especially since the cost of each missile was just about that of a manned tacship.

Atago was not concerned with any of that – if Cavite's fall was delayed much longer, Atago's own fall would be guaranteed.

Still accelerating, the first missile missed the fort by only 500 meters – its operator was very skilled. The shock wave flattened what ruins were still standing near Strongpoint Sh'aarl't for almost a kilometer.

Sten was getting out of his command chair when the missile landed. He found himself sprawled flat against a wall two meters away, in blackness. A generator hummed, and secondary lighting went on. Sten was seeing double. Dust motes hung in the air.

He stumbled back to the board. 'All stations. Report!'

And, amazingly, they did.

The impact, of course, had been even more severe up in the turrets. Tapia was bleeding from the nose and ears. But her cannon was still battle-worthy, as were Turrets A and D. The video to Kilgour's antipersonnel turret was out, but there was still an audio link to the center.

By the time Sten had his status, Foss had analyzed what had hit them.

'Very nice,' Sten said. Ears still ringing, he and everyone else in the fort were talking very loudly. 'What happens if they hit us direct?'

'No prog available,' Foss said.

'Very nice indeed. Can you give us any warning?'

'Not when they launch. But they'll be bringing those two monitors on and off station to fire. It'll take 'em some time to reload. As soon as they get on-station, I'll hit the buzzer.

'Speaking of which,' Foss said, looking at a screen, 'that other clot's getting ready to try his luck.'

Sten had time to order all turret crews down into the ready rooms before the second missile hit. This one missed by almost a full kilometer, and the shock was no worse than, Sten estimated, getting punched by Alex.

The gun crews recovered and clattered back up the ladders into the turrets. There were targets waiting for them. Atago had started the second stage, sending assault units forward just when she saw the fort's turrets turtle up. Behind the tracks moved waves of assault infantry.

But her plan became a bloody stalemate. The monitor's rounds did drive Sten's sailors from their guns. But they also destroyed anything around the fort that could have been used as cover for the tracks.

And the monitors took a very long time to reload and fire. There was not time enough for the tracks to close on the fort after the missile exploded before Strongpoint Sh'aarl't was blasting back.

They had reached a stalemate. It wasn't livable inside the fort, but it was survivable. And then two things occurred:

The seventh round from a monitor hit about 175 meters from the fort. The blast was enough to smash the lock on the second, unmanned and inoperable, anti-personnel quad projectile turret. The turret popped up – and stayed up. And on Sten's central control board, no warning light went on.

The second thing was that Tahn Superior Private Heebner got lost.

Chapter Sixty-Seven

Private Heebner would never be used on a recruiting poster. He was short – barely within the Tahn minimum-height requirements – somewhat bowlegged, and had a bit of a potbelly. Not only that, his attitude wasn't very heroic, either.

Heebner had been conscripted from his father's orchards most reluctantly. But he knew better than to express that reluctance to the recruiting officer – the Tahn had Draconian penalties for and loose interpretations of draft resistance. He became even more reluctant when the classification clerk at the induction center informed Heebner that the military had no equivalent for 'Fruit, Tree, Manual Gatherer of' and promptly made him a prospective infantryman.

Heebner endured the physical and mental batterings of training quietly in the rear rank. Since he expected nothing, he wasn't as disappointed as some other recruits who discovered that an active duty battalion was run just as brutally as basic training. All Heebner wanted was to do the minimum necessary to keep his squad sergeant from striking him, to stay alive, and to go home.

The private was slightly proud of himself for having survived this much of the war. He had an eye for good cover, excellent fear reactions, and an unwillingness to volunteer – mostly. Heebner had made a brilliant discovery during training. Volunteer duties were mostly in two categories – the extremely hazardous and the extremely dirty. Dirty frequently meant safe.

Heebner specialized in getting on those kind of details – digging holes for any purpose, bringing rations up through the muck, unloading gravsleds, and so forth, since he had learned that they generally weren't done under fire. And so he had survived.

His willingness to accept the drakh details even got him promoted one notch. Heebner now had to be wary – if he continued doing well, they might make him a noncommissioned officer. Which meant, to Heebner, a bigger target. He was contemplating whether he should commit some minor offense – enough to get him reduced in rank but not enough to earn a beating from his sergeant.

That morning the company his squad was part of had been ordered into the attack against the cursed Imperial fort. The Tahn infantry had nicknamed it AshHome: attacking the fort was a virtual certainty that one's cremated remains would be sent out on the next ship – assuming that one's remains were recovered. Many Tahn bodies lay unrescued in the mire around the fort, buried and then resurrected by exploding rounds.

Superior Private Heebner was lagging just behind the line of advancing troops when Tapia opened fire on the two assault tracks supporting his company. He dived for cover, heard shouts from his sergeant to keep moving, picked himself up – and a round from the monitor slammed in. Heebner went down again, stunned. He was still out when his squad advanced – straight into a burst from Alex's antipersonnel quad mounts.

Heebner staggered back to consciousness and his feet. Behind him the tracks billowed greasy smoke. There was no sign of his squad or company. Most of them were dead. Heebner's mind told him that there was no point continuing the attack if everyone else had given up. He should return to his own lines.

He waded through the mire, concentrating on not falling down again. Cannon rounds splattered nearby, and Heebner ate dirt.

Not dirt, he corrected himself. He was lying against metal. But no one was shooting at him. And there were no cascades of mud falling on him from exploding shells.

Heebner took stock – and moaned in horror. Somehow he had gotten turned around. Instead of finding his way back to his own lines, the Tahn private was lying on the low mound that was the Imperial fort. Next to him was the shiny, if dented, barrel of a gun turret. Heebner considered prayer. But there were no bullets slashing at him. He was lying next to the unmanned antipersonnel turret, the one that the monitor's seventh round had blown open.

Very well. He could just wait here until night and then escape. And then he remembered that great spaceship somewhere up there. One of those shells would spread him like oil over the fort's carapace. Another realization – he could see a gap between the four muzzles sticking out of the turret and the turret itself. He crawled toward it. The blast had bent back the guns' bullet shield.

Sheer panic impelled Heebner to take the next step. He slid through and thunked down onto concrete. As he landed, his brain began working again. You just entered this fort. Where there are Imperials who probably have fangs the size of pruning hooks?

And then another round from the monitor slammed in, and Heebner was out for close to an hour.

He came fuzzily awake, surprised that he was still alive and not resident in one of the Empire's cooking pots. Heebner, like most of the uneducated Tahn soldiers, believed that the Imperial troops ceremonially ate their enemies.

But he was alive. Uninjured.

And thirsty. He drank from his canteen.

He was hungry, too. His company had attacked carrying only ammunition.

Heebner looked around the inside of the turret. There were lockers against the turret. He explored them. Gas suits . . . radiation suits . . . and emergency rations. Heebner fumbled a pak open and sampled. He smiled. Meat. It was something that a Tahn of his class would be permitted only once or twice a year. The next pak was also meat. It joined its brother in his stomach. The third was beans. Heebner sniffed at them, then set the pak aside. Other cans went into his combat pack.

What now?

More of his brain, possibly stimulated by the beef, woke up. They told us this fort was full of soldiers. Why, then, is this position not manned? Was it hit?

There were no signs of damage to the walls.

Heebner found that he had two choices – either he could remain where he was, or he could flee. If he stayed in the turret, eventually that monstrous cannon would kill him.

If he fled back toward the Tahn lines, there would be questions. Why was he the only survivor of his squad? Had he hid? Had he avoided the attack? The penalties for cowardice under fire were most barbaric.

Wait. If he came back with some valuable information, they might not punish him. Such as?

Of course. Fellow soldiers could use this gap in the turret to take the fort! But wait. If all you return with is a way into the fort, won't your officers expect you to guide the assault formation?

Heebner grimaced. That could be an excellent way to become dead. He brightened. If he returned with some very interesting piece of information, they would send him up to higher headquarters with it, while other unfortunates made the attack.

What could he bring back?

The hatchway leading down into the bowels of the fort was nearby. Heebner undogged it and climbed downward.

The ladder ended in a large room with bunks. Heebner looked wistfully at one of them. Even though it smelled, it was still better than anything he had slept on since he had landed on Cavite.

A large room with bunks . . . a large, deserted room? How many Imperials are in this fort, he wondered? He found the courage to investigate.

Heebner went out of the ready room into a central passageway. Seconds later, another shell from the monitor earthquaked down. It must have missed by a considerable distance. Heebner heard the clatter of feet and peered out. A group of Imperials ran out of another ready room and climbed up into one of the main turrets. Heebner counted. Only ten? How many people *were* there, anyway?

Was it possible that there were only a handful of Imperials holding back the Tahn? So it would appear.

That was enough for Heebner. This would be valuable information. Enough to keep him from being sent forward again. The intelligence might be valuable enough, he hoped, for him to report to company headquarters instead of to his platoon leader. If his company commander still lived. This could be an excellent way to stay out of the assault.

Superior Private Heebner made his way out of the fort, made the nightmare journey back to his own lines, and reported.

And found himself standing in front of Lady Atago, more terrified than he had been inside the fort. He was not required to make the final assault on Strongpoint Sh'aarl't. Instead, he was promoted to fire team leader, given a medal, and reassigned to the rear.

Heebner was safe. That was enough. It did not matter to him that he wasn't mentioned in the livies trumpeting the reduction of the Imperial fort.

That honor went to Tahn Assault Captain Santol, a far more heroic-looking Tahn. And if it was an honor, he earned it.

Chapter Sixty-Eight

Sten wondered what would come next when the monitors' shellfire stopped. He wondered if they would run out of projectiles but rather dully hoped that both ships had chamber explosions.

Worry about what comes next when it comes next, he said, and ordered dinner – breakfast? lunch? – up for his people. He rotated a third of the crews down to the mess hall to eat. After everyone was fed, he planned to go to fifty percent alert and let at least some of his sailors sleep.

It didn't work that way.

Contreras stepped off the ladder from the command level to the ready room and burped. A full belly led her to consider other luxuries. Sleep . . . a bath . . . a clean uniform . . . hell, she told herself, why not wish for everything. Like a discharge, spending her accumulated pay on a tourist world where the most primitive machine was a bicycle, and falling in love with a handsome officer. Officer? She caught herself. Too long in the service, woman. Clot the military. A rich civilian.

A smile crept across her lips just as the Tahn projectile blew most of her chest away.

The Tahn assault teams had managed to approach the fort

without being seen. Since the fort's computer still showed the jammed antipersonnel carrier as being housed, the warning sensors showed no movement in that sector. Actually the beams were being returned – bouncing – off the turret, returning to the transmitter and being automatically disregarded as part of ground clutter.

Lady Atago's analysis from Private Heebner's report was very correct, giving about an eighty-five percent chance that the area beyond that jammed turret would be in a dead zone.

Captain Santol's navigation had been exact – the assault elements closed in on the fort along that sector, no more than two abreast. Between the shifts for eating and the sailors' exhaustion, the Tahn weren't noticed on any of the visual screens still active.

Once inside the turret, Captain Santol put two trusted sergeants in front, armed with riot weapons. Behind them were grenadiers and one tripod-mounted heavy projectile weapon, and then Captain Santol and his senior sergeant behind them.

Contreras wasn't the first to die – two sailors had been jumped from the rear and garrotted. But she was the first to be shot.

The explosion clanged down the corridors of the fort. Sten bolted up, and his plate spattered beans and beef across the deck. Accidental discharge . . . like hell, he realized, as he saw Tahn soldiers scuttling forward on one of the command center's internal screens.

He slammed the alarm and opened a mike.

'All personnel.' His voice was quite calm. 'There are Tahn troops inside the fort. All personnel, secure entry to your areas. Alex?'

'Sir?' Even on the com there was a bit of a brogue.

'Can you see how these clots got in?'

There was a pause. 'Tha's naught on the screens, sir. Ah'll bet tha'll hae come in frae' a turret.'

That left two possibilities: Either of the two inoperable turrets – one, the second antipersonnel quad projectile turret; two, the second Turret B – could be breached. But the computer showed both secure.

'Turret C,' Sten ordered. 'Local control. Target – Tahn infantry approaching the fort. Fire at will.'

He switched to another channel.

'Turrets A and D. Send five troops down to secure your ready rooms. There are no friendlies moving. Kilgour. If you've got anybody loose, get them to the command center.'

'On th' way. Wait.'

Alex should have stayed at the antipersonnel turret. But it took only one person to fire the quad projectile weapon. He left that one and, with six others, went looking for blood.

Sixteen sailors manning Turret A went out of their turret, headed toward the Tahn. The two forces met in a corridor. The battle was very quick – and very lethal. The AM2 rounds from the willyguns mostly missed. But hitting the concrete walls of the corridor, they exploded, sending concrete shrapnel shotgunning into the Tahn.

Captain Santol lost two squads before he could get a crew-served weapon firing. And then the sixteen sailors went down in a swelter of gore as projectiles whined and ricocheted.

Santol waved a squad forward, over the bodies and up into the turret. The rest of the sailors assigned to Turret A died there.

A second maneuver element of the Tahn tore into the element from Turret D. The sailors fought bravely – but weren't a match for the experienced Tahn soldiers.

Sten swore as he watched on a screen.

The Tahn were between his command center and the still-fighting Turret C. Sten had Foss and three computer clerks for an assault element. This would be stupidity, not nobility. But again – he had no options.

The Tahn assault company was spread out through the fort's corridors. They were good, Sten had to admit. Their tactic was to spray fire around a corner, send one man diving across the corridor for security, put two men in place as guards, and move on. And still another Tahn company was filing in through the damaged personnel turret.

Then the counterattack hit.

This was not Kilgour's pathetic strike force of seven, which was still moving down the long tube that led to the fort's center. This attack came from underneath – from the storage spaces.

There were five humans, including the two Tahn brothers. They were led by the spindar, Mr Willie Sutton. They were pushing in front of them a small gravpallet. On it there were fifteen or so tall metal cylinders. Emergency oxygen tanks.

The counterattack came out of an unnoticed hatchway, halfway down a corridor. At the far end was Captain Santol and his command group.

Sutton was bellowing like a berserk siren as he rumbled forward.

'Shoot them! Shoot them down,' Santol shouted, and projectiles crashed down the corridor.

The six Imperial sailors were cut down in the blast. The gravpallet drifted on another ten meters before it slowed to a stop.

Santol ran toward the bodies, a reaction team behind him. There would be more Imperials coming out of that hatch.

He slid around the gravsled . . . and Sutton reared up in front of him. Scales were ripped away, and ichor oozed from his wounds and mouth. The spindar loomed to his full height over the Tahn officer.

Santol's pistol was coming up, but late, too late, as claws sprang out of Sutton's forearm and bludgeoned forward, ripping away most of the Tahn's face. Santol screamed and went down.

His soldiers were firing. Sutton staggered back, against the wall, then forward again. From somewhere, he pulled a miniwillygun, brought it up, and fired – not at the Tahn but behind them, at the gravpallet. The round tore a cylinder open. Oxygen hissed, and then a ricocheting round sparked.

The corridor exploded, catching the Tahn in a miniature firestorm created by the exploding oxygen. Half of Santol's company died along with their commander. The disoriented survivors fell back toward the entrance.

Kilgour was waiting at a cross-tube. Again, the Tahn were not expecting an ambush. They fell back still farther.

It was the best chance Sten would have.

He found the nearest wall com. 'All stations. All stations. This is Sten. Evac to entry. I say again. Evac to entry.'

He and his four people linked up with Alex's crew and the one troop that had been left in the AP turret, and set up a rear guard.

It was not necessary. The CO of the second Tahn assault company had ordered most of the soldiers out of the fort. They would regroup and counterattack.

By the time they did, Tapia's entire crew had made it to the fort's exit.

They went back down the underground passage leading to the flattened maintenance shed, splashing through the deep muck. The shed was gone, but the hatch still operated.

Sten stood by it, taking a head count as his surviving sailors wearily climbed out. There were thirty-two left.

He formed them up and started across the flattened wastes toward the Imperial perimeter. Half a kilometer away, Sten took a small transmitter from his belt, snapped off the two safety locks, and pressed a switch.

Three minutes later, det charges would go, and Strongpoint Sh'aarl't – or Sutton, or Tige, or whoever – was going to be a large crater in the ground.

The Tahn could have the privilege of naming it.

Chapter Sixty-Nine

Two hours before dawn, Tanz Sullamora's shielded gravsled was cleared to land in the ruins of Arundel Castle.

There were only two man-made objects above ground. One was a transportable shielded landing dome, very common on radioactive mining planets but most incongruous in the heart of the Empire. The second was a very tall flagpole. At its peak hung two flags – the gleaming standard of the Empire and, below it, the Emperor's house banner, gold with the letters 'AM2' superimposed over the negative element's atomic structure.

All Imperial broadcasts showed the ruins and the flag as their opening and closing shots. The symbol may have been obvious – but it signified. The Emperor, like the Empire itself, may have been hard-hit, but he was still standing fast and fighting.

Rad-suited guardsmen led Sullamora, also in anti-radiation gear, from his ship through decon showers and into one of the drop shafts leading down toward the Imperial command center below the palace ruins.

At the shaft base, Sullamora clambered out of his suit, was decontaminated once more, and was ushered into the center. Two Gurkhas escorted the merchant prince down long paneled corridors that, even at this hour, were filled with scurrying officers and techs. Sullamora caught tantalizing glimpses, through portals that slid open and shut, of prog boards, huge computer screens, and war rooms.

He did not know that his route led through what the Emperor called a dog and pony show. The work was real, and the staff beings were busy – but everything he saw was nonvital standard procedures such as recruiting, training status, finance, and so forth.

The Emperor's own suite had also been carefully decorated to leave visitors with certain impressions. There were many anterooms, capable of holding any delegation or delegate isolated until the Emperor was ready to meet. The walls were gray, and the furniture was two shades above Spartan. Wallscreens showed mysterious, unexplained maps and projections that would be replaced periodically with equally unknown charts and graph. The Emperor's quirky sense of humor had decided that some of them were battle plans from wars fought thousands of years previously. Thus far, no one had found him out.

The Emperor's own quarters were a large bedroom, a kitchen that resembled a warship's mess area, a conference room, a monstrous computer center/briefing room, and a personal library. These were also fairly simply furnished, not so much to continue the command center image but because the Emperor had little real interest in the tide of pomp and thrice-gorgeous ceremony.

The wallscreens normally showed scenes from the windows of one or another of the Emperor's vacation homes. But now three images formed a motif throughout his rooms: the ruins of Arundel above him, a shot from space showing the Tahn home world of Heath, and a still of the twenty-seven-member ruling Tahn Council. The three images, he explained, helped focus his attention.

Sullamora spent only a few minutes in an anteroom before being escorted into the Emperor's library.

The Emperor looked and was very tired. He indicated a sideboard that held refreshments. Sullamora declined. The Emperor started, without preamble. 'Tanz, I've just requisitioned ten of your high-speed liners.'

Sullamora's eyes widened, but the capitalist managed to bury any other reaction. The Emperor, after all, had called him by his first name.

'Sir, any of my resources are yours. You have only to ask.'

'No drakh,' the Emperor agreed. Then he asked, seemingly irrelevantly, 'How long have you been arming your merchant ships?'

'Pardon, Your Majesty? Almost all of my ships carry weapons.'

'Come on, Sullamora. It's been a long night, and I'd like to get my head down before dawn. You've got some ships booming around out there that're armed better'n my frigates.'

'I did,' Sullamora admitted, 'take the liberty of increasing the weaponry on some of my vessels. Those, you understand, that were routed near any of the Tahn galaxies.'

'Good thinking,' the Emperor said, and Sullamora relaxed. 'And that's why I'm grabbing ten of them. I'll tell you why shortly. The other reason I wanted this meeting is that I'm requisitioning *you*.'

Sullamora's response was a not particularly intellectual 'Heh?'

'From twenty minutes ago, you're now my minister of ship production. You'll have a seat on my private cabinet.'

Sullamora was startled. He hadn't even known that the Emperor *had* a private cabinet.

'I want you to build ships for me. I don't care which contractors build them or how. Your orders will be A-Plus category. You have Priority One on any raw materials or personnel you need. I need more warships. Yesterday. I don't have time for all this bidding, bitching, and backbiting that's been going on. Pour yourself a drink. I'll have some tea.'

Sullamora followed orders.

'We are hurting,' the Emperor continued to Sullamora's back. 'The Tahn are taking out my fleets faster than I can commission them. You're going to change all that.'

'Thank you for the honor, Your Majesty. What kind of administration do I have?'

'I don't care. Bring in all those hucksters and sharpies from your own companies if you want.'

'What will my budget be?'

'You tell me when you're running out of credits, and I'll get you some more.'

'What about the accounting oversight?'

'There won't be any. But if I catch you stealing too much from me, or buying junk, I'll kill you. Personally.'

The Emperor was not smiling at all.

Sullamora changed the subject slightly. 'Sir. May I ask you something?'

'GA.'

'You said you'd explain why you need ten of my liners.'

'I shall. This is ears-only, Tanz.' He paused. 'I made a bunch of mistakes when this war started. One of them was thinking that my people out in the Fringe Worlds were better than they were.'

'But, sir . . . you sent the First Guards out there.'

'I did. And they're my best.'

'And they're winning.'

'The clot they are. They're getting their ass whipped. The Guard – what's left of it – is hanging on to a teeny little perimeter of one world. About a week from now, they'll be overrun and destroyed.'

Sullamora swallowed. This was not what the livies had been telling him.

'I put the Guard out there to hold the Caltor System, because sooner or later things are going to change, and I'm going to need a jumping-off point to invade the Tahn systems.

'I blew it. I thought that I'd get more backup from my allies than I have. I also didn't know the Tahn were stamping out fleets of warships like cheap plas toys. Mistakes. Now I've got to save what I can.

'There's a whole bunch of Imperial civilians on the capital world of Caltor, Cavite. I want your liners in to get them out. Get them out – and some other people I'll need.'

The Emperor read Sullamora's face and smiled grimly. 'Things look different when you're on the inside, Tanz. You're going to see a lot more ruin and damnation in the next few days.'

Sullamora recovered. And asked the big question. 'Are we going to win this war?'

The Emperor sighed. This was a question he was getting a little tired of. 'Yes. Eventually.'

Eventually, Sullamora thought. He took that to mean that the Emperor was very unsure of things. 'When we do . . .'

'When we do, I shall make very damned sure that the Tahn systems have a very different form of government. I do not ever want them to return to haunt me.'

Sullamora smiled. 'War to the knife, and that to the hilt!'

'That wasn't what I was saying. I want the way the Tahn run their government changed. I don't have any quarrel with their people. I'm going to try to win this war without dusting any planets, without carpet bombing, or any of the rest. People don't start wars – governments do.'

Sullamora looked at the Emperor. He thought himself to be a historian. And just as he collected heroic art, he admired heroic history. He sort of remembered a statement a heroic Earth sea admiral had made: 'Moderation in war is absurdity.'

He wholly agreed with that. Of course, he wasn't enough of a historian to know that the admiral in question had never commanded his fleet in anything other than a minor skirmish, or that by the time the next war occurred both he and the superships he had ordered built had been obsolete and retired.

'I see, Your Highness,' he said coldly.

The Emperor did not understand Sullamora's frigidity. 'When the war is over, you'll be given the appropriate awards. I assume some sort of regency appointment might be in order, covering the entire Tahn areas.'

Sullamora suddenly felt that he and the Emperor were speaking entirely separate languages.

He stood, leaving his drink barely tasted, and bowed deeply, formally. 'I thank you, Your Highness. I shall be prepared to assume my new position within the week.'

He wheeled and exited.

The Emperor stared after him. Then he stood, walked around his desk, picked up Sullamora's drink, and sipped at it thoughtfully. Possibly, he thought, Sr. Sullamora and I may not be communicating on the same wavelength.

So?

He set the drink back down, went back to his desk, and keyed the com on for the latest disaster reports. He was worried about his Empire. If he held it together – and in spite of his bluffness, the Eternal Emperor was starting to wonder – he could worry about individual people later.

The hell he could, he realized.

He put the com on hold and activated a very special computer. There was one individual he had to talk to. Even though that conversation would be one-sided.

Chapter Seventy

General Ian Mahoney looked at his reflection in the shattered bits of mirror and considered.

Contrary to what two of the Emperor's favorite and long-dead doggerelists – Mahoney vaguely remembered their names as Silbert and Gullivan – there were *two* models of a modern major general. One was that of the general, immaculate in full-dress uniform, posing, three-quarter profile, some sort of harvesting cutter in hand, in front of his assembled troops, all of them dripping medals. The second would be the same general, in combat coveralls, willygun smoking – they did that only in the livies – grenades hanging from his harness, cheering his men forward into some sort of breach or other, in the face of onrushing hordes of Evil Sorts.

Major General Ian Mahoney was neither.

He was wearing combat coveralls, and he did have a willygun slung over one shoulder. But the seat of his coveralls was ripped out; his willygun, thanks be to his security, hadn't been fired – yet; and his coveralls were stained in mud, pink, and mauve.

The Tahn had finally run cross-locations on the command transmissions, found Mahoney's command center, and sent in an obliteration air strike.

Tahn tacships had either suppressed the few anti-aircraft launchers around Mahoney's headquarters or absorbed the few missiles left in their launch racks. Mahoney's headquarters was left naked.

Mahoney had been bodily yanked from his command track seconds before a Tahn missile hit it. He had gone down – into the muck of the street. That accounted for the mud.

As the second wave of Tahn tacships came in, he had pelted for shelter – any shelter. He had found it, diving facefirst into a semi-ruined women's emporium. Into, specifically, the shatter of the makeup department. That explained the pink and mauve.

The emporium had a huge basement, which Mahoney found convenient for his new headquarters. Backup com links were brought in, and Mahoney went back to fighting his war, morosely scowling at his reflection in the shatter of a mirror lying nearby.

A tech clattered into the room. 'Two messages sir. From ImpCen. And your G4 said you'd need this.'

ImpCen: Imperial central headquarters. Prime World. And the case the tech held contained one of Mahoney's most hated security tools.

He looked at the messages. The first was a conventional fiche. What was unconventional about it was the case that the tech had brought in with him. That case, set to a fingerprint lock, contained single-use code pads. These were pads that the encipher wrote his message onto, and the receiver would decipher using a duplicate of that same pad. After one use, both sheets of that pad would be destroyed. It was a very old, but still completely unbreakable, code system.

And Mahoney hated coding almost as much as he loathed formal parades.

The other message had been transcribed onto a rather different receptacle. Mahoney's signal branch had only half a dozen of them; they were the ultimate in security, reception fiches sealed into a small plas box. Whatever had been transmitted onto that fiche could be seen only by Mahoney himself. There was a single indentation on the box, keyed to Mahoney's thumb poreprints. Once Mahoney put his thumb in the notch, whatever was on the fiche would begin broadcasting. If he removed it, or thirty seconds after the message ended – whichever came first – the fiche would self-destruct.

Mahoney knew that these messages were important – and almost certainly catastrophic. The first, encoded onto the single-use pad, would most likely be a set of orders. He ignored it for the moment and instead jabbed his thumb down onto the plas box.

Suddenly, in the cellar, standing on a pile of half-burnt dresses, stood the Eternal Emperor. It was a holographic projection, of course.

'Ian,' the cast began, 'we're in a world of hurt. I know you've thumbed this before you've decoded your orders, so I'll give it to you fast.

'I can't back you up.

'I don't have the ships, and I don't have the troops to send forward.

'I guess you've probably already figured that as a possibility. Hell, a probability – since there haven't been any good guys in your skies for quite a while.

'Real brief, here's what your orders are: I want the First Guards to hold on to Cavite until the last bullet. Only when all possible means of resistance have been exhausted do you have my permission to surrender. Any elements of the Guards that can evade, escape, and continue the struggle as guerrillas have permission to carry on the fight. I may not be able to keep the clottin' Tahn from treating them as partisans, but I'll do my best. You probably expected that.

'I'm sending in ten fast liners to pick up the civilians that are still on Cavite. Get them out. And I want you out with them.

'This is the hard part for you, Ian. I'm going to have to sacrifice your division. But I am not going to sacrifice what the First Guards really is.

'You've got probably six E-days until the liners show up, from the time you've received this. I want you to pull out a cadre. Your best noncoms, officers, and specialists are to be on those liners.

The First Guards Division will die on Cavite. But there will be a new First Guards. We'll reform the division on Prime World, and send it out to fight again.

'I said "we," and I meant "we." You will be the commander of the new First Guards. Which means that I want you on one of those liners.

'That is an order, General Mahoney. I don't expect you to like it, or to like me. But that is what is going to happen. And I expect you to follow orders.'

The holograph whirled about itself and disappeared. Mahoney stared at the open space where it had been.

Then he opened his code case and took out the single-use pad – actually a small computer that self-destructed its programming as it went.

Sorry, Your Eternal Emperorship, he thought. I'll follow orders. All of them except the last one.

If you're going to let my Guards die, there is no way in hell I won't be with them.

Chapter Seventy-One

Sten and the remnants of his command made it back into the dubious safety of the Imperial perimeter without incident.

He faced a future that was without options. Sten knew that his ragtag band would be resupplied, rearmed, and fed back into the meat grinder as the Tahn continued their attacks. He was morosely wondering who would be the last to die. That was the future – to be killed, wounded, or captured.

Sten was as unused to defeat as the Empire itself. But there were no options.

He was only mildly surprised when the officer in charge of the repple-depple gave him unexpected orders. His detachment was ordered to turn in all weaponry except their individual arms and stand by for a special assignment.

Sten himself was to report to Mahoney's tactical operations center. Before reporting, he managed to scrounge a few liters of water for a shave and a joygirl's bath, and found a fairly clean combat suit that was pretty close to his size.

The TOC was still in the basement of the emporium. Mahoney finished briefing a handful of officers, all of whom looked as battered as their general, and motioned Sten into a small office that had been the emporium's dispatch room.

Waiting for them was Admiral van Doorman.

Mahoney tersely brought Sten current. The ten liners were inbound to pick up the Imperial civilians and 'selected elements' of the First Guards. They were escorted by four destroyers – all that could be spared – and were, so far, undetected by any Tahn patrol. Their ETA was four days away.

Suddenly the 23rd Fleet needed its technicians again. There were only four ships still spaceworthy: two destroyers, including Halldor's ship, the *Husha*; one elderly picket ship; and the *Swampscott*.

They were to be made as combat-worthy as possible, immediately. Sten's surviving techs, highly experienced at improvisation, would be assigned to the *Swampscott*.

Just assigned the cruiser, Sten wondered? And he also wondered if he would get an explanation.

Mahoney was about to give him one, when van Doorman spoke for the first time. 'General, this man is still under my command. I'd prefer . . .'

Mahoney stared at the haggard naval officer, then nodded and exited.

Van Doorman leaned against the side of a desk, staring into emptiness. His voice was nearly a monotone. 'The problem we all seem to face, Commander, is that the older we get, the less we like things to change.'

Sten thought he was beyond surprise – but he was wrong.

'I was very proud of my fleet. I knew that we didn't have the most modern equipment, and that because we were so far from the Empire we didn't always get the finest sailors. But I knew that we were a strong fighting force.

'Yes,' van Doorman mused. 'It's obvious I thought a lot of things. So when a young flash shows up and tells me that all I have are spit-and-polish marionettes, and my command structure is rigid, bureaucratic, obsolete, and blind, I did not take kindly to that officer.'

'Sir, I never said—'

'Just your presence was sufficient,' van Doorman said, a slight note of anger entering his voice. 'I have made it a rule to never apologize, Commander. And I do not propose to alter that rule. However. The reason I want you, and whatever's left of your command, assigned to the *Swampscott* is that I know the Tahn will hit us hard when we attempt to withdraw with those liners. I assume heavy casualties. Very likely including myself.'

A safe assumption, Sten thought.

'I have appointed you as weapons officer of the *Swampscott*. According to the conventional chain of command, you would be fourth in charge, under the XO, the navigating officer, and the engineering officer. This is not a time for convention,' van Doorman went on, his voice flat once more. 'I have informed all appropriate officers that, in the event of my being incapacitated, you are to assume command of the *Swampscott*.

'Very good, Commander. I was wondering if I would be able to penetrate your poker face.

'The reason is that I no longer have any faith whatsoever in those officers I chose to promote to their present position. I think I selected them more for their social compatibilty and sycophancy than command ability. And I am not sure that any of them can handle crisis adequately. Do you understand?'

'Yessir.'

'I have also informed Commander Halldor that, even though he has a certain amount of time in grade over you, if I become a casualty you are to assume command of my fleet.

'My fleet,' van Doorman said in mild wonderment. 'Two DDs, one museum piece, and a hulk.

'Those are your orders, Commander. I assume if I survive the withdrawal, I shall face a general court martial. Very well. Perhaps it is warranted. But I am not going to end my career with total defeat. Make sure the *Swampscott* is fought like a combat ship, and not some tired old man's private toy.' Van Doorman's voice broke, and he turned his back on Sten.

Sten came to attention, the interview evidently ended.

'Oh, Commander. One more thing. Personal. My daughter sends her greetings.'

'Thank you, sir. How *is* Brijit doing?'

'She is still healthy. Still working with her new . . . friend.' His next words were nearly inaudible. 'Another thing I shall never understand.'

Sten, with nothing to say, saluted the old man's back and got out.

Chapter Seventy-Two

The four ships that were now the 23rd Fleet had gone underground along with the troops and the civilians. The two destroyers were hidden about two kilometers apart in a widened subway tunnel. The picket ship was camouflaged in a ruined hangar. But the ponderous *Swampscott* had been more difficult to hide.

Sten wondered if the engineer who had come up with the *Swampscott*'s eventual hiding place was still alive. He would like to have bought the man a beer or six – if there was still any beer in Cavite City.

Two of the massive bomb craters from the Tahn attack on Empire Day had been widened, deepened, concrete-floored, and connected. Under cover of night, electronic masking, and a probe by a Guards battalion, the *Swampscott* was moved into those craters. The hole was then roofed with lightweight beams, and a skin was sprayed over them. Plas was then poured and configured to exactly resemble the craters. None of the Tahn surveillance satellites or overflights by their spy ships spotted the change.

Sten figured that he would probably have carte blanche when he reported to the *Swampscott*. He was right. His immediate superiors, van Doorman's appointees, surmised that Sten was the new man and, true benders and scrapers, believed that his every thought was a general order.

Sten carefully scattered the survivors of his own command through every department of the *Swampscott*. If the drakh came down – and Sten agreed with van Doorman that it would – at least there would be one or two reliable beings he could depend on in every section.

He moved the combat information center, which was also the secondary command location and his duty station, from its location in the second, rearmost 'pagoda.' He buried it deep in the guts of the ship, finding a certain amount of satisfaction in taking over what had previously been the *Swampscott*'s officers' dining room.

He also suggested – which became an order – to van Doorman's executive officer that perhaps the ship might be stripped for combat. Somehow, the *Swampscott* still had its beautiful wooden paneling, ruminant-hide upholstery, and fine and flammable dining gear in officers' country.

The loudest objections, of course, came not from the officers but from their flunkies. Sten gleefully reassigned the waiters, bartenders, and batmen from their lead-swinging positions to the undermanned gun sites.

This was a great deal of fun for Sten – until he remembered that sooner or later this hulk would have to go into combat. He estimated that the *Swampscott* would last for four seconds in battle against a Tahn cruiser. Half that, if they were unfortunate enough to face the *Forez* or *Kiso*.

But he had to take his satisfactions where he could get them.

Sten had, at General Mahoney's request, detached Kilgour and put him as coordinator of civilian movement.

When – and if – the liners showed up, they would have only moments on the ground to load the refugees. And both Mahoney and van Doorman agreed that in this area, there was no room for either ego or proper precedent.

Therefore, Kilgour was ordered into civilian clothes and officially given the rank of deputy mayor of Cavite City. Whoever had held that post previously had either died or disappeared, as had the mayor himself.

Kilgour wondered why he had so much support – certain officers and noncoms of the First Guards had been put under his command. Neither he nor anyone else in the Guards – beyond Mahoney's own chief of staff and the heads of his G-sections – knew that Mahoney was systematically stripping his best out of the division to be sent to safety as cadres for the new unit.

And no one except Ian Mahoney knew that their command general was about to violate orders from the Emperor and stay behind on Cavite to die with the remnants of his division.

At first Kilgour thought it would be a hoot to have vastly higher-ranked officers under his command. The hoot was there, but a very minor part of his job.

Alex Kilgour got very little sleep as the civilians were winkled out of their shelters, broken down into hundred-person loading elements, and assigned cargo orders. Each of them was permitted what he, she, or it wore. No more – including toilet articles.

Kilgour stood in one of the assembly areas. There were two scared children hanging onto either leg and a very adorable baby in his arms – a baby, Kilgour realized, that was piddling on his carefully looted expensive tweeds. And he was trying to listen to, regulate, and order from several conversations.

'. . . my Deirdre hasn't shown up, and I'm very . . .'

'. . . Mr Kilgour, we need to discuss which city records should be removed with . . .'

'. . . I wan' my mommie . . .'

'. . . your behavior is simply incomprehensible, and I want to know the name of your superior, immediately . . .'

'. . . since y' be't th' boss, is there anything me an' some of my mates can do to help with . . .'

'. . . since you're our representative, I would like to protest the heartless way that those soldiers . . .'

'. . . when we reach safety, my lawyers will be most interested in the fact that . . .'

'Where's Mommie?'

Kilgour rather desperately wanted to be somewhere safe, like on the front lines facing a Tahn human wave assault.

The blurt transmission came through – the rescue force was twelve hours away from Cavite.

Sten was in the engine room of the *Swampscott*, trying to figure out why the ship's second drive unit was not delivering full power.

He was crouched under one of the drive tubes, listening to the monotonous swearing of the second engineer – who was not a van Doorman appointee and who *was* competent – trying to meter unmetered feed lines when he realized that he had been due at a command conference five minutes before.

He slithered out and ran for a port. There would be no time to change out of his grease-soaked coveralls.

Outside, on the concrete, he looked around for the gravsled that was supposedly assigned just to him. The driver had taken a break and was grabbing a quick meal. It took Sten another ten minutes to hunt the woman down.

Sten was very late by the time the sled lifted and hissed down a communications trench toward Mahoney's TOC. Very late – but still alive.

The Tahn missile was a blind launch.

The Tahn knew, of course, that the Imperial Forces inside Cavite City had gone underground. But they had little hard intelligence on exactly where the vital centers were.

Since they had a plethora and a half of available weaponry, they fired into the perimeter at random. The Imperial stronghold was narrow enough so that almost anything would do some damage.

Assembled under the ruined emporium were the top-ranking Imperial officers. Mahoney knew the dangers of having most command elements in one place – but it was necessary for him to give a final face-to-face briefing.

The Tahn missile was sent in, nap of the earth, across the front lines. It was not detected by any of the Guards' countermissile batteries. Two kilometers inside the lines, following its programming, it lifted and looked for a target.

There wasn't much. The missile might have gone random, reverting to its basic instructions, and smashed in somewhere close to the perimeter's center if its receivers hadn't picked up a broadcast fragment.

The broadcast came from one of Mahoney's brigade officers, who had sent a 'Received-Acknowledged' signal on his belt transponder before entering the TOC.

But that was enough for the missile to target.

Mahoney was beginning. 'Six hours from now, most of you will be on your way out. Here's what's going to happen—'

And then the hardened rocket smashed through the upper floors of the emporium, through the shielding atop the basement, and exploded, centimeters above the basement itself.

Sten arrived to a charnel house.

The emporium was a smoking disaster. One of Mahoney's bodyguards stumbled toward him, leaking blood and muttering incoherently. Sten burst past him, down into the basement.

He found death and dying. Major General Ian Mahoney lay on his side, his jaw smashed, his face covered in gore, slowly suffocating.

Sten's fingers curled, and his knife slid out of his arm and into his hand, as he rolled Mahoney onto his back. Very carefully, his knife V-incisioned into Mahoney's throat, cutting through the windpipe about three centimeters. He made another cut, V'd to meet the first, then thumbed the tissue out of the tracheotomy.

Mahoney was breathing again, with a gargle and bubble of blood.

Sten grabbed a power cord, cut it through, and ripped the center wires out of the cover. That hollow cover was forced into Mahoney's windpipe, and then Sten covered the incision with the outer foil cover, a dressing sealant from Mahoney's own aidpak.

Mahoney would live – if his other wounds were treated.

He *would* live. Ironically, since Mahoney had planned to stay and die with his Guardsmen. Instead, he would be evacuated as a casualty on the liners.

Sten stood as med people ran into the building.

He took stock.

Fleet Admiral Xavier Rijn van Doorman grinned down at him.

Sten thought that the admiral really didn't have that much to smile about, since the top of his brain case was missing, and gray tissue – almost matching the late admiral's hair color – was leaking out. Also, van Doorman was missing certain components, such as his right arm, his left hand, and, more importantly, his body from the rib cage downward. What little was left of his body was strung on a ruptured pipe.

I suppose I have a ship, Sten thought to himself. Now let's see if van Doorman's flunkies follow their orders.

He didn't have to worry about that – the XO, nav officer, and chief engineer were also dead in the ruins.

Commander Sten was now in charge of the 23rd Fleet.

Two hours later, the rescue liners signaled that they were approaching Cavite.

Chapter Seventy-Three

For three days the air around Cavite City somewhat resembled gray noodle soup. It was part of the deception plan for the evacuation. Not only did the liners have to slip through the Tahn patrols beyond the Fringe Worlds – which they had successfully done – but then they had to land and remain undetected long enough to load the evacuees.

The Tahn total air superiority helped slightly. Since there were seldom any Imperial ships in the air, the Tahn aerial monitors and scanners were only cursorily checked.

The boil of smoke and haze over the Empire's perimeter radically reduced visual observation, and the 'noodle soup' blanked almost all other detectors.

The 'soup' was chaff, an invention that even predated the Emperor himself. Chaff originally had been thin strips of aluminum, designed to block radar screens. It was cut in lengths one-half that of the wavelength it was intended to interfere with and was dropped from aircraft. On a detector screen the chaff showed up as a solid, impermeable cloud.

This chaff was far more sophisticated, capable of blocking not only radar but infrared and laser sensors. And it was nearly invisible – many thousands of the strips could be fed through the eye of a needle.

Blasted into the upper atmosphere, the canisters exploded, and the strands drifted slowly down toward Cavite City. They may have been almost invisible, but they did not make breathing any more of a pleasure.

The Tahn had gone to full alert when their sensors suddenly became inactive, but as time passed, they decided that this latest tactic was merely a ploy to slow down the inevitable final assault on the city. They certainly did not need sensors – they knew where the Empire's troops were. And so the chaff clouds became nothing more than an annoyance.

And then other alarms went off.

Offplanet patrols suddenly reported enemy forces. The screens showed, unbelievably, that two full Imperial fleets were heading toward Cavite, fleets that Tahn strategic intelligence said could not exist.

The Tahn ships went to general quarters and lifted for space.

Intelligence was quite correct – the only Imperial squadron in that sector of space was being held in reserve. The Tahn were being 'attacked' by the four destroyers that had escorted the liners into the Fringe Worlds. Four destroyers and nearly a thousand small, unmanned drones.

The drones were Spoof missiles packed with electronics that gave them the signature in every range except visual of full-size warships.

And for once the Empire was lucky.

Atago brought her ships into battle formation and moved in for the attack.

And the liners roared down toward Cavite City.

They were, of course, immediately seen and reported by Tahn infantrymen, but by the time the reports reached Atago, she was six hours off Cavite. And she had worries far more serious than what she thought were transports reinforcing the Empire's ground forces.

She would not discover what the Imperial attack fleets actually were for another hour.

Seven hours to evacuate a world . . .

The blunt torpedoes that were Sullamora's commandeered liners settled down onto Cavite Base, their bulk crushing the debris under them.

Then Kilgour's evac scheme went into motion. He had organized the civilians into fifty-person groups, each group salted with guardsmen and women that would be part of the new, to-be-formed division. Civilians – Kilgour had dubbed them evaks – brought only what they could carry in small daypaks, which were no more than sandbags equipped with slings. In the last few hours, the civilians had been staged forward to any shelter close to Cavite City's field. The shelters were mostly improvised – and many noncombatants died under the periodic Tahn bombardments.

Sten paced on the bridge of the *Swampscott*. All screens were active, showing the scurry toward the liners and the sky above that might lead them to safety.

Sten felt naked on that bridge – it was one of the two pagodas on the *Swampscott* that stood outside the ship's armor. It felt more like a stage set for a livie than a command center. It stretched two stories tall, with huge screens on all sides. Foss, whom Sten had field-commissioned and put in charge of the ship's C3 section, was more than twenty meters away from him.

Sten watched the swarm and prayed to a god still unknown to him that somehow everyone would board before the Tahn came in. He also found space in his prayers that Alex would be one of those on board as he watched the inexorable tickdown on a chronometer that told him when the *Swampscott*, and the liners, must lift.

And while he was at it, he made another request to the heavens – that Brijit would be among the civilians. He had seen General Mahoney, unconscious in his bubble pakked stretcher, loaded onto a liner.

The timer moved down through final seconds.

The screens showed Cavite Field, bare and empty, gray under drifting smoke clouds, with flashes of fire from incoming Tahn rockets.

Warrant officer Alex Kilgour stood beside him. 'Ah hae them, lad. Thae's all 'board't.'

Sten touched the com switch on his chest. 'All ships. This is the *Swampscott*. Lift!'

Dust boiled across the shattered concrete as the liners took off on Yukawa drive.

'On command . . . main drive . . . three . . . two . . . one . . . Mark!'

And the liners and the four ships remaining of the 23rd Fleet vanished.

Below them, the Tahn final assault began.

Fewer than 2,000 soldiers of the First Guards held the thin perimeter. Their best had, under orders, been evacuated on the liners. They were commanded by Mahoney's chief of staff, who, violating the same orders that Mahoney had planned to break, had remained behind with his soldiers.

The Tahn assaulted in wave attacks.

And were slaughtered.

The First Guards died on Cavite.

But they fulfilled the prophecy that Sten's first training sergeant had made years earlier: 'I've fought for the Empire on a hundred different worlds, and I'll fight on a hundred more before some skeek burns me down . . . But I'll be the most expensive piece of meat he ever butchered.'

Three Tahn landing forces had invaded Cavite. One had already been shattered. The other two made the final assault on Cavite City.

They won.

But they also ceased to exist as fighting units.

Brijit van Doorman was *not* among the evacuees.

Supreme triage had been done with the casualties, and those who were dying or, more cruelly, could never be restructured enough to be fit for combat were left behind.

And someone had to stay behind to keep them alive. Dr. Morrison volunteered.

As did Brijit.

The first Tahn shock grenade shattered two orderlies who were posted near the entry to the underground hospital. Then the door exploded inward, and a Tahn combat squad burst into the ward.

Dr. Morrison, her empty hands spread, stood in front of them. 'These are wounded people,' she said slowly and calmly. 'They need help. They are not soldiers.'

'Stand aside,' ordered the Tahn captain commanding the squad. He lifted his weapon.

'These are not combat soldiers,' Morrison started. 'There are no resistants or arms—'

The burst from the Tahn officer's gun blew Morrison nearly in half.

Brijit screamed and hurtled at the captain.

He hip-swiveled and fired again.

Three rounds cut Brijit in half.

The officer lowered his weapon and turned to a noncom. 'The Imperial whore said there is no one here capable of bearing arms. They are not necessary for us.'

The sergeant saluted and raised his flamer.

Chapter Seventy-Four

Lady Atago, although not a believer in ceremony, had positioned things very nicely. She was not able to take the surrender from General Mahoney as planned. That really did not matter. She thought that her livie 'cast to Heath would be equally dramatic.

Atago stood in front of the *Forez*, grounded in the center of Cavite Field. To one side, guards chivvied endless lines of surrendered Imperial soldiers.

She expected the 'cast to be sent directly to the Tahn Council. Instead, her broadcast was intercepted by Lord Fehrle. He stood in formal robes, very small on her monitor.

Lady Atago covered her surprise and reported.

'My congratulations,' the image of Fehrle said. 'But this is not enough.'

'I apologize,' she said. 'What more could be required?'

'You have won a victory, lady. But the Empire has made much of their warriors on Cavite. Heralding them as martyrs and signposts of the eventual victory, and so forth.'

'I am aware of their propaganda 'casts.'

'Then I am surprised that you have not already made the appropriate response,' Fehrle said. 'There must be no iota of victory in this defeat. The forces on Cavite must be shown as totally destroyed.'

'They are, Lord.'

'They are not,' Fehrle corrected. 'If one single Imperial soldier returns to the Empire, somehow their information specialists will find a way to turn that into an accomplishment.'

'Let them. We still hold the Fringe Worlds.'

'Do not dictate policy to me, Lady Atago. Here are your orders.

Pursue those ships that evacuated the Imperial survivors. And destroy them. Only if there are no – I repeat, *no* – survivors will the Emperor be properly shamed.'

Atago started to speak, then rethought. 'Very well. I shall follow your orders.'

The monitor screen went blank, and Lady Atago strode toward her battleship. She would follow orders – but soon, she realized, there must come a reckoning with those rulers of the Tahn who were more interested in paper achievements than in real victories.

Chapter Seventy-Five

Two of the Empire's destroyers survived the spoof attack, broke contact, and set a deceptive orbit that rendezvoused them with the escaping liners.

Fact – the fast liners were moving at many multiples of lightspeed. But to Sten it felt as if they were in one of his least favorite nightmares, fleeing some unknown monstrosity through waist-deep mud. Another illogical perception he had was that the Tahn ships were coming after them, even though there was no particularly valid military reason for them to pursue the shattered elements under Sten's command.

The first casualty – of sorts – was the underpowered picket ship. Less than two hours off Cavite, it was already faltering far to the rear.

If there had been room or time for humanity, Sten would have ordered one of his two destroyers to take off the picket ship's crew and blow it up. But he was sadly lacking in either department.

He found himself with the very cold-blooded thought that the picket ship, limping farther and farther to the rear, still might be of use. If the Tahn *were* after him, the rust bucket might provide an early warning.

Cold-blooded – but there were too many corpses from the past few months. All Sten could do was try to keep the living alive.

He put the two modern Imperial destroyers in front of the liners, Y-ed to either side of the three columns of ships. There were more Tahn ships potentially to worry about than the ones that might be coming up on the tail end of the convoy.

Commander Halldor's *Husha* and the other 23rd Fleet destroyer were positioned as rear guards.

The *Swampscott* flew two-thirds back and above the liners. Sten was very grateful that Sullamora had very experienced crews on the liners – at least he didn't have to concern himself with proper station keeping. He had more than enough troubles of his own.

Spaceships in stardrive, being relatively nonstressed, did not creak.

The *Swampscott* creaked.

They also did not feel as if they were about to tear themselves apart.

Every frame on the *Swampscott* shuddered as if a largish giant outside was working out with a sledgehammer.

'And we're only at full power,' Tapia growled. She touched the large red lever controlling engine power. It was marked QUARTER, HALF, and FULL SPEED. Then there was a manual safety lock. If that was lifted, the *Swampscott* would, at least in theory, go to WAR EMERGENCY power, guaranteed to strain and destroy its engines if applied for longer than minutes.

Sten, Kilgour, and Tapia were in the *Swampscott*'s main engine control room. Sten had immediately promoted the ship's second engineer to chief and assigned Tapia to him. He semi-trusted the man but had privately told Tapia that if the man broke, she was to relieve him at once.

'And if he gives me lip?'

Sten had looked pointedly at the miniwillygun holstered on her hip and said nothing.

Warrant Officer Kilgour would run the central weapons station in the *Swampscott*'s second pagoda. Just below his station was the cruiser's CIC and second control room. The rest of the men and women from Sten's tacships were scattered throughout the ship.

Sten had decided to promote Foss to ensign. He had also told Kilgour that warrant rank or not, the Scot was to assume command of the *Swampscott* if Sten was killed or disabled. He guessed he had the authority. If not, that was something to hassle about when and if they reached safety.

For the moment, there didn't seem to be anything for him to do. The crew was at general quarters – modified. Half of them were permitted to sleep or eat. The food was mainly sandwiches and caff brought to the stations. Those who chose to sleep curled up beside their positions.

Sten turned the bridge over to Foss – the ship was on a preset plot – while he and Kilgour made the rounds.

The engine room was hot and greasy and smelled. The late van Doorman probably would have fainted seeing his carefully polished metalwork smeared, the gleaming white walls scarred and spattered. But spit-shining was something else there wasn't time for. Just keeping the *Swampscott*'s engines running was herculean.

Sten looked around the engine spaces. Tapia and the engineer had everything running as smoothly as possible. He started toward a companionway.

'Commander,' Tapia said, rather awkwardly. 'Can I ask you something?'

'GA.'

'Uhh . . .'

Kilgour took the hint and went up the steps to the deck above. Sten waited.

'You remember – back at the fort – when I said I wanted a transfer? I was being funny then. Now I'm serious. When we park this clotting rust bucket, I want reassignment.'

Sten wondered – was Tapia starting to crack?

'Ensign,' he said. 'If we get this time bomb back, all of us'll get reassigned. Hard to run a tacdiv when you don't have ships. My turn. Why?'

'I just checked Imperial regs.'

'And?'

'And they said you get your ass in a crack if you go to bed with your commanding officer.'

'Oh,' Sten managed.

Tapia grinned, kissed him, and disappeared down a corridor.

Sten thoughtfully went up the ladder and joined Alex.

'Tch,' Alex clucked. 'Hold still, lad.'

He swabbed Sten's chin with an arm of his coverall. 'Th' lads dinnae need t' ken th' old man's been flirtin't wi' th' help.'

'Mr Kilgour. You're being insubordinate.'

'Hush, youngster. Or Ah'll buss y' myself.'

The com overhead snarled into life.

'Captain to the bridge. Captain to the bridge. We have contact!'
Sten and Alex ran for their battle stations.

Contact was not the correct description.

The skipper of the picket ship had seconds to goggle at the screen, and then the Tahn were on him.

Two destroyers launched at the picket ship without altering course.

The ship's captain snapped the com open.

'*Swampscott . . . Swampscott . . .* this is the *Dean*. Two Tahn—'

And the missiles obliterated the picket ship.

The Tahn fleet knew they were closing on the liners. They spread out into attack formation and moved in.

Commander Rey Halldor may have been a clot, but he knew how and, more importantly, when to die. Without waiting for orders, he sent the *Husha* and its sister ship arcing up and back, toward the oncoming Tahn.

The Tahn were in a crescent formation, screening destroyers in front and to the sides. Just behind were seven heavy cruisers and then the two battleships, the *Forez* and the *Kiso*.

Halldor's second destroyer died at once.

But the *Husha*, incredibly, broke through the Tahn screen.

Halldor ordered all missiles to be launched and the racks to be set on automatic load launch. The *Husha* spat rockets from every tube, rockets that were set on fire-and-forget mode.

The *Husha* spun wildly as it took its first hit near the stern. A Tahn shipkilling missile targeted the *Husha* and homed. It struck the *Husha* amidships, blowing it apart. Probably Halldor and his men were already quite dead before they got their revenge.

Two Tahn destroyers took hits in areas vital enough to send them leaking out of battle. And then three of Halldor's missiles found a heavy cruiser.

For an instant it looked as if the Tahn ship's outer skin was transparent, then it turned flame-red as the cruiser was racked by explosions. And then there was absolutely nothing where the ship had been.

The 23rd Fleet still had teeth in its final moments of life.

Sten thought he could still see the blips where his destroyers had been on the screen, even though the ships had died seconds earlier.

Probably an after-image, he thought.

Sten had wondered what gave people the guts to throw themselves at death, to give the suicidal orders instead of running. And he also wondered, if that situation ever came up, whether he would have enough *cojones* to do it himself.

But he never formally made the Big Decision. There were too many other orders to blurt out.

'Navigation. Interception orbit.'

'Aye, sir. Computed.'

'Mark! Engines.'

'Engine room, sir.'

'Full emergency power. Now! Mr Foss. Everyone into suits.'

'Yessir.'

'Weapons . . . clot that. Give me all hands.'

Foss turned the com onto the shipwide circuit.

'This is the captain. We're going in. All weapons stations, prepare to revert to individual control.'

Foss had Sten's suit in front of him. Sten forced his legs in and dragged the shoulders and headpiece on.

'We are now attacking,' he said, choosing his words carefully, 'a Tahn battlefleet. There are at least two battleships with the fleet. We are going to kill them.' He should have found something noble to end his 'cast with, but his mind refused to come up with an 'England Expects,' and he snapped the com link off. 'Foss. I want the CO of the destroyers.'

A screen brightened, showing the bridge of one of the Imperial ships.

'Captain,' Sten began without preamble, 'the convoy's yours. We're going to try to slow down the bad guys.'

'Sir, I request—'

'Negative. You have your orders. Stay with the liners. *Swampscott*, out. Foss! Damage control.'

'This is damage control, Skipper,' came the drawl. 'What do you need?' Sten found a moment to regret not knowing that officer – anybody who could sound that relaxed would be valuable.

'Dump the air.'

'It's gone.'

The suits would make the men more awkward, but the vacuum would lessen the damage from a potential hit.

'Weapons! Are we in range?'

'A wee bit longer, Commander.'

And the *Swampscott* went into its first – and final – battle.

*

Possibly the Tahn had become cocky. Or, more likely, they found it impossible to take seriously the bloated hulk that was charging at them.

The *Swampscott* may have been a disaster of space architecture and a ship long overdue for the boneyard – but it was very heavily armed. It had a Bell laser system forward, Goblin launchers fore and aft, secondary laser stations scattered around the ship, and chainguns running the length of those horrible-looking hull bulges. The ship's main armament consisted of long-obsolete Vydal anti-ship missiles. There were two of them, mounted amidships, between the pagodas that were the command centers.

Kilgour watched the three blips representing Tahn destroyers arc toward him and thumb-activated the Bell assault laser in the ship's nose. The laser was as obsolete as the ship it was mounted on, being not only robot-guided but equipped with verbal responses.

'Enemy ship in range,' the toneless synthesized voice said. Kilgour touched the ENGAGE key.

The laser blast ravened the length of the Tahn destroyer, and the weapons system decided that the target was no longer in existence. Without consulting Kilgour, it switched to a second destroyer and opened up.

'Target destroyed . . . second target under attack,' the voice said, almost as an afterthought.

The laser ripped most of that second destroyer's power room into fragments.

'Second target injured . . . am correcting aim.'

Kilgour slammed the OVERRIDE and NEW TARGET keys. The destroyer was out of battle, and that was enough.

Possibly miffed at being told what to do by a human, the laser switched to stutter mode and lacerated the length of the third destroyer before reporting.

Three down, Alex thought. No more'n a zillion to go.

The *Swampscott* was through the destroyer screen, headed for the heart of the Tahn fleet.

There were three weapons not controlled by Kilgour. They were the huge Kali missiles designed for Sten's tacships. There had been three of them left in the tac division's armory, and Foss and Kilgour had jury-rigged rack mounts for them on the *Swampscott*. Foss had sworn there was no way to run the control circuitry into the weapons control center – it would be easier for him to set up a control helmet/center on the bridge itself.

Sten was fairly sure that Foss was lying, wanting to actually shoot back instead of just being a behind-the-scenes electronics wizard. But he didn't care. Alex would have more than enough hassle trying to make some sense of the elderly and frequently contradictory weapons-control systems already mounted.

Foss had the control helmet plug rigged into his spacesuit: Sten stared at the central screen and blanched. The monstrous *Kiso* filled the screen, and Sten thought they were about to collide before he realized that Foss had the screen at full magnification.

'Sir,' Foss said. 'I have a Kali on standby. Target . . . target . . . target acquired.'

'Launch,' Sten ordered, with no expectations.

The Kali wobbled away from the *Swampscott* without the initial guidance the proper launch tube would have provided. Then it straightened, went to full power, and dived toward the *Kiso*.

And the *Swampscott* took its first hit.

The Tahn missile tore through the skin of the bridge, went out of control, and then exploded less than fifty meters away from the ship. The blast was close enough to smash the entire bridge.

All that Sten knew was a stunning impact, finding himself hurled through the air to slam against a console and staring straight up at what should have been steel to see – see, without sensors – the Tahn destroyer's nose light as it fired a second missile.

His headphones crackled.

'Stand by.' It was Kilgour. 'We have an incoming . . . target acquired . . . ha-ho. Gotcha.'

A Fox missile took out the Tahn rocket. Directly behind it, Kilgour had sent a Goblin. The Goblin scattered fragments of the Tahn ship across a wide area of space.

Sten wove to his feet and looked around the ruins of the bridge. Everyone was dead, down, or hurled out into space.

He recovered and keyed his mike. 'This is the captain. Switching command to CIC. Damage control . . . seal the bridge.'

He stumbled toward a hatch, undogged, and went through it.

Outside, in space, the Kali missile circled aimlessly. It had been given its aim point, but the operator had not completed his procedure. The Kali waited for further orders.

The bridge was a still life – 'Technocracy, with Corpses' – for a moment, and then a figure moved.

It was Foss.

He looked down at the scrap metal where his legs had been. His suit had already sealed itself, surgically amputating the few bits of ligament and flesh.

Foss felt no pain.

He dragged himself on his hands toward the control panel. It was still semi-alive. He switched to a still-undamaged tertiary system and became his missile once more.

The Kali surged toward the *Kiso*.

The Tahn anti-missile officer had seen the hit on the *Swampscott*, seen the Kali begin its aimless orbiting, and told the *Kiso*'s target acquisition systems to ignore the now-harmless missile.

The Kali came alive! The Tahn officer's hand was moving toward his computer's controls when it hit.

The missile struck the *Kiso* in its drivetubes, ripping apart the AM2 fuel storage and sending the antimatter cascading toward the ship's bow.

The *Kiso* vanished in one hellish, soundless explosion.

Foss had time to see the flash light the inside of the bridge, to watch it turn red, and to realize that the red was his own blood, spraying across his suit's faceplate, before his eyes looked beyond anything and he sagged forward onto his controls.

Before Sten reached the CIC, his new command center, the *Swampscott*, took three more hits.

Sten struggled on, praying there would still be something left to command.

Most unusual, he thought, seeing one of the corridors twist and warp in front of him. I am hallucinating. But I am not wounded.

He was not hallucinating. One of the Tahn rockets had hit near one of the ship's mainframes, and the *Swampscott* was bent and twisted.

Sten forced his way through the warped steel tube. His mind recorded observations as his ship rocked around him and explosions sent shock waves through the hull:

Here was a casualty clearing station. Shock blast had killed everyone inside it but left them frozen. Here was one of Sten's med officers, his arms still in the access holes of a surgical bubblepak. Behind him were his corpsmen standing ready. And the casualty inside the pak.

All dead.

Here was an antifire-foam-flooded compartment, where the sensors had evidently gone wild and dumped foam on a fire that could not exist. Sten saw three suited forms struggling toward the exit through the foam but had no time to help them.

A temporary damage-control station, where an officer – Sten

recognized the black-anodized suit arms that were used to denote command rank – was calmly ordering damage teams into action. Sten wondered if that was the drawling, unruffleable control officer he had been on the com with earlier.

And then he found the hatchway into the CIC, undogged the two hatches, and returned to command of the *Swampscott*.

Corns chattered at him, and specialists tried to keep the chaos in some sort of order:

'Forward Goblin launchers do not respond to inquiry. No verbal reports from stations.'

'Secondary engine room reports damage now under control.'

'All controls to forward laser station fail to respond.'

There wasn't much left of the *Swampscott* to command. But still, filling a screen – and not a magnified view this time – was the bulk of the *Forez*. Lady Atago's flagship.

The battleship was vomiting fire, firing everything – anything – to stop the *Swampscott*.

There was an extremely unauthorized broadcast: 'Ah hae y' noo, lass.' The chortle came from the weapons station on the deck above. Then Kilgour launched two Vydals, one slaved to the missile under his control, and sent them surely homing into the *Forez*.

Fire fed on oxygen, and flame and explosion mushroomed down the corridors of the *Forez*. The explosion tore a wall chart from a bulkhead and sent it pinwheeling into Admiral Deska. His eviscerated corpse spun back into Lady Atago, smashing her helmet into a control panel.

She would not return to awareness until long after the battle ended. But command switched smoothly to the *Forez*'s own CO. The battle continued.

The next strike was on the *Swampscott*.

It was deadly, crashing through the armor plating into the ship's main engine room before the weapons officer commanding it touched the DET switch.

A hell of sudden fire filled the engine room and then disappeared.

Tapia had been swearing at the engine temperature gauges, praying that they were lying and knowing they were not, when the rocket exploded. A tiny bit of shrapnel cut through a superpressure hydraulic line. Hydraulic fluid razored out at more than 10,000 feet per second.

The fluid cut Tapia in half as neatly as a surgical saw.

The *Swampscott* went dead in space, still holding its original speed and course.

The two ships, the *Forez* and the *Swampscott*, slid toward each other. None of the Tahn warships could chance firing – the odds of a missile hitting the wrong target were too great.

The battleship loomed up toward the *Swampscott*.

And the cruiser's chaingunners found a target.

The chainguns that lined the two hideous midships bulges were useful only against ground troops or close-range in-atmosphere targets. But now, in deep space, the gunners had a target.

They held their firing keys down; their shells yammered toward the *Forez* and tore the battleship's sides open as if they were tinfoil.

Sten stood on his command deck wordlessly. There was nothing left for him to order.

Another explosion rocked the *Swampscott*, and Sten fought to stay on his feet.

A hatch slammed open, and Kilgour dropped down into the CIC. 'Tha's nae left f'r me to do ae there,' he explained. 'Shall we b' boardin't th' clot?' He still sounded unconcerned.

A larger blast shattered around them, and Sten was down, losing consciousness for bare seconds. He recovered groggily and got back to his feet.

Where was his CIC officer?

Oh. There. Lying with a splinter of steel through his faceplate.

Sten numbly saw that there were still two screens alive in the CIC. One showed the fast-vanishing drives of the convoy, the other, the gutted hulk of the *Forez*, still vomiting fire at him.

Where was Alex? He might know what to do.

Sten stumbled over a suit. Kilgour lay sprawled at his feet. Sten bent and touched monitors. All showed zero.

Sten wove toward a still-functioning com panel. His gloved fingers found a switch, and he began broadcasting.

'Y . . . Y . . . Y . . .'

The universal signal for surrender.

And would they never stop? And would they never receive?

The *Forez* ceased fire.

Sten slumped down on the deck and waited for the Tahn boarding party. Maybe they wouldn't board. Maybe they would just stand off and obliterate his ship.

And Sten did not care what they did.

He was very tired of the killing.

STEN 5:
REVENGE OF
THE DAMNED

To
Frank Lupo
Scholar, bon vivant, gentleman
and
part-time werewolf

Note

The titles of the books are taken from the Earth nation of Japan, which at one time in its feudal history formalized the art of sword fighting, much as it formalized all else. It was called *kenjutsu*. *Ma-ai* is the threshold where the combatants meet. *Suki* is the opportunity to begin the fight. *Kobo-ichi* describes the offensive and defensive engagements. *Zanshin* is final domination.

—AC and CRB

BOOK ONE

MA-AI

Chapter One

He tugged at the last piece of rubble, wincing as rough masonry bit into soft fingertips. Straining under the weight, he lifted it to knee height, then staggered a few paces and dropped the mass onto a pile.

Senior Captain (Intelligence) Lo Prek stepped back to review his work. Only a large, twisted steel door remained. The Tahn officer had labored for hours clearing that door. Beyond it, he hoped, was the key to the puzzle he had been fitting together for more years than he cared to remember.

He hesitated a few minutes as if afraid that he would be disappointed. Almost daintily, Prek wiped his face with a silk handkerchief, which he then returned to his uniform sleeve. For a Tahn, Prek was a tall man and painfully slender. His body was all angles of jutting bone topped by a long horse-like face with small eyes set too far apart and a short nose that left him with an overly long upper lip.

Prek unclipped a small laser torch from his harness and began cutting through the door. Prek was not the kind of man who hummed to himself while he worked or who used a string of favorite obscenities when the task became momentarily difficult. At his former post, where he had worked for almost his entire career, he had been notorious – even among Tahn – for insisting on absolute silence and complete dedication to even the smallest job. He did not allow his mind to wander when performing rote and insisted on the same from his underlings. The joke at his old bureau was that if Prek had his way, every intelligence clerk would have a monitor surgically implanted in his brain as a requirement for employment.

Prek had heard the joke, and although he did not see any humor in it, he acknowledged its truth. Captain Prek knew he had an obsessive personality. He did not particularly like it or dislike it. It was just so. It was a character weakness that he had learned to use to his benefit.

There was a shriek of metal as the door sagged under its own weight and then crashed to the floor. Prek reclipped the torch and stepped inside the record center of the Imperial Navy's defeated 23rd Fleet. If the Tahn had gods, Prek would have whispered a prayer. He had traveled very far and taken many chances to come to this point. If Prek was correct, in this room he would pick up the trail of the man who had murdered his brother.

STEN, (NI). Commander Imperial Navy. Last known post: OIC, 23rd Division TacDiv, asngd Imperial 23rd Fleet. Prev: Cmdr, Imperial Personal Bodyguard. Prev: Records show assigned to various Guards units. NOTE: IntelEst these records fraudulent, prob Cat. 1. STEN actually assigned various Imperial Intelligence duties. GENERAL DESCRIPTION: Species: Human. Sex: Male. Age: Unknown. Records destroyed. Estimated first quarter of life span. Place of Birth: Unknown. Height: Slightly below Imperial norm. Body: Well formed, low body fat, high muscle ratio. Hair: Blk. Eyes: Blk. General Health: Excellent. Distinguishing Marks or Characteristics: None. Family: Unknown. Interests: Unknown. Friends: Unknown.

Prek was not dismayed when he saw the shattered ruins inside. File vaults had been twisted into bizarre shapes by intense heat. There were large spots of white ash scattered uniformly about where office dividers and furniture had once stood. As he walked, his boots stirred up a fine dust that drifted upward and clogged his nose and throat. He fitted a rebreather into place and began combing through the litter of what had once been the 23rd Fleet.

Once his heart jumped when he found a tiny scrap of microfilm lying under a steel joist. He slid it into the slot of his reader and then felt like crying when he saw that it was nothing more than part of a bill for general office supplies.

Prek berated himself for his reaction. Yes, his mission was personal. But his only hope for success was if he behaved like a complete professional.

Prek reorganized himself. He went all the way back to the beginning – to the outlines of what might have been the desk of the chief clerk of the records center. He began sifting through the rubble, starting in the middle and slowly working out to the edges. He was looking for much more than the chance minutiae of one man's life, he reminded himself. Even more valuable would be to discover the pattern of record storage. Prek knew that every office had its own individual logic. Things might have changed over the years as chief clerks came and went, but there would always be the trace of the first being who had received and filed the first and then the second and then the thousandth document.

The Tahn captain was convinced that once he had determined the procedural map, he would find his man.

Although they had worked in private industry, Prek's parents had also been lifelong bureaucrats. They had been equally dull in personality and unattractive in appearance. True, they had both been intelligent people, but their intelligence was what a personnel psych might have called 'highly focused.' Prek was ten years old when his brother, Thuy, was born. From the moment the infant had drawn its first breath, the family knew it was blessed with a golden boy.

Thuy was everything his family was not. To begin with, he was beautiful. Blond, curly hair. Blue eyes. And a physique like an Adonis even as he entered puberty. He was quick-witted and consumed with curiosity about everything. Thuy also saw humor in nearly any stituation. It was hard to be around him long and not be infected by his cheery outlook on life.

Far from being jealous, Lo had loved his young brother more than anything in the world. He had lavished all his attention on him, going so far as to strap himself financially so that the boy could have the benefit of the very best education the Tahn System could offer.

The investment had proved to be well placed. Thuy was instantly snapped up by the diplomatic corps, a situation that allowed him to blossom even more. The only arguments any of his superiors had ever had concerning him was who the young Tahn's mentor *really* was.

And so, when the delicate peace negotiations with the Eternal Emperor were undertaken, Thuy had instantly been assigned to accompany Lord Kirghiz and the other Tahn representatives as a junior diplomatic officer. It was to be a career assignment, which everyone agreed would be just the beginning of a rich career.

The Imperial and Tahn fleets met under the blinding pulsar shadow of NG 467H. The initial negotiations went quickly and well. Everyone believed that an agreement beneficial to the Tahn was only a formality away. The Eternal Emperor had invited the Tahn dignitaries aboard for a treaty celebration. Lord Kirghiz had quickly picked the Tahn who would accompany them. Included among them had been Thuy.

No Tahn knew what exactly had transpired next.

Prek believed the facts spoke for themselves.

Every Tahn who had boarded the *Normandie* died in a horrible bloodbath as they sat at the Emperor's banquet table.

The Eternal Emperor, through his toady judges and special prosecutors, had claimed that the Tahn had merely been the tragic victims of a plot against himself. As far as any Tahn – especially Prek – was concerned, that was too obvious a lie even to comment on. And the only answer to the lie and the treachery was a war of vengeance. It was a war to the death, to the last ounce of air and the last drop of blood.

It was a war that Prek believed in as intensely as did every other Tahn. But the larger war merely underscored his own private battle.

Prek did not remember when he had learned of his brother's death. He had been sitting in his office at Tahn Intelligence headquarters, and his superior had entered. The next thing he knew, Lo found himself sitting up in a hospital bed. Four months had passed. During that time, he was told, he had been a virtual catatonic. War was at hand, and so Lo had been declared 'cured' and sent back to work.

It was then that his private war began. Prek examined every dot of information surrounding the deaths of his brother and the other Tahn diplomats. And gradually he had determined which beings had been responsible. He had not included the Emperor. That would be pointless. To go for the Emperor would be not only impossible but the act of an insane man. No. Go for the possible: the men who had actually wielded the knives or fired the guns. Sten, Prek firmly believed, was one of those men.

He had obtained a copy of Sten's military record, a tissue of lies, he was sure, but at least a beginning point in forming a profile of the man. The official record showed a man who had held a series of slightly above average posts, who had won a little more than his share of military awards and honors, and who had been promoted regularly. Then, suddenly, for no apparent reason, his career had taken a sharp upturn. For no readily apparent reason, he had been appointed head of the Emperor's bodyguards. That had been followed by another sudden shift from the army to the navy and a promotion to commander.

Prek believed the promotion was because of special service to the Emperor. Sten's record was a fake. Actually, Prek thought, Sten had been a valued intelligence agent. The shift to the navy and, ultimately, to his command of four tacships had been a reward for services rendered. Those services, Prek was sure, included the murder of his brother.

Prek had tracked Sten forward to the final battle for Cavite City, where enormous casualties had been suffered on both sides. Tahn records indicated that Sten had probably died in that battle, although his remains had never been found. There had been some out-of-the-ordinary official effort to determine Sten's fate because of 'criminal actions instigated by said Imperial officer' prior to the battle for Cavite.

Prek did not believe Sten was dead. His profile showed him to be a man who would do anything to survive. Prek also did not believe that Sten was serving elsewhere. He was an officer who would always be in the forefront of battle, and he was also the kind of hero the Eternal Emperor liked to feed into his propaganda machine.

No. Sten was alive. And Prek was determined to run him to the ground. He would find the man and then . . . The Tahn brushed that thought from his mind. He could not allow emotion to interfere with the hunt.

Senior Captain (Intelligence) Lo Prek was right.

Sten *was* alive.

Chapter Two

Two emaciated, shaven-headed men crouched, motionless, in the thigh-deep muck.

One of them had been Commander Sten, formerly commanding officer of the now-destroyed Imperial Cruiser *Swampscott*. Sten had assumed command of the obsolete rust-bucket in the final retreat from Cavite and had fought a desperate rearguard action against an entire Tahn fleet. One ultramodern Tahn battleship had been destroyed by the *Swampscott*'s missiles and a second had been crippled beyond repair, even as the Tahn blasts shattered the cruiser. In the final moments, Sten had opened his com and sent a surrender signal. He had collapsed long before the Tahn boarded the hulk that had been a fighting ship. That almost certainly had saved his life.

Seconds after Sten went out, Warrant Officer Alex Kilgour, a heavy-world thug, ex-Mantis Section assassin, and Sten's best friend struggled back to consciousness. He bloodily registered, on the *Swampscott*'s single functioning screen, Tahn tacships closing in. He foggily thought that the Tahn, barbarians, 'ae th' Campbell class,' would not properly honor the man who had destroyed the nucleus of a Tahn fleet. More likely, Sten would be pitched out the nearest lock into space.

'Tha' dinnae be braw nor kosher,' he muttered. Kilgour wove his way to a sprawled body, unsealed the suit, and tore away the corpse's ID tags. He checked a wall-mounted pressure readout. There were still a few pounds of atmosphere remaining in the CIC. Sten's suit came open, air hissing out, and his ID tags were replaced. Kilgour heard/felt the crashing as the Tahn blew a lock open and decided that it might be expedient for him to be unconscious as well.

Fewer than thirty gore-spattered, shocked Imperial sailors were transferred from the wreck of the *Swampscott* to the hold of a Tahn assault transport. Among them was one Firecontrolman 1st Class Samuel Horatio.

Sten.

Fed and watered only as an afterthought, their wounds left untreated, twenty-seven survived to be unloaded on a swampworld that the Tahn had grudgingly decided would be a war prisoner planet.

The Tahn believed that the highest death a being could find was in a battle. Cowardice or surrender were unthinkable. According to their belief, any Imperial soldier or sailor unlucky enough to be captured should have begged for instant death. But they were also sophisticated enough to realize grudgingly that other cultures felt differently and that such assistance to the dishonored might be misinterpreted. And so they let their captives live. For a while.

The Tahn saw no reason why, if prisoners were a burden to the

Tahn, that burden should not be repaid. Repaid in sweat: slave labor.

Medical care: If the prisoners included med personnel, they had a medic. No supplies were provided. Any Imperial medical supplies captured were confiscated.

Shelter: Prisoners were permitted, on their own time, using any nonessential items permitted by the camp officers, to build shelter.

Working hours: At any task assigned, no limitations on hours or numbers of shifts.

Food: For humans, a tasteless slab that purported to provide the necessary nutrients. Except that a hardworking human needed about 3,600 calories per day. Prisoners were provided less than 1,000. Similar ratios and lack of taste were followed for the ET prisoners.

Since the prisoners were shamed beings, of course their guards were also soldiers in disgrace. Some of them were crafty, who reasoned that shame in a guard unit was better than death in an assault regiment. There were a few – a very few – guards who had previously been trusties on one of the Tahn's own prison worlds.

The rules for prisoners were simple: Stand at attention when any guard talks to you, even if you were a general and he or she was a private. Run to obey any order. Failure to obey: death. Failure to complete a task in the time and manner assigned: death. Minor infractions: beatings, solitary confinement, starvation.

In the Tahn POW camps, only the hard survived.

Sten and Alex had been prisoners for over three years.

Their rules were simple:

Never forget that the war cannot last forever.

Never forget you are a soldier.

Always help your fellow prisoner.

Always eat anything offered.

Both of them wished they had been brought up religious – faith in any or all gods kept prisoners alive. They had seen what happened to other prisoners, those who had given up hope, those who thought they could not filter through animal excrement for bits of grain, those who rebelled, and those who thought they could lone-wolf it.

After three years, all of them were long dead.

Sten and Alex had survived.

Their previous training in the supersecret, survive-anything Mantis Section of the Empire's Mercury Corps might have helped. Sten also knew clotting well that having Alex to back his act had saved him. Kilgour privately felt the same. And there was a third item: Sten was armed.

Years earlier, before he had entered Imperial service, Sten had constructed a weapon – a tiny knife. Double-edged and needle-sharp, hand-formed from an exotic crystal, its edge would cut through any known metal or mineral. The knife was sheathed *in* Sten's arm, its release muscle-controlled. It was a very deadly weapon – although, in their captivity, it had been used mostly as a tool.

That night it would assist in their escape.

There had been very few escapes from the Tahn POW camps. At first those who had tried had been executed after recapture, and recaptured they almost always were. The first problem – getting out of a camp or fleeing from a work gang – was not that hard. Getting off the world itself was almost insurmountable. Some had made it as stowaways – or at least the prisoners hoped the escapees had succeeded. Others escaped and went to ground, living an outlaw existence only marginally better than life in the camps, hoping that the war would eventually end and they would be rescued.

Within the last year there had been a policy change – prisoners attempting an escape were not immediately murdered. Instead they were purged to a mining world, a world where, the guards gleefully told them, a prisoner's life span was measured in hours.

Sten and Alex had made four escape attempts in the three years they had been prisoners. Two tunnels had been discovered in the digging, a third attempt to go over the camp wire had been aborted when their ladder was found, and the most recent had been abandoned when no one could come up with what to do once they were beyond the wire.

This one, however, would succeed.

There was movement in the reeds nearby. Alex pounced and came up with a muddy, squirming, squealing rodent. Instantly Sten had the small box he held open, and the water animal was popped inside and closed into darkness. Very good.

'You two! Up!' a guard's voice boomed.

Sten and Alex came to attention.

'Making love? Sloughing?'

'Nossir. We're hunting, sir.'

'Hunting? For reeks?'

'Yessir.'

'We shoulda killed you all,' the guard observed, and spat accurately and automatically in Sten's face. 'Form up.'

Sten didn't bother to wipe the spittle. He and Alex waded out of the paddy to the dike, into line with ten other prisoners. The column stumbled into motion, heading back toward the camp. There were three guards, only one of whom was carrying a projectile weapon; they knew that none of those walking dead were a threat. Sten held the box as steady as possible and made soothing noises. He did not want his new pet to go off before it was time.

The reek – an odoriferous water animal with unusable fur, rank flesh, and spray musk glands below its tail – was the final tool for their escape.

Chapter Three

The prisoner-of-war camps had two command structures. The guards were the most visible. But the camp was actually run by the prisoners. In some camps the commanders were the strong and the brutal. Those anarchies were deathcamps, where a prisoner was as likely to die at the hands of his fellows as by a guard.

Sten's camp was still military. He and Alex were at least partially responsible for that.

The two had fought their way back to health during long delirium months. Then one day Sten was well enough to make a major discovery – not only was he known by the rather clottish name of Horatio, but Warrant Officer Kilgour outranked him. Somehow, he knew that had been carefully plotted by Alex back in the CIC of the *Swampscott*.

But regardless, rank would prevail. Those who felt the 'war is over' or they 'don't have to listen to any clottin' sojers who got us in the drakh in the first place" were reasoned with. If that did not work, other methods were applied. Sten might have been a skeleton, but he was one who knew many, many degrees beyond the third. And Kilgour, from the three-gee world of Edinburgh, was still the strongest being in the camp – even including the camp executive officer, Battery Commander (Lieutenant Colonel) Virunga.

The N'Ranya were not particularly civilized-looking primates who had developed as tree-dwelling carnivores. They had recently been recognized as the Empire's pre-eminent artillery experts – their ancestry had given them an instinctual understanding of geometry and trigonometry. Their 300-kilo-plus body weight did not hurt their ability to handle heavy shells, either.

Colonel Virunga had been badly wounded before he was captured and still hulked around the compound with a limp and a cane. Very few people who survived Sten and Alex thought it wise to argue with the colonel's orders. The Imperial camp commander was a thin, wispy woman, General Bridger, who had reactivated herself out of retirement when her world was invaded and led the last-ditch stand. Her only goal was to stay alive long enough to see the Imperial standard raised over the camp, and then she would allow herself to die.

At dusk, after Sten and Alex had forced down the appalling evening ration, she and Colonel Virunga said their goodbyes.

'Mr Kilgour, Horatio,' she said, 'I hope I shall never see either of you again.'

Kilgour grinned. 'Ah hae th' sam't dream, ma'am.'

Virunga stepped forward. It took a while to understand the N'Ranya speech patterns – they thought speech mostly a waste of time and so verbalized only enough words to make the meaning clear.

'Hope . . . luck . . . When . . . free . . . do not forget.'

They would not. Sten and Alex saluted, then began their moves.

Under orders, without explanation, other prisoners had begun what Sten called 'two in, one out, one in, three out.' In small groups they filtered toward one of the camp's few privies, one that 'co-incidentally' sat less than three meters from the inner perimeter. Sten and Alex joined them; the small box with the reek inside hung around Sten's neck, concealed by a ragged towel. It would be impossible for either of the guards in the towers nearby to keep track of how many prisoners went into the privy and how many came out.

The privy sat over a deep and dank excrement-filled pit. The building itself was a shed, with a water trough down one side and the privy seats – circular holes cut into a long slab-cut lumber box – on the other. Sten and Alex clambered *into* one of those holes. On either side of the box, on the inside, they had hammered in spikes a few days earlier.

Both of them had root fiber nose plugs stuffed in place. The plugs did no good whatsoever. Just hang on, Sten thought. Do no faint. Do not think whether that arachnid that's crawling up your arm is poisonous. Just hang on.

Finally the curfew siren shrieked, and the prisoner sounds subsided. Footsteps thudded, and one privy door opened. The guards, for olfactory reasons, only checked cursorily.

It would have been best for Sten and Alex to wait until the middle of the night before moving, but they had kilometers to travel before dawn. At full dark, they levered themselves out of their hiding places and grimaced at each other.

The next step was up to Colonel Virunga.

It started with shouts and screams and laughter. Sten and Alex saw the searchlight sweep over the cracks in the privy roof, toward one of the barracks. They slid out the privy door.

In theory, they should not have been able to go any farther. The camp was sealed with an inner barrier of wire, a ten-meter-wide 'no-go' passage, and then the outer wire.

The tower guards swept the compound with visual searchlights, far more dangerous light-amplification scopes, and focused-noise sensors. By assignment, one guard should have been on each detector.

But the guards were lazy. Why, after all, was it necessary for three men to work a tower, especially at night? There was no escape from the camp. Even if one of the Imperials managed to get out, there was nowhere for him to go – the peasants surrounding the camp were promised large rewards for the return of any escapees in any condition, no questions to be asked. And even if an Imperial managed to slip past the farmers, where would he go? He was still marooned on a world far inside the Tahn galaxies.

And so a bright guard had figured a way to slave all three sensors to a single unit. Only one guard was required to monitor all three of them.

So when Virunga ordered the carefully orchestrated ruckus to start inside one of the barracks and a guard swung his spotlight, all sensors on that tower pointed away from the two scuttling blobs of darkness that went to the wire.

There were three strands of wire to cut before Sten and Alex could slip through into the no-go passage, three razored strips of plas. Sten's knife would make that simple. But those dangling strands would be spotted within a few minutes. And so, very carefully, Alex had collected over the past several cycles twelve metalloid spikes.

Sten's knife nerve-twitched out of its fleshy sheath. Very gently he punched two holes side by side on a razor strip. Alex pushed the spikes through them, then used his enormous strength to force the spikes into the plas barrier posts. With the strip thus nailed in place, Sten cut the wire. One . . . two . . . three . . . slip through the gap . . . repin the wire . . . and they were in the no-go passageway.

Across that, and again they cut and replaced the wire.

For the first time in three years Sten and Alex were outside the prison camp, without guards.

The temptation to leap up and run was almost overwhelming. But instead they crawled slowly onward, fingers feathering in front of them, expecting sensors and screaming alarms.

There were none.

They had escaped.

All that remained was getting offworld.

Chapter Four

'Now . . . where the hell is that clottin' sentry?' Sten whispered.

'Dinna be fashin' Horrie, m' lad,' Alex growled.

Horrie. Somehow Alex not only had managed to make Sten a lower-rank but had found a diminutive for Horatio.

'You'll pay.'

'Aye,' Alex said. 'But th' repayment ae a' obligation dinna be ae gay ae th' incurrin't ae it.'

Sten did not answer. He stared at the dispatch ship, sitting less than 100 meters from their hilltop hiding place.

Sten and Alex had discovered a potential way off the planet when they were assigned to a work detail on the prison world's landing field. They had both observed and noted a small four-man dispatch ship, once state of the art but now used for shuttle missions between worlds. The ship might have been obsolete, but it had both Yukawa and Anti-Matter Two drives. All they had to do was steal the ship.

Once Sten and Alex were beyond the camp's wire, it should have been simple for them to sneak the few kilometers from the camp to the landing field. But it took more hours than they had allowed. Neither of them realized that one of the corollary effects of malnutrition was night blindness.

And so, in spite of their Mantis skills, they found themselves stumbling through the dark as if they were untrained civilians. Only their reflexive abilities from Mantis on night and silence moves kept them from being discovered as they crept past the peasant farms surrounding the prison camp.

'While we be hain't ae sec,' Alex said, 'whidny y' be likin't Ae tellin't th' aboot th' spotted snakes?'

'If you do that, I shall assassinate you.'

'Th' lad hae nae sense a' humor,' Alex complained to the sleeping reek in the tiny box in front of them. 'An' here com't thae ace boon coon.'

Below them, the sentry ambled across their field of view.

The airfield security was complex: a roving sentry, a wire barricade, a clear zone patrolled by watch animals, a second wire barricade, and internal electronic security.

With the sentry's passage logged and timed, Sten and Alex went forward. They crawled just to the first wire barricade. Alex patted the small box.

'Nae, y' wee't stinkard, go thou an' earn th' rent.'

He flipped the top open, and the reek sprang out. Fuddled by its new environment, it wandered through the wire, into the clear zone. Then it sat, licking its fur, wondering where water would be, and waking up. Its slow thought processes were broken by a snarl.

The caracajou – three meters on three dimensions of furcovered lethality – waddled forward. The skunk bear was angry, which was the normal disposition of its species. But the crossbreeding and mutation to which the Tahn had subjected its forebearers made the mammal even angrier. It dully reasoned that two-legs was its only enemy, and somehow it was forced to be kindly to those two-legs who fed it yet destroy any other two-legs. Also, it was kept from breeding and from finding its own territory.

This caracajou had spent five years of its life walking up and down a wire-defined corridor, with nothing to release its anxieties.

And then, suddenly, there was the reek.

The skunk bear bounded forward – according to instincts and general piss-off.

The reek – also according to instincts and general piss-off – whirled, curled its worm tail over its back, and sprayed.

The spray from its anal glands hit the caracajou on its muzzle. Instantly the creature rose to its hind paws, howled, and, trying to scrub the awful smell from its nostrils, stumbled away, one set of conditioning saying find shelter, the second saying find the two-legs that can help.

The reek, satisfied, hissed and scuttled off.

'Th' stink't tool work't,' Alex whispered.

Sten was busy. Once again the barrier wire was drilled, pinned, and then, after the two crawled past, replaced.

The ship sat in sleek blackness, less than fifty meters away. Neither man went forward. Alex slowly reached inside his ragged tunic, took out four segmented hollow tubes, each less than one centimeter in diameter, and put them together. That made a blow-pipe nearly a meter long. At its far end, Alex clipped on a pierced fish bladder, which was filled with finely pulverized metal dust.

Kilgour put the tube to his lips, aimed the blowpipe at a bush, and blew. The invisible dust drifted out, collected around the bush, and settled. Both men went nose into the dirt and thought *invisible*. Minutes later, the Tahn patrol charged up. Then they stopped and milled about.

In their initial casing of the escape, Sten and Alex had noted that inside the field's perimeter were electronic detectors. They theorized that from a distance the detectors would be fairly simple: probably radar-based. This was, after all, a world far behind the front lines.

The Tahn corporal commanding the patrol lifted his com.

'Watch . . . this is Rover. We are in the suspect area, clear.'

'Rover . . . Watch. Are there any signs of intrusion?'

'This is Rover. Hold.'

The overage and overweight corporal used his torch to scan the ground. 'Rover. Nothing.'

'This is Watch. Are you sure? Sensors still show presence in area.'

'Clot if I know,' the corporal complained. 'But there's clottin' nothing we can see.'

'Rover, this is Watch. Maintain correct com procedure. Your inspection of site recorded . . . your report logged that no intrusion has been made. Return to guard post. Watch. Over.'

'Clottin' wonderful,' the corporal grumbled. 'If there's nobody out here, we done something wrong. If there's somebody out here, we're gonna get the nail. Clot. Detail . . . form up.'

The Tahn guards doubled away.

Very, very good, Sten thought. The metallic spray that Alex had blown onto a bush had obviously registered on the nearest sensor. An alert squad had been sent out and had found nothing. Yet the sensor continued to show the presence of something alien. Therefore, that sensor's reports would be ignored until a repair person fixed that sensor.

And Sten and Alex had free passage to the dispatch ship.

The port was not locked. Alex went to the rear of the ship, while Sten headed for the control room. The unanswered question was whether he could fly it.

The controls were very, very simple.

Sten was in the pilot's chair, touching controls, when Alex rumbled into the tiny command center.

'Tha's nae fuel,' he said.

Sten muttered four unmentionables and touched computer keys. Yes, there was fuel. Enough to lift them off into space. Enough to boost them into stardrive. Enough fuel to . . .

He fingered keys on the navcomputer. Enough to take them out of Tahn space?

Negative.

He slammed the control panel off and spun. 'And all of this is for nothing.'

'Nae, nae, lad,' Alex said. 'Ah hae checked the fuelin't records. This ship'll gae a' topoff in three days. All we hae t' do is seal it, gae back through th' wire, an' then home, an' wait f'r it aye beat. Can we noo come back again?'

Go back through the wire. Go back through the paddies. Go back to the three-year-long hell of the prison camp.

They could not.

But they did.

Sten and Alex slid through the wire, through the guards, and into the camp and their barracks close to dawn. All they wanted was to drift back among the sleeping prisoners and get a few moments of sleep. Instead, they found the prisoners awake.

The explanation came quickly.

The furor that Colonel Virunga had set up to cover their escape had provoked revenge. Revenge was a surprise roll call for all prisoners, with the guards checking each Imperial by name, finger- and poreprint, and visual recognition. There was no way for Virunga or any other prisoners to be able to cover that intensive a check.

Of course, the guards knew, Sten and Alex could not have escaped – their check of the perimeter proved that. But the two must be hidden somewhere, preparing to escape. Perhaps digging a tunnel.

It did not matter.

Colonel Virunga gave Sten and Alex the word: When they re-appeared, they were to be purged. Along with Colonel Virunga – he somehow had to be connected with their non-appearance.

Sten and Alex eyed each other. They would never be able to make the second attempt to get that dispatch ship. Their next destination would be the mining world and death.

They were wrong – courtesy of the supreme rulers of the Tahn.

Chapter Five

The twenty-seven members of the Tahn High Council slumped in bored inattention as their elder secretary droned through another day's legislation.

'. . . HCB No. 069-387. Titled: Negative Pensions. Arguments for: A graduated tax on guaranteed incomes for retirees – not to exceed 115 percent – will relieve a heavy burden on the state and result in key military enlistments. Arguments against: None.'

The elder secretary did not bother to look up as he asked the routine question. 'Opposed?' There was the usual silence. 'Then it's unanimous.'

'Next. HCB No. 434-102. Titled: Fuel Allotments. Subsection Medical Emergencies. Arguments for increase: The commandeering of private emergency vehicles for military use without compensa- tion is proving an undue hardship on an already overburdened civilian health care system. Staff recommendation: No increase.'

Once again the routine question. And once again silence indicated unanimity. It was the way the business of governing had always been done. However, the lords and ladies of the Tahn High Council were hardly mere rubber stamps for their chairman, Lord Fehrle. On the contrary, each member had very strong opinions and powerful allies. Otherwise, they would not have been named to the council.

Lord Fehrle was their chairman as the result of a delicate balancing act. Over the years he had shored up his position through key appointments. For instance, he had recently raised Lady Atago from associate status to full member. True, she was a military hero. Still, she had her detractors.

He glanced over at Colonel Pastour as the secretary mumbled on. Sometimes he thought his decision to support the old colonel's appointment a mistake. It was not that the industrialist was outwardly difficult. He just seemed to have a way of asking innocent questions that were difficult to answer. More importantly, he was, as time went by, becoming a voice Fehrle could not always depend on.

Hmmm. How to deal with Pastour? The problem was that Pastour not only was a successful industrialist, he was also a miracle worker in finding new bodies to hurl at the Empire. He also carried the expenses of many regiments out of pocket. Perhaps it would be better to live with the old man for a while longer.

Then there was Lord Wichman. Absolutely loyal. Absolutely committed. That was his problem. He was an absolutist who knew nothing of the art of compromise. It was a fault that several times had nearly upset Fehrle's balancing act.

Compromise was the key to Tahn politics. All proposals were discussed in labored detail before any meeting. All viewpoints were considered and, whenever possible, included in the eventual program under consideration. With rare exceptions, all decisions were therefore unanimous.

Unanimity was as necessary to the Tahn as breathing. They were a warrior race who had suffered humiliating defeat in their ancient past and had been forced to flee across eons past the fringes of the Empire to their present home. It was a place no one wanted except for the natives, who proved reluctant to move aside for the Tahn. Genocide convinced them of their faulty logic.

Slowly the Tahn rebuilt themselves, and in the rebuilding of their warrior society they created a new racial purpose. They would never again flee. And someday they would revenge their humiliation. Meanwhile, it was necessary to prove themselves.

They turned to their neighbors. First one, then another, and then more and more fell to the Tahn. They used two skills for those victories: a native genius for negotiation as a screen for bloody intent, and a resolve to win at all costs. At times their wars required a sacrifice of up to eighty percent of their military. After each war the Tahn quickly regrouped and struck out again.

It was only a matter of time before they bumped into the Eternal Emperor. The result once again was war.

'. . . HCB No. 525–117. Untitled. No arguments. Opposed?'

The silence was broken.

'Not opposed, exactly. But I do have one question.'

The other twenty-six members of the council were startled out of their boredom into absolute shock. First, an untitled High Council bill was always a personal proposal from a council member. Such a bill would not even be presented if there was the slightest controversy. Second, and even more shocking, was the identity of the questioner.

It was not Pastour for once. It was Wichman. And the number 525 meant that it was Pastour's bill. All the members of the council leaned forward, eyes glittering in anticipation of a battle of a different sort. Only Fehrle, as chairman, and Lady Atago remained aloof. Atago had a soldier's disdain for politics of any kind.

Pastour leaned back in his seat, waiting.

'Now, as I understand the proposal,' Wichman said, 'we are creating a program in which we will rely on prisoners of war to build our weapons. Am I right so far?'

'Poorly put,' Pastour said, 'but basically correct. What is your question?'

'Simply this: A soldier who surrenders is a coward. True?' Pastour nodded in agreement. 'Cowardice is an infectious thing. I fear we may be taking a grave risk with the morale of our own work force.'

Pastour snorted. 'There is no risk at all,' he said. 'If you had bothered to read my plan, you would not have asked the question.'

'I read your proposal,' Wichman said flatly. 'And I still ask it.'

Pastour sighed. He realized that Wichman was intentionally putting him on the spot. He wondered what kind of compromise he would have to offer and whether it would doom the success of his plan.

'Then you certainly deserve an answer,' he said, trying and failing to keep an edge of sarcasm out of his voice. 'The problem we seek to address is simply described but thus far difficult to solve.

'We have factories and material in barely sufficient quantities to fight this war. But we have less than half of the work force required to man the machines.

'I'm mainly a businessman. I see a problem, I immediately assume there is some way to fix it. A lot of times the solution is found in another problem. And with luck, you can fix two things at once.'

'Such as?'

'I looked for a surplus of people. I found it in our prisoner-of-war camps. But that is only the tip of the matter. Our worst shortages are in the technical skills. So, not just any POW would do. Where to find the largest pool of untapped skills? Among the troublemakers, of course. Especially the habitual troublemakers.'

'Where is the logic in that? A difficult prisoner equals a skilled being?' Wichman asked.

'The logic is simple. If these prisoners are still alive after all this time, then our prison officials must have had good reason not to have them killed. Those were my instincts, and after study, my instincts proved correct.

'Regardless. I'm satisfied, and as far as I know, my lord, so are the other members of the council.'

Wichman ignored that. 'So you're guaranteeing us that this program of yours will solve the problem.'

'I'm not guaranteeing anything,' Pastour gritted out. That was one trap he would not spring. 'First off, the program is experimental. If it doesn't work, it affects nothing, especially since I am paying for it out of my own pocket.'

'Good. Very good. You have answered almost all of my questions. But I still have one small worry.'

'Which is?'

'The staffing of the first prison. I note a lack of hard experience in this field.'

Here it is at last, Pastour thought. Wichman wanted a man in some key position. Was it someone Pastour's people could live with? There was no time to find out. He had to make up his mind quickly.

'Perhaps you could help in that area, my lord,' he purred.

'Delighted,' Wichman said.

There was immediate relaxation around the table.

'Once again,' the elder secretary said, 'is anyone opposed?'

In an instant HCB No. 525–177 was law. Lady Atago put another check mark on her agenda. There were half a dozen items to go before it was her turn to face the Tahn High Council. Although it would be her debut report as a full member of the body, she was not nervous at all.

Atago had a list of facts to present on the war. It did not matter to her whether the facts underscored gloom or optimism. The emotions the report elicited from her colleagues was not her concern.

It was plain to her that they were quickly approaching a crucial point in the war. And it should have been equally clear to the others that the way events played out in the near future would determine the eventual winner and loser. She was confident, however, that the plan she and Lord Fehrle had already partially implemented would assure the Tahn of final victory.

'. . . a special report from Lady Atago . . . I'm sure we will all . . .'

Atago did not bother listening to the routine platitudes from the elder secretary. When she heard her name, she stood.

She was an imposing figure even among a group of beings not easily impressed, and she was well aware of that fact. She was much taller than most Tahn, and she wore her hair in a dark spill almost to her waist. Her eyes were large, her lips generous, and she had a lush body set off perfectly by her tight-fitting uniform.

Only the very stupid were fooled by her sensuous looks. Lady Atago's sole passion was war.

'My lords, my ladies,' she said. 'You will have my full report before you shortly, so I won't bore you with a lengthy summary of its contents. You can review the facts later at your leisure. Here, in brief, is where we find ourselves:

'From the beginning, we have managed to always take the war to the enemy. We have won vast areas from the Empire.

'There are two key reasons for our success. First: We are always willing to risk all. Second: The very size of the Emperor's military machine has worked to our advantage. By the time his forces react, it has been too late. This is an advantage we are about to lose.'

That got Lady Atago the full attention of the council.

'Here are the basic reasons,' she went on. 'One: At this moment in time, each success brings an equal burden. Our supply lines are stretched well beyond any safety factor. We are wasting valuable resources garrisoning new territories. Two: The Emperor's intensive efforts to shift from a peacetime to a wartime industrial economy are about to bear fruit. Soon we will not only be outgunned but outmaneuvered because of the sheer size and number of his fleets.'

She paused to let that sink in. Then it was time to spell out the plan.

'Before this can happen, we need to find a place to sink our knife. Lord Fehrle and I are confident we have found it.'

Atago palmed a switch, and the far wall shimmered into a vidscreen. The council members leaned forward when they saw the starmaps. They were looking at two systems in relative proximity. There was nothing that unusual about them – except that they were deep inside the Empire.

The first system, Lady Atago explained, was called Al-Sufi, a major depot for Anti-Matter Two, the fuel that powered the Empire – and the Tahn. It was not necessary for Atago to explain that the Eternal Emperor's control of all AM2 made him the ultimate ruler.

'Obviously, Al-Sufi is a prime target,' she said. 'For some time now, we have been building up our forces in that area. And if we captured it, the setback to the Emperor would probably be fatal.'

'Isn't that also obvious to the Emperor?' Pastour asked.

'We hope so,' Lady Atago said. 'Because the build-up I spoke of is only on paper. It is a shadow build-up. A fake.'

'I don't understand,' Wichman said.

'Without arousing suspicion, we have allowed the Imperial Forces to believe that we intend to attack Al-Sufi. And we have confirmed reports that the Emperor is responding with an equal build-up at Al-Sufi. Now, let me show you our *real* target!'

They saw a tight view of the second system, Durer. It was also a well-known area, as important to industry and transport as Al-Sufi was to the handling and storage of AM2.

'As you can see, the build-up at Al-Sufi has left Durer exposed. It is ours for the taking.'

It was not necessary to explain to the others what that would do. A warrior race could instantly see when the enemy had been outflanked.

From Durer the Tahn High Council could see the beating red heart of the Empire. All they had to do was give Lady Atago permission to use her dirk.

The vote was unanimous.

Chapter Six

General Ian Mahoney hobbled down the long paneled corridor, gritting his teeth in pain as he tried to keep up with the two Gurkhas who were escorting him to the quarters of the Eternal Emperor. He imagined he could feel the plas and metal brackets grating against the bones they were supposed to support.

A door hissed open, and someone rushed out, almost colliding with Mahoney. He cursed at his clumsiness as he nearly fell. Ian, he told himself, you have the gait of a three-legged horse at a steeplechase. Mahoney recovered and moved on. He was deep in the bowels of Arundel Castle, or what was left of it, anyway. Aboveground what had once been an oversize replica of a graceful Earth castle was blackened ruins – victim of a surprise nuclear attack by the Tahn. Even now, there were still pockets of intense radiation.

The Tahn had hoped to wipe out the Emperor with one daring attack on Prime World. They could not know that the castle was an elaborate facade for the bombproof Imperial nerve center many kilometers beneath the surface. The Emperor ground their failure in many times a day. Every news broadcast emanating from Arundel began and ended with a shot of the ruins. Two flags fluttered bravely overhead. One was the shining standard of the Empire. Beneath it was the Emperor's household banner: gold, with the letters 'AM2' superimposed over the null element's atomic structure. Mahoney could almost imagine the Emperor's chuckle over that far from subtle bit of propaganda.

He had mixed feelings about seeing his old boss and, he guessed, friend. Careful, Mahoney, he warned himself. Being a friend of the Eternal Emperor was a decidedly mixed blessing. It was friendship, more than duty, that had led him to his present rotten state of being.

The Tahn's final assault on Cavite had left him shattered and nearly dead. He had no idea how he had survived, although he expected it had something to do with his protégé, young Sten. Mahoney had come to woozy consciousness many months later and immediately had had second thoughts about the highly over-rated business of living. Over the next few years he went under the surgeons' laser scalpel more times than any being ought to have to remember. He supposed they had performed what any casual observer would have called a major medical miracle, piecing him back together to a semi-whole.

Despite their efforts, Mahoney felt many more years than his middle age. What was hardest to get used to was not the nagging pain. It was his face. One side displayed what he had once believed to be the dignified gullies and edges of a long and interesting life. The other was baby-bottom smooth. The doctors had assured him that the plasflesh was programmed to gradually match the elder side. Mahoney did not believe them – although he had to admit that four months ago his jaw had not worked, either. Now it did, after a painful fashion.

Mahoney did not have the faintest idea why the Emperor had requested his presence. He suspected they were still friends enough that the Emperor might want to personally break the news to him that he was getting the old heave-ho into early retirement. What the clot, half pension for a two-star general was not bad. Besides, he could always get another job, couldn't he?

Give it a rest, Ian. Killing people is not considered one of the more desirable skills in private industry.

He came back to reality when the Gurkhas stopped in front of an unmarked door. They motioned for him to place his thumb against the security beam. It beeped satisfaction, and the door hummed open.

Mahoney stepped into the Emperor's suite. There was no one there to greet him, just gray walls and Spartan furniture. Mahoney figured his first guess had been right. He was for the old heave-ho.

Then another door opened, and Mahoney was suddenly over-whelmed by kitchen smells and kitchen heat. It was like being inside an immense Irish meat pie. And there was the muscular figure of the Eternal Emperor standing in the doorway. He looked Mahoney up and down as if measuring him for the pie. Old soldier's habit tried to pull Mahoney's creaking bones to attention. Then the Emperor smiled.

'Mahoney,' he said. 'You look like a man who could use a stiff Scotch.'

'I tell you, Mahoney, this Tahn business has given me a whole new outlook on life. When I finally get them out of my hair, things are going to be different. I don't know if you know it or not, but the job of Eternal Emperor is not all it's cracked up to be.'

Mahoney grinned a crooked grin. 'Uneasy lies the head, and all that,' he said.

The Emperor looked up from his chopping board. 'Do I detect a note of cynicism?' he asked. 'Careful, Mahoney. I have the power of Scotch.'

'Beg your pardon, boss. My most grievous error.'

They were in the Eternal Emperor's kitchen, which looked like a ship's wardroom mess area. The Emperor was not happy about that, preferring his old kitchen with its mixture of antique cooking gear and redesigned modern equipment. But this, he had told Mahoney, was adequate for his current needs. Besides, he had not had much time lately to fool around with cooking.

Mahoney was sitting at a stainless-steel table, a double shot glass in his hand. The Emperor was on the other side, preparing a dinner that he had promised Mahoney was perfectly suited to a war motif.

He called it 'nuked hen.' Between them was a quart of the home-distilled spirits that the Emperor thought might be pretty close to Scotch. The Emperor topped their glasses up and took a sip before going back to his task. As he worked, he talked, shifting back and forth between subjects with a logic unique to him.

'I don't remember the real name of this dish,' he said. 'It was part of a whole phony Louisiana cooking fad that went back even before my time.'

Mahoney guessed that Louisiana was a province on ancient Earth.

'Apparently some people thought food wasn't food unless you burned the clot out of it. It didn't make sense to me, but I've learned over the years not to be too quick about judging folk beliefs. So I tried a few things.'

'And it was all delicious, right?' Mahoney asked.

'No. It was all terrible,' the Emperor said. 'First, I thought it was me. I burned everything. My granddad would have killed me if he had seen all the food I wasted. Finally, I worked out a few ground rules. You just can't go around burning *anything*.'

'Like potatoes,' Mahoney said. 'A man wouldn't want to burn a potato.'

The Eternal Emperor gave Mahoney a strange look. 'Who was talking about potatoes?'

Mahoney just shook his head. He lifted his glass and worked the edge between his lips. He tilted his head back and drank it down. He was beginning to feel a lot better. He refilled his glass.

'I was just being silly,' he said.

The Emperor grew silent for a few minutes, going on automatic. Using his fingers and the hollow of his palm as measuring spoons, he dumped the following ingredients into a bowl: a pinch of fresh cayenne; two fingers of ground salt, ground pepper; a palm of dried sage, and finely diced horse-radish. He moved the bowl over to his big black range. Already sitting beside it was a bottle of vodka, fresh-squeezed lime juice, a half cup of capers, and a tub of butter.

The Emperor took a fat Cornish game hen out of a cold box and placed it on the metal table. He found a slim-bladed boning knife, tested the edge, and then nodded in satisfaction. He turned the hen over, back side up, and started his first cut alongisde the spine. He paused for a second, then laid the knife down.

'Let me run something down to you, Mahoney,' he said. 'See if it comes out to you the same way it does to me.'

Mahoney leaned forward, interested. Maybe he would finally learn why he was really there.

'You familiar with the Al-Sufi System?'

Mahoney nodded. 'Big AM2 depot, among other things,' he said. 'We've got, what, maybe one-third of all our AM2 stored there?'

'That's the place,' the Emperor said. 'And lately I've been getting reports of a big Tahn build-up in that area. Not all at once. But a real gradual shifting of fleets from one sector to another. We're also picking up a lot of radio chatter from supply ships.'

Mahoney nodded in professional sympathy. 'Those buggers are all alike,' he said. 'Tahn or Imperial. Can't follow even the simplest rules of security.' He worked on his drink, thinking. 'So, what's the problem? If we *know* they're going to hit us, then we've got the fight half-won before the first shot is even fired.'

'That's so,' the Emperor said. Then he picked up his knife again, leaving the whole subject hanging. 'You might want to watch this,

Ian,' he said. 'Boning a hen is easy when you know how, but you can chop the clot out of it and yourself if you don't.'

Very carefully, the Emperor cut on either side of the spine. He pushed a finger through the slit and pulled the bone up through the carcass. Next, he laid the hen flat, placed a hand on either side of spine, and crunched down with his weight.

'See what I mean?' he said as he lifted the breastbone out.

'I'm impressed,' Mahoney said. 'But never mind that. I've got the idea *you* aren't too impressed with this intelligence you've been getting on the Tahn.'

The Emperor moved over to his range and fired up a burner.

'You guessed right,' he said. 'But I don't blame my intelligence people. I think the Tahn have something entirely different in mind for us.'

'Such as?'

'Al-Sufi has a neighbor. Durer.'

'I've heard of it, vaguely.'

'You put a dog's leg on Al-Sufi,' the Emperor said, 'and you'll find Durer on a bearing just about at the dog's big toe.'

Mahoney remembered and grunted in surprise. 'Why, that's only . . .'

'If you stood on Durer,' the Emperor said, 'you could just about reach here with a good healthy spit.'

That would have been one mighty spit, but Mahoney basically agreed.

'Assuming you're right,' Mahoney said, 'and the Tahn are trying to make us respond to shadows, then if they took Durer, we could kiss any forces we have at Al-Sufi a fond but regretful farewell. To say nothing of the fact that we'd have zed between us and the Tahn.'

'Interesting, isn't it?'

'What do you plan to do about it?'

'First, I'm going to burn the clot out of this hen,' the Emperor said, turning to his range. 'The whole trick is getting your pan hot enough.'

Mahoney leaned closer to watch, figuring that what was on the menu had everything to do with the Emperor's plans for the Tahn.

The Emperor turned the flame up as high as it would go and then slammed on a heavy cast-iron pan. In a few moments, the pan began to smoke, and fans in the duct above the range whirred on. A few moments more, and the pan stopped smoking.

'Check the air just above the fan,' the Emperor said. 'It's getting wavery, right?'

'Right.'

'As the pan gets hotter, the air will wave faster and faster until the whole interior is a steady haze.'

The haze came right on schedule.

'So it's ready now?' Mahoney asked.

'Almost. But not quite. This is the place most people foul up. In a minute or two, the haze will clear and the bottom of the pan should look like white ash.'

As soon as the ashen look appeared, the Emperor motioned for Mahoney to duck back. Then he dipped out a big chunk of butter, dumped it into the pan, and moved out of the way. Mahoney could see why as flames flashed above the pan. As soon as they died down, the Emperor moved swiftly forward and poured the spices out of the bowl and into the pan. He gave the mixture a few stirs in one direction, then the other. Next he tossed in the Cornish game hen. A column of smoke steamed upward in a roar.

'I give it about five minutes each side,' the Emperor said. 'Then I spread capers all over it and toss the hen into the oven for twenty minutes or so to finish it off.'

'I sort of get the idea,' Mahoney said, 'that you're in the process of heating up a pan for the Tahn.'

The Emperor thought that was pretty funny. He chuckled to himself as he dumped the thoroughly blackened hen into a baking dish. On went the capers, and into the oven it went – at 350 degrees. He cranked the flames down on the range, shoved the pan of drippings back on the fire, and stirred in two Imperial glugs of vodka and a quarter glug of lime juice. He would use the mixture to glaze the hen when it came out of the oven.

'You're right,' the Emperor finally said. 'I've been playing the same game with them. On paper I've been moving forces from all over the map to the Al-Sufi region.'

'But actually, they'll be waiting for the Tahn at Durer,' Mahoney said.

'That's the plan,' the Emperor said.

Mahoney was silent for a moment.

'Question, boss. What if there really is a Tahn build-up at Al-Sufi? What if we're wrong?'

The Emperor busied himself with some spears of asparagus. He planned to steam them in a little thyme butter and dry white wine.

'I've been wrong before,' he said.

'But can you afford to be wrong this time?'

'No,' the Eternal Emperor said, 'I can't. That's why you're here.'

He fished into his pocket and handed over a small black jewelry case. Mahoney opened it. Inside were two rank tabs – the rank tabs of a fleet marshal.

'When the attack comes,' the Emperor said, 'I want you leading my fleets.'

Mahoney just stared at the stars resting on velvet. He could not help but remember the last time he had gotten his orders straight from the Emperor. Those had been the orders that had led him to Cavite.

'Will you do it for me?' the Emperor pressed.

Fleet Marshal Ian Mahoney had difficulty finding his voice. He assumed command of the fleets at Durer with a simple nod.

Chapter Seven

The huge Tahn prison transport ship hissed down onto Heath, the capital world of the Tahn systems. After proper security was set, ports whined open and the prisoners debarked.

Sten and Alex marveled as they clanked down a gangway wearing heavy, archaic, and useless leg and arm irons, with weighted plas chains between them. They had expected to be unloaded onto the Tahn mining deathworld. Instead—

'W' been here before,' Alex whispered, using that motionless mouth and jaw whisper that all professional prisoners learn.

'Yeah.'

Lord Pastour's dictate might have come from the all-highest, but the Tahn bureaucrats still found a way to take their half kilo of flesh. A single Tahn transport was dispatched to all the prison worlds to pick up those incorrigible war prisoners who were to be purged into the new prison. It was a slow, filthy transport.

Therefore, when the transport unloaded, the best and the sneakiest did not appear such as they clanked out, smelling like drakh, unbathed, uncombed, surly, and snarling.

The only measure of respect they had, although none of the prisoners realized it, was that armed Tahn soldiers flanked their passage through the streets of Heath at five-meter intervals. Those guards were the combat element of an entire Tahn assault division whose deployment to a combat zone had been delayed by three weeks merely so that a motley 1,000 scruffy men, women, and beings could be led to their new prison.

Sten clanked forward, head down, hands down, shuffling as the chains clanked – the perfect picture of a properly programmed prisoner. But his eyes flicked from side to side, observing as subtly as Alex's commentary had been delivered.

'Clottin' Heath,' he whispered.

'Na,' Alex whispered back. 'Th' last time we bein't on this world thae were gladdins an' parties.'

'Try war, you clot.'

And Alex observed the city with new eyes.

The last – and only – time they had been on Heath had been under cover, with instructions to find a murderer and extract him. But that had been years before, and just as Sten had suggested, war had ground Heath into grayness.

There were few vehicles to be seen – fuel was restricted to necessary military movements. The streets were deserted. Shops were boarded up or, worse, had few items in their windows. The rare Tahn civilian they saw either disappeared quickly from the streets or, seeing the soldiery, raised one ragged, whining cheer into the cold air and then scurried on about his or her business.

Their route led them through narrow streets, the streets climbing upward.

Sten's psywar mind analyzed: If you have the worst enemy scum in your hands, would you not arrange a triumphal parade? With all your citizens spitting and cheering because we have the barbarians in our hands? With full livie coverage? Of course you would. Why haven't the Tahn done that?

Exploratory thinking: They don't think like I do. Possible. They can't muster the citizens on call. Wrong – any totalitarian state can do that. Maybe they don't want to show how badly the war is hurting them if they are presenting Heath as being the proud center of their culture and don't want off-worlders to see the reality. Most interesting, and worth considering—

Sten's analysis was cut off as the column of prisoners was shouted to a halt and screaming Tahn soldiers ordered them to attention. Sten expected to see a float of combat cars move across the street in front of him. Instead, there was one cloaked officer, with flanking guards on foot, riding some kind of animal transport.

'What's that?'

'Clottin' hell,' Alex whispered. 'A bleedin' horse.'

'Horse?'

'Aye. A Earth critter, w' nae th' brains ae a Campbell, tha' bites you an' is best used ae pet chow.'

Sten was about to inquire further, but the officer in charge of the column ordered them forward again, and for the first time he looked up the cobbled narrow street.

His guts clamped shut.

At the top of the rise was a huge stone building. It sat atop the hill like a great gray monster, its towering walls reaching upward, capped by a ruined octagonal pinnacle that still reached some 200 meters toward the overcast sky.

Alex, too, was staring.

'Lad,' he managed. 'Ah dinnae think't th' Tahn are takin' us to church. Tha' be't our new home!'

Chapter Eight

Koldyeze Cathedral had not been constructed by the Tahn. Their only religion was a vague sort of belief, unworshiped, in racial identity and racial destiny.

Koldyeze had been the Vatican for the first settlers on Heath, monotheistic, agrarian communards. They had spent nearly two centuries building their church atop the highest hill in their tiny capital.

Those settlers stood less than no chance when the first Tahn, then more roving barbarians than the self-declared culture they later became, smashed down on them. They were forcibly absorbed by the Tahn, their language forbidden to be spoken, written, or taught, their dress ridiculed, and their religion driven underground and finally out of existence.

The Tahn might not have been religious, but they were superstitious. No one quite knew what to do with the looming cathedral, and so it was surrounded with barbed fencing and posted for hundreds of years. Seventy-five years before, an out-of-control tacship had smashed off the spire's crown, and storms had battered the ruins.

But Koldyeze Cathedral was still a mighty work of man.

It was cruciform in design, stretching along its longer axis nearly two kilometers and along the shorter axis one kilometer. The center of the cross was the sanctuary and, above it, the remains of the bell tower. The shorter arms of the cross were roofed, but the longer arms held courtyards in their centers.

Koldyeze had been built as a self-sufficient religious community, even though the churchmen were not at all withdrawn from their society. When the Tahn had ordered Koldyeze abandoned, the pacifistic communards had systematically closed it down, sealing passageways and chambers as they went.

To the Tahn, Koldyeze seemed ideally suited to become a prison. Activating it required no drain on scarce building materials. The power drain from Heath's grid should be minimal. The assigned prisoners would provide the work crews to make the complex livable.

The northernmost short arm, where the main entrance to Koldyeze had been located, was sealed off from the other wings, and the chambers around its courtyard were set up as guard and administration quarters. The passage from the guard courtyard into the center sanctuary was set with detectors and triple gates.

Four rows of fencing with mines and detectors between each row surrounded Koldyeze.

Then, even though the security precautions were not complete, Koldyeze was ready for prisoners. The outer perimeter, after all, was sealed – and none of the Imperials could fly. Further anti-escape measures would be added as time went by.

The Tahn believed that Koldyeze was escape-proof.

The Imperial prisoners straggling through the thick stone and steel gates looked about them and believed that somehow, somewhere, a clever being could manage to find freedom.

And there was no reason at all why it could not be one of them.

Chapter Nine

Inside the courtyard, the Imperial prisoners were shouted and pummeled into a formation. Most interesting, Sten thought, as he analyzed the guards.

They looked much as he had expected and experienced in his previous camp: overmuscled bullyboys, semi-crippled ex-combatants, and soldiers too old or too young to be assigned to the front.

Their obscenities and threats were also the same.

But none of them carried whips. They were armed with truncheons or stun rods – which seemed mere pattypaw weapons to the thoroughly brutalized prisoners. No projectile weapons were being waved about. And no one had been slammed to the ground with a rifle butt, which was the standard Tahn request for attention.

The main shouter wore the rank tabs of a police major. He was a hulk of a man whose broad leather belt was losing its battle with his paunch. As he roared orders, one hand kept creeping toward his holstered pistol, then was forced away. The man's face was amazingly scarred.

'Tha' be't ae screw,' Alex whispered, lips motionless, 'thae hae plac'd second in a wee brawl wi' ae bear.'

Eventually the formation looked adequate, and Colonel Virunga limped to his place at its front. That had been one of the few cheery notes of the long crawl through space on the prison ship: Virunga was senior Imperial officer and would therefore be in command of the prisoners in the new camp.

Virunga eyed his command and started to bring them to attention. Then he caught himself.

Standing ostentatiously away from the prisoners was a single defiant being. He – she? it? – was about a meter and a half in height and squatted on his thick lower legs as if early in his race's evolution there had been a tail provided for tripodal security. His upper arms were almost as large as his lower legs, ending in enormous bone-appearing gauntlets and incongruously slender fingers.

The being had no neck, its shoulders flowing into a tapering skull that ended in a dozen pink tendrils that Virunga guessed were its sensory organs. The being had once been fat, with sleek fur. Now its ragged pelt draped down in toga-like folds over its body.

Colonel Virunga had been denied access to the prisoners' records aboard ship, and of course there had not been time to meet every one of the purged prisoners. But he wondered how he had missed that one.

'Form up, troop.'

'I am not a troop, and I shall not form up,' the being squeaked. 'I am Lay Reader Cristata, I am a civilian, I endorse neither the Empire nor the Tahn, and I am being unjustly held and forced to be a part of this machinery of death.'

Virunga goggled. Did Cristata think that any of them had volunteered to be POWs? Even more wonderment: How had that paragon of resistance managed to survive in a prison camp so long?

The police major trumpeted incoherently, and two guards leapt toward Cristata, batons ready. But before they could pummel him to the ground, a large man wearing the tatters of an infantryman's combat coveralls grabbed Cristata by his harness and dragged him bodily into the formation. Evidently the use of force satisfied Cristata's objections, because he then remained meekly where planted.

'Formation . . . ten-hut.'

Virunga about-faced, leaned on his cane, and stared up at a balcony on the third level. He could see two faces looking down at him from behind the barred, clear plas doors.

He waited for the prisoners' new lords and masters to make their appearance.

Chapter Ten

Police Colonel Derzhin was, in his own mind, despite his rank, neither a cop nor a military officer. Many years before, long before the war with the Empire, he had been a junior lieutenant in the Tahn ranks, assigned to a survey ship. Somehow one of the emergency oxygen containers on the ship's bridge had exploded, killing all four of the ranking officers and, worse, destroying the ship's navcomputer. Derzhin, the sole surviving officer, had taken command and managed – mostly by luck, he thought – to limp to an inhabited world.

The Tahn livies must have been hurting for a hero that week, because they made much of the lieutenant. Derzhin received a couple of hero medals and a promotion, but that did not aim him toward a career in the military. A year later, after the publicity had been forgotten, Derzhin quietly bought his way out of the service. His medals got him a lower-management job in one of Pastour's corporations.

Derzhin was promoted rapidly as he showed a rare talent for the proper utilization of personnel and available resources. Pastour once said that Derzhin could be put on an asteroid with six anthropoids and two hammers and, within a year, would have a prototype ship in the sky and three variant models on the production line.

Derzhin maintained his commission in the inactive reserve for the social clout it gave him in the business community. He was not, of course, anti-military. He *was* a Tahn. He never questioned his race's moral rectitude or the rightness of the war.

But he would rather not have been brought back into the military by the general call-up at its beginning. Nor was Pastour happy to lose his talents.

When Pastour realized that a very valuable, highly trained resource – the Imperial prisoners – was being wasted through high-principled flummery and saw a proper utilization for that resource, he immediately set out to get Derzhin to run the project.

He recognized that no executive, no matter how qualified, could instantly become a warden, and so he gave Derzhin backup.

His backup was Security Major Avrenti. Avrenti, too, was not a warden – experienced prison administrators were in high demand. Avrenti was one of the Tahn Empire's most skilled counter-sabotage specialists. Anyone who could prevent the planting of a minuscule bomb or the contamination of a war material or who could identify a potential saboteur long before he became active should have had no trouble keeping known malcontents imprisoned within a known and heavily guarded area.

Avrenti was physically unremarkable. Anyone who met him casually would forget his face minutes after his departure. He would have made an excellent spy. He was soft-spoken and nonargumentative, preferring to win through reason and persistence. His one affectation was his wearing of archaic eyeglasses. When anyone asked why he had never had corrective surgery, implants, or replacements, he professed a dislike for medicos. Actually, he had vision very close to normal. He used his glasses as a stall, giving him time to consider the proper answer or policy, just as other beings used fingering devices, writing instruments, or the careful preparation and consumption of stimulants.

The two men looked down at their charges.

'I imagine,' Derzhin said finally, 'that I am expected to make some kind of speech.'

'That seems to be requisite for a warden,' Avrenti agreed.

Derzhin smiled slightly. 'You know, Major, that part of business requires an ability to speak publicly.'

'One of the many reasons I preferred to remain what I am,' Avrenti said.

'Yes. I have spoken to lords and drunken roustabouts, but I cannot recollect ever having addressed war prisoners.'

Avrenti did not comment.

'Actually,' Derzhin mused, 'it should be quite simple. All I need to do is suggest that they are here to work for the greater glory of the Tahn. If they perform, they shall be rewarded with seeing the next sunrise. If they resist, or attempt to escape . . . even an Imperial should see the logic in that.'

Again Avrenti was silent.

'Do you agree, Major? Is that the correct approach? You are more familiar with military thinking than I.'

'I can be of little assistance,' the major said. 'I do not understand the mind of a soldier who can find himself in the hands of the enemy and not seek self-extinction at the first opportunity.'

Derzhin kept his expression and tone of voice quite neutral. 'There is that, of course.'

And he opened the balcony doors and stepped out.

Police Major Genrikh slammed back into his quarters, wanting to feel out of control.

He held the solid wood door ready to crash closed – then caught himself. He pushed it shut softly. Then he tore off his Sam Browne belt, intending to hurl it. Again he stopped.

He had just witnessed a nightmare.

But should he give in to it? What was the likelihood that his quarters were not bugged? None. Genrikh would have bugged himself.

Instead, he carefully hung his harness over a chair, opened a cabinet, extracted a bottle, checked the bottle to see whether its level had been marked, drank deeply, and sank back on his bunk.

This was going to be a disaster.

Then he cheered himself. Hadn't he been warned? Hadn't he been told, first by Lord Wichman's cut-out, then when he was duly if privately honored by a presence with the lord himself?

But still.

Genrikh ground his teeth against his bottleneck, producing a singularly unpleasant noise. He had spent half a lifetime as an expert penologist. He knew the way to handle the subbeings that committed crimes. Crime to him was anything that contradicted the Way of the Tahn, which he defined as anything that his current superior ordered.

Genrikh's mother was a whore; his father was a question mark. He had fantasized, growing up, that his father was a rising officer whose forced marriage had made him seek happiness in other quarters. That did not mean that he saw his mother as a fairy princess – but Genrikh's dreams were never very coherent.

Genrikh grew up feeling himself an outcast and fearing that someday he would be revealed for what he was and scorned. He was indeed scorned by his compatriots – scorned for being the first to toady to the newest bully, for being the first to inform on any minor offense, for being the first to volunteer for any superior-suggested idea.

He was the ideal prison official.

Genrikh, in spite of his obsessive concern with others' morals, had no problem acquiring anything and everything he could within the prison system. He was in his own dim-witted way a truly immoral being.

Needless to say, he rose rapidly in the Tahn prison system, so rapidly that he was chosen for greater things. Before the war, the Tahn Council had seen the emergence of unions among their exploited workers and had instantly realized the necessity to destroy anybody that did not represent their own best interests.

Genrikh was a natural choice to head company unions or to act as a strikebreaker or an informer.

But even the embryonic unions within the Tahn systems had eventually put out the word: Anyone matching Genrikh's description was pure trouble – trouble that, if it was convenient, should be deposited in the nearest paddy with many, many puncture wounds.

Genrikh's ultimate controller, Lord Wichman, chose not to discard his thug. Instead, he made him head of his personal bodyguard while trying to find a new place to deploy the man. Wichman knew that Genrikh was absolutely loyal to him. The man was ideal to insert into Pastour's scheme, no matter what it *really* was.

Genrikh, now calm, sipped from his bottle and considered what he would have done had he been appointed commandant of the prison. A good thing to think about. He smiled to himself. Because very, very soon he *would* be the commandant.

Yes.

You are in front of an assemblage of not only criminals but cowards and traitors, he told himself. Genrikh thought that anyone who did not kowtow to the Tahn was a traitor.

All right. You want technicians, he mused. But first you must bring them under control. Yes. Bring them into the courtyard at attention. Then select, at random, 100 of the Imperials – there were a thousand in that courtyard – and have them beaten to death.

No, he corrected himself. Select that 100 and then require the *others* to kill them. Kill them or be killed. Yes. That would produce the correct attitude.

Housing? Food? Nonsense. Let them live in fields and eat roots. Wasn't the clotting Empire rich with people, none of whom would *really* fight until they died? The resource should be exploited like cattle – use them until they drop, because there are many, many possible replacements.

Ah, well. Very soon Colonel Derzhin would learn his error and disappear.

Major Genrikh closed his eyes and began planning just exactly how he would be arranging *his* prison.

Chapter Eleven

After Colonel Derzhin's speech, the prisoners were marched from the guards' courtyard through the shattered sanctuary into their own area, brought to attention, and dismissed. They exploded out into the cathedral, exploring their new home.

For the first time in their long captivity, they were in a prison too large for them. The worst thing about jail to non-institutionalized beings was the complete lack of privacy. There was never a moment to be alone. But now 1,000 malnourished beings, quartered in a complex intended to house 15,000 individuals, scattered to the winds.

Sten and Alex held a conference in the courtyard.

'Mr Kilgour?'

'Aye, Firecontrolman Horrie?'

'Where's the best way to get out of this tomb?'

'Ah hae nae certainty. But Ah'd hazard th' east or west wing, or aught near th' sanctuary. Best luck, th' west wing, bein't near'st th' cliff edge.'

'Right.'

And they started looking for their own quarters in the southernmost, longest arm of the cathedral.

Escapers they were. Experienced escapers. Experienced enough to realize that under no circumstances did they want to have their own living quarters near the center of activities. They had once started a tunnel in their own bunkroom and learned the impossibility of peace and quiet when every twenty minutes bags of dirt, tunnelers, or guards were busting through.

After some searching, they found the place.

'Dinnae tha' be bonnie?' Alex asked happily.

Sten looked around the room. It was perfect. He mentally wrote the 'For Rent' ad:

LARGE ROOM. 20 meters x 15 meters. Room to swing a cat. Bring own cat. Rats provided. Formerly office of moderate-level religious official of probably now-defunct order. Room includes VU, but without intrusive searchlights at night. SECOND STORY, avoiding prospective tunnelers, sports players from floor below, yet also two floors below roof, preventing annoyances from guards on roof, escapers on roof, rats on roof, or rain, considering roof only semipresent. INCLUDES: Remains of four beds, which possibly may be reconstructed into two bunks. Various dangling pieces of plas and metal. Ruins of desk. V/thick walls, not only soundproofed but may contain interesting passageways. POWER: Single bulb from ceiling, apparently wired into circuit. WATER: A close walk to nearby dispersing point. A REAL FIXER-UPPER. *Once visited, never left.*

Yes, Sten thought, and stopped being cute. Now, how the clot are we gonna get out of here? Alex was tapping the walls, checking for bugs. There were obviously none, and there was no way a shotgun mike could be trained on them through the chamber's tiny windows.

'Hae y' a call, Horrie, on our wee head screw?'

'Not yet.'

'Ah. Noo, thae's why Ah be't a' warrant an y' be't a low fire-controlman. Ah ken th' man.'

'I never argued you've got a future career in prisons,' Sten said.

'Ah'm wee, nae slickit nae cowerin't, an Ah can still smash y',' Alex said. 'Close th' yap, an listen: We're goin't t' be treated nice, ae long a' we dot-an'-carry f'r th' man. Now, m' question be: Do we cooperate?'

Kilgour was suddenly serious, and Sten was no longer a fire-controlman named Horatio. And he spoke as a commander and as Alex's CO.

'Yes,' he said. 'The clot is talking about using us in war industry. That's the stupidest idea I've heard lately.'

'We can hae fun wi' that,' Alex agreed.

'And as soon as we can, we're going out.'

'We?'

'I don't know anybody here but you and Virunga. There may be doubles, there may be stoolies, there may be agents.'

'Thae e'en may be Campbells.'

'Don't bet on it. Even the Tahn have some standards.'

'Y' hae ideas on how we'll blow th' place?'

'That's what you're for, Mr Kilgour. That's why you're a warrant and I'm a clottin' firecontrol man.'

Alex grinned, and the two fell back into their roles just as there was a thud on the door that might have been a gorilla knock. It was just about that – and it was also the senior officer, Colonel Virunga. Both men came to attention.

Virunga had little time for preambles.

'Tahn have made it . . . clear . . . cooperate. Drakh. Promise under duress . . . meaningless.'

Sten and Alex did not need to show their agreement.

'Drakh. Drakh.'

Sten's eyebrows lifted. He had never heard the N'ranya repeat a word. He must be quite angry.

'Duty . . . soldier . . . escape. Resist. Am I correct?'

A repeat – and a full sentence!

'Yessir.'

'Knew . . . agree. Why you're now Big X.'

Alex started to say something, and Sten waved him to silence.

'Colonel. You can't do this to me!'

'Just did.'

'Goddammit. Why?'

The chain of command in any prison was complex and often unspoken, even in a military prisoner-of-war camp. Big X was part of that secret command link. The title was eons old, dating back to a time even before the Empire. Big X was the head of *all* escape attempts in a camp. His authority was absolute. Part of the hypno-training that all recruits into Imperial service received was 'how to behave if you are captured.' That conditioning included the obvious: Reveal nothing of military value until physically or mentally forced; do not volunteer services unless ordered; remember that although you are a prisoner you are still at war and are expected to continue to fight by any means available.

Continue to fight.

Escape.

Big X's orders, within the very narrow confines of escape attempts, superseded all others, including those of the senior Imperial officer. And once he was appointed, his authority was absolute. Big X, the head of the escape committee in any camp, could be any rank, private to fleet marshal. It was a dubious honor. If Big X was revealed to the captors, of course he would be skedded for immediate death, brainburn, or, at the very least, transport to a deathcamp.

That was not Sten's objection.

The real objection was that Big X was normally picked because he or she was the most accomplished escaper or resister in a camp. But because all escape attempts had to be registered with his committee, he or she was honor-bound *not* to personally participate in any escape.

Colonel Virunga, by appointing Sten, had also ensured that he was doomed to be a POW until the end of the war. Or until the Tahn discovered the identity of Big X and had him killed.

Virunga answered Sten's question. 'Because . . . trust. Known quantity. These others? Unknown.'

There was no possible argument. Virunga saluted once more and left. Sten and Alex looked at each other. Neither of them could find any obscenities sufficient to the occasion, and neither of them felt that tears would be appreciated.

Very well, Sten thought. If I can't be a personal pain in the butt to the Tahn, I'm going to create me 999 surrogates that'll give the Tahn a rough way to go.

Nine hundred and ninety-eight, he corrected himself, looking at Alex. If I'm gonna be stuck here in this clottin' ruin for the rest of the war, I'm gonna have at least one other clot for company.

Chapter Twelve

Senior Captain (Intelligence) Lo Prek stared at the battered mail fiche on his desk.

A normal human being might have cheered, exulted at closing on his enemy, or snarled in happy rage.

But to Prek, the mail fiche merely verified what he had known: Commander Sten was not only still alive but within Prek's reach.

He had come up with a unique method to check his theory, a method that did not require either approval from his superiors or any out-of-the-ordinary efforts from Intelligence. He had merely prepared a letter.

The letter was packeted in a routine drop to one of the Tahn deep-cover agents within the Empire. The agent was instructed to deposit the letter normally and use a return address of one of his safe houses.

The agent followed orders.

The letter purported to be from one Mik Davis. It was quite a chatty missive.

Davis, according to the letter, had gone through basic training with Sten. 'Of course you don't remember me,' the letter began.

I got washed real quick and never got to the Guards. Instead they made me a baker. Guess, probably, they were right.

Anyway, nothing much happened to me. I served my term, making dough, and got out before the war started.

Got married – got three ankle-biters now – and started my own business. Guess what it is – prog you do – a bakery.

Compute you're laughing – but I'm making a credit or six. Guess I can't kick on what bennies I got from the service.

Anyway, here I am out in nowhere and I saw this old fiche, talking about some captain named Sten who's up there running the Imperial bodyguards. I always knew you were gonna rise to the top like yeast.

I told my lady, and she thought I was blowing smoke when I said I knew you back when. I decided I'd drop a line, and maybe you'd have time to get back to me.

Do me a real favor, if you would. Just scribble out a mini-note so my lady doesn't think I'm a complete liar.

No way I can do paybacks, unless you show up on Ulthor-13, and we'll take you out for the best feed this planet's got. But I'd really appreciate it.

> Yours from a long time back,
> Mik Davis

That letter put Prek in a no-lose situation. If the letter was answered, he knew that Sten was still in the ranks of the Empire. If it went unanswered, he knew the same. It would have been delivered at least. Prek had a far greater faith in the Empire's mail system than did any of its citizens.

Instead, the mail fiche bounced, being returned to the Tahn agent in a packet with a very somber, very official, and very formal note.

Dear <u>Citizen</u> Davis

Unfortunately your <u>personal letter</u> to <u>Commander Sten</u> is undeliverable.

Imperial records show that <u>Commander Sten</u> is carried on <u>Imperial Navy</u> records as <u>Missing in Action</u>, during <u>Engagements in the Fringe Worlds</u>.

If you desire any further information, please communicate with . . .

Sympathetically . . .

Captain Prek felt that he had begun his self-assigned mission in an adequate manner.

Sten was not only alive but within reach.

A prisoner.

Prek refused to admit that Sten could have died of wounds or been killed in captivity. He was still alive.

He *must* still be alive.

Prek keyed his computer to begin a directory search for the records of all Imperial prisoners of war captured in the conquest of the Fringe Worlds. He felt he was getting very close to the murderer of his brother.

BOOK TWO

SUKI

Chapter Thirteen

The first escape attempt was go-for-broke.

Captain Michele St. Clair had watched closely for two weeks as the first working parties were formed, assigned tasks, and marched down into Heath. She thought she saw a possibility.

The procedure was rigid: After morning roll call, Major Genrikh would order X number of prisoners for Y number of outside duties. They would be broken down into gangs inside the prisoners' courtyard, and Tahn guards would take charge. Each detail would have, on the average, one noncom per ten prisoners and three guards per five POWs. The Tahn were being very careful.

The ethics of the work gangs were still being debated by the prisoners, a debate, that St. Clair took no part in. The debate ran as follows: Participation, even unwillingly, contributed to the enemy. Nonparticipation, on the other hand, could contribute to the prisoner's own death. St. Clair thought both points nonsense – she knew that the eventual boredom of being in the prison would make people volunteer for any detail that was not actually pulling a trigger. And personally she was all in favor of the outside gangs. Once outside the cathedral, the possibilities of successful escape would be . . . she did not try to work out the exact odds, but she did not have to.

Michele St. Clair had grown up with an instinctive appreciation for the odds and was quite content with the comfortable, if somewhat hazardous, living a 'gambler's share' gave her.

St. Clair, very young, had considered the various careers available on her native world, one of the Empire's main trans-shipment centers. Whoring or crewing on a spacecraft she saw as a mug's game, and running a bar kept one from being a moving target. St.

Clair had been a professional gambler from the time she was tall enough to shove a bet across to a croupier.

She learned how to play a straight game against the suckers and how to shave the odds if she was playing with cheaters. She knew when to get her money down, when to cut her losses, when to fold a bet and get offworld, and, maybe most importantly, when to stay out of the game itself. She was broke many times and rich many more. But the credits themselves were meaningless to her, as to other professionals. They were just markers on how well she was doing.

She had a hundred names on a thousand worlds, and nicknames, as well. All of them related her to the same sort of animal – a sleek, good-looking minor predator.

But for some years the odds had been coming back on her.

Since she preferred to gamble with the wealthy, she maintained a host of identities, all of them well-to-do if a little mysterious. She was very fond of one of them – that of a purchasing agent for the Imperial Navy. Since she had a certain respect for the laws of the Empire, she actually was an officer in the Empire. Standby reserve, of course.

Unfortunately, St. Clair paid no attention to politics. When war broke out, she was systematically cleaning out an upper-class tourist world in her military role, a tourist world with a medium-size garrison on it. St. Clair grudgingly admitted that she might have done too good a job setting up her various identities as unblowable, because no one would believe that she was not actually a first lieutenant, Imperial Navy. Her cover was so well constructed that three months later she was promoted to captain and reassigned as executive officer on a transport.

The convoy her ship was part of was ambushed by a Tahn deep-strike destroyer force, and Michele St. Clair found herself a prisoner of war.

Fortunately, St. Clair was, like all gamblers, an inveterate optimist. In the first prison camp she started running the odds again. What were the odds of surviving as a POW? She saw a gravsled carrying away bodies, shuddered, and estimated ninety-ten – against.

What were the odds of improving her lot by collaborating? Two other calculations were required: Could the Tahn win the war? Sixty-two-thirty-eight – against. The Empire: sixty-forty – in favor. Now, collaboration: seventy-three-twenty-seven – against.

Option: Escape.

St. Clair did not run odds on the likelihood of her getting free.

That would have meant factoring in the failed escape attempts of others, and she knew damned well that she was superior to any of those other clots. Proof: They were soldiers or sailors, and she was not.

Michele St. Clair found a new career. And a new nickname – the Lucky Eel. She had made more than twenty attempts to escape, almost all of them solo. And while she had never succeeded in being free longer than four days, she also had never been executed. Somehow the commandant was feeling kindly, she had a convincing excuse for not being where she should have been, or she managed to get away from the chaos before the sorting out started.

Captain St. Clair was ready for her twenty-first attempt.

Observing the work details, she had noticed an absolute consistency to their actions. Buried in the middle of a thirty-man work gang, she hummed happily to herself, watching that routine play out once more.

Shuffle . . . shuffle . . . then wait as each work gang was singly processed through each of the three gates in the center sanctuary, being swept and counted at each gate. Then each detail moved across the guards' courtyard to the outer gate and waited until that gate came open.

Her gang started through the process. As they were herded across the inner courtyard, St. Clair worked her way to the outside of the knot of prisoners.

The outer gate was opened, and the gang went through. It was time.

St. Clair had noticed that as each gang exited the cathedral, the Tahn guards would turn, come to attention, and salute the colors hanging on either side of the Koldyeze's entrance.

Five seconds of inattention.

More than enough.

As the guards saluted, St. Clair elbowed a prisoner aside and darted for the edge of the path that wound downward toward the city. Six to three, she had thought, they won't see me. Five to two there'll be an incline I can scramble down. Eight to one, even if it's a cliff I can spot a ledge or something I can drop to and get out of the line of fire.

One meter short of the edge, St. Clair realized that she had made another sucker bet and slid to a stop.

The edge of the path dropped straight down for more than 100 meters. All the outcroppings she could see were obviously rotten. St. Clair had no interest in ostentatious suicide.

There were shouts behind her, and a projectile *snap*-CRACK-d past her head. St. Clair put her hands straight up, turned around, and looked at the guards hurtling toward her.

'And sixteen to three I'll never learn how to fly,' she managed before a rifle butt drove into her stomach and sent her down.

Sweat beading on his forehead, Alex fiddled at the lock, trying for what seemed the hundredth time to coax the strange-looking eyehook key his people had fashioned over the little nipple of metal he could feel inside. He had already turned three wheel gears, and according to theory he had just one more to go.

The key slipped, and it was all Alex could do to bury an almighty great shout of 'Clot!' Instead, he wiped the sweat sting out of his eyes, bent his creaking spine, and eased the key back inside.

Behind him, his two companions chatted on, presumably critiquing Alex's efforts. He did not know that for sure, because the entire conversation was taking place in silence.

'Patience, lads,' Alex said, although he had not heard anyone complaining. 'Ah'm a wee tickle away.'

'Not to worry,' the big blond man said aloud. 'Kraulshavn and I aren't the hurrying kind.'

Kraulshavn looked up at his largish friend, Sorensen, waiting for a translation. Sorensen's fingers signed swiftly, and Kraulshavn nodded his head in vigorous agreement. Alex shifted his attention momentarily from the lock to Kraulshavn. There was more finger wagging.

'Whae's he sayin'?'

'That if you are even close to being correct about the contents of the room, the wait will be well worth it.'

Alex grunted his answer and tickled on with his eyehook key.

Kraulshavn and Sorensen were hands down the strangest pair that Alex and Sten had thus far roped into their growing organization.

Sorensen was the epitome of a corn-fed farm boy, with slabs of muscle, pale skin that flushed at the least effort, and a grammar-book way of speaking. He also did not appear to be blessed with a great deal of native brightness. But Alex knew from his days in Mantis how strange a breed Sorensen was. Beings like him had made up a valuable part of several Mantis teams Alex and Sten had been on. They were living battle computers. Their innocent looks and surface slowness concerning immediate things about them hid a massive calculating brain. In fact, Alex strongly suspected that Sorensen *was* a surviving member of a blown Mantis Team or maybe still active on a deep-cover run. There was no sense in asking, because Sorensen would not answer. Even more nagging than that was the fact that if Sorensen was Mantis and Alex knew the being's private code word, they would have themselves the damnedest walking, talking battle computer. Which might help on the odds a bit. He shot Sorensen another sizing-up look.

Like his brothers and sisters, Sorensen knew zip about his fellow beings. His people were perfect marks for any con man or traveling carny. In fact, the Imperial governor-general of their homeworld had been forced to pass strict laws forbidding carnivals, circuses, or anything even vaguely connected with hustle artists. On the other hand, if Sorensen was shown a distance point, he could instantly calculate the range, trajectory, wind speed, and relative gravitational tug that any projectile might encounter on its way to its target.

Those talents made Sorensen a valuable find. Doubling his value was the man's friendship with Kraulshavn.

Alex felt the eyehook catch. Gently he twisted and felt the gear wheel sliding smoothly until it clicked into place with its gearmates. Inside, the gears should have been lined up, exposing the pie-shaped wedge cut into them. Quickly, Alex pulled out the eyehook and inserted a heavy bar key. A few minor fumbles and the gears fell back with a heavy *thunk*. On the other side of the door Alex could hear a counterweight shift, and he stepped back to let the door creak open on its heavy hinges.

Kraulshavn signed what Alex took to be a 'congratulations' at him. A little dip at the end by the being's nimble fingers, however, looked suspiciously like 'dummy.' Alex shot Sorensen a glance. The big man was looking blandly innocent.

'Ah'm sussin' a wee joker frae y'r mate,' Alex said.

'There was not one single joke in anything he said, Mr Kilgour,' Sorensen protested.

He turned to Kraulshavn, spelling out Alex's comments. Kraulshavn's mouth opened in a round merry O. He covered it with a delicate furry hand, hiding his silent giggle. Alex had to grin.

'Na. He's nae a joker. Noo our Kraulshavn. 'Kay. Waggle thae a' th' lad. In yon room thae may be't a wee haunt.'

'Ghosts?' Even Sorensen was incredulous at that. Karulshavn signed back what was a blatant suggestion where Alex could put his 'wee haunt.'

Alex just shrugged. 'Aye. Ye be't doubters. But th' Tahn hae tales thae'll kink y'r curlies.'

With that, he walked inside. Despite their strongly expressed doubts, Sorensen and Kraulshavn hesitated a long moment before they followed.

Kraulshavn had particular reason to hesitate.

Like any reasonable and sophisticated adult Struth, Kraulshavn viewed stories of the spirit world with imperious amusement, as something to look down one's beak at. Even so, ghost stories were an important and ancient signing tradition in his society. Nestlings barely able to put a few symbols together were told simple tales of ghastly elegance. In the deep past, fear of the unknown had been a valuable tool for a hen to keep her featherless, spindly hatchlings safe.

The Struth had originated on a barren and hostile world that to a nervous observer might have seemed to be entirely populated by creatures with fangs and claws and talons and sharp beaks. That was just true enough to require some fairly tricky skills to avoid being on someone else's menu.

In Struth prehistory, they had once been a species facing extinction. Originally beings of the air, they were a little bit too large to hide and too small to defend themselves. The Struth were also handicapped by poor hearing – limited to the ultrafrequency sounds the leaders and guards of the rookeries used to guide their brothers and sisters. The advantage of that was they could not be heard by any potential enemies. Unfortunately, that meant the Struth also could not hear said enemies approaching.

The Struth were down to a few great rookeries when they finally fled to a small subcontinent. It was a place of small animals with sweet flesh, luscious fruits, and no natural enemies at all – a Struth paradise. And as contented Struth generations passed, they became much larger and heavier and lost the ability to fly. Their small wing claws developed into graceful feathered 'hands,' good for mutual grooming, plucking fruit, wielding a large stick or rock to fell game, and, more importantly, speaking.

Paradise, however, could not last forever. Maintaining a large rookery in their new homeland became quickly impossible as the sheer size of the Struth suggested a brighter future in small co-operative groups that would put far less stress on the food supply. That also meant that a sophisticated communication system was essential.

Signing was born. At first it was limited to a few basics: *Tasty creature under rock. You lift. I take. We share.* Soon, however, it became a swift and complex language. A superior signer had greater status than a Struth with a beautiful tail-feather display. Eventually, a Struth philosopher could collapse the most intricate idea into a few symbols of great simplicity. The gentle Struth were on the verge of evolving their signing language into written form when disaster struck.

A land bridge had formed between their paradise and a much greater landmass. At first only a few weaker animals fled across it. They were soon followed by a trickle and then a flood of grazing creatures. The carnivores were right behind. The Struth were easy prey. After thousands of years of relative safety, they were a top-of-the-menu item again. Once again they faced extinction.

But that time they had greater resources to fall back on. The two key talents they had developed post migration were cooperation and language. The Struth split into even smaller groups. They learned to build their nests in the most difficult terrain. They formed two-Struth teams to gather food. That proved to be an ideal number with which to deal with any enemy. One Struth would always be at watch while the other worked. If escape was impossible, the two of them together could kill the attacker.

Smaller rookeries, however, meant that the hatchlings had to be left unguarded for long periods. The question was how to keep the young in their safe nests. The answer was simple: Scare the clot out of them. The ghost story was invented. Struth tales of the spirit world always involved a young hatchling who ignored the warnings of his parents and more cautious siblings and ventured out of the nest. He was always eaten. A favorite villain was the Talon Thing that swooped out of the sky and carried away the little Struth to its own nest, where smaller Talon Things waited to eat the little Struth alive. Another was Big Fang. That beast, it was said, hid in the brush all day, waiting for groups of disobedient Struth young. Big Fang would catch them at play, quickly eating his fill and then hamstringing the others so they could not run away. Big Fang could then seek out his pack mates and return for a feast.

The ghost stories worked. The hatchlings stayed in their nests until they were old enough to bond with other Struth. Eventually the Struth grew tired of hiding in rocky hills from creatures they had realized were not nearly as bright as themselves. The Struth came out of the hills and began killing the carnivores. They killed them until there were no more left. Then they crossed the land bridge and began killing all over again. In two centuries, the Struth were kings of their small planet. Unlike many other races on countless other worlds, when the Struth had run out of common enemies, they did not begin seeing a replacement among their own numbers. Instead, they returned to being the peaceful Struth again, whose greatest joy was in the elegant symbols – both written and signed – that they used to communicate with.

When they were finally discovered by the Empire, the Struth language had reached the giddy heights of the purest of pure maths. Their computer hardware, for instance, was primitive compared with Imperial standards. But the programs they wrote were so simple that they barely taxed the capacity of the most dim-witted Struth machine.

As software artists, they were instant hits, commanding premium salaries and the most luxurious perks. There was one requirement, however, written into every Struth contract with the outside. They must always be hired in twos. Otherwise, they would have no one else to sign with. Struth had been known to die of loneliness.

Kraulshavn was not near death when Sorensen found him at their previous prison camp. But day by day he was wasting away. Kraulshavn had been working as a civilian on an Imperial military contract when the Tahn had invaded. His companion was killed in the first fighting. Somehow Kraulshavn had survived.

Sorensen thought the little Struth was the most mournful being he had ever met. Sorensen's great calculating brain and Kraulshavn's elegant way of thinking made them natural friends. It was easy for a being like Sorensen to learn the signing language, and soon he was wagging away with Kraulshavn like a native Struth. Kraulshavn began eating again and taking an interest in life.

They soon teamed up permanently and made one nearly successful attempt to escape. They were just getting ready for another when they were transported to Koldyeze.

When Kilgour found them, he knew instantly that they were the solution to a seemingly impossible problem. What the organization needed more than anything else was a computer capable of reducing endless years of calculating drudgery to a few hours. With such a computer, the chances of escape would soar geometrically.

Sorensen and Kraulshavn had assured him that the solution was simple. All they had to accomplish was two things. Step one: Reinvent the chip. With that, they could build a tiny-brained computer. Step two: Invent a language that said little brain could deal with without blowing its circuits.

When Alex stumbled upon the large room with the tricky sliding gear lock, he was pretty sure that among its contents was the answer to step one.

When the creators of Koldyeze had considered the early plans for the cathedral, they had paid particular attention to the stained-glass windows that would grace the structure. They quickly discovered that it was an art form that had been lost thousands of years before. Yes, they could create adequate stained glass with modern scientific techniques. But no matter how much they experimented, what they produced paled when compared with the great works of the past.

So it was to the ancient past that the monks of Koldyeze went to find their answer, and find it they did in the writings of a goldsmith named Rugerus. They carefully copied every detail of the methodology. They disdained modern glass-cutting lasers for a tool of heated iron. To smooth the edges of the glass designs, they used a notched tool called a grozing iron. For color, they included in their palette gold and silver salts and precious gems ground to dust.

The room to which Alex had led Sorensen and Kraulshavn was one of the workshops the monks of Koldyeze had labored in for many generations. It was cloaked in dust and cluttered with hundreds of bewildering objects and substances. But little by little they began to pick them out.

Kraulshavn wagged his fingers excitedly when he pulled aside a tarp and revealed neatly stacked sheets of thick glass. He pulled one sheet from a stack and kept pushing it in Kilgour's face. Alex gently brushed him aside.

'Thae be glass. Ah've peeped glass afore. Why's th' feathery one all flutter, young Sorensen?'

'He says glass is what the Struth used in some of their early computers.'

Alex considered that for a moment. 'Aye. Thae'll be a decent breadboard. 'Tis a start.'

As the other two beings continued their search, he wondered how they could etch the glass to hold the circuitry. He would have to get the scroungers busy coming up with a decent glass-eating caustic.

There was sudden excited motion from Kraulshavn. Kilgour found him trying to tug a small barrel from beneath a teetering mess of other barrels. Alex added a little heavy-world weight, and they soon had it out. They popped the lid, and Alex's mouth gaped. Inside was what had to be flakes of pure gold.

'Clottin' figures. Shake down a wee monk, and ye'll find gold about.' Kilgour had always been an instinctive anti-cleric. He was even more so after his and Sten's dealings with the three pontiffs of the Lupus Cluster.

Kraulshavn signed at the flakes and then pointed to the glass. Alex had to chortle. They had found their circuitry.

When they were done, they might have a dullwit for a computer, but it surely was going to be a clotting valuable dullwit.

But before they could scrabble through the mounds of dust and debris to see what other treasures they could find, what seemed like every alarm on Heath went off.

By the time Alex joined Sten on a battlement overlooking the prisoners' yard, he had managed to retrieve his stomach and somewhat untangle his nerves. Sten motioned him over, and he saw what all the shooting and shouting had been about.

The two of them watched as the bloody and limp figure of St. Clair was dragged through the three gates and toward the area that the Tahn had already designated as a 'punishment chamber.'

'Who is it?' Sten asked.

'Dunno. Ah'll find out. She looks t' be still alive.'

Neither of them paid much attention to the prisoner. They were waiting for the next whiplash.

It was not long in coming.

The prison speakers crackled. 'All prisoners! Your immediate attention. This is Colonel Derzhin. One of your number has attempted to escape. She was completely unsuccessful. As I guaranteed when I spoke before, this attempt shall not go unpunished.'

Sten held his breath.

'The prisoner shall be kept in isolation for thirty days. Diet shall be minimal.

'But this is not sufficient.'

'Now's th' clanger,' Alex said.

'All prisoners are ordered lockdown in their cells for twenty-four hours. Since no work can be performed in that time, no rations shall be issued. You have ten minutes to return to your cells. At the end of that time, any prisoners outside their cells shall be fired upon.'

The speaker went dead.

Sten and Alex looked at each other.

'Clottin' hell,' Alex marveled. 'A bleedin' philanthropist.'

'Yeah,' Sten agreed as the two men doubled toward their chamber.

'All the same. I want the word out. The next hero that tries a cowboy run like that won't have legs to run on.'

'Ah'll see thae's nae mistranslation, Skipper.'

Chapter Fourteen

But there had to be more to Sten's plans than just ordering, 'Back off, Buckwheat.' Because if he did not get the camp's escape efforts organized very soon, the provable crazies in the cathedral would ignore his orders.

Escaping as an art form – and given the nature of Koldyeze, any escape would have to be pretty arty – required a great deal more than punching a hole in the ground or lashing a ladder together. It required a formidable conspiracy.

Drawn out, an escape organization would resemble two equilateral triangles set point to point. At the top of the first were the watchers and security people. Then a lesser number of carpenters, tinbashers, and so forth. After them, a still smaller number of artists and specialists.

Probably none of them would be among the escapers.

All their work would go to Big X – the escape organization's head. He would filter material down through the ranks of the actual escapers to the tunnelers or the people working on the physical escape.

And security had to be perfect. Not only did each level have to be protected from exposure, the manner of escape itself had to be a total secret to almost everyone.

As Alex put it: 'I' y' ken me strollin' aboot th' compound wearin' a purple chemise wi' a light standard stick't oot m' arse, Ah dinnae wan' to hear anybody say aught but how bonny the weather is.'

The biggest problem was not with the Tahn guards – Sten had already allowed for their presence. The danger lay in those prisoners who were unknown. Having a measure of respect for Tahn

Intelligence, Sten was absolutely sure there would be at least one double among the prisoners. Probably more. But he – or they – must be found quickly and disappeared. The Imperial prisoners would define that death as execution for treason – the Tahn would call it murder and make reprisals. Sten was forced to use Alex and his hooligans as a cut-out, even though there was a good possibility that he might be putting his friend very decidedly into harm's way. But he had to start recruiting.

Another problem: There would be prisoners who for their own reasons would want nothing to do with whatever Sten planned as the main escape attempt: claustrophobes, solitaries, or simply prisoners who had figured out a single-person way to get out. All those attempts had to be registered to make sure escapers did not cross each other's routes and destroy two or more plans at once. Sten thought he would be lucky if he heard about half the plans – he was just as unknown and suspect to the other prisoners as they were to him.

Sten was glooming over evening rations in their cell and was very glad to hear the shuffle at the door that interrupted him. He was not so glad when he turned and saw who it was.

Lay Reader Cristata crouched in the doorway.

Cristata, since that initial formation, had not become any less of a pain in the fundament. At every formation he insisted he was a civilian and did not belong in the prison, and at every formation he had to be plopped into place. He refused any work detail; *any* task assigned by a uniformed person was assisting the war effort. Naturally, he refused to salute any Tahn guard as required. So far he had not ended up in isolation, but sooner or later . . . Not that Cristata was disliked. The squat being was the first to volunteer to mess-cook. He set up the ludicrous assemblage of medical gear available as a dispensary. He had no objection to latrine cleaning whatsoever. Any sick prisoner would have Cristata hovering over him or her night and day.

Sten wondered what he wanted. Probably he had just discovered their rations were issued in uniform packs and felt that was military. But why was he not ruining Colonel Virunga's meal?

'Yes?'

'May I enter?'

Sten waved him in. Cristata closed the door behind him.

'I understand you are the individual in charge' – Cristata shuddered a bit – 'of the escape attempts.'

Sten mumbled neutrally. Could *Cristata* be a Tahn agent? Not a chance.

'My beings have decided that I should be the one to reserve an area.'

'You want to escape?'

'Why not? How else can I remove myself from this abhorrence of uniforms and regulations? There are four of us who plan to depart this place of testing for freedom.'

'How?'

'We are constructing a tunnel.'

'A tunnel?' Sten looked at Cristata's slender, delicate fingers.

Cristata caught his glance. He extended the armor gauntlet of his wrist, and muscles bulged – very hefty muscles, Sten noted. The fingers retracted, and thick claws slid out.

'In my necessities in dealing with the material world,' Cristata said, 'I function as a mining engineer.'

Sten grinned. 'The Tahn don't know that, of course,'

'I thought, since they forced me to obey their ludicrous orders, there was little sin in not disclosing my mammon-profession and the excavating implements the Great One gave my race.'

'Where are you planning to go out?'

'We have removed a section of paving from the ground level of the east wing. We plan to dig directly out from there.'

Sten mentally pictured Koldyeze. 'That is going to be a very long tunnel. That's just about the farthest point from the cliff edge.'

'That is also our observation. We estimate, and have prayed for guidance to be correct, the location gives us a place unlikely to be examined too closely.'

'How long until you go?'

'Soon, I think. The digging has been easy, and since we are tunneling under the foundation of the cathedral most of the way, not much shoring has been necessary. At the moment I estimate we are nearing the inner wall.'

Sten was jolted. The progress was incredible. 'Clotting great!'

'I wish you would not use obscenities in my presence.'

'Right. Sorry. What support do you need?'

'None.'

'None? Assuming that you get out, what comes next? You aren't exactly – no offense – a lookalike for any Tahn I've seen.'

'We shall proceed directly into open country. There we propose to dig a shelter and slowly make the farmers of the area aware of our presence.'

'What makes you think they won't dump you for the reward?'

'You must have faith,' Cristata said. 'Now . . . may I return to my dedications? We have four new sick ones in the bay.'

'Sure. Let us know if you'll need a diversion or anything.'

'I doubt it.'

'Oh. Yeah. May your, uh, Great One be with you.'

'He is.'

And Cristata ambled out.

Platoon Sergeant Ibn Bakr was perfect, Kilgour thought, especially considering the still-underfed state of the prisoners. He marveled at the infantryman's bulk and repressed the urge to check the man's teeth as if he were buying a Percheron or to look at his pads to make sure he could support the full weight of a howdah. Ibn Bakr could, Alex thought, have fit into any combat livie as the ultimate hero/crunchie, or maybe the hero's first sergeant.

'Mr. Kilgour,' the bulk said.

Clottin' hell. H' can e'en talk.

'I want to volunteer for the committee.'

The word 'escape,' of course, was never spoken by anyone unnecessarily under threat of bashing.

'An' we accept, lad,' Alex said heartily. He had fond dreams of maybe finding three more like the sergeant, and they would just rip the old pinnacle off the cathedral and use it as a battering ram through the gates. *All* the gates. 'We'll be needin't a braw tank like you. Digging . . . carrying . . . holding up the world.'

'Umm . . . Mr Kilgour, that wasn't what I wanted to do.'

Alex's dreams wisped away. 'Aye?'

'I assume,' Ibn Bakr went on, 'that we'll be altering uniforms to look like civvies, screwsuits and that, right?'

'You want to be a clottin' *seamstress*!'

'Is there something wrong with that?' The ham that hung at the end of Ibn Bakr's arm knotted into a fist.

Kilgour, deciding the sergeant might be a handful even for a heavy-worlder like himself, regrouped. 'Nae a' all, nae a' all.'

'I can do needlepoint, knitting, crewel, petit point, crossstitch, featherwork, lace, Carrickmacross, quillwork, broderie anglaise—'

'Tha'll do, Sergeant. Ah'm appalled – tha's nae th' word – o'erwhelmed ae thae talents. Be standin't bye, an' we'll hae materials f'r ye in a wee bit.'

The sergeant saluted and left.

Kilgour stared after him and sighed mightily.

*

The evening formation stunned the Imperial prisoners. They had assembled at the siren blast, counted, and stood warily, staring at a five-meter-high stack of plas crates nearby and wondering what new Tahn screwing the crates presaged.

Camp Commandant Derzhin had taken the count from Colonel Virunga and said he had an announcement. It was short and shocking.

'Prisoners, the Tahn find your work to be acceptable.'

Clot, Sten thought. We'd better step up the sabotage program.

'As a reward, I have authorized the issuance of your Prisoner's Aid parcels. That is all. Colonel Virunga, take charge of your men.'

Virunga saluted like a being in a trance.

The prisoners were equally amazed.

'I din' know there *was* parcels,' somebody muttered ungrammatically.

Sten knew what they were; in the three-plus years of captivity, a softhearted camp officer – who had been quickly shipped off to a combat unit – had issued the boxes once.

Prisoner's Aid was a neutral society, overseen by the ostensibly neutral Manabi and intended to give POWs on both sides some rights, some method of appeal, and most importantly support. The Tahn ignored the first two goals of the society but encouraged the latter. Each parcel contained supplementary rations, vitamins, minerals, and replacement clothing for ten prisoners. Sten wondered if the kindly little old ladies – that was how he pictured them – ever realized that those scarves, gloves, and tidbits in the parcels almost never reached the prisoners they were meant for. If the parcels were not sidetracked by the Tahn supply system itself, the prisoner guards would ensure that the prisoners never saw them. The one parcel that Sten had seen had been most thoroughly picked through long before it was sent into the gates.

'Food,' someone whispered.

The formation swayed forward a little.

Virunga blinked back to awareness only seconds before his military formation turned into a food riot.

'Formation! Ten-hut!'

Military discipline took over – at least for a moment.

'Three volunteers . . . break down . . . parcels. Cristata . . . Kilgour . . . Horatio!'

Lay Reader Cristata muttered but evidently decided that task was allowable and waddled forwrd, Sten and Alex behind him.

'Sir,' Sten said. 'Request that—'

Virunga interrupted him. 'Quite right . . . forgot . . . task. One more being! Sarn't Major Isby!'

The supply specialist swung out on his crutches toward Virunga. In an age when few injuries were permanent, Isby was a man with only one leg. That he had lost it through medical inattention was one atrocity to be chalked up to the Tahn. But it could be explained away as an excusable oversight during wartime. There could be no explanation for not providing him with a new one. The only war crime trials the Tahn were counting on would be overseen by them.

'Rest . . . dismissed! Distribute parcels . . . two hours.'

The formation broke up, but none of the prisoners left the courtyard. They intended to watch – very closely – just how the parcels were divided. At least all three of the 'volunteers' were trusted by the prisoners – more or less.

Sten glanced at Alex, who nodded. Alex would take Colonel Virunga aside and give him a very interesting piece of information that had been learned during his and Sten's pre-Tahn War Mantis training. If that bit of information still applied, those Prisoner's Aid parcels might prove very useful.

Sten, thinking hopeful thoughts about the continuity of sneakiness, saluted Virunga and hurried away. He did indeed have another task.

The two guards snarled at Sten. He kept well back. They unlocked the cell door and snarled once more. A moment later St. Clair walked out, squinting at the light – walked, not tottered or stumbled. During the month of isolation, her bruises had mostly healed. She was even skinnier than before – half rationpaks and water had done that – but, Sten noted, must have maintained some kind of exercise regimen in the cramped isolation cell.

'Next time,' the Tahn said, 'it'll be worse.'

'There won't be a next time,' St. Clair said. The guard pushed her away, down the corridor, and banged the cell door closed.

St. Clair stopped in front of Sten. 'My welcoming committee.'

'Call it that,' Sten said.

'What's been happening in the big wide world?'

'Not much worth talking about.'

'So the war's still not over. And by the way, why aren't you calling me by my rank, Firecontrolman?'

'Sorry. Captain.'

'Forget it. I'm just up to here with clottin' screws. Thanks for the welcome. Now I want to see if the 'freshers are on yet.'

They were in a deserted section of the corridor.

'We have something to talk about first,' Sten said.

'GA.'

'You tried to get out solo. A real cowboy move.'

'So?'

'No more. Any escape attempt's gotta be registered and approved by the committee.'

'Not mine,' St. Clair said. 'Committees screw things up. Committees start war. I like my own company.'

'This isn't a debate, Captain. It's an order.'

St. Clair leaned back against the wall. 'You're Big X?'

'You have it.'

'Nice meeting you. But as I said—'

'Listen to me, Captain. Read my lips. I don't give a damn if you want to try a single run. Anybody who's got any way out of this coffin has my blessings. But I am going to know about it and approve it – before you go.'

St. Clair allowed herself six deep breaths before she said anything. She smiled. 'Again, my apologies. I'll follow orders. Of course. Whatever you and your committee want.'

'Cute, Captain St. Clair. And I think you're blowing smoke at me. Those are my orders. You will follow them!'

'And if I don't?'

Sten spoke very quietly. 'Then I'll kill you.'

St. Clair's face was impassive.

'One more thing, Captain. Just to keep you out of trouble, I'm appointing you my chief scrounger.'

'Scrounger? I'm not familiar—'

'Thief.'

St. Clair bristled. 'I am a gambler. Not a clotting burglar!'

'I don't see the difference.'

Again St. Clair buried her anger. 'Is there anything else, Firecontrolman?'

'Not right now.'

'Then you're dismissed!'

Sten came to attention and saluted her.

St. Clair waited until Sten had rounded a corner, then gave herself the luxury of a silent snarl of rage. Then her face pokered, and she started looking for her long-overdue shower.

Outside in the courtyard, the distribution of the Prisoner's Aid parcels was under way. Sten noticed that as each crate was opened

Alex would remove one or maybe two packs and set them unobtrusively aside. Good. Then he saw, leaning against one of the half-ruined columns, what had to be the Empire's oldest warrant officer. The man looked like the grandfather Sten had never known. He was holding a small pack of what Sten guessed were biscuits and an equally tiny pack of fruit spread. Part of his share from the parcels. The man was crying.

Sten shuddered.

It was time they all went home.

Chapter Fifteen

Big X was flexing his muscles.

Through his cut-outs, Sten had deployed the surveyors. The surveyors were reluctant prisoners who were given improvised metric rules and told to measure everything and anything. Sten was trying to find out what he had to work with and work from. Since there were no plans that he could find or steal for Koldyeze, he would make his own.

The details reported back. A hallway measured so many meters wide, long, and tall. The rooms branching off that hallway measured B meters wide, long, and tall. The wing itself measured C meters wide, long, and tall. And none of the figures matched in Sten's mind. He wished desperately that Alex and his team could move a little faster on the computer. What the clot! Probably wouldn't work, anyway.

Sten tossed aside the bits of paper he had been figuring on. Later for that drakh. In the meantime, which meant on the morrow, he was on a work detail.

The work detail was commanded by someone who seemed to be the first of the Tahn quislings.

Chief Warrant Officer Rinaldi Hernandes seemed to call everyone 'my friend' – except the Tahn guards, whom he referred to, with a completely obsequious bow, as 'honorable sirs.'

'My friends,' he cajoled. 'Come, now. Lift together. We can do this.'

'Doing this' was muscling a huge generator that should have had a McLean sled to raise it up a ramp into a cargo ship.

'You aren't trying, my friends,' he said. 'I am disappointed that I shall have to report you to our commandant when we return. Remember, we are being given a fair day's ration, and we should be prepared to deliver a fair day's work.'

Sten grunted, along with twenty others, and slowly the generator groaned up the ramp into place. He, like the others on the work crew, hated Hernandes. Suddenly Sten realized that in spite of the constant threat, no one assigned to Mr Hernandes's work crews had ever been reported for anything.

Interesting.

The generator loaded, the prisoners sagged in exhaustion. Hernandes walked among them, patting, joking, and ignoring the muttered obscenities he heard.

'That wasn't bad, my friends. Come on. The shift's barely begun. Come on. We've got to show our honorable masters we're as good as they are.'

The prisoners groaned to their feet. The next task was simpler: loading crates into another offbound ship.

Sten realized he was spending less time watching Hernandes than watching Heath's spaceport. Which ship could be stowed away on? Which ship was outbound for where? What were the security measures taken once a ship was loaded?

He humped a crate up a laddered ramp. Hernandes was standing at the ship's cargo door in his typically baggy oversized coveralls.

'Hi-diddle-diddle,' the officer chanted. 'Right up the middle, friend. We've got to get this ship loaded and off-world.'

Definitely, Sten thought, a traitor. But isn't he a little obvious to be an agent?

'There are troops freezing on an arctic world,' Hernandes went on. 'We've got to make sure they have what they need.'

Sten glowered at the warrant officer and continued on, part of the antlike procession, into the ship's hold, where he dumped the crate he was carrying. And then he stared at the loading slip on its side: *Uniforms, tropical, working dress.*

He quickly scanned some slips on other crates: *Recreational equipment, E-normal environment (lowcaloric); Rations, beasts of burden (not for Tahn Consumption); Livies, medical, educational, avoidance of social diseases; Livies, counselatory, what to do when your mate leaves; Spores, seedable, rock garden, for issue to general officers and above.*

That should have had an interesting effect on any Tahn crunchie – on whatever frozen world the ship was bound for – who had to unload or consume any of the crates.

As he made his way back toward the ramp, Sten looked at Mr Hernandes a bit differently. To make sure, he bumped against him. Mr Hernandes's coveralls clanked.

'Careful of what you're doing, my friend,' the grandfatherly warrant officer cautioned.

'See me tonight,' Sten ordered in a low voice.

'I beg your pardon?'

'Big X,' Sten said. What the clot. If he was blown, he was now thoroughly blown.

He was not.

In case Hernandes was wired, Sten had him strip searched and then, finding he was clean, took him for a long and aimless walk down one of the wing's corridors.

Rinaldi Hernandes was a building tradesman, a general contractor who had been a master plumber, carpenter, plasman, ceramic specialist, and so forth, who had joined the service at the beginning of the conflict. He had been assigned to the Imperial construction units – for once the grinding bureaucracy that was the military had put a square peg into a square hole.

Hernandes desperately hated the Tahn. His only grandchild had been killed at the beginning of the war. Then Hernandes himself had been captured. He had survived and, during the years of his captivity, resisted – resisted in ways that would keep him alive until the time came when he had a weapon in his hands and could kill.

'Although, my friend,' he said sheepishly, 'since I've never killed anyone in my life, I really don't know what I would do.'

In the meantime, he had learned the Tahn worlds and sent shipments intended for garrisons to the front, and vice versa. He had stolen and then destroyed any protruding bits of military hardware that he could. He had surreptitiously tugged connections loose wherever he could when he was permitted aboard any Tahn ship.

Hernandes hated the Tahn so thoroughly that he was willing to sacrifice the opinion of his fellow prisoners. So they believed he was a quisling, a traitor, a double. Perhaps they might even kill him. That was the risk that Hernandes was willing to take. In the meantime, he was as trusted by the Tahn as any Imperial prisoner could be. He often wondered, he told Sten, how many – if any – Tahn he had killed. He had never seen any of them die.

Maybe he was not really accomplishing anything.

Sten thought that perhaps Mr Rinaldi Hernandes had killed more Tahn than any Imperial battleship.

And now he had his jack-of-all-trades.

Big clottin' deal, Sten thought. I'm assembling all these troopies. Giving them a mission.

But so far I haven't come up with any mission.

Chapter Sixteen

L'n thumbed back on the joystick. There was a soft whirr as the feeder machine came to life and then two sharp clicks as the tubes dropped into the slots in front of her. She gave a quick double-check glance to make sure there was a pos and neg symbol on each of them, then toggled the joystick forward. The tubes slid slowly toward each other, then gave a quick jump as they mated.

She bent closer to look at the seal. It was so apparently perfect that she could barely see the nth of a hairline where the tubes joined.

All those movements were accomplished in nearly absolute darkness. In fact, it was so dark in the testing room that any other being would have started feeling like a claustrophobe after a few minutes. He would have felt completely cut off from the rest of the world, sensing only the form of his own body. To L'n it was a little bit better than twilight.

She toggled left to apply stress to the seal, pressing down to activate an electric field. Outwardly the seam was still apparently perfect, but L'n's light-actinic eyes could see a dark red stain. The seam was badly flawed. L'n giggled and toggled right to drop the tubes into the discard bin. After only a few hours on shift, the bin was nearly full of rejects. So much for the Tahn's boasts of superefficiency.

L'n liked to think that someday far in the future a really bright historian would trace the Tahn's eventual defeat at the hands of the Emperor right back to the discard bin under her worktable. For the hundredth time L'n smiled at her little private joke, then toggled back to call for the next two pipes. Her small, delicately pointed left ear turned to catch the sound of the machine whirring into life. Instead, there was a loud shout just outside the room. Her ear curled back on itself in pain. What the clot? The shouting went on. It was Cloric, the Tahn work boss. She could not hear what was being said, but somebody was definitely getting it. If Cloric held to form – and she had no reason to believe that he would not – the shouts would eventually lapse into incoherence, followed by heavy blows.

Whoever it was, L'n felt very sorry for him. Still, what could she do about it? She turned back to her work, trying to push the sounds outside her mind. It was a process that seemed to be getting easier every day. That frightened L'n more than anything else – more than Cloric, or the other Tahn, or the war itself. Because until a few years before, violence had not even been a word in L'n's vocabulary.

It was not that L'n came from a race of pacifists. On the contrary, on a scale of amoebic jelly to outright beasts, the Kerrs rated fairly high on the fierce side. They were a slender, soft-furred folk with large, limpid eyes; delicate, highly sensitive ears; and a long, agile balancing tail. The Kerrs' original homeworld was mostly covered by dense forests. They inhabited the middle levels, where light was as scarce as the food supply on the top tier.

Like many forest beings, L'n's forebearers were intensely jealous of their privacy. The only time a Kerr experienced a feeling even close to loneliness was during estrus. It was a trait that would stay with them through the ages, just like their passion for light.

An artist, L'n had been nearing the height of her powers when she decided to emigrate from her home system. It was a very bold – or foolish – thing for a Kerr to do. She was abandoning the warmth of personal privacy for what seemed to her friends and family a hostile and patently ugly life on the outside. But the artist side of L'n knew – as sure as she knew the conceptual beauty of polarized light – that the price of continued privacy was too high.

To reach the next level in her art, she needed knowledge, a knowledge that could be found only in the great 'outside.'

L'n thought she was just on the verge of finding her way, when the Tahn struck. She was in her biaxial period, and her strange light paintings were beginning to find a wider audience.

Audience. That was a strange word. There was no equivalent in the Kerr language. It made a being think of large, smelly crowds, pushing in, closer and closer . . . L'n learned to deal with audiences. In fact, she was even starting to like being the center of one.

She had also made her first 'outside' friend. His name was Hansen. Lance Corporal Hansen, a very large and, at first, very frightening human. When she had met him and Hansen had grasped her small hands in his and grunted on in his ugly low-toned human voice about her light paintings, it was all she could do to keep herself from taking a shrieking leap for the studio's rafters. But she had steeled herself, listened as politely as she could, and then ushered him out the door. L'n had spent hours that night trying to comb the smell of him out of her fur.

Months later, it was one of the things she liked about him the most. He was with her every minute he could spare, admiring her work, criticizing it in ways that turned out to be helpful, and hovering over her when she had a showing – keeping the crowds at a more comfortable distance.

When the Tahn had invaded, Hansen had fought his way to her studio, dragged her from it, and then fought his way back to his lines. They reached safety only moments before the battle-shocked Imperial Forces surrendered. Even then, the Tahn had kept their missiles thundering in.

Hansen and L'n were caught in one such explosion. Sometime later, L'n came to. How very odd. She was barely wounded – while Hansen was messily dead.

L'n had learned many things since she had left her home system. One of them was lying. The Tahn had mistaken her for a member of the Imperial Forces. L'n did not correct them. Out on the streets she could hear them killing the civilians.

The last thing she learned was after Hansen died. L'n learned what it was like to be lonely.

The seam on the next pair of tubes glowed a faint orange. Adequate. Clot! She toggled it to the appropriate bin.

Outside, the shouting had stopped. Instead of heavy blows, she could hear muttering. What was going on?

*

Chetwynd had heard the brouhaha clear across the hangar-sized factory. He quickly checked his guards and their work parties. Everything *seemed* okay. Wait. Something or someone was missing.

He maneuvered his enormous bulk around a chattering machine and took off at a dead run. Chetwynd dodged the waving jaws of a forklift, skittered around a corner, and came to a stop. It was Cloric – again. The man's face was flushed with anger, and his eyes were bulging out from the intensity of his shouting. It was almost orgasmic. The object of his affection, Chetwynd noticed, was a much smaller man – an Imperial prisoner of war. The reason for Cloric's anger was instantly apparent. The two men were standing in the middle of a large jumbled pile of hydraulic tubing that spilled across the floor. Behind them was the bank of doors to the test labs. On one lab a red light burned, showing that it was in use.

Chetwynd assumed a casual pose and strolled over. Whether he intervened would depend on only a few simple factors. On the one hand, the prisoner might have done something wrong or, even worse, sneaky. In which case Chetwynd would shrug his shoulders and abandon the prisoner to his fate. On the other hand, Cloric had a reputation even among the most callous of the guards as a person who lashed out for no apparent reason. Not that anyone really cared; it was just considered unprofessional. Chetwynd had a more important reason to be concerned. As he was the shift commander, the prisoners were ultimately his responsibility. And the word had come strongly down that there was a severe shortage of labor, and therefore the prisoners had suddenly gained value. They were not to be wasted. If Cloric were allowed to run amok, they would quickly run out of people for the work parties.

There was one other reason. Chetwynd knew first-hand what it was like to be a prisoner.

Cloric finally spotted him and went on the defensive without a pause.

'I can handle this, Chetwynd.'

'Snarl at me once more, Cloric, and I'll show you what *I* can handle.'

Cloric took in the mastodon that was Chetwynd. Cloric was big but not *that* big. Chetwynd had at least fifty kilos on him, a great deal of which was muscle. And although as the boss of the work gangs he was not Cloric's immediate superior, Chetwynd had a great deal of clout, even with the muckity-mucks of factory security. The source of the clout was a bit of a mystery, although talk was that Chetwynd was a dispenser of many favors. As for what he got in return, even Cloric was not dumb enough to ask.

All those thoughts took a great deal of time to lumber through the man's mind. Chetwynd waited patiently and was rewarded with a slump of shoulders and a stubborn but still hangdog expression.

'He was tryin' somethin',' Cloric muttered, waving at the prisoner and the jumble of tubing. 'See. He's got all the good ones mixed up with the bad ones.'

Chetwynd did not bother letting Cloric finish explaining. It would take much too long and consist mostly of lies. The prisoner, he was sure, would be much more creative. He turned to the man, who had been looking back and forth as they talked, obviously wondering what was going to happen to him. The prisoner was Sten.

'What do you have to say for yourself?' Chetwynd asked.

'It was sort of an accident,' Sten said. 'See, I was moving the reject bin out of the way, and the officer grabbed my shoulder. Scared the clot out of me, I can tell you. Knocked over that bin and the other—'

'That's a lie,' Cloric protested. 'I was watchin' him the whole time. He was gonna mix 'em together. I could tell.'

'But sir,' Sten said. 'Did you actually *see* me doing anything like that? Where were you standing?'

Cloric was so confused by Chetwynd's presence that he found himself actually discussing the matter with the prisoner instead of smacking him for his insolence. He pointed to a position about twenty meters away; he had obviously been lurking behind a gravlift. Sten studied the indicated spot with great seriousness. After a moment, he shook his head.

'No, sir. I hate to disagree with you, but I don't think you could have seen much over there. Those plascrates would have been in the way.'

'They were at first,' Cloric said, 'but I moved some, see?' He pointed at a gap in a large stack of crates waiting for shipment.

'Gee, sir. That is pretty good,' Sten reluctantly admitted. 'But wouldn't my back have been turned to you, sir?'

Chetwynd waved them both to silence. The discussion was not getting them anywhere. Besides, there was something else preying on his mind. The prisoner looked very familiar. He could not quite put his finger on it, but he was sure he knew the man from someplace. And that someplace was cop!

'Don't I know you?' he asked.

Sten peered up at him. He, too, saw a vague kind of familiarity, but he kept it hidden. 'No, sir. The prisoner doesn't believe so, sir.'

Chetwynd looked closer. He could not shake the feeling that somewhere, sometime he had seen the man in the uniform of a Tahn cop. But what was he doing there acting like an Imperial prisoner? If Chetwynd was right, then the man was a snoop, and he and Cloric could find themselves in deep drakh.

'What's your name?'

'The prisoner's name is Horatio, sir,' Sten said.

He was worried. Chetwynd's face had finally clicked into position. It was when he and Alex had been on the trail of that little bomber, Dynsman. Sten remembered clearly the attack of the gurion. The thing had rushed through the surf at them on its six legs, its tooth-lined stomach reaching out of its body at them. And the whole time, the man in front of him had lolled laughing on the beach, surrounded by a score of lovely female prisoners. Sten and Alex had been posing as Tahn prison guards, so they really could not blame Chetwynd for his lack of concern for their fate. He wondered how Chetwynd had ever gotten off the prison planet. More importantly, how in the clot had he gone from prisoner to boss guard?

Wars produced strange things, Sten had noticed. He had also noticed that those things were rarely funny.

'Okay, Horatio. We'll let this go. This time. Next time your butt is ground meat!'

'Thank you, sir,' Sten said with some amazement.

Before Cloric could protest, Chetwynd raised a hand to silence him.

'Get these parts loaded,' he told Sten. 'We'll run 'em back through again.'

'Yessir. Right away, sir.'

Sten was a blur of eager motion as he began picking up the scattered tubing as Chetwynd and Cloric walked away.

'Whyn't you let me thump him?' Cloric asked. 'He deserved it.'

'Probably,' Chetwynd said. 'But do us both a favor. Keep your eye on him. But your hands off. Got me?'

Cloric nodded. He did not know what was going on, and he was pretty sure he did not want to find out. As for Chetwynd, he still thought he recognized Sten. But the cop business was probably pure foolishness. Probably. Still, he was not taking any chances.

*

L'n went at her rote tasks with new interest. She even hummed a Kerr lullaby to herself as she worked. She had been startled and badly frightened when the man Horatio had slipped into her lab. She almost had not flipped on the small blue light that was just barely comfortable to her eyes but would have allowed Horatio to see. For a moment she had almost let him bump around in the dark while she found a place to hide.

But the man had stayed perfectly still and whispered her name. Finally, she had responded. Without hesitation, the man walked directly to her, as if he could see in the dark as well as she could.

Horatio seemed to understand her right away. He made soothing noises at her and talked about things that interested her, like the geometric pattern and colors produced when light was refracted in a certain, special way. He said he had heard about her art, although he had not actually ever seen one of her light paintings. He promised to help her set up a studio at the prison.

He had also asked her for help. Not in *return* for any favors he would do. Of that she was quite sure. L'n had the idea that Horatio would provide the studio no matter what she did.

Why did she trust him? Well, he had trusted her, hadn't he? He had confessed that he was Big X. That information alone was a death warrant in her hands. And the things that he had asked her to do also depended on his absolute trust in her.

She would be the forger. She would use her many skills as an artist to produce fake Tahn documents and ID cards and a host of other things the prisoners would need when and if they escaped.

L'n had only one hesitation. There was no way she could escape with them. In the Tahn sunlight, she was blind.

Hansen had said – no. Not Hansen, she corrected herself. Silly me. Horatio had said that as Big X he could not escape, either. So they would work together and help the others.

L'n liked that. She also liked the second thing he had asked her. It also involved danger, but not as much. He wanted her to do a little sabotage, to approve as many sections of flawed tubing as she could. *That* would be a pleasure. In fact, she had thought about it before but had been afraid to try it.

Since she had met Horatio, she was not afraid anymore.

Chapter Seventeen

The third gate in the center sanctuary opened, and Security Major Avrenti stalked into the prisoners' courtyard.

The base of the triangle – the support for the escapers – went into operation.

Sergeant Major Isby leaned on his stool and lifted the bandage away from the stump of his leg to get a little more of the dim sun above.

Lance Corporal Morrison, on the second-level balcony, dropped his propaganda leaflet.

Major F'rella, at the far end of the prisoners' courtyard, curled one tentacle under – another Tahn recorded as entering – and, with her second brain, continued puzzling over whether that unusual archaic Earth tune written by someone named Weill could be polyphonically hummed using six of her eight lungs.

Technician Blevens yelped – supposedly at the heat of the caldron he had just touched – and dropped the caldron on the floor of the prisoners' kitchen.

The *klang* rang through the courtyard.

And the word was out.

'Great One protect us,' Cristata said. 'And now it is time to go.'

Instantly Markiewicz dropped her improvised spade and began slithering backward, away from the face of the tunnel. She, like any sensible tunneler who might have to pass inspection at a moment's notice, worked naked.

Cristata grabbed her legs and helped yank her back toward the nearest way station. He looked at her body, interestedly. He was wondering why some of the religious humans he had met saw shame in a body without covering. And suddenly he had a flash. Of course. They realized that their bodies should have been fur rather than pale flesh. They were ashamed of what they should have been instead of what they were.

Cristata, finding that thought worthy of his next meditation with the Great One and thanking the Great One for one more enlightenment, scurried back up the shaft after Markiewicz.

Markiewicz tugged on her coverall, and then they burst out of the tunnel, into the courtyard, as the paving stones slid away and then closed. Two soldiers dropped a very smelly basket of lichens over the stones and busied themselves peeling them for the evening meal.

Sorensen was lowering the eighteenth plate of glass into position, with Kraulshavn waggling final instructions, when the boot thudded against the door. The plate came back up and went hastily down onto the table beside them while Kraulshavn signed frantically for clues.

Tahn. They're approaching.

Clots!

Kraulshavn pulled at the cord hanging close to him, and the ties of a mattress cover, fastened to the rafters above them, came open. Dust clouded down around them.

All the pieces they had worked on that day would have to be laboriously cleaned and sterilized before the project could continue.

Sorensen swore as the two beings slid out the door of the workshop, into the corridor, and closed the door behind them. Their waiting watchman relocked the door, then covered it with more dust blown from a small bellows. He took one final precaution: Just in case the Tahn checked the corridor with heat detectors, he drooped a length of live lighting wire from the overhead so that it dangled across the cell door. Burn marks had already been artistically painted on the door, and the wire occasionally spit sparks. Any heat pickup would, everyone hoped, be attributed to that continuing short.

The watchman wondered what the clot the two beings were doing inside that workshop. But as Mr Kilgour had reminded him, that was na' his t' fash aboot. He headed for the courtyard.

What was going on inside the workshop was the slow, laborious construction of the computer that Sten needed.

Dreamers often wondered what would happen if they could appear in another, earlier time and build some sort of common tool that would make them gods, or even kings. The problem they never considered was that almost all technology required six steps of tooling before that trick item showed up.

And so Sten's computer had to begin with a chip – a series of chips.

No one would have recognized what Sorensen and Kraulshavn were constructing as a computer chip, however.

Their 'chips' were cubes, almost a third of a meter to any side. For simplicity's sake, they had decided to use a basic design of a twenty-four-layer chip. Each layer was a slab of glass. Each slab had the circuitry scratched on its surface and then acid-etched. Where each resister, diode, or whatever belonged, an open space was left. Full-scale components were either built or stolen by the working parties. The circuitry was then 'wired' as molten silver was poured into the acid etching. The chips' connecting legs were hand constructed of gold and wired in. Twenty-four of those plates made up each chip.

They had twelve chips ready and were about a third of the way through their task.

Both Sorensen and Kraulshavn wondered where Alex planned to put together their computer. He had not told them, and they recognized that as yet they had no need to know. They also wondered what Kilgour was planning to use for a storage facility. Another impossibility – but somehow they thought that there would be, when the time was right, an answer.

Security Major Avrenti paced through the prison corridors. He growled at the prisoners, ignoring greetings and the obligatory shouts as the Imperials ordered themselves to attention as he entered each chamber.

He imagined himself a psychic octopus, each strand of his being wisping out, trying to get the feel of his charges.

Were they hostile – indications of a potential riot? Were they smug, hiding a secret joke – indications of an escape in the planning? Were they sullen – hope abandoned? Avrenti continued his tour.

Kilgour watched the Tahn stroll down a corridor and stepped back out of sight.

'What's he doing?' one of his cohorts whispered.

'Ah dinnae ken,' Alex replied. 'Hae y' aye rec'lect tha' any ae th' Tahn be psychic?'

'Clottin' hope not.'

'We'll dinnae take th' chance,' Alex decided.

Avrenti finished his inspection and exited the prisoners' quarters into their courtyard. He paused a moment, waiting for some kind of impression. Then he saw, in the courtyard's center, a medium-sized – each way – Imperial painting the courtyard. His paint had been made from wallplaster soaked in water. His brush was a knotted rag. He was painting what appeared to be a star.

Avrenti walked up to him.

The Imperial – Avrenti searched his mental fiche and remembered him as one Kalguard or Kilgour, a minor, unimportant being – seemed oblivious to the Tahn.

'What are you doing?'

The Imperial bolted to attention, whitewash splattering. Avrenti frowned – some of the droplets had landed on his tunic.

'Ah 'polgize,' Kilgour stammered. 'Ah dinnae ken y' creep.'

Avrenti barely understood what the Imperial was saying but took it as an apology. 'What are you doing?'

'Keepin't th' Campbells off.'

'The Campbells?'

'Aye.'

'What, may I ask, are they? Or it?'

'Thae'll weird, dread six-leggit beasties whae live on treacheries an' soup.'

'Nonsense,' Avrenti snorted. 'I've never seen anything like that.'

'Aye,' Kilgour agreed. 'M' star's ae worker, ain' it?'

Avrenti looked closely at the Imperial. There was not a trace of a smile on the prisoner's face. 'Yes. Carry on.'

'Aye, sir.'

Kilgour went back to painting his star, and Avrenti went out through the three gates, his mind intent on whether he should alert Commandant Derzhin to the possibility that some of the Imperials might need psychiatric care.

Alex finished his paint job, walked three times around it, then started back for his quarters. Very well, he thought. Tha' Avrenti's noo psychic. He's just most intent. He'll hae two watchers on him when' ever he com't through th' gates frae noo on.

Chapter Eighteen

Tanz Sullamora was at his repose. He sat confidently in the anteroom to the Emperor's suite, waiting patiently and confidently to be summoned. Back straight, legs crossed, brow furrowed in thought, he was the definite portrait of a great industrial baron. A man to be reckoned with. A man who had the ear of the mighty.

The Eternal Emperor strode into the room and, without even glancing at Sullamora, walked over to the small service bar and pulled out a bottle and two glasses.

'Tanz, old friend,' the Emperor said. 'You need a drink.'

Sullamora was startled. He felt his careful pose starting to collapse about him. He had sworn to himself that he would set the tone of the meeting. Sullamora had definite ideas about what constituted Imperial behavior. Unfortunately, the Emperor did not go along with him.

'Uh . . . no. I mean, no, thank you. It's a little early.'

'Trust me, Tanz. When I say you need a drink, I mean it.'

Numbly, Sullamora took the glass. 'Is there some, ah, difficulty?'

'"Difficulty" isn't the word I had in mind. "Disaster" would be better. Ship production has gone all to hell.'

Sullamora sat up even straighter. That was a serious charge. He had been put in charge of all shipbuilding in the Empire for the duration of the war.

'But that isn't so,' he sputtered. 'I mean – uh, the latest figures, Your Majesty, uh . . .'

'Bull. I say ship production is dangerously off. And it's no wonder. All that labor unrest at the six plants in the Cairenes. Slowdowns. Wildcat strikes. I tell you they're endangering the progress of the war, and it has to stop!'

That really startled Sullamora. The factories of the Cairenes were his most efficient. He started to protest, but the Emperor waved him to silence.

'I'm not blaming you, Tanz. My lord, no one could expect one man – even a man as efficient as you – to keep abreast of *all* the developments. And I plan to say so at the livie news conference tomorrow.'

'News conference? What news conference? I wasn't informed – that is to say . . .' Sullamora stumbled into muteness.

He choked down his drink, all his confidence gone. Maybe the Emperor was right. But how could he have missed something like that? The Cairenes. Labor unrest. Wildcast strikes. Slowdowns. Profits in peril. It was a capitalist's greatest nightmare.

Watching him closely, the Emperor refilled the man's glass. He let Sullamora torture himself just a little longer. There was absolutely nothing the Eternal Emperor did not know about the military-industrial establishment and how to keep it under his very heavy thumb. 'You gotta keep them off balance,' he had once told Mahoney. 'To them, cost overrun is just another word for paradise.'

Finally he took pity on the man – but just a little bit. He started laughing. Sullamora looked up at him, totally bewildered and unmanned.

'Don't you get it, Tanz? This is just one of my little ploys.'

'You mean it's a joke?' Sullamora sputtered.

'No joke. I've never been more serious. Look. I lay this out at the news conference. Announce that I've called for an investigation by the Imperial Labor Commission.'

'What labor commission?'

'Clot, you're thick sometimes. There's no such animal. I'm just saying there is. Like the labor unrest and declining shipbuilding figure stuff. By the time the Tahn figure out that I'm lying through my teeth, you should be able to crank out minimum twelve more ships that they won't be aware of.'

Sullamora lifted his eyebrows. 'Ah, now I understand.' It had something to do with the rumored buildup, he realized. Where, no one was sure. Although, now that he thought of it, maybe the rumors were also part of the Emperor's unroyal-like and very slippery planning.

'There's something coming, isn't there, sir?' he asked. 'Something big. Is it anything you can tell me about?'

'No offense, Tanz, but that's a negative. I've got to play these cards *really* close to my chest. If the Tahn get even a hint, we're in a world of drakh.'

That was something Sullamora finally could understand. He was an old hand at playing shadow games with business rivals, although rarely did those games result in more than a little bloodshed.

'This much I can tell you,' the Emperor continued. 'If this works out, the war will be over in four years. Five tops. If I can smack them, and smack them good, they may never really recover.

'Oh, they can keep fighting for a while. But it'll be all over but final surrender. On *my* terms.'

Even Sullamora's frigid soul had to shudder at that thought. He would hate to be on the receiving end of a contract dictated by the Emperor.

'Of course, I *do* expect a few immediate benefits. Such as the signal that will be sent to any of my wavering allies and the fence sitters.'

After a moment he added in a near whisper, 'I think it's the fence sitters that irritate me the most.'

Sullamora felt his mouth go dry. He felt he should say something, but for some reason he was suddenly afraid. And then the moment passed. The Emperor took Sullamora's glass and put it and the bottle away. Sullamora was being dismissed.

'Plan on a five-minute speech tomorrow, Tanz,' the Emperor said. 'My flack can get together with your flack tonight. Put what I want you to say in your own words.'

Sullamora rose. He started to say his good-byes, then paused. With some amusement, the Emperor watched the other man screw up his courage to speak. He kept silent, deciding not to help him.

'I've, uh . . . Ah. Your Majesty, I've been wondering,' Sullamora finally got out.

'Yes?' The Emperor's voice was flat; he was still not helping.

'After the war, uh . . . What do you plan to do?'

'Get very drunk,' the Emperor said. 'It's a good habit to get into before you count the dead.'

'No, sir. That's not what I meant . . . uh, sir. See, I've been talking to the other members of the privy council, and . . . What I mean to say is . . . What do you intend to do with us?'

The Emperor had created the privy council just after the outbreak of war. On it he had placed Sullamora and several other beings important to his cause. In theory they were supposed to advise him. The Eternal Emperor had never meant to listen to them. It was just his way of making them feel important and keeping them out of his hair. Like the Imperial Parliament. The Eternal Emperor was a great believer in the trappings of democracy. It was one of the essential underpinnings of an absolute monarchy.

He pretended to consider Sullamora's question.

'I don't know,' he said. 'Disband the council, I guess. Why?'

'Well, we think that if we've been of use to you during war, then think what we can do during peace. I mean, there are certain concerns we have, Your Majesty, that it would be impossible for you to be aware of.'

Riigght, the Emperor thought. I'll bet you'd just love that. No way was he going to have an advisory body with any kind of official recognition. But why tell Sullamora that? He also tucked aside the man's comment that the privy council members had even been suggesting such a thing among themselves. Perhaps he had better start keeping closer track of them.

The Eternal Emperor smiled his most charming smile. 'That *is* a thought, Tanz,' he said. 'I'll be sure to keep it in mind.'

He wore the smile until Sullamora had exited. The smile disappeared when the door closed.

Chapter Nineteen

The Tahn had unwittingly provided the prisoners of Koldyeze with the ideal hiding place for their reinvented computer: the general-purpose sanitation facility. The Tahn had approached the problem of sanitation for so many prisoners with typical single-minded efficiency. Thirteen cells had been turned into one huge room by the simple application of sledgehammers to the walls. One area was devoted to lavatory facilities. Another contained half a dozen gigantic and ancient industrial washing machines. A third was to be used for showering. And on another were nearly 100 washbasins.

Above those were an equal number of large mirrors sunk into the stone wall.

Alex had replaced thirty-six of them with the mirror-surfaced chips that made up the computer. They swung out on hinges designed by Hernandes after pictures he recalled from a course he had taken on 'Ancient Engineers' in his student days. They were linked together by cryogenic wire scavenged by St. Clair from the motor coils of abandoned gravsleds.

Next problem: software. Despite the size of the computer, it was a basic pea brain. It would not be able to handle too many facts at a time, much less compare and analyze them against a mounting pile of data being gathered by Sten's surveyors, scavengers, and work-party spies.

The solution required two very different but equally elegant minds: Sorensen and Kraulshavn. The big farm boy boiled everything down to the smallest possible level of expression. That reduced everything by about eighty percent. Still too much. Then Kraulshavn performed the impossible. He created a symbol language in which a single squiggle might represent a hundred screens of data. The written language of the ancient Chinese was a mere glimmer of Kraulshavn's art.

Next came the difficult problem of communication with the electronic moron. In such primitive conditions, how did one send and receive symbols? Oddly enough, the answer came rather simply. Why not a spark transmitter? Sten had asked. Alex had just gaped at him a moment and then put his little team to work on it. They quickly broke Kraulshavn's symbol language down into dots and dashes. A simple key – a spring device manipulated by hand – was used to transmit. A tiny speaker was used to receive the computer's buzzing response.

The memory banks had created the biggest problem. No one had been able to offer even a silly suggestion for storing the data. Alex had lied to Kraulshavn and Sorensen, telling them that he had the solution in mind and urging them to press on with the computer. As the online date grew closer and closer, Alex found himself growing increasingly frustrated.

Ibn Bakr gave him the answer. The big tailor needed to age cloth to make Tahn peasant costumes. He used a mild caustic in near-boiling-temperature water and washed the cloth over and over again in one of the huge industrial washing machines. One day Alex found himself considering the problem as he stood in front of the machine, hypnotized by the twin agitators chugging back and forth. His jaw dropped as he realized he was staring at the answer. If he played with the gearing . . . spooled wire from one spindle to another . . . reversed the polarity of the wire . . . then fed the data from the computer to the wire . . . Voilà! After several thousand years, Kilgour had reinvented the wire recorder.

Finally the big moment had come. Sten and Alex hovered over Sorensen and Kraulshavn as they got ready to fire up the computer. Sorensen wagged his fingers for Kraulshavn to start. The being shook its head. *No.* Finger wagging came back.

'What's the problem?' Sten asked.

'He says it needs a name.' Sorensen laughed. 'Otherwise it won't know who we're talking to.'

Sten buried a groan of impatience. It was obviously important to Kraulshavn. The last thing he needed was a big pouting bird for a programmer.

'How about Brainerd?' Sten suggested. 'Wasn't he the guy way back when who got us all into this computer mess?'

Sorensen ran it through for Kraulshavn. No problem. Brainerd it was. Feathered appendages manipulated the key. Tiny sparks began rhythmically leaping between the gap. Sten imagined the dot-dash symbols flowing along the wire. Unconsciously he found himself leaning over the small speaker, waiting for the crackling response of the computer.

Nothing. More flying fingers. More sparks.

'Come on, you little clot,' Sten breathed. 'Wake the hell up . . . Come on . . . Come on . . . Speak to us . . .'

There was a crackling stutter. Then silence.

'Clot! What the hell's wrong with it?'

'Patience, young Horrie,' Alex said. 'Maybe the wee beastie is afeared to wake up.'

After all the time and energy invested, Sten failed to see any humor in the situation. He was all for putting the boot into it – and he did not mean the electronic variety. A big, heavy leather boot was more along his line of thinking.

The one-sided conversation continued for many more long minutes. Finally, Kraulshavn leaned back. There was some finger wagging, silent quizzing from Sorensen, then more finger wagging.

'What's he saying?' Sten asked.

'It doesn't like its name,' Sorensen said. 'He says we should try something else.'

'I don't clotting care what we clotting call it,' Sten gritted out.

The big washing machine/wire recorder *gaaronked* its agreement in the background.

'Call it anything you like. Call it gaaronk-gaaronk for all I give a clot!'

Sorensen nodded quite seriously. Fingers translated. Kraulshavn responded.

'Well?' Sten finally asked.

'Kraulshavn thinks one Gaaronk will be sufficient,' Sorensen said.

And before Sten could kill someone, the sparking started again. Almost instantly there was a return crackle. It was hesitant at first, and then there was one long stream of crackling. Kraulshavn bent his head to the speaker, listening. Then his fingers flashed at Sorensen. The big farm boy turned his innocent face to Sten.

'It's awake,' he said. 'It likes Gaaronk just fine!'

Chapter Twenty

Cristata had passed the word that he wished to see Big X after the last roll call – which meant after all prisoners were securely locked into their cells.

Sten pulled on the tatters of a dark coverall and picked the lock on his cell. By that time, the lock tumblers were so used to being picked that a sharp smack on the doorjamb probably would have sprung the lock. He ran down the corridors and stairs toward the ground without worrying about guards – the few patrols that the Tahn ran inside Koldyeze's wings at night were large and noisy.

He picked the lock that led out into the courtyard and waited. He was following instructions.

Cristata's emissary had told him to wait until the large search beam – the one that was slightly blue – swept across the courtyard.

He was to count six, because there was an amplified light beam behind it. 'Then walk – do not run – *walk* twenty-six paces toward 1430 hours, assuming that the search beam is at twelve.'

He paced the requisite number of paces, then stood, slightly hidden behind a ruined column, feeling stupid and waiting for the search beam to pick him up on its next sweep. Instead, the paving stones next to his feet slid away, and Cristata's tendrils probed out.

'If you wish,' he said, 'you could jump down beside me.'

Sten wished – and jumped.

He found himself in a narrow pit next to the furry being. The paving stones – Sten realized they were a very clever trapdoor – slid noiselessly closed above him.

After a moment there was a spark, and then there was light. The lamp Cristata held was a small pannier with what looked a great deal like one of the prisoners' standard rations floating in its center, surrounded by liquid.

Cristata explained that the lamp was just what Sten thought it to be – they had boiled extra rationpaks until they yielded fat, then used the fat for fuel and the packs themselves as wicks.

'But that is not what I wished to show you. Come with me.'

Cristata, without waiting for a response, dropped down into a narrower pit that Sten had not noticed and disappeared.

Sten followed.

The pit dropped about two meters and then, Sten could see, opened into a tunnel. The tunnel was completely boarded and reinforced, top, bottom, and sides.

Crawling through it was hardly claustrophobic – it was more like moving down a small but perfectly engineered corridor that led slowly but certainly downward.

At what Sten estimated were twenty-five-meter intervals, the passageway opened up into small but equally well built way stations.

It was, Sten thought, something that would take humans five years to engineer – or longer. But there was no one in the tunnel except the flailing fur-covered rump of Cristata moving ahead of him. Then the lay reader's rump wiggled and then vanished.

Sten crawled on and found himself at the lip of a larger, rocky chamber.

In it were Cristata and three humans. Sten vaguely recognized them as fellow prisoners. He levered himself over the edge and settled onto a granite boulder. There was complete silence except for the hissing of the fat lamp.

'Well, sir? What do you think?'

The question was asked by a woman wearing the stripes of a lance bombardier – Markiewicz, Sten remembered. He answered honestly.

'I've dug some tunnels,' he said. 'But this is the best one I've ever seen. You've done a clot – sorry. An excellent job.'

'In the spirit of the Great One,' Cristata intoned. 'By his leave only.'

'In the spirit of the Great One,' the other three said. What the hell, Sten thought. So Cristata was converting the masses. If believing in whatever Cristata did could produce a tunnel like that, Sten was ready to be baptized himself.

'I'm impressed, as I said,' Sten said. 'But I've already said that you people can have any help we can give. Why'd you decide to show it to me?'

Cristata's facial tendrils wiggled. 'Because,' he said, 'we appear to have a problem.' His tendrils indicated. Sten looked: The large rocky chamber, he realized, was composed on three sides of roughly cemented chunks of rock – what must have been the cathedral's foundations. But directly in front was one very large, very solid piece of stone, like unto a wall.

Sten figured out why Cristata had brought him down there. It was not pride. They needed help.

If Sten had not been Big X, he might have been more cooperative. But he had several thousand other people to consider, and so he put on his blandest face.

'You need help in getting through that clotting – beg pardon – rock?'

'We do,' Markewiecz said.

'I could have more diggers come in,' Sten said. 'But it'd still take about a thousand years to chisel through that beast. And blasting, I'm thinking, is contraindicated.'

The humans slumped. But Cristata had no reaction.

'But I think we might be able to help,' Sten went on.

Cristata's tendrils wriggled once more. 'When a more senior reader offered to deliver what might be considered the less interesting – forgive me, Great One – portions of the lesson, portions which were my duty under normal circumstances, normally there were what I have heard called tradesies involved.'

'There are,' Sten said.

'We are listening.'

We, Sten wondered, far underground. *We* meaning Cristata and his converts, or we and his Great One? Sten considered the tons of rock, earth, and stone above his head and decided this was not the place to be terribly agnostic.

Sten was not offering a pigless poke.

Kraulshavn and Sorensen's computer had already begun *gaaronk*ing through the surveyors' figures. And yes, indeed, there were big missing spaces between what the measurements produced and what Koldyeze looked like.

Most interesting were the cheapjack echosondes the surveyors had run. Some of Avrenti's supersensitive anti-tunneling microphones had somehow ended up in the hands of Kilgour's thieves. Those had then been implanted in the stone courtyard, and an impulse had been introduced. The impulse was generally a somewhat unconnected chunk of stone atop the cathedral's battlements. When said chunk of stone came crashing down, of course as a result of natural causes, the crash was recorded at various points and fed through Gaaronk.

The crashes did not match – and showed that, mysteriously, there was a lot of unknown there underneath Koldyeze. Empty unknown there.

Cellars.

That was Sten's oinker in the sack.

'If,' he began, 'I can show you a way around or through this rock, your tunnel is no longer going to be exclusive.'

The three humans growled.

'Continue,' Cristata said.

'I would like to use the tunnel to take more escapers out.'

'How many?'

'I don't know. But you four would be the first. And you would have all the assistance my organization could provide.'

'We have all the aid we need from the Great One,' Cristata said. His converts nodded in agreement.

Sten felt slightly sorry for what he was doing, but as yet there was no other viable escape plan in motion. And Sten remembered once again that warrant officer crying over his parcel.

'We'll give you more diggers. Diggers working under your direction. And nothing will be done without your knowledge and approval.'

'Do we have any choice?'

Sten did not bother to answer.

Markiewicz glanced at Cristata and answered for the four of them. 'It appears as if the Great One wishes this.'

It was unanimous.

Sten sort of hated to give them what looked to be the answer, because it was simple.

Dig down.

Disbelieving – except for Cristata, who reasoned that somehow the Great One was speaking through Sten – they did.

Many days later, they broke through into the cellars of Koldyeze. And that, for Cristata, created an even larger problem.

Once again Sten went out and down late at night, then shinnied down from that small rocky chamber into caverns. High stone-ceilinged caverns that led on into darkness. Caverns that were flagstone-floored, with pillars stretching up. Caverns that, Cristata pointed out, held all the temptations of Xanadu.

Sten took a quick torchlight inventory, whistled, and agreed. Evidently the simple, monotheistic agrarian communards who had originally built Koldyeze had planned for some very rainy days. And they had planned on spending those rainy days in more than ascetic meditation. There were chambers with large barrels. Sten thumped them, and they appeared to still have liquid in them. He ran his finger along the barrel staves and tasted alcohol.

Other chambers held foodpaks; still others, clothing.

'And we have not fully explored these chambers,' Cristata went on gloomily. 'But it would appear that whoever stored these substances enjoyed life.'

Sten eyed the foodpaks hungrily – and stopped thinking about what a meal composed of real food could do for him. Instead, he made plans.

Cristata – personally – would make a full survey of the cellars. What was in them would be told to Colonel Virunga and Mr. Hernandes only. The last thing Sten needed was for that tunnel, which looked to be their only salvation, to get blown because a bunch of tunnelers started looking fat, well dressed, and – worst case – drunk. The assigned tunnelers from the X organization would be conducted into the rocky chamber blindfolded and then taken through the cellars to the working face. Only Cristata and his converts would know what those cellars of plenty held. They would be kept secret for emergency rations and to help the escapers get into shape.

And Sten hoped most sincerely that none of Cristata's true believers would suffer a lapse of faith and a subsequent big mouth.

Chapter Twenty-One

Senior Captain Lo Prek sat nervously on the edge of his bunk, trying to decipher the radio chatter between the freighter captain and traffic control. The mysteries of naval patter were beyond him, but he could tell from the tone of the captain's voice that all did not bode well.

Prek had wrangled passage on a ship carrying low-priority materials for the Tahn factories. Already the ship's flight had been interrupted or rerouted half a dozen times since he had started his journey many cycles before. And from the captain's whining, he was sure it was about to happen again.

He squirmed impatiently on the bunk, almost welcoming the bite of the metal edge into his skinny haunches. He felt helpless. There was nothing he could do or say to hurry the journey. He had already called in the few favors that were owed him to get the short amount of leave that had been approved. And he had almost begged to get permission to travel on the puny freighter. Permission had been granted grudgingly – possibly out of guilt.

Prek knew that he was not a man anyone liked. He was super-efficient. Super-obedient. Single-minded at his work. Never asking for any rewards for a job well done. Being non-competitive, he had also never harmed anyone in his life. Still, he was not liked. There was something about him . . . and Prek knew and accepted it, just as he accepted the guilt that caused in his fellow officers. For a change, he had used that guilt. Acting completely out of character, he had molded it to his own advantage. Normally, even the thought of something like that would have disgusted Prek.

But not this time. Because this time he was sure he had found Sten – or, at least, where Sten was hiding.

There was a new prisoner-of-war camp. For troublemakers. For survivors. It was on Heath at a place called Koldyeze.

Prek listened to the resignation in the freighter captain's voice. There would be another delay. Another reprieve for his enemy.

Chapter Twenty-Two

The prisoner work detail, surrounded by their Tahn guards, clattered back toward Koldyeze. Just in front of them the cobbled street wound upward toward the prison.

'I'm waiting,' Sten said.

'Shut up. You'll see,' St. Clair whispered.

'Deee-tail . . . halt,' Chetwynd bellowed.

The prisoners clumped to a stop. On either side of the road rose abandoned slum apartments.

'Five minutes. Rest. Be grateful.'

Sten goggled as all the guards, including Chetwynd, ostentatiously turned their backs and the detail dissolved, scampering into the buildings like so many rodents.

'What in the—'

'Come on,' St. Clair urged, nearly dragging Sten into a doorway.

'Didn't I say I had a surprise?' she went on.

'GA, Captain. And quick.'

'Don't give me orders. Look. You know how to search a room?'

'I do,' Sten said.

'Okay. We're going upstairs. You look for things. I'll talk.'

They went up the rickety stairs, and Sten followed her instructions.

'What am I looking for?'

'Anything we can use. And anything the Tahn can sell. We got ourselves a business going, Big X.'

Indeed they did.

The slum quarters had never been that well populated – the apartments were entirely too close to Koldyeze. And the periodic draft sweeps the Tahn made for their military started, of course, in the poor sections of Heath.

St. Clair had followed orders – if she was to be the scrounger, she would be a clotting good one. And the way to get things was, of course, on the outside. In spite of her total loathing for anything resembling manual labor, she had volunteered for every work gang going. She did not know exactly what to look for, but she knew there was something out there.

What was out there were the guards. And St. Clair knew that any being who was willing to batten on the miseries of others was corruptible. She had tested her theory – and her teeth – when she had found a jeweled tunic pin in some trash.

She had offered it to the nearest and – by estimate from body weight – greediest guard. He had snatched and examined it.

'Are there others?' he had asked.

'I guess so,' St. Clair said innocently, waving a hand around at the multistory buildings. 'It'd be interesting to look.'

'Wouldn't it?'

The guard grinned. 'Whyn't you an' the others go have a look?'

Within minutes, Captain St. Clair had the rest of the detail worming through the nearest apartment. That looked as if it could develop into something. Within two days she felt less like a corrupter and more like the corrupted. The 'looting break' became an instant ritual for most of the work details on their way back to Koldyeze.

St. Clair stopped her explanation and marveled at Sten. He was listening intently while quartering the room like a bloodhound. He started at the far wall and quartered outward. Each piece of broken furniture was picked up or tapped for hidden compartments. The rags that had been clothes were swiftly patted down, then held up to see if they still could be used. The ripped mattress was kneaded for any interesting lumps. There were two pictures lying on the floor in their broken frames. Both of them were torn apart. Then Sten set to work knuckle rapping on the walls.

'I said to look for things,' she said.

'That's what I'm doing.'

'Pretty clottin' thorough, mister. What were you when you were a civilian? Some kind of burglar?'

'No,' Sten said. He certainly had no intention of explaining to anyone, least of all to St. Clair, whom he trusted about as much as a Tahn, that his search was the product of thorough Mantis training. 'Here we go,' he said.

St. Clair stared – it looked as if Sten had pulled a sliver of metal from his arm and then knifed through a wall switch. The sliver disappeared, and Sten's fingers emerged with a wad of credits. St. Clair inhaled sharply.

'Money. Tahn money.'

'Right. Now, go on out, Captain.'

'What are you—'

'That's an order! Move!'

St. Clair found herself outside the broken door. A moment later, Sten stepped out beside her.

'Very good, Captain,' he said. 'Now. Here's the drill. Anything the guards want – play-pretties, alk, drugs – give it to them.'

'Give?'

'Give. Money goes to me.'

'Nice racket,' St. Clair said cynically.

Sten paused. 'You know, troop – you got a bad attitude. You keep a log. Report what you bring in to Colonel Virunga. Or don't you trust him, either?'

'I trust him,' St. Clair said grudgingly.

'Fine. I also want civilian clothes. Anything electronic. Wire. Tape. If you find any weapons—' Sten stopped and thought. A prisoner found with a weapon on him would be for the high jump – as would, most likely, the entire work detail. 'Weapons – you stash them. Report to me, and we'll arrange to get them in the gate.'

'Detail! Reassemble!'

'Let's go.'

Sten clattered back down the steps. St. Clair followed, looking at his back and wondering several things.

Chetwynd was waiting in the street outside.

'You!'

Sten snapped to attention. 'Sir!'

'What was your name again?'

'Horatio, sir.'

'You sure you don't remember me?'

'Nossir!'

'Before the war, I worked the ports,' Chetwynd went on. 'Maybe you used to be a merchant sailor?'

'Nossir! I was never offworld before I joined up, sir.'

Chetwynd scratched his chin. 'Clot. I dunno. Maybe you got a twin brother somewhere. You two got anything?'

St. Clair felt Sten's fingers touch her hand. As an experienced gambler, she palmed the object, then held it out.

'Credits,' Chetwynd said. 'Very good. Very good, indeed. Maybe next time I'm in charge of the detail, and you two want to go off and . . .' He snickered. 'I can make it a long enough rest break.'

St. Clair thought fondly of how she could thank Chetwynd as she smiled and ran back toward the detail. Drawing and quartering, she decided, was far too easy. Bed Sten? She would rather make love to a mark.

Chapter Twenty-Three

The supersecret of the Prisoner's Aid parcels was that they were neither quite wholly altruistic nor neutral.

Mercury Corps – Intelligence – field operatives, which of course included Mantis, flag officers, and skippers of long-range penetration units or ships were given the secret orally when a mission suggested they might be captured.

A few items in each crate were loaded. For instance:

One key item to look for was any foodstuff that supposedly had been produced by a paternally named firm, such as Grandfather's Caff, Dronemaster's R'lrx, Packguru's Scented Tofu, and so forth. All the firms were quite legitimate, but the foodstuffs packaged were designed to be as close to inedible as the Emperor's most devious chemists could make them. Even a prison guard should have had little interest in them.

There was nothing out of the ordinary in their contents, but each of those cans contained something potentially useful for an escaper. Microwire saws were buried in the rim of the pak. Needle-size engraving tools were in others. Still other paks had miniature printed circuit boards sealed in the double layer that made up the pak's base. It would take a cursing prisoner two days to break the seal apart – but that might also prevent discovery even with a thorough inspection. There were other interesting devices in other cans. All the materials used would never show up on detectors.

All metals – such as the pins and needles in the archaic sewing kits – were magnetized and could be used in compasses.

The clothes themselves were indelibly marked with a black-white X on the front and rear. There was no reason for a prison official to object to issuing them – they certainly could never be used for any kind of escape. The X's were actually *almost* indelible. Each parcel contained small single-use artificial sweetener packs, artificial sweetener that was in fact tasteless. The sweetener was intended to be dissolved in water, and the clothing soaked in it. Four hours later, the X's would vanish and the POW would be left with a garment that, given enough tailoring skill, might be converted into an acceptable civilian-looking garment for his escape.

No one outside Imperial Intelligence knew about that – certainly not the gentle Manabi. It was a violation of every POW convention and any civilized ethos. And, of course, it had been the personal scheme of Fleet Marshal Ian Mahoney in the days when he had headed Imperial Intelligence.

Even the legitimate items in the aid parcels had their own, non-legitimate purposes.

For one thing, the foodpaks were very useful for one of Kilgour's intelligence schemes.

This one he had mentally dubbed 'Seduction of the Innocent/ Reward for the Wicked (Wee Free Division).'

By that point he had selected the agents for the operation, choosing the friendliest and most open prisoners he could find. Each of them was ordered to choose a guard or two, then try to make friends with that screw.

To accomplish that, the 'seducers' were given access to anything any of the prisoners had. If a guard fancied a ring, somehow he would be given it. If a guard needed someone to talk to, there would always be a sympathetic ear or auditory apparatus the seducer could provide. The only limit was sexual involvement – not because Kilgour had any particular moral qualms but because he was an experienced enough spymaster to realize that pillow talk usually was not significant and that there was the constant danger of the seducer eventually becoming the seducee. There were five primary goals:

1. Can this guard be corrupted?
2. Can this guard be blackmailed?
3. Discover everything about camp security, from the personalities of the guards to the location of sensors to shift assignments.
4. Find out everything and anything about Heath, from what can be ordered in a restaurant (escapers, unaware of civilian shortages, have been blown ordering a nonexistent item) through travel restrictions and requirements to current slang and civilian dress.
5. Are there ways to get offplanet? If so, what are they, and what are the problems?

There were also other requirements.

There was a tap on the door to Alex and Sten's cell. Kilgour beamed and bellowed, 'Thae's noo need t' beat, sir. We're a' home.'

The door opened, and Mr. N'chlos peered in.

Sten and Alex shot to attention, as prison orders required.

'No, no,' the young man said shyly. 'You don't have to do that around me.'

'Just showin' a wee note ae respect, sir.'

Kilgour was most proud of his work so far.

The heavy-worlder had noticed N'chlos watching him when he was on a work party. Kilgour was fairly sure the interest was not romantic. He was more sure after he had single-lifted a chunk of concrete rubble away after three other prisoners had struggled unsuccessfully to move it. He had also seen that the guard was undermuscled, even for a man trying to grow on the Tahn guard rations. Alex was absolutely sure after hearing a couple of guards make sarcastic comments about N'chlos and his weakness.

Alex had waited until he and N'chlos were away from the rest of the detail, then heaved a monstrous beam out of the roadway the crew was clearing. Apropos of nothing and seemingly talking to thin air, he had said, 'Thae's a bit ae a' trick there.'

The guard had asked, and Kilgour had shown him just a bit about body leverage: lifting from the legs, not the back, putting the entire force of one's shoulders into an effort, and so forth. N'chlos had never learned any of that.

Kilgour had generously offered to show him some other tricks yet had never suggested that N'chlos was anything other than a fine figure of a Tahn. N'chlos fell into the habit of dropping by Kilgour's cell when he was on walking patrol inside the prisoners' quarters.

The young man had quite a taste for caff, heavily sweetened

with Earth sugar. Kilgour then had an unlimited draw from the aid parcels.

Sten had never before been permitted in the cell when N'chlos visited. There was a reason, Kilgour had told him. He said he might need a distraction.

'A brew, lad,' Alex said, lighting a small fat stove and putting on the blackened, hammered-out tin they used to cook with. N'chlos sat down on one of the stools Alex had constructed.

''N how goes th' war?' Alex asked.

'They just cut the ration points again,' N'chlos gloomed. 'Even for us.'

'Shameful,' Kilgour said. 'An' curious t' boot.'

'Something about those who fight the hardest deserve the most.'

'Speakin't frank, Ah considers tha' a bit of ae error. Meanin' no criticism. Dinnae th lords ken th' folks on th' home front be fightin't thae own way ae war?'

N'chlos shifted and unbuttoned the top button of his tunic. Damned right, Sten thought. He, too, was sweltering. In the cell below theirs three men were stoking a plas-fed jerry-rigged furnace.

'Bleedin't hot,' Kilgour said sympathetically. 'Canne y' take off thae tunic?'

'It's against orders.'

'Clot,' Alex swore. 'A wee soldier should know whae orders are to be followed an' when. Mak't comfortable, sir. I' thae lead-booted sergeant comes, we'll hear his clumpin't in time.'

N'chlos took off his combat belt and holstered his stun rod and, his tunic-jacket after looking doubtfully at Sten, who was carefully positioned across the room. He looked for someplace to hang the jacket and spotted a peg – the only peg – driven into the cell wall very close to the door.

'C'mon, lad, Ah mean, sir. Caff's on.'

N'chlos hung up the tunic and reseated himself.

'Y' were sayin't afore Ah interrupted?'

'Oh. Yes. Sometimes I think I should put in for a transfer. To a line unit.'

'Sir, once't Ah thought th' same, an ne'ever harked t' m' poor crippl't brother. War dinnae be bonnie, sir. Lookit th' spot Ah'm in noo.'

'*I* wouldn't want to be a POW,' N'chlos said frankly.

'True. An' thae's nae th' worst thae can happen.' Kilgour paused. 'E'en when y'hae no fightin't, thae's little joy. F'r instance, dinnae Ah tell you ae the spotted snakes?'

'I don't think so.'

Kilgour spared a mini-smile for Sten, and Sten glowered back. The clot had trapped him, well and truly.

'I' was ae Earth. Ae a wee isle called Borneo.'

'You've been to *Earth*!' N'chlos was astonished.

'Aye. lad. Th' service broadin't thae background. At any rate, an' t' go on, Ah'd jus' taken' o'er a wee detachment ae troops.'

'I didn't know Imperial warrant officers did that.'

'Special circumstances,' Alex went on. 'An' so Ah calls th' sarn't major in, an Ah asks, "Sarn't Major, whae's thae worst problem?" 'An' he say't, "Spotted snakes!"

'An' Ah says, "Spotted snakes?"

'An' he says, "Spotted snakes, sir."'

At that point the cell door opened silently, and an arm – St. Clair's arm – snaked in. Her hand lifted N'chlos's tunic off the peg, and tunic and arm vanished.

'Here's th' caff, sir. Anyhoot, Ah'm looki't ae th' fiche on m' new unit, an' it's awful. Thae's desertion, thae's a crime sheet thae long, thae's social diseases up th' gumpstump – m' command's a wreck!

'So, Ah call't th' unit t'gether an' questions m' men on whae's th' problem.

'An' they chorus, "Ae's th' spotted snakes, sir."

'"Spotted snakes?" Ah asks.

'"Aye, sir. Spotted snakes," they chorus.

'An' thae explain't thae's all these spotted snakes in th' jungle. Ah did say th' detachment wae in th' center ae a braw jungle, dinnae Ah?'

Outside, Sten hoped, N'chlos's tunic was being searched. His soldier book and any other papers were tossed to the prison's fastest runner, who darted downstairs to a cell where L'n waited.

His papers were scrutinized and memorized by her artistically eidetic memory, to be reproduced later.

The tunic was measured, and all uniform buttons had wax impressions made, also for reproduction. The stun rod's measurements were taken just in case someone needed to build a phony weapon.

Within minutes the escape committee would have all the essentials on the off chance that an escaper might want or need to look like a guard. Or maybe to use N'chlos as a cover identity.

Unless, of course, N'chlos turned around, realized his uniform was missing, and shouted an alert.

But in the meantime Sten squirmed under Alex's story.

'An' aye,' Kilgour went on. 'Thae wee spotted snakes. All over th' place. Wee fierce lads w' a braw deadly poison. Crawl in th' fightin' positions an' bites, crawl in th' tents an' bites, crawl in the mess an' bites. Awful creatures. Som'at hae be done.

'So Ah considers an' then orders up aye formation. An' comit out, an th' men gasp, seein't Ah'm holdin' a spotted snake.

'An' Ah say, "Listen't up, men. Ah hae here a spotted snake, aye?"

'An' th' men chorus back, "Aye sir, ae spotted snake."

'"Now, Ah'm goin't t' show you th' solution to thae spotted snakes. Ae's by th' numbers. Wi' th' count ae one, y' securit th' snake wi' your right hand. Wi' th' count ae two, y' secure th' snake wi' your left hand as well. Wi' th' count ae three, y' slid't y'r right hand up t' its wee head, an *pop*, on th' count ae four, y' snappit th' snake's head off wi' y'r thumb!"

'An' th' men's eyes goggle, an then they go t' war.

'F'r th' next two weeks, thae's all y' hear around th' detachment. *Pop . . . pop . . . pop . . . pop.* Thae's wee snake heads lyin't all around.

'An th' morale picks up, an' thae's noo more deserters, an' thae's nae crime sheet, an' e'en the pox rate drops a notch.

'M' problem's solved. An' then, one day, Ah'm visitin' th' dispensary.

'An' thae's one puir lad lying't thae, an' he's swathed in bandages. Head t' foot. Bandages.

'An' Ah ask't "Whae happen?"

'An' he croakit, "Spotted snakes, sir!"

'"Spotted snakes," Ah says.

'"Aye, sir. Spotted snakes."

'"G'on lad," Ah says.'

Alex was looking a little worried – then the door opened again, and the same silent arm replaced the tunic and weapons belt. Alex hesitated, then put his story – if that was what it was – back on track. Sten was trying to remember just what the most painful and slowest method of execution he knew of was and was determined to apply it to his warrant officer.

'"Sir," th' lad in bandages goes on. "Y' know how y' told us how t' deal wi' th' spotted snakes?"

'"Aye, spotted snakes. But Ah dinnae ken—"

'"Ah'm tryin't t' tell you. Ah'm in m' fightin' position ae stand-to th' other night. An' thae wee furrit object wi' spots slides in m' hole. An' just like y' ordered, Mr Kilgour, on th' count ae one Ah grabs it wi' m' right hand, on th' count ae two Ah grabs it wi' m' left hand, on th' count ae three Ah slides m' hand up, an' on th' count ae four Ah *pop* . . . an' sir, can y' fancy m' sittin' thae wi' m' thumb up a tiger's arse?"'

There was dead, complete silence.

Finally N'chlos spoke. 'That is the worst clotting joke I have ever heard.'

And for the first and only time, Sten found himself in complete agreement with a Tahn.

St. Clair peered into the gloom, watching her strange roommate begin sketching – working from memory only – the Tahn identification card directly onto a photosensitive plate. She had wanted to object when Sten had ordered her to pair up with the shy Kerr, but she had swallowed her protest. She did not want to give the clot the satisfaction of knowing her objections. It had nothing to do with the fact that L'n was not human. St. Clair just preferred to be alone. She had always been solo, had always depended on her own wits, with never the thought of responsibility for another being to hold her back. St. Clair survived by taking chances, by not hesitating. And L'n was the kind of being that made those cold feelings difficult.

Also, there was some logic to the pairing. As the main scrounger, it was better for her to deal directly with the little Kerr artist. But it took some getting used to. L'n needed darkness to be comfortable, and outside the cell she was almost helpless in the bright Tahn sun. Gradually St. Clair had found herself automatically helping L'n with little things: guiding her to mess; finding tools lost in the glare of the late afternoon sun; pulling her back to reality when she became hypnotized by some freak manifestation of light.

In short, St. Clair found herself liking another living being. L'n was becoming that strangest of all animals – a friend.

It took some work, especially the way L'n went on about that bastard Horatio, who was so full of his own authority. The way L'n talked, the man was practically a saint. And then St. Clair heard the story about Lance Corporal Hansen, and she understood Hansen and Sten had become one person – an interchangeable hero. It was all L'n could do to hold on to her sanity living in the squalor and dense crowding of the prison camp. She yearned for the peaceful forests of her homeworld. L'n spent longer and longer periods of time lost in those memories. And the hard reality of the camp was becoming more and more difficult. Without Sten – or at least the idea of Sten – L'n would eventually cross over into silent madness.

St. Clair had made herself a promise to change that. If it was the last thing she did before she escaped, she would coax L'n into standing on her own.

'Tell me, L'n,' she said. 'You're interested in light. Have you ever seen that famous light tower on Prime World?'

L'n stopped in midsketch. 'You mean the one built by those two Milchens? Marr and Senn, I think they're called.'

'Yeah.'

'Just pictures,' she said. 'Not in person.'

'Oh. You've never been to Prime World. When this is over, maybe we can go see it together.'

'Oh, I've been to Prime World before. In fact, when I was there, I heard there was going to be a big party at the tower. Now, *that* would have been something to see!'

'Why didn't you go?' St. Clair asked.

'I wasn't invited.'

St. Clair was incredulous. 'Why the clot not? You coulda crashed it easy. I did it a couple of times! At a Marr and Senn party, nobody could possibly know if you're legit or not.'

L'n sighed, a little hopeless, a tinge jealous. 'Crash a party . . . I've dreamed of doing something like that. You know, the new L'n. Bold. Determined. Daring. Sweeping into a party like I owned it. Making everybody think I've just got to be somebody famous because of the way I carry myself. But afraid to ask and show their ignorance.' She shook her head. 'Not a chance. They'd take one look at these big ugly eyes of mine and know right off I'm a nobody.'

St. Clair was stunned. 'What are you talking about? Ugly eyes?'

L'n shrugged. It was a shrug of someone resigned to an uncomfortable truth.

'I'm telling you, girl,' St. Clair finally said. 'You and I have got a lot of work to do. And we're going to start with your notions of ugly and work right up to party crashing.'

L'n giggled as if St. Clair had just made a joke. But St. Clair knew better. She had just made a promise. And St. Clair was a woman of her word.

Chapter Twenty-Four

'Count complete,' Virunga announced, echoing Isby's report. Then he pivoted, saluted Genrikh, and bellowed, 'All prisoners present.' He paused just a beat. 'Sir.'

Even Genrikh could not find a reason to prolong the afternoon roll call. He nodded and stalked toward the administration area. Virunga saluted his absence, about-faced and shouted again: 'Unit . . . dis-missed!'

The semi-rabble became a babble of conversation, and the prisoners headed toward their quarters, mess kits, and the evening meal.

Sten, who had more important plans, slid toward the stairs and Virunga's chambers – and, head in a tunnel, he nearly walked into Chetwynd, who was waiting and smiling down at him.

'Prisoner Horatio.'

'Sir!'

'That's not your name.'

'Pardon, sir. My mother would be surprised.'

'Not too bad. I just remembered where I saw you before. Dru.'

'Bless you.'

'Knock off the drakh. I don't have a lot of time. Dru. Prison world. I was running a happy knot of villains, harvesting mollusks. And you and that tub Kilgour showed up in screwsuits. To harvest some weasel named . . . hell, what was it? Dunstan . . . no. Dyntsman.'

Chetwynd's memory was excellent. Good enough to kill him.

'Sir. No offense, sir. But how could I—'

'How could you be a Tahn screw then and a POW now? Try this. You're Imperial Intelligence. When the war started, you got caught up in the net. Maybe your cover was firecontrolman. Maybe you grabbed it out of the hat when the drakh came down. Hell if I know.'

Sten calculated. Could he kill Chetwynd now? Here? Negative. He could disappear before the body was found, but there would be reprisals. Second question: Could he stall Chetwynd from reporting this interesting piece of information to Avrenti long enough to arrange some species of fatal accident, preferably outside Koldyeze's walls? Possibly.

'Speak up, prisoner.'

'I can't, sir. Anything I say'd get me tossed into solitary.'

'Very good,' Chetwynd said approvingly. 'If you'd started burbling that I was a flip case, I would've had to smash you a few times and toss you in the cells. And might've started wondering about whether my mind's finally going. But . . .' Chetwynd smiled. 'Now all I have to do is figure how to play the card. Or whether to play it at all.'

'The prisoner does not understand.'

'The prisoner surer'n hell *does* understand. I'm a screw right now. But my sentence's still on remand. These clottin' Tahn can yank my privileges and have me back on Dru – or off to one of the deathworlds – for any reason or no reason at all.

'So I got to figure this some more.

'And, just so you don't start trying to arrange some kinda incident that'd go and change my lovely body, I'll give you a further piece of my thinking. I like to back winners.'

Chetwynd was a far more subtle man than he appeared, Sten realized.

'The war isn't going well?'

'The war's goin' just fine. So far.' Chetwynd said. 'We – clot. I'm even startin' to talk like a screw. The Tahn are poundin' you Imperials like you're drums. Question I got is how long. I go out the gate an' I see gravsleds grounded 'cause fuel's rationed. I see us scroungin' through the rubble for recyclables. I got to figure if the drakh's like this here on Heath, what's it like on the other worlds?

'You like my figuring? Maybe I shoulda been an analyst, huh? My thinkin' goes on – if the Tahn don't win some kinda flat-out battle real quick, the grinder's gonna go on. And there's more of you than there is of us.

'So maybe the war don't go like the lords and ladies want it. And maybe – sooprise – Heath's got a little different system of government. Like maybe we're payin' our taxes to Prime World.

'I'm thinkin' – in a case like that – Mr Chetwynd might not get a little gold star by havin' set up some hero intelligence type to get his brain scanned and then burned. Might end up bein' some kind of war criminal.

'Wouldn't like that at all.

'Like I said, I back winners. So . . . least till things change, and I can get a better idea on what game we're playin', and with whose deck . . . I'm planning on doing just what I been doing about you. Nothing.

'That's all, prisoner.'

Sten was about to make a decision he hated.

Even in escaping, there was strategy and there was tactics. Tactics – find possible escape route, build possible escape route, equip escapers – was very easy.

The strategy was the agony.

A POW's duties did not end with his or her capture. He or she was still a combatant. The war still had to be fought – even inside a POW camp. Everyone in Koldyeze not only had been hypno-conditioned during training but had accepted that with his continued resistance.

Part of that resistance was escape.

Escape did far more than get the poor sorry prisoner to home base and, hopefully, returned to war – it continued the war while it was being carried out. Each prisoner who was a pain in the butt to his captors took one or more potential enemy soldiers away from the lines and made them into guards. The bigger the pain in the butt, the more he or she decreased the available fighting strength. The fine line to walk, of course, was gauging at what point the enemy would decide that a bullet was more economically feasible.

Thus far, the prisoners of Koldyeze had done an excellent job of continuing the war and their own lives.

Cristata's tunnel might change all that.

That was Sten's decision, one that Colonel Virunga gave his opinion on and then qualified it.

Once the tunnel punched out beyond the walls, there were two choices for escape – mass or planned.

A mass attempt would mean that everyone who could fit down that hole would burst out onto Heath.

The end result?

Certainly all troops and auxiliaries on Heath would be yanked from their normal duties to hunt down the escapers. Other units, headed for battle, could well be diverted onto Heath. The end result would be that most, if not all, of the escapers would be rounded up.

And then murdered.

It was also very likely that the entire POW complement of Koldyeze would be slaughtered in reprisal.

That was Virunga's recommended option. Go for broke. We are all soldiers – and we all accept the risks.

Sten chose the second option, even though at best he was condemning people who had worked long hours on the tunnel to staying in captivity, denying them even the slightest possibility of making it to freedom.

The second option was to filter out a handful of completely prepared escapers, given every bit of kit the X organization could provide, from forged papers to money.

Sten did not reach his decision for any humanitarian reasons. Or, at least, so he told himself.

There had been almost no successful escapes by prisoners of the Tahn – at least very few that he had heard of. If Koldyeze broke out en masse – and the escapers were captured, given a show trial, and executed – that would effectively dampen any resistance, let alone further escape attempts from any of the other camps scattered through the Tahn worlds.

Better that one escaper make his or her home run all the way from the heart of the Tahn Empire – and the success be promoted.

Virunga grunted in displeasure. 'I delegated . . . your decision. Now. Who goes?'

Painful strategy turned into more painful tactics. Sten would have to play God.

It was easier to start with the exclusions. Virunga, of course. He could not – and would not consider – abandon the beings in his charge.

Sten and Alex – Big X was banned.

Other beings who could not blend into the essentially human population of Heath. The crippled.

Who *could* make an attempt – and probably get killed in the process? Sten had only the original thousand prisoners, plus the various additions, to choose among.

Cristata and his three converts. It was their plan. Sten hoped to force the four into accepting some assistance and a plan more rational than flinging themselves on the mercy of country peasants.

Ibn Bakr and his partner.

Sten grimaced. St. Clair. He liked her about as much as she reciprocated. But if there was to be one solo attempt, he thought she probably had the best chance of anyone.

Hernandes. If anybody deserved to go out, it was he. Also, Sten figured that Hernandes's continuing sabotage operations were due to get blown, and Hernandes due for the high jump.

Completely unsure whether he had made the right decision, or even if he had made the correct choices, Sten left Virunga's room to begin the laying on of hands.

Naturally enough, nothing worked out as Sten had thought.

'My friend,' Hernandes said slowly. 'Thank you. But . . . I shall not be going out through the tunnel. I dislike enclosed spaces.'

Sten, having more than a bit of a tendency toward claustrophobia, understood that. But Hernandes continued.

'Probably what you've said is correct. Probably I've run the game about as far as I can. But I don't *know* that. Do you understand?'

No. Sten did not.

'I'll try it another way. Assume that I manage to wiggle down that tunnel without making an exhibition of myself. Further assume that I am able to disappear into the unwashed of Heath and, using your – I am sure – most clever plan, return to the Empire. That is all very well and good.

'But what then would happen to me? I assume that I would be pridefully exhibited across the Empire as someone who managed to – capital letters please – Find Freedom.

'I would be far too valuable to ever get assigned to combat once more. Isn't that probably correct?'

'You assume a helluva lot in how far you'd get,' Sten said. 'But you're right.'

'My granddaughter died. As I told you. And I am not convinced that a full repayment has been made.

'Now do you understand?'

Sten did. There had been more than a couple of times when Imperial orders and duty had fallen second to personal vengeance.

And so he made apologies to CWO Hernandes – and made mental allowances that when Hernandes was caught by the Tahn, none of Koldyeze's secrets would be exposed.

Similarly, Sten went zero for zero with Lay Reader Cristata.

He had come up with – he thought – a severely clever plan for the three humans and one nonhumanoid. Rather than vanish into a guaranteed-hostile countryside, they should, Sten proposed, stay inside the capital city of Heath. Cristata should present himself as an absolute convert to the cause of the Tahn. He should become a street preacher, loudly espousing how, in seeing the way his own world had been 'liberated,' he had come to know the true evil of the Empire.

It would take a long time, Sten knew, for people to question a true believer if that true believer was telling them that everything they did was correct.

'But that would be a lie,' Cristata pointed out, and his acolytes nodded.

Sten practiced jaw clenching and unclenching as a substitute for answering.

'The Great One would withdraw his support if we taught such a lie,' Cristata went on. 'Also, I do not see what good we could do by remaining within this city, within this place of regimentation and uniforms.'

'You could stay alive,' Sten offered.

'Life is given and taken away by the Great One. It matters little which is the gift.'

More jaw clenching.

'Also, you have failed to understand the teachings of the Great One. Only those who live close to the earth, who have avoided false mammon-professions and have realized that the duty of us all is to feed and help others, could understand and give us shelter.'

Sten, remembering a long-ago time when he and his Mantis Team had been chased cross-country for several days by some supposedly uninvolved peasants, did not respond.

'I had hopes, Horatio,' Cristata finished sadly, 'that you were understanding my message and would become one of us. You did not.

'But we can still pray that those who will take advantage of what the Great One has given us will find truth within their own hearts and, once they return to freedom, will preach the light.'

The best that Sten could hope for as he excused himself was that Cristata and his three friends would be sufficiently obvious to take the heat off the real escapers and find an easy and clean death.

St. Clair waited until the door closed behind Sten before she looked at L'n. Even in the dimness, she could see L'n's 'hands' twitching.

'But you must go,' L'n started without preamble.

Yes, St. Clair thought. I must go. I'm starting to go mad here.

This would be escape number twenty-two? Or was it twenty-four? She had set the previous attempts at twenty-one but really did not want to know if she had tried more and failed in more.

This one had to succeed.

Because otherwise St. Clair could see herself, quite coldly and calmly, doing a run at the wire during assembly and getting killed.

Thus far she had avoided forcing herself to play in a rigged game because it was the only one in town. But the odds on staying cold and waiting until the numbers were right were becoming more and more slender.

And L'n?

At least she would have Sten to fall back on. She would survive, St. Clair told herself.

Besides, she was not an orphan. She was the Eel. A lone survivor and gambler. She needed no one and nothing.

Didn't she?

Chapter Twenty-Five

The brilliance of Lady Atago was the same as that of the Tahn – and that of their failure.

In war, their plans were carefully worked out down to the last detail. If those plans went awry in midbattle, the Tahn were also geniuses at improvisation. They could – and did – cobble together units made up of the most disparate elements, pitch them into the front lines, and win.

The culturally programmed willingness of their warriors to die in place rather than yield did not hurt, of course. But what the Tahn lacked was the ability to modify a plan once the seal of approval was on it.

And so Lady Atago paced a battle chamber, her boot-heels clicking against the emptiness.

She should have been busy briefing the twelve battlefleet commanders, giving final and full details for the attack on Durer, step by step. The battle chamber was fully equipped to show, on its hemispheric domed screen, any detail from the overall strategic advance to the disposition of the lowliest patrol craft.

Instead Atago had been informed, in the highest code, to postpone that meeting and stand by.

Further orders – EYES ONLY – said that the head of the Tahn Council, Lord Fehrle, requested the privilege of conferring with the commander of the fleets at her convenience.

Atago did not bother sending anything other than a routine confirmation. Nor did she arrange to be waiting when Fehrle's battleship broke out of AM2 drive and warped alongside.

The side people and staff officers could provide the panoply. Atago was worried. Something was about to go very, very wrong.

She was very correct.

Fehrle entered the chamber, greeted Atago with all the formality her office required, and then dismissed his aides.

Lady Atago, maintaining propriety, asked if Lord Fehrle wished the honor of seeing her plans for the upcoming engagement.

'No,' Fehrle said. 'I am well aware, and certainly approve of them.'

Then why are you here? Atago thought.

'The council has met, and is committed to the grand plan. In fact, they wish to increase its strategic impact.'

Atago smelled a – no, several reeks. Reflexively she palmed a switch, and the projection of the attack against the Durer System sprang across the night galaxy simulation of the chamber above them. But neither Tahn looked at it.

'Perhaps I don't understand,' Lady Atago said flatly.

'We have realized, through your brilliant planning and analysis,' Fehrle went on, 'that your attack should be implemented massively.'

He turned to the screen and picked up the control.

'Here,' he said. 'Twelve battlefleets shall attack through emptiness toward the Durer System. Over here, the feint against the Al-Sufi System will engage the Imperial Forces in the cluster until far too late.'

Atago did not even bother responding.

'The strike, as we have all agreed, is for the heart of the Empire. Therefore, after full analysis and discussion, we of the council have agreed that we should expand this plan, both because of its brilliance and because of its perfection to the Tahn ideal.'

'Which means?'

'We feel that those fleets which have been kept in reserve could be better committed to the full battle. We shall not worry about our flanks but rather practice a policy of leapfrogging ahead. Any ship, unit, or fleet which becomes engaged shall drop out of the main thrust. Other units will drive through or around them, toward the main goal.'

'The main goal, Lord,' Atago said, 'was to secure the Durer systems and use them as a springboard for the final assault.'

'An easily achieved objective,' Lord Fehrle said. 'One which could conceivably require us to slow and regroup. The council has decided to leapfrog Durer and make the final assault.'

Go for broke.

'Suppose,' Atago said, looking at the display overhead, 'that the Imperial Forces that will flank us, in and around Al-Sufi, succeed in breaking free? And then attack the main thrust toward Prime World?'

'That will not happen,' Fehrle said with a note of impatience. 'We are confident that your plan of deception will make them defend the non-goal until far, far too late. Also—' He paused. 'We have a further reinforcement of that deception.'

'Go on.'

'There is another reason,' Fehrle said. 'Lady Atago, this war has gone on far beyond our most pessimistic projections. We simply do not have the AM2 resources to luxuriate in any battle pause.'

Lady Atago, at that moment in time, could conceivably have provided reasons why Fehrle's battle plan – she knew better than to think it was the creation of the council – was an ill-conceived one, a roll of the dice when the dice could very well be loaded toward the house.

But she was a Tahn – and kept silent.

'There are two other modifications to your plan,' Fehrle said. 'The diversion which you have cleverly created against Al-Sufi. There is only one thing lacking. That force must be commanded by someone that the Empire feels to be our absolute best. Our most feared strategist.'

Lady Atago felt her cheeks redden, her hand move toward her personal weapon, and fought to keep herself under control.

'I am honored,' she managed, and was surprised that her voice was not shaking. 'But if I am to command the diversionary attack, who then will take charge of my twelve fleets – correction, my twelve, and those additional elements the council had decided to add to the attack?'

'Since this is an all-out effort,' Lord Fehrle said, 'we that command the attack should seamlessly represent the force of our Empire.'

Lady Atago managed the formal bow to the Will of the Tahn, the formal salute to her replacement, Lord Fehrle, and then she broke.

Somehow she was out of the battle chamber and in her own quarters before she exploded into rage and words that even a Tahn dockwalloper would have admired.

She calmed.

She took out her personal weapon.

Yes, her honor was besmirched. But not, she realized, by her own doing. Injustice had been done. That was the way. Such things had happened. She had risen above many wrongs. Just as her race had. Beyond those was victory. Very well, she would accept orders. She would command that deception fleet. She would do more, far more, than any timeserver would have accomplished. And she would stand by, ready to assist.

Because she knew that her plan would work – even with the idiot modifications of Lord Fehrle. But after Durer was obliterated, as the combined Tahn fleets struck toward Prime, Lord Fehrle would discover just how hard it was to truly lead rather than merely replace the battle leader and become a last-minute figurehead.

For the final victory, she knew Fehrle would need her help.

And she planned to make him pay most dearly for that, after the defeat of the Empire.

Chapter Twenty-Six

One-third of a meter to go. Sten could almost feel the cold blackness of the Tahn night just beyond the skim of earth on the other side of the tunnel. It pulled at him relentlessly, like an immense moon at the high tide of freedom. All he had to do was scrape away a little more dirt and he would be out. His long years as a Tahn prisoner would be over – leaving only his own survival to worry about.

He turned back, choking on the acrid air thick with fat-lamp smoke. It bit into his eyes, making them tear. He wiped the tears away with a sleeve and surveyed his troops, the men, women, and beings he had handpicked for the escape.

'Motley' was a distinct compliment. Some, like Cristata and his three converts, were dressed in the rough pale green and brown of Tahn peasants. Ibn Bakr had put all his sewing talents into his uniform and that of his partner, a tiny woman whose name Sten vaguely recalled as Alis. Bakr was dressed in what appeared to be the glitter of a full admiral. Alis's uniform was just slightly less so.

Actually, they were posing as the stationmaster of a gravtrain and his assistant. They had identification and papers showing that they were on an inspection tour of all the main hub stations of Heath. Sten had laughed when Ibn Bakr had first shown him the sketches of what he and Alis would wear. He was instantly sorry when he saw Ibn Bakr's hangdog expression – there was nothing so mournful as a giant with his chops dragging on the ground. And then Ibn Bakr had explained about the Tahn love of uniforms and how the lowliest office tended to have some of the most glittering clothes.

'You should see the head garbage collector,' Ibn Bakr said.

Sten closed his eyes against the glare and decided that was something he would just as soon skip.

The other members of the escape team were dressed somewhere in between Cristata and Ibn Bakr, ranging from farmers to shop-keepers to grunts to medium – and low-level Tahn officers.

One other standout was St. Clair. She was dressed in boots and a camo cloth jumpsuit so form-fitting that Sten found himself waver between lust and dislike. She had a small matching bag slung over her shoulder. Tucked into it were a change of clothing and the super-lightweight camping gear favored by wealthy Tahn sportsmen and women. What St. Clair was relying on was that twice a year a very rare and very tasty tuber appeared in the ground on Heath. The tubers were so prized that only the nobility and the very rich were permitted to gather them. So twice a year the sports world turned out to comb the forests and meadows of Heath for those tubers. The locations where they could be found were as jealously guarded as the trout streams the Eternal Emperor had restocked on Earth.

St. Clair was posing as one of those hunters. She was convinced she could go to ground with ease and wait for just the right opportunity to get off Heath. Sten was not too sure. Still, he had turned down St. Clair's bet – even though the odds she offered were fairly juicy.

Sten observed it all in semi-silence, waiting for the lay reader and his followers to finish their prayers for 'the Great One' to look with favor on their efforts. The only words Sten could make out were the 'ahhhmens' sighed by the three each time Cristata paused. Finally he finished and waddled over to Sten, plucking at the dirt clogging his fur. Every centimeter of his squat form was purposeful and somber. Only the sensitive tendrils ringing his nose squirmed with what Sten was sure was excitement.

'The spirit of the Great One is with us,' Cristata said. 'He told us it was nearly time to go.'

Sten buried any sarcastic remarks that came to mind. After many thousands of tons of digging and shoring, who was he to criticize another being's beliefs? Besides, maybe it was some kind of 'Great One' who had given Sten a nutball like Cristata in the first place. Would he have ever found the cellars that honeycomb Koldyeze otherwise? As far as Sten was concerned, it the Great One wanted the credit, he could clottin' have it.

So, instead, Sten grinned a weak grin and said, 'Fine. Uh . . . Next time you talk . . . uh, tell him, or it, or whatever, I said thanks.'

Cristata took no offense at all. He understood that Sten meant none.

There was a rumbling sound from the far end, and everyone pressed up against either side of the tunnel as Alex came around a corner hauling an enormous load of supplies on three trained-together carts, the same carts that had been used to move rubble back from the tunnel's face. The heavy-worlder moved with ease, as if he were pulling a few tots in a wagon. When a wooden wheel stuck in a rut, he simply lifted the front end of the train up and shifted it to an easier path. He was hauling at least a ton and a half of gear.

'Thae be the last of it, Horrie, lad,' he said, stepping away as a few of the others began unloading his cargo and stacking the supplies at one point of the hollowed-out eye that was the tunnel's face. He glanced around at the faces in the small crowd, nodding pleasantly – a man without a nervous bone in his body. Then he casually moved over to Sten and leaned close to whisper.

'Ah dinnae like this, lad,' he said. 'Thae all appear dead t' me. Noo, ae we could only teach a few Mantis tricks . . . Aye. Thae they'd hae a hope.'

Sten shook his head. 'This dress rehearsal went as smooth as anyone could want,' he said. 'And as for teaching them any tricks . . . All they'd do is learn enough to be confident amateurs. Clot! Might as well kill them all right there, save the Tahn the pleasure.'

'Still, lad. Ah'd feel bonnier ae they kenned a few more wee tricks ae th' craft.'

'Believe me, Alex,' Sten said. 'They're better off this way. It's sort of like a style of fighting I read about. A few thousand years ago, they used to pile troops into these big clumsy aircraft. They'd load 'em down with maybe fifty kilos of gear, strap this big silk bag around them, and kick 'em out the door when they were maybe two three klicks up.'

Alex looked at Sten in shocked disbelief. 'Th' puir wee lads. Musta had Campbells f'r officers. Atrocity committin' Huns! Pushin't boys oot t' squash 'em ae thae be't bloody bugs.'

'Weellll . . . That wasn't their intention. See, the silk bags were supposed to open, and the soldiers were supposed to float gently to the ground.

'Anyway, they used to train these airborne troopers for the jumps. Some of the toughest training of that era.'

'Ah should hope so,' Alex said, still a little shocked.

'Funny thing is,' Sten pressed on, 'when the drakh really hit the fan, sometimes they used to just grab any old grunt, put a sack on him, and toss him out just like the fully trained types. And you know what? There was no difference in the casualty rate. Just as many trained troopies ate it as the grunts who were still wet behind the ears.'

'Ah dinnae believe it,' Alex said.

Sten surveyed the nervous beings jammed into the tunnel and thought about what terrible things surely awaited them once they crawled out of the safety of Koldyeze.

'I *want* to,' he said. 'They go out in two nights.'

Virunga put the word out during the morning mess. He wanted to see Sten. Urgently. Sten moved casually across the crowded central yard, weaving his way through small garden plots and exercising prisoners. He stopped here and there to chat, to laugh at the right moments, and to scowl and shake his head in disbelief at others. It was an elaborate and constantly changing ritual he had to perform, else a Tahn stoolie might start taking note of how often a lowly firecontrolman visited the camp CO.

All the while, his mind churned with possibilities. Some news of how the war was going? Badly for the Tahn, he hoped. With a great stretch of luck, Virunga might be calling him in to report the greatest success in Koldyeze so far. Maybe, just maybe, they had managed to plant what Alex called 'the Golden Worm.'

They had spent an enormous amount of time and effort figuring out a way to suborn a petty bureaucrat named Fahstr. She was the middle-aged chief clerk in charge of pay vouchers. Every Tahn feared her. Even Derzhin, the camp commandant, walked softly around her. At the slightest insult, a pay voucher could be lost forever. And it would take another three small forevers to get it back. What was worse, if she felt particularly nasty, she would misinterpret the coding, and a Tahn victim might find himself docked a whopping chunk for back taxes – whether he owed any or not.

The problem was that Fahstr was seemingly incorruptible. No matter how hard they leaned on N'chlos and their other tame guards, they could not find a single weakness. The woman was fat – but did not particularly favor any type of food. She was obviously sexless, which Alex had remarked was a good thing, because he did not want to be the man who asked for volunteers. She seemed to revel in living a Spartan life, so money was out. How to get to her? It was important, because Fahstr was the key to planting the Golden Worm.

St. Clair stumbled onto the answer. She had gotten herself assigned to a janitorial shift at the payroll office, figuring that a woman of her experience certainly ought to be able to spot another's weaknesses. If nothing else, she might be able to scrounge a few cleaning fluids that might be put to more interesting use.

St. Clair had bumped around the office for half a day before she saw it. As the other clerks kept their eyes glued to their duties, afraid even to lift their heads and be seen not working, Fahstr had spent the entire morning enjoying herself.

It was an emotion that was difficult to recognize right off. Because to Fahstr, enjoyment seemed to be slamming away at her computer board and gritting out a long string of obscenities that almost made St. Clair blush, interspersed with occasional screams of what seemed to be victory. St. Clair finally sidled over to the computer to see what was going on. A bewildering stream of figures swirled on the screen, then firmed. Shouts of disgust came from Fahstr to be followed by more hammering at the keyboard. More figures. More cursing. Then it slowly dawned on St. Clair. The figures on the screen were algorithms. There was a game going on. And the game was bridge.

St. Clair had not just found a weakness. She had found a gaping wound.

'Typical bridge freak,' she had told Sten later. 'Including her charming disposition. There isn't a thing in this universe the woman cares for except bridge. She hates people. But to enjoy bridge, you gotta have people.'

'She's got her computer,' Sten said. 'It can give her any kind of game she wants. At any level.'

'You sure aren't a cardplayer,' St. Clair had said. 'To enjoy cards you have to see your opponent squirm. Especially bridge-type cardplayers. You can't see blood when you beat the bejesus out of a computer.'

'So you hinted broadly that you might know something about this – uh, what was it called?'

'Bridge. And as for hinting broadly, clot that. I told her right off that I had been watching her. Couldn't help myself, I said.'

'And she didn't get ticked? I would have figured she'd have cut you off at the knees for even daring to talk to her.'

'No way,' St. Clair said. 'Bridge players can't help themselves. She understood right off. Especially when I told her I was fleet champ.'

'Fleet what? Of what? There's no such thing!'

'So? She doesn't know that. Or care. Especially since I allowed that although she might be good, I could wipe the ground with her.'

Grudgingly, Sten had to admire that. From what he could gather, there was no way the type of fanatic St. Clair was describing could turn down such a challenge.

'Okay, you get tight with her. Win a few games. Lose a few to keep her interested. Then you find out what it takes to get her over on our side.'

'Don't need to.' St. Clair sniffed. 'We're programming the computer to partner up with each of us. I got complete access to that thing any time you want.'

Sten had instantly put Kraulshavn and Sorensen to work on the Golden Worm. They had completed it a week before and, with St. Clair's expertise, had coded it into a cut-throat north-south pair of hands.

All St. Clair had been waiting for was the chance to plant it. The problem was that time was running out. She was going out the next night. If she did not succeed in planting it immediately, they would have to start all over again. But after the escape, the bloody reprisals might make the whole thing pointless. Because the Golden Worm was their only hope to keep the Tahn from cutting all their throats.

Sten walked into Virunga's cell. There was only the old man to greet him. From the dark, solemn look on his face, Sten knew there was something very wrong. He assumed it had to do with failure. And that failure involved the Golden Worm.

'They caught her,' he said flatly, meaning St. Clair.

'No,' Virunga said. 'She . . . was successful. But . . . there is another . . . matter.'

Sten decided to quit guessing and let Virunga tell it.

'As you know . . . St. Clair has complete . . . access. To the computer.'

Sten nodded. Fahstr pretty much let St. Clair noodle at will on the Tahn computer in her spare time. To have an opponent of any worth, St. Clair needed time to toy with new bridge strategies. But that had not seemed important to Sten.

The only records in there were the mundane details of Koldyeze life: Tahn payroll and personnel and the basic files of the prisoner. Sten could see little value in snooping and pooping in that area.

'St. Clair has . . . noticed something,' Virunga said, interrupting Sten's thoughts.

He went on to explain: As St. Clair logged in and out of the computer, using Fahstr's code name, she had become familiar with the other people who used the same system and with how frequently they used it. Then another code name had popped up recently. It not only did not seem to belong to anyone in the camp, it was searching through the records with a regular one-plus-one-plus-one pattern that was slower than clot but guaranteed not to miss a single detail.

St. Clair had become curious about who that person was and what he or she was looking for.

'And did she find out?' Sten finally asked.

'Not the . . . seeker,' Virunga said. 'Only what was . . . sought.'

'Okay. So what was the person looking for?'

'You,' Virunga said.

That rocked Sten back. 'But how . . .'

Virunga told him the rest of it. The unknown person was

searching the records for someone matching Sten's description. It was a methodical search designed to see through any disguise or assumed identity. It was only a matter of time before Sten's file popped up.

Virunga assumed – with very good reason – that whoever was looking for Sten did not plan on throwing his or her arms around him and greeting him with a shower of gifts and kisses.

Bottom line:

'You . . . and Kilgour must . . . go!'

There was no argument from Sten. He and Alex would go out with the others. All he had to do was get his escape team together one last time and fill them in on what he hoped was the final hitch in their plans.

The news was greeted with silence by the others. They took a quick look into the roles they were supposed to play, checked to see how Alex and Sten would affect them, saw there was no problem, and just shrugged. The more, the merrier.

Then St. Clair stood up and announced there would be one other change in plans. She was no longer going out solo. She was taking L'n with her.

'That's the stupidest idea I ever heard of,' Sten blurted out before Alex could dig an elbow into his ribs and suggest a more diplomatic way of dealing with St. Clair. Later on, Alex explained that Sten should have hesitated first – then told the woman she was around the bend.

'Just the same,' St. Clair responded. 'That's the way it's going to be.'

Before Sten could do something so foolish as try to forbid St. Clair, she played her ace.

'Don't bother trying to stop me. We're both going out tomorrow night – one way or another. Through the tunnel with the rest of you. Or under the wire.'

Sten had no choice but to give in. If St. Clair did another cowboy run, she would blow whatever chance the tunnelers had – and Sten was pretty sure that nothing he could come up with short of murder would stop her. But he always wondered why St. Clair had decided on that course of action. As far as he was concerned, it was way out of character – because with L'n along, St. Clair would certainly get caught. He wondered what St. Clair thought she would get out of it – because personal gain could be her only reason.

He was wrong on both counts. For once in her life St. Clair was not being selfish. She knew what the news of Sten's escape would do to L'n. Without the crutch of her ideal, L'n was doomed. Second, although St. Clair could not know it, L'n's presence would save both their lives.

Sten curled his fingers, and the knife leapt into his hand. He smoothly cut through the dirt, carefully easing it away at first and then clawing at it with growing impatience. Then the night air bit through, chilling them all to the bone, drying the sweat, and clearing the smoke-laden air.

Sten found himself tumbling through. He came to his feet – numb and a little in shock. Below Koldyeze he could see the dim outline of the city with the blackout lights gleaming here and there. And then he felt Alex come out from behind him, grabbing him around the shoulders and pushing him on.

They were free.

Chapter Twenty-Seven

Durer was a major victory.

The general history fiche, to which all Imperial worlds subscribing to the Imperial education scheme subjected their secondary-level students, portrayed the battle in a few, sweeping arrow strokes.

At this time, the attack was made . . . here. A red arrow, moving across systems. It was backed by a secondary attack . . . here. It was met . . . here. A blue arrow.

The results were . . . this.

The more curious might acquire a specialty fiche and, given access to a battle chamber, project more details of the battle.

At that point, the bewilderment would begin.

First, Durer was variously called the Durer–Al-Sufi Battles, the

First Imperial Counterattack, the Second Tahn Offensive, Fleet Encounters of the Midstages of the Tahn War, and so forth, into degenerative and confusing accounts of the ships involved.

Still more confusing for the eager student were the accounts of anyone and everyone involved in that battle.

The battle(s) became a favorite study of both amateurs and professionals, all of them seeking a perspective that would enable them to understand what had happened during those weeks and, possibly more important to historians, to see some grandness in what otherwise appeared to be a bloody, blind-folded brawl in which several million people had died.

They would look for that understanding and perspective in vain.

Because that perspective never existed.

A Mantis Section captain named Bet sat in a spacesuit, watching what looked like the entire Tahn Navy float toward her, and wished that Vulcan had given her a god or six to pray for.

The Emperor had coppered his bets. Yes, he believed that the real attack would be made on Durer. Al-Sufi would be nothing more than a feint. He had so allocated his forces under Fleet Marshal Ian Mahoney.

But still . . .

Light-years beyond Durer drifted what appeared to be the ruined hulks of some Tahn destroyers. A complete flotilla thereof.

They were just exactly that.

What the Tahn did not know was that the flotilla had been ambushed many, many months earlier in an entirely different galaxy by an Imperial battlefleet. Their screams for help had been blanketed and had never been received on any Tahn world. To the Tahn, the flotilla had simply disappeared, probably doing something or other terribly heroic.

The hulks had been recovered, and strong-stomached salvors had cleaned out the ship interiors. Then those destroyers had been given shielded power sources, sophisticated sensors, and shielded com beams and positioned in place, beyond Durer.

They had been crewed with Mantis teams and given orders to sit and wait.

Bet and her team, and other teams, had done just that, fighting against boredom and the feeling that they were being stuck in nowhere for a meaningless mission.

All the teams viewed the assignment as a glory run and swore at the head of Mantis Section for the medal- and obituary-winning idea. Why hadn't far more sophisticated and unmanned sensors been used?

The head of Mantis was not to blame. The idea was completely that of the Eternal Emperor and Fleet Marshal Ian Mahoney. Certainly those zoot capri sensors could have been scattered in front of where they felt the Tahn forces would make their real attack. But suppose one of those sensors was found? Would the Tahn not conceivably guess that the Imperial Forces were waiting?

Instead, it appeared far less logical for the Empire to have some dumb troops inhabiting hulks. Plus, cynically, Mahoney pointed out that it would be very unlikely for any Mantis troopie to surrender and be deprogrammable, unlike the average machine.

Cursing, smelling, and sweating, the teams waited.

And then the sensors lit.

More Tahn fleets than even Bet's high-level briefing had suggested swam through space toward her hulks.

Bet burst-transmitted the information, then shut down. Her view of the battle – if there was going to be one – was complete. All she had to do was hope that none of the Tahn battleships or destroyers passing – almost within visual range – bothered to investigate her wreck for survivors.

The Eternal Emperor sat aboard the *Normandie*, his personal yacht/ command ship. The ship was as far forward – and three more light-years – as he could logically go without potentially becoming involved in his own battle. His battle chamber was set to give full and complete reports of any and all intelligence forthcoming.

The Emperor figured that Mahoney would very rapidly become involved in the grind of the battle. The Emperor hoped to be able to stand off and help if Mahoney lost track of the grand strategy.

He was earnestly lying to himself when he said that he had no intention of stepping in. He had done everything possible.

The Tahn were moving into his trap quite nicely, the preliminary intelligence reports said – although he was astonished that somehow, somewhere, the anticipated twelve attacking fleets had become more than twenty. He had them cold. On toast. This, he thought to himself, is the beginning of the end. Or, his non-linear alter ego whispered, the end of the beginning at least.

Bet me, Engineer H. E. Raschid thought. Suppose it's the end of the end?

And so he stood ready to save Mahoney's – and his own – cookies.

Unfortunately robot Tahn ships, intended only to blank off transmissions between the Al-Sufi and Durer systems, slipped through the Imperial perimeter, and the Eternal Emperor found himself sitting in the most sophisticated war analysis room ever installed on a spaceship, listening to static and watching pixels of misinformation interspersed with scattered bursts that showed either the Tahn or the Empire victorious and advancing or defeated and retreating on all fronts.

Durer, for the handful of Imperial tacships and destroyers assigned to hold and defend the system, was a very short battle.

There would be seven survivors of the eighty-nine ships that moved against the attacking Tahn fleets. Their orders were to stop the Tahn attack, to prevent landings on Durer, and finally to exert the maximum number of casualties possible.

They were, unknowingly, a suicide force.

The ships that had been assigned to Durer had been mainline attack units – neither obsolete nor state of the art. The Empire planned to maintain as long as possible the deception that Durer was underguarded and not expecting an attack.

The Emperor had therefore made the correct assignments, knowing he was sending people to their deaths.

'The Price of Empire,' it might have been called if the Eternal Emperor had not been several centuries beyond believing such grandiose statements. Those were for the rubes, not the rulers. Besides, this was not the first time, the most murderous time, or certainly the last . . .

The Durer units' tactics were well-planned. One flotilla of destroyers came in on the same plane as the incoming Tahn. Two other flotillas waited above the system ecliptic until the forward elements of the Tahn were engaged. Then they dived 'down' for the heart of the enemy. Shortly afterward, six wings of tacships came up from 'below,' each tacship under independent command with orders to find targets of opportunity.

All the sailors had done a fast head count of the enemy, realized they were doomed, and – at least for the most part – determined to make their dying quite expensive.

Very noble.

Unfortunately, such noble determination worked very seldom, and mostly in livies.

When the enemy had total numerical superiority, all the tactics in the world would not let the attacker get within killing range.

So it was with the ships from Durer.

The obvious flotilla vanished in long-range missile blasts from the incoming Tahn cruisers long out of their engagement range.

The two high flotillas got in among the fold – but for only seconds. Those thirty-two destroyers barely had time to acquire targets and make first launches before they, too, vanished. Results: Destroyed, four Tahn destroyers, five Tahn logistical support craft. Damaged: two Tahn cruisers, three Tahn logships.

On a battle chamber, or from a grand fleet projection, that left the space beyond Durer cluttered with trash, which the deadly little tacships would have been able to swim through unobserved and deal death.

Battle chambers and grand projections crunched lightyears into centimeters. The reality was that the destruction of the Durer ships left whirling wreckage across some twenty light-years. A destroyer's screen, particularly one that was programmed to ignore destroyed targets, showed something different.

A raider, a guerrilla, a pirate – and that was what the tacships were – could not exist on a battlefield.

Perhaps the tacship commanders were overeager. Perhaps the Tahn were expecting an attack from 'below.' Perhaps they had bad luck.

No one would ever know.

There were no survivors from those ships.

The Imperial propaganda made much of their doomed attack and made several posthumous awards of the highest degree. Propaganda also said how effective they were: Two Tahn battleships had been destroyed, and one crippled. One Tahn cruiser destroyed, two crippled. Four Tahn destroyers crippled.

Postwar analysis: One destroyer smashed. One cruiser lightly damaged.

But by then no one wanted to be reminded of the war, let alone the fact that some of their dead heroes had died *trying* to be heroic instead of succeeding.

Lady Atago's original strategy had been for one fleet to bombard Durer, a second to invade, and a third to be kept in reserve.

Command on Durer expected something similar.

Ready for the last grand stand, they were surprised when the Tahn fleets swept through the system, well outside engagement range.

And maybe they were a little disappointed, at least at first. After all, when someone screwed his courage to the sticking point only to find it not needed, it took awhile for the stupidity and the adrenaline to subside.

But the disappointment did not last very long as the Imperial Forces on Durer realized that they were alive, that they were likely to stay alive for a while, that the battle was being fought without them, and that they were in ringside seats for it.

That was perhaps why so many of the personal memoirs of the Durer-Al-Sufi battle(s) were done by Imperial troops on Durer.

They lived to dictate them.

Lord Fehrle admired perfection on the bridge of his command ship as the first four fleets swept, almost unopposed, out of the Durer System. Ahead of them were rich industrial worlds and then the heart of the Empire. And thus far, the Tahn casualties had been insignificant.

Once again he pointed out to himself the necessity for an overseer. No matter how inspired, the man or woman who was in charge of a task needed someone over him or her, someone who could step back, uninvolved, and see whether that task was destined to be a success, a failure, or, Fehrle thought, able to be taken beyond its humbler goals.

Lady Atago is most brilliant, he thought. But thanks to our system, there will always be someone beyond those brilliant leaders in the field, those who can think, those who can say: Here. Here is the grandness you have overlooked.

Fehrle was basking in that grandness when the Kali missile blew his command ship in half.

Fleet Marshal Ian Mahoney was not at all surprised when the robot Tahn ships sent his big picture communications into la-la land. He had sort of expected something like that to happen.

In spite of the frownings and suggestions from his highly trained and educated specialists, Mahoney had insisted on setting up a series of links – blocked and tight – with specific ships in each of the fleets under his command. Each broadcast came into a separate receiver, manned by an individual tech who was trained to report, not to interpret.

Probably, Mahoney thought, he was being an imbecile and trying to maintain the illusion that he was still a hands-on field officer. Probably all this drakh was going to confuse the hell out of him, make him get obsessed with trivia and lose whatever half-assed strategy he had to fight their battle.

On first contact, that was exactly what was going on.

And then the battle chamber became a kaleidoscope, all his computers started recycling previous information, and his interpreters found themselves with nothing to interpret.

Mahoney told them to keep interpreting, shut off the com links, and started listening to the field reports.

It was a stupid way to try to win.

The Tahn had opened the battle believing that they were masters of deception, without allowing themselves much of a margin for error. That was the single biggest error.

But there were many other mistakes that they made.

One of the largest – uncredited by historians because there were no visible heroes – was the failure of the Tahn automatic mine fields.

The Tahn, unlike the Empire, had spent many, many man-centuries developing those unglamorous objects that just sat and lurked until something made them explode. But once they had developed mines that could not only be rapidly deployed but had the sophistication to distinguish friendly from enemy targets and maneuver en masse by command, they had relaxed.

Some years earlier, a young tacship commander named Sten had discovered a fairly nasty way to subvert those mines. The Tahn, who were in the middle of other worries, never realized that. Sten had routinely sent a report through on his discovery.

That discovery, made by someone who at that moment was slowly crawling down the intermittently floodlit slope of a Tahn prison camp, was critical.

The Tahn had liberally sowed their mines between Al-Sufi and Durer, expecting them to serve not only as a block against the inevitable counterattack but as an early warning system.

Imperial destroyers, part of the fleets lurking in emptiness between and beyond the Al-Sufi and Durer systems, had long ago seen the minelayers seeding their deadliness, registered the mine fields, and then rendered them completely harmless, one by one. The effort was massive and successful. Any specialists who had made a small mistake defusing the devices would not be recognized until after the battle.

To the Tahn, the Imperial fleets lanced out of nowhere. Their battle computers, however, quickly analyzed the attack. Conventional. Tacships were screening the attack, with cruiser anti-ship killers in the forward screen. Behind them came destroyers and then a conventional structure – destroyers, cruisers, battleships, and tacship carriers.

The computers provided the proper response, and the Tahn admirals complied.

The Imperial Forces, however, were not what they had expected.

Mahoney knew good and well that he was a little untrained for grand strategy. Maybe he could have come up with some kind of superplan. He had done a little private research before leaving Prime on what kinds of things grand strategists did to make their living.

The record was kind of grim.

The one-roll-of-the-dice generals had as great a failure rate as success, from Darius to Phillip to von Schlieffen to Giap to M'Khee to P'ra T'ong. Mahoney, figuring he was not even in their class, decided to run war the way he knew how – which was to keep it simple and keep it unexpected.

The tacships were what they appeared onscreen. Mahoney figured that with the confusion he planned behind them, they would have a good chance not only of survival but of wreaking some damage.

Those cruisers were in fact lumbering, unmanned transports with false electronic signatures. Their missiles were set up on a launch-and-forget basis – and were so primitive that they had best be forgotten unless some complete incompetent stumbled into their trajectory.

The destroyers were also false. They were phony-signatured Kali missiles, modified for long range.

After them came the real warriors.

The battle opened.

The tacships swarmed.

The 'cruisers' were quickly converted into gas clouds, and the Tahn felt reinforced as to their superiority. Their acquisition gear turned to the destroyers just as those 'destroyers' went to full drive and homed on capital ships.

Warriors generally made an assumption: Someone who was attacking behaved in a certain manner. When a dangerous swordsman turned into a berserker, or a bomber into a kamikaze, it took a while to readjust.

The readjustment cost the Tahn most of their cover destroyers and threw the lead three fleets' battle array into disorder.

That was not a disaster. Admiral P'riser, who had automatically assumed overall command of the battle when Lord Fehrle's ship fell out of communication, ordered the three stalled fleets to engage and the banked fleets behind them to attack through.

The arrow sped onward.

Lord Fehrle glummed inside his suit helmet as technicians swarmed around the control chamber of the crippled command ship.

Go here and do this, he thought. He could order, he realized, any of the people around him to breathe space on general principles. Or he could program commands for the fleets he commanded.

Neither of those options would change his situation – the battle was out of his hands, he was getting absolutely no information as to what was going on, and his ship was spinning in emptiness far behind the lines of battle.

The fact that there was a good possibility that the ship would explode in hours or become a vanished derelict was hardly important to his thinking.

Lady Atago's ships dove in against the Al-Sufi worlds almost unopposed.

Six outbound convoys loaded with AM2 were cut out and seized. Their escorts were quickly smashed.

Lady Atago, following orders, had determined that the feint against Al-Sufi would be as deadly and determined as she could make it.

Her attack ships swept destruction across storage worlds, creating havoc and hell that would take generations to rebuild.

Then, in the midst of a battle of triumph, Lady Atago realized what had happened.

She was wreaking havoc not because of her brilliance but because Al-Sufi was nearly undefended. Her success was merely that the Imperials had made no plans for *any* Tahn attack against the systems.

Which could only mean that her grand plan against Durer had been found out. The Tahn fleets were advancing into a trap.

Lady Atago had no hesitations at all. Less of a person, less of a Tahn, would have let Lord Fehrle and the never-to-be-sufficiently-damned civilians take the blame as they would have taken the credit.

Instead, she diverted and drove her swiftest battleships toward the Durer systems, broadcasting an alarm on all frequencies.

It was, by then, quite too late.

*

The man's name was Mason. And, from his no-rank-tabbed flight coverall to the scar seaming his face, he looked to be a killer.

He had been that – a highly decorated tacship commander, seconded after a crippling injury to flight school, and more recently Sten's nemesis. His injuries prevented him from ever skippering a tacship again. But the war had promoted Mason. He was a one-star admiral, commanding a fast light-destroyer squadron.

He ran it as he had run his tacship flotilla. His crews hated him. He insisted on obedience, dedication, and originality. An error of omission or oversight produced a very rapid court martial.

The story was that one of his destroyers had bounced a Tahn ship that turned out to be filled with Imperial prisoners. One of Mason's bosuns had seen the cheering rescued exprisoners streaming through the air lock and then bellowed 'Get back, clots! Don't you know when you're well off?'

Mason was permitted to be in command for only one reason. His flotilla had the highest kill ratio of any equivalent unit in *any* of the Imperial fleets.

Now he led his destroyers, scattered in fingers-four formation, into the rear of the Tahn fleets.

Eleven Imperial fleets had been hidden far beyond Durer, with orders to attack only after the Tahn were initially engaged.

A surprise.

More of a surprise was their make-up. Sullamora's shipyards in the Cairenes, supposedly shattered with labor problems, had done very well. The Emperor had expected twelve more battleships to be ready.

Instead, thirty heavies attacked the Tahn – ships that were not leaky botch jobs but supersophisticated engines of destruction, completely unknown to the Tahn.

The slaughter began.

Even if, somehow, an all-bands receiver could have listened in on the battles, coherency would have been a joke:

'Samsun, Samsun . . . I have a target . . . damage report as . . . incoming observed . . . six Tahn ships now without power and . . . launch, you clottin' bastard . . . Samsun, are you receiving . . . units, stand by for . . . change orbit, Eight, you're acquired . . . I have a launch from . . . Samsun, this is Whitway. Do you receive this station . . . this is an all-stations broadcast . . . Nostrand units, redeploy to Sectors one by thirteen . . . *squaawk* . . . Allah give us strength . . . Samsun, Samsun . . . Kee-rist, did you see that one go up? . . . All units, this is . . . Samsun, Samsun . . . do you receive . . .'

Four broadcasts, all set en clair:
To Fleet Marshal Ian Mahoney:
'Comm One, Comm One, this is Liberty Seven. There ain't nothin' left to shoot at . . .'
To Lady Atago:
'Unknown approaching units . . . this is the Tahn battleship *H'rama*. We have you ID'd as friendly. Do not continue your present orbit, over. Request you stand by for recovery assistance.'
To Lord Fehrle – unreceived:
'Command . . . Command . . . this is P'riser. Plan Heartstrike canceled. Plan W'mon activated.'
To all Tahn ships:
'All units. All units. Begin retirement. Support, if possible, friendly units under drive.'
In eyes-only code, Fleet Marshal Ian Mahoney to the Eternal Emperor:
'Tahn seared. Repeat, all Tahn seared. Question – how to serve? Second question – what wine?'

Confused though it might have been from its name to its step-by-step execution, there were some completely obvious conclusions from the battle(s) of Durer-Al-Sufi:
The Tahn had been smashed.
Their major war-winning offensive had been blunted and turned back.
The nearly-total destruction of the Tahn's finest units meant that it would be years before they could mount another such offensive.
The Emperor hoped – and knew he was full of hopes – that those conclusions were equally evident to the Tahn.
It might have been the beginning of the end – but getting there was still going to be a long, bloody, and certainly not foreordained process.
And the Eternal Emperor could afford to make no other mistakes.

BOOK THREE

KOBO-ICHI

Chapter Twenty-Eight

The Tahn reeled back from the awful blow of Durer like a man struck in the stomach with a lead-weighted bat. They were left doubled over, mouth gaping, lungs emptied of air and blood hammering at the temples, threatening to hemorrhage at the ears.

They were caught in that long, frozen moment in history that even casual students would point at eons later and say, 'Here was the turning point. Here was where priorities needed to be re-examined, strategy revamped, scenarios rethought.'

Because, as an ancient philosopher once said, 'It ain't over till it's over.' Or as the Eternal Emperor might have put it; stealing from one of his favorite political thinkers, 'Winning isn't everything. But losing isn't anything.'

Durer-Al-Sufi was lost. That was a tired fact almost as soon as it was over. But not the war. Another tired fact, viscerally understood by the Tahn. The trick was to make the mind understand what the gut was thinking without ripping open the gut and spreading out the entrails. History was a blackened landscape of great kingdoms that murdered the oracle to seek the message. That was a mistake the Tahn could not and did not make.

They turned inward, fighting every instinct to find fault, to point the blame. They turned inward to find strength but were confronted with the frozen poles of their culture: a north where defeat could not even be contemplated, and a south where every facet of Tahn life had to be controlled and molded to official will – all spinning on an axis of hatred for anything un-Tahn. And they had no Shackleton or Perry to lead the way. Only Lord Fehrle – the man who had presided over the second greatest defeat of their history.

Fehrle was no coward. After the defeat, he did not commit ritual suicide. Instead, he returned to Heath, fully expecting to be stripped of all honors, executed, his name excised from Tahn history. If his people needed to work out their rage on his quivering corpse, then so be it.

Instead, he was seen in his usual position of prominence – with the other members of the Tahn High Council lined up exactly around him as before – during a news broadcast covering the appointment of a governor-general to a newly won Tahn territory. It was an event noted with interest by every skilled Tahn watcher who knew about Durer. The Eternal Emperor – the most skilled of them all – grunted to himself when he reviewed the fiche. Fehrle's survival was not something he had expected.

When he had learned that the Tahn lord had personally led the expedition, he had thought the man's political destruction would be an added bonus to all that twisted metal and those blasted bodies. Still, there was an advantage to press for there and the Eternal Emperor went all out for it.

When the Emperor struck out and connected with that loaded bat, the only thought his enemy had as he reeled back from the blow was that no one could know about Durer. Even that old cynic, Pastour, realized that it was not the time for recriminations or political infighting. When he had heard the news, he had vomited, wiped his lips, then hurried to the emergency High Council meeting, determined to keep his colleagues from removing Fehrle and then committing bureaucracide in the resultant fight over who would lead the council.

Even in normal times there were too many factions with too many self-serving interests to declare a clear winner. Given time, a consensus might be hammered out the way a cooper formed the hoops of an enormous barrel whose contents could not be contained under the normal laws of volume.

Pastour had a glimmering, even at that moment, that the only conceivable choice would have to be Lady Atago, as much as he disliked the woman. When the day came to replace Fehrle, she would be the only knight in white armor left. Because although Durer had permanently blackened Fehrle, it would have the opposite effect on Atago. To survive as a coherent people, the Tahn needed their heroes – like the ancient Persians needed the myth of Jamshid. Pastour went to the meeting armed with every diplomatic and political skill he could command.

Surprisingly, it did not take much argument. The others were as stunned and gasping as he was. All of them knew, without coaxing, that if news of Durer leaked out to the populace, the war with the Empire was lost. The first order issued was for a total clampdown on anything and anyone involved with Durer.

Even in a society where news was not just controlled but rationed, the order was carried out on an unprecedented scale. An enormous amount of credits, energy, and manpower was hurled at the task. It was a gag order with no journalistic equivalent. Scholars, looking for descriptive comparisons, would have to turn to human-wave assault battles – like Thermopylae, the Russian Summer offensive of 1943, the Yalu, or the Imperial disaster of Saragossa during the Mueller Wars.

The destroyed ships and personnel were removed from all files and logs. All survivors were seized and incarcerated, as were the friends and families of the dead and wounded. Behind-the-lines suppliers found themselves mysteriously reassigned to barren regions. Even minor officials were visited at night and grilled for any speck of information that might be damaging. Then the interrogators themselves were grilled. On and on it went as the Tahn searched out and purged every kink and crook in the line of the vast plumbing system that was the Tahn bureaucracy.

The Tahn even launched a crash Manhattan-style program to develop and fix in place the greatest jamming system ever conceived. And even that leaked as the Eternal Emperor turned up the volume of propaganda.

If the Tahn blackout effort had no known historical precedent, neither did the Emperor's effort to broadcast it. With his right hand, the Emperor directed his fleets and armies to take instant advantage of the vacuum left by the Tahn. With his left, he orchestrated a massive propaganda machine. He turned the equivalent of small suns into radio beacons, heralding to the many galaxies the news of the great Tahn defeat.

The Emperor attacked with information as if it were the spearhead of an invasion force of thousands of ships and millions of troops. And the more he turned up the volume, the more desperately the Tahn fought to shut it out. He pushed them to the point that, even for their barren souls, so many civil liberties were suspended that life was nearly intolerable.

The grim, bitter mood spread downward from the High Council to the lowest sub-altern and petty official. No one knew what had happened, but everyone feared for himself. Even the simplest of decisions was left unmade in case it might disturb a superior. In actual fact, that was a wise way of behaving. Because the smallest change *would* upset a superior, who was equally in fear for his own hide. Added to that were increasing shortages. All the empty warehouses seemed even emptier after Durer. And as for AM2, there just was none available for any purpose other than military, and even there, each use was carefully judged and the proper forms filed with the appropriate signatures willing to take the blame in case of error.

Yes, the Tahn had turned inward after Durer. And it was the Eternal Emperor's official policy to shove their heads up until 'they gag on the hair at the back of their throats.'

Chapter Twenty-Nine

Police Major Genrikh's heart jumped when he heard the hunters hooting in the woods. Their quarry had been flushed. He whisper/prayed to himself that it would not be a false alarm. Ever since the escape, Genrikh and his men had been rushed from one tiny rut in the road to another, responding to even vague rumors that a POW had been spotted. As far as Genrikh was concerned, the entire effort to bring the prisoners to ground had been hamstrung by his superiors' insistence on a total blackout of the news of the escape.

Normally, any matter requiring secrecy would be second nature to Genrikh. But he and the other teams of hunters had been handed the messiest end of the stick. The blackout meant that it was nearly impossible to pick any *real* locus to start from and then connect the dots until the quarry could be found, circled, and then flushed into waiting Tahn guns. There had been a few successes, but not nearly enough.

The only part of his orders that he liked was that any prisoner found was to be killed on the spot. There was to be no sizing up or interrogation, just a heavy-caliber projectile in the back of the head. That this shut down the possibility of one find leading to another did not bother Genrikh at all. He was not a man who enjoyed the confusion of many flavors.

The hooting from his tracking team grew louder. Genrikh took a deep breath, loosening his grip on his weapon. He did not have to turn to see if his men were in place. He could feel the tension drawing them tighter to him. Genrikh prepared himself for disappointment.

The odds were that when the quarry broke the treeline, it would turn out to just be some lost farm animal, wall-eyed with fear. Then all they would be left with to satisfy their frustration was to gun the animal into a bloody pulp.

His weapon came up at the same time he saw motion just inside the trees. Around him he could hear the others doing the same, sounding like a rustle in a dry wind. There! Over there!

Two figures shadowed away from the brush, hesitated, then started shambling runs across the meadow for the other side. In two heartbeats his mind registered that they were (a) human, (b) one tall, one short, (c) prisoners. He squeezed the trigger, and then all hell erupted as his men also opened up. The combined fire caught the prisoners only five or six steps from the trees. They gave massive, loose-limbed jolts and then were hurled aside as if swept away by a fire hose. There was echoing silence and then another swift *brrrp* of fire, and the bodies jerked and jumped on the ground.

There was a clash of magazines changing, and then Genrikh and his men were on their feet, sprinting for the large splash of red and white gore. He almost lost his footing in blood-slick grass as he skidded up to the first body. It was the big man. He kicked the corpse over. The features were twisted but clear – Ibn Bakr. Then the smaller prisoner – Alis.

Genrikh turned to congratulate his team of killers. He was greeted by beaming faces with shy, almost childlike grins. Except for one.

Lo Prek looked down at Ibn Bakr's face and cursed his soul for not being the man he wanted to see lying there. Once again Sten had slipped the net.

Virunga sat in a slatted metal chair designed for discomfort. Every aching joint in his crippled legs told him that he had been kept waiting outside the commandant's office for days. From the sounds of the prisoners shuffling through the courtyard outside, he knew it could have been no more than four hours. Virunga had spent too many years as a prisoner of the Tahn not to know the game

Derzhin was playing. The wait was a routine softening-up process. Still, being familiar with the game did not make it any easier to play.

From the moment he had been summoned, the old self-doubts had come rushing in. Could he stand up to torture? He had before, hadn't he? Yes. But could he do it again? All right. Let's get past the torture part. (I can't. Please, I can't. Shut up! You have to.) What about the mind gaming? He had never gone one on one with Avrenti, Derzhin's expert in black work. But he had measured him. The man would be good. Virunga thought he was better. (Clot! There you go with a negative again! Eliminate 'thought.' Substitute 'knew.' Yes. That's better.) Try a new tack. A course with fresher breezes.

You have questions, Virunga. Put it on them. Make them answer. Don't give them time to gain the upper ground. Hit them with your questions. Questions, like . . . After the escape . . . why were there no reprisals?

Virunga and Sten had factored reprisals into the escape equation. There was nothing they could do about the immediate actions of the Tahn. In the first red flash of anger, there were sure to be victims, beatings, rations cut off, and personal belongings ripped to shreds in the search for the escape hatch. There was nothing they could do about that. But a moment later, when cooler heads prevailed, the planning would pay off. There were too many careers at stake in Koldyeze. Too many questions would trigger a hunt for scapegoats – careless guards, officers with questionable loyalties. The Tahn would be cautious, knowing that it would give enemies an opening to pin blame on the blameless. And there would be the ultimate threat that the crisis would spill over, flooding out the gates and catching the politicians who had put all the rotten eggs in the rickety basket that was Koldyeze.

Just to make sure, Sten and Virunga had stacked the deck, slipped a fifth ace in the cards. The fifth ace was the Golden Worm St. Clair had planted in the Koldyeze computer. It was a virus that day by day would monkey with the production figures. A decimal point slipped. A minus turned to a plus. And, voilà! Koldyeze would be able to boast far higher successes than even the most optimistic Tahn could dream of. Derzhin would have absolute proof that the POW camp was an experiment that was working.

There were too many lists of failures on the Tahn Empire's slate to ignore such a glowing success. The virus had a second function built into it. As time went by, it was eating away key areas of memory in the computer. In time, no Tahn would know up from down at Koldyeze – just that everything looked really good as long as one did not look that hard.

The expected first rash of reprisals came the instant the Tahn realized there were POWs suddenly among the missing. They had shut down the camp with a mailed glove. There were interrogations, beatings, and a few deaths. But the Tahn never found the secret of the catacombs and the tunnel that led to the hill outside. And then, almost as quickly as it had begun, the interrogations came to a halt.

It was just as well. Virunga was at the point of breaking out the ancient weapons he and Sten had found in one of the catacomb vaults. Such an action would have been suicidal. But briefly satisfying.

Virunga's goons reported the comings and goings of the camp hierarchy. There were many hushed meetings and whisperings to other, faceless Tahn over com lines. Virunga could feel some kind of crisis mounting. And then it stopped, just at the moment when he expected the pustule to burst. A sudden gloom engulfed the camp, affecting every Tahn from the top on down. The prisoners were surprised by a loosening up of attitudes. It was as if they were all being handled a little gingerly, with just a hint of fearful respect. Something had happened, of that Virunga was certain. Some huge event that he would read about in the history books – assuming he survived. But no one had the slightest idea what it was. Especially the Tahn.

Virunga started to attention as the door to the commandant's office swung open. A cold-faced guard nodded to his two fellows standing on either side of the prisoner. A hard object jammed into his side, and Virunga caught his breath from the pain. He pushed the annoyance from his mind, positioned his crutches, and creaked up on his haunches. He shifted position, jammed the crutches forward, and leaned into them with his massive weight. He swung his body at the door as if the guard were not there. It was not physical strength but the sheer force of Virunga's immense dignity that made the guard step aside.

The atmosphere in the room was forcedly mild. Avrenti was slumped in a chair in a corner, seemingly riffling through some minor papers. The commandant, Derzhin, was standing at the window, his back to Virunga, gazing outside as if witnessing something of mild interest. Virunga came to a halt in the middle of the room. He did not look left or right or hint for a chair to hold his crippled body. He just stood there, leaning into his crutches, waiting silently for the game to begin.

After a very long time, Derzhin turned away from the window. He seemed to note Virunga's presence for the first time.

'Ah, Colonel. Thank you for coming.'

Virunga did not give him the pleasure of responding. But Derzhin did not seem to notice. He crossed to his desk and sat down. He picked up a printout, studied it, then replaced it. He tapped his fingers on his desk as if trying to remember why he had called Virunga.

'I have some information about the . . . uh . . . shall we say lost members of your command.'

Despite himself, Virunga stiffened. It was as if an arctic wind had suddenly cut through the thick fur guarding his spine. 'Yes?'

He did not trust himself to say more.

'Forgive me, Colonel, but I am forced to bear grim news. From your point of view, that is. They've been caught. Every single one.'

Virunga sighed, a little relieved. It was over, then. Okay, they were captured. Now he would have to make sure of their treatment.

'I . . . wish to . . . see them. At once. To assure . . . they are . . . treated in accordance . . . with the laws . . . of wartime.'

Out of the corner of his eye, he saw Avrenti sneer.

'I'm afraid that will be impossible, Colonel,' Derzhin said.

'You . . . refuse?'

'No. I wouldn't be so rude. The fact of the matter is, there is little to see. All of them are dead.'

Virunga found himself gasping. His twin hearts thundered. His ears rang from the sudden pressure. 'What? Dead? How could—'

Shouts came from the courtyard outside. At first it was just a few voices. Then it grew in size and panic and anger. Derzhin smiled at him and waved him forward. Somehow, Virunga found himself leaning on his crutches, staring out the window. At first all he saw was a crowd of prisoners swarming around something in the center of the courtyard. Then he saw an old flatbed truck with a team of horses hitched to the front. On the truck was a contingent of Tahn guards. And Genrikh. They seemed to be unloading something – or somethings – pulling whatever it was from dripping gunnysacks and hurling it to the ground.

And then it was as if Virunga had suddenly acquired telescopic sight. He saw what they were unloading. Arms . . . and legs . . . and heads. The butchered bodies of Ibn Bakr and Alis.

Chapter Thirty

Chetwynd, spaceport/waterfront thug, labor organizer, convicted felon, political prisoner, and now somewhere between a trusty and a pardoned guard at Koldyeze, contemplated the angles as he bull-dozed his way down the dockside toward a needed and, he felt, richly deserved double quill.

Chetwynd had matured beyond the hustler who knew he knew what was going on – which was what had put him on a prison planet in the first place – into a hustler who knew he did not know what was happening.

Not that the change had produced much difference in Chetwynd's behavior.

What should have happened after the mass break from Koldyeze was suitable retributions. Derzhin should have been lowered by a head, Avrenti should have been transferred to a penal battalion, Genrikh should have been given command of the prison, and draconian measures should have been meted out. Chetwynd had already sounded out connections for another assignment – anything to avoid being sent back to Dru and being chased by gurions. Instead, nothing happened.

Nothing much, at any rate.

Two escapees had been nailed, dragged back, and blasted. But the others?

Nothing. Even through the guards' rumor mill.

More important than those vanished POWs was the fact that little had changed at Koldyeze. Things and people continued in their measured course. Chetwynd cursed in an aside at his wasted credits supplying that worm Genrikh's seemingly inexhaustible pit with alk to create a note of sympathy when the drakh came down.

Another angle that he had not figured out was what had happened to his richly beloved government, out there beyond somewhere. Chetwynd had been thinking aloud when he had told Sten that the Tahn needed a fast, vast victory. But, he realized later, it was so.

Something, out there in the far beyond – and Chetwynd was not sure where or what – had happened. Something that the Tahn were not pleased with.

His union might have been smashed when Chetwynd was convicted and sentenced to a prison world, but his contacts were not. There were still friends around. Friends . . . acquaintances . . . enemies . . . people he had knocked over gravsleds with as a boy. The labels did not matter – growing up on the wrong side of the power structure of Heath created a life-long alliance. Us against Them. At least so long as it was profitable.

Heath was suddenly the transshipment point for strange cargoes – materials, tools, and shipwrights – to the previously unheard of Erebus System, and medical supplies and personnel by the kiloton to other worlds where Tahn hospitals were not based.

The far beyond, which meant the Empire, had not been kind to the Tahn, Chetwynd reasoned. That was another card he did not know how to play yet.

He stopped just outside the entrance to the Khag, the prime bar on Heath if one wanted anything illegal, immoral, unavailable, or beyond priorities – and his headquarters. Filled with his cronies.

Chetwynd put on a brave leader face and entered.

He bought a round for his boyos.

He sipped the shot he wanted to slug down.

He held court, awarded and withheld approval, granted or with-held favors – and told the latest joke:

'A mister finally gets the vid. He's on the list. Through priorities. His gravsled is fin'ly available.

'He goes bug. 'Bout time. Paid for it six years ago. When is he gonna get it?

'Salesclot says four years down. Whitsl-cycle. Fourth day.

'Mister asks that be in the morning or afternoon?

'Salesman says, "Mister, that be four years away! Why do you care if it's morning or night?"

'"Cause I got the plumber coming in the morning . . ."'

During the laughter he blasted down the rest of the shot and waved for another.

Court business over with, his cronies drifted away to let the great man be alone with his thoughts. Chetwynd, rerunning the angles, was not pleased to have his concentration broken by two boiler-suited, drakh-reeking dock scrapers sliding into his booth. He was about to summon ancillary thugs for the slaughter when he recognized them and sprayed his mouthful of quill across the booth.

Alex smiled at him in sympathy. 'Dinnae be wastin' thae lifewater, lad. Tha'll come ae time when y' regret it.'

Sten was motioning for the barmaid. 'Chien,' he said, 'you look like you need a carafe.'

Chetwynd did. 'I thought all of you'd be heading for the woods,' he managed, proud of not having asked any of the usual boring questions or made any of the expected responses.

'Can't speak for the others,' Sten said. 'But I'm a city boy. Scared of the dark, out there in the bushes.'

'The bully patrols check in here regular,' Chetwynd said.

'Ah hae nae problem,' Kilgour said. 'We're sittin' wi' our respect'd friend. Kickin't thae gong around.'

Chetwynd grudged defeat. He could shout and scream – and the two escapees would be taken. He would be eligible for some kind of reward. However, he thought, if the official word is that all these clots were shot attempting to escape, how would my masters explain two suddenly alive Imperials?

'Besides,' Sten said, reading Chetwynd's thinking, 'we'd both be up for brain scan – and both of us have been spending five minutes a day thinking about how much we love you.'

Chetwynd did not believe that – he did not figure that anyone, even these obviously talented Imperial Intelligence types, could precondition themselves to provide false information to the Tahn torturers. The problem was, his belly rumbled, he did not think the Tahn believed that.

'Excellent, cheenas. There are back rooms. There are 'freshers. You two stink. But first – what are you looking for?'

Sten explained. They had slid out the prison and gone to ground with no escape route or anything other than the most superficial false ID. They wanted identification – not false. They wanted to become real citizens of Heath. Sten – correctly – assumed that as the manpower barrel drained, the Tahn were drafting the young, the out of work, the criminal, and the dissident – all of which sounded as if they could be friends of Chetwynd.

Sten and Alex planned to replace any two of Chetwynd's cronies who were up for the high jump. They then would volunteer for the Tahn military. Certainly no one would look for two Imperials in the service. Chetwynd's cohorts could then go on about their business. 'Ah'm assumin't,' Alex added, 'thae y' noo hae problems gie'in a bein' another name.'

Once in the military Sten and Alex knew they could go through training easily, volunteer for a combat assignment, and then slither through the lines, ground or spatial, to make their home run.

At that point, Chetwynd started gurgling. Not in protest, Sten realized, but in laughter.

'Cheenas, cheenas,' he finally said. 'Now I see why you Imperials ended up in this war in the first place.'

He stood waving – and Sten's knife slid out of his arm. Two barmaids bounced up.

'My friends,' Chetwynd said, 'need almost everything. They want a quiet room. Baths. Two baths. Each. Food. From my private supplies. Any alk they order. And someone to rub their backs.' He turned back to Sten and Alex. 'Women satisfactory?'

There was no dissent – Kilgour and Sten were gaping.

'Clean ones. And another pitcher now.'

Chetwynd sat back down. For the first time in days, his angles coincided, and he knew what to do next.

'You want me to do all that, in the vague hopes that you two orphans can get home? Cheenas, let me tell you. All of my people are so safe from this war, it is disgusting. Your deal is the worst I've heard of late.

'Correction. The only worse one I can think of is if I recaptured you two clots.

'Now. Shall I tell you what is going to happen?

'There are chambers below this hellhole. You will disappear into them. You will be fattened and battened, dighted and knighted until a certain date.

'When I order, you shall be moved quietly through the streets to a certain place, where I shall introduce you to a charming man named Wild. Jon Wild.'

Chetwynd was most surprised when first Sten and then Alex started laughing. Jon Wild was the urbane smuggler they had carefully cultivated years ago, before the beginning of the war. Sten had promised Wild to leave his operation alone provided that Wild smuggled no war goods into the Tahn Empire and was willing to provide intelligence. When the war had started, Wild's home base of Romney had been destroyed, and Sten assumed that Wild and his people had stuck around a little too long even though the warehouses were empty and there were no bodies in the ruins.

Maybe he had spent too long being one of the emperor's café society toughs in Mantis Section – but Sten was privately delighted that Wild and his operation were surviving comfortably.

'We know him,' Sten said. 'Go ahead.'

Sails somewhat sagging, Chetwynd finished. Wild would take them out of the Tahn systems and deliver them to a neutral world. They would be provided with whatever money and identity they needed to get to an Imperial world from there.

'I'll finish,' Sten broke in. 'Since you obviously assume that we are connected, you would like a little gold carat in your fiche, so that when the Empire lands on Heath you don't get stuck in my old cell on Koldyeze.'

'Of course.'

And Chetwynd never realized how much that response meant to men who had spent years hearing of defeat and death.

Chapter Thirty-One

Tanz Sullamora had constructed his fishing retreat in a time when he not only still believed in heroes but imagined the Eternal Emperor as the leader of any laughing band of handsome devils. It was built out of his desire to emulate the Emperor in every way.

The Emperor loved cooking, so Sullamora slavishly copied his recipes and presented them at elaborate banquets for his friends. Except that everything tasted like drakh – which Sullamora, having no palate, did not know, and he was too rich and powerful a businessman for his friends to tell him.

Then there was fishing. The Emperor loved fishing to such a point that he had invested over 300 years of effort and a large fortune to re-create a fishing camp on the banks of the Umpqua River in the ancient region of Oregon on the planet Earth. Sullamora built his own camp – on a vastly smaller scale – many kilometers upstream from the Emperor. He threw himself into fishing with great enthusiasm and no talent at all.

For several years he would celebrate the end of any difficult business negotiations by taking off – with great fanfare – to the wilds of Oregon to relax on the banks of his retreat. After a suitable period he would return, boasting to everyone within hearing distance about how relaxed he was and about how a being could not really know his own inner nature until he had tested himself against a canny salmon fighting to escape his hook. What he did not admit to anyone, much less himself, was that he hated everything to do with fishing. After his first trip he hired gillies to catch the salmon for him, and after another trip he even refused to eat his catch and fed the fish to his servants and aides instead.

Not only that, he found himself going quietly mad in the silence of the Oregon forest. He began hating every minute he spent at his rustic retreat – which, like the Emperor's, at first consisted of only a few rough-board buildings that blended into the environment. There was nothing to see but green, nothing to hear but the bubbling of the river. And to him the air was disgusting, with its smells of ripe river mud, decaying plants, and too-virile pollen. Sullamora missed the bustle of the deal and the sharp smells of adrenaline and fear.

But the fishing retreat was not something he could just let go of. He could not just sell or abandon it. Somehow, he was sure, there would be a great deal of whispering, secret smiles, and a loss of face. Sullamora compensated by inviting more and more of his friends and business acquaintances to his camp by the banks of the Umpqua.

The rough-board structures were replaced by larger and larger gleaming metal buildings filled with humming machinery. The small landing pad became a large private port that could handle nearly a hundred vehicles. And the quiet times in between deals took on a loud, festive air, with more and more elaborate entertainments.

The final step took Sullamora and the retreat full circle. As his hero worship of the Emperor diminished and disenchantment set in, the camp became once again a quiet place. A place where odd alliances could be made and deals could be struck in secret. A place where the art of fishing took on a whole different meaning.

Sullamora used the excuse of a loose boot tab to stop and let his five companions stroll on through the trees. He glanced up at them, listening, measuring. The conversation was quiet and light. But Sullamora could sense the underlying tension, as if each being were waiting for someone to declare himself, to speak first about matters that concerned them all – and their solution. And the longer it took, the more wary each became.

Sullamora swallowed at the knot of fear in his throat. It was becoming increasingly apparent that it might be Sullamora who had to speak up first. And if he did so, and he was wrong about his companions, he would be very quickly humiliated, crushed, and then . . .

The Emperor's privy council was like a man who suffered from obesity: bloated with all the rich meals but terrified that the next banquet was about to be canceled.

For most beings in the Empire, the war with the Tahn had created hardships of historic proportions. But for the six members of the council, it had been a time of historic profits and opportunity. And after the stunning Imperial victory at Durer they were faced with not only an end to the enormous profits but huge losses as the Emperor looked about for the means to pay the butcher's bill.

And at the moment, it appeared the first place the Emperor would look was at his six lords of industry: Volmer – mass media; Malperin – agriculture, chemicals, and pharmaceuticals; Lovett – banking; the Kraa twins – mines, mills, and foundries; Kyes – artificial intelligence; and finally, Sullamora – ships and trade.

Sullamora had approached his duties as a member of the Emperor's private cabinet with a great deal of reluctance and cynicism. Until the moment the Emperor had appointed him to the council – in a chilling and, for Sullamora, revealing conversation – he had not even been aware of its existence. And the appointment had been made in a half-hearted way when Sullamora had questioned the Emperor's strategy in dealing with the Tahn if and when they were defeated.

The Emperor was planning to remove the government and eliminate all vestiges of the Tahn culture, then to follow up with a massive rebuilding program. Sullamora saw that as pure weakness and foolishness. All Tahn should have to suffer for what they had wrought. Besides, the beings who had loyally supported the Emperor from the very beginning would therefore have to forgo vast potential profits. That did not make sense, and Sullamora said so – although he put it as a carefully worded suggestion, not a criticism.

When he had first met with his colleagues of the privy council, Sullamora had kept all that to himself. Groping for direction, he had bided his time until he had taken each member's pulse a hundred times and had their profiles drawn and redrawn as many times more by key people in his psych division.

Looked at from afar – something Tanz was not capable of doing – the privy council presented a strange but accurate portrait of the Empire itself: an odd kind of blend of vigorous entrepreneurism and dynastic capitalism. Seen up close, it was a confusing puzzle of wildly different interests and goals. Little by little, however, Sullamora gradually uncovered a common note.

Volmer was the most vocal of the group. Usually, when the others danced about a point, it was Volmer who tended to be openly and harshly critical of the latest Imperial policy they were deploring. That did not mean that anyone – much less Sullamora – trusted him.

As head of one of the oldest family dynasties in the Empire as well as the chieftain of the largest news-gathering, polit-prop, and advertising companies in the many systems that made up the Empire, Volmer was the least vulnerable of the six. He also had a private reputation among the various companies that made up his barony as a bit of a waffler, a man who would encourage his underlings to take hard stands when it suited him and then leave them hanging if the wind switched direction. Still, as the war dragged on and when even an idiot could see what a hollow shell the privy council in fact was, Sullamora was sure Volmer was moving out of the swamp of his own indecision onto the firmer ground shared by his colleagues.

It was the raw, open greed of the Kraa twins that made Sullamora put them in his potential allies column. They had a deserved reputation as the most corrupt, vicious, self-serving beings in the brutal world of high-stakes business. The two women were second-generation mega-rich. Their father had been a wildcat miner who had parlayed a minor fortune in Imperium X into a virtual empire consisting of minerals, exotic and common, and whole systems whose sole occupation was the milling and smelting of the same. Their father had been a canny man whose word had been his religion.

Upon his death, the twins had instantly dissolved the religion and sent his high priests howling into the wilderness, where they then had their economic assassins hunt them down one by one. The Kraa twins delighted in nasty plots and wild schemes that took their fortunes on wild roller coaster rides from treble profits to near bankruptcy and back again. Although they had been born identical twins, fifty years of indulgent living had stamped out two entirely different-looking beings. One was gross and banded with bulge after bulge of greasy fat. The other could best be described as anorexic – bones jutting nearly through pasty, unhealthy flesh. But appearance was the only difference. In everything else they thought and acted as one, seemingly taking turns as the dominant twin. Sullamora noted with minor interest their first names and then wisely forgot them. To think of them as anything but one was a fatal mistake too many others had made.

It was to Sullamora's credit that he saw the Kraa twins as the easiest members of the council to manipulate. With the Kraas, one only had to hoist the carrot and they would follow. If they did not, they had more than enough vulnerable spots to probe. And one did not have to be subtle about it.

Malperin, on the other hand, had only one area of vulnerability. She was a woman with an exterior *and* interior of ten-point steel. She was the ultimate chief operating officer, armed with academic degrees and hands-on management experience that stretched for three small forevers. It did not matter what kind of company she was called upon to manage, be it toy widgets or sophisticated electronics. In her case, it was an ability that was a two-headed coin. Because her viewpoint was necessarily fixed on the upper level, she had no feeling or gut instincts about specifics. That almost meant she had no loyalties to things, only to procedures.

It was for that reason that the Emperor had tapped her to head up ACP, one of the most bizarre but vital mega-corporations going. Even an industrial historian's eyes would glaze over tracing the hydra head back to its beginnings. Suffice it to say that in a bewildering series of small fish somehow swallowing big fish swallowing whole schools of other fish actions, ACP came tentatively into being. It was a tacked-together conglomerate that operated millions upon millions of kilometers of farms and ranches, oversaw massive vats of brewing chemicals and gases of every nature, and also produced most of the basic important drugs and medicines in the Empire. It was a company born of business warfare, and it never got better after that. Each division was bred and educated to hate and distrust the others. The situation had been threatening to spin out of control when the Tahn war broke out. At any other time the Eternal Emperor would have let matters take their course. ACP was a dinosaur doomed to extinction. But there was no way that he could allow evolution to take its course while fighting a war. The only solution was to suggest strongly – read 'you'd clottin' better or die' – that the various boards of directors go outside ACP for a chief operating officer.

After a great deal of squabbling and threatening, Malperin was picked. To firm up her position, the Emperor also named her to his private cabinet. That would give her temporary prestige. But as the war seemed to be winding down, Malperin was beginning to realize that her overlong honeymoon at ACP was as good as over. She would also have to be stupid not to realize that at any moment the Emperor could and *would* withdraw his support and let economic gravity settle the rest. Malperin was not stupid. She did not look upon her future gladly.

The next to last member of the privy council was the money man, Lovett. Like Volmer, he was from a great family dynasty. There were Lovetts who had acted as financial go-betweens in some of the Eternal Emperor's earliest business dealings. The newest Lovett scion was handsome, dashing, and daring.

Tragically, through a series of misfortunes, he was the last member of his clan, and he had taken over the helm of the banking empire upon his mother's death. He was also the wildest of wild cards, who refused to listen to his advisers and had a habit of taking large and unnecessary risks. Some said it was out of remembered gratitude to the Lovetts that the Emperor had stepped in. Others said that it was because the Lovett banks were too integral to the Emperor's plans to be allowed to collapse and that it had been purely in self-interest that the Emperor had reacted. Both were right. And so history would someday record that on such and such a date Lovett became the youngest being ever to head up the Imperial Monetary Foundation, a non-profit organization whose charter was to play banker to the poorest systems in the Empire. In short, it was a position of extreme glitter and no substance at all. Sullamora grinned to himself, knowing that Lovett had *just* figured that out. Tanz Sullamora saw Lovett as the easiest one of all to manipulate.

If Lovett was paper, Kyes was stone. Kyes was a Grb'chev, one of the saddest creations of the gods of madness. He was a tall, slender, vaguely humanoid being of immense dignity, just entering his 121st year. His coloring was silver leaning toward white, except for a triangular slash of scarlet that rode across his bony skull. When he spoke, his limbs were animated and his eyes flashed with impatient intelligence. But in repose, the face slackened, the eyes went blank, and the great splash of red pulsed like an infection that had reached crisis. Kyes was two separate beings with one dominant will and a weaker, genetically suicidal other. The Grb'chev were the result of an odd form of symbiotic bonding. Before the bonding, when the Grb'chev were merely tall and slender and very white, with no red 'birthmark' on their skulls, there was nothing to distinguish the race except for their great stupidity and even greater genetic luck. They had brains that were no more than a large pimple on the end of a spinal stalk. They favored a particular type of fruit that was edible only when the pollen was most active. The pollen was deadly poison to anything, including the Grb'chev. The Grb'chev developed an exotic system of nasal filters topped by super-efficient sinuses that gradually bulged out their heads until they were oversize.

They also developed an immune system that was impenetrable to any form of virus and bacteria on their homeworld. Left on their own, the Grb'chev would have spun out their destinies of exceedingly stupid, exceedingly lucky beings who spent most of their waking hours gaping, scratching, and eating fruit. But although stupid did not bother nature one bit, happy seemed to give it problems. Enter, stage right, a lowly virus looking for a home. It was a virus that had only one ability to brag about: it could mutate its protein sheath to pierce any genetic structure, no matter how invulnerable. Usually that meant the instant infection and almost as instant extinction of any living forms it encountered. It was a closed-end deal, so that although the virus could giggle on into virus paradise, it could never be anything more than what it was, a wolf with changeable clothing.

It encountered something different in the Grb'chev. As quickly as it cast off its sheath and fitted on another, the Grb'chev's immune system threw up another shield. The virus finally found its home in the sinuses, the most recent addition to what made a Grb'chev a Grb'chev. The mutating virus met cells in the middle of their own transition. They met and formed an entity consisting entirely of brain cells, nerves, and nerve receptors, an entity operating with – but separately from – the bodily parts and functions. The brain cells were also far stronger and more durable than any main body cells. The closest cells one could compare them with were cancer cells. In short, they were immortal.

Next came awareness. And after that, despair. Because the Grb'chev came complete: an efficient fuel and waste-disposal system. Smooth locomotion. An ability to easily duplicate the Grb'chev structure as many times as necessary. And a perfect time clock that spelled out beginning, middle, a long senility, and an end. When Kyes entered his 121st year, he knew he had no more than five more years of awareness before the agonizingly slow deterioration of intelligence led to his ending up as a vegetable that gaped, bubbled, and then died.

In his hundred-plus years of adult-active life, Kyes believed that he had eliminated all the seven deadly sins from his system one by one. Ninety years before, he had rolled out of a prestigious institution armed with a degree in artificial intelligence, a sheaf of job offers, and a double sheaf of ideas. He ignored the job offers and struck out on his own. Twenty-five years later he was richer than any being's wildest dreams. He was also famous for the hundreds of vital patents he personally owned and the lean-mean company he had created that could identify and exploit any fad in the most faddish of fields years before his competitors. Kyes was good. And he was arrogant – as he had every right to be.

Then the big boys got together, kicked sand in his face, and took his company, wealth, and arrogance away from him. Kyes disappeared for fifteen years. But when he returned, he was a remade being. He had spent every second of every waking day studying his old foes. As he learned their weaknesses, he eliminated weaknesses of his own. He came on stage again quietly. He was still creative and inventive, but he buried his inventions in masses of partnerships and cut-out companies. Just before his hundredth birthday, Kyes found himself the master of the greatest computer, robotic, and artificial intelligence conglomerate ever known. He was famous again, sought after for his views and insights. He even met the Eternal Emperor and had reason to believe that he had met him on as nearly an equal level as possible. Had not Kyes been one of the first beings the Emperor had come to for advice in his dealings with the mechanics of the Tahn conflict? And was he not one of the first appointees to the privy council?

And then, little by little, Kyes began to believe that he was being used. After that, he began noticing that his firm was becoming more and more dependent on the Emperor's contracts. He had enjoyed enormous expansion in the past few years, but he was beginning to realize just how delicate the expansion was. A frown from the Emperor would mean starting all over again. Except that with only five years left, to start again would be impossible.

Kyes became obsessed with newly realized vulnerability. He could see no way of stopping it. It seemed as inevitable as the winding down of his biological clock. Then he began thinking about the Emperor. The *Eternal* Emperor. And he realized there was nothing empty about either word in the title.

Kyes met envy face-to-face. And it was just about then that Tanz Sullamora began whispering in his ear.

After Durer, the whispering was replaced by louder and louder mutterings of discontent. At first, Sullamora just complained about how the Emperor's busy schedule prevented him from consulting his privy council for their thoughts on how to deal with the depression that was sure to follow after the war. The others not only agreed but became encouraged to complain that the few times they *had* been consulted, their advice had been ignored.

'Take me, for instance,' Volmer had said. 'The last time I spoke with the Emperor I strongly suggested that we had to start planning for the future right now. A good propaganda campaign isn't created overnight.

'We've got to come up with our message. Target our audience. Tailor the message for the various target groups. And then deliver it in a carefully orchestrated way.'

The message, as Volmer saw it, was: 'Hope through sacrifice. Each of us is going to be called upon to sacrifice for the good of the Empire. And of our children. And our children's children.'

'I like it,' Lovett had said, immediately thinking about some ideas he had concerning interest rates pegged to inflation, with a high floor to take care of any unexpected deflation. 'What did he say?'

Volmer frowned. 'He asked me what *I* was planning to sacrifice. He said for a message like that to work, people would want to see their leaders do a little suffering . . . Suffering, what a negative word! Sacrifice is much easier to sell . . . Anyway, I told him flat out that was an insane idea. Why, if people see us hurting—' he waved, including his colleagues in the gesture '—what would they have to hope for? Destroys the whole concept.'

He found no disagreement in that.

Each of the other members had similar horror stories. Malperin wanted wage controls but no ceiling on prices. The Kraas wanted 'more enlightened' pollution and safety laws. Sullamora wanted a one-sided tariff arrangement to shield his merchant empire. And as for Kyes, well, Kyes did not say anything for some time. The others wondered at that for a while, disturbed that the Grb'chev was not reaching in for his share of the pie. What they did not know was that Kyes, with one huge exception, already had all that he wanted. And he figured that if he ever thought of anything else, he was quite capable of getting it on his own, without the benefit of Imperial intervention. Still, there was *the* exception . . .

Several meetings went by before he moved his first pawn. He opened on the king's bishop side. And when he spoke, everyone was respectfully silent, waiting for him to finally declare himself. They were not disappointed.

'Perhaps we are doing our Emperor a disservice,' he said slowly, as if he were thinking out loud. Every member of the council knew better. 'From his point of view, perhaps we are firing ideas at him from all directions. He has *so* much on his mind now. How can he pick here and there when he can see no whole?'

His colleagues nodded wisely, merely to mark time until Kyes got the rest of it out.

'Let's make things simpler for him,' Kyes said. 'We need to speak as one. To present a coherent view. And then have the authority to enact the needed reforms. With the Emperor's concurrence, of course,' he added quickly.

'Emperor's concurrence . . . of course,' everyone muttered.

What Kyes proposed was deceptively simple. The privy council would call upon the Parliament and then the Emperor to create a quasi-public agency – consisting of members of the sitting council, to start with – that could act independently of the whims and fads and pressure of any special-interest group.

Said agency would take the long view of the economy, carefully managing the AM2 pump to control the strength of the Imperial credit, keep a close eye on vital industrial and agricultural supplies, make sure that the government always spoke with one voice, and serve as a much needed check and balance between the competing views of business and the public good.

There was no disagreement. Sullamora, the man with the most direct clout with Parliament, would take point. The first step would be approached cautiously. The skeleton of the proposed agency would be buried in a 'sense of Parliament' resolution which, once enacted, would be difficult for the Emperor to shoot down without causing a very loud fuss. The trick was to keep anyone – especially the Emperor's back-bench toadies – from even guessing that something was up. The privy council decided to praise Caesar rather than to damn him. The praise took the form of a lengthy document profusely congratulating the Emperor for his victory over the Tahn at Durer and calling for Empirewide support of the Emperor to carry the victory forward to a final surrender and then beyond. Even on the surface, it was not an empty document. It was worded in such a way to make even the fence sitters who had been the bane of the emperor for some time to back his act. If approved, and Sullamora's people went out and twisted every arm and tentacle available to assure its passage, the resolution would break the back of the neutrals.

Sullamora knew that would ensure the Emperor's support. He also had his experts put together a swampland section that committed Parliament to 'render every assistance' to the Emperor in his 'brave and lonely struggle.' The independent agency was the gator hiding in the swamp.

Sullamora's analysts pored over the document and finally agreed that there was no way anyone could ever spot the gator amid obfuscations no one would bother to read. As one patriarch of the Parliament once put it, 'If everyone knew what they're voting on, we'd never get out of here.' When the big moment came, Sullamora personally planned to present the resolution in a speech punched up to the nth degree by a team provided by Volmer. It was pure-dee guaranteed to be welcomed with thunderous applause.

Sullamora paced back and forth in the small anteroom, waiting to be called to the speaker's rostrum. As he paced, he rehearsed the speech in his head, punching out at the air with his right hand to mark the rhythms. A door hissed open behind him, and Sullamora turned, mildly surprised. The call was five minutes early. But instead of seeing the huge jolly figure of the Parliament's sergeant at arms, he found himself gaping down at a small, dark man with a large curved knife hanging from his uniform belt. It was a Gurkha, one of the Emperor's personal bodyguards. The Gurkha gave him a small, barely polite bow and handed him a message. It was a summons. The Eternal Emperor had spotted the gator.

The Emperor was a study in casualness, feet propped up on his antique desk, a drink before him, another in front of Tanz Sullamora, and a bottle between them. He even picked up his drink frequently as he talked, seeming to take a sip and then replace the glass on the desk. Sullamora noted that the level never went down.

'. . . I appreciate your good intentions, Tanz,' the Emperor was saying. 'And I plan to personally thank each member of my cabinet for going to all this thought and effort. But . . .'

He let the word sit there for a moment while he took another sip of his drink. From that moment on, Sullamora knew the conversation would be one he would take to his grave – or, at least, to his memoirs.

'I don't go for this independent agency concept,' the Emperor

finally said. He raised a polite hand as if Sullamora would protest
– not that he would ever *dare* to. 'I know you may think I'm being
shortsighted, but these kinds of things have a way of taking on a
life of their own. The fact of the matter is, I'm a one-man show.
Always have been. Hope to always be. You fellows are talking
about taking the long view. Well, I have to tell you, from where I
sit, there is no way your view can be long enough.'

He waited, encouraging comment from Sullamora.

'There was no disrespect intended,' Sullamora said. 'But we just
can't see how one person – no matter how good – can handle
everything himself. What we're offering here, sir, is a chance for
you to take advantage of the experience of some of the best minds
under your rule.'

The Emperor pretended to think about that for a moment. Then
he nodded to Sullamora.

'Okay. Let's run through this and see if maybe I'm wrong. I
suppose we all agree on what we're facing once this is over. Once
the Tahn agree to my terms, we turn off the war machine. And
then we immediately face one holy mother of a depression. I doubt
there has ever been a depression the potential size of what we're
talking about.

'All your shipbuilding factories, for instance. They'll come to a
halt. We've got enough ships of the line now for ten long lifetimes.
The same goes for every other area of the economy. The torque
will be tremendous. A whole lot of great big axles churning away,
with no place to go.'

'We've got ideas that specifically—'

'I've heard of them,' the Emperor snapped. 'And they don't wash.
You want me to raise the AM2 tax from two mills to three or
maybe four. But what you can't seem to get through your heads is
that if you take money out of people's pockets, there's no way they
can buy what little you'll be able to produce.

'It's not war that has destroyed the great empires of history. It's
money, or the mishandling of same. When the soldiers' job is over,
you've got this big whopping bill. And you've got interest running
on that big mother of a bill. And you better not make the mistake
of not paying it off. Otherwise, next time you need to fight, the
money people will drag their feet and jack up the interest on what
little they will lend you. Same with the little guy whose life we put
on the line. If he comes home to misery, he's not gonna be too
thrilled about fighting for you next time out, no matter how worthy
you tell him the cause is.

'Personally, I'm thinking about pulling in my horns. Reducing the tax to peacetime levels. One mill. No more. And maybe after a while a temporary decrease to two-thirds of a mill. That way the local governments can pop on a quarter-mill tax of their own to pay back their share of what this stupid war cost.'

Sullamora gasped at that idea. 'At least we can increase the AM2 output,' he said. 'That'll bring in more taxes. Besides making it cheaper for us all to operate.'

'Sure it will,' the Eternal Emperor said. 'It will also kick hell out of the value of the credit. People will be walking around with wheelbarrows of the stuff to buy a glass of beer.'

Sullamora did not know what a wheelbarrow was, but he got the general drift. 'You mentioned beer,' he said. 'Now, there's a way to make money nobody can object to. A tax on beer. A tax on narcotics. A tax on joy—'

'Used to be called a sin tax,' the Emperor said dryly. 'Another dumb idea. Between me and the Tahn, we have killed and mutilated more beings than I like to think about. What we're left with is a pretty miserable group.

'Now, the beings in this group may not agree on a lot. But if we let them, misery will be the first hammer they'll pick up. And they'll hit us with it, Tanz. I guarantee you that.

'No. This is a time to start encouraging a little *more* sin, if anything. Lots of spectacle. And as close to free as dammit.'

That made no sense at all to Sullamora. The Emperor pretended not to notice and moved on.

'And speaking of keeping people happy,' he said. 'You realize that we're all talking about some major increases in wages, don't you? And if you want to sell anything, a major *decrease* in prices.

'In fact, since a lot of my fellow capitalists are usually pretty slow to get the drift of these kinds of things, I'm considering some pretty heavy-duty legislation on the subject.'

'How – how can you possibly see that?' Sullamora sputtered out.

'Simple. Fewer people to work equals higher wages. Lower prices means more productivity providing things those people can now afford. And lots of cheap material to build those things from. For anyone with vision, that is. Take all those ships of yours, Tanz,' the Emperor said, slipping the dirk between Sullamora's ribs. Sullamora realized that the Emperor planned on sticking him with a lot of those soon-to-be-useless warships. 'With a little creative retooling, you'll have plenty of scrap of just about any kind of material going to build some useful products.'

'Like what?' Sullamora asked in a bare whisper.

The Eternal Emperor shrugged. 'Beats the clot out of me. You've got R&D geniuses. Put 'em to work making some new things to cook food with instead of frying people. Should be easy.

'Hell, Tanz. The more I think about it, we're talking about *real* opportunity here. Almost makes me wish I didn't have this stupid job. A guy with a little brains, a bit of money, and a lot energy could make himself a great big pile out of all this.'

Sullamora had to ask the question. 'Do you really believe that?'

'Sure I do,' the Emperor said. 'At least I know *I* could, although you probably think that's just big talk. Fact is, most emperors think the same way. There was a queen, way back when, who used to say pretty much the same thing to her advisers.

'She used to tell them that if somehow she were plucked from her throne and dropped in nothing but her petticoats on any desolate coast, it wouldn't take her long to be running things again. Some of her advisers used to laugh about that behind her back.

'Her name was Elizabeth. Elizabeth the First. Ever hear of her?'

Tanz Sullamora shook his head, knowing his audience was coming to a close.

'She must have been really something,' the Emperor mused on. 'Some historians think she was the greatest ruler ever. Maybe they're right.'

A small wild thought crossed Sullamora's mind. He wondered what had happened to the advisers. The ones who laughed. Had they ever thought about . . .

'Of course, she was pretty quick with the ax,' the Eternal Emperor said, and it was almost as if he were reading Sullamora's mind. The ship baron rose quickly to his feet, nearly knocking over his drink.

'Excuse me, sir,' he stammered. 'But I think . . .'

'Are you all right?' the Emperor asked, giving Sullamora a strange, puzzled look. But maybe Tanz was just imagining that. He made an excuse about feeling slightly ill and, after being dismissed, hurried for the door. Just as it hissed open, the Emperor called his name. Sullamora forced himself to turn back.

'Yes, sir?'

'No more surprises, okay, Tanz?' the Emperor said. 'I don't like surprises.'

Tanz Sullamora gasped out a promise and hurried away, vowing to break that promise the first chance he had.

*

He spoke uninterrupted for a full hour. The members of the privy council listened in cold silence as he related in complete detail his conversation with the Emperor. Sullamora did not color his account in any way or attempt to paint himself as being larger or bolder than he had in fact been. These were businessbeings who had no patience for hyperbole. Just the facts was what they wanted, and just the facts was what they got.

The silence went on after he had finished. It seemed like an eternity as each one filled in the blanks and thought over the personal consequences of what the Eternal Emperor was planning to do.

Volmer was the first to break. 'But – but – we're looking at disaster here. Doesn't he understand . . . My God! We've got to stop him!'

And then the impact of what he had just said hit him like a padded club, and he flushed and stuttered back into silence. After an appropriate pause, Tanz Sullamora made a suggestion. He said that maybe they could all benefit from a walk in the woods.

'A walk in the woods' was an ancient political phrase that had originally meant 'to seek a meeting of the minds,' for a representative of one camp to convince another that both had to swallow some very evil-tasting medicine. It meant a method of reaching a difficult decision without the pressures of the outside world.

Tanz Sullamora meant something similar when he proposed the walk. Except, in his case, there was obviously already a meeting of the minds. He was sure they all knew what had to be done but were afraid to be the first to suggest it. Sullamora was ninety percent correct.

The members of the council walked many kilometers, weaving through the trees and pausing here and there to sniff the air or listen to a bird's song. Pretending interest. Pretending pleasure in the simple things. Inside, each being's guts roiled with acid. Finally, it was Kyes who broached the subject.

'Volmer was right,' he said. 'I see no other solution. Perhaps it's just as well. The man is obviously out of touch with reality.'

Everyone nodded, relieved that it had finally been said. Everyone except Volmer. The man was shocked, frightened. To him, his blurted remark was being twisted and turned into something he was not willing to deal with. Volmer might have thought regicide, might even have blurted regicide. But it was being tossed back at him as bloody-handed treason.

'What are you saying? My God, I don't want any . . . Look,

we're all under a lot of pressure. We're not thinking clearly. Let's all just take our lumps like beings and get back to it. Okay? It's time to go home, right? Get back to business?'

Sullamora came in like a snake. He draped a soothing arm over Volmer's shoulder. He patted his back, ruffled his hair, and steered him slightly away from the others. 'A misunderstanding . . . not what he meant . . . Speaking metaphorically . . .' And on and on. Volmer was grabbing at his phrases like a drowning man, agreeing, subsiding, and becoming calm again.

As Sullamora ushered the man through the door of the main building, he looked back at the others. They were all staring after him. The bargain had been struck, the deal made.

Sullamora laughed at some weak joke Volmer had made and pounded his back in manly appreciation – thinking, as he did it, that that was the first place the knife would have to fall.

Chapter Thirty-Two

The rest of Sten and Alex's escape was not the stuff lives were made from. True to his word, Chetwynd tucked the pair away in the lap of luxury, which consisted of an oversize bed with sheets and unlimited time to spend in it – alone and asleep.

It also meant being vermin-free for the first time in years. Being able to bathe in clean water any time they wanted. And there was food! Calories and glutinous calories of it! At first the foods were simple, so as not to stress their battered digestive systems. And finally there was the ecstasy of being able to walk away from a meal leaving food still on the plate.

The various joygirls and boys who offered other services might have been disappointed at the lack of response, but as Kilgour explained for the both of them, 'Ah'd need a splint, but thanks f'r thinki't ah me.'

Chetwynd left them alone. He knew how long it took for a prisoner to realize he was more than a stubborn survival machine.

Eventually the two were moved out of Heath, hidden below a ton and a half of metal scrap stacked on an ancient, bailing-wire-maintained gravsled onto, Sten guessed, the private estate of some Tahn muckety. Chetwynd declined to provide information, of course.

The tiny smuggling ship hovered, Yukawa drive humming. Sten and Alex were bundled aboard, and the ship lifted off-world and vanished into AM2 drive.

Somewhere the ship rendezvoused with its mother transport, and Sr. Jon Wild greeted them.

He had, he told them, gotten off Romney just in time. The feeling that expert crooks get that the heat was breathing down their necks had prickled his spine – and Wild had ordered an evacuation. He had lost seven ships and his base, but all of his people and, more importantly, his goods were saved. And anyone, he explained, rubbing his fingers together meaningfully, 'can acquire a ship and a place to land it.'

He was most delighted to be able to move them to safety, he explained. He owed Sten.

Some time before, a small convoy of his had gotten jumped inside the Imperial sector. The next stage would have been confiscation of ships and cargo and appropriate measures for the crew and Wild.

'There was some mention of prison planets,' he went on. 'Or for those of us considered rehabilitatable they offered some horror called penal battalions. I did not ask for details.'

Sten had been Wild's ace. In honest bewilderment he wondered to his captors why they would interfere with an Imperial Intelligence operation. He had been met with loud laughter.

'I suggested they check with their own G, S, or whatever letter they use for the section. Shortly thereafter, to some surprise, the spyboys reported that I was a gentleman born to the colors.

'I am very grateful that you filed the proper paperwork, young man.'

With grudging apologies, Wild and his people were freed and continued on about their own, quite profitable business providing Tahn luxuries for rich Imperials, and vice versa.

'I estimate that if this war continues another . . . oh, give it ten years, I should be able to go legitimate.' Wild shuddered slightly at the concept. 'So indeed, Commander, or whatever your rank is, you shall be treated, during this passage, as if you were the illegitimate son of the Emperor himself.'

The remainder of the voyage was marked by a slow, steady increase in their waistbands, some occasional sweaty moments as patrols, either Tahn or Imperial, were evaded, and more sleep.

Sten figured they were returning to something close to normal after seeing Alex duck into a cabin with one of Wild's more shapely officers.

By the time they were landed on an Imperial base that coincidentally was in a system where Wild 'had some interesting people to meet,' both ex-POWs would have made lousy propaganda fodder. They should have been bearded. Haggard. Emaciated. Scarred. Ready to testify to the monstrous inhumanity of the Tahn and the ability to tough it out that brave Imperial soldiers had.

The propaganda mills were not even alerted.

Both men knew far too much to allow the public prints near them. They were shuttled to Prime World, and the Empire's most skilled debriefers worked them over using every skill and technique they had short of mindprobe. Sten had been there once, thank you, and would rather not repeat the experience.

By the time Intelligence grudgingly decided that whatever else of value was inside their now-bruised and exhausted brain cells, Sten and Kilgour felt as if they had been crucified by Tahn torturers.

And then the real surprises began.

Both Sten and Alex expected various medals. Not because they necessarily thought they had done anything particularly heroic in captivity, except getting the clot out of it – for which accomplishment they would have cheerfully accepted free alk for the rest of their lifetime instead of a gong – but because when any war got nasty, the survivors tended to collect bits of tin as they survived.

Those they received.

Both of them expected promotions – and had theorized on the long run back whether they would be kicked up one or more grades.

Those they did not receive – yet.

Their orders were quite similar:

STEN (NI) (WITHHELD) Ordered to (WITHHELD) following (WITHHELD) leave time, authorized travel to (WITHHELD). Upon return to duty, you will report to (WITHHELD) for further orders. Conditions of reporting for further duty will be communicated to you by (WITHHELD) date.

KILGOUR, ALEX (WITHHELD) Ordered to (WITHHELD)

following (WITHHELD) leave time, authorized travel to planet of EDINBURGH and other systems as desired. Upon return to duty, you will report to (WITHHELD) for further orders. Conditions of reporting for further duty will be communicated to you by (WITHHELD) date.

Sten and Alex looked at each other. Somebody up there had plans for their future. Probability: unpleasant. But there was little that could be done about it short of deserting. And both of them had spent enough time on the run.

The second step was to collect their back pay, which would amount to a small fortune.

One of the few productive pastimes the Tahn POWs had was figuring out how much money they were due and how they would spend it.

The Empire paid its military somewhat differently than had governments of the past. A soldier's paycheck was either given to him in cash on pay period or banked in a civilian bank and allowed to draw whatever interest or non-interest it paid, bank to be determined by individual.

That was *not* done because of any particular kindness the Emperor felt toward each grunt. There were three very simple reasons that, one drunken evening eons before, the emperor had outlined for Mahoney:

1. This is a capitalist Empire. I think. Therefore, money in circulation is healthier than money sitting in anybody's vault.
2. I understand a lot of things. I can sketch you out, if you're interested, the mathematical correlation of the nine basic forces of the universe. I don't understand economics, and nobody else does, either. Therefore, I ain't gonna get involved.
3. Banks what get my troopies' money are very, very rational people. Which means they do what I clottin' tell them, when I tell them, or else suddenly they're on the 'Not Recommended For Military Deposit' list.

And so, when Sten and Alex paraded into the Prime World bank that for years had been favored, for some lost reason, by Mercury Corps and Mantis Section operatives, they expected to be greeted politely, as if they were stockholders.

They did not expect to be ushered into the office of the bank president and informed they were now majority stockholders. And if it would please the gentlemen, now that they were . . . ahem, available, would they be interested in advising the current members of the board on future investment possibilities?

Sten gurgled.

Kilgour, however, rose to the occasion. He reached for a cheroot – real tobacco, it would appear – from a humidor, struck it on the president's desk, leaving scars across what looked like real wood, and inhaled. He managed to bury the subsequent coughing spasm and called for a printout on both of their accounts.

They were not just well-to-do.

They were rich.

Both of them had significant holdings in the most formidable corporations of the Empire. Plus a percentage in exotic metals. Plus a percentage in war bonds. Plus . . .

Sten goggled at about page thirty-six of the printout. He was most grateful that the bank president had excused himself.

'Uh . . . Kilgour. I own a world.'

Kilgour was equally bemused. 'Ah nae hae thae . . . but it appears Ah'll hae the richest estate ae Edinburgh. Ah can afford to r'store th' family castle.'

'You have a castle?'

'Noo Ah do.'

And both of them understood, just as the fawning banker returned with the contents of a certain safety deposit box, which, he said, was to be given to them personally and privately. Again, he withdrew.

They opened the box, found a fiche, and booted it up.

Gypsy Ida's less than conventionally lovely face appeared onscreen.

Ida was a former member of Sten and Alex's Mantis Team. She was a hustler, an investor, and one of the best pilots Sten had ever flown beside.

She had disappeared from the service years before but as she was leaving she had somehow tapped into her ex-teammates' bank accounts and invested, invested, invested – leaving them most comfortable.

The sound cut on: 'Y'r clots, you know. Howinhell'd you two ever manage to get captured? Kilgour, you're as dumb as you are fat. Sten, why'd you listen to the clot?

'Anyway.

'I accessed your credits when I heard you were missing. Knew there weren't any Tahn smart enough to waste you on sight, and figured that you'd live.

'Hope now that you're listening to this and it ain't your heirs and assignees and the war's over.

'I started filtering all those credits you had sitting there and took care of you two clots.

'Near as I can figure, there ain't nothing that can go wrong, unless maybe the Emperor surrendered – an' by the way, you got holdings in the Tahn worlds if that happened – that can keep you from being rich-rich.

'Reason I'm putting this on fiche, instead of bein' there when you see how good care I took care of you, is . . . aw, drakh, I went and listened to somebody, and, well, they want me to go do something out there somewhere.

'So that's the way it is.

'I guess 'cause I'm dumb I miss the old days.'

Ida's image fell silent, and Sten was appalled to see what looked like a tear well up in her eye. Fortunately the image lasted only for a moment, as suddenly the Rom stood, turned, and hoisted her skirt. What looked like two oversize loaves of bread – pan point of view – went onscreen.

And the screen blanked.

'Th' lass still dinnae wear knickers,' Alex managed.

Somehow they made the correct noises to the banker and, each clutching a full briefcase that proved, with full details, that he was rich-rich, went for the closest bar.

A day or so later, after sobering up, they made the correct noises at each other. Sorry to split up, mate, but that's the way the service works. Hell, it's a small world. Maybe we'll get lucky again and get paired.

Sten drank Kilgour aboard the ship headed for the world of Edinburgh and contemplated.

First he wanted a quiet place to figure out where he was going to spend his leave – whatever amount that WITHHELD figure was giving him before something else happened.

Not to mention that planet that he appeared to own. Planet? he thought. Nobody *owns* a planet. That's disgusting. But maybe he did. If so, he would like to see what his real estate looked like. Preferably with a friend.

He headed for a com and called the police.

Specifically, he called Prime World Homicide and asked for a Lisa Haines. Years earlier, she and Sten had been quite seriously in love before Sten had been reassigned into the maze that took him into the Tahn War and captivity. He sort of hoped, just maybe, she was still solo and remembered him. The copshop advised that yes, a Lisa Haines was still a police person. And that they would accept a message for her. But she was unfortunately not available at the moment.

'When do you expect her?'

'That information is not available,' the synthesized voice began, and then suddenly the screen blanked, and a second, human voice came on. A very polite one.

'This is Message Center. You were trying to contact Captain Lisa Haines. We are prepared to relay a message . . . however, please stand by. We are experiencing difficulties receiving you. Do not break the transmission. An operator will be with you in moments when the signal is corrected.'

Sten, out of sheer habit and training, never stood inside camera range of any com. He was therefore unseen when the red RECEIVING light glowed on. Shortly thereafter, he was some meters away, appearing to be in the middle of a bargaining session with a shopkeeper when two heavy set men with close-cropped hair thundered toward the com booth.

Security thugs, he made them for. He paid for whatever it was he was bargaining for and slipped into the crowd.

Lisa had been caught up in the war. Obviously she was somewhere in the bowels of Intelligence. Message Center, indeed. Sten grimaced. It looked as if he were about to spend a solitary leave, at least until he ran across some local talent. Speaking of which, he headed for a library to find out if his real estate *included* local talent.

It did not – or so, at least, the various star fiches he consulted suggested.

The world's name was Smallbridge. About .87 E-size, commensurate gravity, E-normal atmosphere, three AU from a dying yellow star. Climate tropical to subarctic. Flora/Fauna . . .

The slender report from the Imperial Survey Mission that said that there was nothing particularly interesting about the world of Smallbridge – then called Survey World XM-Y-1134 and many other numerals and letters – other than extensive members of the Orchidae family, giant specimens of Polypodiosida . . . blur . . . blur . . . insect life . . . blur . . . blur . . . non-malevolent . . . water potable, with following blur blur presences . . . following water-dwelling species found edible, worthy of possible commercial exploration . . . fauna . . . nothing that would try to eat Sten, with the exception of a small, rather shy catlike creature that might try to nail him if he were passed out in front of its den – maybe. Nothing else of interest – which meant, to the survey crew, that nothing had tried to kill them. NO BEINGS OF HIGHER DEVELOPMENT OBSERVED.

Sten appeared to be owner of an eight-tenths-scale Eden, if one that seemed never to have progressed very far.

Now, what had man done to screw it up after discovery? After all, somebody had given Survey World Whatever-it-was a name. Sten fed in the fiche from his own files.

The answer was – nobody. It had been acquired by an entrepreneur who had made his fortune doing something that nobody had ever thought of and had then decided he had a corner on entrepreneuring. He had named the world, built himself and, Sten gathered, his paid companions in joy a rather wonderful mansion, added a state-of-the-art spaceport, and then gone bankrupt trying to make a second, third, and so on fortune.

Once again – an Eden.

Sten swore a rather surprised oath in Low Tahn, suggesting that the hearer's mother had private parts that could accommodate a battalion – and jerked away from the screen, hearing a giggle.

The giggle came from a very young, very tall, very blond woman sitting at the computer table next to him.

'You understood?' he asked.

'I understood.'

Sten, all too aware that his somewhat limited social graces probably had not been improved by his time as a POW, made himself blush and apologized.

The woman, who introduced herself as Kim Lavransdotter, explained. She spoke High, Low, Medium, and War Tahn. She was a researcher and historian, doctor of this in Tahn culture and that in Tahn history, and very pleased that her studies had been honored by a request to come to Prime World and work with Imperial Social Analysis.

'Maybe I shouldn't tell you this,' she said, looking worried. 'I guess we've got some kind of feed into Intelligence, even though they never say anything.'

Sten reassured her.

He had clearances. Right up to and including 'Eyes Only – Imperial Staff,' although he did not tell her quite that much.

She was very beautiful.

And Sten was very lonely.

He offered to buy her a caff.

She stayed very beautiful.

Sten bought her dinner.

The next day, he took her with him to look up some old friends – Marr and Senn, in their crystal light tower.

She charmed them.

She continued to charm Sten.

And she *was* very beautiful, he noted the next morning as he studied her, lying naked beside him.

Perhaps . . .

Sten felt very lucky that it happened that Kim was well overdue for a vacation and thought that going with him to Smallbridge was perfect. She had never known anyone who owned his own planet, let alone the racing yacht that took them there.

He should have realized.

But he did not.

Perhaps Sten's perceptions were still dulled from the time in prison. Or perhaps it was Kim. Or perhaps it was Small-bridge itself.

Eden . . . from its arctic slopes to the long sandy beaches on its islands, with waves that curled in perfectly and endlessly. The fruit was delicious; the mansion was lavish, roboticized, and seemingly equipped with any liquor or food that could be conceived of.

Even that catlike predator turned out to be moderately friendly and more interested in lifeboat emergency rations than a human arm.

As they lazed and explored, Sten was learning.

Lavransdotter, he realized, deserved however many degrees she had and then some. She was an expert on the Tahn. Even Sten, who thought he had learned, by the whip, everything there was to know about the warrior culture, learned. And his hatred subsided. He almost felt sorry for any single Tahn, crippled by his or her background and his or her culture.

Almost, but not quite.

After the last Tahn lord had been destroyed and their culture and works lay in ruins, he might be willing to concede that the Tahn would be eligible to join the civilized races.

Almost, but not quite.

And so the leave passed, dreaming days and nights.

Sten should have realized.

But he did not.

Not until the morning, when a remote from his spaceport buzzed and he came awake. Kim yawned, her head pillowed on his upper thigh, snorted, and went back to sleep.

Sten stretched and flipped a screen on.

He looked at the huge ship that sat on his tarmac, dwarfing the yacht, snarled, and was on his feet. He glowered at Kim as she woke again, stretched, and smiled.

'What's your rank?'

Kim's smile stayed in place. 'Very good, Sten. Colonel.'

'Mercury Corps?'

'Mercury Corps.'

The huge ship sitting in the spaceport was the *Normandie*. The Eternal Emperor's personal yacht.

'Where,' Sten wondered aloud, 'did I ever get the idea that somehow, someway, I am so charming and clottin' attractive that, sitting in a library, the world's most beautiful woman just *happens* to fall in love with me?'

'You sell yourself short,' Kim said.

'Thanks. But why you?'

'The Eternal Emperor said to tell you – when or if you figured it out – that the best kind of dictionary is one you sleep with.'

'Aw . . . clot!'

'It is a hell of a war,' Kim sympathized. 'Now . . . shall we get dressed and report?'

Chapter Thirty-Three

Sten glowered his way up the ramp to the *Normandie*, saluted the OOD, snarled at Kim as she tried to say goodbye, and stomped off, following, as requested, a snappily uniformed aide.

He barely noticed the interesting fact that there were eight Gurkhas at the salute as he boarded, other than that they looked inordinately dumb wearing white gloves.

As the aide led him into a paneled conference room, the *Normandie*'s Yukawa drive hissed, and the ship lifted.

Sten was not all that surprised to find Warrant Officer Alex Kilgour in the room. Alex was grunting – loudly.

'Clottin' Emperor. Clottin' hae me, ae Ah'm supervisin't thae unloadin't ae cargo ae marble f'r my dinin't chambers. Clottin' lairds wi' nae clottin' understandin't ae naught.

'Clottin' chop m' leave wi'out clottin' sayin't ae word, an' next week wae the openin't ae shootin't season!'

He paused in his diatribe long enough to register Sten.

'Boss. Sorry the clottin' pismire scragged you, ae well. Clottin' Emperor. Whae w' need't here is ae some sanity an' nae a little anarchy.'

That was a little much. Sten's fingers flashed in Mantis sign language: *Shaddup, clot. The room's bugged!*

Kilgour sneered. 'Clot him, clot his snoops an aye th' Empire! Ah'll speakit ae Ah wan'. Wha'es the clot t' do? Send us back twa Heath?'

'That, in fact, is very much what I had in mind.'

The dry voice, of course, came from the Eternal Emperor.

Fleet Marshal Ian Mahoney let the outrage from the babble of politicians die into silence. He walked to the conference room's window and looked pointedly overhead.

Twelve Imperial superbattleships hung over the capital city of Gorj, their screens ringing the ships.

Mahoney turned back to the assembled rulers of Gorj.

'I shall reiterate the situation. Gorj determined to stand neutral in this war. The Emperor respects that decision.

'However, under the original treaty signed between the Emperor and Gorj, your world requested our support and aid if, at any time in the future, Gorj was threatened with attack.

'You agreed in that treaty that Gorj would provide any necessary logistical aid to that support.

'The Empire has determined that Gorj is imminently in danger of being seized by the Tahn. This shall not be allowed to happen.

'In exchange for our securing your independence, all we are requesting is access to three of your primary spaceports and the necessary real estate to develop basing for Imperial maintenance crews.'

'And if we don't willingly let you take over those ports?'

'There is,' Mahoney went on, 'recognized by Imperial law, either the rights of force majeure or eminent domain. The Empire will, of course, make proper restitution.'

'The Tahn have made no signs of attacking us!'

'They are very subtle,' Mahoney said. He was starting to feel most diplomatic, even though he had wanted to start the meeting with: Look, guys. You clowns are sitting here, right on the edges of the Tahn Empire. You've gotten all the goodies from staying neutral. Too bad you've got the only populated and developed worlds handy for us to grab.

'We'll protest this!' another politician said.

'You have every right. The Imperial Court of Admiralty, I might advise, has a case backload of some seventeen years.'

'This is morally reprehensible! We'll have our military forces mobilized immediately.'

Mahoney nodded politely, glanced again at the hovering fleet, and picked up his gold-braided hat from the table. 'You have six hours to reach a decision. Good day, gentleman.'

The war had gone on long enough for fine moral principles to become quite corroded.

At the moment all the wallscreens in the huge auditorium showed what appeared to be a rather obese walrus sloshing in a powered swimming tank.

The 'walrus' was Rykor, easily the Empire's most skilled psychologist.

The auditorium was filled with her top advisers and the elite of the Empire's propaganda machine.

Rykor sprayed foam from her whiskers – the speakers around the auditorium squealed – and made her summation. 'I am hardly equipped to specifically tell any of you gentlebeings how to do the job. All the various suggestions and proposals you saw onscreen will be made available to you. If you choose to use any of them, we would be flattered and honored.

'And, of course, none of the possible gray or black operations can be discussed at this gathering.

'But, overall, your thrust should be twofold:

'One. The victory in the Durer worlds is the beginning of the end. Those who serve the Empire well in hastening victory will be well rewarded.

'Two. What life under the Tahn means, particularly to a non-Tahn, should be developed. Worlds recaptured from the Tahn will be instantly available for visit by any accredited livie crew or journalist. Accreditation policy, I have been advised, shall be most liberal.

'Thank you. In our seminars, we shall attempt to further develop some more cohesive strategies.'

A woman stood in the middle of the audience. 'What about the Tahn? What direction will Imperial propaganda take?'

'Again, I am not discussing gray or black areas. It shall be quite simple. Large 'cast units will be established on the fringes of the Tahn Empire and relocated forward as we continue recapturing systems. Information broadcast to the Tahn shall consist of exactly what is going on.'

'Even if we lose another battle?'

'Even so. We are attempting to prove to the Tahn citizenry that their own leaders *never* tell the truth.'

'What about subversion attempts?'

'Yes. I assume you mean atrocity leaflets, livies showing the corruption of the home front, and so forth. I have some exact orders from the Eternal Emperor. I might word them a little more politely, but . . . he said that we are not in the business of preventing the bum fodder shortage for the Tahn.

'Thank you.'

'As I see it,' the young man said, 'our race has a single problem.'

Sr. Ecu, senior diplomat of the Manabi, floated above the immaculate floor of the deserted factory, his three-meter-long tail snaking gently below him.

'Ah,' he hummed in his most neutral tone.

'You would understand it, I hope.' the young man said.

Ecu's wings waved what might have been taken as slight encouragement.

'We see our race as a single being. Stretching from the days of stone on a planet known as Earth, when we ruled by racial right, through the days when a stronger race invaded, defeated, and almost destroyed us. But for centuries, we endured.

'When we emigrated to our own system, we determined that never again would we be creatures of the moment. History and our racial memory would provide the answers.

'We determined to take the long-range view.

'That was our first error: We neglected to wonder how this day's bread could be provided.

'Secondarily, we forgot that those who sit upon the fence become targets for both sides.

'The end result? We built factories before the war, and then the war begins. We refuse to build war materials. And no one is interested in anything else.

'Except for those,' the young man spit. 'Those who wish us to work on speculation. With a ninety-ten split. Ninety for them, who are the smokedancers, ten for us, simply because we are willing to build and beat their drums.

'And then those others, the Tahn, who we have been assured time and again have no quarrel with us, insist on being able to port and supply their ships and satisfy the demands of their crewmen to confirm our neutrality; who levy a tax against us because they realize that we wish to support them; and so on and so forth.

'Such might be livable. We have resources enough to support our workers who have nothing to do. We have tolerance enough for those who sell their services and bodies to the Tahn.

'But what will come after?'

The Manabi were known and used throughout the Empire as diplomats. They were air-floating beings who were completely neutral – and were, therefore, ideal for the crafts of state. It was completely unknown that just after the Tahn War began, Sr. Ecu had declared the Manabi support for the Empire – not because they thought the Emperor was the epitome of civilization but because they saw the defeat of the Empire as a collapse into barbarism. That support was known to the Manabi collective intelligence, the Eternal Emperor, and no one else. To the Tahn, the neutral systems, and the Empire itself, they remained as they were – the perfect statesbeings.

'What will come after,' Sr. Ecu began, 'is an unknown. I can only wish that your use of the past and your belief in racial identity provide you the path. Also, I thank you for your confidences and sympathize with your problems.

'But the reason I am here has nothing to do with any of them. I was requested by a representative of the Eternal Emperor to deliver the following:

'"The Emperor has noted the plight of the Five Nations and is deeply distressed. He will therefore provide a doubling of the treaty-allocated amount of Anti-Matter Two to your worlds and deeply hopes that your problems thereby become alleviated."'

Sr. Ecu was very impressed by the young man, whose expression changed only three times during his announcement. Possibly, he wondered, after some epochs, humans might become capable.

'What are the strings?'

'Pardon?'

'The attachments. The obligations.'

'None.'

'I do not believe that,' the young man said.

'I was so instructed that you would not,' Sr Ecu went on. 'I was finally instructed that your ports should prepare for the arrival of six Imperial energy ships within six E-days of my arrival in your system.'

Sr. Ecu, having delivered his message and received no answer for the moment, lifted, and his huge black and red-tinted body floated away toward his ship.

He wondered just how long it would take the Five Nations to renounce their neutrality and declare for the Empire. It was a pity, he decided, that he did not understand what was called gambling and could not think of anyone to perform that activity with.

Sr. Ecu thought that he was becoming a bit degenerate – and worried because he was not worried about it.

Fire Team Leader Heebner was a happy man in what appeared to be a desperate situation.

Sometime earlier he had been very unhappy in everything. Drafted into the Tahn forces and sent into combat when he would have been much happier pruning in his family's orchards, he had been most unfortunate/fortunate.

His unit wiped out, he had stumbled into a stubborn Imperial stronghold – and back out. He had informed his superiors of that way in – and had not been required to participate in the following bloody assault.

Instead, he had been promoted and given a nice safe assignment.

Not, as he had imagined, on something like recruiting duty but, to justify his new and staggering rank, as noncommissioned officer in charge of an SAA site on the Tahn superfortress world of Etan. A decorated soldier, his missile site was high atop a mountain, a post of honor, where he would be the first to engage any Imperial units stupid enough to attack Etan.

Heebner, already experienced at being shot at, rapidly and correctly redefined his post of honor.

He was a target.

And targets got hit.

Heebner was not quite sure what to do about the situation. Nor did he know how to order his soldiers in a proper military manner so that he would not be relieved and sent back to a frontline assault unit.

More importantly, he had no idea where his own retreat route should lie if his missile site *should* be attacked.

Heebner, once again, was very lucky.

His troops were for the most part volunteers from one of the Tahn Troops of Eager Youth, who were determined to show their leader, a hero of the Battle of Cavite and the scout who showed the very heroic, very noble, very decorated, and very dead Assault Captain Santol the way to assault that Imperial stronghold, that they were worthy of his trust.

The translation was that they made their own rules, slightly stricter than the brutal Tahn regulations; made their own living conditions, most Spartan; and made their own schedule. Fire Team Leader Heebner had only to wander out of his quarters at some appropriate hour, make appropriate remarks, and then go about his business.

Heebner was also lucky that he had no particular interest in luxurious quarters, the perks of rank, or the indulgences of command. His Troops of Eager Youth admired his Spartan life. It was, truly, the Way of the Tahn.

The fact was that Heebner was just too stupid to realize what he could have taken advantage of.

Since it seemed that his command was self-running, Heebner spent his hours wandering below the crags, looking for a nice safe place to hide when the drakh came down. He was very interested to discover one day that below his missile site was what looked to be several long-untenanted hectares of fruit trees.

Heebner's smallish mind flickered interest. He mentioned that there did not seem to be any pruning tools in the site's armory. His befuddled assistant decided that somehow, someway, the hero of Cavite was planning to teach them something, perhaps to think in other categories.

Two shifts later, Fire Team Leader Heebner was provided with hooks, clips, lifts, and baskets. He happily disappeared downslope with them. His Eager Youth determined that when the time was right, they would learn what he was doing.

Another stroke of fortune:

Etan's commanding admiral, one Molk, happened to be interested in the art of fruit. He wondered why a certain strategically placed missile base had requested what appeared to be farming implements and decided to place a surprise visit to said base.

The Eager Youth, all prostrate in honor, sent Admiral Molk down the crags, together with his bodyguard, to see what their most honored commander was preparing.

Heebner was counting buds, his lips moving silently, trying to determine which branch should be pruned short and where, when he heard the crash of boot-heels coming toward him.

Molk also was a very lucky Tahn.

Because it was approximately at that moment that six Imperial fleets hammered Etan.

Impregnable fortresses, like impregnable generals, got lazy. If the enemy would be insane to attack them, of course only the insane *would* attack. And so they rested on their ever-fattening behinds. Spit-scared attackers, on the other hand, did not.

The Imperial admiral in charge of the fleets was most disappointed that there were no Tahn capital ships on Etan. After the disaster of Durer, they had all been withdrawn to Heath for reassignment.

Nevertheless, major damage was done in the series of smashing attacks. Fire Team Leader Heebner's missile site was obliterated in the first strike; fortunately for him and for his fruit trees, a non-nuclear missile was used.

That hardly mattered for his Eager Youth. There were three survivors. And those, all terribly burned, lived for only minutes after the strike.

When the fire, smoke, and earthquake shakes died away, six Tahn cruisers, twelve destroyers, and many auxiliaries and transports were shattered on their landing grounds.

Etan was still impregnable.

But with no significant warships based on the world, and with the Imperial-forces severing Etan's supply routes, it did not matter. Etan could do whatever it chose to do until the war came to an end.

Several hundred other Tahn citadels were isolated, rendered impotent, and ignored in the same operation.

Not that Fire Team Leader Heebner had nothing to do. He was very busy – instructing Commanding Admiral Molk on the proper way to grow fruit.

It was a very important task. All the Tahn isolated and forgotten on Etan had to eat.

After nine months of humble instruction, Admiral Molk requested that Heebner begin calling him Yuki.

Admiral Mason defined diplomacy as a word occuring somewhere in a dictionary between dildo and dissidence. That explained his response when the supposedly neutral convoy complained: '*Imperial units . . . Imperial units . . . do not understand your order to stand by for boarding. We are from the Umed systems. Repeat, Umed systems. We are allies of the Empire. Our cargo is necessary energy supplies. Please respond, over.*'

Mason, were he polite, could have responded over the com or boarded and delivered the same information.

The Umed systems, allies of the Empire indeed – on paper – were provided with X quanity of AM2. According to information received from spies, the systems practiced severe rationing. Nearly twenty percent of their allocated AM2 was not utilized in any known way. It was instead very profitably sold to the Tahn.

Such would have been the response – from a polite man.

Mason, instead, responded: '*Umed ships. All Umed ships. You have seven minutes remaining. Stand by for boarding. Any resistance will be met with maximum force. All Umed ships. All Umed crewmen. Prepare to abandon ship. Your ships and their cargo have been seized. Imperial Strike Force Mason clear.*'

It was to be hoped that Admiral Mason would not survive the war and thus require that the Emperor deal with his vagaries.

'Cut it,' Haines ordered.

The soldier nodded, touched the button of his flamer, and seared through the main power cable that led into the shabby apartment building above them.

'Good. Go!' Haines shouted.

Burdened by a stun rod in one hand, a willygun in the other, plus two separate ranks, Major (Imperial Forces-Mercury Corps-Reserve-Temporary) and Captain (Imperial Police-Prime-Homicide-Permanent) Lisa Haines led the raid upstairs. Two Security mastodons sent the door crashing down, neatly timed so that Haines did not miss a step going into the apartment.

The gray-haired old woman sat up in bed, befuddled, grabbing the ruins of what once might have been a lace nightie around her skinny shoulders.

'Imperial Intelligence,' Haines intoned, pro forma. 'Andrea Hayyl. You are under arrest as a suspected agent of an enemy power. You are advised that you can be detained for as long as six cycles without benefit of court or attorney. You are also advised that you may be subjected to wartime interrogation techniques authorized by the proper conventions.

'You are also advised that any cooperation you extend voluntarily will be recorded, and be of extreme importance as evidence when you are brought to trial.'

The thugs, without needing any orders, had the old woman out and down the stairs in seconds.

The search team came in.

As expected, the transmitter was found in seconds, amateurishly hidden in a false-drawered dresser that might have been the old woman's prized antique.

That was one more.

Haines left the evidence team shooting pictures and went down the stairs.

Six thus far. Two more to go.

More than 12,000 raids were made by Imperial Intelligence at nearly the same time. Years had been spent identifying deep-cover Tahn agents assigned to capital worlds. And then, nearly simultaneously, they were taken.

Haines was disgusted with herself and her job, even more than after the officially sanctioned 'disappearences' she had been witness to after the failure of Hakone's conspiracy, the conspiracy that had begun the war.

The agents would be isolated and then given a simple choice: either be doubled or be executed. Wartime penalties for espionage never changed.

The ploy worked. Almost instantly, Tahn Intelligence began receiving completely false information. The few agents the Empire had missed, who continued to feed correct data, were siberiaed as having been doubled. Eventually they were trapped, tried, and executed, along with those agents who had decided to remain true patriots to their cause.

The end result was that the Tahn's own lovingly developed spy network became one of the most lethal weapons the Empire had.

Chapter Thirty-Four

Chief Warrant Officer Alex Kilgour went into something approaching battle shock when he realized that not only had he bad-mouthed the Eternal Emperor, his Eternal boss, and been overheard, but he actually was in the presence of said Emperor.

The Emperor allowed himself a wintery smile. 'Thank you for your input, Mr Kilgour. Perhaps you would be interested in stepping into the next chamber, where more information shall be provided.'

Alex numbly saluted and stiff-legged through the indicated hatchway, which hissed open and then shut behind him.

'In times like these,' the Emperor observed, 'you tend to allow yourself cheap little shots as I just did. Pour the stregg, my friend.'

Sten, equally obedient, went to a sideboard and decanted two shots of the probably hydrazine-based Bhor liquor he had introduced the Eternal Emperor to years earlier.

The Emperor was in an easy chair, his feet propped on a tabletop, when Sten delivered the drink.

'Chin-chin,' he toasted. Sten just mumbled and drank.

'Yes, indeed,' the Emperor began, 'I want you two thugs back on Heath.'

'Yessir,' Sten said after the stregg had finished replumbing his plumbing. 'However . . . when I left there were people that were real . . . interested in me.'

'No longer,' the Emperor said. 'Somebody who must've been taken by the charm of your smile planted a virus in the Tahn central computer. Seems that neither someone named Sten nor someone called Firecontrolman Horatio ever existed. No ID, no prison record, no *nada*.

'Any idea who your unknown benefactor could be?'

Sten had less than none.

'Light a votive candle to the patron saint of computer programmers. Whoever that is.

'However. If such circumstances are correct, would you be willing to go back to Heath? That's an honest question. You've already figured out, I assume, what your next assignment would be if you tell me to clot off.'

Sten had not so figured. 'Uh,' he hazarded, 'in charge of some garbage scow somewhere.'

'Admirals don't run drakhbuckets.'

'Huh?' was all Sten could get out.

The Emperor smiled. 'You're most unobservant, Sten. Think. How many of my Gurkhas, looking stupid and uncomfortable in white gloves, were on the ramp when you boarded?'

Eight, Sten suddenly remembered.

'Exactly,' the Emperor said. 'Four clots to pipe you aboard when you're a working slob. Eight when you put up your star.'

Sten, uninvited, got up, poured himself another shot of stregg, drank it down, and refilled his shot glass while recovering.

'If you don't go back to Heath, you'll get a destroyer squadron, and you can go out there and be one more dashing leader who'll get some nice medals and whom I'll be publicly proud of in the livies.

'Sten, the one thing I don't have a shortage of is heroes. What I don't have is somebody who knows what's going on on the bad guys' home turf.'

A destroyer squadron, Sten thought. And a star. That was a bit beyond Sten's dreams. Years ago, he had decided to be career military. At the end of the line, he had figured, was, if not a gravestone, some kind of honorable wound and retirement as colonel – maybe, with his naval training added, commodore.

The Emperor filled his own glass and stayed silent.

Sure, Sten's mind went on, I could do some serious ass kicking on the Tahn. I know how what passes for their mind works. I could turn any Tahn ship or formation under a battle-wagon every which way but loose. But like the Emperor just said, I'm not the only one who could do that.

'Why?' he asked, his face and tone as blank as it would have been to any Tahn guard.

'The agents I have on Heath are button counters. Maybe. The clotting nets I have are low-level and, I suspect, doubled by the

Tahn. That's one problem. Your tubby cohort can shake them out, if he's willing to go back.

'I need someone in place on Heath as *my* agent. We've reached, like the man said, if not the beginning of the end, the end of the beginning. I'm looking for somebody who can be a spy – and who can sit and talk like he's a diplomat.

'I am not praising you, by the by. You're at least a century too young and several assignments too gory to be my dream square peg. Mahoney, back when you first met him on Vulcan – don't jump, I did a little refresher course – would be ideal. But he's a little long in the tooth and too clottin' good as a fleet marshal to waste on Heath.

'No offense.

'And I've wasted enough time jacking my jaws while you think about it. Decision time.'

Sten had already made it. Not only could he probably do more good on Heath than as a bucko destroyer leader, but there were certain things there he wanted to deal with personally. Such as the prisoners in Koldyeze.

'Thank you, Admiral,' the Emperor said without waiting for a verbalization. 'My intelligence types will brief you and set up the insertion plan.'

Sten got up. 'I think I'd rather use my own way to get in.'

'Your option. Like I said, the only boss you've got this time is me. All orders that you get will be mine. How you carry them out – and even if you do or not – is your option. You're the man in place. Oh, yeah, before I forget. Mahoney had something that might be of help. He said there was a POW at Koldyeze. I think his name was Sorensen. Is that right?'

Sten nodded, remembering the big, smiling face of the farmbeing. He and Alex had debated for hours whether Sorensen was a Mantis battle computer.

'Fine,' the Emperor said. 'Mahoney said to tell you that Sorensen's code word is "Saider." Whatever that's worth.'

If the drakh came down at Koldyeze, it would be worth a lot. Sten smiled to himself, but the Emperor was not through yet.

'One favor?'

Sten waited.

'If you decide to overthrow the clottin' government, don't put some anthropoid who likes stregg and can't speak the same language I do in. Or if you do, let me know first. 'Kay?'

Sten found himself saluting a rapidly closing hatchway.

All he had to do was get the detailed briefing, listen to Kilgour tell him why it was a good idea to go back to Heath, and then track down Wild and let him know the time for fence-sitting neutral smugglers was over.

Chapter Thirty-Five

Volmer, Publishing Baron and member of the Emperor's privy council, was very proud of his complex mind.

He could sit, completely invisible, at the far end of a roaring Barbary hell, one of the rowdiest of the rowdy dock bars in Prime World's port city of Soward, and do some serious thinking, undisturbed by the noise and unnoticed by the occupants.

On one level, he was contemplating what the evening might provide. Volmer had never heard the expression 'polymorphously perverse' and would have been grandly irked if he had heard it applied – after, of course, he had looked up the meaning of 'polymorphous.'

But that was one level of Volmer. Rich beyond comprehension and able to pay for safe, clean, comfortable sex of whatever category, he found it more interesting to look for it in the gutter. Volmer found it fully as satisfying to end up jackrolled in a gutter, Murphied, or badgered as it was to wake up next to an incredibly beautiful and insatiable sex object. That was his secret life, which only the top two percent of his reporters knew and laughed about. He had once heard a rumor that the Eternal Emperor did the same – and canned six journalists for being unable to verify it. But regardless, at least once a month Volmer gave his bodyguards and staff two days off and slipped away, in the appropriate disguise, through a hidden exit of his mansion to slink, disguised as 'one of the people,' onto the wild side.

He thought that he was able to blend seamlessly into the sexual underworld and that he was accepted as nothing more than a mysterious man. Actually, he had been accepted as a sicko mark. But just recently another rumor had cropped up – a rumor that would be acted upon that very night.

The second layer of Volmer's mind was pondering the recent meeting on Earth with Sullamora and the others. He had reacted, he thought, perhaps a little too quickly. Perhaps Sullamora and the others had considered their future problems more carefully than he had. Perhaps he should have been silent, or perhaps expressed more interest – if, he suddenly realized, he had even heard them correctly. Perhaps he had jumped to some incorrect conclusions. Volmer rewarded himself for considering all possibilities, even one that might not be the most ego-rewarding.

That kind of thinking, he added, was what had made him as successful and respected a media baron as he was.

He never knew that his staff referred to him as 'Old Ademony-Kademony,' a term lost in journalism's prehistory meaning a waffler who can never make up his mind on anything.

But if he was correct in his understanding, he went on, would he be better off informing the Emperor of his suspicions? Well, not suspicions. Actually there was not that much to report to the Emperor. Suppose he had misunderstood what Sullamora and the others were saying. Would he not appear as a prize ass, some kind of hysteroid, if he *did* trouble his Emperor with what had gone on?

Perhaps, he concluded, he should do nothing. Perhaps he should reapproach Tanz and let the situation develop.

Yes. That was the way to behave.

Satisfied that once again he had reached the decision to juggle, he turned his primary focus to the pleasures of the evening.

He listened with interest to the handsome young man who appeared at the bar beside him, discussing some dizzying possibilities as to sex partners, not the least of which was the young man himself. Volmer thought that a possibility – but he was more intrigued with what the young man told him about certain most unusual events that were occurring among the staff of a certain hospital, centering on that hospital's cold room.

The handsome young man was available, indeed. But not as a whore. The young man's services were available, in fact, at a much higher price, specifically to take care of annoyances.

The rumor that had spread recently about the sicko mark was that he was more than what he appeared. He was, in fact, a deep-cover copper. Why else had some of Soward's more eminent sex hustlers been arrested, charged, and convicted sans deal in the last month?

The rumor – no one knew where it came from – made perfect sense.

And for that reason it was logical for the underworld bosses, each of whom thought he was much more lethal and in charge than he in fact was, to put out an open contract on the mark. The handsome young man proposed to fill that contract.

Two hours later, as Volmer listened drunkenly and fascinatedly to the young man's descriptions of necro-pleasures, he was skillfully sandbagged below his left ear, his pockets ransacked, his jewels and half boots stolen; then the unconscious body was tipped over the railing to thud soddenly down four levels to the concrete below.

When the body was discovered and reported two days later, Tanz Sullamora expressed appropriate shock. He announced that he would, out of pocket, have his shipping security patrols widen their assignments beyond the yards themselves. That terrible incident had no doubt occurred because Volmer, a respected hands-on newsperson, was conducting his own investigation of the corruption sapping the war effort. Sullamora even posted a reward for the apprehension of the lethal muggers who had killed his friend.

Chapter Thirty-Six

The four Tahn officers glowered at St. Clair. Even in the glitter of their full-dress uniforms they were looming, ominous. Without even checking rank tabs, she knew from the cut of their tunics and the gleaming custom willyguns strapped to their waists that they were higher-ups. They almost filled the small anteroom with their presence, and St. Clair had to wrestle with the urge to bolt. Their faces were set in the automatic brutish threat mode that high Tahn officials wore to get their way.

Instead of running, St. Clair greeted them with her priciest smile.

'Gentlebeings,' she said. 'Check your guns and credit at the door.' And with that, she waved them into the main lounge of the K'ton Klub, the most exclusive and successful gambling hell in the Chaboya District of Heath.

And it's mine, all mine, St. Clair gloated as she watched the smooth, muscular hunk she had hired as her head host go into his little bowing and scraping act that eliminated all the sting from what the Tahn officers would have to go through to enter her members-only club. In a matter of seconds their rank would be verified, ability to pay checked, and weapons and cloaks tagged and locked away. Then they would be putting their fingerprints to a membership contract that would put the K'ton Klub first in line of debtors if there was any hint of financial difficulties. All that was accomplished with smiles and jokes guaranteed to crack even the thick varnish of gloom that the Tahn seemed to prefer in public.

Moments later, the door leading to the ground-floor casino hushed open and the four laughing Tahn officers were plunging into the boisterous throng of marks anxious to eat, drink, and gamble their souls away to St. Clair, because the next day they might find themselves volunteered as targets for an Imperial cruiser.

There was a tinkling of old-fashioned mechanical bells, announcing more customers. St. Clair motioned for her host to take over. From that time of night on, the customers would mostly consist of regulars that St. Clair would not have to sus out.

St. Clair followed the Tahn into the casino. It was time to check out the action. Not that she had to go too far to check – the joint was jumping. By the time the night was over, St. Clair figured, she would have another record take in the till.

The K'ton Klub was one of many multi-storied casinos that made up the Chaboya District's gambling strip. But there were two, no, three, big differences between her club and the others: (1) The percentages were honest. (2) The percentages were honest. (3) The percentages were honest. From long experience, St. Clair knew that the rake-in from the house's built-in edge was more than enough profit for any fool. Every time her competitors skinned a mark, they lost that same mark permanently to St. Clair.

It was dishonesty in fact that had brought the K'ton Klub into her hands. The previous owner, like most of the other casino operators in the district, had been unable to swim against the new economic tide created by the war. As shortages tightened the supply and power screws, the casinos, instead of finding new ways to keep the customers happy, racked up the gambling machines' percentages until it was nearly impossible to win, then pulled in their heads, cutting back hours until many of them finally just shut their doors and walked away.

If St. Clair had been looking at the situation purely from a business point of view, instead of trying to find a nice comfortable way of hiding out in plain view until she and L'n were rescued, she still would have sized up the situation the same.

War brought shortages, true. But looked at another way, the shortages meant that the price of things simply went up. More importantly, the sin business always boomed during war. That was an economic curve on a chart that St. Clair had memorized before she had any curves of her own.

St. Clair had plucked the club off the tree within weeks after she and L'n had made their escape.

They had spent very little time in the actual escape itself. St. Clair had abandoned her plan to be a rich-bitch tuber hunter as soon as she had decided that L'n's only chance of survival was as her escape partner. She would have to trust to luck and play the situation by ear. There was no forged ID card that might fit the number of situations St. Clair and L'n might meet – so she did not carry any.

Bluff would be her calling card.

As soon as they had exited the tunnel, she headed for the nearest gravtrain station. Acting imperious as all hell, she had browbeaten the ticket clerk into selling her an unauthorized first-class seat on a train heading directly into the center of town.

'Travel permit? Ration card? My good man, I explained to you that I lost them, didn't I? I suppose you expect me to grovel in my carelessness, now, don't you? Very well, then. If that gives you satisfaction, I am now groveling! See me grovel?' She put her hands together as if in prayer and gave him a slight bow. 'There! I hope that makes you happy! Now sell me the damned tickets!'

Her non-groveling grovel act scared the holy bejesus out of the clerk. From her clothes, she was obviously richer than hell. Either that or joygirl to a Tahn officer whose rank he did not even want to guess at. He sold her the tickets, not even asking why she needed two of them. He supposed it had something to do with the strange pink little furry creature accompanying her. Maybe rich types always bought seats for their pets.

St. Clair and L'n were just taking deep, shuddering breaths of relief as the gravtrain's generators wound up to a high keen, when they heard the station speakers crackle into life. There was a series of sharp, barked orders. The keen died down to a low hum. Then they heard heavy footsteps. St. Clair swore she would not look up as she heard someone in obvious authority grilling the passenger just in front of her. She felt L'n quiver in fear. Absently she ran her fingers through L'n's smooth fur, trying to calm her, but it was hopeless.

Authority Figure shouted. Passenger wailed. L'n choked back a low moan. And St. Clair found herself looking up against her will – straight into the eyes of a black-uniformed Tahn thug.

She would never forget those eyes. They were the color of a bottom-feeding fish. They took her in. Then L'n. Then her again. Fish Eyes dropped the papers into the passenger's lap and walked straight back toward her. St. Clair forced out what she hoped was an in-character haughty smile. She prepared to reach into her jumper suit pockets and fumble for nonexistent papers.

The man stopped in front of her. He leaned forward. Then, surprise of all surprises, he grinned, exposing a horrible row of black and yellow stumps.

'Chook-um, chook-um,' he said. 'Chook-um, chook-um.' And he began stroking and tickling L'n!

'I say! What a great pet! What is it? Some kind of cat? I love cats! The wife and I must own thirty or forty of the little buggers. Ha! I should say they own us.'

And all the while he kept stroking and tickling L'n. St. Clair burbled something between a laugh and a sob, thinking all the while, Purr, you clot, purr, to L'n.

'Yes,' she said. 'A cat. A type of one, anyway. Very rare breed . . .'

At that moment L'n started purring, saving her life and St. Clair's in what was probably the only actual case of interspecies telepathy ever to occur in the Empire's history.

And once she started purring, she never stopped. She purred through the entire conversation. St. Clair lied. Fish Eyes bought. And a little while later, he waved her down when she tried to look for the papers that were not there and exited a happy Tahn with a great story to tell his nice Tahn wife.

'You can stop purring now,' St. Clair finally whispered to L'n.

'Not on your life,' L'n whispered back. 'The kid plans to keep purring for at least the next fifty-sixty years. And you will, too, if you know what's good for you.'

And St. Clair realized that L'n did not understand that she had been mistaken for a pet. Oh, well. She would wait awhile before she let her furry friend in on it. But, oh, God, was there going to be an explosion when she found out.

Later, after St. Clair had explained and then scraped her friend off the ceiling of the compartment, she just had to ask it. 'Did you know how to purr before?'

'No,' L'n had said. 'I've never even *heard* of a cat, either!'

'Then how . . .'

L'n gave a shrug of a furry pink shoulder. 'I don't know. I just reached down inside and . . . purred, dammit! Now, will you shut up about it, before I show you what I can do with teeth?'

It was the turning point in the life of the once-shy being called L'n. And there would be no going back.

As soon as they reached the center of the city, St. Clair instinctively gravitated toward Chaboya. In any area where sin was largely ignored and corruption was waist deep, cops tended to ignore most of the evildoers and their victims. The crackdowns usually came against well-known types who had not coughed up enough to stay in business. Credits changed hands, and then it was back to business as usual.

St. Clair found a dive for them to hole up in and then hit the streets. For the first day or two she fooled around with a few penny-ante shell games just to get warmed up and increase her stash of credits. Then she hit the casinos. Unnoticed, she filtered through them one by one, dropping a little here, picking up a little there, always keeping a low profile. She found what she was looking for at the K'ton Klub. From the thin crowds and the peeling plas walls, she knew it was close to folding. She played small-time dice machines for a while, watching the crowds.

She identified the owner right off. He was an older, handsome man who tended to dress a bit too flashily. She noticed that he spent little time on the floor, appearing only when another obviously high-stakes flash gambler occasionally showed up.

He would personally greet him, then they would disappear upstairs to what St. Clair just *knew* was a big-time game. It was time to strike. She invested a healthy chunk of her stake for the flashiest, sexiest outfit she could find, then re-entered the club, looking for all the world like a bored professional anxious to find some action.

The owner spotted her right off. A little flirting followed, and teasing remarks were exchanged. Mild sexual innuendo was used on each side to check out the gambler in the other. An invitation was offered.

A little later she found herself being ushered into the owner's office. As soon as she entered the room, she knew she was home. In the center of the table was the pot. And it did not consist of the funny money the Tahn laughingly called credits. Instead, there were rare gems and exotic heavy mineral baubles. And there were also stacks of parchment-like papers that could only be Imperial bonds and real estate deeds.

One week of around-the-clock playing later, she was bowing the owner out of his own office, holding *his* deed to the club. All the objects that made up the pot were also hers. She expected a bit of a strong-arm bluff from the man. And she was prepared for it – St. Clair had a minipistol hidden in the voluminous sleeve of her blouse. Oddly enough, the man did not seem to mind all that much. He said he had been thinking it was time to move on, and the cards that they all worshiped had confirmed that.

There was one other deed on the table that proved to be of far greater value than was obvious at first glance. It was for the seemingly worthless cargo of a freighter – a museum ship stranded by the war in midtour.

As soon as she and L'n had cracked the rusted hold and entered, St. Clair had smelled money. Inside was a traveling exhibit of ancient Earth-style casinos: mechanical gambling machines, crap tables, bingo machines, roulette wheels, decks of *real* paper playing cards. And vidbooks after stacks of vidbooks on how the old folks had lost their money thousands of years before.

St. Clair stripped the K'ton Klub down to the ground floor, then installed the machines. The lure of honest percentages and old-fashioned gambling drew customers like beasts to carrion. The marks were sure they could not be cheated because there was little electronics involved. Things that went *crank-crank, whirr* were considered far more trustworthy and ruled by the laws of a kind nature than were computers that talked to one, fooled with one, and toyed with reality livie-style, all the while gulping away at one's credits.

From the very beginning, St. Clair decided that the place would be as exclusive as possible. Instead of garish, lighted signs outside, she had only a small glowing plaque on the front door reading 'The K'ton Klub. Members only.'

St. Clair congratulated herself as she slinked through the more drably dressed customers who made up the crowds on the ground floor. She noted the things that were going right and, just as importantly, what was going wrong – if anything. The room was ringed with the one-armed bandits she had salvaged off the museum ship. On this floor they were one of the biggest money-makers, second only to the dice tables and followed by chuck-a-luck and the marathon bingo games that featured a pot that grew each day until no simple-minded blue-collar type mark could resist laying his credits down.

To keep a bit of class and social strata awe going, the center of the room was occupied by a raised, roped-off platform where there was always a high-stakes whist game going. To encourage a constant supply of whist players, St. Clair charged only a minimum fee per chair and took no house percentage at all.

Sexily uniformed servers constantly moved through the crowd, offering cocktails, narcotics, and snacks. In peacetime it would all have been free, but now the marks were so grateful that there was anything available at all that they gladly paid. There were two ways a customer could go from there. A mark could either exit to the street – after passing through a brothel where joyboys and joygirls hustled whatever credits remained – or he or she could climb the stairs to the next casino, where the price soared along with the class of the clientele.

The previous owner had had a somewhat similar setup, with three working casinos on each floor and a nightclub restaurant on top. However, he had used entrances and elevators to separate the poor marks from the middle class and the middle class from the rich. One of the first things St. Clair did when she took over was eliminate the elevators and the separate entrances. Everyone had to go the same way to get to the top, and without exception, money was left on each floor.

St. Clair climbed the stairs, making sure at each level that the bouncers were properly culling the credit-level chaff from the wheat. The second casino leaned toward roulette and higher-stakes card games and crap tables. The next floor was invitation-only straight card games, mostly poker, whist, t'rang, bezique, and bridge.

The nightclub was on the top floor. There was no cover, no minimum. It was St. Clair's idea. The prices she charged for food, drink, and sex with the entertainers who swung that way were astronomical, even for those inflationary times. Everything else about the nightclub was L'n's.

She had designed it so that the mark and his mate would be

overwhelmed as soon as they entered. It hit St. Clair even though she had known what to expect.

She was overwhelmed by the multicolored lights that dipped, dodged, swirled, and smoked, grabbing the viewer's mind in a soft glove and delivering him or her into the arms of the entertainers who danced and sang and cavorted on three stages. The moment L'n had spotted the dusty room jammed with creaky, high-tech seats, she had known she was on the verge of discovering a new art form, a living art form that would call into play all the powerful talents she had spent so many years developing. She used light sources of all types but seemed to get the most out of the more natural effects of resistor-based vacuum bulbs, and especially candles and torches whose burning centers she captured on moveable mirrors, split with prisms, and then re-formed again to be cast any place she chose.

L'n controlled everything from a computer console in a dark corner of the club near the door that led to their private quarters and offices. At first she had curtained off the console area. But as she grew more confident, she had the curtain removed. If one looked in her direction, she could be seen playing at the board with all the flair and drama of a concert pianist.

St. Clair edged around the room so as not to disturb the audience. Spotting her, L'n toggled a few switches, spun a control wheel, then joysticked the lights to a higher crescendo. Then she motioned with her head to the door.

Someone was waiting in the office. St. Clair mimed a 'who is it?' but L'n merely smiled. It was all very mysterious.

She went through into the hallway and marched to the office door. She did not remember it opening. But it must have, because standing in the middle of the room was Horatio, an immense grin on his face. St. Clair shouted and sobbed and hurled herself across the room into his arms. And she was kissing his neck, and hair, and anything else she could find. And Horatio was doing the same until the sudden heat in her loins brought her back to reality. Of all the men she had ever met, this guy was way up there on her hatred list. The slimy so-and-so was probably there to . . .

St. Clair shoved him roughly away, eyes blazing, finger stabbing into his chest. 'Listen here, you son of a bitch,' she said. 'I'm not in your clottin' military, remember? I'm a civilian. And you guys can't touch one mill of our hard-earned. Got it, buster?'

Sten gaped. What the clot did he care? Besides, he was as confused about what had just happened as she was. What was with this woman, anyway?

'Fine with me,' he said.

'I suppose you think you're here to rescue me,' St. Clair said. 'Well, think again, bud! I've got transponders blaring out a coded SOS, here we are, on half the Tahn freighters in the merchant marine.

'Although I don't know what's taking those clots so long. I've got a sweet thing going here. And a hell of a deal to offer. Why, we've got customers who are generals and admirals, and—'

'I know,' Sten said. 'We got your message.'

'Say clottin' what? What are you blabbering about? Who got what message? When?'

And then St. Clair got it. Sten smiled, admiring how lovely she still looked even with her jaw nearly brushing the floor in surprise.

'Let's start all over,' he said. 'First off, the introduction. If anyone calls me Horatio, or Horrie, or whatever starts with an H again, I'll kill them. My name is Sten. So much for boy meets girl. Now, where do you want to go from here?'

St. Clair started to say something terribly biting and terribly clever. She had about six well-tested ways to emasculate this insufferable little . . . Except that was somebody else, wasn't it? That was—

She bit off the remark. She just looked up at Sten, waiting.

It was a good thing the office desk was a museum relic. Because what happened next had probably happened to it many times before.

Chapter Thirty-Seven

His name was Chapelle.

Until recently, he had been a landing controller at one of the Empire's busiest spaceports. Like most controllers, he was very young and very intense. The pressures of his career guaranteed burnout by the age of forty. Unlike most controllers, his entire life was spaceports. He spent all of his offshift times haunting the port. He had walked the hills around the port time and again. He had been through all the buildings around that port. He boasted – only to himself, since Chapelle was a neurotically shy man – that even if all radar, laser ranging, and the port's other artificial GCA systems went out, he could land a ship by mind and voice. He could visualize 'his' spaceport from any angle, under any weather conditions.

Chapelle's proudest possessions were two holographs. One was of the Imperial yacht *Normandie* settling onto 'his' field, and the other was an autographed portrait of the Eternal Emperor. His leader, whom he had brought safely to a landing. Of course, the portrait was machine-autographed and had been routinely provided by the Emperor's flack as part of another show-the-flag tour.

Chapelle had *known* he was being recognized for his abilities when he was unexpectedly promoted and transferred to the main port on Prime World.

Immediately he began the same self-education program he had used before. Perhaps his superior did not understand what he was doing. Or perhaps Chapelle's obsession was becoming worse. It did not matter. The supervisor had mildly suggested that Chapelle might consider taking some time off, with no loss in status at all. But . . . he seemed so very intense. Perhaps he might consider consulting a specialist. Chapelle had barely kept himself from striking the man. Perhaps his supervisor was right – about being too dedicated. Of course he was not right about Chapelle needing psychological help. Yes, he would take the time off.

At that point, Tanz Sullamora's agents discovered Chapelle's lovely profile.

Chapelle, feeling rested, was ready to return to work when the fax in his high-stack apartment complex delivered a notice, placing Chapelle on extended unpaid leave. Chapelle found the guts to vid his department and ask why.

'The reason is sealed.'

Sealed, Chapelle wondered. Why? Who could do such a thing? Who had the right? No one . . . except . . . and his eyes found the smiling portrait on the wall.

Why?

He was the Emperor's most dedicated subject. Had he not, after all, saved the *Normandie* from a possible crash?

Chapelle sat for hours in the tiny apartment, staring at that picture. He barely picked at the meager, welfare-provided rations that slid out of the dining slot. There had to be something wrong.

He determined to visit the library. Perhaps he needed to know more about his Emperor.

While he was away, his apartment was visited.

Several hours passed after he returned before he noticed. That portrait, the portrait he had always thought was smiling benevolently at him, had a cruel edge to it. The twinkle in the Emperor's eye was not that of a kindly leader, but that of someone who thought it humorous to play a meaningless practical joke on his most loyal subject. Yes. Perhaps he was wrong about his Emperor. The histories he had read suggested that the Emperor was more than the universe's paterfamilias.

He needed to learn more.

And again his apartment was visited. And again the picture of the Emperor was changed.

It was, Chapelle recognized, the face of all evil. He had been a fool. He would have served the Empire better if he had allowed the *Normandie* to crash.

That night, the voices began.

Chapter Thirty-Eight

It should have been a routine meeting, Kilgour's third for the day. All he had to do was be sitting quietly in the dispatch clerk's efficiency apartment when the man returned. After the man recovered, Kilgour would apologize for letting the man, one of Tahn Counterintelligence's most valued agents, fall out of contact. But, he would explain, the man's control had been desperately needed in a fighting sector, and unfortunately, there was a bit of disarray. Now he, Senior Specialist Fohch, was reactivating the man.

Nothing would change. He should continue to report any

anti-Tahn sentiments at his workplace and, most importantly, describe exactly how those affected the efficiency of his plant. There was no more important part of the war effort than the continued production of Imperium X, which was used for shielding Anti-Matter Two.

The only change, Kilgour would be delighted to inform the man, was that his superiors had authorized an increase in the small retainer paid to the dispatch clerk. And once final victory over the Empire had been achieved, appropriate medals would be awarded to men and women like him, who performed vital duties far from the fighting front but were as responsible for that soon-to-arrive victory as the most decorated hero.

Et cetera, et cetera, et cetera.

Certainly there was no need to confuse the poor man with reality. If he felt happy being a fink for Tahn CI on his fellow workers, Kilgour would offer nothing but support.

So it was up the emergency slide, pick the window's friction catch, and inside. Perhaps, he hoped, the man would have a bit of alk chilled. Spymasterin't, Kilgour thought, could get thirsty.

There was a half-empty container of something that tasted like soya wine. Kilgour gagged but continued sipping as he wandered around the apartment, gloved hands routinely lifting, moving, and checking.

He lifted a lamp and *tsked* sadly. Then he replaced the flask in the reefer and went back out the window, leaving no trace that he had ever been in the room.

Kilgour wandered back toward the nearest transit dump point, considering possibilities.

Most interestin', he thought. Thae's little if any safety here. An th' puir workers boil out frae th' tubes like salmon up a weir.

Pity should a wee dispatch clerk who just happens to hae a bug in his apartment which nae should be there happen to come a gainer in front ae the outgoing.

It was. He did.

And Kilgour headed for the next address. Nae too shabby. Thirty agents so far. Five gone, three lost nerve, and two doubled. The rest were all humming away, happily back in harness, reporting what they were told to, to whichever spy service Alex thought appropriate for them to be employed by.

Sten briefly admired his reflection in the large mirror. He looked rather dashing, he thought, in evening wear, even if it was a shade too flashy for his personal tastes. But big-time gangsters were never known for their subtlety. He minutely adjusted a shirt stud, sipped brandy, and leaned back, waiting for Connl to make the next move.

It appeared to be a straightforward deal. Connl had a warehouse, custom-sealed, full of the high-protein glop the Tahn military used to augment its ship rations.

Sten wished to purchase said glop.

A straightforward deal – on the black market.

How Connl had come into possession of the glop was not Sten's concern.

Sten had made his offer, calculated to be several units per kilo above what Connl could get from other black market commodity dealers and far above what the Tahn would be willing to pay.

He was also willing to pay in hard Imperial credits.

The details of Durer still were not known. But the entrepreneurs had heard bad things. Plus they were not particularly thrilled doing deals in the already inflationary and good-faith-based Tahn currency. Even if the Tahn managed to win, would Imperial credits be worthless? No one thought that would happen.

Plus Imperial credits were weatherproof. Buried under the gazebo in one's estate, they would be safe from wear, tear, and rodents. The fact that possession of those credits made the owner subject for the high jump worried no one. At worst, bribery would be called for.

Connl ran a fingertip around his snifter. 'Interesting offer you've made. May I ask an intrusive question?'

'You may ask.'

'There have been some interesting stories about your background.'

'I've heard some of them.'

'Connections straight into the Tahn Council itself, I've heard. A man with a private army, somebody told me. Very, very interesting.'

'Perhaps one or two of them might be factual,' Sten suggested.

'Perhaps.' Connl did not press it; he had asked merely to gauge Sten's reaction. He had gotten, of course, none.

'To return to business. You don't have the reputation of being foolish. So I assume you have an idea of the actual market value of my hi-pro.'

'I do. Quoted this morning, for delivery, of seventy-five units per kiloton.'

'Yet you offer eighty. Interesting. If you are not a fool, then neither am I. Offer accepted.'

Connl was paid within the hour and went on his way, somewhat delighted. He had made a huge profit, and he had never had to put his hands on that slimy hi-pro to make it. He also had figured out what Sten's game was. The man was actually trying to corner the market. Once he had a sufficiency, he would turn the screws.

Connl determined to reinvest. His half-mill warehouse of hi-pro was, of course, worth nearly three-quarters. He would adjust his price accordingly.

The end result of Sten's maneuver: Even less high-protein additive was available to the Tahn at any price. Plus he had done his bit to destabilize the currency. Those credits, if not buried, would go back into circulation and further devaluate the Tahn unit.

L'n was curled up on a silken pillow, looking terminally cute and asleep. Her ear sonared on the conversation at the table next to her.

The four Tahn officers were playing an incredibly complex game with counters, multiple sets of dice, and variable rules, a game that could only have been invented, let alone played to the point of expertise, by military types trying to while away long, boring hours on patrol.

Such was the case.

And it made the game a status symbol – anyone who knew the rules, let alone how to win, was of course intelligent, part of the Tahn hierarchy, and probably noble to boot.

The game went on.

And the officers talked, paying no attention to St. Clair's pet napping beside them.

The conversation was most interesting. Such and so had been relieved through no fault of her own. X Unit would never be deployed to Y Sector on time, not with the shortage in medium weapons. And did you hear about poor Admiral Whoosis? His new flagship's the *Sabac*. That's the first of the Amtung class, y' know. What a pile! TA can't pick up more than six targets without going into program reject. Power room, he told me's got leaks from the drive. Good thing he's a hero sort.

There was laughter, and the game and conversation droned on, L'n filing every bit of the hard intelligence for transmission to the Empire.

Kilgour dropped from the skylight onto the top crate in the huge stack. He looked around the deserted warehouse, laid out his tactics, and went into motion.

The warehouse was a ration outshipping point. Each crate contained fifty cases of rations. Each case held one day's rations for ten combatants.

Kilgour had in his overall pockets six cans. Each of them would be inserted into a different ration case, and the case and crate would be resealed without notice.

The poor sod getting that particular can would not be happy. Not that there was anything lethal in the cans. Each of them contained exactly what it was supposed to and was as edible as military food ever became. There was, however, a small addition to each can.

Puir, wee, slikit beastie, Alex thought sentimentally.

Not that the cans contained an entire mouse.

Just its tail.

Kilgour wondered how long the rumor would take to spread as to just what those war profiteerin' clots were feeding the poor frontline fighters.

Not long at all, he knew.

'A pint, cheena?' Sten suggested.

Chetwynd, feeling most proud, merely looked up and smiled. 'I'm drinking brandy these days.'

'Life's been good to you?'

'Life's been acceptable,' Chetwynd said neutrally.

The two men stared at each other as the barmaid delivered drinks, was paid, smirked at the two, and wobbled back to the bar.

'So you made it,' Chetwynd said then.

'So I made it,' Sten agreed.

'Did my, uh, message get delivered?'

'It did. At the highest level.'

'And?'

Sten answered by sliding a case across the table. Chetwynd glanced to either side, snapped the case open a crack, and then, at light-speed, closed it.

'Someone,' he said, 'out there likes me.'

Sten smiled. 'We love you, Chetwynd.'

The case was stuffed full of Tahn money.

'And what am I expected to do with this?'

'Whatever you want. An estate in the country, if that's what turns you over.'

'Nah. I've learned.'

Chetwynd *had* learned. He had spent time re-establishing contacts and making them very happy. He had a chubby finger in almost anything crooked that went on around Heath's spaceports. He had even begun making most vague noises about unions. But this time he was not messing with the longshoremen, having realized that someone with a size twenty-six neck and a size three hat who got political might be easily replaceable. Instead, he was listening with great sympathy to the dispatchers, ramp rats, controllers, and bookkeepers around the spaceports. Technicians were hard to retrain.

'That's nice,' Sten said. 'A suggestion. Are you still a loyal prison guard?'

'I've thought about—'

'Don't,' Sten ordered. 'That gives you a nice solid ID. Keeps you from getting sent back to Dru.'

Chetwynd shuddered, then understood. 'You want a pipeline into Koldyeze?'

'You have learned.'

'Anything else. Mister?' Chetwynd spit.

'None. Just keep on keeping on. I'll be in touch every now and then. If you need more gelt, just ask.'

Chetwynd considered. 'How deep's your purse?'

'How wide is the Empire?'

That was a correct answer. Sten was prepared to give Chetwynd, or any other Tahn, a limitless amount of units – flawlessly counterfeited units that would further inflate the economy. Every five thousandth bill had its serial number duplicated. When two bills, perfect examples of Tahn currency, showed up at bank clearinghouses, there would be hell to pay – further lessening the Tahn's willingness to trust their own monetary system.

Sten got up. 'Oh. There was one other thing. Don't have me tailed. And don't show up at my nice safe home.' He reached across and tweaked Chetwynd's cheek. 'I want you to be my back-street girl. You'd look clottin' stupid with a tag around your toe.'

And Sten was gone.

St. Clair systematically laid the markers, scrawled in various stages of desperation and sobriety, across her desk. The young woman on the settee sobbed convulsively.

'Come, now,' St. Clair said. She crossed to the side bar, poured a drink, and waited while the woman choked it down.

'Are you all right?'

The woman nodded.

'Let's look at it from my point of view,' St. Clair began. 'Of course you didn't know what you were doing. Mayd, I've gotten myself into the same kind of problem. When I was young.'

There were perhaps no more than three or four years between the two women. But St. Clair knew how to play the script.

'And you can't pay.

'And if you ask for units from your family, you'll be out in the cold. Your father doesn't sound like the understanding type.

'If this were the livies, I would be twisting my mustaches and – what would I be doing? Suggesting that you become available, since you are very young and very attractive, to some of my older guests? Or maybe stealing the family gems? No. I have it. You should deliver all your family secrets into my keeping. Blackmail, that's how the livies play it.

'No wonder I haven't seen a livie in years.

'I am certainly a loyal Tahn. And would do none of those sillinesses.

'Mayd, I like to think of you as my friend. I have always been honored that a woman of your caste honors my establishment with your presence. The fact that you have had unspeakable luck on the tables doesn't change that.

'But . . .' St. Clair sighed and swept the markers into a pile. 'I am also a businesswoman. I frankly don't know what to do.

'I can tear these markers up—' She paused and Mayd looked at her hopefully. 'But then I would be forced to bar you from being allowed here ever again.

'Still worse, I would be forced by my agreement to mention what happened to the Casino Owners' Security Block. That could be embarrassing if you were blacklisted in all of Heath's establishments.'

St. Clair pretended deep thought. 'Wait. I have an idea. I am a gambler. As you are. But, well, I like an edge. As you did.'

The woman blushed, not wanting to remember the time that she had tried to introduce a set of shaved dice into a game.

'Your father's conglomerate produces rare metals. I have been interested in taking a plunge in business investments. Maybe you could tell me how your father's business is doing. Nothing specific, of course. But strange things that help an investor. For instance, I know that a lot of the metals go outsystem. But where?'

Mayd looked at St. Clair's smiling, open face. 'That won't work, Michele,' she wailed. 'I don't know anything about business. You just asked about where the metals go. I can't tell you. All I know is that Daddy keeps complaining about having to go somewhere called Aira . . . Airabus, where it's nasty and cold and Daddy says they don't treat a nobleman the way he deserves.

'You see? I'd like to cooperate, but I don't *know* anything.'

Erebus. The long-secret shipyard system of the Tahn. That information was worth, to the Emperor, a year's income.

'Oh, well,' St. Clair said. 'We tried. Look. Here's what we'll do. I'll keep these markers. And I'll personally guarantee you an open line for, say, ten thousand more units. Your luck is due to change – and maybe next time I'll be asking *you* for markers. Mayd, this is on my personal guarantee.

'Do me a favor. One gambler to another? Stop doubling the bet when you're losing. The way to come out on top is to double up when you're *winning*.'

Mayd behaved as if St. Clair had presented the six lost commandments to her. St. Clair knew that it would not matter; all she had to figure out was how to keep the woman so confused that she never remembered when she had lost the next ten grand.

It was too good to be true.

'It's ta braw t' b't true,' Kilgour muttered to himself as he glowered across into the park from his position under an abandoned gravsled – abandoned, he was realizing, because of a total hemorrhage in its lubrication system as the oil soaked through his rather becoming, he thought, suit.

The contact had come most skillfully, Alex admitted.

One of his agents – very trusted, at least until twelve minutes earlier – had asked if Kilgour would be interested in talking to a certain minor bureaucrat in the Tahn naval payroll department. The man was upset, the agent said, evidently because he had been passed over for a promotion. He was prepared to deliver – for hard Imperial credits – the payroll roster for any naval unit anywhere in the Tahn Empire.

The meet had been set up twice, and blown twice, supposedly because of the bureaucrat's paranoia. Third time lucky.

They were to meet in a certain park – which looked, to Alex's country eyes, more like a vacant lot – minutes before curfew. The money would be passed in exchange for a complete roster of Tahn Council operations personnel.

The bureaucrat had said that if anyone else was in the park at the time of the meet, he would vanish once again.

Too good, indeed.

Kilgour had shown up hours earlier and cased the park and surrounding buildings. He found it most interesting that the apartments surrounding the park appeared to be very interested in livie transmissions, and all of them could afford new 'cast antennas on their roofs.

He had then rented himself an alky. He had bought the man two bottles of cheap plonk and said there would be two more if the man drank them in the park.

Then Kilgour had crawled under the gravsled and waited.

An hour before the meet, a handful of very battered vehicles had settled around the square. They lacked anodizing or washing but were equipped with very shiny McLean generators.

Oh, well.

Kilgour wanted to stick around until the bureaucrat showed up, then see about seven zillion Tahn Counterintelligence thugs swoop on that poor alky, passed out on his bench, and attempt to grill him.

But the last act was usually anticlimactic. Kilgour slid – literally – out from under the gravsled and then low-crawled around the corner away from the scene.

Nice try, lads. But nae Oscar.

Kilgour wondered who clottin' Oscar was, anyway, then headed back to the K'ton Klub and degreasing.

It took three tries before Senior Captain (Intelligence) Lo Prek was received by Lord Wichman.

The first attempt had been rejected after he had scared holy clot out of Wichman. Wichman's adjutant – so he had dubbed his executive secretary – had informed his boss that a certain captain in Intelligence wished to see the lord.

Wichman, even though honest to the point of caricature, had still turned pale. Intelligence officers, so it was said, could find guilt in their mothers if so required – and make the bones confess on vid.

The captain did not, however, have an official sanction.

His request was ignored.

When the second request was made, Wichman ordered his secretary to check into the background of the officer.

He scanned the fiche with interest, admiring Lo Prek's commendations and obvious ability. But he still saw no reason why he should waste his valuable time.

The third time Lo Prek was lucky. Wichman was bored and not interested in viewing the latest industrial projections – down – or in why things would improve shortly.

Lo Prek might have been a monomaniac, but he also knew how to present his case.

Wichman listened in increasing fascination.

The captain was determined that one man, formerly a POW in Pastour's vacation prison, was on the loose on Heath. He had already committed many depredations before being captured. Depredations, hell. Defeats.

Perhaps. A bit grandiose, but perhaps . . .

Now that individual – Sten – was loose and underground in Heath's society. He would strike again. Already, Lo Prek said, there were instances of sabotage, espionage, and generally anti-war sentiments abroad.

Wichman scanned the microfiche that Lo Prek had presented and marveled. This single Tahn officer, technically over leave from his assigned unit, had managed to collect this amount of data without any resources except what he could borrow.

Fascinating.

Wichman reached a decision. He thought Lo Prek to be a loon. The Imperial, whatever his name was, either had never existed or had gotten drowned in a ditch somewhere. But it could be very useful to have such a dedicated person around collecting evidence of anything that had gone wrong – what he had once heard the never-to-be-sufficiently-damned Emperor call a stonebucket.

Wichman looked up from the screen and smiled. 'Captain, I think that I can definitely use a man of your caliber.'

Chapter Thirty-Nine

Admiral Mason's destroyer squadron made a full-power bounce on an entire planet. The planet was the Tahn home-world of Heath. The ships' noses were already heat-glowing from the atmosphere by the time the first alarms went off.

Anti-aircraft crews who were more accustomed to ceremonial posturings and polishing brass fittings scrambled for battle stations trying to remember real-world target acquisition and launch procedures. Several crews lost minutes tracking down the officer with the input code for the armed missile loaders.

Civilian block wardens dug into dresser drawers for their arm bands and hard hats, fumbling through their time-passed briefings to find out what exactly they were supposed to do.

The invasion alert hammered out on a thousand channels, then rescinded, then rescreamed. Heath's workers sheep-panicked to the shelters that had never been anything more than the subject of jokes, following drills that were considered one more way to get in trouble with the police if one did not instantly obey.

The three interceptor squadrons around the capital, more familiar with providing ceremonial escort to VIP ships, took fifteen full minutes to get into the air.

By the time the first missile came out of its tube and the first gun opened fire, the destroyers were out-atmosphere and under full emergency AM2 drive.

The raid was a carefully designed one-time affair. Mason's flotilla, equipped with every known ECM and spoofer, bulging with additional supply containers, and using Tahn codes broken after the debacle around Durer, took weeks to slither through the Tahn Empire.

The Eternal Emperor was making two statements.

The first was made by Mason's DD, the *Burke*, as it launched a lovingly tailored monster missile.

The missile was a slim needle, set with offset fins front and rear. Its AM2 drive unit had come from a Kali ship-killer and nearly-instantaneously flashed the missile to full speed. The warhead, many tons of nonnuclear explosive, was buried far behind the nose cone, which was a solid mass of Imperium X.

Six separate guidance systems, using everything from inertial navigation to a pre-war street map of the capital, made sure the missile would not miss.

It did not, impacting squarely in the center of the Tahn Council chambers. And nothing much happened.

The watch commander in charge of the palace's guards had time to pick himself up from the ground where the initial shock had dropped him, recover, and grin to his second.

'Clottin' Imperials. All that trouble to drop a dud that—'

That went off.

The missile had driven nearly 300 meters underground, its Imperium X nose cone crumpling, before the detonator went off.

The explosion, far underground, created a cavern.

The original design was eons old and had been set aside as a peculiar footnote when the age of nuclear overkill had arrived. Its original designer, one Barnes Wallis, had originally described it as an 'earthquake bomb,' an incorrect if impressive label. More exactly, the bomb was intended to 'camouflet' – to dive deep below the earth without breaking the surface. And then to detonate.

A more exact description was a 'hangman's drop.'

That is exactly what happened. The entire Tahn Council palace fell through the 'gallows trap.'

All that remained was a stinking hole whose perimeter was littered with the stone ruins of the Tahn's proudest symbol of power.

The strike had been ordered for the early hours of the morning, and so only a handful of Tahn noblemen died, and those low-ranking. Not only was the palace communication system destroyed, but the standby relay stations below the palace vanished.

The Emperor had not intended the strike to kill the Tahn Council. He preferred them alive, worried, and having to explain to the Tahn just how the unthinkable – an Imperial strike on Heath itself – could not only have been thought but carried out. Also, he wanted them alive to consider that he had proved he could kill them any time he felt like it. Even fanatics like those who ruled the Tahn Empire might think about that.

The second statement was made by the rest of Mason's destroyers as they contour-flew over the city, launch bays spewing thousands of tiny incendiaries.

Carpet bombing.

The Emperor might have told Sullamora he would try not to win by mass slaughter. But his histrionic speech one cycle after the war had begun might have been more accurate, when he promised the Tahn that eventually their own skies would be flame.

The heart of Heath exploded in a firestorm. The city center – and everything in it – melted. People outside – who probably were already doomed from the radiation generated by the missile's impact – disappeared. The pavement ran like liquid. Oxygen was sucked out of even the filtered shelters. Ponds, fountains, and one lake boiled dry in an instant. The firestorm, reaching thousands of meters into the sky, created a tornado nearly a kilometer in diameter, swirling carnage and rubble at speeds over 200 kph.

Fire departments, disaster agencies, and hospitals were buried in a tidal wave of catastrophe – those which survived the fire itself.

The city center of Heath burned for nearly a week.

Half a million people were dead.

The Emperor's second statement was self-evident.

Chapter Forty

Pastour felt dirty, smelly, and just plain angry as he and his bodyguards exited the shelter. From the distance, he could hear the dying wail of all-clear sirens. Another clotting false alarm. In the three days since the bombing raid, at least two dozen false alarms had sent him, his bodyguards, and his entire household staff scurrying into the cramped bomb shelter about twenty meters under his garden. He was sick of feeling like a small rodent that bolted for a hole at even the hint of a predator's shadow. It was especially humiliating when the shadow turned out to be that of something innocuous, like a poor flying berry-eating creature.

He stopped just outside the steel door that covered the tunnel entrance to the shelter. Most of his staff headed straight for the comforts of the square-built structure he called home. As a man who had grown up in the greasy squalor that the Tahn called factories and had then fought his way to the executive suite, Pastour treasured his privacy over almost all else. He had constructed his home many years before on the edge of the industrial slum near the outskirts of Heath. Despite the grimness of the surroundings, Pastour believed it was important not to lose touch with his roots. That was definitely un-Tahnlike but was also probably the secret to his immense success.

A former factory slave himself, Pastour liked to believe that he knew how to get the most out of his workers. His industrial competitors used only the stick. Pastour had accepted that necessity.

It had always been done that way. But he had also reinvented the carrot.

In a Pastour factory, the worker was treated with a comparative measure of respect, with healthy bonuses for the most ingenious or the hardest workers. It was not out of kindness. It was pure calculation – like his plan to put POWs to work for the Tahn cause at Koldyeze. His factories were far from being utopias. In most other systems the conditions would have been considered barbaric. Even Prime World capitalists would have been shamed into shutting them down. On other worlds the workers themselves would have gone after them with bombs and guns. Still, if there ever was going to be a Tahn future history, Pastour would someday be judged 'enlightened.'

Therefore, the house had been built, in his words, 'right among 'em.' Still, he had a need for privacy. So he had his architect design a multi-storied home that presented four blank walls to its neighbors. It was constructed around a sprawling courtyard, complete with paths, fountains, and, right in the center, a small-domed structure containing his garden.

He had almost lost the garden when he had become a full member of the High Council. A minus side of the perks and influence he had gained was the insistence that each council member 'shall cause to be constructed or personally construct a facility which shall be capable of withstanding . . .' mumblemumblemumble and other legal jargon that bottomlined out that he had to tear out his garden and put in a bomb shelter capable of standing up to a nearly direct nuke hit.

Pastour had actually been toying with telling Lord Fehrle where he could put the great honor he was about to bestow upon his proud Tahn brow, when he came up with a solution.

Armed with his pet architect, a great wad of credits, and a lot of heavy string pulling, Pastour had weaseled the military out of its heaviest-duty laser cutters and gravjacks. It still took months of cutting and burrowing to lift out the entire courtyard, ground and all. Then the shelter was constructed to the meanest standards possible – Pastour had no intention of wasting any credits on such foolishness. And the courtyard and his treasured greenhouse were lowered over it and sealed in place.

He glanced around, still noting the accomplishment with a bit of pride. True, there were a few flaws. Drainage had proved to be a problem, but he had tacked together a barely adequate system that dumped into the neighborhood sewer system. There was a tendency for it to flood the street, but Pastour did not mind taking on the burden of the pumping and the cleanups that followed a heavy storm.

He acknowledged the salute from his chief guard, who reported that the shelter had been secured and that they were ready to escort him inside the house. Pastour impatiently waved them away. Over the past three days of scares, the situation had become routine – something that did nothing to make it easier on Pastour. They would insist that he go inside while they doubled-checked with Security Central – a process that could take hours. Pastour would refuse, sending them all reluctantly away while he instead retired to the solitude of his greenhouse. There were purposely no means of communication once inside, and Pastour sometimes spent many hours roaming the aisles of hydroponic pans, where all he had to listen to was the soft hum of the recycling pumps and the buzz of the sunlamps.

That day was no different. The exchange had almost become formal. Once again Pastour won, and once again the guards went sullenly away, and once again Pastour stormed through the door of his greenhouse and peace.

But once inside, the scowl faded and the wrinkles of anger softened into the permanent grin lines that wreathed Pastour's face. Today, however, it was quieter than usual inside. He shrugged. It was probably because his machines did not have to work nearly so hard to maintain the false atmosphere inside. The same bombs that had killed and maimed so many of his fellow Tahn had also briefly left behind a more accommodating world for his beloved plants.

He moved along a row of legume vines, picking off dead leaves, replacing flailing tendrils on their support nets, and generally taking note of the small differences that only a careful gardener saw in his progeny.

Pastour was just turning the far corner of the center aisle when he realized that it was not the hum of pumps that he was missing. It was the whine of the supersensitive pollen-carrying insects that he had imported across vast distances at no small expense.

The insects darted for cover the moment they sensed an alien presence. They knew Pastour; he was no longer considered a threat. Ergo . . . someone else . . .

'Be very careful, Colonel,' the man said. 'You would be advised to rethink anything you're planning to do next.'

It was better than good advice. Because as soon as Pastour saw Sten and the deadly weapon aimed at his gut, his first reaction was to throw himself on the man, pummeling and shrieking for help as hard and as loud as he could. He rethought. After murder, kidnapping seemed the next most obvious fate. Pastour relaxed. If kidnapping was the intent, then talk and negotiations must follow. Pastour was good at both. Therefore, outward calm was in order.

Sten watched the thinking process carefully. A moment before Pastour knew that he had reached a decision, Sten allowed the weapon to droop. He leaned against a tool bench and motioned for Pastour to perch on a gardening sledge. Pastour obeyed. He looked about curiously, wondering how Sten could possibly have penetrated his elaborate human and electronic security system. Then he spotted the grate lying beside the half-meter-wide mouth of the greenhouse main drain. Pastour could not help laughing.

'I knew that clottin' bomb shelter was a rotten idea,' he chortled.

Sten did not see what was so funny, but Pastour just said never mind. It would take too long to explain.

'How do you plan getting us both out of here?' he asked instead. 'I'm much too old to crawl through that thing.' He pointed at the drain.

'Don't worry.' Sten said. 'You're staying right here.'

Pastour frowned. Was it assassination, after all? Was the man a maniac? Did he plan to toy with him first and then kill him? No. There was nothing maniacal about the young man.

'So what do you have in mind?'

'Talk. That's all. It was my boss's idea.'

Pastour raised an eyebrow. Boss?

'You know him as the Eternal Emperor. Anyway, he suggested we chat. See if we can come to some sort of understanding.'

Pastour was beginning to doubt himself. Maybe the man *was* nuts. How to handle this? He warned himself that whatever he said next, he must be sure not to condescend. Before he could form his thoughts into words, Sten casually reached into a tunic pocket, pulled something out, and tossed it on the floor next to Pastour. The Tahn picked it up, glanced at it, and was jolted back. It bore the Emperor's personal seal! Pastour did not need to have it checked to know the seal was genuine.

Sten was exactly who he had said he was, an emissary of the Eternal Emperor. Questions flooded into Pastour's mind. Then one huge, glaring one wiped the others away: Why me? And he became very, very angry. Did the Eternal Emperor see some supposed flaw in his character? Did the man think he was a traitor?

'All my boss wants,' Sten said, as if sensing what was going on in Pastour's mind, 'is to let you know that he is aware of you. He said to consider this nothing more than the opening of a dialogue.'

'And just what does he expect me to do or say?' The words were etched in heavy frost.

'Nothing right now,' Sten said.

'Is anyone else being contacted?' By 'anyone else' he meant other members of the High Council.

'Just you.'

Sten allowed a long silence to follow. He wanted Pastour firm in his anger. He wanted hatred to build. Because when the shift came, confusion would follow. And then he set the hook.

'How did you like the little party my boss threw the other night?'

Pastour squirmed, knowing that Sten was referring to the bombing raid. To him the raid had been a sign that the Emperor could strike at will. And Sten's presence in his private garden only underscored that fact. Still . . .

'If the Emperor believes his cowardly attack on innocent people will in any way weaken our resolve . . .'

'You're sounding like a politician, Colonel,' Sten said. 'I hope that's not what you really think. Because if it is, you might as well kiss a lot more of your innocents goodbye.'

'You didn't answer my first question,' Pastour came back. 'Or, if you were, you were just being glib. I don't like glib. Once again, what does he expect from me?'

'If you think my boss wants you to turn traitor,' Sten said, 'you're dead wrong. If you were a traitor, you'd be no use to him at all.'

'And what use does he see in me?'

'At some point in time,' Sten went on, 'you people are going to realize that this thing is over. That you've lost. And when that happens, the Emperor would like to have someone sensible to deal with.'

Pastour knew that Sten was talking about surrender. How odd, he thought. The word doesn't make me angry. The lack of feeling disturbed him. What kind of a Tahn was he? Surrender? It should have been unthinkable. Instead, it seemed . . . inevitable. 'Go on,' he said.

And by those two words, Sten knew he had struck pay dirt.

'There's not that much more. Except to say that a great deal of grief can be avoided if some sort of Tahn government survives. The Emperor is betting that it will be you.'

Pastour nodded. Survival was something he knew a great deal about – unlike most of his brothers and sisters on the council.

'What else?'

Sten hesitated. What he was going to say next had nothing to do with his instructions. Then he plunged headfirst. 'Koldyeze.'

'What about it?' Pastour was puzzled.

'The Emperor is worried about the prisoners there,' he said, lying, lying, lying. 'He hopes that no matter what happens, they'll be treated humanely. And since the place was your idea to start with . . .'

Now it made sense to Pastour. He had heard that the Eternal Emperor had some strange ideas about the treatment of the lower classes. Even prisoners of war. Why the man bothered with the plight of cowards, he had no idea. Still, what would it cost him?

'Tell your Emperor that he need not concern himself about their fates. I'll do my best for them. As long as he doesn't interpret this as some kind of concession. Or acknowledgment from me that anything but his final defeat and humiliation is—'

Sten laughed and raised a weak hand, calling for surrender. Pastour could not help laughing with him. There he was, sounding like a politico again. Sten straightened up and headed for the mouth of the drain.

'Are you just going to leave me here?' Pastour asked. 'How do you know I won't instantly call the guard?'

'There's a lot more lives at stake here than mine,' was all Sten said. And then he dropped out of sight.

Pastour only had to think about that for a second. The man was right. He kicked the grate back in place and returned to tending his garden.

Chapter Forty-One

A historical atlas fiche, equipped with a time tick, would show the Imperial assault on the Tahn Empire as if the war were a liquid projector. The red – or whatever color – representing the Tahn conquests would ebb back as the color assigned to the Empire and its allies flowed smoothly forward, excepting, of course, those blotches representing fortress worlds like Etan that had been isolated and left to rot.

That would suggest that the average Imperial grunt also had an idea of how the war was going.

He, she, or whatever did not.

The sailors loaded supplies and ammunition, boarded ship, and transited in minor fear and major boredom to a certain point, where they off-loaded supplies on a ramp and off-loaded ammunition through launching tubes.

The soldiers trained, boarded ship, transited in major fear to a drop or landing point, and attacked. When the last Tahn lay dead, they returned to their base or were moved to a new location where they built a new base, trained, and tried to find ways to burn off the sickening realization that the only end to it all was death, wounding, madness, or victory.

Seeing the next sunrise became the only major victory.

It took twenty years, fortunately, for a statistician to come up with the cheery news that during the war against the Tahn, a combat troop could expect to survive no more than thirty personal days in battle.

Also fortunately, very few Imperials experienced those thirty days back to back.

But there were exceptions, just as, contrary to what that 'liquid projector' showed, there were disasters.

One was the landing on Pel/e.

The Pel/e systems were priority one to the Emperor's strategists. They were at the midpoint of a galactic arm that was a longtime part of the Tahn Empire. Once the systems were taken, the Empire would have a base, a striking point to search and find the long-sought secret Tahn shipbuilding system.

The always hard-luck Eighth Guards were chosen for the 'honor' of the assault. After two weeks of prior bombardment, the Imperial Navy advised that all Tahn resistance was battered bloody. The assault transports went in. The first wave was shattered in-atmosphere. The second made it to the ground – and then the Tahn opened fire.

Imperial strategists and psychologists had blundered. Because the Tahn used a rigid military and social structure, it was assumed that once the command elements were destroyed or out of contact, the soldiers themselves would stop fighting, commit suicide, or at the worst fight ineffectually.

The ignored statistic, known to the Empire before the war began, was that the Tahn used far fewer officers and noncoms per serving soldier than did *any* of the regular Imperial units. And so the Tahn regrouped, by squads, by fire teams, by pickup combat elements, and fought back.

Conquering the Pel/e systems was supposed to have taken two E-months and required only the Eighth Guards to accomplish. Final victory took two *E-years* before the last Tahn element was killed. Six divisions were used in the process, and it became SOP for a new division to spend time on one of the Pel/e worlds getting final live-fire training before being committed to a frontal assault.

The Eighth Guards was shattered. Two commanding generals were relieved, and the unit took eighty-three percent casualties before being pulled from combat. Its colors were cased, the guardsmen were reassigned to other units, and the unit was rebuilt from scratch.

That was disaster enough. What made it worse was that the assaults on Pel/e were made before St. Clair discovered that the secret shipyards were in the Erebus System – half an empire away from Pel/e.

Seventy-five thousand Imperial deaths. One and a quarter million Tahn corpses. In a completely meaningless battle.

Six battlefleets hit Erebus under the flag of Fleet Marshal Ian Mahoney.

So-called panacea targets – hit here and the war's gonna come to an end the day before yesterday – were normally a joke, useful only when a space force was arguing for larger appropriations that would probably bankrupt every other service if made.

Also, those glamour targets usually got hit once and once only. If the factory was trashed, they would not have to worry about it ever, ever, ever producing nasty widgets anymore.

The fact was always ignored that after a war, when the bean counters went in to figure out how effective the bombs had been, they learned that said factory probably was not trashed that badly and that concerted effort brought it back online within a few months.

Erebus looked to be such a panacea target.

Mahoney, coming from a more realistic background than most of the skyjocks serving under him, approached things differently.

The Erebus System was a bastard target, defended by every onworld weapon and heavily armed spacecraft the Tahn could afford to divert from mainline combat. And the pilots and missile crews fought to the death.

Mahoney made sure it was a real death.

His first strike took thirty percent casualties. There were splintered destroyers and tacships broken on the ground of Fundy, the Erebus System's main world, and more hulks spewing debris out in space.

He sent his ships in again the next day.

Twenty-eight percent casualties.

There were ship crews who broke and refused the attack order. Mahoney calmly ordered their courts-martial and relieved any skipper who hesitated at his orders.

Then he threw his guts up in his cabin, washed his face, and sent more men and women to their deaths.

After six days of hammering, the Tahn had nothing left to fight back with.

Mahoney sent in his battleships, monitors, and cruisers.

Three battlewagons and two of the ponderous cruisers went down – but the Erebus shipworks appeared to be permanently out of business.

Mahoney ordered the strike repeated the next day.

He had to relieve a fleet admiral for objecting.

But the attack ships went in again. And still a third time.

The worlds of Erebus looked to be suitable parking lots.

But just to make sure, against all conventions of war, Mahoney had the worlds dusted.

The factories of Erebus might go back to work – but every worker assigned to them would glow in the dark.

The First Guards, Mahoney's old command – now led by Major General Galkin – spearheaded the landing on Naha.

By that point they knew how to fight the Tahn:

Don't shoot at the civilians – they've got their own set of problems. Get them to the rear. Don't believe that *anything* isn't booby-trapped, from the ceremonial flag to the ugly plas casting of Lord Fehrle that'd make a great souvenir.

A Tahn can be anywhere. In a crater beside the road. Tied into a tree. Sited in a weapons position in the base of a statue. Waiting for days inside a burnt-out track, waiting for the chance to kill any Imperial within range, whether fighting man or woman, clerk, or civilian. And very competent at his or her trade of slaughter.

Eventually, Naha fell, in spite of the fact that the final days of the resistance were personally commanded by Lady Atago. The casualty rate was twice what had been expected, and the battle lasted three times longer than expected – expected that was, by staff people. The line grunts thought themselves damn lucky and damn good to have gotten off that lightly.

Naha gave the Empire the long-needed major base inside the Tahn worlds.

Now the real hammering would begin.

Chapter Forty-Two

Even an experienced Tahn watcher might have drawn some wrong conclusions if he had observed the meeting between Lord Fehrle and the leaders of the two major factions on the High Council, Wichman and Pastour. If a hidden camera had captured them sitting at ease in Fehrle's darkened study, the Tahn watcher would have been most interested in who was *not* present. Meaning Lady Atago, Fehrle's heir apparent. The expert would make the instant assumption that new alliances were being struck and that Atago was on the way out, obviously because Fehrle perceived her new hero status as a threat.

The expert would have been wrong on both counts. Yes, it was true that Fehrle had thought of her when he had issued the invitation to Wichman and Pastour. It was because of her 'white knight' image that he pointedly ignored her.

He did not want what he was about to propose to tarnish her image in any way. If he fell, he wanted her to be able to pick up his sword wearing armor that was mirror-bright. Fehrle was about to suggest a plan that assumed and depended upon the corruption and disloyalty of his own people. Atago would be enraged at his even suggesting that such a thing existed. It was a fact that Atago's simple soldier's mind could not accept.

Wichman would argue, it was true, but he could eventually be convinced. With the help of Pastour, the realist, Fehrle would have no difficulty at all.

Lord Fehrle served his guests with his own hands, helping them with their choice of delicacies on the tray and building them drinks. And as they ate and drank, he talked, setting the background: There were traitors everywhere, spies at every level, and fools who leaked vital information to enemy agents. To make his point, he vastly overstated the situation.

As expected, Wichman was shocked and immediately called for a heroic medicine-style purge to remove the poisons of disloyalty. What he had not expected was Pastour's reaction. The man sat in silence, his face growing bleaker with every word. Had Fehrle misguessed? Instead of support, would Pastour take on the role of an Atago and back Wichman's call for a bloodletting? If so, Fehrle would have to do some fast reanalysis of the situation or his plan would never get off the ground.

What he did not realize was that Pastour was suffering from a nearly terminal case of guilty conscience. Did Fehrle suspect him? Were there guards waiting with drawn guns just behind the door? If so, why did the man keep looking over at him, as if he were looking for help? Gradually, he realized that was exactly what Fehrle wanted. But help doing what? What the clot! He already had his genitalia on the table. Maybe it was time to dare the knife.

'Forgive me, my lord,' he said. 'Along with you, and my Lord Wichman, I certainly deplore the situation you are outlining. We should take drastic action. But . . .'

'Go on,' Fehrle said a little sharply, trying to prod the man into giving him an opening.

'But . . . perhaps there is some way we can make use of some of these people first.'

Wichman almost exploded at that. He came halfway to his feet. 'How dare—'

'Exactly my thinking,' Fehrle said.

Wichman thumped back down. 'What? Oh, yeah! Good idea. Uh . . . right!' Then the poor bewildered man could not help himself any longer. 'Clot! What am I saying? What's a good idea?'

Fehrle and Pastour laughed, and Wichman, after a moment, had the good grace to laugh with them. They had more drinks while Fehrle laid it out for them.

He did have a way of making use of the leakers, but in a contorted way that even the Eternal Emperor would have admired. In fact, he had taken the whole plan right out of the Emperor's book.

Fehrle planned to pull hope out of the ashes of the ruins of the High Council's palace. They had all been puzzled at the Emperor's behavior after they had launched their own sneak attack on his headquarters in the opening blow of the war. The Emperor had immediately flooded the airways with an endless series of propaganda portraits showing him shaking his fist at the Tahn in defiance. At first it had seemed like empty gesturing. What did that accomplish? Immediately after that, they were surprised at how many of his straying allies returned to the Emperor's camp. There was nothing empty about the campaign at all. It brought in badly needed ships and troops in a swell of public opinion.

Fehrle was proposing the same thing, but on a much larger scale. He wanted to launch a grand tour of twenty-two systems in which he would personally appear with the leaders of said systems, giving the Emperor the finger at every opportunity.

The lonely Tahn, fighting on despite the odds against the warmongering running dog Imperialist giant. Vowing to win against all odds. That sort of thing. Privately, he would use a heavy cudgel to stiffen the spine of their allies. He would convince them all to dig into the trenches and fight to the last being. If it worked, any victory the Emperor hoped for would come at an exceedingly high price that Fehrle doubted he would be willing to pay.

Wichman loved it. Pastour, grudgingly, admitted there might be some wisdom in it. Still, he remembered the bloodbath of the bombing raid on the city and the strange appearance of Sten in his heavily guarded domain. If the Emperor could do all that at will . . .

'I fear for your life, my lord,' he finally said. 'What is to prevent the Emperor from learning of your plan and then attacking when you least expect it? If you were assassinated, I'm not sure how the people would behave.'

'I *want* the Emperor to learn about it,' Fehrle said.

Once again, Wichman was surprised. Pastour, however, got it right away. Fehrle would have his staff plan two itineraries. The first would show the tour commencing on Arbroath. On the surface, that would seem like a logical choice, since the Arbroath were totally loyal to the Tahn. They would grovel at Fehrle's knees and praise him, making for wonderful propaganda. That itinerary would be leaked. In reality, Arbroath was a rotten jumping-off point. The people were so stupidly and blindly loyal that they would fight on anyway until they were all dead.

The real stepping-off point would be Cormarthen. Pastour saw the wisdom in that right off. The people there were wild rebels – a semi-Celtic splinter cult whose sole motivation for aiding the Tahn was their unreasoning hatred of the Empire. When the war was over – assuming the Tahn won – they were sure to instantly turn on their allies. In fact, after the string of recent defeats they were already wavering. Fehrle planned to put a stop to that immediately. On day one of the twenty-two system tour he would be able to present his people with a diplomatic victory.

The rest of the tour would be plotted the same way. False clues would be planted with the Imperialists while Fehrle maddeningly popped up at the least expected places to flip off the Eternal Emperor.

Pastour and Wichman pledged enthusiastic support. They would work on their own people as well as lobby the other factions. Fehrle was guaranteed unanimous acceptance when the proposal was formally presented to the High Council.

While Fehrle and Wichman were congratulating each other on the yet-to-be success, Pastour remembered Sten. And Koldyeze. He had thought about the young man's odd request. He had recently seen a way not only to make good his promise but to bump the value of the pot 1,000 percent.

During the course of the conflict the Tahn had taken millions of prisoners of all kinds. But a very few of those prisoners presented special difficulties.

They were the important diplomats, politicians, and high-ranking officers who had fallen into Tahn hands. Even the instinctive Tahn disdain for prisoners did not allow them to treat those beings with anything other than kid gloves – relatively speaking. The problem had been finding the proper guards with at least a modicum of political reality.

At the moment, that was impossible. The prisoners were spread out in camps all over the Tahn Empire.

What Pastour wanted to do was to solve that problem at one stroke. He would place them all at Koldyeze. Then he would personally oversee their treatment through his emissaries. There was also an even greater advantage in putting all his rocks in one stonebucket. If and when the Tahn were defeated, Pastour would have heavy-duty trading stock to strike his bargain for peace with the Emperor.

Obviously he could not word any of that exactly the same way if he wanted to bring Fehrle and Wichman to his side. Instead, he appealed to their blood lust.

'If we had them all in one place,' he said as he came to the end of his explanation, 'we'd only need one gun to hold against their heads.'

'And if the Emperor refuses us,' Wichman broke in, 'we kill them all. I like it!'

Fehrle also added his support.

When Pastour went home some time later, a little warm and tiddly from the drink and the companionship, he thought fondly about how well the Tahn system of government worked. A few well-chosen words – out of hearing from the squabble of conflicting viewpoints of the public – and the correct measures were taken to ensure the future of the race. It made him feel proud and patriotic.

The next day, when he was sober, he would plan his next moves at Koldyeze.

Chapter Forty-Three

Sten was fairly disgusted with the Tahn. What, after all, was an evil empire without an internal conspiracy or six? The Tahn were short on dissidents. Those few enemies of the regime seemed to have gotten policed up years earlier, and their dissidence was mainly made up of the idea that maybe the Tahn Council ought to say please before conquering somebody. From the limited leaks he had been able to get from Tahn CI, the current treason seemed to consist of street gossips or poor sods who complained about having to work a double shift without getting a food break.

Sneakiness abhorred a vacuum, and so Sten and Kilgour went to work, building themselves a good list of traitorous swine. They decided, just to keep things interesting, that it would be a military conspiracy.

There were three requirements:

1. The conspiring officer had to have complained about how the war was going. Even a recorded mutter into a shaving mirror made the officer eligible. So, in that manner, Admiral Whoosis on the *Sabac* made the grade.
2. The conspiring officer had to be highly respected.
3. The conspiring officer had to have served in combat, on a front-line world, or, during peacetime, on a world where there was an Imperial presence.

It was not necessary that the eager conspirator actually be anything other than a rabid believer in the Tahn right to grab anything around from anyone weaker. As a matter of fact, Sten did not want anyone like that. People with real politics made him nervous – even if he had been able to find any.

Once Sten and Kilgour had the list, they put it up on a computer screen and started cross-connecting the conspiracy. The officers chosen for links needed no particular qualifications, except that their absence would not improve Tahn efficiency. That was, for instance, how the third assistant paymaster general, the Tahn Counter-intelligence number two, and the chief of the chaplain's acolyte division became dangerous threats.

Once Kilgour had the list all neat and tidy, it went out on a burst transmission to the Imperial base station located somewhere they never knew for appropriate usage.

Most of the conspiracy list was handled by Alex. Sten had another problem: Lord Fehrle's 'show the flag' tour. It did not make any sense. Not that the tour made no sense – but everybody seemed to know about it. Either Tahn Security was composed of numbwits – which Sten did not dare let himself believe – or else everyone connected with the tour was suffering from terminal oral diarrhea.

He sent through the reports of when Fehrle was going, where Fehrle was going from the Arbroath worlds onward, what he would eat and drink, where he would be banqueted, and whom he would meet straight on to the Empire. All graded Category Two or lower, ranging from reliable source, personally received, down to outhouse rumor. But none of it was Category One: accepted by this station as truth.

Then one afternoon Chetwynd sent word, through the cut-outs, that he wanted a meet.

They fenced recreationally for a couple of drinks. Wasn't it about time that Chetwynd's credit allowance was increased? Couldn't he be more helpful to the cause if Sten gave him some idea as to what was happening next? Had he heard anything about a new offensive failing? Then he got down to it.

'One a' my longtime cheenas hit on somethin' you might find interesting. He's one of my best agents, y' know.'

'A thief, in other words.'

Chetwynd looked ponderously injured. 'Clot, Sten, don't be so suspicious. The clot's a hard-core freedom fighter.'

'I stand corrected. A *good* thief.'

'He was out last night. Around the 23YXL area of the port. Y' know, that's where most of the bonded warehouses are. He was looking for good intelligence and—' Chetwynd chuckled and drank '—anything else that wasn't riveted down.

'Came on this warehouse. Security up the yahoo. Which was interestin'. He got up on the rooftop and snaked in. All of a sudden couple Tahn plainclothes come out from behind a vent. Damn near popped him.

'He come off that roof and said the place was crawlin' with rozzers. Funny – he said he knew a couple of 'em. CI, they was.

'Dunno what's in that warehouse. But thought you might want to be tipped the wink.'

Chetwynd waited. Sten dug out a wad of credits and passed them across. They were not given with any pretense on either side that they were intended for Chetwynd's organization. Maybe Chetwynd's tier ranger, if he was indeed a longtime cheena, might see a little of it. But probably not.

Kilgour swept the warehouse with a palm-size set of available-light binocs and hissed through his teeth. 'Thae tub's wae bein't conservative. Thae's more screws around yon ware-house thae a Campbell hae fleas.'

There were other interesting things happening. A ship had landed about half a kilometer beyond the warehouse. Sten ID'd it as being a standard armed transport – but with very non-standard security around it. The ship sat on an absolutely bare stretch of tarmac. There were three, no, four rings of guards around it, uniformed

soldiery, each bashing his beat in a military manner. Between the
rings, searchlights mounted on portable towers on the field's edges
swept the darkness.

'The ship's bein't loaded,' Kilgour whispered. 'An' by a braw
crew ae stevedores.'

He passed the binocs to Sten, who looked and nodded.

'The only civilian thing about them is they ain't in step.'

Fascinating. Not only did the warehouse obviously hold something enormously valuable – which made it enormously interesting
for Imperial Intelligence – it was being loaded by soldiers in the
dead of night. Sten rather wanted to pry open one or another of
those unmarked crates. They were being loaded very carefully, he
noted, as if they contained delicate merchandise.

Kilgour, mumbling, had a tiny multifunction computer dug out
of his boot and was tapping keys and staring intently at the ship.
Sten concentrated on the warehouse and put his Mantis joint-casing
skills to work.

Can we sneak in? Not unless somebody happens to come up
with an invisibility suit. Can we go in over the roof? We've got to
be sneakier than Chetwynd's boyo. Unlikely. Under? No time to
play caver – at the rate they're moving, the ship will be loaded by
dawn. What about a simple walk-up? Pretending to be some kind
of warehouse inspector? A superior officer? Negative on both. Not
that we can't get out if we're blown – but I have this feeling I'm
not going to want anybody to know we were here. Join the loading
party? Nope. Ten-man teams. Even the Tahn noncoms would notice
if there were more spear-carriers than the number of fingers on
each hand.

'Ah think w' kin do it, boss,' Kilgour broke in. 'Ah've been
runnin't a timer on thae guards. There are lapses. An' thae searchlights dinnae cross-sweep like thae should.'

Sten stared at the completely bare expanse between the building
they crouched next to and the ship and gulped in a cowardly
manner. 'Choreograph it, Mr Kilgour.'

Five minutes later:

'On thae count . . . be followin't mah twinkli't toes . . . three
. . . two . . . now!'

And the two black-clad men trotted out toward the ship.

'Sixteen . . . seventeen . . . down, boss! One, two, three, four,
five . . . up. Twenty paces . . . down!'

They became part of the tarmac as the searchlight beam passed
very close to them.

'Eleven, twelve, now! Three, four, five . . . six and freeze!'

The only music they 'danced' to as they crossed the field was their own hoarse breathing.

'The skid, boss. Straight for it an' look like a shock absorber. Two, one, on th' way, lad!'

Sten flattened himself next to the huge, grease-stained landing skid, wondering if he actually did look like an oleo strut.

'Na,' Alex growled in his ear, 'if Ah'm right, we'll be doublin't up thae gangplank shortly. Y' ken thae ramp watch is posted behin' an' under thae ramp. Lookit like he nae like thae glare when the beams hit him. So be goin't up softly, wee Sten. W' dinnae want thae thunder ae y' hooves alertin' him.'

'And if there's a watch *inside* the ship?'

'We'll say we're solicitin' frae the home f'r wayward banshee bairns an' scoot wi' a smile. Three . . . two . . . hit it!'

Running on tiptoe up a ramp – even a cleated ramp – was interesting. *Pointe*, uphill, was straining.

They made it through the port. Kilgour was lucky – there was no interior boarding watch posted.

Sten extended his hands, palm up. *Well?* Kilgour shrugged, then spotted an order board and grabbed it. Assuming a worried expression, he waved them forward into the heart of the ship.

Actually, it was more of a private joke – nobody ever interfered with a man who looked upset and was carrying a clipboard – than a practical disguise. Both of them knew full well that no sailor worthy of his hangover would board until three blasts after the final call. The passageways were deserted. There was clattering from what probably was a galley and some drunken snores from a berthing compartment, but nothing else.

Sten noted that the ship was very, very clean – freshly refinished. Either it was run by a bully captain, or high-level passengers were expected.

They found the hatchways leading down to the hold and slid down the ladders. The hold was a little over half-full. The loadmaster and his assistants were bellowing instructions to the laden soldiers as to what went where and why the clot was doing it wrong.

Sten and Kilgour found a pile of not yet secured crates near the forward area of the hold, and Sten deployed a pry bar quietly.

The first crate held dinnerware – expensive dinnerwear with the Tahn Council crest embossed on it. Sten thoughtfully opened more crates.

The sixth was the tip-off. It contained ceremonial robes made of a material that no Tahn would have seen for years and years. And each robe's left breast area was embroidered in gold and silver with a small three-headed dragon. Kilgour's eyes widened, and he applauded silently.

The crate's top was replaced, and Sten and Alex went back the way they came, dancing a pas de deux past the searchlights and guards.

Neither of them needed a short course in heraldry to know what that triple-headed dragon was. The natives of Cormarthen were too well known for carrying that emblem wherever their intransigence led them and for putting that emblem on everything, including, some theorized, their toilet paper.

So, as Sten had predicted, Fehrle was not going anywhere near Arbroath or the other supposed systems. But he – or some other muckety on the council – *was* making a grand tour. And Sten thought the Emperor might be vaguely interested in knowing what Fehrle's *real* itinerary appeared to be.

Chapter Forty-Four

The Eternal Emperor *was* interested.

He just was not quite sure what to do about having the facts on Lord Fehrle's wanderings. Actually, he corrected himself, he knew quite well what to do about it. The problem was *how* to do it.

Damn, but he missed Mahoney. If the flaky Mick were still head of his Intelligence – Mercury Corps – the Emperor would merely have had to hint heavily. But his current intelligence chief happened to be a tolerably straightforward man. Which meant too moral to be a good spy. Clot, he swore. Why'd I promote Mahoney?

The Eternal Emperor's fingers were on the decanter of stregg.

They hesitated, then went to the concoction he called Scotch. He needed a bit of brainpower, not blind instinct.

Icing a fellow ruler was acceptable only in fiction – historical fiction. And even then it had better be hand to hand, the Emperor thought glumly. If Hank Doo had personally clunked Beckett with the nearest mace instead of sniveling about things to his clotpole court, he might have gotten a better press.

It was not that any politician found assassination *morally* abhorrent. But it made them nervous to think that the fellow across the negotiating table might actually take things personally. Killing millions of citizens was one thing – but wasting one of his own class? The boss class? Shameful, indeed.

After thought, the Emperor put the operation in motion. It never had a name nor any permanent fiche, even in the most classified files of the war.

The Emperor requested the specifications, to include the signature in all ranges from visual to output drive, of the most current Tahn battleships. Since Fehrle's profile showed that he liked to travel in style, he would use the newest, most modern class available – regardless of whether that ship would be better deployed in combat instead of being used for transportation.

Intelligence showed that the Tahn were building three new super-battleships. One was – ? – in commission, one was in shakedown, and the third was nearing completion.

Mercury Corps technicians were given instructions to prepare a detonator that would explode the charge only when the active signature of that particular class of ship was within range. They had only days to build that detonator – Lord Fehrle's tour was almost ready to begin.

There was no problem. The technicians were – self-described – so used to doing the impossible with the improbable under circumstances that were preposterous that they felt capable of doing everything with nothing.

Explosive charges were prepared. Sixteen of them. The requirement was to provide a cased, nondeteriorating, small amount of explosive with the given CLASSIFIED detonator, capable of destroying a large object, such as a Tahn battleship, when it came within close range.

Sixteen was not an arbitrary choice. Cormarthen's capital port had sixteen pilot ships.

Mantis operatives were given those sixteen charges and inserted on Cormarthen.

All the pilot boats were booby-trapped, and the Mantis people withdrew without contact. They would have felt shamed if anything else had happened. They expressed no curiosity as to what was in the casing or what it was supposed to do and to whom at what date. They would find out – if the operation worked – in the privacy of their own bars or barracks. Very conceivably not until after the war ended.

The entire amount of 'paperwork' on the operation against the ruler of the Tahn occupied one fiche. That fiche was hand delivered to the Eternal Emperor and destroyed. He then sent his Mercury computer experts back through the system, ensuring that there were no backup, ghost, or FYI copies of the fiche.

Satisfied, he poured himself a stregg and waited.

Lord Fehrle's battleship, the *Conemaugh*, cut AM2 drive power and, under Yukawa drive, closed on Cormarthen. The ship's commander felt proud that his navigators had been able to pinpoint within 0.10 AU. Six ships were reported coming out-atmosphere: the pilot boat and appropriate escorts.

The commander so notified Lord Fehrle, who was in his cabin making final adjustments on one of the dragon-breasted robes he would wear.

While Fehrle's staff diplomats were on the com with the escort ships, the pilot craft closed to a forward lock without ceremony. On contact, the bomb went off.

Mercury demolition experts had planned for the blast to remove the entire nose section of the Tahn battleship. But because the *Conemaugh* was new, its fire-control circuits were still under test. Back-up systems were not what they should have been. And so the blast ravened through the hull and then down into the drive system.

The AM2 fuel detonated.

The *Conemaugh* no longer existed – nor did the pilot boat, two of the approaching Cormarthen ships, and six of the Tahn warships escorting Lord Fehrle.

The Emperor, as he had promised some years earlier, was getting very personal about things.

BOOK FOUR

ZANSHIN

Chapter Forty-Five

It was the Rangers versus the Blues in what every sports commentator in the Empire agreed was the gravball match of the decade. One hundred thousand beings were packed defecating-organ to elbow in Lovett Arena to see if the home-planet Rangers would revenge themselves on the dreaded Blues, who had whipped the Rangers for the gravball championship three E-years in a row. Despite the war, billions upon billions more – including, it was said, the Eternal Emperor himself – were watching the match on their home livie screens.

So far, the game had lived up to expectations. At the bottom of the fifth and final period, the score was fifty-three all after a series of seesaw duels that had marked the four hours of play. In the last period, Naismith, the big red-uniformed Ranger center, had fought his way four times through and around the Blues' heavy-gravity hotspots until he was within scoring distance. And each time the Blues had rallied, blocking the light-gravity lanes and driving the Rangers back onto their own territory. The game had been so fiercely contested that every hotspot on either side had been racked up to a full penalty three gees.

Rabbaj, the Blues' center, took the ball. Forwards veed out from him, hunting for a weakness in the Rangers' defense. Blue guards took up position near the light-grav lanes in their own territory. Then it was Rabbaj! Shooting past his own forwards, feinting left at a hotspot, then driving through a hole in the line. Then he was in the clear. An undefended light-grav lane just ahead! And beyond that, the tantalizing splash of red that marked the Rangers' goal line! The home crowd groaned. They were looking into the maw of a fourth humiliating defeat. A heartbeat,

and Rabbaj was into the light-grav lane and jumping . . . jumping
. . . jumping—

Tanz Sullamora palmed the switch that chopped the sound and
blacked out the big windows that overlooked the playing field. He
shook an angry finger at his colleagues on the privy council.

'I'm the one taking all the risks,' he said, his voice shaking in
fury. 'We all vote Volmer has to go. Fine. But then I'm the one
who has to do it. We all agree on the plan. Wonderful. Except once
again, it's good old Tanz who sticks his neck out with Chapelle.'

'We're all behind you, my friend,' Malperin murmured. 'I don't
see what the problem is. If you fall, we all fall. We agreed on that,
didn't we?'

'Sure,' one of the Kraa twins soothed. 'Me 'n' my sister been
with you from the start, Tanz. All the way in or not at all is our
motto.'

Sullamora snorted at this. There were few businessbeings who
were more notorious than the Kraas when it came to backstabbing.
He looked over at Kyes for support, but the silvery eminence did
not seem to be paying attention. Instead, he was lolling in one of
the huge, ornate overstuffed armchairs, staring at the blank window
as if he were still watching the in-progress gravball match. Sullamora
slumped down in frustration and choked back a fat drink. The
other members of the council were silent, staring around the owner's
suite in pretended curiosity at the baroque-upon-baroque setting.

One of Lovett's more eccentric ancestors had built the enormous
all-weather arena. It had no equal on Prime World. It could be
converted within a few days to play host to any event from agricultural fairs to high-speed boat races. The seating was designed
so that even the poorest fan could see the action. And looming
over all of it was the imposing dome that was the owner's suite.
Several hundred 'close friends' could easily be entertained in that
suite, although the multitude of garish paintings, stuffed animal
heads, rickety statuary, and oddly formed furniture tended to make
even two people feel claustrophobic. It produced the kind of atmosphere that would bring out the violence in even the most committed
pacifist.

Perhaps that was what was making Sullamora behave so out of
character, allowing his anger to be seen by his peers. Or maybe it
was because he was suddenly feeling very vulnerable. The way
things stood, if the plan failed, only Sullamora would take the
blame. The others were clean. Nothing could be traced to them.
Adding to the pressure was that this was most certainly the last

time the members would be able to meet out of public view without arousing suspicion. The match between the Rangers and the Blues was likely to be their last excuse.

It was Kyes who finally broke the silence. He went right for the bottom line. 'What do you require of us, Tanz?'

Sullamora acknowledged him with a nod and fished six cards out of his pocket. He skimmed them across the table like a dealer, one for each being at the table and one for himself. The cards were made of indestructible plas. Kyes was the first to slide his card into the viewing slot in front of him. A small port opened in front of him, and words lit up on a tiny screen. The others did the same with their cards.

WE, THE MEMBERS OF THE PRIVY COUNCIL, AFTER DUE CONSID-
ERATION, HAVE COME TO THE RELUCTANT CONCLUSION THAT THE
ETERNAL EMPEROR HAS BECOME INCREASINGLY AND DANGER-
OUSLY UNSTABLE. THEREFORE, WE HAVE DETERMINED TO TAKE
THE FOLLOWING ACTIONS . . .

It was the preamble to assassination. And at the bottom were six places for the signature prints of each being at the table. Once the marks were made, there would be no turning back. And each conspirator would be equally culpable.

There was a long moment. Once again it was Kyes who went first. He smiled and made his mark. One by one the others did the same.

Chapelle would be activated.

Out on the playing field, the home crowd happily rioted. The defeated Blue team was retreating behind a phalanx of armored cops. Naismith was being hoisted on his teammates' shoulders. And the celebrating fans poured out of the stadium for a glorious night of rapine, looting, drinking, and general head-busting.

Honor had been restored.

Chapter Forty-Six

'Got a question. Sir,' Fleet Marshal Mahoney growled. 'And a request. Sir.'

'GA,' the Eternal Emperor said.

'First. What's the official Imperial policy on torture?'

'Bad thing. Don't get caught doing it.'

Mahoney nodded. 'You mind if I brainburn this clot a little bit? Slow? Promise not to get caught doing it.'

'Tsk. And she appears to have such a bright future.'

'Future,' Mahoney snarled. 'Listen to this drakh.'

He read aloud from the news dispatch on the video display. '"Suddenly the smile vanished, and I was reminded that this man is the Empire's fiercest fighter, a leader who sends millions of men and thousands of ships into battle, a strategist whose very presence in a sector has caused the Tahn to surrender in droves."'

'Droves,' Mahoney said. 'I got more POW interrogators than I do POWs.'

'Yeah,' the Emperor agreed. 'I would've said hordes. Better word.'

Mahoney went on. '"Now we're preparing for the grand offensive,"' Fleet Marshal Mahoney said in a steely voice. '"Against the Fringe Worlds. I got thrown the hell out of there and didn't like it. I promised that one day I would return.

'"Now we're going back.

'"We have the Tahn reeling in all sectors. This should be the death blow. It will be a long and a hard struggle. But this will put us within sight of the end."'

'Drakh, drakh, drakh, charming wife, Spartan but well-chosen quarters, idolized by aides, men hold him in awe, dedicated to the welfare of his grunts. Drakh.

'The hack that wrote that deserves torture.'

'*Por que?*' the Emperor asked.

Mahoney started to snap, then caught himself. Okay. The Emperor's getting cute. Getting up, he went to the sideboard and reached for the Scotch. He changed his mind in mid-reach and poured a blast of stregg.

'Okay, boss,' he said, reseating himself. 'I'm the straight man. You aren't upset that this writer seems to have bashed security in talking about where we're gonna strike next.

'And this is the first time I've heard about this general offensive. Ignore that. Let's get into the small stuff. Like I never met this hack in my life. And where'd that charming wife come from?'

Mahoney cogitated – then swore. 'Boss, you're not really gonna do this to me, are you?'

'Sure am,' the Emperor said. 'We need a real hero-type general, and your name came out of the hopper. By the way, you think that story's bad, you ought to see what the *real* credit-dreadfuls are doing. How about the fact that you're a real fighting leader – you still carry a hand weapon everywhere. And the story about when you were a young lieutenant in charge of some outpost somewhere and the ration ship was delayed and for six months you fed your troops out of your own pocket? Real admirable. Especially considering you came from a poor but honest family.'

Mahoney's father and grandfather before him had first been fairly high ranking officers and then made comfortable second and third careers in civilian megacorporations.

'I say again my last. Why?'

'Maybe the twinkle in your Irish eyes,' the Emperor suggested. 'Or maybe because I've got the Tahn in a reactive situation and am grinding it in.

'By the way. That wasn't a breach of security. We – or rather you – *are* going against the Fringe Worlds. With every ship and troopie I can strip out of other sectors. And I want the Tahn to know about it.

'Their prestige isn't doing too good these days, what with Lord Fehrle happening to have gotten dead and their legions getting obliterated.

'The Tahn believe in symbols. I'm giving them one.

'Every clottin' 'cast that goes out is talking about how important those clottin' Fringe Worlds are to the Empire and to me personally. There is no way those imbeciles aren't going to take the bait.'

The Emperor, having made one of his longer private statements, found it necessary to have a drink or two.

'So I'm part of the symbol?'

'Yep. You'll notice, if you do any reading besides Op orders, that I went and stole colorful bits from at least three old-time generals. And the hype is going to get worse.

'You see, Mahoney, we're going to win. Soon.

'Which brings up the question of what we're going to do with all these clottin' Tahn worlds. Rykor had a suggestion. Seems there's some types who respect the clot out of somebody who beats hell out of them.'

Mahoney shook his head. 'Don't understand that, sir. My dad always said the only people who fight and make up are tinkers and Englishmen. Whatever they are.'

'Yeah. That's the way I've always operated, too,' the Emperor agreed. 'But we aren't Tahn.

'So you're going out to the Fringe Worlds. The Tahn are going to throw everything at you they can, and you're going to be my little Imperial meat grinder.

'Couple of side notes that might help you. We'll use Naha as a forward strike base into the Tahn worlds. So you'll be able to access a good left hook if you need it.

'Another thing. Seems there's this terrible conspiracy going on in the Tahn worlds.'

Mahoney looked interested, if disbelieving.

'Said conspiracy is composed of a whole cluster of Tahn officers who maybe have been recorded as not being happy with the way the war's not being run.

'We can thank our friend Sten for discovering all these quote traitors endquote.'

Both men grinned – unpleasantly.

'He built me a conspiracy and sent it forward. Now, some of my – pardon, the Tahn's – most trusted agents are leaking that conspiracy back. Category One intelligence and all that.

'Where were we?

'Oh, yeah. You've just finished slaughtering every Tahn that shows up in the Fringe Worlds with a chip on her shoulder. So next, when we make the final assault into the Tahn worlds themselves, you'll be in charge.

'Don't plan on any long vacations after the war's over, either. Because I'm going to put you in as – hell, maybe I'll call it governor-general – for their whole stinkin' ex-empire. At which point you'll have ten years or so trying to teach the Tahn how to pretend they're human.'

Mahoney meditated. Finally, he laughed. 'Great stew, boss. Now all we have to do is catch the rabbit.'

'Exactly,' the Emperor agreed. 'Do me a favor, Ian. Don't get your butt whipped out there in the Fringe Worlds. I don't want to have to start planning from day one all over.'

Chapter Forty-Seven

The members of the Tahn High Council gloomed their way to order. The elder secretary droned through the final draft of Lord Fehrle's official obituary. When he finished, the first order of business would be the vote for approval and then scheduling it for broadcast.

The second order of business would be the vote for Fehrle's successor. What would happen next was anybody's guess.

The king is dead, Pastour thought sourly. Long live the king.

He looked at the tight, guarded faces of his twenty-six colleagues. They were all holding their cards nipple-close to their chests. But Pastour already knew the outcome. He had counted the votes. Wichman's faction of nine was backing Atago. No surprise there. Wichman was in love with the trappings of war. And even among the military-minded Tahn, no single being shone more as a soldier than the Lady Atago.

The second faction – of equal size – favored a troika composed of various candidates but with Atago, Wichman, and Pastour mentioned most often. That left Pastour and his faction: another nine votes, nine swing votes to be played any way he chose. But there was no question in Pastour's mind on how to play the hand. All he had to do was wait through the endless droning of the late Lord Fehrle's accomplishments.

Sten had visited him again in his garden a few nights after Fehrle's death. Pastour did not know how he had gotten in – Sten had not used the drain again. The clot just seemed to appear out of the shadows of one of Pastour's most prized trees. As soon as he had spotted him, Pastour's Tahn emotions had jumped like a crown fire from frightened surprise to pure hating anger over Fehrle's assassination.

'Don't be stupid, Colonel,' Sten had warned him. 'The last thing your people need right now is a stupid man for a leader. A dead stupid man.'

Pastour had pulled himself back. 'What do you want this time?'

Sten had relaxed then. He had tucked his weapon away and hoisted himself up on his perch. It was a casual action, but Pastour realized that it was carefully calculated to eliminate any hint of threat from his body language.

'First of all, I heard about the changes at Koldyeze. I wanted to thank you for that.'

Pastour shrugged. 'There's nothing to thank me for. Nothing you said influenced me. It was the logical course.'

'If that's how you want to think about it, Colonel, fine. We were just worried about some friends. Doesn't matter how they were taken care of. Just as long as it was done.

'Although I did notice some refinements from our discussion. A lot of new faces. Important new faces. I assume you're planning to use them as a hole card. If so, I've got to warn you. It won't work.'

Pastour could not help showing his curiosity. 'Are you telling me that if we held a gun to their heads, we couldn't win *some* concessions from your Emperor?'

'It'll just make him hit you harder,' Sten said. 'Believe me. I speak from long and very personal experience. The only thing you get out of the Emperor if you threaten him is a lot of bloody stumps.'

Pastour understood. That was also the way of the Tahn. Perhaps that was where they had gone wrong years before. The public image of the Emperor was kindly, concerned, that of a vigorous and handsome young uncle with wisdom well beyond his visible age. But that was obviously a falsehood. Perhaps the Emperor was more Tahnlike than the Tahn themselves.

Pastour wondered how bloody the Emperor's vengeance would be if the prisoners – especially the important prisoners – of Koldyeze came to harm. Pastour shuddered for his people. He knew what *he* would do if he were in the Emperor's place.

He pulled himself back. Sten was studying him as if he were seeing Pastour's thoughts form and dissolve and reform.

'Koldyeze is not why you're here,' Pastour said flatly.

'No. That's only part of it.'

Sten slid off his perch and started pacing up and down the aisle, casually peering at the plants in their hydroponic trays. 'The Emperor is concerned about what's going to happen to you people next. Now that Fehrle is dead. Who's going to take over? Who will he have to deal with?'

'I imagine he would be,' Pastour said, not bothering to hide his sarcasm. 'I suppose he thinks we're just going to roll over and play dead. Like those old livies. The warrior chieftain is killed. The tribe loses its heart to fight. Another war won and over.'

'If you think that,' Sten said, 'then you really don't know my boss. I imagine what's really on his mind is how many more of you he'll have to kill before you people finally realize you've lost.

'You do know you've lost, don't you?'

The question caught Pastour by surprise – mainly because he had been dodging it in his own mind for some time. And now he had to answer it. It was as if a great black storm cloud had been ripped open and he was standing under its emotional deluge. Defeat. Surrender. Humiliation. But, yes. They had lost. It was over, but there was nothing Pastour could do to stop the insanity. He could not bring himself to speak and only nodded.

'Then all you can do now is fight for what happens after the surrender,' Sten said. 'Peace with honor and all that diplomatic double-talk. What your people need very badly is a true leader who can deal with the Emperor and still guard the honor of the Tahn.'

'And the Emperor thinks that person is me? Not a chance. I haven't the votes – assuming I was willing, of course.'

'Assuming you were willing,' Sten agreed. Both men realized that Pastour had just stepped over the line with that hedging phrase.

'Here's how the Emperor sees it,' Sten continued. 'The only clear leader anyone can hang a reputation on is Lady Atago. But she has too many enemies on the council to win the vote.

'Second is for there to be some kind of patched-together leadership group of compromise candidates. Say, Atago and one each from the major factions. I imagine your name would be on any such list.'

Pastour knew it would. 'And third?'

'There is no third,' Sten said. 'Only those two choices. And frankly, the way I personally see it, nothing ever came of group leadership. It tends to lead to costly blunders. No one is ever willing to take the blame, so nothing is ever done. Or you end up with political civil war, with no one in charge.'

'I agree,' Pastour said.

'Then the only logical choice,' Sten said, 'is Lady Atago.'

Pastour could not believe what he was hearing. Sten was right, of course, but why would the Emperor back someone who had to be his greatest and most fervent enemy among the Tahn? Lady Atago was so single-minded that . . . And then he got it. That was just the quality – or weakness, depending on one's point of view – the Emperor needed.

It was like isolating a cancer that then could be simply and easily removed. Atago would lead the Tahn to final defeat. Someone else would hand over the sword. And the Eternal Emperor was betting that someone else would be Pastour.

'He *must* understand that I am no traitor,' Pastour insisted, striking the bargain. 'You must impress that on him.'

'I will,' Sten promised.

Then he turned away, moving toward the shadows. But just before he ducked out of sight, Sten turned back.

'Oh, I almost forgot. How's your health?'

'Excellent,' Pastour said, wondering what the clot Sten was talking about.

'I wouldn't be too sure of that,' Sten said. 'If I were you, after the vote, I'd develop something lingering and nasty enough to warrant a long, well-deserved rest. Out of the line of fire.'

Pastour had still been reacting to that mysterious bit of advice when he had realized that Sten was gone.

The elder secretary had finished reading and was calling for the first order of business. Atago and Wichman were glaring around at the other members of the council, sure they had a bitter fight on their hands. Pastour knew that all the private overtures they had made had been rebuffed and that they were resigned to a rare around-the-table battle. Pastour had carefully kept his people quietly neutral. The word was that they would vote for whoever the clear winner was. But there *could* be no clear winner. As soon as Atago lost the vote, the troika proposal would carry the day.

At least that was the conventional wisdom of the bean counters. The count began on Atago's side of the table. It would move through Pastour and his group, then the troika faction. The first nine 'affirms' went swiftly. Then it was time for Pastour's vote.

'Abstain,' the elder secretary said automatically. 'Next?'

'Excuse me,' Pastour said. 'I haven't spoken yet.'

The elder secretary peered at him, wondering what was going on.

'I don't want to abstain,' Pastour said. 'I want to vote affirmative.'

His words were met by instant shock – and then excitement, as everyone realized what had just happened. There was a babble of voices and a plea for order, and then the vote flashed the rest of the way around the table.

In a moment it was unanimous, and Lady Atago was affirmed as the new leader of the Tahn High Council. The victory came so swiftly and so surprisingly that the gloom dropped from everyone's shoulders. Fehrle was forgotten, and the council members were pounding each other on the shoulders and generally congratulating themselves for their political wisdom.

They had a leader. It was time to face the enemy again.

'One question, my lady,' one member of the council broke in. 'The Imperial news reports are filled with stories about Imperial Fleet Marshal Ian Mahoney. He's sworn to return to the Fringe Worlds. Retake Cavite. How do you plan to deal with him? Or is it too early to say?'

Atago rose to her full, substantial height. Leadership glowed from her like a mythical aura – the stuff heroes were made of.

'I welcome him to try,' Atago said. 'I've beaten him before. Badly. In fact I took Cavite *and* the Fringe Worlds over his blasted and bleeding body. And this time I'd be glad to finish the job.'

There were cheers all around, with one exception: Pastour. He poked up a finger for recognition. Atago could not help giving him a hate-cdgcd glance. She did not know why he had backed her, but she expected that the price would be high. Then she caught herself, and the expression changed to a grim smile.

'Yes, Colonel?'

'Why is the Emperor putting so much importance on the Fringe Worlds? To me they no longer seem to be a particularly strategic target. Are we sure it's not just a ploy? To force us to commit?'

'Of course it is,' Lady Atago said. 'They're making it seem important so that any victory they win there will appear to take on greater meaning than it in fact would have.'

'Then, if we react,' Pastour said, 'aren't we in danger of turning fiction into reality?'

'Only if they beat us,' Atago said. 'And I promise you that can't happen. I've proved it once, and I'll do it again. And we'll turn the Emperor's sword back on himself.'

With that promise, Lady Atago double-thought her way into taking the Emperor's bait. And Pastour fully understood the Emperor's strategy. The only thing still puzzling him was Sten's odd comment about his health.

'Now for the next order of business,' Lady Atago went on. 'I have here a list. A very important list. It was stolen by our agents from Imperial files.'

The council members looked at the printout she was holding in her hand. She was waving it at them like some kind of accusation.

'On it are seventy-two names. Tahn names. Traitors. And I ask full authority to purge them from our midst. And that's only the start. I want to follow their trail to wherever it might lead. No matter how high the traitor, no matter how . . .'

Pastour tried an experimental first cough.

Chapter Forty-Eight

The cafeteria had several advantages, but they were not visible to normal citizens. To them, the large converted storage building stank of grease and the unwashed, and it was up a side street in a very bad part of the port city of Soward. It looked like a very good place to get either ptomaine or a shank inserted between the third and fourth ribs.

That was an accurate summation.

But it did have very definite advantages: It was not automated. Instead, it was run by living beings who really did not care what happened so long as the blood was mopped up afterward. Caff was a tenth-credit, and alk a half-credit. The alk, of course, had never seen an Imperial tax stamp.

Anyone was welcome to hang out as long as he, she, or it wanted.

A cup of caff could be nursed for half a day, and no one would object. It was an excellent place to make an illegal drug deal, plan a job, or just hang out, as an alternative to sitting in one's apartment, letting the four walls close in.

To Chapelle, the cafeteria had still other advantages.

He could stare for hours at the blank concrete building across the street and listen to the voices. Every day he learned of a new iniquity and injustice caused by the Emperor.

Sullamora's operating team had removed the subaudible projectors weeks earlier. Chapelle listened to voices of his own making, and the stories they told were fascinating.

A few days earlier, he had realized that he *had* to do something. Just what, he was not sure. The only possibility he could think of was the cafeteria's other advantage – its proximity to the Democratic Education Center.

Any war, no matter how 'just,' had opponents. Opposition ranged from true pacifism, through a quite logical reluctance to get one's ass shot off for any reason whatsoever, and on into less savory areas.

It was a constant battle for the Emperor to keep his intelligence organizations somewhat under control. Someone who merely thought – or even said – that the Eternal Emperor was full of drakh was not a danger to society, the Emperor had to remind his CI types.

It was a nice theory. At present, however, it was not widely practiced. Freedom of speech, like many other civil liberties, was not encouraged at that time. There were many thousand dissenters, who had merely mildly suggested that the Eternal Emperor did not have all the answers, and were spending the war in internment centers.

The Democratic Education Center was something else entirely. Its philosophy was very simple: that the Empire had overreacted to the Tahn and that more peaceful means could have been used. Before the war the center had lobbied for Imperial funding to establish other centers within the Tahn Empire. The good people of the society believed that truth would win out – once a Tahn, no matter what his class, was shown that his society was inhumane, that society would be changed. Fortunately, funding was not granted, and none of the theorists ended up as missionary stew.

The Tahn being what they were, they had loudly welcomed the existence of the Democratic Education Centers as long as they were all located on Imperial worlds. And they had promptly used the organization as a front.

All the active agents had been rounded up at that point, of course. But the center continued to exist – at the Emperor's teeth-gritted acceptance. The organization provided an excellent means of locating future dissidents and was riddled with Imperial Intelligence operatives. Imperial Intelligence did not realize that if it were not for their own agents, the center would have gone bankrupt years earlier. Even a front organization required regular dues paying, and very few of the center's members were considered politically employable at anything above the janitorial level.

Chapelle had known of the center for some time. How he had learned about it, he was not sure. The information, of course, had been planted in an early subaudible broadcast.

Not that Sullamora actually wanted Chapelle to join the organization. But once the man had reached that decision, the fourth stage of his education could begin.

The problem was that Chapelle appeared to be somewhat brighter than Sullamora's profile would have suggested. Even though Chapelle was a näif, he had somehow thought that the evil Emperor's agents might have penetrated the center. His walking through that door, Chapelle knew, would be his death. The Emperor would use that as an excuse to grab and torture Chapelle and then put him into a lethal chamber, just as the voices had told him had happened to millions of others.

But there appeared to be no alternative, Chapelle brooded.

Realizing there was somebody standing beside his table, Chapelle brought himself back and cowered. Not that he had ever been threatened in the cafeteria – the other patrons realized that it was very unlikely that Chapelle had anything worth stealing. Plus there was a certain sheen in his eye that suggested that even pushing the man around for sport could produce unpleasant ramifications.

The man did not belong in this dive, Chapelle thought; in fact, he belonged even less than Chapelle did. He was older. Gray-haired. Soberly and expensively dressed. Chapelle wondered why the man had not been instantly jackrolled, then eyed the bulging muscles and the barely visible scar on the man's neck. No. The man was not an easy target.

The man looked sternly at Chapelle. 'You don't belong here,' he said flatly.

Chapelle stammered – and the man suddenly smiled.

'I don't, either. But I seem to have a problem.'

Somehow, unasked, he was sitting across from Chapelle.

'My problem is that I'm lost.' He laughed – a rich bass laugh that showed a man who had learned the vagaries of the world and appreciated them. 'I thought that just because I still had that built-in compass I could find my way around a city. Wrong again, Colonel General Suvorov.'

Chapelle gaped. 'You're a *general*?'

'Forty years. Pioneer Development Corps. Retired. Guess it's a courtesy title now. At least the clottin' Empire hasn't figured out a way to take *that* away from me, too. Or at least not yet.

'At any rate, I'm new here on Prime World. Thought I knew my way around. Got lost. Looked for somebody who might be able to help. Everybody I saw looked like the only help they'd give me is into a dark alley.

'Except you.'

Chapelle was embarrassed.

'I'd be grateful,' the man who called himself Suvorov said, 'if I could get a guide back to the nearest pneumostation and out of this slum.'

Chapelle was only too grateful to volunteer.

At the station Suvorov checked the schedule and muttered. 'Typical. Very typical.' He elaborated – the first pneumo-subway run out to where he had rented quarters was an hour away. 'Talk about your bureaucracies. Makes sense not to schedule runs out to where people who can pay live. But not when you've blocked all the gravcabs out of business.

'Wartime contingencies.

'You know, Sr. Chapelle, and I probably shouldn't be saying this to a stranger, but this is sure a good example of the way the Emperor thinks.'

Chapelle nodded eagerly.

'Although,' Suvorov went on, 'you'd have to have been out on some of the Pioneer Sectors to see what it's really like. Out where there aren't any laws. Except the kind one person makes.

'And out there, you better not talk too loudly about things like that.

'Guess I was lucky. All that happened to me was I got requested to resign. And then the agrofarm I'd built up got requisitioned by the Imperial Quartermaster Corps.

'Why I'm here on Prime. Hoping I'd be able to get my toady rep to do something. Should've known better. He's been bought and sold so many times, he ought to have his soul in for a rebuild.

'Sorry. Man doesn't respect somebody whining.'

During the wait, it was very natural for Suvorov to buy Chapelle a meal at a very expensive restaurant – and express amazement when he found out that Chapelle was an ex-landing controller.

'Did a lot of things. Have to, when you're out on the frontiers. But I could never handle all the things you people have to keep in your mind.' He paused. 'Not prying . . . but what the hell are you doing stuck down there in that slum? You don't have to answer.'

Chapelle did, of course.

Suvorov was aghast. 'Guess you feel sorry for yourself for not having shoes till you run across the man with prosthetics,' he said. 'You really got the shaft.'

He ordered a second bottle of wine.

Chapelle, being a near-teetotaler even when he had credits, got a little drunk. And so did Suvorov.

'You know, Chapelle,' he said over dessert. 'One thing I'm sorry I never had was a son. Nothing left behind once I'm gone.

'Clotting Emperor – sorry for the language – is going to make sure of that.'

They had brandies, and he called for the bill.

Outside the restaurant, Suvorov looked at Chapelle and apologized. He had gotten his guide and new friend drunk. It sure as hell would not be safe for the young man to go down those mean streets in his condition.

Chapelle should come stay with him. Hell, that clotting mansion he was leasing had room for a whole recon force.

Chapelle, stomach and mind full, found it easy to agree.

He also found it easy to agree the next day when Suvorov suggested that Chapelle might consider staying on. 'Guess we both know I need a guide around this clotting planet. Besides, you're easy to talk to, son.

'I really like what you've been telling me about the Emperor. Learning a lot, I am.'

Six weeks later Suvorov presented Chapelle with a willygun – and showed him the previously sealed shooting gallery below the mansion.

Chapter Forty-Nine

Lady Atago's headquarters/home was as Spartan and single-purpose as her mind. The furnishings were sparse and deliberately uncomfortable. It was not a place for lounging but for quick decision making. Aides came with their reports, sat on hard nervous edges for her decision or comments, and then were quickly gone, to be replaced by others.

The only thing on her desk was a small, framed fading fax print of the Eternal Emperor. She kept it there to focus herself constantly on her enemy. Atago would have been mildly surprised to learn that her opponent had done something similar; her picture had recently gone up in place of Lord Fehrle's in the Eternal Emperor's office.

On the far black-glass wall was a constantly changing map of the disputed areas. The Imperial positions were in red, the Tahn in green. The green areas had been swiftly dwindling of late, pinching in from the sides, with a red spearhead driving toward the Fringe Worlds. Even Erebus, that distant system Lady Atago had single-handedly turned into one of the great war factories of history, was firmly in Imperial control.

In any age Lady Atago would have been considered a military genius. And since Fehrle's death she had been poring over the battle map, desperately searching for an unexpected blow that would reverse the tide.

Although she had never heard of the man, Atago would have known and approved of Napoleon's decision to land 35,000 troops in Egypt, seemingly far from the main contest. And she would have been dismayed at his failed attempts to flank Britain in Ireland. The reasoning was sound; it was only the application that had gone wrong. And, as happened to many great generals, it was the details that were overwhelming her. The only thing that was clear to her was that whatever the target, she had to set the stage first. She needed a victory, and she needed it badly.

The only place she could see such a victory coming was in the Fringe Worlds. The most frustrating thing about that was that she had to wait for the Emperor to play the card before she could attempt to trump him. And Lady Atago was too much of a Tahn to be good at playing a waiting game.

Adding to that frustration was the constant barking of her aides, calling her attention to this, bemoaning that, and continually demanding that she concentrate on the bottom line. Early that morning, for example, her financial advisers had descended, warning her of the empty treasury and waving demands for payments from allies and neutrals alike.

'Tell them to wait,' she had said angrily. 'I haven't heard of any Imperial bankers dunning the Emperor. And this war has to be costing him five or six times what it's costing us.'

'That's different,' one adviser had said. 'The Emperor has a financial history. We don't. Besides, he's fighting on borrowed funds at three percent interest. We're fighting at upwards of fifty percent.'

Lady Atago did not know whether to scream for the adviser's instant execution or to cry, although crying was something no Tahn did easily. It wounded her soldier's soul that this conflict could boil down to something so filthy as money. But the advisers assured her that all was not lost.

After the Fringe Worlds battle – assuming victory – they would be able to bargain for much better terms, and the money tap would be turned on again. But for the time being, the only thing she could do was order the seizure, stripping, and selling of everything of value.

Her advisers did not dare tell her that there was almost nothing left. Even the plas inner walls and insulation in the meanest of Tahn dwellings had already been carried away by the tax collectors and sold for scrap.

And so, blocked from action at every corner, Lady Atago turned inward. If she could not yet fight, she would put the Tahn house in order. At the top of her agenda was the leaked list of seventy-two traitors. She attacked the problem with cold glee. The Tahn military police were already sweeping them up.

Along with the seventy-two they were arresting anyone connected with those foul beings. Not only that, but more and more names were surfacing daily. Lady Atago realized that some of the victims were innocent – their names appeared merely because they had made the wrong enemies. But that was a fact she was willing to live with. Besides, she had a list of those who were providing the names. She was already ordering police visits to those homes. Filling the jails and military tribunals with suspects was providing an outlet for her frustrations. It was a new and different kind of body count, and she pursued it with relish.

And so it was a flushed and glowing Lady Atago who ushered Wichman into her office. If only the livies could capture this, he had thought as she greeted him. She was beautiful and sensuous and deadly – every millimeter of her tall, flowing form was that of a great Tahn hero. To see her, to be near her, was to realize that the current difficulties were momentary, that victory must eventually fall to the righteous.

The purpose of Lord Wichman's visit was to aid Atago in ferreting out wrong-thinkers. He came armed with Lo Prek's steadily mounting evidence of criminality and corruption on Heath.

Lo Prek had examined thousands of police and intelligence log entries and had sifted out evidence that Heath was in the grip of a wave of crime and dissidence. Moreover, he had tracked many of the crimes that appeared to be minor hooliganisms back to the bureaucracies and officials responsible. That many of the tarnished were in fact blameless did not matter, because Lo Prek had uncovered a pattern that led to the flawless conclusion that an Imperial conspiracy was behind the crime wave.

Lo Prek was correct in every detail, including the fact that Sten was not only behind that conspiracy but directing it. That was the only point that Wichman disbelieved and for the moment withheld from Lady Atago. When Lo Prek had haltingly spelled out his findings, Wichman had only buried a smile at the man's obsession.

If the carrot of the mythical Sten produced such results, Wichman would only encourage him. Just because Lo Prek was insane, it did not necessarily follow that he was stupid.

As Lady Atago leafed through the printout with growing enthusiasm, Wichman congratulated himself on his foresight in roping Lo Prek into his organization.

'This is exactly what we need, my lord,' Atago said. 'I admire your dedication. If only a few others . . . I must confess, some of the members of the High Council are disappointing me.

'They only do what is absolutely necessary. They take nothing upon themselves. No extra effort. Sometimes I wonder if they expect me to fight this whole thing alone.'

Wichman preened but quickly made half-hearted noises of support for his colleagues. Lady Atago waved him down.

'Take Pastour, for example,' she said. 'He's practically gone into retirement. I know he's ill, but . . . Oh, well. I suppose we should be grateful for his support. And at least he's continuing his work at Koldyeze. An amazingly successful program. Personally, I never held out much for it. Expecting prisoners – cowards and malcontents all – to perform that well. In fact, according to the latest data, all previous performance records have been broken.'

The data she was referring to had all come from Sten and Virunga's Golden Worm. Mickied figures were hiding what was in reality a dismal performance that had only worsened as the Tahn shipped captured dignitaries to Koldyeze.

The thought of Koldyeze darkened Wichman's mood. It did not help that the people he had placed there grudgingly supported the data that so impressed Lady Atago. Still, he firmly believed that if he were in control at Koldyeze, he would be able to find far better uses for the prisoners. Especially now that it housed the best and the brightest of the Imperial prisoners. Sometimes he was awakened by dreams of what he would do to them. He never remembered the details of the dreams, only that they were pleasurable.

Lady Atago brought him back to his good mood and the business at hand. 'I wonder if I could impose myself on you, my lord?'

Wichman made self-deprecating sounds. Atago ignored him. She tapped the report compiled by Lo Prek.

'I would like you to assume command of this program,' she said. 'I've not been pleased with the results of the sweeps so far. So many seem to be slipping through the net.

'I have been finding myself distrusting the officials responsible for carrying out my aims. And from the information you have gathered here, I may have good reason. There may be more than laziness and inefficiency behind their lack of performance.'

Wichman did not know what to say. He was too overcome by emotion. To think that his efforts met favor with a hero the like of Lady Atago! He gladly accepted the new responsibilities. Also, not too far in the back of his mind was the realization of just how much power had been handed him.

Just as he was regaining his composure and was about to thank her, Atago broke in with a new thought.

'There seems to be one thing missing, however,' she said as she folded up Lo Prek's study. 'There is a clearly indicated trail here. But it seems to stop short. It's as if something, or someone, has been left out.'

Lady Atago was right. The only part of the report Wichman had excised was the man Lo Prek believed responsible for the conspiracy: Sten. Wichman took a deep breath and then plunged in. He explained about Lo Prek and about the little being's belief that the person behind it all was also the being responsible for the murder of his brother. Lady Atago nodded as he talked. Lo Prek was clearly mad, but as a Tahn she could understand his obsession for revenge.

'Who is this man?' she finally asked.

Wichman told her.

Lady Atago frowned. The name was familiar. 'Sten?' she asked. 'Would that be a Commander Sten?'

Wichman said it was but wondered how she knew the rank. But he did not ask, because her face had suddenly gone blank. As if she was remembering something.

The Forez *was vomiting fire. Firing everything – anything – to stop the* Swampscott. *Lady Atago leaned over Admiral Deska, gaping in amazement at the damage the enemy ship was taking. There seemed to be little left, and even as she watched, huge hunks of the* Swampscott *were being hurled away into space as Deska's guns and missiles hammered, hammered, hammered. But still, the* Swampscott's *chainguns kept firing. Wild communications, monitored by her probes, told her that Commander Sten was the ship's CO. Over and over, Deska killed the ship, but it kept coming in.*

Then she heard the strangest voice mocking her. 'Ah hae y' noo, lass.' She would never know that the voice was that of Sten's second in command, Alex Kilgour. And then the chortle became two Vydals spearing out from the oddness that was the Swampscott. *The* Forez *was racked by the explosion. The blast tore a wall chart from a bulkhead and sent it spinning into Admiral Deska. His eviscerated corpse slammed into her, and she was falling back – back, back, into darkness. Later, when she had resumed consciousness, she had fought off her nurses and sent a boarding party to the* Swampscott. *She wanted the names of everyone aboard the ship – living or dead.*

Atago personally checked through the ID discs until she found the correct one. Sten. And then she carefully wiped the blood away to make sure.

'The man's insane, all right,' Lady Atago finally said to Wichman. 'Sten is dead. I killed him myself.'

Then she remembered something else.

'Twice.' The word was a whisper.

'Pardon, my lady?'

'Twice. I killed him once before. And then he came back. And I killed him again.' She shuddered, pushing away the ghosts.

A moment later, Wichman found himself being ushered gently out the door. He left, his ardor for his heroine uncooled. Still, he could not help wondering at the demons, or demon, who troubled Lady Atago's sleep.

Chapter Fifty

Sten forced his body to fit the slight depression that was the only cover for 100 meters on either side of him. The prison searchlight swept across the barren landscape, methodically exploding deep shadows into light. To Sten, it seemed to hesitate a beat just before it crossed over his curled form. It was as if a living mind, rather than a computer, controlled it. Sten felt himself tense as insane thoughts flashed through his mind: Did someone know he was there? A gloating someone who was toying with him? Had there been a tip-off? Would the light suddenly stop on him, and then a dozen laughing Tahn guards jump out of the darkness to drag him into Koldyeze for a few years of solitary confinement, periodic torture, and then execution? Sten ran an old Mantis Section mantra through his mind and felt his pulse slow to normal and his breathing ease.

The light passed over him without incident.

Sten lifted his head and peered into the darkness. He pushed his senses up the series of gradual rises and then the steep hill that led to the rear of Koldyeze and his own private back entrance. Nothing.

Still, he could feel his hackles rise at the thought of pulling aside the camouflage that covered the entrance and re-entering the tunnel.

Then he would crawl into the catacombs beneath Koldyeze. And finally he would be back in prison!

Alex had protested when Sten announced his plan to personally touch base with Virunga. There was nothing to worry about, Sten had reassured his friend. He would be in and out before dawn.

'Y'r stir-crazy a' me, lad,' Alex had said. 'Ah nae hae kenned th' hae wee symptoms. When Ah wae but kilt-hem high, m' mum gie me three warnings: Nae play a' cards wi' ae bonny lass—' At that he had shot St. Clair a grin full of Kilgour charm. '—nae eat ae a place called Campbell's, and nae go inta a room wi' brawny bars ae its door!'

Clot! Sten thought. Kilgour's mum was right! What was he thinking of? His body temperature dropped to zero at even the prospect of another long stretch of forced confinement. It was at that point, as he hesitated between going on and calling the whole thing off, that he heard footsteps. And then humming. It was a Tahn sentry. Freezing was no trouble at all.

Sten hugged the depression, turning his head just slightly to the side so that he could see – a cautious hunter's peep he had learned in Mantis basic. You never tested your quarry's instincts by looking directly at him.

Only to the sides of him, young Sten, he warned himself, and then only for a tick at a time. He saw that the sentry's path would bisect his hiding place only a half meter or so from his head. The sentry's steps were slow, ambling.

He or she was badly trained, lazy, or just plain vanilla stupid. As the sentry approached, the humming grew louder. Sten, recognizing it as a popular Tahn war-crossed lover's ballad always in demand from the lower-class crowds at St. Clair's club, chose a combination of all three.

Then he felt a heavy boot-heel crush his fingers and resisted the temptation to snatch his outstretched hand away. The sentry paused, and agony smashed up Sten's arm as the Tahn turned slightly to the side – grinding Sten's fingers even further – and stopped.

There was the fumbling of a heavy greatcoat and then blinding pain as the sentry shifted most of the weight to the foot, jamming Sten's hand into the ground. Sudden relief flooded in as the Tahn stepped away, still fumbling with clothing, then more pain as the blood forced itself through crushed capillaries and veins.

Sten sensed that the sentry's back was turned to him. His head rose slightly, and he saw something large and pale peering at him. It was the sentry's naked behind.

From the splashing sounds on the ground, it was pretty obvious what she was doing. As she rose from the squatting position, adjusting her uniform, Sten curled his fingers, and his knife dropped from the surgical sheath in his arm. Its slim coldness in his palm comforted him.

Then he sensed startled motion. He had been discovered! Sten shot up like a great sea beast with a head full of glittering fangs rising above the surface of the water.

Numb fingers of one hand reached for her throat, and his knife hand drove at her abdomen. For one brief flash, Sten saw the sentry's face. She was young, no more than sixteen. And slender – no, skinny. So skinny that she looked like a poor, scrawny bird with flapping greatcoat wings. The eyes that widened just before death were filled with innocence and terror. A child, but a child who was about to die just the same.

It was prudence, not pity, that saved the girl's life. It was because there was no time to hide the body that Sten held back just before the knife plunged its needle length into her. Instead, he took a chance that his numbed fingers would work before she could scream.

He pinched the artery that cut off the flow of blood to her brain and then caught her in his arms as she collapsed. He lowered her carefully to the ground, fished in his pocket for a bester grenade, pulled the pin, covered, and blanked her memory.

There would be hell to pay when her sergeant found her on his next rounds. She would be cuddled up softly on the ground, sleeping the sleep of the blessed. The beating the sergeant would administer for sleeping on duty would be awful. But what were a few cracked ribs compared to a pile of pale guts glistening in the starlight?

Sten made sure the young sentry was comfortable, then slithered on up the hill, the ghost of her song humming softly in his head.

The chair groaned in protest as Virunga's 300-kilo-plus body rocked in mirth. Sten was catching him up on the war news. Although he tried not to paint a too-glowing picture of things, he could not help pumping up a morsel into a soufflé here and there for the hope-starved N'Ranya.

There was also a great deal of information about Sten's current activities on Heath that he was forced to censor on a need-to-know basis. And so, when he had the opportunity to embellish, he did, knowing that Virunga would do some censoring of his own when he filled in the others on Sten's visit. At the moment Sten was telling his old CO about St. Clair and L'n's adventures, exaggerating only a bit.

'. . . and so, there they were, General Lunga, his two aides, and at least a dozen joys of both sexes, and a couple in between, when they get the call.

'Priority One. Ears only. And all that rot. So the general shoos the whole shebang out. Punches in a supersecure line on his porta-com, and half a belch later he's on a direct to some muckity-muck aide to Atago herself.

'The aide double-checks. Is everything A-okay? No keen little ears hiding in a closet? The general looks around, then gives the guy an all-clear. The general gets his orders. He's to get his big-brass Tahn butt to the Fringe Worlds not yesterday but the day before yesterday. Big things are coming down.

'The general does a little lightweight protesting. Already heavy duties and that sort of thing. Meaning brass or no, he expects to get his previously reported butt shot off out there.

'There's a big long discussion. Pros and cons of ship and troop movements. A small shouting match. The general loses and storms out, his two boot shiners in tow.

'Of course, what he doesn't realize is that we've taken the whole thing down. Heard every word!'

'The . . . room . . . bugged,' Virunga said flatly, knowledgeably.

'Not a chance,' Sten said. 'That room is permanently leased for the general's pleasures. His people run a sweep through before he comes and after he leaves.'

'So how—'

'L'n,' Sten said. 'She heard the whole thing. The entire time the general was talking, she was curled up in the corner. Right in plain sight. You see, the general thinks she's just a pet. A largish, pinkish, cattish-type pet.'

Virunga laughed again. But then the laughter cut off in mid-chortle. 'Are . . . you positive all . . . this is good for . . . her? L'n is so . . .' His words trailed off not out of linguistic patterns but because of a lack of vocabulary for what L'n had to be witnessing daily.

'Innocent? Sheltered? Sensitive?' Sten filled it in for him. Virunga nodded.

'Not anymore,' Sten said. 'You wouldn't believe the change. She made the jump from Koldyeze to freedom and landed on all four of her pretty little feet. Even Michele – I mean, St. Clair – is surprised how she's blossomed. She sounds like a dockworker now.

Or a pro thief. It's cheena, and sus, and a pretty good use of drakh
and clot when she needs them.'

Virunga marveled at that. He was soaking up everything Sten
said as if he were personally living each word. After his own years
as a prisoner of war, Sten understood that, just as he knew that in
a few days the euphoria would die and be replaced by deep depression. And the great walls of Koldyeze would press in even more.
Then Virunga – along with the others whom he chose to tell about
Sten – would start doubting if he would ever live to be free again.
And the chances were, Sten thought, that the doubters would be
right. He knew the war would end soon, but he could offer no
guarantees on the fate of the Koldyeze prisoners in the melee that
was sure to precede the Tahn's last fighting gasp.

But Sten had a plan – a plan that would do more than just
relieve a little of the depression. It was a plan designed not only
to save as many prisoners' lives as possible but also to hand any
Imperial invasion force a small edge in the battle for Heath. It
would not be a fifth ace. No, not that good. But it just might be
a fifth face card of some kind. And there was a glimmer that it
might even fill an inside straight.

You gotta quit thinking like Michele, Sten told himself. I mean,
St. Clair. Like an imp, her lush form popped into his mind. Soft
fingers. Even softer lips. Tingling whispers in his ear. Knock it off,
Commander. Uh, Admiral, that is. Keep your mind on business.
Remember, you're a high-ranking officer now.

Still, Admiral Sten had to bury a grin and cross one leg over
the other. Thankfully, Virunga interrupted his thoughts.

'What . . . was . . . name of . . . Michele's – I mean . . . St.
Clair's . . . casino again?'

Sten looked closer at Virunga. Had he guessed? The blank
expression on the big, beetle-browed face gave no clue.

'The K'ton Klub,' Sten said. 'Why?'

'Oh . . . I just . . . didn't know . . . the young woman had . . .
knowledge of . . . music.'

'I didn't know you did, either,' Sten said, mildly surprised.

'Yes . . . Oh . . . yes. I do. Although I . . . cannot . . . enjoy any
longer.' He tapped his ears. 'Tone-deaf . . . now. An old . . . artillery-
being's . . . complaint. The guns . . . deadened . . . the ears. But when
. . . I was . . . young. I very much . . . enjoyed the . . . music. I even
. . . played . . .' He fingered an imaginary instrument. 'A little . . .
The saxophone. Not . . . the synth-sax . . . But . . . with the . . .
reed. A real . . . reed. It sounded . . . so . . . Ah. I cannot . . . describe.'

There was silence as Battery Commander (Lieutenant Colonel) Virunga briefly recalled a time before he gave up the wail of the saxophone for the thunder of guns.

More clottin' music. Sten thought. There must have been something catching at Koldyeze. Something in the air.

In a way he was correct. There was something in the air at Koldyeze. A great deal had happened since his chat with Pastour. To begin with, the prison was quickly becoming jammed with prisoners – of every variety, from high-ranking officers, to diplomats, to even a few captured provincial governors. The Tahn were heaping all their golden eggs in one big stone-walled basket.

And Pastour had heeded Sten's words about their treatment. Along with the prisoners, he had filtered in a small contingent of his own loyal officials. All of them had been placed in key positions. A stern warning went out that all inter-Empire laws involving prisoners of war must be adhered to down to the finest point. The clampdown was so severe that even Avrenti and Genrikh – especially Genrikh – were afraid to move.

Pastour had also set up a personal office inside Koldyeze. And he had made a habit of unannounced visits in which shaking transgressors would be lined up outside his office and called in one by one to be dealt with personally.

On top of all that, the awful losses the Tahn had suffered made it increasingly difficult for Derzhin to keep the prisoner-guard ratio at any kind of rational level. He was down to recruiting the very young or the very old. Supply shortages had also undermined the guards' morale. At home, and even on the job, their rations were at starvation level. And the treasure trove of foodstuffs and other materials that Cristata and Sten had discovered in the catacombs not only kept the prisoners from suffering equally but left them plenty for generous bribes.

It was so bewildering to many of those untrained Tahn that they seemed puzzled about whose side they were really on. If there were two sides to a troubling incident, the new breed of guards instinctively sided with the prisoners. The prisoners fed them, didn't they? They even gave them a little for their families, didn't they?

Besides, even Lady Atago's thought police could not squash the rumors that the war would end soon – and not in the Tahn's favor. Like Chetwynd, many of the new guards had decided to copper their bets and look out for their own hides.

There was something in the wind, all right, but Sten was hoping it would not all turn to flying drakh when the Tahn hit the fan.

And that was why Sten had slipped back into Koldyeze. He wanted to give Virunga something to throw back.

He had told Virunga that Sorensen was Mantis and a battle computer, plus given Virunga Sorensen's activating code word. Now Gaaronk would be a backup computer. As for what Sorensen could be used for:

'Do you ever get up on the walls to snoop around?'

'A few . . . times. It is . . . difficult . . . with my . . . injuries.' Virunga gripped his cane tighter.

'When you look at the city, what do you see?'

Virunga laughed. '. . . Lately . . . some big . . . holes in . . . ground. Our bombers . . . did . . . well!'

'Too right,' Sten agreed. 'But that's not what I meant. I mean as an old artillerybeing. What do you see when you see the city?'

Virunga's giant brows furrowed, his eyes nearly bushing out of sight. Then he gave another laugh – more like a bark, really.

'Koldyeze . . . is the highest . . . point,' he said. 'If . . . I had my . . . guns . . .' He lapsed into a brief dream of shells falling on Heath. His shells. Then he snapped into alertness. Sten could see coordinates flashing across his eyes. There were many targets of opportunity. He stirred in excitement, remembering the stored weapons hidden in the catacombs.

'I . . . can get . . . the guns,' he said. 'They're . . . much out of . . . date. But . . . I can . . . fix them.'

He blinked out of his planning and stared at Sten. There were no ifs or hows or buts in his next question.

'When? Just . . . tell me . . . when?'

Sten came to his feet and walked over to the N'Ranya. He gave the big slab of furry muscle and bone that Virunga called a shoulder a hard squeeze. 'I'll get word to you,' he said. 'You just be ready.'

Virunga merely nodded. But Sten could tell that in his mind, Virunga was a battery commander again, and he was already moving up his guns.

Chapter Fifty-One

Sten slipped out of Koldyeze just before dawn. As planned, he hid in the rubble surrounding the ancient monastery and waited for the lines of sleepy workers to stagger out of the slums and join the long labor lines that were marched off to the factories each day. Sten skipped the first two formations.

He was much too clean-cut for the ragged bands of obvious textile dye workers. The third group was a little cleaner, a little better dressed. From the conversations he big-eared after he joined them, most of those Tahn workers toiled at pharmaceutical vats or were janitorial crews for the munitions works.

By the time anyone woke up enough to wonder who the new guy might be, they were already in the center of the city, and Sten broke off to mingle with a marketing crowd. He bought a string bag and a greasy blob of some kind of animal protein and elbowed his way into a lane of Tahn who were vaguely pressing toward the direction of Chaboya and the K'ton Klub. Two more turns, a dive down an alley, and he would be home with a nice cold brew.

There was a stirring in the crowd ahead of him, then puzzled muttering. Before Sten had a chance to figure out what was going on, the crowd moved around the corner – to be greeted by a long line of green-uniformed Tahn cops spread out across the street, blocking the way. Sten's heart jumped orbit, and he whirled, crushing toes and ignoring protests. And as he whirled, another long green line snaked across the street, barring the back door. He was trapped in a Tahn sweep!

The beefy cops pressed in, their stun rods held at port arms, their black faceshields jutting forward. The crowd was strangely

– Sten thought – silent, the muttering turning to a puzzled lowing with a few barks of pain as someone ran afoul of a stun rod.

Then phalanxes broke off from the main cop lines and speared through the crowd. Sten noticed from the rank tabs that the phalanxes were composed entirely of sergeants. Their eyes had purposeful hunters' looks as they scanned faces in the crowd, picking individuals out with a shout. 'You! You! You!' Before any of the unfortunates had a hope of reacting, they were muscled into the wedge and swept away.

Sten was trying to back off, to slip close to a wall and then tunnel out through the mass of Tahn around him. Just as his elbow dug back, expecting more soft flesh but finding the hardness of a wall, an enormous sergeant spotted him. The cop thrust his stun rod out like a bludgeon, screaming, 'You!'

And before he knew it, Sten was being strong-armed into the wedge and carried off to clot knew where.

More than a million bodies were crammed into Heath's gigantic central square. The late-morning sun was turning hotter, and the crowd was packed so densely that the stink from their sweating bodies rose like fog from a primordial swamp.

Vidscreens many stories high had been set up on three sides. On the fourth was a towering porta-stage, behind it the blackened hole and ruins of all that was left of the Tahn High Council's palace after the Imperial bombing raid.

Sten's group was trotted around the edges of the crowd to its front, and huge placards were thrust into their hands. Still waiting for the ax to fall, Sten glanced at the sign he held. 'Down With Imperialist Hegemony!' it screamed in thick, blood-red letters.

A big sergeant threatened with a stun rod. 'Wave the sign!' he screamed like a basic-training drill instructor.

'Oh. Okay,' Sten said. And he waved the sign.

'Cheer for victory!' the sergeant advised him at the top of his lungs.

'Sure,' Sten said.

And he began cheering for victory. Taking a clue from the others, he pumped his sign up and down vigorously. To begin with, he confined himself to bellows about nothing. Then, as the crowd's voice grew into an incomprehensible roar, Sten started relaxing. He was not in trouble at all. All he had to do was stand there and demonstrate for the Tahn livie camera crews, hear whatever speech he was supposed to listen to, and then go home when it was over. No problem. So he would be a couple of hours late.

Then he remembered the peculiar habit all totalitarian speakers had of railing on for half the day, and corrected that to maybe five or six hours late. It would be wearying, but he had undergone far worse on many other cesspools – such as the Lupus Cluster, where the phrase 'papal bull' took on new meaning. So he decided to enjoy himself a little and mixed in a few obscenities with his bellows.

Five hours later Sten realized he had yet to cure himself of optimism. The crowd was still screaming – even louder than before – and any sign of weariness was quickly prodded out of them by roving cops with stun rods set on blister. And on the stage there was still no sign of activity.

Then from the distance he heard a howling sound that triggered his old infantryman's instincts, and he hunched his shoulders and pulled his neck in just before a black tacship squadron popped up over the horizon behind the ruined palace and thundered over the crowd so low that it gave the lie to the fact that there were no nerves in bone marrow.

It was all Sten could do to keep from flinging himself to the ground as that squadron was followed by another and then another, and then the whole sky became black as a thick fleet of battle-wagons came between the sun and the ground in an awesome display of Tahn military might.

Even Sten was impressed at first, but then he began noticing things. There was something visibly and obviously out of kilter if one picked any single ship out of the mass. They were all creaky, battered, and old, with signs of hasty repairs, leaking fuel lines, and thick armor plate warted over gaping battle scars. But apparently only Sten noticed that, because the tone of the crowd changed from enforced duty to thrill.

A moment later, the sky cleared and Sten found his professional cynicism washing away, to be replaced by cold fear as he saw three of the biggest and most awesome battleships ever built parade into view. Their hulls were sleek and as black as a null star. The many artistically crafted ports hinted at firepower that would make the editors of *Jane's* weep in frustration at not having a picture and breakdown for their new fiche. Sten was only beginning to guess what those ports hid when the ships rumbled overhead and then passed from view.

The crowd's voice was momentarily stilled by pride and awe. Even the cops were quiet, their eyes glazed with patriotic fervor. It was like a religious experience, Sten thought. The Tahn's Great Spirit obviously loved things that went bang. Sten wondered wryly what Lay Reader Cristata would make of it.

A low hum broke off his thoughts, and Sten found himself craning back around along with the rest of the crowd to find its source. It came from the ashes of the palace.

He stared in fascination as something blazing white lifted from the ruins. It was shaped like an enormous spoked wheel, and it hovered just above the ruins for a few minutes, as if waiting for the last of the ashes to be repelled by the purity of the white and shower to the ground. Finally, it rose about half a kilometer above the ruins, then smoothly moved toward the stage.

Sten's head stalked back along with a million-plus others as a huge port slid open and a large black capsule appeared. The capsule broke away and settled silently down until it nearly touched the stage. There was a series of sharp cracks, and then red pods shot out and the capsule grounded, its legs taking up the weight.

Silence. Not a mutter or a whisper from the crowd. Then martial music trumpeted from giant vidscreen speakers. A portion of the capsule's smooth skin broke away, revealing a yawning arced doorway. Uniformed Tahn guardsmen marched swiftly out, their boots reaching knee level and then slamming down in unison.

They took positions around the stage. Sten noted swiftly that their weapons were not ceremonial and were kept at edgy ready. He saw officers among them – probably Intelligence – scanning the ground, looking for any hint of trouble. There was none. The crowd was firmly in the arms of its leaders. Music swelled louder, and first one and then another member of the Tahn High Council appeared.

As they spread out on stage, Sten automatically checked their positions against his small mental library of vidpics of the council, making what he could of who was in favor and who was not by where they stood.

Except for the absence of Pastour and Lord Wichman's spot directly to the right of the empty center place of honor, he could detect no difference. He quit trying as soon as he saw the first of the combat-clad Tahn soldiers wheel out of the doorway: the man towered well above the others on the stage. He was joined by another and then another, all equally tall. The squad formed up, and as Sten remembered where he had seen those troopers before. Lady Atago stepped out behind them. Her personal guardsmen were probably among the few Tahn in the empire who were taller than Atago.

The crowd erupted into a howl of greeting as the guardsmen marched her to the place of honor, then withdrew. But not very far, Sten saw. They were hovering right behind and on either side, ready to throw themselves around her as living shields if necessary.

Lady Atago stretched both arms over her head, and the cheers of the crowd became even louder – so loud that they echoplexed and howled as the vidscreen speakers picked up the reverb. For a moment, although he was surrounded by many times more than a million beings, Sten felt completely alone.

He remembered the last time he had seen Lady Atago. It had been back on Cavite in the early days of the war. She had worn a red cloak and green tunic, just as she did now. And she stood barely 150 meters away. He remembered that brief moment when he had shifted the willygun until the green tunic was centered in the cross hairs. He had inhaled, let out half that breath, and taken up the slack on the trigger. In a moment an AM2 round would blow a fist-sized hole in that tunic. And then Atago's bodyguards were moving like a corps de ballet, closing around their charge – and all Sten could see was the white of their uniforms instead of the red and the green.

To this day, Sten was not sure whether he had missed the shot out of cowardice or lost an opportunity. As he watched her, he cursed himself for both. It did not matter which side of the coin came down. Both were losers. And he could not help wondering what would have happened if he had succeeded. Who would be standing on the stage now? Wichman? Pastour? Anyone at all?

On the stage, Lady Atago had lowered her arms and let the cheers wash over her. Then she raised them again, asking for silence. She got it.

'Thank you, my fellow Tahn,' she began, 'for joining us in this celebration.'

Sten saw not a flicker among the rapt faces around him. To the crowd there was no incongruity in the fact that they had not joined anything voluntarily. And what was there to celebrate?

'These are trying times for us, my people,' Atago continued. 'Our resolve is being tested more than in any other era after the Great Shame. And it is this resolve of ours – this dedication to victory basic to our Tahn way of life – that we celebrate today.

'But there is more than just resolve that makes up the Tahn genetic code. There is also the absolute willingness to sacrifice all to preserve—'

She waited, and then the final word snapped out of the speakers like a metal-tipped whip.

'Honor!'

'*Honor!*' the crowd screamed back. '*Honor!*'

'Yes, honor,' Lady Atago said. 'Let no outlander mistake the meaning of this word to the Tahn. To us it is not just a phrase requiring sacrifice for the future of our children and their children's children. Because we would sacrifice all for honor. And we are willing to die to the last Tahn lest our honor be fouled.'

Again she held the moment, bowing her head.

'For without honor there can be no future,' she went on. 'Without honor the Tahn are extinct as a race. And if we all die to fulfill this unique and holy vision of ourselves, what does it matter? We may all be gone, but we still will have left our mark on history.

'And a thousand years from now – and a thousand after that – beings will read of us and marvel at the standard for honor we set. And they will curse themselves for their weaknesses and damn themselves as cowards because no living thing will ever achieve that mark again. But they all died, their children may protest. And their parents will nod, yes. But they died for . . . *honor!*'

It took a half hour for the crowd to calm down before Lady Atago could go on. They shouted and wept and hugged one another and passed children from shoulder to shoulder so they could reach out and touch history.

Lady Atago kept very still during that time, letting the wave of sound wash over her, seemingly unaffected. Her face was stern – and waiting.

'And so, my fellow Tahn,' she continued when the time was right. 'I have called you here to celebrate. To celebrate and to rededicate ourselves to honor.

'It will not be easy. We face a formidable foe. A foe who will not be satisfied until the last of us has been ground up for his bread and meat. We have won great victories against this foe, and we have suffered great losses.

'But it does not matter. I welcome this foe. As you all should. Because we are fortunate to live in a time of our ultimate test. This foe has forced us to confront our own weaknesses. And when it is over, we will be strong and pure and good. Or all of us will be dead . . .

'. . . for honor.' The last words came softly, like a prayer. The crowd was silent, as if sensing what was to come.

Lady Atago slowly raised her hands to the clear Tahn skies. The odd thought crossed Sten's mind that not once had Lady Atago mentioned the Eternal Emperor by name. It was a speechmaking tactic that he immediately mentally wrote down in his little Mantis book of propaganda tricks.

'I pledge to you this, my fellow Tahn. I will hurl at our foe every bolt you build me. I will track him to the Fringe Worlds. I will hunt him out of his coward's lair in Cavite. And then I will follow him wherever he flees to.

'I pledge you battle, my fellow Tahn. I pledge you victory. Swift and sweet. But I may not be up to your measure. Some weakness in me may make my aim go astray.

'And so . . . if in the end I fail you . . . If I cannot give you the victory you deserve . . .'

There was a long, last wait . . .

'I pledge you honor!'

Sten barely noticed the tumult around him. The crowd was insane, but that did not matter. Because he was witnessing a rare thing: a leader who was addressing her people – and believing every word she said.

Since Sten had set off for Koldyeze, the K'ton Klub had closed, reopened, and then closed again. In a few hours it would reopen once more, and Alex and St. Clair and L'n were waiting anxiously at a table in the empty nightclub.

To cover their anxiety, they were doing what soldiers have been doing ever since beings had picked up a rock and learned to throw it at others. In short, they were grousing and wondering what foolishness they would be asked to do next.

'Look, I don't mean to complain,' St. Clair was saying. 'Business is great, and I'm also enjoying beating the snakesnot out of the Tahn. But I'm a bottom-line kind of a person.'

'True,' L'n said. She said it a little too quickly but presented a guileless pink furry face to St. Clair's quick questioning look.

'Whae be y'r wee problem, lass?' Alex asked.

'Lately I don't feel like we're getting anywhere. We're wrecking their money. Fine and good. We're fouling up production. Messing with their morale. Stealing their secrets. And being a general pain in the tush. This is great. As it should be. We're hurting them bad.'

'I don't see what your problem is,' L'n said. 'What more do you want?'

'I want to hear them yell ouch,' St. Clair said. 'I mean, how bad are we *really* hurting them?'

'Aye,' Alex said, tapping the table thoughtfully. 'Ah ken whae y' mean.'

'You do?' asked the unsuspecting L'n, who still had a few innocent bits left in her.

Alex nodded wisely. ''Tis ae old malady,' he said. 'How much hurt hurts. Aye. An old tale, lass. Let Kilgour tell y' how old.'

And Alex settled back to tell a suspicious St. Clair and an intrigued L'n his story.

'Ae gran'sire ae mine wae trappin't. Ae Eart'. Bleakit an' cold an' a'. Been oot ae th' wilderness aye weeks an' months.

'An' one day, thae was a wee town. Nae, no e'en a town. A village. Thae see't thae great pourit ae snow comin't toward them. An' thae thinki't ae's a bear or some' at.

'M' grandsire, 'twere.

'Lookin't f'r ae dentist.

'Turns oot, thae's a diploma-mill quack ae thae village. An' m' gran'sire sits doon ae th' chair, an' thae dentist lookit ae' his teeth an' say, "Aye, thae's got to coom oot. But ae nae hae anesthesia." 'M' grandsire say, "Dinnae fash. Pull it."

'An so, wi' great gruntin' ae groanin't, thae dentist yankit thae tooth. An' he's sweatin', an m' grandsire's sweatin't.

'An' thae quack say't, "Dinnae thae be th' greatest pain y've ever felt?"

'M' grandsire says, "Nae. Thae's naught."

'Wi' considerable astonishment, thae dentist say, "Whae's worse?"

'M' grandsire, explain't. "Last week, Ah come down wi' th' runs. S' bad, Ah canne mak't oot m' cabin t' thae backhouse. So, Ah drap m' trews ae th' snowbank, right outside m' door. An' Ah forget Ah was cleanin't m' bear traps before thae snow fell, an' Ah left a wee trap set right where't Ah be crouchin't.

'"Which Ah'm remindit aboot when thae trap closit.

'"Snapit closit on m' balls."

'"Good Lord," thae dentist sae. "Y'r right. Thae's th' biggest pain ae all."

'"Nae, nae, lad," m' grandsire say. "Th' biggest pain ae all wae when Ah come to the *end* ae th' chain . . ."'

His punch line was greeted by the usual cold, stony silence. But only from St. Clair. L'n was on the floor with laughter. Alex gave her a huge, fond smile.

'I don't get it,' St. Clair said flatly.

'You – you don't?' L'n gasped through laughter. 'Why not? It's

– so simple that it's—' She broke off to compose herself. 'Look. A bear trap has this big long chain.'

'I know that,' St. Clair said, a little miffed.

'And one end of the chain is staked to the ground. And on the other end is – well, the bear trap. And, see, when the jaws snapped shut, they caught Alex's great-great-whatever-grandfather by the scrotum.'

She erupted into laughter again. St. Clair just glared at her. Alex thought she was absolutely wonderful.

'But – see, that still wasn't what really hurt the most,' L'n went on. 'What really hurt was—'

'I don't want to hear it again,' St. Clair said. 'Please!'

Alex got to his feet and strode around the table to L'n. He patted her fondly on the shoulder. She was a being after his own heart. Kilgour had found himself a duck.

'Do you know any more like that?' L'n asked hopefully.

'A few, lass. Just a few. D'ya e'er ken thae one aboot th' spotted snake?'

'Nooo . . . I don't think so. Why don't you—'

'Don't get him started, L'n,' Sten's voice boomed from across the room. 'Or you'll wish you were back in a Koldyeze cooler.'

The three turned to see their wandering boy. Poor Sten. His hair was wild, his eyes were glazed, and his clothes drooped from him like wet gunnysack material. And as he walked toward them, he moved with a footsore limp.

'What the clot happened?' St. Clair asked.

Sten sighed and shook his head. He slumped into a seat and made desperate pointing gestures at a gaping mouth. Alex handed him a throat-soothing brew. Sten gulped it straight down in less than four swallows. He slammed the mug on the table. Alex refilled it. Sten chugged only about half of it. Then he belched and took a tentative sip.

'Well?' St. Clair prompted.

'For a while there,' Sten said, 'I thought I was for the high jump. I got picked up in a Tahn sweep.'

His three companions started. Sten waved them back down again.

'They just needed some clean-cut types to stand in front of a demonstration to wave signs at a livie crew. We all stood there in the sun for five hours or so, and then Lady Atago came out to make general nice and urged us to commit suicide. We all thought this over for a bit and said that was okay, but can we go home now?

'No such luck. Atago said stick around there's gonna be a show.

And we were treated to eleven more hours of traitors confessing their sins on the big screen and then getting themselves geeked for our pleasure.'

'Any traitors in particular? L'n asked.

'The ones we made up. Toward the end there, I almost felt sorry for them.'

'Thae'll no be blame in pity, young Sten,' Alex said, 'so long a' y' dinnae make a habit ae it.'

Sten did not comment. Instead he did a little gentle whining for food, and while he ate, he filled them in on his mission to Koldyeze.

'What do we do next?' St. Clair asked.

'Right now there's not much more we can do. We keep our agent network nit and tiddy. Feed the corruption meter whenever the flag pops up. And make general low-profile pains of ourselves.'

'Clottin' boring,' L'n said. 'Where's all the romance and pulse throbbing you promised? Intrigue! Danger! Clandestine action! I didn't sign on to be bored, cheena!'

Everybody laughed.

'I'm afraid that's what's in the cards for a little while,' Sten said. 'We've done all we can to this point. Now we have to wait for events to catch up to us. Big events. That we have no control over. Like in the Fringe Worlds. And Cavite.'

He got up and refilled everyone's glass with brew.

'Although I hate to confess this, it's sorta like Alex's story,' he went on. 'We've got the Tahn by the scrotum in the jaws of a big steel trap. But they still don't know they're hurting yet.

'So we gotta wait until they reach the end of the chain.'

Chapter Fifty-Two

The empire had learned – at least slightly – from the slaughter in the Pel/e systems.

Fleet Marshal Ian Mahoney looked at the pre-invasion bombard-ment plans for the Fringe Worlds and snarled, 'Double it.'

'Double what, sir?'

'Everything.'

His staff looked at the overheads and followed orders. Twice the conceivable amount of ordnance was scheduled for delivery on the Fringe Worlds, and then, once more, Mahoney told them to double *that*.

He doubted that it would work – but then, Mahoney had never been convinced that putting a man where a bomb or a bullet might go necessarily worked.

But he would do the best he could.

He would have liked to have leveled the worlds as he had done to the Erebus System – but there were civilians resident. Mahoney wondered how many of them had survived not just the Tahn conquest but the subsequent occupation.

Had he his druthers – but he did not.

Finally there came a day when there was no return fire taken on any of the Fringe Worlds selected for invasion.

Mahoney ordered the assault.

He acted knowing that the Tahn defenders would come out of the rubble as if all the firepower expended had been so many fire-works.

He was quite correct – which was why Mahoney chose to disobey orders.

According to the Eternal Emperor and his psych staff, Mahoney's return to the Fringe Worlds was what the Emperor insisted on calling, using jargon unknown to anyone around him, a 'photo opportunity.' Whatever the clot a photo was did not matter – his propagandists went into motion.

Before Mahoney's battlewagon lifted with the fleets toward the Fringe Worlds, several chaingun galleries had been stripped of weaponry and converted into press suites. As many livie crews and journalists as could fit were packed in.

The battleship was supposed to land on Cavite, center of the Fringe Worlds, in the fourth wave. Assumption: First wave gets slaughtered, second wave takes casualties but holds, third wave consolidates, and we can land some camera-beings in the fourth wave. Bangs will still be banging, but nobody's going to get killed.

Least of all Ian Mahoney as he strode nobly down the ramps of his battleship and made a noble statement that he had returned or declared this world open or whatever noble statement he chose. Noble statement-type propagandists were assigned to his staff.

Unfortunately, on L-Day, H-hour, Mahoney was nowhere near his command ship.

He was strapped into a troop capsule on an assault transport next to the First Guards' command sergeant major, a noncom whose body, guardsmen thought, had been replaced sixteen times, bit by bit over the decades, but whose brain had never been modified after the CSM had been declared clinically dead a century or so before.

Mahoney had forgotten how much it hurt when the transport, just in-atmosphere, blew its twenty assault capsules down toward the surface below. He had also forgotten just how many times 'down' changed places as the capsule dived toward the robot homer below.

Just before impact, he and the sergeant major forced grins at each other: See, we're used to this drakh. Neither of them realized how much his own smile resembled the rictus of a corpse or thought about it as the capsule slammed down in the usual semi-controlled crash. Semi-controlled was defined as less than fifteen percent incapacitating injuries on landing.

The minicharges exploded and the capsule's walls blew off. The straps came free, and Mahoney grabbed his willygun and stumbled out into the rubble of Cavite.

There were various reports as to what noble pronunciations on the order of 'I have returned' or '*Lafayette nous arrivons*' Mahoney made as his boots crashed down. They were all tissues of lies.

His first observation: 'I forgot how much this clottin' armpit world smells like an open— Incoming!'

And Mahoney chewed gravel as the missile smashed down bare meters away.

The First Guards had been singled out for the 'honor' of being the first to land on Cavite by Mahoney. Years before, the division had been wiped out holding Cavite in the opening of the Tahn War. Only a handful of noncoms, officers, and technicians had been evacked during the retreat at the Eternal Emperor's personal orders. They had been used as a cadre to reform the unit with fresh blood and then sent back into combat.

Mahoney thought they deserved the 'privilege' of revenge. He might have been a little battle-happy in his thinking. There were no more than a dozen guardsmen who had been on Cavite – the grinding down of the Tahn had ground the division, as well. In addition, they still had not finished training the replacements after the Naha.

The 'honor' that all the combat-experienced troops would have liked was a return to Prime, a nice parade, and the next half century spent garrisoning some R&R world. Two beats after the first *wheep-crack* past his or her ear, even the most gung-ho replacement agreed with that idea.

But the Guards pushed on, day by bloody day, across the planet and into Cavite City. The battle was a reversal of their bitter defeat – now they had complete air and space superiority and an unlimited amount of weaponry and ammunition.

Not that the Tahn defenders surrendered. *K'akomit'r*, in their language, meant both 'I give up' and 'I do not exist.'

Most of them chose just that – fighting to the last round, then suiciding with a grenade or charging armor with an improvised spear. Mahoney saw one stubby Tahn private, surrounded, tap-arm a grenade on the ground and then tuck it under his combat helmet. By that time he and the other battered guardsmen around him thought the subsequent explosion the best joke of the day.

Less than an hour later, one of Mahoney's aides, one who *had* landed on the battleship, found the fleet marshal and handed him a message.

EYES ONLY, from the Eternal Emperor. The message was in an old Mantis code that Mahoney could decipher blindfolded and in a typhoon. It read:

QUIT PLAYING GAMES AND GET BACK TO WORK.

Mahoney growled, stripped his combat vest of grenades and magazines, threw them to a nearby guardsman, and headed back to maps, computers, and projections.

Lady Atago fulfilled her vow.

Every Tahn fleet that was combat-worthy was grouped and launched at the Fringe Worlds. She ruthlessly stripped reserve and home defense squadrons of all warships and sent them into battle.

The slogans were chanted, and the livies were ominous with takeoff after takeoff.

The Empire's defeat was certain.

It was very *un*certain to a nameless Tahn supply officer who sat in the cramped cubicle of his obsolete battle cruiser. Finally he shut off the com that was still broadcasting inspirational messages from the council and stared at his screens.

He keyed to the bottom line of all of them.

CREW: 50% of mandated personnel. 11% rated 'Trained.' 4% 'Station-trained.'
SUPPLIES: 71% required for mission accomplishment including return to base.
ARMAMENT: 11% bunker capacity chainguns; 34% tube capacity missiles.
SYSTEMS: 61% functional.

As he watched, the 'sixty-one percent' hesitated, then changed to 'fifty-eight percent' as, somewhere in the guts of the ship, another weapons system succumbed to cumulative wear.

The livies that showed the Tahn going off into the final battle were supposedly broadcast live. Atago, no fool, was not about to allow that.

Accidents, after all, could happen. And accidents were most demoralizing even to the thoroughly conditioned Tahn populace – which was why the livies showing the takeoff of those three brand new superbattleships that had chilled Sten were never seen.

One of them – the replacement for Atago's obsolescent and battered *Forez* – was not scheduled for the assault.

But the other two were.

One, the *Panipat*, lifted up to twenty meters away from its massive docking cradle before losing two Yukawa drive units and almost crashing. Only skillful pilotage brought it back down, seemingly undamaged. Immediate system analysis showed, however, that not only were the two drive units out, but *all* other units would be failure-prone. Also, the AM2 drive would produce no more than fifty percent capacity.

There were no explanations – except that all three ships had been slammed together, even more hastily built than were the usual Tahn warships. Plus, in a time when all strategic materials were in critical shortage, compromises had been made.

The new *Forez*-class ships might have looked awesome. But there was not a lot of them there.

The third ship, the *Gogra*, lifted successfully. Out-atmosphere from Heath, the ship's commander ordered the ship and its four escorting cruisers into AM2 drive.

Someone blundered.

The *Gogra* and one cruiser managed to collide. Collisions, in the macro-distances of space, never happened.

This one did.

There were no survivors from either ship, so no explanations as to exactly what had gone wrong were ever available.

Just beyond detection range of the Fringe Worlds, the Tahn fleets three-pronged for the assault, becoming the first, second, and third attack forces. The formations, timing, and deployment would have produced, from any pre-war Tahn admiral, relief of at least half of the ships' captains and probably a tenth reminded of their 'honor' and given one projectile round.

But there were not very many prewar Tahn admirals, let alone ship captains, left. Their bodies were desiccated in space, filmed across the bulkheads of shattered ships, or were simply a no-longer-visible contribution to entropy.

But war was the fine art of making do with what one had.

Plus the Tahn knew that destiny was on their side.

Destiny, of course, was generally on the same side as God.

And so the Tahn fleets attacked the big battalions.

The Tahn second attack force never made it to the Fringe Worlds.

Admiral Mason, commanding six destroyer squadrons from the bridge of a brand-new cruiser, was waiting. His ships were lying doggo, barely within detector range of each other, as the Tahn came in. The first DD making contact linked up, and Mason sent in all ships in carefully and endlessly rehearsed attack formations.

They broke the Tahn on the first sweep, then went independent. Mason's skippers might have been drilled to the point of brainburn, but secretly each of them was proud to serve under a killer like Mason – even if he was a complete clot, he still put them 'in harm's way.'

The Tahn battleship that was flagship for the second force center was killed by at least three launches from three separate ships, and all command of the ragtag fleets was gone.

At that point Mason grudgingly reported to his superior – and nine full Imperial fleets came in to finish the job.

One Tahn cruiser, eleven destroyers, and a handful of auxiliaries, all damaged, survived to break off and limp back to Heath.

Admiral Mason had to admit that his ships had performed adequately.

*

A full sector away, Fleet Admiral Ferrari fought his battle almost perfectly.

He had had more than enough time, since Intelligence had alerted him that the Tahn fleets had launched, to prepare himself.

He had run endless progs on several screens as to what exactly the oncoming first attack force would do. He even had an Imperial Intelligence strategic/tactical bio-fiche on the Tahn admiral in command. Some clot named Hsi, Ferrari thought, who's been piloting a bureaucracy for most of the war. Now, what did he do to get himself beached? He consulted another bio-fiche – one that, although Ferrari never knew it, had come from Sten and St. Clair's intelligence.

'The gentleman,' Ferrari thought aloud, 'appears to have managed to lurk up on four Imperial fleets way back when and make them unhappy. That should not mean that . . . mmh. Perhaps he has well-connected friends? No. Ah. Here is the tiny malfeasance. Appears to have lost control of his units during the midpoint of the battle. Incurred casualties. Mercy.'

Ferrari smiled to himself. So the clot did not know his midgame.

Ferrari blanked all the progs. They were all incorrect. He *knew* where Hsi would attack.

Admiral Hsi had planned to use the 'clutter' of the Sulu systems to mask his approach on the Caltor System and Cavite itself. There was no way that even the sophisticated Imperial detectors could pick up his fleets before they attacked.

Hsi had not calculated that the reverse was also true – the Tahn detectors showed the Sulu systems as a blur of asteroids.

They did not pick out Ferrari's waiting fleets until the last few seconds. Ferrari was slightly disappointed; he had hoped that the Tahn would come in even closer before he began the battle.

But it was enough – and he ordered action.

Looked at from 'above,' two-dimensionally, Ferrari's fleets came laterally across the spearhead of the Tahn force – what had been known as 'crossing the tee.' All Imperial weapons could acquire targets, but the Tahn weapons systems were 'masked' by their own formation.

Ferrari hammered in on them. The battle, at that point, went from chess to the greater subtlety of battle-axes at one meter as the Imperial fleets slaughtered Hsi.

Hsi ordered his force to break off battle, retire, and regroup.

Ferrari sent his units after them, and the battle continued, a blind melee in the emptiness between systems.

Ferrari won, quite handily. Again, only a few Tahn ships survived.

But he had made one mistake.

When he had decided to go after Hsi, he had neglected to inform Mahoney, who was trying to coordinate the battle from Cavite, of his decision. He had left a large, undefended hole in the perimeter around the Fringe Worlds. And through that hole, three E-days later, poured the Tahn's third attack force.

There were no Imperial combat fleets between it and Cavite.

Someone once said that most heroes could be explained simply as sane people deciding to do something that was completely insane.

William Bishop the Forty-third would have defined the action that won him the Galactic Cross and his second star as something that only a nut who had managed to convince himself he was not a nut would have even begun.

So far, Bishop had not had that bad a war.

He had originally been a guardsman, an infantry sergeant who had gotten his share of gongs for ducking at the appropriate moment in the appropriate place. Realizing that if he went into places where people were shooting at him, eventually they were going to connect, he had volunteered for flight training.

His intentions were to graduate and then push big ugly clot transports around the sky until his time came up, then work quietly on his own abstruse mathematical figures. The only other medal he wanted was some kind of long service without getting caught doing anything too terrible award.

He was a natural pilot.

When he had graduated as part of Sten's flight training class, he had gotten the assignment he had wanted.

But things had caught up with him.

Perhaps it was that no one could believe that a man with that many medals, who looked like that much of a commando, had no interest in seeing any more combat. Or perhaps someone with a sense of history had looked up who William Bishop the First was.

But in any event, Bishop not only had been forcibly transferred from his REMF supply wagon to an assault transport but had been given more and more promotions.

Currently he was a one-star admiral in charge of two divisions of assault craft. Worse yet, he had been hand selected to be in charge of the Cavite landings.

A man could get dead doing things like that, he had thought. Going in.

But so far, not much had happened – not much, at least to

Bishop's mind. The air-to-space missiles, the Tahn tacships, and the occasional suicide attack had been discounted.

Bishop was determined that it was not that bad a war. Survive this, he thought, and all I have to make it through is the final landing on Heath.

That produced a wince and another train of thought. It was more important to wonder whether Fermat was not right, after all. In the meantime, his assault ships went in on Cavite, their support transports cross-loaded, and the handful of combat craft kept the Tahn mosquitoes away.

At that point, the alarms shrilled.

Bishop found himself on the bridge of his assault command ship, looking at the incoming reports that input and then blanked as the oncoming Tahn third attack force came in.

Bishop then realized that he was a psychopath.

His orders were most clear. 'Com . . . close beam to Com-Escort. Commander, stand by for orders.'

'Admiral, we're getting—'

'We're getting hit by the whole clottin' Tahn spaceforce. I know. I noticed. Orders, I said. I want your ships out of orbit and headed out. Now.'

'Toward what?'

Bishop groaned to himself. 'Do you have a breakdown on the incoming Tahn?'

'Uh . . . that's an affirm. We have seven BBs, several tacship launchers, twenty-eight cruisers . . . you want more, Billy?'

'Negative. That's about what I show. Orders . . .' He motioned to his nav officer. 'Stand by for relay. Contact orbit will be for the third – no, fourth battleship in line. Relay—'

His paling navigator nodded.

'—on transmit. Activate on a ten-second tick – from now.'

'Further orders. Sir?'

Bishop stared into the screen at his escort commander. 'Hell, no. You need any more?'

'Guess not. You know any good prayers, Billy?'

Bishop shook his head.

And the attack began.

One armored assault command ship. One cruiser. Twelve destroyers. Eleven escort ships. And seventeen tacships.

Attacking four Tahn combat fleets.

It was insane.

*

It *was* insane.

The Tahn admiral in charge of the third attack force saw the handful of ships incoming on a collision orbit and realized that he had fallen into a trap.

No one would attack like that. Not unless, behind those absurd attackers, was the full force of the Empire.

The admiral admired the temerity of the attackers. They could, truly, be Tahn. To be willing to die merely to pin down the Tahn fleets for a few moments, moments enough for the yet-to-be-detected Imperial battleships to strike.

The admiral issued a string of orders.

Break contact and re-form. Go back, beyond the Sulu systems. We shall let the Empire strike against emptiness, then come in again from the flank.

Four Tahn fleets fled back into emptiness. For the most logical of reasons.

The admiral in question never had a chance to realize what had happened and what had not happened, because his reassembly point happened to be only light-minutes from the orbital path of Ferrari's fleets, returning from the destruction of Hsi.

There were no surviving Tahn ships.

Bishop looked at the receding Tahn fleets, retracted all those last words he had been muttering, and, reflexively, looked over his shoulder.

There was nothing 'over his shoulder' or 'behind' him on the screens.

William Bishop the Forty-third, not believing in bluffs, in what had happened, or, more importantly, in what had *not* happened, returned to his orbit off Cavite, seriously thinking about the virtues of early retirement and then perhaps joining an intensely religious monastery.

Lady Atago stood in the litter of disaster and read the onscreen message, sent en clair from General Lunga's command post on Cavite:

> Imperial units have broken through. Contact lost with fighting elements. Last reports say all positions resisting to last man. This post now three combatants, no remaining ammunition. Will attack. Repeat. Will attack. My apologies to the council and to my race for failure.
>
> Lunga

Atago turned away. She had her own honor – and her own pledge – to fulfill.

Chapter Fifty-Three

Without ceremony, the new *Forez* hurtled into space.

Lady Atago might have been the ultimate Tahn, but she had been more than grudgingly acquiescent to the Tahn's cultural love of ceremonies.

There were rituals for warriors choosing to go into battle, seeking the final victory of death: the touching of the home-world's earth to one's temple. A last sip of pure water. An oath over one's personal weapon, preferably one that had been in the family for generations. Exact instructions as to how the memory of the about-to-fall hero(ine) was to be honored.

Lady Atago chose to die in her own fashion.

The livie crews could cobble together some kind of scene from stock footage. In fact, she imagined, they probably were already hard at work doing just that.

Atago did not care.

After lift, the *Forez*'s second officer had turned to her, eyes glistening, and stammered something about it all being a dream. The old and the new, culminating in a moment of history.

Atago puzzled at him for a second. Old and new? Oh. Yes. She remembered. The officer had been something or other on the old *Forez*, which was now probably being cut apart and recast into something or other. Atago did not know or care. A ship, like a weapon, was a tool and nothing more.

But she managed a frosty smile and a nod of agreement to the officer. If those were the thoughts he chose to carry into emptiness, so be it.

Atago was busy with her final plans – such as they were.

Any culture that managed to admire the slaughter of other beings also lionized the fighter who went to war in a hopeless cause. But to qualify for legend, that fighter also had to accomplish something by his death, even if it was nothing more than keeping the bad guys out of a pass for an hour or so.

That had been true even on ancient Earth. For instance, before Roland was an acceptable hero, his pig-headedness at Roncesvalles had to be changed from a minor ambush by irked Basques to a grand last stand against several million Saracens. Custer and his people *had* to be doing something worthwhile instead of what they actually were to get to Little Big Horn – drunk, untrained, ignoring intelligence, and having less than no idea of what they would do when they got wherever they were going.

There was an exception: the kamikazes – Second Global War – who went out to die with only the forlorn illogic that somehow their deaths would work magic and change history. Other cultures had tried to explain by claiming they were psycho-cases, drunk, or using drugs. Only their home culture had made them into heroes.

The Tahn would have understood the kamikazes quite thoroughly.

Lady Atago's 'battle plan' was to drive directly for Cavite. Somehow the *Forez* would battle through the surrounding Imperial fleets and somehow attack Cavite itself. Of course they would all die.

But somehow that would turn the war.

The crew believed. Perhaps a bit of Lady Atago's own emotions did as well.

But more important to Atago was her honor and her expiation of failure. She had done something – and had no idea what – wrong. The war should have been over already. And the Tahn victorious. To consider anything else was impossible.

'Impossible' was also the word for her plan.

The never-to-lift-again *Panipat* was stripped of its missiles, armaments, supplies, and the few crew members who were properly trained.

But even so, the *Forez* launched with only eighty percent of full complement. They had, however, almost 175 percent more than the specified systems basic load for all weapons systems – weapons systems that had seen, at best, a single test firing during the ship's trial passage from shipyard to Heath.

A battleship was normally escorted by a fairly largish fleet

– cruisers, destroyers, ECM ships, tacship carriers, and half a horde of auxiliaries.

The *Forez* attacked the Empire with one cruiser and seventeen destroyers.

Ensign Gilmer thought himself a clever man.

He came from a family that had served in the Empire's military for generations. Such service was obligatory for any Gilmer's first career. Ensign Gilmer had groaned into adulthood with the knowledge that he was sooner or later going to have to go out there and play with people who probably had evil intentions. But it was either that or disinheritance, a far worse fate.

He had hoped, without success, that at the very least the war with the clotting Tahn would end before his tender pink body saw its majority. No luck.

Gilmer joined up.

But he had a plan that would not only make his somewhat suspicious elders realize that Gilmer was true to the tradition but keep said pink body unscathed.

He volunteered for picket ships.

His fellow graduates at the academy were in awe – they had never expected the flaky Gilmer to become a firebrand. Picket ships, after all. Out in front of the rest of the fleet. Waiting for the enemy to come at them, *in force*.

Picket ships were even more suicidal than tacships.

A being could get killed doing that.

Gilmer took their admiration badly – the same way he had handled their earlier polite contempt – and gloated to himself.

Gilmer had been sent to hack one day in his first year at the academy and spent it doing some interesting research: looking for a future home. He discovered that picket ships indeed were in front of everyone. But unlike the tacships, intended to shoot and scoot, picket ships just scooted. He ran a stat analysis on their casualties, all the way back to the Mueller Wars. Most interesting: less than two percent. Lower, even, than a transport. So much for cadet wisdom. And most of the losses, he discovered by wading through endless fiches on accident boards, had been due to inept pilotage.

Gilmer was a superb spacepilot. Everyone agreed on that.

And so he went off to war.

His picket ship was not a happy one. The twelve beings in his crew hated Gilmer's guts – not that there was anything concrete they could dislike him for. The ship was tautly run. Promotions and punishments were handed down promptly and according to regs. But there was something wrong.

Gilmer had not been pleased when his picket ship had been attached to a flotilla assigned to the Pioneer Sectors invasion. But thus far he had kept well out of danger. He had flashed first contact reports, in fact, on several Tahn ships trying lone-wolf runs against the Empire, which should have gotten him a respectable gong or two to take into civilian life and his planned new career as a livie producer.

And he could see that the Empire was winning.

A few more weeks, and then it would be over. He planned for his ship to need a massive quarterly that would keep it out of the final battle against Heath.

Therefore, Gilmer, that clever man, was not pleased when a screen lit, showing a single incoming blip at full drive.

He enlarged the scope, cutting to a sensor he had planted several light-years away, and then gurgled as the monstrous bulk of the *Forez* swam at him. It was, a second screen told him, not an illusion. The *Forez*'s orbit, indeed, would pass less than one light-minute away!

His com team was already yammering its close-beam report back to the fleet. Gilmer slammed full power, programmed a random evasion pattern, and looked for something else to do. Frantically he ordered a weapons panel up and then blind-launched two missiles.

The four missiles with which the picket boat was armed were about as useless as a weapon could be. They were single-lobe homers less than a meter long. In theory, they were to be used to stop an enemy picket boat or maybe even a tacship from sucking up a defenseless ship. In fact, they were intended to give the picket boat crewmen something to do before death if they were inept enough to be caught.

Gilmer gnawed his knuckles, waiting to stupidly fulfill one of the family's *other* traditions: death in battle.

But nothing happened.

None of the Tahn ships bothered to launch against his ship, let alone go in pursuit.

Gilmer then knew he was not only a superb pilot but a master tactician as well. For a moment he even considered staying on in the military after the war. No, he caught himself. Don't be arrogant. Take the big medal they're going to give you and be content.

He did at least receive the medal. And it was a very large one.

*

The picket boat survived for one reason: Lady Atago *wanted* the Empire to know she was attacking – and to come out to face her. Perhaps that picket boat had given the alert a little earlier than she would have liked, but no battle was ever fought exactly to plan.

She did not even notice when one of the picket ship's missiles actually hit the *Forez*.

A junior damage-control officer saw a screen report a hit somewhere near the ship's stern. Damage was through the outer skin of the ship, and an unknown object had lodged in the baffling just next to the second skin before exploding. The damage-control officer tapped keys, dumping fire retardant into the baffling area, ordered the evacuation of the storeroom next to the impact area, and also filled that compartment with retardant.

He wondered what had hit them, then concentrated on other screens.

Mahoney paced his command center.

He was angry.

Again, he looked at the screen. Great, he thought. So some Tahn clot in some kind of new battlewagon wants to count coup before we put him away. Real noble, he thought. Nobody ever told him, Mahoney's thoughts ran, that ain't the way modern war gets fought. All that happens is they wait for you to ride out and then open up with the machine guns.

Pity some people who don't want to be heroes generally get killed in the process. Clotting clot, he thought, as his mouth routined moving entire fleets out against the doomed ship. Maybe part of his anger, he thought with a flicker of humor, was that way down deep he thought counting coup *was* a better way of making war than machine slaughter.

A tech shouted at him, and Mahoney whirled.

'Who the hell trained you to report like—'

And Mahoney gaped, staring at the screen the tech sat in front of.

On it was Lady Atago.

'What the hell is that?'

'Broadcast on all channels from that incoming Tahn ship. It's a still. No audio, no other vid.'

'Holy Kee-rist,' Mahoney swore. 'Com link. Immediate. Sealed beam to Prime. X-ray code.'

That code would put the cast straight through to the Eternal Emperor.

Not only had his carefully planned trap of the Fringe Worlds attack nailed the kits, but now the mother dire wolf was on her way.

Two tacship flotillas made the first attack. The first bored in, straight on, hoping that their angle of attack would, roughly, keep some of the weaponry masked. Their orders were simple: Kill the battleship.

That was incorrect – the *Forez*'s target acquisition systems had been designed to pick up attackers from any angle, and the weapons systems to have the same launch capabilities.

The tacships should have been obliterated light-years beyond even the screening destroyers.

The ships were hit – and hard. Five out of twenty-five survived the battle. But they were not obliterated, and it took a while for the twenty to go out.

The first disaster should have been a nasty little surprise. For the first time, the Tahn had built a battleship fitted with four internal hangars, housing sixteen tacships.

Ports slid open, and the tacships struck.

But the war had been hard on Tahn pilots; it had been especially lethal for the young beings who chose to strap themselves into the semi-guided missiles called tacships. The sixteen pilots had, combined, less than 8,000 real E-hours' experience. Before the war, that would have qualified a Tahn as graduate trainee and nothing more.

The Tahn tacship pilots scorned such niceties as evasive tactics and spoofs – not that they would have been capable of running them, especially against the highly experienced Imperial officers they faced, all of whom had thousand-thousand-mission stares and steel teeth.

The tacships lived for only seconds before ceasing to exist. They made only one hit – and that was on one of their own destroyers. But the clutter of missiles fired served nicely to fragment the already nearly chaotic Tahn battle formation.

Atago, standing on the bridge, kept her face immobile. She had not expected much from the tacships – but this was absurd. But it *was*. She issued further orders.

The chief weapons officer had already decided on the system. He ordered a massive Nach'kal launch – self-homing ship-to-ship missiles, medium range.

The second disaster was the inept, un- or undertrained Tahn weaponeers. Computer simulation did not equal combat reality.

Acquisition techs misreported targets, and aimers 'lost' aim points or, worse, missiles themselves after launch. Gunners fumbled through firing sequences that should have been genetically imprinted by then. Loaders hit the wrong buttons and sent missiles back into storage bays or made them jam half-loaded.

The third disaster was the new untried weapons systems themselves. The Nach'kal launch should have been 100 percent. In fact, less than seventy-one percent of the tubes fired.

Others refused to admit that they had been loaded or had acquirable targets or simply sat there. One entire bank of launchers went on automatic – but did not order the missile's drive systems to activate after launch. Several dozen Nach'kals were jettisoned into space before a volunteer short-circuited the bank's computer – electrocuting himself in the process.

But the tacships took hits even as they launched their Kali ship-killers.

One hit the *Forez*, exploding in a now-empty tacship hangar bay. Damage-control crews fought their way into the roaring fire and managed to damp the flames in minutes.

And then the first flotilla was trying to get out.

Five made it.

But the Tahn's attention was taken up by the second flotilla. Their orders were to kill the escorts.

They mostly did.

The Tahn destroyers maneuvered frantically under individual control. After the disaster of the Nach'kal launch, the *Forez*'s weapons officer was reluctant to give them support. Nine destroyers incandesced before the officer ordered the launch.

Twenty operator-guided long-range shipkillers spit out from the *Forez* and went looking for targets.

The flotilla, under tight control, spewed Fox countermissiles and Goblins keyed to home on the large Tahn ship-killing missiles. The operators, confused, lost targets and control. The missiles, told they were no longer in contact, obediently self-destructed.

The Imperial tacships came in again. Four of them struck for the cruiser.

Three of them hit the old ship, and it shuddered and broke in half. The halves, orbiting aimlessly but still moving at their initial velocity, were next sighted three E-years later by a survey ship. By then, it was of course far too late for the handful of Tahn who had survived the initial explosion.

The tacships broke once more and headed for home.

They had done enough.

Waiting in the wings were the heavies.

Atago ordered the first launch against the incoming Imperial ships at extreme long range.

Twelve self-guiding monsters floated out of their ports, and then their AM2 drives cut in. Each of them had multiple guided warheads with enough KT to kill a city the size of Heath's capital. The missiles, so new that they had not even been given a code name by Imperial Intelligence, worked superbly.

They ignored, as per last-minute instructions, any of the destroyers screening the larger Imperial ships, homed, and exploded. Their warheads had been instructed to *not* split on final acquisition. They disobeyed.

But the effect was still grim enough:

Two Imperial battleships destroyed.

One put out of action and later scrapped.

One cruiser destroyed.

One cruiser badly damaged.

Four cruisers forced out of battle.

Mahoney had been correct in anticipating the damage potential of the berserker.

Seconds later, in-range, the Imperial ships launched.

More than 30 Kalis, each operator-guided, homed on the *Forez*.

It was a confusion – Kalis were homed on each other, were operator-lost, and were even lost in sympathetic explosions after nearby missiles went off.

But the huge area of space occupied by the *Forez* and its escorts was a hell of explosions.

The remaining Tahn destroyers were dead or smashed out of battle.

The *Forez* itself took two hits.

But it was still coming in, still under full drive – and still firing.

The weapons officer was slightly pleased.

Recognizing the incompetence of his weapons crews, he had come up with a plan. The Nach'kal missiles were aimed for the incoming Imperial ships, but with little expectation of success. Also, they were set on rapid fire.

More effective were the close-range weapons: the ballistically aimed Don rockets and the volley-fired Mirkas. Even the chainguns were yammering at the Kalis when they got in range. The explosions were wreaking havoc with his electronics and sensors – but his ship was still alive.

The three hits were acceptable. One had taken out a combat information center near the stern – but there was a secondary center. Another had blasted the Nach'kal's main computer. No loss there. The third shattered the crew living spaces. No one should have been in them, anyway. The fires would soon be brought under control, he assumed. Besides, that was a task for damage control.

The fourth Kali, from the Imperial second launch, smashed into the *Forez* at that moment. A quarter of the Leviathan died in seconds as the nuclear blast ravened.

The bridge's lights died. Atago heard a suppressed shriek in the blackness. Then the secondary lights went on. She scanned faces. Who was the weakling?

There was no clue.

'Admiral,' she snapped to the *Forez*'s CO. 'Damage?'

It took a long moment. Half the bridge's screens were out or blinking nonsense. But eventually she had her information:

Engine Room: Capable of fifty percent drive. Yukawa drive units defunct.

Weapons: Percentages . . . percentages . . . Atago scanned on. Not good. The long-range missile system was dead. But she still had most of the shipkillers and even some of the Nach'kal systems left. The close-range systems had about twenty percent capability.

Casualties . . . Atago turned away. That was meaningless. She could still fight.

Another screen showed that the *Forez* would be within the heart of the Imperial fleet in minutes.

Atago's honor would be redeemed.

One of the more pointless and trivial pastimes military historians always had was trying to discover the specific person who got credit/blame for killing a great warrior/tyrant. Arguments as to whether von Richtofen was shot down by a fellow in-atmosphere pilot named Brown or potted out of the sky by a nameless Australian grunt were endlessly boring. Another Earth example: Which atmo-pilot had actually assassinated an admiral named Yamamoto – Lanphier or Barber?

More recently: Was Mordechi, battle leader of the Mueller, really killed in hand-to-hand combat by the mortally wounded Colonel Meinertzhagen, or did he in fact stumble on top of an anti-personnel mine?

So it was with Lady Atago and the *Forez*.

There were two main claimants.

One was a destroyer weapons officer named Bryennius. She had launched her Kali and then let it go 'dead' in space, directly in the orbital trajectory she had calculated for the oncoming *Forez*. At the right second she brought the missile alive and aimed it at the heart of the Tahn battleship.

The other was a particularly skilled tacship commander named Alexis. He had decided to fight his mosquito battle at the same time as the big boys and had tracked the *Forez*. When he assumed that the Tahn had other things on their minds, such as the recent three hits, he had launched his own Kali. He had screened it against the close-range rocket and chaingun fire by punting all eight of his Goblin XII missiles in front of the shipkiller.

Neither one of them was the hero, even though both Kalis were hits.

The historians, not for the first time, were wrong.

Lady Atago and the *Forez* were killed by Ensign Gilmer.

Or maybe the *Forez* killed herself.

The tiny hit on the *Forez*, hours before the battle had begun, had come from the tiny missile launched from Gilmer's picket ship.

It had, as the damage control computer said, only punctured the ship's outer skin. But it had not just lodged in the baffling. A small rip was made in the inner skin.

The compartment having been evacuated, no one noticed.

It was also not noticed that:

The fire retardant system between the ship's skins failed to operate.

The storage compartment's retardant system had never been filled.

The fire alarm itself was out of circuit, as was the alarm system for that entire subsector.

And there was a fire.

It was quite a small one, glowing, barely a spark. If the hole in the center skin had been larger, the fire would have gone out in the resultant vacuum. But the ship's atmosphere system kept pumping air into the compartment.

That was enough to feed the spark.

The spark grew. Flickered.

The compartment walls should have been treated with retardant. They were not. They were also made of a relatively low-temp synthetic. The compartment itself had non-manifested crates of waste rags.

The compartment walls melted – but not into the other corridor, where the fire could have been seen. Instead, it spread down the ship's side, toward the stern.

The damage-control computer still reported that nothing was wrong.

Finally the fire ravened, gutting through compartments. Crew members died before they could scream. Maybe, at that point, one of the computers made a report. If so, it went unnoticed in the heat of battle.

Eventually the blaze hit a firebreak. Two huge chambers ringed the ship, one above and one below the AM2 fuel storage. The chambers not only were filled with a completely inert and non-flammable material but were given multiple anti-blast, anti-radiation, anti-anything drop shields.

They did not drop when the outer wall went down.

Nor was the nonflammable substance perfection.

The *Forez* exploded microseconds before the two Kalis struck what had once been matter and now was energy.

Lady Atago might not have been that disappointed with her death. She had not reached the heart of the enemy, but she was firmly in command of her ship and about to issue an order – still in complete control.

But nearly instantaneously, she ceased to exist.

Along with more than 5,000 other crew members.

There were worse ways to die in a war.

Lady Atago had been responsible for many millions of people discovering almost all of them.

Chapter Fifty-Four

Lady Atago died with her honor intact. The living paid with their own. Her symbolic act of heroism backblasted all down the line, exploding every joint in the pipe of authority. Leadership collapsed in shame and despair, and the mob took to the streets, looking for someone to blame. The mob declared the season open on anyone wearing a uniform or even the lowliest badge of officialdom.

Sailors were dragged out of port bars and beaten to death. Thousands upon thousands gathered outside military posts to wail and grieve and tear their hair and then hurl themselves against the wire until they broke through. The soldiers fired on them, but only half-heartedly. Hundreds died, but still the crowds kept attacking. Many soldiers stripped off their uniforms and joined the mobs, leading the hunt for their officers. Police stations were set on fire, and the fleeing cops were pursued and hammered into gel with fists and feet. Postal workers were stoned to death on their rounds. Conductors were hauled out of their trains and hanged from light stanchions, then their bodies set ablaze to scream and struggle as living effigies. Many members of the Tahn High Council hid in their homes, beating their breasts in self-blame and remorse, not lifting a finger or even considering calling for help as their furious fellow citizens killed first their guards, then their servants, then their families, and finally them.

When the mob could find no one in authority left to slaughter, they turned on the merchants – most of whom had used their capitalist good sense to flee – looting the stores and shops, smashing open warehouses, and destroying everything they could not carry away. Huge columns of smoke and angry flames erupted across Heath, as if the planet had been thrown back in time to the volcanic age.

Only Chaboya – and the K'ton Klub – was left strangely alone. Sten and Alex had planned well. Each time a mob was tempted to invade the sin district, their agents steered the crowd away with shouted promises of softer and more deserving victims. Backed up by St. Clair and L'n, the two of them monitored the rioting from the rooftop nightclub. The big com unit they had smuggled into the club was alive with the back-and-forth chatter of their agents as first one target and then another fell. Heath was being prepped for invasion.

The rioting had raged for two weeks before Mahoney finally breached the last of the Tahn defenses. Sten and Alex got the word at midday. Suddenly all the radio chatter was swept away under the weight of Mahoney's wide-banded broadcast. He and Sten had decided before that there would be no time for a series of scrambled hide-and-seek broadcasts. Mahoney figured that a big planetwide bellow was sufficient cover.

'At that point,' he had said, 'I couldn't give a clot who knows I'm coming. And if I yell loud enough, the Tahn should have enough drakh in their shorts that they won't have the foggiest idea who I'm talking to. So. Soon as I say the word, you trigger the operation.'

'What'll we call it?' Sten asked.

'Oh, I dunno. How about Operation Black Cat?'

'Isn't that supposed to be bad luck?'

Mahoney had given him a wolfish grin. 'I was thinkin' more of the dead kind. That you drag across a grave.'

Sten did not have to ask whose grave Mahoney had in mind.

Alex and Sten had tumbled to their feet as soon as the com unit fell silent. They waited for agonizing seconds. Then the message came through. 'Institute Black Cat. Repeat. Institute Operation Black Cat. Are ya listenin', lad? Repeat. Institute Black . . .'

Sten bleated a fast 'I hear you,' and the signal cut-off in mid-message. He turned to his staff of three. They stood there, gaping, not believing that after all that time the end was finally there. They were all staring at him – even Alex – waiting for him to speak. Sten searched for something historical-sounding, something that an admiral would say. And right then and there Sten decided he would not be that kind of admiral. Clot history!

'You know what to do, people,' was all he said. And his staff of three jumped into motion.

St. Clair and L'n would immediately put the word out to their key agents. Alex would notify Chetwynd to get his big crook's behind to Koldyeze and stand by.

Sten would take care of Pastour himself. He dialed in the code, toggled the broadcaster timer to peep and out, peep and out, and then punched the button that would send the message to Pastour.

The chief bodyguard, Lemay, found Pastour working peacefully in his garden. The man's hands were shaking as he handed his superior the coded message. Lemay had no idea what it said, but he had been told to keep a twenty-four-hour watch on the basement com. Anything that came across was to be brought instantly to Pastour's attention. The man had failed in his duty. Lemay was the most loyal member of Pastour's personal staff and had spent the last two weeks in terror for his boss. Oddly, the mob never came to Pastour's door, so the terror was for nothing. Still, it had exhausted him, and he had fallen asleep on shift. The message came and went unnoticed, for how long, he did not know. For that slip-up he firmly believed he should have died if Pastour chose it. That the message was finally brought to his attention by a new member of the guard made his crime seem even worse. For that he should have died twice. The fact that the new guard was in Lemay's professional opinion a weasel and a worm did not help the matter.

He anxiously explained all that to Pastour, making no excuses and fully expecting the ultimate punishment. Then he realized that his colonel was not paying attention. Pastour read the message for the fourth time. His face was pale, his body cold. All the mental bracing for that moment was no help. Pastour was to make his way to Koldyeze as quickly as possible. There he and the most trusted members of his staff were to hold in position. They were to make sure that no prisoner was harmed as they waited for the Imperials to land. And then Pastour was to surrender for his people. For a moment Pastour thought he would prefer death over what was to come. Then he remembered Lady Atago and what her death had brought on. The moment passed, and Pastour gave Lemay his orders.

Sergeant Major Schour had the honor of being the first member of the Imperial invasion force to address a Tahn peasant. Schour's transport was part of the rear perimeter of the First Guards landing fleet that touched down just outside Heath.

Her lieutenant had chosen a nice soft green field. Sergeant Major Schour was the first trooper off. She lumbered down the ramp on short, muscular legs, willygun at the ready, eyes searching for some sign of enemy activity.

'Get out of my tubers!' a voice rasped out.

The sergeant major spun, fingers tightening on her trigger. Then her mouth fell open. Standing in front of her was a small, brawny figure dressed in the rough pale green and brown of a Tahn peasant. Pink tendrils wriggled angrily from what Schour imagined was the being's nose. The peasant in question was heatedly waving a hoe at the bewildered noncom. Schour noticed that the being was fur-bearing and had enormous forearms that ended in strong, stubby claws.

'What the clot did you say?' was all Schour could get out.

'Don't swear in my presence,' Lay Reader Cristata said. 'The Great One does not tolerate swearing!'

'I'm s-s-sorry,' Schour stuttered. 'But what—'

She broke off in bewilderment as more 'peasants' appeared. Three of them, all wearing the same pale green and brown, were obviously Imperials. The others were Tahn. Peaceful Tahn. Sten would have been at first massively surprised and then equally massively amused that everything had gone according to plan for Cristata. The lay reader not only had successfully escaped but had converted an entire Tahn peasant village.

'Are you going to remove yourself from our tubers, or are you going to force me to complain to your superiors?' Cristata asked.

All the amazed Schour could do was blurt, 'Don't you know there's a war on?'

Cristata sniffed, unconcerned. 'War – like governments – is for the lower orders,' he said. 'Both are forbidden. We who bask in the glory of the Great One do not participate in these mundane matters.'

The other peasants muttered in agreement, waving their hoes for emphasis. All Schour could do was gape and sweat and stutter. Cristata took pity on her. He put down his hoe and walked to Schour's side.

'You look very tired,' he sympathized. 'Perhaps this humble follower of the Great One could help you lift this burden from your spirit.'

And Cristata set about adding Sergeant Major Schour of the First Imperial Guards to his flock of converts.

Wichman had always been suspicious of Pastour's sudden illness and decision to reduce his public duties. The reports of Pastour's increased profile at Koldyeze had only added to his suspicions. And so, when the young, fresh-faced guard he had planted on Pastour's staff came to him with the news of the mysterious message and the sudden saddling up of the colonel and his staff to head for the monastery, it did not test his reasoning powers to add one and one and get the obvious two: Pastour was planning to protect the prisoners of Koldyeze. But for what purpose? What did Pastour expect to gain?

As the next piece of the puzzle fell into place, Wichman was filled with loathing. Pastour was a traitor. And he intended to use the prisoners as trading stock to assure his future as a toady for the Emperor.

But what could he, Wichman, do about it? Lady Atago, the last Tahn hero, had fallen. At that moment Wichman imagined Atago beckoning to him. And in his mind, the hero's mantle was passed on. Wichman would pick up her sword. And he pledged that before he died, there would not be one prisoner left alive at Koldyeze.

Senior Captain (Intelligence) Lo Prek ducked into the ruined tenement that lay just below the approach to Koldyeze. He had an assault rifle slung over his shoulder. At his belt was a rationpak. He tugged with all his puny strength at the door that hung from sprung hinges, jamming the entrance to the stairway that led up to the second floor. It finally gave way with a loud shriek that almost stopped his heart.

Lo Prek waited for a moment, breathing in deeply, until his heartbeat returned to normal and the fear was gone. Then he padded up the stairs. On the top floor, he found a gaping hole in the wall where a window once had been. From there he had a clear view of the front entrance of Koldyeze and the narrow cobblestone street that wound up the hill to the old cathedral.

Lo Prek cleared a space and settled in to wait.

That it was probably going to be a long wait did not trouble him at all. It was patience that had allowed him to track his brother's murderer across many years and millions of miles, and now he was sure his moment was near. Lo Prek had added one more factor to Wichman's logic. If there was to be a final fight for Koldyeze, Sten was sure to be there.

Lo Prek would be waiting.

He loaded his weapon and made final adjustments to the sights.

Chapter Fifty-Five

The survival of Koldyeze – and the lives of the many hundreds of VIP internees and POWs inside the walls – was perhaps attributable to the fact that Lieutenant Colonel Virunga had been a bit more of a musician than he had admitted to Sten.

When the young Virunga had become fascinated with reed instruments, to the point that his parents grudgingly paid for the astronomical cost of importing – from Earth – an archaic instrument called the saxophone, he had become part of a rebellion. The N'ranya's music at the time was formalized into a thirty-nine-tone structure, with each musical composition in two parts. Part one began with a certain number of notes, which were then repeated in varying patterns, with the section ending in a different key. Part two rang changes on those notes to finish eventually in the beginning key.

The N'ranya delighted in descending from their trees, gathering in great glades, and listening to those pieces. Virunga's generation found that boring, boring, boring and created other forms of music – music in which not only might a key never be repeated but each musician was permitted endless individual variations as he or she saw fit. They called it *y'zz* and gathered secretly in small clearings to perform the banned music.

Virunga, loving improvisation, was in no trouble when Sten's sonata in the key of freedom, for unaccompanied soloists, went badly awry.

The first movement opened in the cellars below Koldyeze. Combat-experienced prisoners unsealed the long-forgotten weapons in the crypts and trained those who were still sane and healthy enough to use them.

Grudgingly, Virunga let Kraulshavn and Sorensen prepare azimuth cards and range sketches for his soon-to-be-used artillery. He himself spent hours closeted with Derzhin and Avrenti, discussing what was inevitably going to happen – and what must occur. Avrenti, ever the professional, had no trouble realizing that he almost certainly would be serving new masters in short order. And Lord Pastour's increasing presence inside the prison made it easy for Derzhin to give in. The problem was Genrikh and the handful of uncorrupted Tahn guards he had as followers. But it was still not a problem, Virunga thought. His armed prisoners, plus Chetwynd's now-enlightened – translation: corrupted or scared – guards, would be capable of dealing with them.

The first movement closed, as expected, as Imperial ships blasted overhead. The landing was under way. Minutes later, sirens shrilled for an emergency formation and to open the second movement. The prisoners formed up slowly in spite of the screams of the guards. Virunga took the count. His formation leaders reported all prisoners accounted for. An alert Tahn was about to bellow in anger at the huge gaps in the formation. Instead, he found himself trying to shout through the ruins of a windpipe and then collapsed.

The killing had been done by Sorensen. Mahoney's giving Sten Sorensen's code word had done more than merely grant access to his mental battle computer – it also freed Sorensen to exercise some of his other Mantis Team skills.

Police Major Genrikh was standing at the head of the guards' formation, facing the prisoners, when he saw that guard die. He could see other prisoners – armed prisoners – suddenly appearing on battlements and on balconies. He was shouting a command, gun coming up and aiming across the courtyard at Sorensen when Chetwynd moved. Initially, Chetwynd had growled at Sten's orders. By rights, he should have been out on the streets running his teams. He considered further. Suppose things did not go exactly right in the beginning? A being could get killed being the first to fight. Koldyeze seemed a fairly good place to wait until the Empire stabilized things. And there was something else to take care of.

The something else was Genrikh – Genrikh and all the clotting Tahn guards and cops who had bashed Chetwynd around from the time he had first jackrolled a drunk sailor to the present day.

Genrikh took aim – and two anchor cables smashed around him. Then he was kicking, lifted into the air in Chetwynd's bear hug. His shout became a gurgle of blood as Chetwynd's arms tightened, smashing ribs and caving Genrikh's chest in.

Chetwynd pitched Genrikh's body aside and went for the other 'loyal' guards. He dived for the cobblestones as projectile weapons cracked and men went down. The POW marksmen practiced some restraint, killing the rest of Genrikh's bullies no more than two or three times apiece.

Virunga stood motionless, waiting for the slaughter to end. Then he turned his attention to Derzhin and Avrenti. The remainder of the guards fingered their weapons, unsure of what to do.

'It . . . begun. Lay down . . . arms. Return to quarters. Wait further orders. Follow orders . . . no one harmed.'

And so, when Lord Pastour and his escorts arrived, Koldyeze was already in Imperial hands. He was greeted politely and shown to very safe quarters deep in the castle cellars.

That was the end of the second movement.

The third movement should have been nearly pastoral. Imperial ex-prisoners manned Koldyeze's gun towers, the guns turned outward.

All the prisoners had to do was wait inside their prison for eventual relief by the Empire. Any still-fighting Tahn should have been easily discouraged by a few accurate rounds and convinced to go elsewhere to find more meaningful death.

Instead, the third movement opened with the grating of tracks as four heavy tanks rumbled up the cobblestone street toward Koldyeze.

Lord Wichman. And friends.

Those friends consisted of the squadron of heavy tracks, one squadron of recon tracks, a scout company of gravsleds, and nearly a battalion of soldiers. The prisoners of Koldyeze could be very grateful that Wichman had not been able to acquire any tacnukes.

A prisoner team manning one of the watchtowers ran a burst from its chaingun across the bow of the lead track – and the tank's cannon blew the watchtower apart.

The new arrivals were not there for a casual investigation.

Virunga got on the com to Sten.

The rest of the symphony would be *y'zz.*

Sten, even though he had gone through the long, drawn-out defeat in the Fringe Worlds, still had not realized there were so many ways of being told he was clotted.

He stood in the middle of what had formerly been the K'ton Klub's main lounge and was now his com center. Koldyeze was up against it. There was no way that Virunga and the rest of the POWs could hold out against an armored attack. And there appeared to be nothing that could be done. His link with the Imperial Forces around Heath told him their attacks were stalled. They had three days minimum until they broke through. Negative on tac-air. There were still enough AA missiles sited to make any air support run nearly suicidal. And Wichman's units were too close to hazard even an operator-guided missile attack.

He glanced out a window and winced. He did not need a weatherman to tell him that a storm front was closing in. He saw drizzle and fog. Across the room, Kilgour was already at a computer terminal. A wallscreen cleared, and a map appeared. The map showed Heath's capital with five-meter contour lines. The map shifted, and Koldyeze was suddenly at the map's center.

Sten crossed to the map and studied it. The contour lines grouped very close together around Koldyeze, and Sten's leg muscles memory-ached, remembering the number of times he had groaned up that steep cobblestone street when he was a prisoner. Oh-ho.

'Turn that sucker and animate it,' he ordered.

The map changed, and Sten was staring at a lateral projection of Koldyeze showing that outlined, ruined cathedral atop the rise.

'Alex,' he wondered aloud, 'you got any read on what kinda crunchies Wichman's got?'

'Negative, boss. But Ah'll bet it's nae th' Tahn's finest.'

Probably not, Sten thought. 'Spin it again.'

Once more Sten stared 'straight down' at Koldyeze.

He had an idea – of sorts. But he needed one thing.

He asked Kilgour.

'Ah lack exact whae y' need, but Ah hae a wee ersatz.'

'Nobody's looted it?'

'Ah gie m' word, wee Sten. Nae e'en a desperate Tahn'd go near it.'

'You got two gravsleds running?'

'Ah hae.'

And Kilgour was out the door.

Sten, who had planned to spend the last few days of the war sitting in his web being big daddy spider, grabbed the waiting combat harness from the wall and tugged it on.

He looked across the room at St. Clair. She shook her head in disbelief, and he shrugged, then went down the stairs.

Kilgour, already in fighting gear, was waiting outside at the controls of the gravsled. Behind him were two of Chetwynd's agents at the controls of a cargo sled. Both vehicles were battered and battle-damaged but still lift-capable. Sten clambered in, and Alex took off.

'How do you know the stuff's still there?'

'D' ye ken,' Alex went on, 'thae quadrped we noted, aye back th' day we arrived ae Heath?'

Sten thought back – and recalled that four-legged creature ridden by a Tahn officer. 'A hearse?'

'Close, lad. At any rate, dinnae y' wonder whae happens to horses when they die?'

Sten had not.

'The term is renderin't. An' stinkit. Th' recyclin't center's still there an' reekin't. We'll hae our social lubricant.'

Kilgour did not have an order of battle for Wichman's assault unit, but his guess had been correct.

The recon squadron was a recently activated reserve unit made up of soldiers previously invalided out of combat; the gravsled unit had been formed by cadets from one of the Tahn military secondary schools; and the infantrymen had been grabbed from the walking wounded, replacement centers, and transport depots.

The heavy tracks were factory-fresh and intended to be driven directly to the front lines and sent into combat. They were so new that they lacked even a coat of camouflage anodizing. Their crews were civilian – final line inspectors who had been grabbed and given orders by Wichman's people. Only one inspector had objected – and been promptly shot by H'nrich, Wichman's chief of security. The others did what they were told.

They attacked Koldyeze.

The first tank made Sten's plan possible.

The first watchtower destroyed, the tank ground into motion up the cobbled street, its cannon finger probing for a new target. The gunner's sights swept across the second watch-tower on the other side of Koldyeze's gates. There was no sign of motion. The gunner looked for a better target.

Very slowly, the chaingun in that second watchtower swiveled. The skinny man crouching in the gunner's seat turned to the equally emaciated man kneeling beside him. 'Is it loaded?'

'I think so. You figure out how to shoot it?'

'Hell if I know.'

'You know that popgun ain't gonna punch through that tin can down there, don't you?'

'Shaddup. I live a clean life.'

The ex-POW loading the chaingun would have been correct –
under normal circumstances. The anti-personnel rounds in the
chaingun should have spattered off the heavy tank like raindrops.
But the tank's designers had assumed that no clotting driver would
ever be dumb enough to take that track over a pile of rubble and
expose its belly and extremely vulnerable escape hatch.

The scared civilian behind the tank's controls was that dumb.

And the Imperial soldier behind the chaingun's triggers was a
very good shot.

Ten rounds blew the hatch off its locks – *into* the tank's crew
compartment – and then ricocheted. Heavy armor could keep things
in as well as out.

There were two survivors, and they were shot down by riflemen
as they scrambled out the rear hatch for safety.

'Not bad,' the loader said.

'Not bad at all,' the gunner said.

Ten seconds later smoke wisped out of the tank's atmosphere
exhausts, and the track 'brewed up' in flames.

The easy way to take Koldyeze had been cut.

Virunga wondered what his still-unknown attacker would try
next.

Probably an infantry assault.

That indeed was what Wichman had in mind. But his cobbled-
together assault unit was still getting itself organized, and most of
the improvised platoons were nowhere near the line of departure
when whistles shrilled.

About a company of grunts started up the hill. They were quickly
shot down or into shelter. There was no second wave. Instead, they
started building barricades across the streets and creating fighting
positions inside the tenements.

Perfectly fine, Virunga thought. We have no intention of counter-
attacking, and if they turn this into a siege, perhaps we can hold
on until the Imperial Forces arrive.

Perhaps. He went to prepare what he was trying to convince
himself was his artillery.

At twilight, Sten and Alex were crouched on the roof of one of
the tenements, looking for a way in.

Below them, hidden in wreckage, was the larger gravsled, its
cargo slooping and stinking, just as Kilgour had promised.

Sten saw an opportunity to create some chaos.

The cadets manning the gravsleds were evidently trying to attack Koldyeze as if they were Scythians bashing out a Roman legion. Their sleds darted back and forth and up and down, the sleds' gunners occasionally blasting off a burst or two. Good shots. They hit Koldyeze almost every other time.

Sten waited until dark, then flipped on the light-enhancing sights of his sniper rifle. It was a fairly nasty weapon that fired a tiny, shielded AM2 round that on impact would blow a hole in a man's chest that a gravsled could be driven through. But unlike the issue willygun, the heavy sniper rifle used a modified linear accelerator to propel the round. The scope was used not merely to give a precise range and fix on the target but could be turned if the target happened to go behind a wall. On firing, the accelerator would spin the round at the appropriate time – and the gun was quite capable of shooting around a corner.

Sten did not need that much trickery.

He put the scope's cross hairs on a gravsled pilot and blew him out of his seat. When the gunner jumped for the controls, he died, too.

A few seconds later, five gravsleds were orbiting around the ruined streets below Koldyeze aimlessly.

That would provide the necessary chaos.

Kilgour and Sten dropped down the shattered tenement steps and into their own sled and moved slowly forward. Their advance went seemingly unobserved – at least none of the rounds that slammed into the ground nearby seemed particularly aimed.

They reached the still-smoldering tank, and Kilgour steered the sled around it. He turned, free hand question-marked, then pointed down. *Here?* Sten signed: *Ten meters more.* Kilgour obeyed and then grounded the gravsled.

And they almost got themselves killed.

In spite of Virunga's bellows and protests about losing his battle computer and fifty percent of Gaaronk's operators, Sorensen put together an ambush team. He was – at least as far as he knew – the only Mantis operative inside Koldyeze. But there were POWs from other hands-on lethal units who wanted a bit of close-in revenge. They slid out of the cathedral toward the destroyed track.

Sorensen knew that Wichman's forces had to remove that hulk before they could send in more armor. Figuring that combat engineers were few and far between those days, he intended to kill a few recovery specialists.

He saw the gravsled ground and crept toward the two Tahn – he thought – getting out of it. Eyes away, he reminded himself. His backup men flanked him. Sorensen readied the long ceremonial knife he was carrying. He would take the heavier one first. Then—

A flare bloomed on the horizon, and all five men became bushes. The flare sank down, and Sorensen's two targets were alive once more. The smaller man's hands moved to one side, then together, as if holding a package. Patrol sign language, Sorensen realized. Had the Tahn stolen that from the Imperials? He decided to take a chance and hissed sibilantly.

The two men crouch-spun, weapons coming up. But they did not fire.

'ID,' Sorensen whispered.

Sten realized that the whisper was not in Tahn. He assumed that the ambushers must have come out of Koldyeze.

'Imperials.'

'One forward.'

Kilgour rumbled toward Sorensen.

Sorensen's night vision was almost gone – the vitamin-lousy diet the Tahn had fed them ensured that. Even with the added rations from the discovered stores, he still was looking at a blur when Alex recognized him.

'Wee Sorensen,' he whispered.

The accent was enough.

Sorensen waved his team forward and hand question-marked. *Need help?* Sten nodded ostentatiously, then indicated. Two out as security. The rest – start pouring.

Sten lifted the gravsled's nose slightly, and the semi-liquid cargo sloshed out. As Sten shoveled glop out onto the cobblestones, he wondered if it was a lum. Kilgour was always closing letters with some nonsense phrase about somebody's lum reeking. And dead hearse – horse, he corrected – did reek. Kilgour had been quite correct – no one had looted the rendering works. And the liquefied fat from the vats should work very well.

They finished and regrouped. Sten had planned on reentering Koldyeze with Alex through the still-undiscovered tunnel. But obviously Sorensen had a better way.

Sten sent the gravsled, at full power, back down the street. It ricocheted away, caroming off buildings and providing an excellent diversion. Then everyone doubled back toward Koldyeze. Sten had ordered Sorensen's run aborted; he figured that the demolished track would not be recovered by specialists. Wichman's people were more adept at brute force – and Sorensen would be more than a little outgunned.

Sten went through the half-opened main gate, hoping that Koldyeze's water supply was still turned on. He smelled. Smelled like . . . a dead horse.

A very dead horse.

Sten was correct. The ruined track was bulldozed out of the street and through a tenement wall early in the morning by a second heavy tank. Sorensen's ritual butcher knife would not have done much good.

Wichman attacked, predictably at dawn.

And Virunga unmasked his artillery.

It was not much.

The crypt had held four cannon. Real cannon, not lasers or masers: put shell and propellant in one end and yank a handle, and it works – maybe. Virunga thought the cannon were probably intended for some kind of ceremonial use, although that did not explain why they had sights, and ordered the barrels wire-wrapped for reinforcement. Virunga had marveled at the sights. They were primitive. It had been years since he had seen a laser ranging cannon, and then only in a museum.

Working parties had managed to hoist the cannon onto the battlements, and firing apertures had been bashed through the walls and then concealed. Virunga was pretty sure that the recoil mechanism of the cannon was rusted solid. Regardless, he did not plan on taking chances and had ringbolts spotwelded to the cannon and bolted to the cathedral walls themselves. Cables linked the guns to the wall bolts and, hopefully, would prevent the cannon from recoiling straight off the battlements when they were fired.

Virunga had found and trained cannoneers, then dubbed his four popguns 'Battery A.'

'Battery B' was eight multiple-tube rocket launchers, firing solid heads, powered by propellant picked from the projectile rounds stores in the crypts and then hard-packed into containers. At least there was more than enough propellant. Aiming consisted of squinting through a V-sight atop the tubes until the target was more or less aligned and then getting the hell out of the way while someone hit an electrical firing connection. The launchers were crewed and then sited atop other battlements.

'Battery C' was even worse.

Observing that the castle's plumbing seemed built for all eternity, Virunga had ordered sections of pipe to be cut into meter-and-a-half sections and wire-reinforced. He was making mortars. Very, very big mortars.

Micrometers, small inspection telescopes, bubble levels, gears, and knobs had been stolen from the various workshops that the POWs slave-labored for and had been cobbled together to make sights for the mortars.

Virunga discovered that the propellant used in the rifle rounds could be liquefied and cast without harm. He decided to use that powder, cast into round increments, to fire his mortar rounds. The rounds themselves were smaller sections of pipe built up again with wire to approximate the interior dimensions of the mortar tubes. They were hand-grooved so the pipe would shrapnel on impact, but not deeply enough that the round would explode on firing.

Maybe.

The rounds were packed with more propellant. Nitric acid, alk, and mercury were gingerly mixed by self-taught POW chemists to make the horribly dangerous mercury fulminate that would be used to detonate the rounds on impact.

Maybe.

Virunga readied firing positions in the courtyard for the mortars, with high-stacked stone around them in case the bad guys had mortars of their own.

The tiny com units that had been brought to Heath by Sten and smuggled into Koldyeze by Chetwynd were the only modern items Virunga had. They linked the observers to the batteries. In spite of the risk – the observers were located anywhere the streets around Koldyeze could be seen from – there was no shortage of volunteers.

Thirty seconds after the first tank popped into open, Virunga opened fire.

'Battery A. Armor in the open. Acquire targets visually. Fire on individual control.'

The gun commander of the first cannon had one of the recon tracks in his sights. He held his breath and yanked the firing lever. The cannon cracked and slammed back against the cable restraints. The commander stared down at the streets below. The round slammed into a wall about five meters from the recon track.

'Come on down a little bit and right a skosh,' the commander advised the gunner. He was not, needless to say, a trained artillery-being.

The third round ventilated the thinly armored recon track, and its crew bailed out.

Virunga smiled in pleasure.

His other three guns were also firing and hitting.

Down below, the three heavy tracks ground up the street toward the cathedral. One of them took a direct hit from a cannon, but the solid round ricocheted off the track's armor plating.

Sten peered through a battlement's machicolations and swore. He had hoped that somehow Virunga's cannon would have enough power to punch holes in the heavy tracks. The only thing that could stop them, he realized, was his deceased horses.

The tank clattered slowly up the cobblestones toward Koldyeze, infantry moving forward in its shelter. Then the track hit the grease. Its tracks spun uselessly on the cobble-stones. The huge tank slid sideways and back down the hill, slamming into the first hulk.

And then the defenders of Koldyeze got lucky.

Not, of course, that luck was ever mentioned by either Sergeant Major Isby, observing for Battery C, or by the mortar crew. Isby, even though he was a supply specialist, had been given infantry training, which at one time had included artillery/mortar observation. He remembered his lessons quite well.

'Charlie Two,' he broadcast. 'This is Observer Six. Fire Mission. Azimuth 5250 down 30. Distance 3200. Tanks and infantry in the open. Will adjust.'

The sights of the mortar were adjusted, and two still-brawny women, VIP hostages, fitted firing charges onto the mortar bomb and hoisted it up over the mortar's mouth, let go, and ducked away.

The mortar thudded. Sten saw the wobbling pipe climb high into the sky, then turn and drop downward. The first round hit the stalled track directly on top of its engine exhaust plates and exploded. The tank itself blew up, sending its turrets cartwheeling away into the infantry around it.

Once again, the way was blocked.

Isby and the mortar crew, of course, said that the first-round hit proved how good they were. They bragged accordingly. They did not think it worthy of note to mention that they hit nothing else for the rest of that day.

And then the infantry began its assault.

They came in cautiously, keeping to the cover of the tenements and rubble. But they still had to come into the open eventually.

Sten methodically sniped down an entire squad of grunts who were hiding behind what they thought was solid stone. Other marksbeings, now familiar with the projectile sporter weapons they were equipped with, decimated the infantry.

But the siege of Koldyeze was still being lost by the ex-prisoners.

Slowly the ring of Wichman's troops closed on Koldyeze. There was just too many of them.

The single chaingun that survived atop the second watchtower was smashed by three accurate rounds from another heavy tank firing over the corpse of its brother. Tahn soldiers countersniped from positions on the roofs of tenements.

Sten saw a POW lying on the battlement not far from him slump, the top of her head suddenly missing.

'Dinnae y' hope, young Sten,' Alex observed, 'thae our wee Guardsmen aren't takin' long mess breaks?'

Sten hoped that very desperately.

Chief Warrant Officer Rinaldi Hernandes had wondered what would happen if he survived imprisonment long enough to get a weapon in his hands. Could he kill – even beings who had been responsible for his grandchild's death?

He could.

Somewhere Hernandes had found an enormous rifle – nearly as long as he was – that single-fired a round the size of the cheroots he missed desperately. It was an ancient rifle fitted with a museum-quality optical sight.

But it was a very effective antique.

Hernandes held his sights on the target – a Tahn in the gunner's seat of a gravsled. He breathed in deeply. Then he let out half the breath and held. His finger pulled the forward trigger, then moved back to the set trigger. It touched the metal, and the rifle slammed him.

Kilgour had taken one look at Hernandes's weapon and dubbed it a 'dinosaur gun.'

'Because it'd kill a dinosaur,' Sten straight-manned.

'Na, clot. Because it takit a dinosaur to fire the beast.'

It damn near did. The rifle kicked – hard. Hernandes was pretty sure that his shoulder was if not broken at least cracked a lot.

But it was far worse on the arrival end.

The gunner in the gravsled had time enough to notice that he lacked a pelvis before he died.

Hernandes carefully scratched a mark on the stone next to him. That made twenty-seven.

He looked for another target.

Downslope, a Tahn sergeant spotted the movement, sighted, and touched a trigger.

The three-round burst blew Hernandes's abdomen apart.

The decimation went on.

Virunga reflexively ducked when the explosion went off, the blast echoing seemingly endlessly around the courtyard walls.

And then the screams started.

The first of the mortars had exploded. Thirty-one people were dead or maimed around the shattered metal. Medics scurried to help.

Virunga kept his expression untroubled. At least the blast walls had provided an unexpected side benefit and kept the damage moderate. But Virunga knew that the three remaining mortars would be shot on a duck-and-fire principle. Koldyeze, he estimated, could hold no more than another day, at best.

And that night Wichman's forces mined the wall.

Wichman gave precise orders. Even though he was inexperienced at combat, he was learning rapidly.

I could have served better, he realized with resentment. I should have resigned my post for a combat command when this war began. Perhaps . . .

But he was not egotistic enough to think he could have changed things.

But this would be enough: a final revenge against the traitors and a final strike against the Imperials. Koldyeze was to be completely illuminated, both by flares and from six mobile searchlights that one of his aides had scrounged. Chainguns on the recon tracks were to sweep the walls. Any Imperial prisoner who stuck his head up would be slaughtered.

His plan worked.

When he was satisfied that all fire from the cathedral had been suppressed, he sent in the troops with demopacks. Nearly ten tons of high explosive was arranged at the foot of the wall. His next assault, which would occur an hour before dawn, was certain to succeed.

Unfortunately, Lord Wichman did not survive to see whether his tactics were successful.

Sten, outranking Sorensen, pulled the plug on the young man's commando operations. Virunga was right – they could not stand to lose him. Especially not now, with Virunga's cannon firing by calculation, calculation made possible only by Sorensen's mind functioning as a battle computer.

But those orders did not hold true for Sten.

After dusk, he and Alex went out looking for trouble. They went through the Tahn perimeter easily, all the old Mantis moves returning. Beyond the front lines, they split up and began their head-hunting.

Sten carried a miniwillygun with a single magazine of ammunition. If he was blown, he knew better than to imagine he would be able to shoot his way out. He carried four Mantis demolition packs with him, along with two grenades and a Gurkha kukri he had brought back to Heath.

The demopacks were the first to go. With a variable time set on the fuses, they were deposited, one on the deck of a recon track, one in the middle of four parked gravsleds, the third on one of the searchlight's generators, and the final one under what Sten thought was a com trailer.

Large cables led from that trailer into a well-guarded building. Sten found that interesting. He slipped into that building's neighbor and found an appropriate-length section of metal stair banister. On the roof, he positioned the banister across to the guarded building and hand-over-handed his way onto its roof, the rusty metal bending slightly as he went. He crept down the stairs, keeping low and close to the wall.

Lousy blackout, he thought, seeing a gleam of light from the curtained doorway of a room on the second floor. Then he saw the bulk next to it.

H'nrich might have been an excellent bodyguard against normal intruders.

Sten was not normal.

H'nrich's eye registered a flash in the dimness as the kukri came up from below. That was all.

Sten yanked the kukri out of H'nrich's neck – he had pulled the slash so he would not have to worry about a head bouncing around the hallway – caught the sagging, blood-spouting body, and eased it down. He sheathed the kukri, wiped stickiness from his face, and took three deep breaths.

The question was not what was going to happen next but what would happen *next* next. Specifically, would Sten have time to get out with his vital signs vital before the reaction.

Possibly.

He took the two grenades from his webbing and rolled the timer until the X was under his fingers. Ten seconds.

Come on, son. Don't get cowardly now.

His hand blurred the pistol from its holster, and Sten went through the blackout curtain.

There were seven beings in the room. One of them, Sten's mind registered, was wearing a dress uniform, and then he ID'd Lord Wichman as his finger pulled the trigger to its stop and the AM2 rounds spit around the room.

Four rounds tore Wichman's body apart. Sten's free hand lobbed the grenades at the com console, and then he was gone.

There were screams and shouts and somebody outside shooting at something.

Sten was back up the steps, three at a time, almost falling through a broken lift, then on the roof and across. Running. He hit the far edge, eyes telling him he could make the jump, mind saying you ain't no Kilgour, and then he was in the air.

He landed at least a meter on the other side of that third building's parapet. Getting cowardly, he thought once more, and then melted into the night toward Koldyeze.

Sten came back to awaiting catastrophe.

He had seen the searchlights blinding on the walls of Koldyeze, realized that he could not return the way he had come out, and went once more through the tunnel.

Virunga brought him quickly up to speed; they had heard, and seen, the demolition charges being planted. When the Tahn had pulled back, four brave men and women had tried to get to the charges. Their bodies lay only a few meters beyond the gate.

Not, Sten thought privately, that they could have accomplished much. He assumed that the demo charges were not only separately det-timed but booby-trapped as well. The romantic days of putting the fuse seconds before the bang banged were, as ancient as Hernandes's rifle.

'Ordered,' Virunga said, 'all troops back from wall. If Koldyeze doesn't fall on our heads . . . will retake fighting positions after blast.

'Better suggestion?' he asked Sten hopefully.

Sten had none. Neither did Kilgour when he returned an hour later.

They looked for a big rock to hide behind.

*

Wichman might have been dead, but his troops soldiered on.

The blast went off – on schedule.

The shock wave blew down five entire rows of already-shattered tenements. The ground earthquake-shook, and in their still-separate battle two kilometers away, Imperial guardsmen ducked, sure that somebody had set off a nuke. The blast cloud rose more than three kilometers into the clouds despite the continuing drizzle.

The entire front wall of the cruciform-shaped cathedral crumbled, and slid down the hill.

But only six POWs died. Koldyeze had indeed been built to withstand almost anything.

The Tahn mounted what was to be the final attack – and ran instantly into trouble.

The ruins of that front wall made an excellent tank trap – far superior even to Sten's grease. Even the heavies could not grind through the building-high boulders.

Only the gravsleds could provide support for the infantry.

Somewhat surprised that they were still alive, the Imperial defenders boiled out of their holes and found fighting positions.

Gravsled pilots were hit, and the gravsleds orbited out of the battle. The first wave of the Tahn infantry was obliterated.

But the second wave found forward positions and laid down a base of fire.

The third wave attacked, and the gravsleds were able to move in.

The prisoners pulled back. Back and down.

Into the crypts.

'Clottin' convenient place to die,' Kilgour observed, sourly looking around the cellar. 'Thae'll be na need to dig a wee grave.'

Virunga herded the last of the hostages down more stone steps deeper into the subbasements and limped back toward Sten.

Sten had hastily reorganized the surviving fighters into five-man squads and given each one a position to hold: a stairwell, a landing, a portion of the huge basement he himself was in. Anything bullet-resistant had been dragged up as a barricade.

He had not needed to tell his squads they were to hold till the last – none of the Imperial prisoners were stupid enough to believe the Tahn were interested in recapturing them.

Kilgour, three-gee muscles straining, had lifted a stone altar into position for his and Sten's personal last stand. He spread out his remaining grenades and ammunition in front of him.

Sten followed suit.

'Y' know, wee Sten,' Kilgour observed. 'If thae clottin' Tahn hae brain one, thae'll just filter gas down the steps an' be done wi' us. Thae's nae a filtermask t' be had.'

At least, Sten thought, that would be relatively painless.

'Or p'raps,' Kilgour went on relentlessly, 'thae'll just seal us up alive. Thae'll be no bones f'r m' mum t' mourn over. An me a claustrophobe, too.'

Sten showed his teeth in what he realized probably did not much resemble a smile and settled down to wait for death.

It was, surprisingly, a fairly long wait.

They dimly heard the sound of firing from above. Sten wondered. Had the Tahn found some other way down to them? The firing suddenly rose to a dull storm and died away. There was the crack of single shots then.

Sten looked at Kilgour.

'Na,' Alex suggested. 'Thae's too convenient.'

But both of them replaced their grenades and ammo into their harnesses and moved slowly up the steps toward the courtyard. A burst of fire shattered down at them, and they ducked behind the turn in the stairwell.

'Clot,' Alex swore. 'Ah was right. Too convenient.'

Sten waited for the requisite grenade to roll down on them. But instead there came a shout in very bad Tahn.

'Surrender. Weapons no. Hands air in.'

Sten and Alex grinned. And Sten shouted back in Imperial.

'Friends. Imperial. Kiss to be kissed.'

'One up,' came the shout, in Imperial but still suspicious.

Sten shucked his combat harness and, moving very slowly, hands in plain sight, climbed the steps until he saw two battered guardsmen, their red, exhausted eyes glaring through filthy faces. And he kissed them both.

Out of common courtesy, the one with the beard got the first one.

They were rescued.

The relief force was commanded by a one-star general. Imperial forces had mounted a massive armor assault and driven a wedge through the Tahn lines.

They had not stopped to widen that perimeter but had kept on moving, their tracks slamming at full speed through the city of Heath. Gravsleds hovered above them. Gunners opened fire on any movement without checking to see whether the target was a scared civilian or a Tahn soldier. They had hit the remnants of Wichman's forces in the rear and scattered them.

Sten and Alex stood in the courtyard, listening to the general. He was very proud of himself and his men.

Why not? Sten thought in stupid fatigue. After I sleep for about six months, I'll buy him a beer, too. Come to think, I'll buy anybody in this unit as much alk as they can pour down. Or whatever else they take, he amended. He was turning to Kilgour to suggest they find somewhere to collapse – and suddenly the Scotsman's rifle was snapping to his shoulder.

Senior Captain Lo Prek was aiming very carefully. He had followed the assault wave into Koldyeze, and no one had bothered asking who the hell he was.

He had found a position inside Koldyeze itself and waited. Perhaps Sten was outside the walls, or perhaps inside. But he knew that he would have his chance.

He ignored the destruction of Wichman's soldiers and the victorious Imperials. That was not a part of his war.

And at that point he was rewarded, seeing below him the man who had murdered his brother.

As his sights found Sten, his heart thundered and he aimed, knowing he would get only a single shot.

Sten and the Guards general went down as Kilgour fired a long, chattered *snap-burst* that blew apart the cathedral window above them.

Kilgour lowered the rifle.

'What was—' Sten managed, and Alex waved the barrel.

A body slumped forward out of the window and hung, motionless.

'Clottin' sniper,' Kilgour said.

Sten picked himself up. That was it. For him, the war was over.

The body of Senior Captain Lo Prek was eventually picked up by a press gang of Tahn civilians under the direction of an Imperial sanitation expert, loaded onto a gravsled, and taken outside the city. It was cremated, along with several thousand other, equally nameless bodies.

And the war was over.

Chapter Fifty-Six

The surrender document was a small off-white sheet of parchment. There were very few words penned on the document itself, because there were *no* terms. The surrender was unconditional.

From the moment the document was signed and then countersigned, the Tahn would have to depend on the charity and mercy of the Eternal Emperor.

The document sat upon a small linen-covered table. Behind the table sat Ian Mahoney, the Emperor's representative and newly appointed governor-general of what had once been the Tahn Empire. The table and chair were the only furnishings in the yawning main banquet room of the *Normandie*.

It was in that room that the incident that had triggered the war had taken place. On that day it had been crammed with tables laden with delicacies to be enjoyed by the cream of Tahn diplomacy. It was there that an entirely different sort of document was to have been signed: a declaration of peace. And the Emperor himself had presided. But the incident had ended in murder and the betrayal of both camps.

Now the Emperor was nowhere in sight. His deliberate absence was a calculated act to add to the Tahn's humiliation. Instead, there was Mahoney, his two chief aides standing at full attention on either side of him, and, lined up along the walls of the room, the top officers of the Emperor's fleets and armies.

On the far side of the room, partially hidden by a hastily hung curtain, was a livie crew filming the event for Empirewide broadcast.

The main portal hissed open, and Colonel Pastour stepped in. He was the sole surviving member of the Tahn High Council. In a moment he would be just citizen Pastour. The Emperor had decreed that once the surrender had been signed, there would be no ranks or titles permitted in the lands of the Tahn.

As Pastour started the long, slow march toward the table, two other Tahn trailed behind him. One was dressed in the ragged uniform of a customs officer. The other wore that of a postal official. They were the highest Tahn officials anyone could find. Pastour himself, at the demand of the Emperor, wore civilian clothes.

Pastour came to a stop just in front of the table. The only movement in the room was Mahoney's head as it lifted. Two eyes below bushy, forbidding eyebrows bored into him. Pastour hesitated, unsure what to do next. He thought of his people watching on the public-square screens that the Imperials had erected in every major city. He knew it was his duty to abase himself for them. But how much humiliation would be required?

Mahoney slid the document toward him.

'Sign!' was all he said.

Pastour fumbled for a pen and scratched his name. Mahoney flipped the document over and signed his name beneath Pastour's. He handed it to one of his aides. Then he looked up at Pastour, his eyes filled with hate. Oddly, the hate was comforting. *That* Pastour understood.

'That's all,' Mahoney said.

And in total silence, citizen Pastour turned and stumbled away.

Admiral Sten paced back and forth in the passageway. A commentator's voice crackled from speakers mounted on either end of the corridor, analyzing the events that were unfolding for his audience. As Sten paced, he kept glancing at the door that led to the Emperor's stateroom. And any moment, he would be called into his commander in chief's presence. Sten was one of the few people who were aware that the Eternal Emperor *was* aboard the *Normandie*.

'He said it was his damned show,' Mahoney had explained, 'and he planned to have a ringside seat, even if he couldn't allow himself to be there in person.'

Sten understood that, just as he admired the Emperor's willpower in staying away from the ceremony itself. If it were Sten, protocol be damned, he would want to see his enemy squirm close up. But that was not what he was thinking as he paced nervously.

His head was buzzing with questions, which mostly boiled down to, What did the boss want of him next? Sten was sick of anything vaguely involving official violence. He was sick of killing. Sick of manipulations. Sick of giving orders and sick of seeing his fellow beings dying carrying them out. He was wearing his new admiral's uniform for the first time, and he was already sick of that, as well. Sten was fuzzily imagining some kind of life that had nothing to do with the military. He was not sure what he would do with it, but he felt good just wondering.

St. Clair and L'n were in the process of selling the K'ton Club. Maybe he would join them in whatever venture they had in mind. Clot, after the bundle Ida had made for him, he could bankroll streets and streets of nightclubs. Sten in showbiz? Nah. Wouldn't wash. Maybe he should talk to Kilgour. Maybe they could team up and do a little poking around some frontier systems. See what the Indians were up to.

He was casually considering the prospector's life and wondering if St. Clair or Haines might fit in, when the door *whooshed* open and a Gurkha beckoned him inside.

The Eternal Emperor palmed the switch that cut the vidscreen off as Sten entered and came to full attention.

'Knock it off, Admiral,' the Emperor said impatiently, 'I've had it with ceremony. And I hope it doesn't offend your military sensibilities when I inform you that soldiering of any kind is starting to give me a pain in my royal behind.'

Sten laughed, not offended at all, and slumped into a chair. The Emperor got up, fetched a bottle of stregg and two shot glasses, and filled them both to the brim.

'We've got time for one of these and then one more before I chase you out of here,' the Emperor said. 'Soon as those clottin' Tahn clear the *Normandie*, I'm taking off.'

'Going home, sir?' Sten asked.

'No such luck,' the Emperor said. 'I've got a lot of fence mending to do. You know the drill: shake hands, kiss babies, have my picture taken with people I've allowed to think are important, thank my allies for missing every time they tried to stab me in the back, and generally pump up my popularity polls.

'Hell, I won't see Prime World inside of six months. And I'm already fed up with the whole thing. Shows what a rotten attitude I've got.'

He raised his glass in toast. 'Here's to rotten attitudes.'

Sten chinked his glass with his boss's, and the two of them choked back the raw stregg. The Emperor refilled the glasses. One more shot to go, and Sten's time was up. And he was . . . free?

'Look. When I get back is when the real work starts,' the Emperor said, 'and I'm gonna need some help.'

Sten saw his freedom vanishing.

'I've had to rebuild this whole shebang more than once,' the Emperor said, 'but I don't think things have ever been this bad. Don't get me wrong. I know *what* to do. But after this war I'm short of talent to help out.

'Sullamora and his boyos won't do much more than get in my way. All they can see is bottom-line profits. Funny about those types. They have some minor money-making abilities – if you call pirating business savvy. The thing that bothers me is that they don't seem to have any fun doing it.

'Bunch of gloomy clots. And they don't help my mood at all. All right. Forget them. I bring in some young, spirited types like yourself. We bust our scrotums for just fifty or sixty years, and maybe we end up with something looking kind of nice. Something we can be proud of.'

If Sten had been uneasy before, when the 'we' crept into the conversation, he really started getting worried.

'Excuse me, sir,' he broke in, 'but I'm not sure how I can fit into all this.'

The Emperor waved that away. 'You're not to worry about it,' he said. 'I've got some pretty good ideas.'

'It's not that,' Sten said. 'And I don't mean to sound ungrateful. But . . .' He hesitated, then took the plunge. 'You see, I've got some pretty severe doubts about where I want to be in those next fifty or sixty years. And right now, the military doesn't feel like it. Like you said, it feels like a pain in the behind – although mine isn't royal.'

The Emperor laughed. 'So, what are you thinking?'

'I'm not sure,' Sten said. 'I've got leave coming to me. Probably a couple of years' worth if I totted it all up. I thought maybe I'd just kick back and see what happens.'

The Emperor gave Sten a measuring look. Then he smiled and shook his head. He tilted his glass at Sten in a silent toast. The audience was over. Sten drained his glass and got up. He set down the glass and gave the Emperor what he hoped would be his last salute. The Emperor returned it, very formal.

'Within six months,' he predicted, 'you'll be bored out of your skull. I should be back home by then. Look me up.'

Believing that the Emperor was wrong on all counts, Sten wheeled and was out the door.

Chapter Fifty-Seven

The Eternal Emperor clumped down the ramp of the *Normandie*, his Gurkha bodyguards pressed tightly around him. He paused at the bottom, then breathed a silent sigh of relief. As per his orders, there were no welcoming crowds at Soward, Prime World's main spaceport. Instead, a short distance away, there was only his personal gravcar and its escort to take him back to his dreary makeshift quarters beneath the ruins of Arundel.

He would have to do something about that, he reminded himself. Time to give the rebuilding program a boot in the butt. It was not the image of pomp and splendor he missed but the carefully built-in comforts and, above all, privacy. Just to be alone for a little while with one of his nutball projects – like reinventing the varnish used on a Strad violin – would be an immense relief.

At the moment he felt that if one more being asked him for a decision or brought some trouble to his attention, he would break down and sob. The problem was that emperors who sobbed publicly were never eternal. Still, that was exactly what he felt like doing. Just as his face felt as if it was going to fall off from smiling at vidcameras, and his fingers were bleeding from shaking the hands of so many grateful subjects. They were all anxious to tell him what a hero he was.

He thought of another hero and winced, with a small smile. After a decisive battle, one of the man's aides had told him what a great hero he had become. Sure, the new hero had observed. But if I had lost, I would be the greatest villain in our nation's history. What was the guy's name? Who knows. Probably something Prussian. So much for clottin' heroes.

The Eternal Emperor pulled himself together and headed for his gravcar. A few years earlier he would have slept the clock around three or four times, then donned his Raschid identity and gone on a long drunk at the Covenanter, with maybe a tumble with Janiz for old time's sake. But the Covenanter was gone because of treachery. As was Janiz. Both gone, and it was his fault, dammit! He had let it get away from him somehow.

The master of doublethink. Bah! Maybe that's your problem, Engineer Raschid. You overclottin' complicate every clottin' thing. Keep it stupid, simple, and a whole lot of folks might still be breathing – instead of dead or, worse, on their knees, praising your name.

The Eternal Emperor was feeling every year of his 3,000-plus span as he reached the car. Then he saw Tanz Sullamora's smiling face, and he groaned and almost groaned again as Tanz stuck out a hand to be shook. Instead, he took it – gingerly.

'Welcome back, Your Majesty,' Sullamora gushed. 'We're all very proud.'

Sure you are, the Raschid side of him thought. You just can't wait to figure out how to intrigue me out of a few more warehouses full of credits. But the Eternal Emperor side of him made him merely smile and mutter a polite thanks.

'I have one small request,' Sullamora said. 'I know you're anxious to get home, but . . .'

The Emperor raised an eyebrow. He was about to be put out. He was too tired to speak, so he just motioned for Sullamora to continue.

'It's the spaceport employees,' Sullamora said. 'They've been waiting for hours and . . .'

He glanced over where Sullamora was pointing and saw a small mixed-uniform crowd near the main gate. Oh, no! More smiling. More hand shaking. More . . . Ahhh . . .

'I can't handle it, Tanz,' the Emperor said. 'Get Mahoney to do it. He's back on the *Normandie* taking care of some last-minute business. He'll be out in a sec.' He stepped to the door of his gravcar.

'It won't be the same, sir,' Sullamora insisted. 'It's you they want to see. I know these beings aren't *real* fighters and all. But they have done their best in their own ways. So, won't you please . . .'

The Eternal Emperor resigned himself and changed direction for the gate. He wanted to get it over with, so he picked up speed until he had his Gurkhas trotting on their stumpy legs to keep up.

The little crowd broke into cheers as he approached them, and the Emperor, who was too professional to disappoint under such circumstances, painted on his most Imperial smile and started shaking hands. He made sure he asked each being's name as he took the outstretched hand with his right and clasped the elbow with his left. It was a handshake guaranteed to generate warm feelings, and at the same time he could use the elbow hold to move them gently to the side as he pulled back his shaking hand and stepped to the side to take another.

He was about a third of the way down the line when he came to the man with the pale face and too-bright eyes. The Emperor asked the man's name and went into his hand shaking act. He could not make out the nervous mutter he got back so that he could repeat it, so he just grinned more widely and started to withdraw his hand and pass on.

The hands stayed clasped.

The Eternal Emperor had only a heartbeat to puzzle at what was going wrong, and then he saw the pistol coming up in the man's other hand. And he was falling back, trying to get away, but he could not let go as the pistol went *crack-crack-crack-crack* and he knew he was hit but could not feel a thing except maybe that his stomach was bruised and—

The Gurkhas were on Chapelle, slashing with their deadly kukris, and the man was dead even as his trigger finger kept pulling in reflex and the gun was clicking empty. It happened so fast that only then the crowd began to get the idea that something awful was occurring. The first screams began.

Tanz Sullamora stood there for a frozen moment, shaken at being so close to violence, even though it was of his own making. Then he turned and started to drop to one knee before the Emperor's body.

There was only a small bloody splotch on the Emperor's dress uniform to mark where the bullets had penetrated, and for a moment Sullamora was not sure if he had even been hurt.

A minute later, the worry was over. The Eternal Emperor was dead.

Then the privy council turned up the joker in the Emperor's deck.

The bomb implanted in his body exploded. The size of the blast had been determined thousands of years before. Sullamora died. And the Gurkhas. And the sobbing crowd. And anyone and anything within a precise one-eighth of a kilometer.

Odd things happened in all explosions, and that one was no

exception. A week later, a tech from the pathology lab found Chapelle's face. That was all – just his face. There was not a blemish or a mark on it.

Chapelle's face was smiling.

Chapter Fifty-Eight

Mahoney pressed his thumb against the print sensor, and the door to the Eternal Emperor's study hissed open. He hesitated before he entered. This would probably be his last time. There were only a very few beings the sensor would pass, and for an hour or two more Mahoney was one of them.

After that, the memory would be wiped and a new order of permitted presences would be installed. Mahoney knew there was no way his name would be on that exalted list, just as he had known there was something very wrong almost as soon as he had scattered his handful of dirt on the Eternal Emperor's coffin and stepped back to let the others pay their last respects.

The five surviving members of the privy council stood slightly apart from the other mourners on a small grassy knoll, just beyond the screen of rosebushes the gardeners had hastily planted to fulfill the Emperor's burial wishes.

But there was only one rose blossom on the entire span of bushes. It had no hidden meaning, but Mahoney found it strangely apt, and as it drew his attention, he made note of the presence of the Council of Five.

They stood together, but at an apparent measured distance, as if they were afraid to be too close. Not a word was whispered between them, and their faces were stony and guarded. It was as if they had something to feel guilty about, Mahoney thought; then he wiped away the thought as a product of Mick romanticism.

But the image nagged at him, and when he saw the news feed

that night, he marked the announcement that an emergency session of Parliament had been called. Now, what could be odd about that, my friend? Mahoney thought. This is an emergency, isn't it?

Sure it is, Ian, but bless your sweet dumb Irish behind, don't you see it? The session was called by the privy council. Mahoney did not have to be a legal scholar to realize that such an action was well beyond their constitutional authority. All right. So why didn't any member of the Parliament complain? Or, better yet, refuse? Simple. Because it was wired, dear Ian, dear Ian, wired.

The Emperor had been murdered, and Mahoney knew who had done it, and it was not the poor mad fool the livies were going on about in their endlessly recycled analysis. It was not Chapelle.

Sure, Chapelle had pulled the trigger. But the real guilt rested with the five lone figures on the grassy knoll. And there was not a thing Mahoney could do about it because, even if he wanted to, he would not be part of the new order. Just as he knew that the hero of Cavite had better get on his horse and haul butt out of town before they came to *really* thank him.

Mahoney stepped into the clutter of the Eternal Emperor's study for the last time. He was not sure why he had come, except for the mad hope that there would be some clue about what to do next.

He was so used to his old boss having every base covered that it had not quite sunk in yet that this was one contingency that had been impossible to plan for.

Mahoney looked in dismay at the many scattered books on the shelves, some lying open just as the Emperor had left them as he searched for some arcane fact or other.

The study was jammed with the idiosyncrasies of his old boss: from ancient wind-up toys that clattered about with no purpose but to amuse to experimental cooking tools, plas bags of spices he was considering, scattered notes and scrawls, and even music sheets crammed with marginalia. An entire division could not have found a clue there in half a thousand years.

So Mahoney decided to have a drink. What else could he do?

He walked to the Emperor's desk and slid out the drawer where the boss kept his Scotch. He noted that the seal on the bottle was unbroken. That was strange. The Emperor never put an unsealed bottle in his desk. He always took a snort first. Mahoney shrugged, pulled out a shot glass, and reached for the bottle.

As he picked it up, something small and white came unstuck from the bottom and fluttered to the floor. Mahoney stooped over to see what it was. When he saw the scrawling on it, he almost let it drop from his fingers in shock.

Mahoney dropped heavily into a chair. He held the piece of paper before his disbelieving eyes. His face was flushed, sweat leapt from his forehead, and his pulse rate jumped into triple time.

The message was for him. From the Eternal Emperor. And this was all it said:

'Stick around, Ian. I'll be right back.'

STEN 6:
THE RETURN OF
THE EMPEROR

To
Norman Spinrad
(Hippiecommiesymp – Active)
Who helped us walk into this drakh
and
Dennis Foley
(Green Hat – Retired)
Who keeps it from getting more than chin-high

Note

The titles of Books One, Two, and Three are the official ranks Augustus won from the Roman senate to become Emperor. *Princeps* means 'Leading Man.' *Imperator*, 'Military Commander.' This word is the Latin root for Emperor. *Pater Patriae* means 'Father of the Fatherland.'

The title of Book Four translates as 'We About to Die Salute You.' It was the famous cry of the gladiators as they paid respects to their emperor before engaging in the bloodbaths of the ancient circuses.

BOOK ONE

PRINCEPS

Chapter One

The ship bulked monstrous. Each of the decahedron's sides measured nearly a square kilometer.

There was but one man on board. He floated, motionless, in a shallow pool that curved in the center of one compartment. His eyes opened. Blue. Incurious, like a newly born child. Some time passed.

A valve activated, and the liquid drained out of the pool. One side dropped away. The man sat up and lowered his legs to the deck, moving slowly and carefully like an invalid testing himself after a long time bedridden. The deck was warm.

He might have sat there for a moment, an hour, or a day before a voice spoke. It came from everywhere.

'There is food and drink in the next chamber.'

Obediently the man pushed himself to his feet. He swayed, then recovered. On a low stand beside the pool/bed was a blue coverall. He glanced at it briefly, then walked to a wall. It was smooth and blank except for a circular palmswitch. He touched the switch.

The wall became a screen. Vid? Imaging radar? Computer simulation?

Outside lay space/not space. It was black, and it was all colors. It hurt the man's eyes. He palmed the switch once more, and the screen became a wall.

Still naked, he padded through a doorway.

A table was set for one. The dishes were covered. The man lifted one cover and scooped food up with his fingers. He chewed, then swallowed. His expression was still unchanged.

He wiped his fingers on his thigh and walked into another compartment, where he saw a reclining chair with a steel-gleaming helmet on it. Odd tendrils curled from the helmet.

The man sat down and put the helmet on.

There were other people in the room. No. He was outside. He was wearing clothing – some kind of uniform. The other people were all smiling and laughing and trying to touch him. He let them. He heard himself saying words he did not yet understand.

He noted one person amid the throng. He had a very pale face, and his eyes gleamed. The pale-faced man stretched out his hand to shake. Suddenly he drew something metal-shining from his clothing.

The man felt blows in his stomach. Felt himself falling backward. Felt pain. Pain rising until . . . until everything stopped.

The man took off the helmet. He was back in the compartment, back in the reclining chair.

The voice spoke again. 'E-time since deactivation: six years, three months, two days.'

The man's expression changed slightly. A thought drifted through his mind: Wrong. Five years late. Then the thought was discarded as meaningless. What was 'late?' He rose.

'You have ten ship-days before departure.'

The man nodded once. He returned to the mess compartment. He was hungry again.

Chapter Two

It was a quiet little planet in a nondescript system overseen by a dying yellow star. The system had no particular history, was well off any major trade or tourist routes, and rarely had any visitors.

Many E-years before, an Imperial Survey Mission had made a desultory study and found little of interest. The science officer had duly noted that it was about .87 E-size, had commensurate gravity, E-normal atmosphere, and sat three AU from its sun. The climate was tropical to sub-arctic, and the planet supported any number of thriving life forms. The top predator on land was a shy, catlike creature that proved to be of no danger to anyone.

There were also 'No beings of higher development observed.'

The planet was dubbed Survey World XM-Y-1134. And for several hundred years, that was its sole name – although it was unlikely anyone ever asked.

It got a proper name of sorts from a restless entrepreneur who built a mansion in the temperate zone for himself and his hangers-on, then briefly toyed with the idea of turning it into a remote resort. To this end, he had constructed a state-of-the-art spaceport. Whether or not the idea had merit, no one would ever learn. The entrepreneur lost three or four fortunes and came to an obscure, rather sad end.

But the planet didn't mind. It hummed and wobbled busily about its orbit as it had done for several billion years, scratching its fur against a cosmic stump every few hundred millions of years or so – and wiping out any life-forms that had become too prolific and giving another group a start.

The planet's new name was Smallbridge. The source for that name was buried along with the entrepreneur and his conceit.

Sten liked it fine. He had spent more than five years exploring Smallbridge's beaches, marshes, broad plains and deserts, forests and ice floes, sometimes with eager companions, sometimes alone. There had been a few adventures – and more than a few trysts with lovely women. But nothing had stuck. He had encountered no one like the steel-willed Bet of his youth. Or the relentless Lisa Haines. Or the fiery gambler, St. Clair.

In the last year or so, he had found himself just going through the motions of living. He had fallen into a dark mood he couldn't shake.

During rational moments, he would rouse himself. Give himself a good talking to. Call himself all kinds of a rich fool of a clot.

He had everything any being could want, didn't he? Gypsy Ida, his old Mantis teammate, had seen to that. He and Alex Kilgour had exited the Tahn POW camp wealthy beyond their dreams. While they had languished in the Heath slammer, Ida had rolled their ever-growing back pay into one investment after another until the result was two not so smallish fortunes.

Besides the money, Kilgour wound up with the poshest estate on his heavy-world home of Edinburgh.

Sten got his own planet.

Thanks a clot of a lot, Ida. Now, what?

Come on, don't blame the Rom. As Mahoney would have said: 'Don't be kicking over the milk the cow gave.' Mahoney would have reminded Sten that he had plucked him off the factory world of Vulcan, a young Delinq half a breath from being brain-burned. Mahoney would sneer and point out that Sten had crawled through the mud and worse to rise from the ranks as an infantry grunt to a deadly Mantis operative to commander of the Emperor's personal bodyguard to hero of the Tahn wars – and finally to admiral. He would brush over the oceans of gore Sten was personally responsible for and tell him that he was still a young man and just needed to pluck his finger out and get back to business.

But Mahoney was dead.

Sten's old boss, the Eternal Emperor, would have laughed at him, poured a double shot of stregg to put blood in his eye, and sent him off to face a suitable enemy. It wouldn't matter much who the enemy might be. It would be enough that the beings were threatening the peace and security of an empire that had thrived for nearly three thousand years.

But the Emperor, too, was dead.

The last time Sten had seen the Emperor, he had sworn to the man that his career in the military was over. This despite promises of many honors and much important work to come in the aftermath of the Tahn conflict that had nearly bankrupted the Empire.

The Eternal Emperor had scoffed and said Sten was just weary, and understandably so. He said to look him up when he tired of the peaceful life. The Emperor had estimated it would take no longer than six months.

It was one of those rare times when the Eternal Emperor had been wrong. Almost six months to the day, Sten had looked up from blissful idleness in his mansion at Smallbridge, patted the curvaceous naked form nestled against the pillow next to him, and whispered 'no clottin' way' to his absent boss.

A week later, the Eternal Emperor had been assassinated.

It had been one of those stupid things that Sten had dreaded when he commanded the Emperor's bodyguard. No matter what precautions were taken, there was no such thing as absolute safety for a man as public as the Eternal Emperor. Even the fierce loyalty of his Gurkha guards was not complete protection. The little men with the long, curving knives who had kept the Emperor's foes at bay for nearly thirty centuries were helpless under certain circumstances.

The Emperor had returned to Prime World the conquering hero.

Billions upon billions of beings across his far-flung empire had watched on their livies as he stepped from his royal ship and advanced across the tarmac to the phalanx of waiting gravcars that would whisk him home to Arundel.

Tanz Sullamora, the great ship-building industrialist and most trusted member of his privy council, was at his side.

Sten remembered watching the screen in the mansion's vidroom. The newscaster's voice was hoarse from describing the triumphant return. The schedule, he said in a raspy whisper, called for no ceremonies at that moment. The Emperor would board the waiting craft and head for a well-earned rest. In a week or so, a grand celebration of the victory over the Tahn was planned. Beings from all over the Empire would gather to honor their leader. There would be no recriminations, it was said, even against the shakiest of the Emperor's allies.

Sten didn't believe a word of that. He knew his boss too well. There would be a purge. But it would be swift, sure, and hardly a bubble of interruption as the Emperor turned his attention away from war and back to the business of being the chieftain of the greatest capitalist system in history.

But it would still be a good show. The Emperor was master of dazzle and triple speak.

Idly, Sten noted the small group of spaceport employees gathered far to one side of the screen. They were drawn up in what was obviously a receiving line, waiting to shake the hand of the Emperor. Sten was glad his old boss was heading in the opposite direction. Not that there was any *real* danger. What would be the point of attacking the Emperor now that the war was over? Still . . . His instincts always fought his common sense in such situations. Once among the press of flesh, it would be impossible to totally protect the man.

Then he saw Sullamora catch the Emperor's attention and nod to the waiting line. Sten let out an automatic groan. Tanz would be pointing out, he knew, that the spaceport group had been waiting for hours to greet their ruler and should really not be disappointed.

Sure enough, after a moment's hesitation, the Emperor's party turned toward the assembled group. They were moving fast. The Emperor obviously wanted to get this bit of duty over with as quickly as possible. The Gurkhas hustled on stubby legs to keep the shield up.

Then the Emperor was going down the line in that smooth, graceful way he had among his people: the charming, fatherly smile fixed on his young features; the tall, muscular body bounding along from being to being; one hand coming out to shake, the other going for the elbow for a warm double-grip that also moved the greeter swiftly aside, so the next hand could be taken.

Sten had seen a blur of motion. What was happening? He heard the distinctive *crack crack crack* of pistol fire. And the Eternal Emperor was falling back. The camera swirled into mass confusion. Then it cleared – but just for a moment.

He saw the Emperor lying on the tarmac. Sten's heart was still. His breath caught somewhere in his chest. Was he . . . dead?

Then the screen turned to pure burning white, and Sten heard the beginnings of a mighty explosion.

Transmission was cut.

When it was finally restored, Sten had his answer.

The Eternal Emperor had been assassinated.

By a madman, it was said. Some malcontent named Chapelle, who had acted alone out of some insane motive – revenge for an imagined slight, or ambition for an odd sort of immortality.

Along with countless billions of other beings, Sten had been a numb witness to what followed.

It was inconceivable that the Emperor was gone. Although there were few who believed that any living thing could be immortal or even close to it. There were a few odd cells – usually particularly virulent things that destroyed their host, hence themselves – that could theoretically live forever, as well as a few dwellers of the seas and upper atmospheres. But that was nit-picking. For all things, to be alive meant eventual death.

For human beings, this was particularly so. And the Emperor *was* a human being. There was no dispute on that and never would be.

But as long as anyone could remember he had always been there. Whether one agreed or disagreed with his policies, the Emperor was a comforting and permanent presence. Even the most bitter and radical scholars gnashed their teeth as they tracked his reign back century after unbelievable century. It was no accident that the word *eternal* was the official preface to the Emperor's title.

It was also something one didn't dwell on. An ordinary human might live for two hundred years if he were lucky. To think of someone vastly older was frightening.

Sten had personally known the man a great deal of his own allotted span. In apparent age, the Emperor was no more than thirty-five or so. His eyes were youthfully bright. He even made occasional mocking references to his great age. But there was little the Eternal Emperor didn't mock. Nothing was holy to him, especially himself.

Sometimes, however, Sten had seen him overtaken by a great and terrible weariness. It had happened more often toward the end of the Tahn debacle. Deep lines would be etched on his features, and his eyes would suddenly grow so distant that anyone looking *believed* for a moment that the man had seen and been places far beyond any being who had ever lived. And somehow one was sure he would remain long after one's own memory was lost in distant time.

Two days after the assassination, the members of the Emperor's privy council had, one by one, mounted the stage hastily set up in the great grounds around the ruins of Arundel Castle. Only one member did not appear; Tanz Sullamora. Faithful servant to the last, he had died in the explosion that had also wiped out everyone within the one-eighth-of-a-kilometer kill zone. Why Chapelle had found it necessary to set off such an enormous explosion after he slew the Emperor, no one could say. Except that it was the act of an insane man. All else remained part of that mad puzzle, because Chapelle himself had been one of the first victims of his actions.

The five lords of industry stood before the vast throng assembled on the grounds. Prior to their entrance, it had been explained in great detail exactly who and what they were.

There was Kyes, a tall, slender, silver being, who controlled most things involving artificial intelligence. He was a Grb'chev, a vastly bright race, and appeared to be the chief spokesbeing of the privy council. Next was Malperin. She ruled a gargantuan conglomerate that included agriculture, chemical, and pharmaceuticals. Then there was Lovett, scion of a great banking family. Finally, the Kraa twins – one grossly fat, the other painfully thin – who controlled the major mines, mills, and foundries in the Empire. Besides Sullamora, there had once been another member of their group. But Volmer, a media baron, had died in some silly mishap just prior to the end of the war.

Kyes had a dry, light, pleasant voice. It was somber now as he explained that Parliament had cast a unanimous vote urging the five lords to rule in the Emperor's place during this terrible emergency. None of them had sought this awful burden, and none of them certainly felt worthy of the trust beings everywhere were placing in them at that very moment.

But they had been convinced that for the time being there was no other choice. Order must come out of this awesome chaos, and they pledged to do their very best to govern wisely and fairly until the proper moment came – very soon, he hoped – when free elections could be held to determine how exactly the Empire was to be led without the presence of His Majesty, their martyred ruler.

Kyes said he knew this was a weak solution at best, but all of them had racked their brains for tortuous hours and could find no other way out. A commission was being set up – as he spoke, in fact – to study the situation and to make suggestions. He and the other members of the council awaited word from this eminent body of scholarly beings as eagerly as anyone watching and listening. But he had been told that what they were attempting to accomplish had never been done before and might take a great deal of time and reasoned debate.

Kyes counseled patience, then pledged he would carry on in the spirit of the great man who had rescued them all from the threat of enslavement under the Tahn.

One by one the others stepped up to make similar remarks – and to add a bit of detail, such as the date of the funeral, which would be vaster and richer than any funeral that had gone before. New honors were announced to be posthumously bestowed on the Emperor, and a year of mourning was declared. Sten palmed the button that blanked the screen and sat back to reflect.

He did not need his Mantis psywar training to know that he had just witnessed a power grab.

So. The privy council would *reluctantly* govern until free elections could be held. Sten had propped up a few despots in his time with similar empty pledges. He wondered how long it would be before the first coup attempt. And which one would eventually be successful. And then the one after that. And the other – on and on until the entire system collapsed. He supposed there would be constant warfare of greater and greater intensity for the rest of his life.

Ultimate power was at stake. He who controlled the Empire determined the flow of all the Anti-Matter Two – AM2 – the fuel upon which civilization everywhere was based. It was the source of cheap power, the key to all major weaponry, and the sole practical means of interstellar travel. Without AM2, trade would be almost entirely reduced to intrasystem lumbering about on the infinitely practical but painfully slow Yukawa drive engines.

But there was nothing Sten could do about any of it.

The Eternal Emperor was dead. Long live the Emperor.

He would mourn him. Not as a friend. No one could call the Emperor friend. But, as – well, a comrade at arms, then. Sten got drunk and remained drunk for a month, switching from Scotch to stregg and back again – the Emperor's two favorite drinks.

Then he tried to get on with his life.

Sten didn't pay much mind to the chaos the Empire fell into. He only coppered his bets by purchasing all the AM2 he could lay his hands on, and it wasn't long before the shortages began and he was congratulating himself on his foresight. The why of the shortages didn't concern him. He assumed the privy council – in its infinite wisdom – had determined such a course to further line their already heavy pockets.

He dabbled a bit in business, found it far from his liking, then was reduced to an endless series of momentary enthusiasms. Not unlike the Emperor, who had a host of hobbies always in progress. He became a fair cook, although he knew he would never be the Emperor's match. He honed his skills with tools and building things. He took a fling at a few of the lusher fleshpots. When he wearied of that – a little too quickly for comfort, he sometimes thought – he explored and improved Smallbridge.

He and Alex corresponded, always swearing to get together soon, but soon never came. And as the controls on AM2 tightened, travel became more and more impractical, and before he knew it 'soon' wasn't even mentioned in any of their letters.

Ian Mahoney – his only other real friend – quietly retired to the life of a military historian, then died in some silly accident. Sten had heard that he had drowned and that the body had never been found. He supposed there was some irony in such a meaningless death for a man who had managed to survive against impossible odds so many times before. But he didn't see it, or he was too depressed to examine it.

The final year of his self-imposed exile was proving the worst. His bleak moods were constantly on him, as well as a gut-itching paranoia. Whom he should fear, he had no idea. He had no suspects. But he became paranoid just the same. Every residence he set up on Smallbridge was enclosed with increasingly sophisticated and – he had to admit it – eccentric security devices, including some nasty, being-devouring plants he imported from some hellhole whose name he had easily forgotten. They had taken off like mad in the non-threatening environment of Smallbridge. Every once in a while he had to set the perimeter on fire to keep the grove under control.

Lately, he had taken up residence in the northwestern sector of the second-largest land mass in the temperate zone.

Temperate was a weak, nondescript word for this place beside the chain of four mighty lakes. The winds always blew fierce and cold there. The snow lay deep on the ground and bowed the trees of the forest for many months of the year. But for some reason it had a powerful attraction to him – just as it seemed to have for the being-devouring plants, which thrived in the cold, wet climate.

Sten had built several frontier-style domes in the cluster by one of the lakes. One was devoted to a kitchen and pantry where he prepared and stored food, butchered out a little game, or cleaned the strange, bullet-shaped but tasty dwellers of the lake. He grew vegetables in the hydroponic tubs that took up all of one side. The second dome contained his workshop and was crammed with tools and building materials of every variety. He also kept and worked on his weapons there, as well as the snooping devices he was always toying with. The last dome held his living quarters and gymnasium. He spent hours in the gym and outside in the cold, endlessly practicing and honing his Mantis skills.

He lined the walls of his living quarters with real wood cut from his own forest. He built bunks and cabinets and all sorts of things from the same material. When he was done, it looked so homey that he was pleased with himself. Still, something seemed to be missing. He scratched his memory until he came up with an 'aha.' It wanted a fireplace. After several smoky and tortuous attempts, he finally had it. And it was huge, big enough to take a two-meter log. It drew like clot and gave off a wonderfully cheery glow.

A woman who had stayed with him a few months said it reminded her of something she had seen before but couldn't quite make out. Sten pressed her, but all she could remember was that it had involved some item at a shop where 'less expensive things' were sold. From the tone in her voice, Sten got the drift she meant garish and sentimental.

He was so lonely, he let it pass.

A week or so later, he was returning from some errand in the forest. It was a beautiful, gray day, and a light snowfall was drifting down from the skies and through the trees.

Sten hailed the dome, and the woman opened the door to greet him. She was framed in the doorway, with the glowing fire lighting her from behind, and Sten knew then what she had been thinking of. Because now he remembered, as well.

A long time before, his mother had extended her contract for six months to buy a muraliv. A country girl completely lost and out of place in the workshops of Vulcan, she had deeded half a year more of her life for what she believed was a work of art.

It was of a snowy landscape on a frontier world. He remembered the snow drifting down on the little cluster of domes, and the door that always swung open to greet the returning workers from the forest and field – and the bright cheery fire the open door had revealed. It was his mother's dearest treasure. In eight months, it had gone quite still.

Sten had unconsciously recreated the mural.

He made some excuses and hustled the woman on her way. It was silly to blame her for a slight she couldn't know she was committing, but he couldn't bear to have her around anymore.

That was when the gloom reached its absolute bottom. Month after month, he pricked at the wound. He didn't need the walrus-psychologist Rykor to tell him what he was doing. Sten *knew*. But he did it just the same. He even named the four lakes after his long-dead family.

The largest lake, where the domes were clustered, he named Amos, for his father. The next in the chain became Freed, for his mother. Then Ahd and Johs, for his brother and sister.

When that was done, he sat and brooded, hoping his condition was no more than a lingering fever that had to be endured until the viral tide shifted and the fever broke.

Five hundred miles to the north, a bright light winked into being and arced down through the night skies. It steadied a moment above the frozen ground, then sped toward the lakes and Sten's retreat.

Then a globe appeared, hanging amid the stars. Powerful jamming devices hummed into life, bathing Smallbridge in an electronic blanket that comforted and coaxed Sten's alarm system into believing all was well.

A light very much like the first separated from the globe, then sped off in the same direction.

A few klicks from the domes, the battered little spaceboat came to ground, a black splotch against the snow. The port groaned open, and a dark figure exited. After dragging on cold-weather gear and snapping snowshoes to his feet, the man straightened, then hesitated, scanning the skies, an immense, bulky figure, sniffing the air for danger very much like a big Kodiak from distant Earth. Suddenly he saw a light pop above the horizon. It was the other ship, coming fast.

The man turned and hurried across the snow, moving like a nullgrav dancer despite his bulk. He scanned the ground ahead with a practiced eye, setting a zigzag course and not bothering to obscure his tracks. There wasn't time.

Occasionally – for no apparent reason – he sidestepped little pimples in the snow.

Behind him, he heard the other ship settle down, the frozen crust shattering under the weight with little pops and cracks.

At the tree line, the man spotted an almost imperceptible ridge. He stopped. Moaning in frustration, he moved in first one direction, then the other. But the slight ridge seemed to stretch without relief all along the outer edge of the woods. For some reason, the man considered his path blocked.

The port of the other craft hissed open and seven black figures tumbled out. They were already garbed for the terrain. Fingers flew in silent code. Agreement was reached. And they sped off in the man's direction. They moved in a ragged vee, with the tallest being taking point. They skimmed effortlessly across the snow on gravskis, keeping a fast, measured pace.

If anyone had spotted them, there would be no mistake about their business. These were hunters – after very big game.

Their quarry was kneeling beside a drift, his gloves off, digging gently around the ridge. His fists felt like heavy, unwieldy things. He had to stop now and then to pound them back to life against his coat. Behind him, the figures moved on.

Finally there appeared a silver thread so slender that it would be the envy of an arachnid. Snow dust hung from it. The man blew on the thread, puffing out warm moisture that collected and froze. When he thought it was thick enough, he pulled out a tiny little device with just-visible claws. He flipped open the back with a fingernail, revealing little programming holes. He inserted a pin in several of the holes, until the device gave a chirp indicating that it was alive.

The man clicked it shut, breathed a prayer, and slowly . . . so slowly . . . stretched it toward the thread.

A laser blast cracked the frozen air with its heat and blazed a furrow in the snow millimeters from one knee. The man winced but fought back the urge to jerk away or hurry. He knew that if he was wrong, worse things than a charred hole in his corpse would occur.

He had to get to Sten, before Sten got him.

The little claws gripped the thread. The man held his breath, waiting. Another laser blast cracked. The heel of one snowshoe exploded as the lased AM2 round detonated. Finally a chirp from the tiny device said that all was well.

The man plunged across the wire into the woods just as the marksmen found their range. A hole boiled at the spot where he had knelt one breath before.

As he disappeared, the hunting team surged forward, faster. Skimming around the pimples their prey had avoided, they leapt the wire and landed silently on the other side. The leader motioned and the vee divided and the hunters scattered into the woods.

Sten paced the room. He was edgy. He picked up an antique, leather-bound book and he stared at the title, but it didn't register. He dropped it back on the table, strode over to the fire, and poked it up until the flames were hot and leaping. He still felt a little cold, so he tossed on another log.

There was something wrong, but he couldn't make it out. He kept glancing at the bank of security monitors, but all the lights were calming green. Why did he have this feeling that he was being lied to? The hackles were crawling at the back of his neck. One part of his mind said he was behaving like a whiny old being: afraid of the dark, jumping at every noise. Ignore it, that part ordered. But the tiny voice of survival kept up its keening.

Sten palmed the override on the monitors and went to manual scan. Still green. He flipped from sector to sector. Nothing. Disgusted with himself, he put it back on automatic. Just for one heartbeat, the lights seemed to blink yellow, then went to steady green. What was that? He switched back to manual again. Green, goddammit! Then to auto. This time there was no telltale yellow as the lights stayed steady emerald. He must have been imagining things.

He went to the front door, slipped to one side, edged it open and peered out. All he could see was the empty expanse of snow, bright under the hanging moon. He had reflecting devices hidden in several trees within easy view. Sten studied them. He could see his shadow peering out from the edge of the door. There was nothing lurking on either side of the dome.

Feeling like all kinds of a clotting fool, he slipped a miniwillygun from its hiding place in a slot by the door, flipped its safety off and stepped outside.

There was not a sight or a sound out of the ordinary. Sten scanned the area, millimeter by millimeter. Nothing seemed remotely awry. He snapped the safety back on, telling himself that if he was that edgy, he might drop the damned thing and blow off a knee. Still, old habits die hard – and, sometimes, not at all. He slipped the gun into his belt, backed into the dome, and swung the heavy door shut, turning to the fire as inertia carried the door on greased hinges.

He stopped.

Sten hadn't heard the lock click or the thud of the door closing. He probably hadn't pushed hard enough. Yeah. Probably.

He tensed the fingers of his right hand. The muscle sheath that held his surgically implanted knife contracted, and the slender, deadly blade slipped into its resting place in his palm. He curled his fingers around the haft.

Just to keep himself honest, and in tone, Sten sometimes played a game with himself. He would imagine there was someone behind him. A breath would give the lurker away – or a slight motion, a rustle of clothing. Failing that, his old Mantis instructors had pounded into him, any sort of presence added to a space, changed and warped that space. More heat. A shift in pressure. It didn't matter what the change was. One's senses just had to recognize it when it occurred.

Sten spun, dropping away to one side, to avoid any blow. At the same time, he slashed up with his knife. The knife blade was only fifteen molecules thick. It would cut through steel like ripened cheese. Flesh would be no contest at all. If there was an arm bearing a weapon, coming down at him, that arm – its hand still gripped around the weapon – would be neatly sliced off. It would plop to the floor while his enemy stared blankly at him, eyes widening in amazement and then dulling to instant shock as blood spurted from severed arteries. His enemy would be dead in seconds.

Meanwhile, as Sten fell, he would try to spot any other threatening presence. Which way he rolled when he hit the floor would be determined by the angle of the next attack, if any.

Sten slashed empty air. He continued the fall, imagining the first kill, concentrating on the second. More slashing at empty air. Panting, he stood with his feet splayed apart, staring at the almost-closed door. Of course, there was no one about. There never was anymore. The knife disappeared back into his arm.

Grinning and shaking his head, Sten walked to the door to push it the rest of the way shut, idly wondering what he ought to fix himself for dinner.

Just as he touched the knob, the door slammed back at him. The heavy wood caught him flat. He was hurled backward, clawing for balance and trying to twist as he hit the floor to free his knife-hand. He curled into a ball and let himself roll all the way. He rebounded off the wall, and using the force, was coming to his feet and slashing out before the knife had even cleared.

'Dammit, Sten!' the man shouted. 'Stop!'

Sten froze, gaping. What the clot! It couldn't be. It was . . .

'Get your wits about you lad,' ex-Fleet Marshall Ian Mahoney said. 'There's a Mantis team right on my heels. And if I stand here explaining, we're both for the meat locker.

'Move. Now!'

Sten moved.

Sten and Mahoney quick-crawled through the tunnel that snaked from the hidey-hole behind the fireplace toward a small stand of trees about eighty meters from the main dome. It was dimly lit – on purpose. And it contained many bends – also on purpose. They could hear someone breaking away the stones of the fireplace to get at them. Sten tried not to think of the months he had worked on the beast, or of all the heavy rocks he had carried from the edge of the lake to build it.

He was only very thankful to the gods of paranoia that had commanded him to construct a bolt-hole in the face of no apparent danger. When – not if – the hunters broke through, Sten and Mahoney would be dangerous game to follow. The lights would make aim difficult. The many twists and turns would make it even harder. They would also lessen the force of any explosions set off. And the narrowness took away any advantage in numbers.

Of course, there was always gas. But Sten was comforted by the howl of the powerful ventilators constantly pumping in fresh air. The atmosphere of the entire tunnel was recycled in seconds.

They finally reached a dead-end vault where they could stand. Emergency clothing, gear, and weapons were stacked on shelves to one side. The exit was just beyond. With a press of a switch, the port would lift silently away. The exterior was artfully camouflaged with brush, dirt, and rocks. The tunnel emptied into a thick clump of woods near the edge of the frozen lakes.

Sten quickly began donning his gear. He motioned for Mahoney to pick up a pair of gravskis like his. A small explosion rocked the tunnel as the hunters finally broke through the fireplace.

'They'll have this end covered, as well,' Mahoney said.

'I know,' Sten said. He palmed the switch, and cold fresh air flooded in as the port lifted aside. It would close automatically behind them. He pressed a marble-sized bit of impact-explosive under the edge of the switch, a down and dirty booby trap.

'They'll find it,' Mahoney said.

'I know that, too,' Sten said. 'But it'll slow them down.'

'Maybe we ought to—'

Sten raised a hand, cutting Mahoney off. 'No offense,' he said, 'but there isn't a clottin' thing I don't know about tunnels. And exiting same. I had a little experience, if you recall.'

Mahoney shut up. Sten had spent a small lifetime digging under the POW camp at Koldyeze. Actually, as Big X – commander of the escape committee – he had done a lot more than dig.

'Now, give me a hand,' he said.

He pulled the cover off an elderly snowcat, which had been converted to burn combustibles. Together they muscled it over to the exit. Sten flipped the various switches to the 'on' position and set a meandering course on the navigator, then told Mahoney to stand back as he fired the engine.

A great blast and gout of smoke roiled out. Mahoney coughed and wheezed.

'So, we'll not be sneakin' up on them, then,' Mahoney said, dry. Sten silenced him with a glare.

Then he jammed it into gear and leapt to the side. The snowcat jumped forward with a loud roar and in a flash boiled out of the tunnel. Sten peered after it. The tracks churned up huge clouds of snow as the cat plunged forward – straight for a tree. Sparks showered out of its engine ports, eerie against the night. The cat brodied to one side at the last minute. Laser fire smeared the darkness, and several holes appeared in the cat's body.

'Now!' Sten shouted.

And he and Mahoney hurled themselves outside. Sten had just enough time to see one startled hunter whirl back from the cat and raise his weapon.

The hunter jerked, and a neat hole appeared in his forehead. As the hunter slumped down, Mahoney got another shot off at the man's companion, who dodged to one side. By the time she had recovered, Sten and Mahoney were gone. The Mantis operative moved forward, throat-miking hoarse instructions to the team inside the dome. She found the footprints leading deeper into the woods. They wouldn't be difficult to follow. They stood out starkly – almost deep blue – in the moonlight.

Then she sensed something behind her. She half straightened, bringing up her weapon and trying to spin to the side. Then she was lying in the snow, blood gushing from the red grin of her throat.

Sten wiped his blade on her tunic.

'Am I just getting old,' he asked as Mahoney stepped out from behind a tree, 'or are the new kids really just not as good as they used to be?'

Mahoney looked at the corpse of the Mantis operative. As the former chief of Mercury Corps – meaning Mantis, as well – he had mixed feelings about seeing one of his own in such a state. Then he looked at Sten. He was a little older, and there were a few hard lines etched in his face, but he seemed tougher, somehow. Harder. His dark eyes were sunk deeper into his skull. They were a little bitter, but there was still that touch of cynical humor in them. Mahoney saw the slender dirk disappear back into Sten's arm.

As for Sten's question: No. They *weren't* slower.

Mahoney shrugged. 'You've been practicing,' was all he said. 'There's five more. I doubt we'll be so lucky with them, lad,' he said. 'I hope you have a plan.'

'I do,' Sten told him. Without another word he stepped into the bindings of the gravskis, flipped them on, and adjusted the lift so that he hung bare centimeters above the snow. He poled off into the woods, digging the poles in hard just to make sure no one would lose the track.

Mahoney had seen a lot of strange things in his long life, but the thick grove that Sten was leading him through had to be up high on his personal list of the bizarre.

The trees weren't really trees at all, although they took that form. They towered over what, from a distance, appeared to be a gigantic root system at least three meters high before the main trunk started. Up close, the root systems were revealed to be more like immense tubers. They were so huge that Mahoney thought it must have taken centuries for so many leaves to form together to make such large bulbs for water and nutrients. Later he learned that it had only taken a few years.

The branches were furry and appeared almost muscular – if a plant could have muscles. And they looped about like tentacles, although they seemed stiff and relatively sturdy, like wood. The leaves were long, needlelike, and edged with sharp spines, and they were covered with a thin film of moisture. Extremely odd in this climate. Why didn't the moisture freeze?

He reached out a hand to touch.

'Don't,' Sten snapped. Then he saw the puzzled look on Mahoney's face and took pity – but only a little. 'They don't like to be touched,' he said. He pushed on with no other explanation.

As far as Mahoney could tell, they were doing nothing more than traveling in a wide circle. Moving closer to the lake, he thought. With a shrill cry, a large, white bird with leathery wings suddenly bolted for the sky. It circled about in the moonlight, obviously angry.

'They're coming,' Sten said. 'Finally. I was afraid for a moment we'd lost them.'

'Not likely,' Mahoney said. 'Probably talking to their mother.' He pointed to the night sky beyond the bird. He was referring to the command ship, which he assumed was in a stationary orbit – very low, very close.

'We'll have to do something about that, too,' Sten said.

Before Mahoney could ask exactly what, he saw the knife slip into Sten's hand again. Sten moved cautiously toward one of the odd trees. Picking out a low-hanging branch, he inched forward, knife blade gleaming. As his hand neared the branch, Mahoney swore he could see the branch ever so slightly move toward Sten. But the motion was so miniscule, he wasn't sure. The drops of moisture seemed to swell into larger beads, almost dripping like saliva, and the leaves seemed to be rotating so the teeth were facing out.

Sten leapt forward and struck. Moisture boiled from the wound and the branch snapped forward at Sten, trying to curl around him. But he bounded back again, just to the edge of safety. Mahoney felt his blood run cold. The liquid pouring out of the wound hissed and bubbled in the snow.

'That should make him nice and mad,' was all Sten said.

He pressed on, Mahoney in his wake. Sten repeated his attack at least a dozen other times, each time with the same result: the tree lashing out in agony, just missing Sten. For a few moments, it was all painful motion. Limbs squirming, seeking justice; caustic moisture pouring out. But the wounds seemed to heal instantly, and in a few seconds the tree would fall still.

When Sten had first come upon the plants during his travels, he had been instantly repelled by their appearance and attracted by their nature. They possessed a defense system only an ex-Mantis kiddie could love. Something had once found them extremely delicious – hence the sharp leaves and caustic fluid. When attacked, the plant reacted by pouring even nastier fluids into the area where it was bitten. That took about fifteen minutes. Some creatures got around it by developing a tolerance to the normal fluid and just nibbling small areas at a time, moving on to a new section before the plant could react. The plants were a bit like cabbage or tomato.

But the plant species had not stopped there. A drastic change in climate, perhaps, had sent it in search of further means to feed. Why not the beings that ate it? With its super-efficient tuber storage system as a base, it evolved into a carnivore. Oh, it would make do for years at a time on the nutrients in the soil and water, but the flesh and blood of any number of species were its particular dining pleasure.

And now that Sten had gotten their attention with his attacks, they would be laying for whoever or whatever followed. Such as the Mantis team.

Mahoney heard a terrible scream. It was not the kind that cut off abruptly. It went on and on, growing more horrible as long minutes passed. Laser fire cracked. Silence. Mahoney shuddered.

'Now there's four left,' Sten said.

Mahoney didn't answer.

They knelt by the edge of the ice. Their cover was a small outcropping of rock. It was false dawn, and the light was tricky. But Mahoney could make out the tree line on the far side of the lake. It was little less than a kilometer, perhaps a two-minute crossing on their skis, if they didn't stumble.

He and Sten had led the surviving hunters on an all-night chase. Sometimes he thought Sten was trying to lose them. Then he would slow – purposely, he thought – and soon he could hear them on their heels again. By now, he thought they should be tiring. Clot! So was he.

The only good news he could think of was that the Mantis team had yet to be reinforced. There could only be one conclusion. There weren't any beings aboard the command ship to spare.

There had been no time for Mahoney to do more than hazily sketch in what was going on. Nothing about himself. Only the situation at hand.

The privy council was desperate. They had sent out similar teams all over the Empire. Their mission: Capture and return for questioning any being who had been close enough to the Emperor to know his deepest secrets.

Sten was amazed. 'What the clot could I know? Sure, I commanded his bodyguard. And I had clearances up to my eyebrows during the Tahn business. But that's old news. Nothing worth ferreting about. You could stuff it in the small end of nothing and it would still rattle about. They should have saved themselves all the bother and just asked.'

'It's the AM2,' Mahoney said. 'They can't find where our boss has it stashed.'

Sten gobbled. 'But, I thought – I mean, everybody assumes . . .'

'Too right, lad,' Mahoney said. 'And we all assumed wrong. Now the AM2 is running out.'

Sten thought about that for a moment, munching on a dry nutra stick. Then, anxious, he said, 'Alex! They'll be after him, too. We have to—'

'I already took care of that,' Mahoney said. 'I sent warning. Hope he got it. I didn't have much time.'

He waved out at the darkness in the direction of the hunters. No further explanation was needed. Obviously Mahoney had only been half a step ahead when he reached Sten.

'We'll have to get word to Kilgour when we get free,' Mahoney said. 'Tell him where to meet us.'

Sten laughed. 'No need,' he said. 'Alex will know where to find us.'

Mahoney started to ask how, but something cracked deep in the woods.

They moved on.

They were at the edge of Amos Lake, waiting to cross. Sten wanted just a bit more light. Mahoney cursed. The little clot *wanted* to be seen.

A hand gripped his wrist, then was gone.

It was time.

As they rose to make their dash, Mahoney saw a small, black orb in Sten's hand. There was a large red dot imbedded in the center – a pressure switch.

They soared out onto the ice, the wind at their backs so they barely had to pole to keep up the speed. The frigid air tugged at their garments, finding gaps where none in fact could exist. The cold nipped through those gaps with sharp, tiny teeth.

Mahoney thought his lungs were so brittle there was no way any self-respecting oxygen molecules could attach.

Ice gouted just in front of him, hurling up a thick cloud of particles that choked him as he sailed into it. The crack of the laser fire followed the shot. This was bad. The hunters had found them. It was also good. They were at a distance.

The far shore came crashing up at them. Mahoney could see the snow-choked trees just beyond. Without slowing, they plunged onto rocky ground. Mahoney felt the wind knocked from him, but he stayed low, hugging the frozen ground like a lover.

He saw Sten roll until he was lying on the ground, facing the enemy. Mahoney fought for air and dared a look, then ducked as an AM2 round powdered the rock in front of him. But he had just enough time to see the hunters advancing in a broken pattern so he couldn't get off a decent shot. Just to keep them honest, however, he raised his weapon.

The hand went on his wrist again.

'Not now,' Sten whispered.

Mahoney found a safer angle to peer out.

The Mantis team was nearing the center of the lake. He heard motion beside him and looked over to see Sten holding the hard, black ball. His thumb rested on the red spot. The knuckle whitened as he pressed.

Instinctively Mahoney looked out on the lake. But all he saw was hunters coming on. Then there was an ungodly roar as the entire center of the lake lifted up. Sheets of ice the size of small buildings were hurled to the side.

A gleaming white ship arose straight through the center. He saw bodies – or what had to be bodies, from the way they were flailing – spin upward and then plunge into the frigid water.

He didn't know if death was instant, or long and agonizing. If anyone screamed, he wouldn't have been able to hear it over the noise of the rising spacecraft.

Then he saw Sten sitting up and fumbling another nutra stick out of his pack.

Mahoney groaned up himself. He looked worriedly up at the sky. 'There won't be any question of capture, now,' he said. 'And they won't chance another team. If they've even got one. That command ship will just hunt us down and bomb the clot out of us. That's what I'd do, at least.'

'I've been thinking the same thing,' Sten said. 'But we've got that—' He pointed at the white ship hovering obediently over the lake. 'And we've got two spares. Yours, and the team's. Should be enough for a diversion, don't you think?'

Mahoney caught his drift. It might work – just. He started to get up. Sten motioned him back.

'I'm starved,' he said. 'It might be a while before we get another chance. Let's eat.'

Mahoney felt hunger pangs gnawing at his own guts. It was a comforting, being-alive kind of feeling. What the clot!

They ate.

Chapter Three

Laird Kilgour of Kilgour, formerly Chief Warrant Officer Alex Kilgour (First Imperial Guards Division, Retired); formerly CWO A. Kilgour, Detached, Imperial Service, Special Duties; formerly Private-through-Sergeant Kilgour, Mantis Section Operational, various duties from demolitions expert to sniper to clandestine training, to include any duties the late Eternal Emperor wanted performed sub rosa with a maximum of lethality, was holding forth."

'. . . An' aye, th' rain's peltin' doon, f'r days an' days i' comes doon. An' her neighbors tell th' li'l old gran, "Bes' y' flee t' high ground."

'"Nae," she says. 'Ah hae faith. God will take care a' me. Th' Laird wi' provide."'

It was a beautiful evening. The tubby man was sprawled on a settee, his feet on a hassock, his kilt tucked decorously between his legs. Conveniently to his right were his weapons of choice: a full pewter flagon of Old Sheepdip, imported at staggering – staggering to anyone not as rich as Kilgour – expense from Earth and a liter mug of lager.

The fire blazed in a fireplace that was tall enough for three men to stand in at their full height. Outside, a winter storm crashed against the walls of Deacon Brodie's Tavern with all the fury a polar frenzy could produce on the planet Edinburgh, Alex's three-gee home world.

A beautiful evening. Kilgour was on his fourth – no, fifth drink. There were good friends across from him, good friends who also had not yet suffered the complete repertoire of Kilgour's stories. The wee barmaid had shyly wondered if Laird Kilgour might not find the time – later – to escort her home through the muck an' mire.

It was safe and quiet and peaceable. It was just old habits that had Kilgour seated with his back to a wall, and his left hand, resting on his kneecap, was a few centimeters away from a mini-willygun holstered on his upper thigh.

'An th' rain comit doon an' comit doon, an' th' water's risin'. And her pigs are wash' away, squealin't. An' the' coo's swimmin't f'r shelter. An doon th' road comit ae gravcar.

'"Mum," comit th' shout. "Thae's floodin't. Thae must leave!"

'"Nae," she shouts back. "Ah'll noo leave. Th' Laird will provide."

'An' th' water comit up, an' comit up, an' th' rain i' peltin' an comit doon. An' the chickens ae roostin' ae the roof. Floodin't her house t' ae th' first story. An' here comit ae boat. "Missus, now thae *must* leave. We'll save y'!"

'An' agin comit her answer: "Nae, nae. Th' Laird will provide."

'But th' rain keep fallin't. An' th' water keep't risin't. An' coverin't th' second story. An' she's crouchin' ae th' roof, wi' th' chickens, an' here comit ae rescue gravlighter. It hover't o'er th' roof, an' a mon leans oot. "Mum! We're here t'save y'."

'But still she's steadfast. Once again, "Nae, nae. Th' Laird will provide."

'An' th' rain keep fallin't an' th' flood keep't risin't. An' she drowns. Dead an' a'.

'An' she goes oop t' Heaven. An' th' Laird's waitin'. An' th' wee gran lady, she's pissed!

'She gets right i' Th' Good Laird's face, an shouts, "How c'd y', Laird! Th' one time Ah aski't frae help – an ye're nae there."'

The com buzzed. The guvnor answered.

'Alex. F'r you. From your hotel.'

'B'dam',' Alex swore. But he rose. 'Hold m'point. 'Tis nae a good one, nae a long one, but be holdin't it anyway.'

He went behind the bar. He recognized the face onscreen – one of the com operators at the hotel he stayed at when he came to the city.

'This is wee Alex,' he said.

The operator was puzzled. 'Laird Kilgour, this message wa' bounced frae y'r castle. A text transmission. But it seems a bit garbled.'

'Gie it me, man. P'raps the twa ae us can decipher it.'

The operator tapped keys. Across the centerscreen scrolled: XRME TRACD BYDG RRDG, and on for a full page.

Alex's face blanked.

'I'm sorry, Laird. But thae's all thae were.'

'A garble, Ah ken. Ah'll be direct back ae th' hotel. Hae a call frae there.' He forced a smile and cut the link. 'Damned storm! Lost m'connection.'

'They'll try again.'

'Aye. That they shall,' Alex agreed. 'Tell 'em t' hold. Ah'm ta the recycler. Leith needs th' water. An' we'll be needin't another all round.'

The smile fixed on his lips, Alex meandered toward the lavatory. His eyes skipped around the few people in the tavern. No. All known – unless this was a long-range set-up. He thought to add an artistic, drunken stagger as he went into the bathroom.

Then he was moving. Foot braced on the washstand – it would hold his weight. Good. He pushed at the high, seemingly barred window. What looked to be rusted hinges swung smoothly open and the bars fell away. Kilgour wriggled head-first onto the narrow ledge above the alley outside. He chose his pubs – or modified them – for more than cheery companionship, complaisant barmaids, and high-alk service.

He lay motionless for a moment. The ice-needled wind, the driven snow, and the below-zero cold did not exist in his mind. He was looking for movement. Nothing. Most of the message had, indeed, been a garble. Intentionally so, intended to bury the real message. The operative code groups were the second and third. They were old Mantis signals, and decoded as:

MISSION BLOWN. EXTRACT TO RV IMMEDIATELY.

Which posed some very interesting questions. Such as – Kilgour was out of the military. He certainly had no links with the Empire or with the supersecret Mantis Section since his hasty retirement after the assassination.

So: Who was trying to contact him?

Second: Why were they using a common, general code? One that was part of a standard SOI, had been around for many years, and almost certainly had been compromised?

Was Mantis looking for him? Did he want to be found?

Kilgour swore at himself. He was getting sloppy and careless in his declining years. For the past several days he had been feeling that skin-crawl between his shoulder blades that he should have listened to: You are being watched. You are being followed. There are beings about with bad intentions.

But nae, lad. Y'were bein't th' city cock ae th' walk. Doon frae thae aird mors an' coirs, thinkin't th' eyes on ye were naught but thae lassies admirin't ae man ae means.

Enough, Kilgour.

Y'r mither said years gone y'r nae better'n ae purblind ox. Noo, try t' find y'r way out off th' killin't floor.

He had a second for a final mourn. Nac m'friends'll nae hear the last line:

'An' th' Laird looki't ae her, an' he's sore puzzled. "Gran, how can y' say Ah dinnae provide? Ah giv't ae car, ae boat, an ae grav-lighter!"'

With a silent chuckle he slid down the alley to the High Street. He held close to the high gray wall next to him for a few meters, then stepped out suddenly, as if coming from a doorway – a man intent on late business, with nothing else on his mind but his destination and how clottin' miserable the weather was.

Movement. From the shadows across the street.

The first question was: Who was after him?

Kilgour was operating at an advantage and a disadvantage. On a normal E-world, his three-gee muscles might have provided an easy solution, either acrobatic or bloody. Here he was just another man. Of course, his pursuers would be under a disadvantage – unless they, also, came from a high-grav world.

He chanced a look back.

His tail had entered a commercial gravsled. The sled had lifted and was creeping down the street behind him. Kilgour grimaced. If this was a termination attempt, the sled would go to full power, lift over the sidewalk, and scrub him against the high stone wall beside him. An unfortunate accident. He listened, but the sled's McLean generators did not increase their pitch.

So let's see if we can find out who these lads are, he thought.

Three crossings down, he turned onto a narrow street. Very narrow. A close, actually – so steep it was not ramped but was instead a long stairway. Alex moved faster.

The close ended in a small courtyard. Four other lanes opened from it. Kilgour picked one, ducked into its shadows, and held for a moment.

Two figures moved down the stairs. The flurried storm broke, and Kilgour glimpsed them. Clot. He had no strength advantage at all. Either he was being chased by a pair of hyperthyroid Earth gorillas, or his pursuers were wearing fighting armor. Fighting suits were AM2-powered killing machines that turned the properly trained infantryman into something far more lethal than a conventional tracked assault vehicle. Amplified musculature gave the wearer many times the strength and endurance of an unsuited soldier. Their armor was impervious to conventional shoulder weapons and even medium-size shrapnel.

Against a suit, Kilgour was far more impotent than a man from a zero-gee environment would be against Alex.

Two of them. Just wonderful. Och well. *Th' Laird wi' provide . . .*

Kilgour was off, zigging through alleys at a dead run, his mind running at equal speed.

How were they tracking him? Had they planted anything on him? Was his kilt wired? Or that locator? He didn't think so but started to hurl the locator away, then considered.

He came out of the alley warren onto a street. It was very late and the streets were still. Ahead he saw a gravsled land and three other monsters lumber out and up the hill toward him. He went into another alleyway.

Who was after him? Occasionally fighting suits came into the hands of big-time private warlords, but these, Alex thought, appeared to be current Imperial issue. Which meant? That for some reason he had offended the powers that be. Not the planetary officials on Edinburgh – Alex had purchased far too many friends in high places not to have gotten a tip – but off-world.

Worst case? The Empire – or those clottin' imbecile thieves who'd taken it over after the Emperor's death. Assume that, Kilgour. For whatever the privy council's reason, assume that.

Now, he thought. What do they want of me? If they wanted me just dead they would've had plenty of opportunities over the past few days, weeks, or months. There's more'n enough lads still in service who remember how to plant a bomb or look through a crosshairs.

So it's alive, alive-o, then.

If they looked up m'wee record – th' honest one – then they'll noo send a boy for a man's work. So think those lads in thae braw suits are Mantis. They *are* lookin't f'r me. But nae quite the way I thought. An' they're nae suited up because th' grav pulls hard on their wee bones.

So it would be a simple snatch, wi' th' minimum of screekin' an' broken bones. Then off t' th' brainscan.

Ah think not. Ah'll nae hae some psych's slimy fingers pryin't ae m'soul. But I hae nae desire t' put m'back 'gainst a wall, spit on m'sword, an' go down yodelin' like ae Vikin' sarky, or whatever thae dubbed themselves.

The storm was lashing down harder.

Two back of me – driving. Three more backup. Plus there'll be another team in immediate reserve. Solution: drop all five of them before they hae a chance to gurgle f'r help.

Five men. Five of the Empire's best operatives, wearing suits that could have let them walk through the thickest walls of Alex's castle and emerge with their hair unmussed.

Nae problem, lad. Nae problem at all.

Kilgour stayed moving – just fast enough to keep the Mantis people after him, but not fast enough for them to blow the whistle and think he was on a full-tilt run.

His path wound through the back alleys of the city. His pursuers may have been in suits, but Alex had grown up familiar with the cobblestones that the idiotically tradition-minded builders of the city – God bless them to the twelfth generation – had installed when Edinburgh was first colonized.

First a wee rope . . .

He found it – a coil of 5 mm wire, hanging from a building site. Alex grabbed it and pulled. He had, he estimated, nearly sixty meters of wire. A bit too much.

His route became more direct, heading back toward the heart of the city. The cobbles were steep and the muck on either side of the road greasy. He led his pursuers back to the High Street, then went into the open. He doubled up the center of the street, stopped, and turned. Now his pursuers were in the open, as well.

They'll be thinkin' Ah'm armed. But noo wi' this. Imperial issue an' all. He knelt, pistol in right hand, left hand cupped around his right, left arm just behind the elbow on his knee . . . breathe in . . . out . . . hold . . . squeeze.

The willygun cracked. The bullet was a 1 mm ball of AM2, shielded by Imperium. AM2 – spaceship power. The round struck one of the suited men in a leg – and the leg exploded. AM2 was not a conventional infantry round.

B'dam, Alex thought in some surprise. Moren' one hundred meters an' Ah hit somethin'. Sten'll nae believe it . . . Four left . . . Now the gloves were off. Return fire spattered around him. Kilgour assumed they were using more conventional weapons – and still trying to take him alive. One block up was his street.

The wire was knotted securely to a lamppost, half a meter off the ground. The Mantis operatives were bounding, ten meters to a leap, up the rise toward him. Alex went down 'his' street at a run. At a skate, actually.

The narrow alley was at a fifty-degree angle – and icy. There was no way anyone could walk, let alone run down it. Kilgour could not – but he used that cable as a steadying ski tow in reverse, swearing as he felt the insulation sear his hands. He braked, stumbled, nearly skidded, and recovered.

Two Mantis operatives were leaping down the alley toward him. They touched down – on slippery, fifty-degree ice. Even as the pseudomusculature kicked in and they rebounded, their feet had gone out from underneath them. One man smashed into a wall, then skidded, motionless, toward Kilgour. The other man pinwheeled in midair, out of control.

Kilgour shot him through the faceplate as he tumbled past. Then Alex was going back up the way he came, hand-over-hand.

He heard a suitjet blast over the storm and went flat, rolling onto his back. One operative came over the rooftop. Y' panicked and let the power save you, lad. An' noo you're hangin' thae, like a braw cloud. Alex shot the cloud three times in its center. The suit's drive stayed on and rocketed the tiny near-spacecraft straight up and away into the sleet clouds.

One more. One more. Show yourself, lad.

Nothing.

Not knowing – or caring – if the final operative had cracked, had gone to aid his downed teammates, or had lost control of his suit, Alex went up the rest of the way to the High Street. Now all he had to do was get out of the city, offworld, and make his way to a very private rendezvous point, one known but to one other being in the universe.

'Wi' m' left hand. Wi' m' left hand in m' sleep. Wi' m' left hand in m' sleep croonin't ae lullaby to a bairn.'

And Alex Kilgour vanished from the planet of Edinburgh.

Chapter Four

The getting of power had always been a complex thing with complex motives. Socio-historians had written whole libraries on it, analyzing and reanalyzing the past, seeking the perfect formula, saying so and so was the right course to follow, and such and such was obvious folly.

Kin mated with kin to achieve power, producing gibbering heirs to their throne. The threat of such a succession sometimes assured the parents of very long and royal reigns.

Kin also murdered kin, or kept them in chains for decades.

Genocide was another favorite trick, one of the few foolproof methods of achieving majority. The difficulty with genocide, the socio-historians said, was that it needed to be constantly applied to keep the edge.

Politics without murder was also favored – under special circumstances. Power was won in such a case by constant and unceasing compromise. Many voices were heard and views taken into account. Only then would a decision be reached. A little artful lying, and everyone *believed* they had been satisfied. Everyone, in that case, was defined as beings of material importance. A leader only had to make sure those same beings had sufficient bones of imagined progress to toss to their mobs. The rule, there, was that if one had too little, the prospect of more was usually enough to satisfy.

There were other methods, but they tended to follow the same paths.

The most certain way, those historians agreed, was to possess a commodity that beings desired above all else. In ancient times it had been food or water. A well-placed road might accomplish the same end. Sex worked in any era, given the proper circumstances. Whatever the commodity, however, it had to be kept in a safe place and guarded against all possible comers.

The Eternal Emperor had had AM2. It was the ultimate fuel and the cornerstone of his vast Empire. In the past, he had merely to turn the tap one way or the other to maintain complete control. His policies had been supported by the largest military force of any known age. The Emperor had also kept the AM2 in a safe place.

More than six years after his assassination, his killers were unable to find it – and they were about to lose the power they had committed regicide to claim.

Even if they had possessed the key to the Emperor's AM2 treasure chest, it was likely the privy council was headed for disaster.

Times had not been kind.

In the aftermath of the Tahn wars – the largest and most costly conflict in history – the Empire was teetering on the edge of economic chaos. The Eternal Emperor's coffers were nearly bare. The deficit from the tremendous military spending was so enormous that even with the highly favorable interest rates the Emperor had bargained hard for, it would take a century to significantly reduce it, much less pay it off.

When the Emperor was still alive, Tanz Sullamora and the other members of the council had strongly proposed their own solution. It involved freezing wages below the pre-Tahn rate and creating deliberate scarcity of product, forcing sharp increases in the price of goods.

And a hefty surtax on AM2.

Through those means and others, the debt would be quickly paid, and corporate health assured for the ages.

The Emperor had rejected those proposals out of hand. When the Emperor rejected a thing, it was law. With no appeal.

His Majesty's post-war plans called for a directly opposite approach.

The late, never lamented Sr. Sullamora had detailed the Emperor's views to his fellow conspirators without editorializing:

Wages would be allowed to rise to their natural levels. The war had been costly in beingpower – especially, skilled beingpower. This would result in immediate higher costs to business.

Prices, on the other hand, would be frozen, putting goods within easy reach of the newly prosperous populations.

Of course, the war had been a tremendous drain on supplies. To alleviate that, the Emperor fully intended to temporarily *reduce* taxes on AM2 – immediately – making goods and transportation cheaper.

In time, he believed, a balance would be achieved.

Where the lords of industry had once seen a future of sudden and continuous windfalls, they now faced a long period of belt-tightening and careful management of their resources. Unearned perks and hefty bonuses would be a thing of the past. Business would be forced to compete equally and take a long-range view of profitability.

That was unacceptable to the privy council. They voted no – with a gun.

The vote had not been unanimous. Volmer, the young media baron, had been horrified by their plan. He wanted no part of it, despite the fact that he disagreed with the Emperor as much as anyone on the council. Although he had no talent for it, Volmer was a fervent believer in the art of persuasion. But he had always had whole battalions of reporters, political experts, and public relations scientists at his command, constantly feeding his enormous media empire. All that was inherited, so talent wasn't necessary.

Like most heirs, Volmer believed himself a genius. It was his fatal flaw. Even such a dimwit as Volmer should have been able to cipher the precariousness of his situation when he broke with his peers. But the bright light of his own imagined intellect had kept that fact hidden.

The elaborate plot that ensued claimed Volmer as its first victim. The architect of the plot was the Emperor's favorite toady, Tanz Sullamora.

For most of his professional life, Sullamora had licked the Eternal Emperor's boots. For decades, he saw his ruler as a being without visible fault. Certainly, he didn't believe him to be a saint, with gooey feelings for his subjects. He viewed the Emperor as a cold and calculating giant of a CEO, who would use any means to achieve his ends. In that, Sr. Sullamora was absolutely correct.

He erred only by taking it to the extreme. Business was Sullamora's faith, with the Emperor as the high priest. He believed the Emperor infallible, a being who quickly calculated the odds and acted without hesitation. And the result was always the correct one. He also assumed that the Emperor's goals were the same as his own, and those of every other capitalist in the Empire.

To their complete dismay, many others had made the same assumption. But the Eternal Emperor's game was his own. It was his board. His rules. His victory. Alone.

As for infallibility, even the Emperor didn't think that. In fact, when he planned, he assumed error – his own, as well as others. That's why things mostly worked out in his favor. The Eternal Emperor was the master of the long view. 'You tend to get that way,' he used to joke to Mahoney, 'after the first thousand years.'

The Tahn war was the result of one of the Emperor's greatest errors. He knew that more than anyone. But the conflict had been so fierce that he had been forced to be candid – to Sullamora, as well as to others. He started thinking aloud, running the logic down to his trusted advisors. How else could he seek their opinions? He had also revealed self-doubt and admitted his many mistakes.

That was a terrible blow to Tanz Sullamora. His hero was revealed to have feet of definite clay. The corporate halo was tarnished. Sullamora lost his faith.

Murder was his revenge.

To protect himself, he kept the actual details of the plot secret. He guarded his flanks by demanding that his fellow conspirators equally implicate themselves. They had all fixed their prints to documents admitting guilt. Each held a copy of the document, so that betrayal was unthinkable. But the particulars of Volmer's murder, the recruiting of Chapelle, and the subsequent death of the Emperor remained unknown to the other conspirators.

The members of the privy council watched the events at the spaceport unfold on their vidscreens along with the rest of the Empire. And there were no more fascinated viewers. They saw the royal party veer to the receiving line at Soward. They cheered Sullamora as their private hero. They waited in anticipation for the fatal shot. The tension was incredible. In a moment, they would be kings and queens. Then the Emperor died. Mission accomplished!

The explosion that followed surprised them as much as anyone else. The bomb might have been a nice touch. But it was inconceivable that Sullamora would commit suicide. The council members assumed the madman, Chapelle, was merely making sure of his target. Oh, well. Poor Sullamora. Drakh happens.

Although it meant there were more riches to divide, they honestly mourned the man. As the chief of all transport and most major ship building, Tanz Sullamora could not be replaced. They also badly needed his skills at subterfuge, as well as his knowledge of the inner workings of Imperial politics. His death meant that they had to learn on the job.

They didn't learn very well.

The Emperor had stored the AM2 in great depots strategically placed about his Empire. The depots fed great tankers that sped this way and that, depending upon the need and the orders of the Emperor. He alone controlled the amount and the regularity of the fuel.

Defy him, and he would beggar the rebel system or industry. Obey him, and he would see there was always a plentiful supply at a price he deemed fair for his own needs.

The privy council immediately saw the flaw in that system, as far as their own survival was concerned. Not one member would trust any other enough to give away such total control.

So they divided the AM2 up in equal shares, assuring each of their own industries had cheap fuel. They also used it to punish personal enemies and reward, or create, new allies. Power, in other words, was divided four ways.

Occasionally they would all agree that there was a single threat to their future. They would meet, consider, and act.

In the beginning, they went on a spending spree. With all that free fuel, they vastly expanded their holdings, building new factories, gobbling up competitors, or blindsiding corporations whose profits they desired.

The Emperor had priced AM2 on three levels: The cheapest went to developing systems. The next was for public use, so that governments could provide for the basic needs of their various populaces. The third, and highest, was purely commercial.

The privy council set one high price to be paid by everyone, except themselves and their friends. The result was riches beyond even their inflated dreams.

But there was one worm gnawing a great hole in their guts. It was a worm they chose too long to ignore.

The great depots they controlled had to be supplied. But by whom? Or what?

In the past, robot ships – tied together in trains so long they exceeded the imagination – had appeared at the depots filled to the brim with Anti-Matter Two. Many hundreds of years had passed since anyone had asked where they might come from. An assumption replaced the question. Important people knew – important people who followed the Emperor's orders.

Like all assumptions, it rose up and bit the privy council in their collective behinds.

When the Emperor died, the robot ships stopped. At that moment, the AM2 at hand was all they possessed. It would never increase.

It took a long while for that to sink in. The privy council was so busy dealing with the tidal wave of problems – as well as their own guilt – that they just assumed the situation to be temporary.

They sent their underlings to question the bureaucrats at the fuel office. Those poor beings puzzled at them. 'Don't *you* know?' they asked. For a time, the privy council was afraid to admit they didn't.

More underlings were called. Every fiche, every document, every doodle the Emperor had scrawled was searched out and examined.

Nothing.

This was an alarming state of affairs, worthy of panic, or, at least, a little rationing. They only panicked a little – and rationed not at all.

They were secretive beings themselves, they reasoned. It was an art form each had mastered in his or her path to success. Therefore: An emperor had to be the most secretive creature of all. Proof: His long reign – and their momentary failure at figuring his system out.

Many other efforts were launched, each more serious and desperate than the last.

Real panic was beginning to set in.

Finally a study committee had been formed from among their most able executives. The committee's objectives were twofold. One: Find the AM2. Second: Determine exactly the supplies on hand and recommend their disposition until objective number one had been reached.

Unfortunately, the second objective obscured the first for more than a year. If the Emperor had been alive, he would have howled over their folly.

'They tried that with the Seven Sisters,' he would have hooted. 'How much oil do you *really* have, please, sir? Don't lie, now. It isn't in the national interest.'

The council would not have known what the Seven Sisters was all about, or the terrible need to know about something so useless and plentiful as oil. But they would have gotten the drift.

When asked, each member lied – poor-mouthed, as the old wildcatters would have said. The next time they were asked, they were just as likely to inflate the figures. It depended upon the political winds about the conference table.

What about the rest of the Empire? After they had been treated so niggardly, what would the truth gain the council?

Actually, the first outsider who had been questioned soon spread the word. Hoarding fever struck. There was less readily available AM2 than ever before.

Adding to the council's dilemma was a whole host of other problems.

During the Tahn wars, the Emperor constantly had been forced to deal with shaky allies and insistent fence sitters. When the tide turned, all of them swore long and lasting fealty. That, however, did not remove the cause for their previous discontent. The leaders of many of those systems had to deal with unruly populations, beings who had never been that thrilled with the Imperial system and became less so during the war.

Peace did not automatically solve such doubts. The Eternal Emperor had just been turning his attention to these matters when he was slain. The problems would have been exceedingly difficult to solve under any circumstances. It was especially so for his self-appointed heirs. If those allies of the moment had not trusted the Eternal Emperor to have their best interests at heart, then who the clot were these new guys? The council ruled by Parliamentary decree, but most beings in the Empire were cynical about Parliament. They saw it as a mere rubber stamp for Imperial orders. The Eternal Emperor had never discouraged that view.

It was one of the keys to his mystique.

The Emperor had been a student and admirer of some of the ancient czarist policies. The czars were among the last Earth practitioners of rule by godhead. They had millions of peasants who were brutally treated. The czars used the members of their royal court as middle beings. It was they who wielded the lash and kept the rations to starvation level. The peasants did not always submit. History was full of their many violent uprisings. But the peasants always blamed the nobility for their troubles. It was the noble corpses they hung on posts, not the czar's.

He was a father figure. A kind of gentle man who thought only of his poor subjects. It was the nobility who always took advantage of his nature, hiding their evil deeds from him. And if only he *knew* how terrible was their suffering, he would end it instantly. There was not one scrap of truth to this – but it worked.

Except for the last czar, who was openly disdainful of his people.

'That's why he was the last,' the Emperor once told Mahoney.

It was just one of those little lessons of history that the privy council was unaware of. Although if they had known of it, it was doubtful if they would have understood it. Very few business beings understood politics – which was why they made terrible rulers.

Another enormous, festering problem was how to deal with Tahn.

To Kyes, the Kraa twins, and the others, it was simple. The Tahn had been defeated. To the victors go the spoils, and so on.

To that end, the privy council had gutted all their systems. They had hauled off the factories for cannibalization or scrap, seized all resources, and beaten the various populations into submission and slave labor. They also spent a great deal of credits they didn't have to garrison their former enemy. The rape of the Tahn empire produced an instant windfall. But before they had time to congratulate themselves for their brilliance, the privy council saw all that gain going over the dike in an ever-growing flood.

The Eternal Emperor could have told them that tyranny was not cost efficient.

An economic miracle was what the Emperor had in mind. At least, that was how he would have portrayed it. Certainly he had reprisals in mind. The purge would have been massive and complete. He would have wiped out all traces of the culture that had bred the war-loving beings.

But he would have replaced it with something. The will to fight would have been harnessed to the will to compete. Aid every bit as massive as the purge would have been provided. In his thinking, such single-minded beings as the Tahn would eventually produce credits in such plenty that they would soon become one of the most important capitalist centers in his empire.

They would have made wonderful customers of AM2.

Which brought the dilemma of the privy council to full circle.

Where *was* the AM2?

Chapter Five

Kyes saw the storm warnings before his ship touched down at Soward.

Prime World's main spaceport was nearly empty. A five-kilometer corner was a jumble of tugs, and from the pitting and streaks of rust on their bulky sides, they looked as if they had been idle for months.

The few liners he saw were pocked with the viral scale that attacked all deep-space ships and ate steadily away at them if left untended. He saw no work crews about. The once vital, bustling heart of the Empire looked like an ancient harridan who had lost even dim memories of lovers past.

A glistening phalanx of military vehicles was waiting for him. They were in stark contrast to the degeneration afflicting Soward. The tall, silvery being with the red mark of his kind throbbing angrily on his smooth skull slid into the seat of his official gravcar. He motioned the driver to proceed.

As the gravcar and its escorts hummed toward the entrance, they skirted the gaping black roped-off crater torn out by the bomb blast that had taken the Emperor. There had been a serious proposal to build a memorial to the Eternal Emperor at the site. Kyes himself had pressed the measure – as a gesture to the being whose memory he and his colleagues based their own authority upon. There had been no argument. Funds had immediately been approved and a designer set. That had been during his last visit, more than a year ago. As yet, not one iota of work had begun.

He was greeted by more squalor as they cleared the port gates. Empty warehouses. Closed businesses, boarding hanging from the vacant eyes of their windows, where gleaming goods had once enticed an affluent population. Unlicensed beggars and crowds of idle beings eyed him as he passed. A shambling tub of a lout, wearing the rags of a loader, glared at the flags of office fluttering on Kyes's transport. She looked him straight in the eye, then spat on the broken pavement.

Kyes leaned forward to his driver. 'What's happened?' He waved at the desolation around them.

The driver needed no further explanation. 'Don't bother yourself with them, Sr. Kyes,' she snarled. 'They're nothing but slackers. There's plenty of jobs, but they won't take 'em. Just want to suck on the public tit. Now they're whinin' and groanin' 'cause decent, hard-workin' folks are tellin' 'em: "No work, no credits." If the Eternal Emperor – bless him – were still around, he'd straighten 'em out fast.'

The driver stuttered to a stop as she realized that Kyes might take her comments as criticism of the privy council. Then she recovered. A toady's smile wreathed her broad face.

'Not that alla yuz ain't doin' best ya can. These'r terrible times. Terrible times. Wouldn't take on yer job for a fistful a credits. I was tellin' me hub just the other . . .' The driver droned on. Condescension heaped upon forced humility. Kyes shut her out. He also made no objection to her talking, much less the language. It marked her as on the payroll of the Kraas. There were few things the twins even bothered being subtle about.

The reason Kyes was on Prime World after so long an absence was that he had been called to an emergency session of the privy council. The chief of the AM2 commission was scheduled to reveal the full details of his committee's study on the fuel situation. More to the point, he was to spell out exactly when the search for the Emperor's hidden resources was to be concluded.

Kyes hoped there would be better news here than the depressing report he had received shortly before he left for Prime World.

A crucial mission had been blown. That a number of military operatives had been killed in the process didn't concern Kyes. An important confidant of the Eternal Emperor's – one Admiral Sten – and his longtime aide, Alex Kilgour, had eluded the net spread for them.

The idea that had launched the hunt for all of the beings who had been close to the Emperor had not originated with Kyes. Possibly it had been the Kraa twins'. It didn't matter. Kyes had immediately seen that it could be a shortcut solution to his own dilemma. Round them all up, put them under the brainscan, and voila! All the Emperor's secrets would come tumbling out.

It had taken many, many months to lash that idea into action. Kyes had done the lashing. His plight was far more desperate than the others. It still amazed him how much inertia had to be overcome when dealing with a five-member ruling board. He and his colleagues were used to running their own shows, without compromise or consultation. But finally, the Mantis teams had gone out and quickly returned, prey kicking and mewling in their nets. The result: Zed. Zero. Not one tip or hint on the source of the AM2 . . . or anything else.

Kyes had analyzed the long list of suspects, and more and more he had come to admire just how close-mouthed the Emperor had been. Although his analysis came after the fact, it became apparent that only a very few beings might be able to help. None of those had been among the Mantis teams' catches. Two individuals stood out.

One was retired Fleet Marshal Ian Mahoney. He was officially listed as dead. Kyes had reason to doubt that. He had several reasons. The most important was the gut feeling he got studying the man.

The Mercury Corps files pertaining to Mahoney revealed an exceedingly canny individual who would have no difficulty at all in staging his own demise and remaining out of sight for as long as he thought necessary. The only flaw Kyes could find was his unwavering loyalty to the Emperor, a flaw that made Mahoney potentially dangerous – if he was alive. Assuming the death was a cover, that could suggest only one motive for Mahoney's actions: the fleet marshal suspected the privy council of assassinating his old employer.

The second most likely suspect was Admiral Sten, a man who had once commanded the Imperial bodyguard, the Gurkhas – who, oddly, had all resigned their positions immediately following the Emperor's death and returned to their homeland of Nepal on Earth. Sten had been an important but shadowy figure during the Tahn conflict. Kyes had also personally reviewed Sten's files. There were enormous gaps. Very strange. Especially since the gaps seemed to have been ordered by the Emperor himself. Adding to Kyes's suspicions was that the man had suddenly become enormously wealthy, as had his companion, Kilgour, although on a lesser scale. Where did all that money come from? Pay-offs? From the Emperor, himself, perhaps? For what purpose?

Kyes added one and one and got an instant six: Sten must be among the very few that the Emperor had entrusted with his secrets. When the admiral had been located in his distant exile, Kyes had demanded that a crack team be sent to capture him. He had gotten gilt-edged assurances that only the very best would be sent. Obviously he had been fed a sop. After all, how good could those Mantis beings have actually been? Wiped out by one man? Clot!

Kyes had packed his steel teeth for this meeting. Some heavy ass-chewing was in order.

Out on the street, Kyes spotted three beings in dirty orange robes and bare feet. They were making their way through the motley crowd, handing out leaflets and proselytizing. He couldn't hear what they were saying from the soundproof comfort of his car, but he didn't need to. He knew who they were: members of the Cult of the Eternal Emperor.

All over the Empire, there were countless individuals who firmly believed that the Emperor had not died. A few thought it was a plot by his enemies: The Emperor had been kidnapped and was being kept under heavy guard. Others claimed it was a clever ploy by the Emperor himself: He had deliberately staged his death and was hiding out until his subjects realized just how terribly he was needed. Eventually, he would return to restore order.

The cultists were at the absolute extreme. They believed that the Emperor was truly immortal, that he was a holy emissary of the Holy Spheres, who wore a body for convenience to carry around his glowing soul. His death, they said, was self-martyrdom. An offering to the Supreme Ether for all the sins of his mortal subjects. They also firmly believed in his resurrection. The Eternal Emperor, they preached, would soon return to his benign reign, and all would be well again.

Kyes was a kindred spirit of the cultists. Because he, too, believed the Emperor was alive and would return. Kyes was a businessbeing, who had once disdained all thinking based on wishes rather than reason as a weak prop for his mental and economic inferiors. But that was no longer so. If the Eternal Emperor were truly dead, then Kyes was lost. Therefore, he believed. To think otherwise was to risk madness.

There were ancient tales of his own kind that directly addressed the issue of immortality, or, at least, extremely long life. They were part of a Methuselah legend, based on the fatal flaw of his species.

Kyes – and all of the Grb'chev – were the result of the joining of two distinct life forms. One was the body that Kyes walked about in. It was a tall, handsome, silvery creature, whose chief assets were strength, almost miraculous health, and an ability to adapt to and absorb any life-threatening force. It also was as stupid as a tuber.

The second was visible only by the red splash throbbing at his skull. It once had been nothing more than a simple, hardy life form – which could be best compared to a virus. Calling it a virus, however, would not be accurate, only descriptive. Its strengths were extreme virulence, an ability to penetrate the defensive proteins of any cell it encountered, and the potential for developing intelligence. Its chief weakness was a genetic clock that ticked to a stop at the average age of one hundred and twenty-six years.

Kyes should have been 'dead' already, that fine brain nothing more than a small, blackened ball of rotting cells. His body – the handsome frame that performed all the natural functions of the Grb'chev – might continue on for another century or so, but it would be nothing more than a gibbering, drooling shell.

When Kyes had thrown his lot in with the other members of

the privy council, it was not power he sought – but rescue. Riches had no attraction to him. It was life he wanted. Intelligent life.

He cared nothing for the AM2, although he whispered not a hint of that to his colleagues. To reveal his weakness would bring his doom. When the Emperor had been slain and the desperate search launched for the source of the Emperor's never-diminishing fuel cache, Kyes had been looking equally as desperately for something else: What made the Eternal Emperor immortal?

At first he had been as sure of finding it in the Emperor's classified archives as the others were of locating the AM2. But it had proved to be equally as elusive.

When the murderous act had been committed, Kyes had been 121 years old. That meant he had just five years to live. Now a little more than six years had passed – and Kyes was still alive!

In the intervening years he had become a near-hysteric about his mental powers, constantly aware of the clock that was running out. Even the smallest lapse of memory sent him into a panic. A forgotten appointment plunged him into black moods difficult to hide from his peers. That was the chief reason he had stayed away from Prime World for so long.

He had no more notion why he continued to live than he had of the Emperor's greatest secret. No being of his species had ever survived beyond the 126-year natural border.

Well, that wasn't absolutely correct. There had been one, according to that myth – the myth of the Grb'chev Methuselah.

It was during the prehistory of the intertwined life-forms that the legend began. All was conflict and chaos during that long, dark era, the story went. Then along came an individual who was entirely different from the others. The being's name had been lost, which put the reality of his actual existence in extreme doubt but made the legend more compelling.

According to the myth, the being declared his immortality while still an adolescent. And in the hundred or more years that followed, he became noted as a wandering thinker and philosopher who confounded the greatest minds of his time. The year of his death-date, the entire kingdom took up the watch, waiting daily for the heralds to announce his demise. The year passed. Then another. And another. Until his immortality became an accepted fact. That first – and only – long-lived Grb'chev became the ruler of the kingdom. An age of great enlightenment dawned, lasting for many centuries, perhaps a thousand years. From that time on the future of the race was ensured – at least that's what the tale-tellers said.

The last part of the legend was what interested Kyes the most: the prophecy that someday another Methuselah would be born, and that immortal Grb'chev would lead the species to even greater successes.

Lately Kyes wondered if he might be that chosen one.

But this was only during his most hysterical fantasizing. More likely, the extra span he had been allotted was due to nothing more than a small genetic blip. In reality at any moment he would 'die.'

If he was to have any future, Kyes would have to seize it himself. He would find the secret and become the new savior of his kind.

Kyes looked out the window. The car was moving through a working-class neighborhood of tall, drab tenements facing across a broad avenue. The traffic was mostly on foot. The AM2 squeeze prohibited public transport, much less the boxy little flits favored by the lower middle class. Kyes saw a long line snaking out of a soya shop. A tattered sign overhead pegged the cost at ten credits an ounce. The condition of the sign mocked even that outrageous price.

Two armored cops were guarding the entrance of the shop. Kyes saw a woman exit with a bundle under her arms. The crowd immediately began hooting at her, clawing at the package. One big cop moved tentatively forward. Kyes's car glided on before he saw what happened next.

'. . . been like that ever since the food riots,' the driver was saying. 'Course, security costs somethin' fierce, so the prices gotta go up, don't they? But you can't make folks understand that. I was tellin' my hub—'

'What food riots?' Kyes burst through.

'Dincha hear?' The driver craned her neck around, gaping in amazement that a member of the privy council was somehow not in the know.

'I was advised of disturbances,' Kyes said. 'But not . . . riots.'

'Oh, *disturbances*,' the driver said. 'Much better'n riots. That's what they was, all right. Disturbances. Musta had twenty, thirty thousand lazy, filthy types disturbin' drakh all over the place. Cops went easy. Didn't kill more'n half a hundred or so. Course, three, four thousand was shot up some and . . .'

Furious, Kyes tuned out the rest. He had made his views quite plain to his fellow council members. Prime World and all the beings on it were to be handled like gossamer. As the heart of the Empire, it was the last place shortages of any kind should show up. When he had learned of the 'disturbances,' he had made his views even plainer. But the Kraas and the others assured him that all was well. There had been a few small glitches in the supply system, that was all. The supplies and the peace had been restored. Right! It wasn't the lies that disturbed Kyes so much – he was a master dissembler himself. It was the plain wrongheadedness of the matter.

If the privy council could not keep matters under control a few kilometers from its own front door, how could they possibly succeed in ruling a far-flung Empire? And if they failed, Kyes was doomed to something far worse than any hell they could imagine.

A second immesnsely irritating factor: If things were really so awful that basic foods were out of the reach of the local populace, then why were the members of the council flaunting their own wealth?

He groaned aloud when he saw, ahead of him, the spire needling up over the tall buildings of the financial district. It was the newly completed headquarters of the privy council.

'Amazin' as clot, ain't it,' his driver said, mistaking the groan for a belch of admiration. 'You fellas done yourself proud with that buildin'. Nothin' like it on Prime. Specially with the Emperor's old castle wrecked by bombs and all.

'I know yuz ain't seen it yet, but wait'll ya get inside. You got fountains and drakh. With real colored water. And right in the middle they put in this great clottin' tree. Called a rubiginosa, or somethin'. Probably sayin' it wrong. Big mother fig. But the kind you can't eat.'

'Who's idea was it?' Kyes asked – dry, noncommittal.

'Dunno. Designer, I think. What was her name? Uh . . . Ztivo, or somethin' like that. But, boy did she charge an arm and two, three legs. The tree alone's gotta be fifteen, twenty meters tall. Dug it up from someplace on Earth. But they was scared it'ud shrivel up and blow away if they brought here direct, like. So they seasoned it. On three-four different planets. Spent a big bundle of credits on it.

'Musta worked. It's goin' crazy in there! Picked up another two meters, I heard, in the last two-three months. Why, that clottin' tree's the pride and joy of Prime World, I tell you. Ask anybody.'

As the gravcar slowed, Kyes saw a crowd of beggars push forward. A wedge of club-wielding cops beat them back. Certainly, he thought. Ask anybody. Go right ahead.

The AM2 secretary's report was a dry buzz against glass. On the table before him was a one-third-meter stack of readouts, the result of many months labor. He was reading – syllable by maddening syllable – from a précis not much slimmer. His name was Lagguth. But from the glares he was getting from the members of the privy council, it was likely to be changed to something far worse.

Kyes and the others had gathered eagerly around the table. This could possibly be the most important listening session of their lives. So no one objected a whit when Lagguth's aides hauled in the mass of papers. Nor did anyone raise a brow when the preamble went a full hour.

They were in the second hour – a second hour to a group of beings who habitually required their subordinates to sum up all thinking in three sentences or less. If they liked the three sentences, the subordinate could continue. If not, firing was a not indistinct possibility. After the first hour, the AM2 secretary had gone past firing. Executions were being weighed. Kyes had several nasty varieties in mind himself.

But he had caught a different tone than the rest. There was real fear beneath all that buzz. He caught it in the nervous shufflings and newly habitual tics in Lagguth's mannerisms. Kyes stopped listening for the bottom line and started paying attention to the words. They were meaningless. Deliberate bureaucratic nonsense. That added up to stall. Kyes kept his observation to himself. Instead, he began thinking how he might use it.

The Kraas broke first.

The fat one cleared her throat, sounding like distant thunder, loomed her gross bulk forward, and thrust out a chin that was like a heavy-worlder's fist.

'Yer a right bastard, mate,' she said. 'Makin' me piles bleed with all this yetcheta yetch. Me sis's arse bones'r pokin' holes in the sitter. Get to it. Or get summun else in to do the gig!'

Lagguth gleaped. But, it was a puzzled sort of a gleap. He knew he was in trouble. Just not what for.

Lovett translated. 'Get to the clotting point, man. What's the prog?'

Lagguth took a deep and lonely breath. Then he painted a bright smile on his face. 'I'm so sorry, gentle beings,' he said. 'The scientist in me . . . tsk . . . tsk . . . How thoughtless. In the future I shall endeavor—'

The skinny Kraa growled. It was a shrill sound – and not nice. It had the definite note of a committed carnivore.

'Thirteen months,' Lagguth blurted. 'And that's an outside estimate.'

'So, you're telling us, that although your department has had no luck in locating the AM2, you *now* have an estimate of when you will find it. Is that right?' Lovett was a great one for summing up the obvious.

'Yes, Sr. Lovett,' Lagguth said. 'There can be no mistake. Within thirteen months we shall have it.' He patted the thick stack of documentation.

'That certainly sounds promising, if true,' Malperin broke in. She stopped Lagguth's instinctive defense of his work with a wave of her hand. Malperin ruled an immense, cobbled-together conglomerate. She did not rule it well. But she had more than enough steel in her to keep it as long as she liked.

'What is your opinion, Sr. Kyes?' she asked. Malperin dearly loved to shift discussions along, keeping her own views hidden as long as possible. It was Kyes's recent surmise that she actually had none and was waiting to see which way the wind blew before she alighted.

'First, I would like to ask Sr. Lagguth a question,' Kyes said. 'A critical one, I believe.'

Lagguth motioned for him to please ask.

'How much AM2 do we have on hand right now?'

Lagguth sputtered, then began a long abstract discussion. Kyes cut him off before he even reached the pass.

'Let me rephrase,' Kyes said. 'Given current usage, current rationing – how long will the AM2 last?'

'Two years,' Lagguth answered. 'No more.'

The answer jolted the room. Not because it was unexpected. But it was like having a death sentence set, knowing exactly at what moment one would cease to exist. Only Kyes was unaffected. This was a situation he was not unused to.

'Then, if you're wrong about the thirteen months . . .' Malperin began.

'Then it's bleedin' over, mate, less'n a year from then,' the skinny Kraa broke in.

Lagguth could do no more than nod. Only Kyes knew why the man was so frightened. It was because he was lying.

No, not about the two-year supply of AM2. It was the first estimate that was completely fabricated. Thirteen months. Drakh! More like never. Lagguth and his department had no more idea where the Emperor had kept the AM2 than when they started more than six years before. Motive for lying? To keep his clotting head on his shoulders. Wasn't that motive enough?

'Stay with the first figure,' Kyes purred to the skinny Kraa. 'It's pointless to contemplate the leap from the chasm when you have yet to reach the edge.'

Both Kraas stared at him. Despite their brutal features, the stares were not unkind. They had learned to depend on Kyes. They had no way of knowing that from the start, his personal dilemma had forced him into the role of moderate.

'Sr. Lagguth believes it will take thirteen months to locate the AM2 source,' Kyes said. 'This may or may not be the case. But I know how we can be more certain.'

'Yeah? How's that?' Lovett asked.

'I have a new mainframe about to go online. My scientists have been working on it for a number of years. We developed it specifically as a tool for archivists.'

'So?' That was the fat Kraa, the blunter of the two – if that were possible.

'We plan to sell it to governments. It should reduce document search time by forty percent or more.'

There were murmurs around the room. They were catching Kyes's drift, and all he was saying was true. If there was a lie, it was only in his real intentions.

'I propose that Sr. Lagguth and I join forces,' Kyes said, 'assuring us of meeting his stated goal. What do you think? I am quite open to any other suggestions.'

There were none. The deal was done.

As for the other matters – the blown Mantis mission to capture the admiral, the terrible conditions Kyes had witnessed on the streets of Prime World – they were left untouched. Kyes had gotten what he wanted.

Only one other thing came up, and this fairly casually.

'About this clottin' two-year supply business,' the skinny Kraa said.

'Yes?'

'Me 'n Sis, here, think we oughta try and stretch it.'

'More rationing?' Lovett asked. 'I think we've just about—'

'Naw. Don't be puttin' words in me mush. Drakh on that.'

'What then?'

'We take it.'

'From whom?' Kyes could not help but be drawn in by the fascinating discussion.

'Who gives a clot?' the fat Kraa said. 'Somebody that's got a whole lot of it, that's who. Can't be that many.'

'You mean steal it?' Malperin asked, also fascinated. 'Just like that?'

'Why not?' the skinny Kraa said.

Yes. They all agreed. Why not, indeed?

Chapter Six

Sten's first step, once clear of Smallbridge, was to go to ground. Mahoney had a planned refuge – which Sten rejected. Sten had his own very secure hideout. Where – he hoped – Kilgour, if he had been warned in time, would meet him.

The hideout was Farwestern, and there Sten saw first-hand the effect the dwindling of AM2 and the privy council's incompetence at managing what fuel there was.

Farwestern had been – and to a degree, still was – a shipping hub near the center of a galaxy. At one time it had provided everything a shipper could want – from shipyards to chandleries, recworlds to warehousing, hotels to emergency services, all cluttered in a system-wide assemblage of containers. 'Containers' was about the most specific description that could be used, since the entrepreneurs who had gathered around Farwestern used everything from small asteroids to decommissioned and disarmed Imperial warships to house their businesses. Almost anything legal and absolutely anything illegal could be scored in and around Farwestern, including anonymity.

Years earlier Sten and Alex, on one of their Mantis team missions, had run through Farwestern. They found its cheerful anarchy to their liking. Most especially, they fell in love with a small planetoid named Poppajoe. Poppajoe was jointly owned by a pair of rogues named Moretti and Manetti. Having acquired fortunes elsewhere under almost certainly shadowy circumstances, they had discovered Farwestern and decided that there was their home. The question was: what service could they provide that wasn't available? The answer was luxury and invisibility.

They reasoned that there would be beings passing through who would want to be well taken care of and might prefer that their presence not be broadcast. This applied to criminals as well as to executives on their way to make a deal best kept secret until the stock manipulations were complete.

Moretti and Manetti had thrived in peace. In the recent war they had doubled their fortunes. Now times were a little hard. Not bad enough to drive them under, but ticklish. They survived because they were owed so many favors by so many beings, from magnates to tramp skippers.

There were still people who needed the shadows. Moretti and Manetti catered to them. All room entrances were individual. Guests could dine publicly, or remain in their suites. Privacy was guaranteed. Their food was still the finest to be found – fine and simple, from Earthsteak to jellied hypoornin served in its own atmosphere and gravity.

When Sten and Kilgour had run across Poppajoe, they had made a very quiet resolution that if things ever got Very Very Hairy, this would be their private rendezvous point.

As Sten's ship entered the Farwestern system, neither he nor Mahoney looked particularly military. As a matter of fact, neither looked particularly anything.

Beings frequently go to too much trouble when they decide, for whatever reason, that they would rather not be recognized as themselves. All that is necessary – unless the person is unfortunately gifted with the face of a matinee idol or an abnormal body – is to appear (A) unlike who they really are; and (B) like no one in particular. Dress neither poorly nor expensively. Eat what everyone else is eating. Travel neither first class nor steerage. Try to become that mythical entity, the average citizen. Mercury Corps called the tactic, for some unknown reason, a 'Great Lorenzo.'

Sten and Mahoney were now businessmen, successful enough for their corporation to have provided them with fuel and a ship, but not so successful that they had their own pilot, and the ship was a little rundown at the edges. Three days' work at a smuggler's conversion yard had turned Sten's gleaming white yacht into just another commercial/private – but only as long as no one looked at the engines or the com room, or figured out that some of the compartments were much tinier than they should have been, and that behind those bulkheads were enough arms to outfit a small army.

Mahoney had worried that the ship could be traced by its numbers. Sten was glad to find that his ex-boss did not know *everything*. The ship and every serial-numbered item on it was trebly sterile – another product of Sten's professional paranoia that was now paying off.

So they arrived on Poppajoe and were greeted by Messrs. Moretti and Manetti as if they were both long-lost cousins and complete but respected strangers.

Poppajoe may have been surviving, but Farwestern was not. Commercial travel was a trickle. Between the fuel shortages and the cutbacks in the military, even Imperial ships were a rarity. A lot of orbital stations had sealed their ports, and their people had gone dirtside to one of Farwestern's planets or moved on.

'But we will make it,' Moretti explained. 'We're like the old mining town that struck it rich. A group of emigrés moved in and discovered that no one likes to do his own washing. They were willing to provide the services. Eventually the minerals played out and the miners headed for the next strike. However, the laundry-beings stayed – and all became millionaires doing each other's laundry.'

He found that quite funny. Sten did not. What he saw, and had seen from the time he and Mahoney had fled Smallbridge, was the slow grinding down of the Empire. He had felt it going on even in his isolation on Smallbridge, but witnessing it was another thing. Beingkind was pulling in its horns – or was being forced to. Entropy was well and good as a thermodynamic principle. As a social phenomenon it was damned scary.

Mahoney gave him as big a picture as he could – which was hardly complete, he admitted. Worlds, systems, clusters, even some galaxies had slipped out of contact. By choice, rejecting the ham-witted leadership of the council? By war? By – barely conceivable – disease?

As Sten well knew, AM2 had been the skein holding the Empire together. Without the shattering energy release of Anti-Matter Two, star drives were almost impossible to power. And of course, since AM2 had been very inexpensive – price determined by the Emperor – and fairly available – depending on the Emperor, once more – it was easy to take the lazy way out and run anything and everything on the substance. Interstellar communications . . . weaponry . . . factories . . . manufacturing . . . the list ran on.

When the Emperor was murdered the supply of AM2 stopped.

Sten had found that hard to swallow the first time Mahoney had said it. He was still having trouble. Back on Smallbridge, he had assumed that the privy council – for profiteering reasons of their own, as well as base incompetency – had merely been keeping the supply at a trickle.

'Not true,' Mahoney had said. 'They haven't a clue to where the goodies are. That's why the council wanted to pick you up – and anybody else who might've had a private beer with the Emperor – then gently loosen your toenails until you told them The Secret.'

'They're clottin' mad.'

'So they are. Consider this, boy. The *entire universe* is bonkers,' Mahoney said. 'Except for me and thee. Heh . . . heh . . . heh . . . and I'm slippin' away slowly if you don't find a bottle and uncap it.'

Sten followed orders. He drank – heavily – from the bottle before handing it to Ian.

'Ring down for another one. If your prog circuits are DNCing now, it will get far worse.'

Again, Sten followed orders.

'Okay, Mahoney. We are now on the thin edge.'

Mahoney chortled. 'Not even close yet, boy. But proceed.'

There was a tap at the door. 'Y'r order, sir.'

Mahoney was on his feet, a pistol snaking out of his sleeve. 'A little too efficient.' He moved toward the door.

'Relax, Fleet Marshal,' Sten said dryly. 'It's open, Mr Kilgour.'

After a pause, the door came open, and Alex entered pushing a drink tray and wearing a disappointed expression.

'Did I noo hae y'goin' frae e'en a second?' he asked hopefully.

'You gotta do something about the way you talk, man.'

'Thae's some think it charmin',' Alex said, mock-hurt.

Sten and Alex looked at one another.

'How close did they get to you?' Sten asked.

Kilgour told them of the near-ambush and the battle in the icy streets.

'Ah'm assum't,' he said, 'frae the fact th' warnin' wae in gen'ral code, nae whae Sten and I hae set up, y're responsible f'r tippin' me th' wink.'

'I was,' Mahoney said.

'Ah'm also assum't, sir, thae's reason beyon' y'r fas'nation wi' m' girlish legs an' giggle. Who d'ye want iced?'

'Quick thinking, Mr Kilgour. But sit down. You too, Admiral. The debriefing – and the plan – will take awhile. You'll guess the target – correction, targets – as I go along. The suspense will be good for you.'

Mahoney began with what had happened to him from the day of the Emperor's funeral, when he had looked at the Council of Five standing on the grassy knoll that was the Emperor's grave and knew that he was looking at five assassins.

He hesitated, then told them the impossible part. After the funeral, he had gone into the Emperor's study, dug out a bottle of the vile swill the Emperor called Scotch, and planned a quiet, private farewell toast. Stuck to the bottle was a handwritten note:

'Stick around, Ian. I'll be right back.'

It was in the handwriting of the Eternal Emperor.

Mahoney stopped, expecting complete disbelief. He got it, masked on both men's faces by expressions of bright interest – and a slow shift by Sten toward Mahoney's gun-hand.

'That's – very interesting, Fleet Marshal. Sir. How do you suppose it got there? Are you saying the man who got assassinated was a double?'

'No. That was the Emperor.'

'So he somehow survived getting shot a dozen or so times and then being blown up?'

'Don't clot around, Sten. He was dead.'

'Ah. Soo he ris't oot'n th' grave t' leave ye a wee love note?'

'Again, no. He must've left instructions with one of the Gurkhas. Or a palace servant. I asked. Nobody knew anything.'

'Let's ignore how the note got there for a sec, Ian. Are you listening to what you've just been saying? Either you're mad – or else you've joined up with that cult that goes around saying the Emperor has lived forever. And remembering six years plus is a long time for you just to be sticking around. Which is how long it's been.'

'Neither one – or maybe I *am* bonkers. But will you keep listening?'

'Mought's well. Whae's time t' a clottin' hog?' Kilgour said. He poured himself a drink of quill – but still kept a wary eye on Mahoney.

Mahoney went on. He had made his own plans that day. He was going after the privy council.

'Did you consider maybe they'd think you were the type to carry a grudge?' Sten asked.

'I did – and covered my ass.'

Mahoney put in for early retirement. The privy council, in the mad rush to get rid of the bloated and incredibly expensive military after the Tahn wars, was more than willing to let anyone and everyone out, few questions asked. Sten nodded – that was exactly how he and Kilgour had been able to slip into retirement and obscurity.

The council was especially happy to be rid of Mahoney, who was not only the Emperor's best-loved Fleet Marshal, architect of victory, but also once head of Mercury Corps – Imperial Intelligence – for many, many years.

'But I didn't want them to think I was going to create any mischief. I found a cover.'

Mahoney's cover, loudly announced, was that he planned to do a complete biography of the Eternal Emperor, the greatest man who ever lived. That plan fit quite well into the council's martyr-building.

'What I was, of course, doing was building my stone bucket. Hell if I knew what I would do with it – but I had to do it.'

Mahoney dived into the archives – he planned to spend a year or so researching The Early Years. By then he figured the council would have lost interest in him, and he could go for the real target. A little sheepishly, he told Sten and Alex that he had always loved raw research. Maybe if things had been different, and he had not come from a military family he would have ended up poking through archives trying to figure out The Compleat History of the Fork. Or something.

He was not the first, the hundredth, or the millionth person to bio the Emperor. But he discovered something interesting. All of the bios were crocks.

'So what?' Sten asked, disinterested. 'If you were up there on the right hand of God, wouldn't you want everybody to make nice on you?'

'That is not what I meant.' Mahoney said. He had seen a pattern. Biographers were encouraged to write about the Emperor. However, they were mostly of the type who would work hard to either find Deep-seated Humanity in Tamerlane, or else write a psychological biography of the poet Homer.

'Let's say there might have been a great number of sloppy historians. But somehow their work was still encouraged. They won the big contracts. Their fiche were picked up for the livies. And so on and so forth.

'I'm telling you, lads, no one was really encouraged to look at source material – what hasn't somehow, and I quote, vanished in the mists of time, end quote.'

'So what was our late leader trying to hide?'

'Damned near everything, from where he came from to how he got where he is. You might spend a lifetime daring insanity trying to make sense out of the seventeen or eighteen thousand versions of events, each of them seemingly given the Emperor's imprimatur.

'I'll just mention two of the murkiest areas, besides where the clot the AM2 is. First is that the son of a bitch is – or was, anyway, immortal.'

'Drakh. No such animal.'

'Believe it. And the second thing is – he's been killed before.'

'But you just said—'

'I know what I just said. He's died before. Been killed. Various ways. Several accidents. At least two assassinations.'

'And you won't accept a double.'

'I will not. But here is what happened, at least concerning the incidents I was able to document: First, the Emperor dies. Second, there is, immediately afterward, a big goddamned explosion, destroying the body and anything around. Just like that bomb that went off after Chappelle killed the Emperor.'

'*Every* time?'

'Every one I can find. And then – the AM2 stops. Wham. Just like that.

'Then the Emperor comes back. As does the AM2. And things start back to normal.'

'Ian, now you've got me playing loony games on your turf,' Sten said. 'Okay. How long does he usually vanish? Not that I am believing one damned word of what you are saying.'

Mahoney looked worried. 'Accident – perhaps three or four months. Murder – as long as a year or two. Maybe time enough for people to realize how much they need him.'

'Six years an' more hae gone noo,' Alex pointed out.

'I know.'

'But you still believe the Eternal Emperor is gonna appear in a pink cloud or some kind of clottin' seashell in the surf and the world will be happy and gay once more?' Sten scoffed.

'You don't believe me,' Mahoney said, pouring himself a drink. 'Would it help if I let you go through the files? I have them hidden away.'

'No. I still wouldn't believe you. But set that aside. What else did you get?'

'I worked forward. And I got lucky, indeed. Remember your friend Haines?'

Sten did. She had been a homicide cop, and she and Sten had been up to their elbows unraveling the strange assassination plot that had inadvertently sparked the recent Tahn wars. She and Sten had also been lovers.

'She's still a cop. She's still on Prime. Homicide chief now,' Mahoney told Sten.

He had gone to her for permission to access the files on Chapelle, the Emperor's assassin. He'd had the highest clearances – volume one of the biography had been published to great acclaim. 'Complete tissue, of course,' he assured them.

'Anyway, your Haines. She's still as honest as ever, boy.'

Mahoney had asked some questions – and one day Haines had gotten the idea that the ex-Intelligence head was not in his dotage, indulging a private passion.

'She said the only reason she was doing it is because you'd spoken well of me. For a, ahem, clottin' general. You remember a young lad named Volmer?'

Sten did. Volmer was a publishing baron – or, more correctly, the waffling heir to a media empire. Part of the privy council. Murdered one night outside a tawdry ambisexual cruising bar in the port city of Soward. The released story was that he had been planning a series on the corruption around the war effort. A more cynical – and popular – version was that Volmer liked his sex rough and strange and had picked up the wrong hustler.

Haines had something different. She had been stalking a contract killer for about a year – a professional. She didn't give a damn about a triggerman, but wanted to know who had hired him. She got him – and with enough evidence concerning the disappearance of a gang boss to get at least an indictment.

The young man evidently agreed with Haines as to the worth of the evidence. He offered to make a deal. Haines thought that a wonderful idea. She might not care, particularly, if underworld types slaughtered each other on a daily basis. But when they kept leaving the bodies out on the street to worry the citizens – then action had to be taken.

The man offered her something better. He confessed that he had killed Volmer. The word had been that the freako was an under-cover type. There had been an open contract. The killer had filled it – and then found out later whom he had touched.

Haines wanted to know who had paid. The man named an

underworld boss, now deceased. Haines punted him back to his cell, told him to think about corroborative evidence, and tried to figure out what it all meant. The assassin 'suicided' in his cell that night.

'That's all she had?'

'That's all she had.'

'So who terminated Volmer?'

'Perhaps his brothers on the privy council? Maybe Volmer wasn't going along with the program? I don't know – yet. But there was the first member of the council dead.

'Then Sullamora. Blown up with the Emperor.

'Something funny about that lone hit man, Chapelle. He came out of Spaceport Control. I did a little research on him, as well. Seems he felt the Emperor was after him personally.'

'Yeah. I saw the livies, too. A head case.'

'He was that. But he was set up to become one. Somebody – somebody who could have played with his career – arranged for him to get his face shoved in it every time he turned around. To this day nobody knows, for instance, why he suddenly lost his job and ended up on bum row.

'Spaceport Control. Ports, shipping – that was Sullamora's responsibility on the privy council. And now he's dead, too.'

Sten started to pour himself another drink, then thought better of it and walked to the viewpanel and stared out.

'All right, Mahoney. You've got some interesting things. Maybe. And maybe you're a head case like this Chapelle. Maybe all you've got is that thieves fall out. A Mantis op on his second run could tell you that.

'Fill in the blanks. What happened next? And come to think about it, what *happens* next?'

Mahoney told them. About the time he had talked to Haines, he had started feeling a bit insecure. The council, he had realized, had not a clue as to the source of AM2. Mahoney thought it was a matter of time before they started rounding up the usual suspects and probing their brains for this had-to-be-somewhere secret.

'Brainscan's an uncomfortable feeling, I understand. Frequently fatal. So I died. Laundered my investments by somehow getting swindled. Paid the swindler ten percent of the money he stole. Then I drowned. A stupid boating accident. There were whispers that it was because I'd lost my entire fortune.'

Dead and invisible, Mahoney went to work. Part and parcel of his research was looking up all his old service friends, anyone who might have had any knowledge of the Emperor.

'Many of them still serve. And most of them think we are heading for absolute chaos unless the council is removed.'

Sten and Kilgour exchanged looks. Removed. Yes.

'Then . . . then we have access to everything the Emperor left on Prime. I know – knew – that man. He would have hidden the secret somewhere. Hell, for all I know, in one of those glue pots he used trying to make a gutter.'

'Guitar,' Sten corrected absently.

'Because that's the only chance we have,' Mahoney said. 'Probably you were right. Probably I am quite mad believing the Emperor will return. Maybe that he ever did. Indulge an old man's eccentricity.

'But if someone does not do something – this Empire, which maybe it's done things wrong, and even some evils, has still held civilization together for two millennia and longer.

'If nothing's done, it will all vanish in a few life-times.'

Sten was looking closely at Mahoney – a not especially friendly look.

'So you get me out of harm's way, get word to Kilgour. And all you want in return is for us to kill the five beings who happen to rule the known universe.'

Mahoney chose not to see the sarcasm. 'Exactly. No impeachments. No trials. No confusion. Which is why I wanted you, Sten. This is the linchpin to the whole operation. You've done it before. In clean, out clean – with five bodies behind you.'

Sten and Alex sat, wordless, staring out the plate into deep space. They had told Mahoney they had to talk, then thrown him out of their quarters. There had not been much talk. They had capped the alk and called for caff.

Sten ordered his thoughts. Could he somehow take out the privy council? Yes, his Mantis arrogance said. Maybe. It was the 'out clean' that bothered him. Sten had always agreed with his first basic sergeant, who had said he wanted soldiers who would 'help the soldier on the other side die for his country.'

The privy council had tried to kill him – and probably grabbed all of his wealth and pauperized him as well. So? Credits were not important. They could be made as well as lost. As far as the killing – once the shooting had stopped, Sten, who prided himself as being a professional, had bought narcobeers for his ex-enemies on many occasions.

Were the privy council members evil – which would somehow justify their deaths? Define evil, he thought. Evil is . . . what does not work.

Thus, another list:

Was the privy council incompetent? Certainly. Especially if one believed what Mahoney had said. Once more. So? The worlds Sten had lived in, from Vulcan to the Imperial Military itself, were more often than not governed by incompetents.

The Empire was running down. For a third time. So? Sten, veteran of a hundred battles and a thousand-plus worlds, could not visualize that amorphous thing called an Empire.

Another list. This time, a short one.

All Sten had known – like his father and his father before *him* – was the Eternal Emperor. That, in fact, was what Sten thought of when he considered the Empire.

He had sworn an oath. Sworn it twice, in fact. '. . . to defend the Eternal Emperor and the Empire with your life . . . to obey lawful orders given you and to honor and follow the traditions of the Imperial Guard as the Empire requires.' The first had been administered after he had been cold-cocked by Mahoney, eons before, back on Vulcan. But he had retaken the oath when they had commissioned him.

And he had meant it.

If the council members had tried to kill the Emperor – and failed – would he have considered it his duty to hunt them down and, if necessary, kill them? Of course. And did he believe the privy council had killed the Emperor? Yes. Absolutely.

He thought of an old Tahn proverb: 'Duty is heavier than lead, death lighter than a feather.' It did not help.

That oath still stood, as did the duty. Sten felt somewhat embarrassed. He looked across at Kilgour and cleared his throat. Such were not things to be said aloud.

Kilgour was avoiding Sten's glance. 'Ae course, thae's th' option ae findin't ae deep, rich hole, pullin' it in behind us, an' lettin' the universe swing,' he said suddenly.

'I'd just as soon not spend the rest of my life looking over my shoulder.'

'Y'lack confidence, lad. We c'd do't. Nae problem. But if we did, m'mither'd nae hae aught to brag on, come market day. So. Empire-topplin' it is? Sten?'

Sten managed a grin. Better this way. Let the real reasons stay inside. He stuck out his hand.

'Nae, we c'n gie lushed wi' a clear conscience,' Kilgour sighed. He groped for a bottle.

'Ah noo ken whae Ah nae lik't thae livies. Here's a braw decision made. In ae hotel flat by a fat man dressed like ae commercial traveller an' a wee lad resemblin't ae gig'lo. Nae a sword, gleamin't armor or wavin't banner amongst us. Whae a world.'

He drank.

'Nae. How filthy d' we scrag thae' bastards?'

So Sten and Kilgour went into partnership with an ex-Fleet Marshal who both of them considered, privately, a bit round the bend.

Chapter Seven

The man stared at the screen. His hands remained folded in his lap.

'You have not begun the test,' the Voice – for he had begun to capitalize it in his mind – accused.

'What happens if I fail to obey?'

'Information will not be provided. Begin the test.'

'I shall not.'

'Do you have a reason?'

'I have already taken it. Three – no, four sleep periods ago.'

'That is correct. Test complete.'

The screen blanked.

'All test results have been assimilated. Subject determined within acceptable parameters,' the Voice said. Very odd. It was the first time It had spoken as if to someone other than the man.

'You are ready for the next stage,' It told him.

'I have some questions.'

'You may ask. Answers may or may not be provided.'

'I am on a ship. Is there anyone else on board?'

'No.'

'You are a synthesized voice?'

'Self-evident.'

'You said moments ago that I was . . . within acceptable parameters. What would have happened were I not?'

'Answer determined not to be in your best interests.'

'I shall try another way. What constraints did your programmer limit you to?'

'Answers determined not to be in your best interests.'

'Thank you. You answered, however. Another question. Who programmed you?'

Silence except for ship hum.

'Answer will become self-evident within a short period of time,' the Voice said finally. 'Those are questions enough.'

A previously sealed panel opened.

'You will enter that passage. At its end will be a ship. You will board and prepare yourself for takeoff. You may issue two orders, if you feel you know the answers. If you do not, recommendations will be offered.

'First. Should the machines be reactivated?'

'What machines?'

'The recommendation is that they should – given recent circumstances.'

'Recommendation accepted. I guess.'

'Second. Should trans-shipment begin? The recommendation is it should not until you progress further.'

'Accepted. Trans-shipment of what? And whatever it is, how do I communicate with you?'

'Both answers will become self-evident. Proceed to the ship now.'

The man walked down the passageway. At the end, as promised, was the entryway to a small ship. He entered.

Again, the ship was constructed for one person.

He seated himself in a reclining couch. Behind him, the hatch slid shut. He felt motion: stardrive.

'This is a final communication,' the Voice said suddenly. 'There are four separate automated navigation systems on this ship. Each of them is preset for a different destination. On reaching each destination that system will self-destruct and the next system will activate.

'Do not be alarmed.

'Do not attempt to interfere with this system.

'Your final destination and debarkation point will be obvious.

'Good-bye. Good luck.'

The man jolted. The fine hair at the back of his neck lifted.
Good luck? From a machine?

Chapter Eight

The Honjo were a small but firmly committed culture of traders.
Their antecedents went back to the early days of the Empire. They
populated a system some light-years from Durer, the site of one of
the famous Tahn war battles. Their home base was a less than
desirable cluster of stars and planets with little in the way of
commercially important resources.

This was no hindrance to the Honjo. Their distant, oceangoing
ancestors had plied the island trades, and they were ancient masters
at the art of playing middlebeing for any product. Their ships were
of their own design, although constructed in the factories Sullamora
had once owned. They were light, a bit boxy, and made up for
lack of speed by being able to deal with just about any atmosphere
where there might be goods to buy or sell.

The Honjo were also among the most frugal beings in the Empire.
Since their resources were so few, they stockpiled and guarded them
jealously. Especially AM2.

That had been a minor source of irritation to the Eternal Emperor
from time to time. Since the price was pegged on supply – which
he controlled – he was always just a bit touchy about the large
amount they kept squirreled away. Whenever he let the price drop,
the Honjo were the first in line to buy more. But it was only a
petty irritation, and after wrangling with the thick-headed beings
a few times, he let it slide. The Emperor had learned that it was
usually best to ignore eccentrics. The Honjo performed well as
traders, they were mostly honest, and their system was so small as
to be nearly meaningless.

One other thing about the Honjo. They were always quite willing to take offense. Especially when it involved what they perceived as their own property. In short, if pressed, they would fight. They tended not to think about the odds.

When the privy council considered the Honjo, they were all in agreement: When it came to larceny, the Kraas had chosen well.

'Me'n Sis sussed it out,' the fat Kraa said. 'The stingy clots keep it stashed in one place. So, all we's gotta do is send in a fleet. Blow the drakh out of 'em. 'N it's home again, home again, with enough AM2 keep us goin' for more'n a bit.'

'I don't think we ought to be that direct,' Malperin objected.

'No? Why the clot not? Them Honjo's right bastards, and everyone knows it!'

'Good plan, just a touch short on diplomacy,' Lovett chuckled.

Kyes noted that the energy level in the room was far higher than it had been the last time. Was it just because action – *any* kind of action at all – was contemplated? Or was it the thought of armed robbery that was so energizing? Kyes and his fellow businessbeings had participated in countless forms of theft in their long careers. But it was always on paper – kept at a distance, with at least a cloak of respectability thrown over it by their legions of legal experts. This was real! And, Kyes had to admit, extremely exciting. He was as susceptible to the excitement as the rest.

'Try it this way,' he said. 'We send enough ships to do the job, just as our colleagues proposed. Except, we send one small craft far out ahead. Something lightly armed. And not too expensive . . .

'Then, we have the ship deliberately violate the Honjo cluster's borders.'

'That'll piss 'em, sure,' the skinny Kraa said. She liked where he was going. 'Then we just waggle our arses, make 'em shoot . . .'

'And we retaliate! And boom! It's ours!' Lovett finished.

Everyone was pleased with the plan. Oddly, the Kraas had an important caution.

'We need a bleedin' alibi,' the fat one said. 'So's it don't look too planned out, if yer get me drift.'

They did indeed.

'Perhaps we should stage some kind of economic summit?' Malperin suggested. They had never had one before – there was not much economy to contemplate – but they understood the connection.

'Here's what we do,' Malperin said. 'And we can achieve two goals at once. It's about time for a little good news.'

There were murmurs of agreement about the table. The situation was deteriorating so quickly they were all afraid to look it straight in the eye. But as system after system drifted away from their grasp, it always remained at the edge of their vision, like a recurrent nightmare.

Malperin proposed that they release a canned study, showing that the steadily dipping economic curve had bottomed out and was at last turning upward. Simultaneously, they would convene the privy council for the Economic Summit, a summit they would claim would set the course of the Empire for the next six or seven years.

They would play up the summit as the most important event since the death of the Emperor. Full media coverage. Pull out all stops. She also suggested where such a summit could be held, for maximum suspense.

It would be staged on Earth, in Tanz Sullamora's old fishing camp, now revitalized for the use of the council for their most private meetings.

There they would convene, innocently contemplating things of great and holy importance – the public good. At that moment, the Honjo would make their unprovoked attack on the defenseless Imperial ship.

The Kraas figured the booty would fill a spacetrain ten or fifteen kilometers long.

'That's a lot of clottin' AM2,' the skinny one said.

Kyes agreed. It certainly was a clottin' lot of AM2.

Mahoney bounced into Sten's suite, happily singing/humming what he remembered of a medieval ballad: 'Let me something my eyes . . . dah . . . dah . . . dah dah dah day, on the something green hills of Earth . . .'

He crossed to Sten's video display and booted up the news menu:

NEW COURSE FOR EMPIRE

The drop:

BIG 5 TO CONVENE
ECONOMIC SUMMIT
AT HISTORIC RETREAT

Sten read the story closely, Alex hanging over his shoulder.

'We would appear,' Sten said, 'to have acquired a Target Opportunity.'

Mahoney beamed. 'Never could figure why the black hats think there's safety out in the boonies. Maybe because they're usually ex-city punks?'

'Ah dinna ken either,' Kilgour said. 'But gie me a moor w' a wee rock to skulk behin', an' hae f'r a rest, an' Ah'm as happy ae a butcher wi' his mallet.'

'That's it,' Sten said. 'Now . . . let's kill us some politicos!'

Chapter Nine

The privy council's announcement was the trigger for the final meeting of Ian Mahoney's 'conspirators.' They had a single target and a time to hit it.

The 'conspiracy' had already gone on far too long for Mahoney's comfort. As a rule of thumb the less time passed and the less those involved had to meet in any covert operation, the less likelihood that operation would be blown or self-destruct. He mentally put both conspiracy and conspirators in quotes. Because while his plan would ensure that anyone involved was for the high jump if it was exposed, there really was not much to it.

Mahoney had, in his 'research,' looked up many of his old compatriots, as he had told Sten. Once he was conveniently deceased his secret wanderings from galaxy to galaxy had increased. His purpose was simple. Once contact was made with one of his old service acquaintances, the formal dance began. Mahoney set out trying to lead each of them down the primrose path to murder.

Did they agree that things were going to hell in a hand-basket? If so, did they think something could be done about it? *Should* something be done about it? Should something be done about it by the acquaintance? Would he or she be willing to participate?

That leading took time – too much time. All too often danger signals went off in Mahoney's spook-circuited brain, and he broke contact.

What he wanted from each of those serving high-ranking officers and/or civil officials was roughly the same. If the privy council were to be rendered suddenly powerless, what would the officer do? Ideally, Mahoney wanted that officer to mobilize any forces under command to:

1. Maintain public order.
2. Disarm or otherwise deactivate any armed forces still loyal to the privy council, starting with the council's own security apparatus and private armies.
3. To control the media and prevent access to privy council loyalists.
4. To support the formation of an interim caretaker government. Mahoney was fairly vague on what that would be – he thought perhaps a loose federation headed by those members of Parliament who had not been corrupted by the privy council, representatives of dissident systems/galaxies, and others yet to be discovered. The federation could be headed up by the utterly incorruptible Manabi.

Possibly. Mahoney kept saying that 'first we have to catch the rabbit.' The conversation tended to stop there – very few wanted to know the exact mechanics of how the privy council was to be 'rendered powerless.' Knowing the bloody-handed intelligence chief in front of them, they had a fairly good idea it would not be something as civilized as house arrest.

Once – and if – the privy council was dealt with, whatever government replaced them would be operating under two very clear orders: first, to slow the Empire's slipping into chaos; and second, to find the AM2.

Mahoney had a single rule about what the caretaker government would *not* be: military. He didn't think, on reflection, that Ian Mahoney would make that bad a king, nor would some of his longtime friends. And that was exactly why the military would not be allowed near the government, not if he himself felt a bit of the slow crawl of power-madness in his own soul.

But all this took time. Not only because the solicitation toward what, after all, was high treason had to be done carefully, but also because of the incredible layers of bureaucracy between a leader and the people. Mahoney had always prided himself on his own lean and mean command. Anyone serving under him could have near access to the boss. Now he wondered, after having spent hours and days waiting in antechambers for an old friend to even be aware he was out there, if his own machine had been that lean and mean.

Time passing increased the dangers, as did Mahoney's failures. He tried not to blame anyone who wanted no part of the operation. There were those who simply felt the military had no place in politics. Others believed the problems were temporary – that eventually the privy council would improve. What was happening was merely the inevitable chaos of a war's end worsened by the death of the Emperor. Still others did not think the privy council was doing that bad a job – considering the circumstances. And still others had been co-opted by the council. And, Mahoney grudged, there were those – even in his own profession of soldiery – who were moral or physical cowards.

Other than Sten and Kilgour, Mahoney told no one about his private belief that the Emperor would return. Their enterprise looked insane enough without adding proof of psychosis.

He ended with about a thousand beings he felt could be depended on. Now would be the final – and for most of them only – chance to gather for their final plans.

Such a meet was a terrible risk, but Mahoney knew he had to prove to his fellows that there was, in fact, a conspiracy beyond coded transmissions and one dangerous old man. He had reduced the threat of exposure – he hoped – by setting the meeting not only in plain sight, but also near the heart of the beast. It was in the system of Klisura, an entirely military group of worlds. Sten himself had gone through Guard training on the system's main world, years and years gone.

One smaller world had been set up for war games centuries earlier. War games without soldiers, without ships – what Mahoney had heard had been called in ancient times a 'kriegsspiel.' A map exercise, now played with computers and battle chambers. This particular game had been suggested by Fleet Marshal Wentworth, a longtime and completely trusted compatriot of Ian's.

Obviously, so that Mahoney's compatriots could assemble from their Empire-wide posts with as little suspicion as possible, the game had to be universal. It was that.

GIVEN: the current status of military forces (radical disarmament following the end of the Tahn wars); the current economic environment (lessened AM2 fuel availability); and the present political situation (worded more subtly, that a great percentage of the Empire felt the privy council were incapable of leading a goat to a garbage dump).

SITUATION: A sudden, large-scale threat to the Empire, up to and including full war.

REQUIRED: Possible military responses for the first two E-years of such an event.

In short, the game would refight the beginning of the Tahn wars, as if the Emperor were not present and AM2 was available only in limited quantities.

Such a large-scale exercise, even though it involved nothing but troop commanders, had come to the attention of the privy council. They thought the idea of a new, massive bogeyman coming out of nowhere slightly absurd, but there was merit in their military leaders accepting a far more limited future. At first they grudged that the game would be played with a realistic logistical scenario, but eventually they realized that their soldiery should know – even though it was uncomfortable – just how limited the AM2 actually was.

That did mean they required the assemblage and the game itself to be held under the tightest security, which played exactly to Mahoney's desires. Kyes even thought there might be some interesting, if quite minor, concepts developed during the game.

Their hope was bolstered when they learned that Wentworth proposed to include civilians as well as military. The civilians – all of whom, of course, were properly clearanced – included retired military, experts in logistics, and even a handful of rather dreamy-eyed techno-prophets. Kyes was a bit surprised and pleased that the military, which he had always thought as rigid in its thought patterns as any computer, was capable of welcoming outside input.

So the admirals and generals, fleet marshals and intelligence specialists, with their aides and assistants gathered on Klisura XII. As did the civilians, including one elderly, cheerful human male who claimed to be a morale specialist. Mahoney chose the cover name of Stephen Potter.

The game *would* in fact be played out – and played again two or three more times, with different participants. This first game would be composed of Mahoney's conspirators, the following games played by the innocent, who would never know they were providing the most elaborate cover for Mahoney's schemes. It would have been more ideal if it could have been played just once, with the innocent sheep giving cover for the wolves. But too many people knew Ian Mahoney, and he understood there was no way he could keep those in the conspiracy who were inevitably hesitant, skeptical, or wavering in line if he were not there in person to share the risk.

Other arrivals trickled in, gray, quiet beings without faces. They were ex-Mercury Corps operatives, technicians, recruited by Mahoney. They were intended to secure the security.

Mahoney assumed that when the world had been screened by the privy council, part of that had included bugging everything. He was correct. But it was a simple matter for his own techs to find the bugs and key them. None were destroyed – although Mahoney thought it appropriate that some of them were reported to the proper authorities. The proper authorities expressed dismay and disconnected those bugs.

The rest were left in place and fed false information. Sometimes they were given blank time, as if nothing were happening in that particular chamber. Others were fed meetings that had been prescripted and then voice-synthesized, so that General X would be discussing with his staff whether or not transports would be available to move his units, and how much of their basic equipment load could be carried; whereas in fact General X was sitting with Ian Mahoney, talking about how many of his troops could be depended upon, once The Day was announced, to move out and seize barracks held by one of the Kraa twins' private thuggeries, and how many would have to be sent on leave or confined to barracks.

There were a few counter-intelligence agents in attendance. They were quickly ID'd and beeped, their movements tracked constantly. Only one agent found anything suspicious, and he was skillfully terminated before he could either report or get offworld.

Mahoney was disappointed in his enemies – he had seen and run better CI when he was an assistant patrol leader in the Imperial Youth Corps.

Sten and Alex held well in the background. Both of them were quite hot – especially Sten.

All of the conspirators were told when the operation would be mounted. They were further instructed to have their troops on standby on that date, with those orders to be issued as unobstrusively as possible.

There were a few who wanted more. They had faith in Mahoney, to be sure, but they were beings who took very little just on faith. For them, Sten would be trotted onstage. To some, he was little more than a hero of the early stages of the Tahn wars. But the fact that an admiral would be willing to lead, in person, the raid on Earth seemed to satisfy them.

The most suspicious, generally, were those high-rankers with some intelligence background or training. For that reason, most of them had heard of Sten or known him – if not by fiche, then by reputation. In their eyes, he was a thoroughly acceptable head of the murder squad.

Near the end of the gaming Sten collected Mahoney and took him to an ultra-clean room. Quite baldly he asked the fleet marshal if he really believed that all of these beings would swing into motion as ordered when ordered.

'Of course not,' Mahoney snapped. 'As your pet thug might say, I'm mad but I'm hardly daft.

'Assuming you carry out your end . . . prog: seventy-five percent follow their orders and we'll not only have the murderers dead, but the transition of power will be painless.

'Fifty percent . . . it'll be a little bloody. But I still think it'll come off. That's assuming those who get the collywobbles don't try to stop us.

'Less than that . . .

'Less than that, lad, and you'd best have the luck of the heavens and be in excellent running condition.

'Now, Admiral. You're in motion. Collect your assistants and start putting them through whatever rehearsals you need.'

As he and Alex slipped offworld, Sten ran his own prognostication. He had even less faith than Mahoney that the conspiracy, in its entirety, would succeed. There were too many people involved, too much time had passed, and Sten had damn-all confidence in any conspiracy when the conspirators had a vested interest – no matter how loudly denied – in the state. Generals and admirals made lousy dissidents.

But as far as his and Alex's end . . . the murder in a ditch?

Just less, he calculated, than fifty-fifty.

Hell, for a Mantis operative, that was a sure thing. So very well. Eliminate the privy council, and what would happen, would happen. That was for others to decide – after the bodies stopped bouncing.

It was a pity Sten had never met Brigadier Mavis Sims – and never would.

Chapter Ten

Sten was in a thoroughly crappy mood. He shut down PLAY function and removed the helmet. Repressing the urge to punt it across the room, he glowered out at the rain.

Clottin' poor mission briefing, he thought. Suicide run for sure. Sten *was* in a rotten mood – the intelligence data he had fed into the interactive livie machine gave him no more or less details than many, many missions he had already run and survived.

His mood may have been caused by the rain. Here in this forested province called Oregon, the sun seemed proscribed. The degrees of weather ranged from overcast threatening rain through drizzle to downpour to here comes another storm. He sort of wanted a drink. But he and the other team members were now temperance clots until they extracted.

Kilgour broke Sten's mood. Pushing the door to their rented A-frame – a building Sten suspected had been made from real wood – he said cheerily, 'Oop an' away, boss. Y're gettin' fat an' sloppy sittin' here. Time f'r th' old pant-an-wheeze.'

Sten pulled on running shoes, grabbed a rainproof, and they went out into the streets of Coos Bay. The village itself might have been the root of Sten's depression. Old – thousand-year-type old – ruins were one thing. But buildings only a couple of hundred years gone were different. People had lived there before it became a hamlet of rotting, collapsing buildings and shattered streets.

The city, Sten had been told, had once had nearly twenty-thousand inhabitants – farmers, loggers, sea-shippers. That must have been long ago. Now there were less than a thousand. A few fished, some were artists who made their credits off-Earth; there were a few tribal groups existing on their own, internal economy;

and other residents catered to the sprinkling of tourists who arrived intent on the area's big game, a fish they called the salmon. They raved about its fighting qualities and wariness.

At first Sten thought they were talking about some woodsy predator before he realized. He found the salmon tasty, just as he did the area's crabs, oysters, bass, and a very ugly fish they called a sturgeon. Fishing could be worthwhile, he thought. Short-fuse an explosive charge, toss it in a pool, and you had dinner for a platoon. But these people used line as thin as a climbing thread, hand-constructed bits of plas supposed to resemble insects, and a casting rod. Often they merely had themselves photographed with their catch and then released it. Very odd.

'Which way today, boss?'

'Doesn't matter. Ruins, rocks, and trees in any direction.'

Kilgour waved a direction arbitrarily and they ground into motion – starting up a hill, of course.

Run a klick, walk a half kilometer, run ten kilometers. A half hour of exercises, then run back. Standard Imperial dictates for combat troops.

Sten thought further on this depressed province of Oregon. Historically, he had read, it had always been an area of future dreams and present depression. But its current state of decline had three causes: the inhuman – to Sten, at least – climate; the constant drain offworld of its young people who couldn't find work at home; and finally the Eternal Emperor.

That last factor was only three hundred years old. About twenty-five kilometers north of Coos Bay was the mouth of the Umpqua River. The Emperor had decided he wanted to go salmon fishing. He put political influence to bear on the province's politicos. They granted him the river in perpetuity – from headwaters to where it rushed into the ocean. That had cost several fortunes in bribes and promises.

From there it got expensive. Little by little, the residents of all the towns along the river and its tributaries were cozened and bribed to move. They were compensated richly – but still . . .

Once there had been a small town – Redspurt, Reedsport, or some such – at the mouth of the Umpqua. Now it was a ghost town. There were other ruins along the river that had once been inhabited – Scottsburg, Umpqua, Roseburg, and so on.

The Emperor was the Emperor, Sten knew. But for some reason that demonstration of Byzantine power put his teeth on edge. But it was not his to question why, he thought as he crested the hill.

More important – up the Umpqua river was the Emperor's old fishing retreat. And, kilometers beyond that, was Sten's target.

In the days when the late Tanz Sullamora had idolized the Eternal Emperor, he had aped everything about his ruler that he could. The Emperor fished . . . very well then, so would Tanz. But where the Emperor was happy with solitude, the redwoods, and a place to pitch a tent near salmon-fat rapids, Sullamora was miserable. His fishing camp became a lavish country estate, with every sophisticated convenience the plutocrat could afford. Sullamora could not chance the laughter that would come if he simply decided that Earth, fishing, and the wilderness was a busto idea. When the privy council's conspiracy began, Sullamora's estate was a perfect neutral ground/safe house to plot from.

Sullamora may have been splattered into molecular pulp but the validity of his estate continued. That was the target – and there were only a few days left before the privy council arrived. Sten was ready.

Knowing the target and area, he started putting his team together. There was no problem with available, completely trustworthy Imperial gangsters. With the Tahn wars ended, the Mantis squadrons were far overstrength. And those soldiers had not chosen Mantis because of their pacifistic nature. They went looking for adventure. It was simple for Mahoney to sieve for availables. Those he chose were completely known quantities. If there would be betrayal, it would not come from any of them. All knew Mahoney's reputation as former head of Mercury/Mantis. As a good percentage had pre-war service and had magically survived the decimation of the war against the Tahn, Sten was a known and near-legendary commander.

The first question he had for the purported Earth-specialist Mahoney assigned to him was who or what were the natives like? Earth-human. Any ETs? None to speak of. Sten grimaced. That would cut the available pool of talent way down.

He asked the specialist about local fauna and got a bland reply of the 'usual oxygen-based food chain.' Sten punted the 'expert' into outer darkness and put Kilgour into research mode. Kilgour had talents beyond lethality. It did not hurt that he had once served with a Guards ceremonial detachment on Earth itself, before he had found a happy home in covert wet work.

While he waited for Kilgour, Sten began thinking of the Delicate Art of Murder, Multiple Variety. The easiest way to take care of the council would be a missile. Limited-yield nuclear or conventional

– to him it didn't matter. Either way, it wouldn't work. First, the privy council would have the skies and space beyond saturated with warships. It was unlikely a missile would get through. Even if it did – Sullamora's retreat would almost certainly be shielded. And Mahoney had requested no survivors.

What about a ground-to-ground? Launch the missile from a safe range, infiltrate a controller to line-of-site of the lodge, and let him guide the bang on home. Unlikely. It was doubtful the council would put on a public show without covering itself with every possible ECM device.

So it would have to be, Sten thought, the classic Four-H technique: Hit, Hatchet, Hand grenade, and Haul. Or as Kilgour somewhat indelicately dubbed the style: 'Ambush, Axes, an' Arse'oles.'

Then his Mantis conditioning cut in. Sten found himself running through fiche of *Antique Weapons and Tactics*. And, as so often before, he found his plan. A blast from the past – literally. His era's security specialists knew all of the sophisticated techniques going and guarded against them – and frequently forgot to wonder if someone might show up with a bow and arrow instead of a laser.

Kilgour reported, laden with fiche, tapes, and even a few antique natural-history books. They went to work. Within two days Sten had found enough Local Critters to enable him to start handpicking his team. Now they were in place, scattered up and down the coast of Oregon. Ten beings for the Kill Team, three on Intelligence & Recon.

Two of them had gone first – an E-type humanoid male and female. Claiming marriage, claiming retirement, they purchased a dockside café/bar. Cover names: Larry and Faye Archuler.

A third human, claiming to be a wandering artist, drifted into Coos Bay and took a casual labor job on one of the boat-hulled gravsleds used for sportfishing, when he wasn't wandering the hills with his tri-pad. He was actually a nearly competent sketch artist who was fascinated with river wildlife. Cover name: Havell.

Then Sten and Alex had arrived. Sten was now a hard-driving and -driven entrepreneur who had suffered a nervous breakdown. He was accompanied by a male nurse – Kilgour. The story Alex had told in the drinking houses – whining under his breath but sipping caff – was that his boss believed his ancestors came from this section of Old Earth. Kilgour added, however, that he personally considered this obsession just part of his breakdown. Sooner or later, he would decide that the ancestors had come from elsewhere, and they would move on.

Being the head of a successful corporation, even if on medical sabbatical, meant that Sten had to keep in contact with his company. That justified a rather elaborate com. Given the entrepreneur's secretiveness, it also justified his use of code. The code was a fairly available business encryption that Sten assumed the privy council's cryptographers had cracked. But the arrangement of the code groups, as well as the groups themselves, kept Sten in contact with Mahoney and Conspiracy Central. The com was poorly antennaed, and Sten's signals, fortunately brief, blanketed the area, to be received by his teammates.

That corporation really existed. Whatever Sten ordered would be done by the officers of the company. The code was also skillfully rewritten to be believable. Sten, like anyone else who had ever had cipher training, had heard the story of the code that had been blown when the criminal requested five and one half elephants.

Kilgour, while spreading the cover story through the village, had also ID'd the two men who were Imperial Security. One was a village constable, far too knowledgeable to be what he claimed to be. The other was a barkeep who was overly curious. Neither one warranted termination.

Four other men and women of the hit team were living in the ruins of that town at the mouth of the Umpqua. They were highly visible: Montoya, Valdiva, Corum, and Akashi. They claimed to be members of the Cult of the Emperor, making a pilgrimage to every place the Eternal Being had blessed with the presence of his glowing soul. So of course they had to journey upriver to his fishing camp. They did. Some days later, they were seen camping where the Eternal One had cast his fly rod, by one of the Imperial river wardens. They refused to leave. The warden brought in reinforcements. The robed cultists smiled, bowed in surrender to the wardens, boarded the gravsled, and were unceremoniously dumped in Reedsport.

A few days later they were back performing their ceremonies. The warden, a little worried, made some vid calls. He discovered that the cult was completely harmless. The late Eternal Emperor had, in fact, considered them beneficial if aberrant, since their beliefs encouraged charity and good works as well as the Emperor as godhead. Just run them out, came the Warden's orders. When they return, run them out again. You can jail them if you want – if you find a jail in your part of the wilderness. I wouldn't bother, the advice from his superior went. Eventually, from what I've read, they finish whatever rituals they're performing and move on. The warden, who hated the idea of being any kind of a policeman, chose to ignore the cultists.

He had received an inquiry from the Imperial Security station at Sullamora's retreat. Overhead surveillance had seen the cultists. The Security officer heard the explanation, laughed, and disconnected.

The warden became used to the four. They would wave at him in a cordial manner as he passed on patrol. Once he saw a battered gravsled leaving the fishing camp, but it was empty, and he could see no sign of the gravsled having brought any supplies or building materials that would suggest the cultists were settling in for a long stay.

Then they vanished. The warden found himself almost missing the robed men and women, but he was more interested in trying to photograph a pinniped he had never seen before. Seal? Sea lion? He did not know, and the few reference materials he could access gave him no hints. He spent time trying – without success – to take a picture that could be sent to a museum for identification.

The mammal, he assumed, seemed to range from the mouth of the river all the way up to where that estate began, and where he was forbidden entry. He hoped the trigger-happy Security goons at the retreat would not shoot 'her' – for so he romantically assumed the creature to be. He hoped she had brains enough to dive if she spotted any of them.

The multi-sexed creature, in fact, had approximately twice the intelligence of the warden. Cover name: F'lesa.

The warden had no interest in flying creatures, mammalian or avian. He paid no attention to the two batlike creatures flashing around close to Sullamora's estate. Nor did he spot the tiny vidcams hung around their necks. The two 'bats' were beings that, though stupid, were found useful by Mantis for aerial intelligence, putting up with their stupidity. They could talk, but their language consisted of half-verbal, half-instinctual squeaks. Their names were, of course, a problem. On the Imperial payrolls they were carried by service numbers. Mantis troopers gave them paired nicknames – Frick and Frack, Gog and Magog, etc. Sten had worked with a pair of them before. These two: Dum and Dee.

Sten used their aerial intelligence to begin building the 'model' of the target area. It would not, in fact, exist; it would be part of the interactive helmet system. Before shipping for Earth, he had already found every vid that was available of the estate. There was not much.

Kilgour managed to ferret out some old gillies who had worked for Sullamora back when he was convincing himself that fishing was fun. That gave them more data. Still not complete, but enough so each team member could put on a helmet, keyed to respond only to him, and 'practice' the attack. Each being's moves were recorded, fed into Sten's central record, and cycled back out. Even though the helmets gave multi-sensory input, it was still strange. Charge a fence . . . feel the barbed wire in your hands. Climb it. Shoot a guard. Round a corner . . . and everything would go blank. NO RECORD AVAILABLE. A few meters farther on, the simulation would recommence. It was off-putting. Fortunately the combat-experienced Mantis operatives had learned to accept these partially complete rehearsal systems. It was the best they were likely to get, could well improve as more data became available from F'lesa, Dee, or Dum, and was far more secure than actually building a full-scale model for real physical practice.

The cultists, however, grew bored with the dry runs. But they had nothing else to do. They were, in fact invisible – invisible to any above-ground or aerial observer, scanning on any length known. The cultists 'ceremonies' had been elaborate. They had dug a slant tunnel ten meters down, then built a large chamber. Into that had gone the weaponry and gear from the gravsled shipment. No one was happy that the sled had even been seen by the warden as it left, but accidents happened.

Now the four waited.

That underground chamber would be the assembly point for the assault.

There were two final members of the team: N'Ran, huge – three hundred kilos average – somewhat anthropoid beings who had become the Empire's best artillerymen. During the Tahn wars, inevitably some N'Ran became curious, adventuresome, and Mantis. Sten was delighted to have them along. Not only could they easily tote the Phase One elements of the attack in one hand, but they would be his weaponeers, as well.

Mahoney did a double take when Sten said he was using two N'Ran. 'Apes? No, lad. They'll not be taken for bears either.'

Sten pointed out their cover. Centuries before, there had been absurd legends of a creature called Big Foot. If spotted, they would be legendary creatures. Sten made sure, when he arrived in Coos Bay, that the legend was reactivated and told his two mythical monsters to lie low but leave chubby footprints if they must. The two N'Ran were waiting, living rough in the forested mountains near the Umpqua.

Sten panted back from his run in a different mood entirely. He considered his work and found it good – or at least acceptable. Privately he thought the odds might even be better than fifty-fifty. He was ready. Then he felt a crawl down his spine and shivered. The weather? Perhaps. But he instantly began a complete run-through of his plans for the nineteenth time.

Four days before The Day the rest of Sten's accomplices arrived – provided by the privy council itself.

Sten's accomplices were the Imperial media. The privy council wanted the maximum amount of publicity from their assemblage. The members handpicked the loudest, dumbest pseudojournalists they could find, journalists guaranteed to lap up every communique from the council as gospel. Legitimate reporters were not encouraged to apply to the press pool.

The council was pleased by the interest. The members thought it was because they were starting to turn the tide of public opinion. They did not realize that the interest was due to their seclusiveness. When a leader hid in what was dubbed by vid people 'The Rose Garden,' anything he said or did was of note and had nothing to do with whether the public thought him either an angel or an Attila.

The 'press' streamed onto Earth. Immediately, they were disappointed. They would not be allowed inside the estate. They were given quarters in hastily thrown-up military campaign huts. Their superiors started snarling. Report. Report what? The council has not arrived yet. Report anything.

A real reporter or analyst might have filed 'What Might This All Mean' pieces, or just filed background. Not the hacks on Earth. They surged out, looking for stories. Stories to them meant 'color': the Benevolence of the Late Tanz Sullamora; the Little Known Estate he Kept on Earth Where he Communed with Nature and the Eternal Emperor; The Sadness of his Death.

That well soon ran dry, and the hacks became desperate. The Beauty of Oregon (tourist trade would be sure to go up). The Unusual Creatures of Earth. The Colorful Folk of the Rugged Seacoast. On and on. Some ass even wanted to interview Sten, without the foggiest as to a newspeg. He was declined, with a smile.

Every gravsled that could be rented was – from the shattered city of San Francisco north to the glacier regions. They dripped vidcams, engineers, and reporters, and were everywhere.

Imperial Security pulled in its horns and disregarded any

satellite, aerial, or sensor intelligence from anywhere except the immediate compound. When the privy council arrived that would take care of things. They would have those damned people back in one place, being spoon-fed whatever the council wanted them to have. Certainly there was no particular reason to overload the sec-computers with meaningless data.

Thirty-six hours . . . Sten moved.

A single, completely meaningless code word was broadcast. Mahoney would receive it – and know the team was on its way in. From then on, until they accomplished the mission, there would be no contact possible. The signal was picked up in the hills and ruins, and his team was in motion. With one exception: Kilgour. That crawl up Sten's spine was still there. He gave orders.

Kilgour was detached from the hit team. Ten beings would go in instead of eleven.

Alex gave a good imitation of ground zero after a multi-KT warhead impacted. He slammed the table – and the two-inch-thick hardwood shattered. Kilgour recovered. His face went back down the spectrum from purple.

'Why?'

'I want you on the back door. That's an order.'

'Y'no ken. Y'r no an' adm'ral, and Ah'm no a warrant. Nae more. Laird Kilgour ae Kilgour deman's – and will hae – an explanation.'

Sten explained. He felt as if someone were watching over his shoulder.

'Best we abort,' Kilgour suggested. 'Ah'll no argue wi' invis'ble clottin' spirits. Or replan.'

'No time for that,' Sten said. 'And I don't have any better ideas. I don't see what's wrong with what I've got – logically. Abort? When will we have another chance?'

'A' these years,' Kilgour said, hurt. 'An' y'll noo gie me th' chance t' keep you frae gettin' dead.' Then he tried another approach: 'M'gun'll do more i' th' fray than back i' th' clottin' RP.'

Sten did not answer.

Alex stared at Sten for a long time. 'Thae's the feelin'? Strong, is't?'

Sten nodded.

Kilgour sighed. 'Best y'd be right, lad. I' you're wrong – you an' me'll hae a dustup a'ter th' extraction i' you're not.'

He stamped out into the rain.

*

Sten and the others made their way to the bunker in the Emperor's camp. They left thin cover stories behind – they would be in, out, and gone within forty-eight hours, so an elaborate story was not needed. Or else . . .

A ship had entered Earth's atmosphere a day earlier, planetfall calculated to occur in one of the inevitable, momentary holes in the satellite coverage. 'Ship' was not a correct description. Two tacships had been slaved together.

Just off the Oregon coast the ships were separated. One was allowed to rest on the bottom, fifty-plus fathoms down. Its controls were set to respond to a transponder in the hands of an angry, worried, and now-scared Kilgour, hidden near the beach.

The pilot of the second ship received a signal. He surfaced and opened a hatch. Dum and Dee darted in, and seconds later, F'lesa flopped into the ship. F'lesa had found all that could be discovered from the water, and Sten could not chance any transmission from Dum and Dee's vidcams, no matter how useful they might be as aerial warning devices.

The tacship submerged. Some time that night, taking advantage of another hole, it would escape Earth's atmosphere.

The mission was hot and running . . .

Chapter Eleven

The sensor/transmitter was the equivalent of a moron with a megaphone. It, and a power pack, were planted in an eons-old satellite in high orbit over Earth, part of the sky junk that made navigation on- and offworld so interesting. A tech had boarded the satellite just days after the summit had been announced. He positioned the bug, turned it on, took a moment to marvel at the primitive machines – clottin' light-optic computers – and was gone.

The transmitter waited, ignoring the flurry of ships approaching the planet. Too small. Too few.

Then it woke. *Ships . . . many ships . . . many big ships.*

It bleated twice on the assigned frequency, then fused into a solid lump of plas.

Sten shut the receiver down and tossed it into the pile in the center of the bunker. 'Our customers are on the way. Shall we?'

The team grabbed packs and headed for the ramped tunnel. All of them wore phototropic uniforms that would also give some shielding against pickup by thermal sensors. They weaseled their gear, including the long, heavy cylinders in padded, shoulder-strapped cases, into the open.

Havell touched a button, and a dim light shone from his notepad as he checked the satellite sked. 'Clean for an hour and a half. Then we've got an overhead and an Eye.'

'Still – use overhead cover,' Sten ordered.

Valdiva whispered a question: 'These, umm, bears you mentioned? Are they nocturnal?'

One N'ran rumbled a laugh. 'No . . . but hugging contest . . . interesting.'

Hugging? The bear would place third. Not to mention, Sten thought, what other instruments of death they were carrying. The cylinders with their sights and mounts – plus each being carried a combat knife, a single-shot completely suppressed projectile weapon, three types of grenades, and heavy, short-barreled 'shotguns,' drum-fed weapons that scattered highly explosive AM2 pellets as their charge. An excellent weapon for a barroom discussion.

Sten looked back at their hidey-hole and decided, not for the first time, that he was a perfectly lousy burrowing animal. If he had to buy it, he would prefer it be in the open.

They started off into the darkness.

In ten hours an incendiary charge in the pile of discarded gear, ration tins, and civilian clothing would go off. All of the team members, excepting the N'ran, had worn membrane gloves since they had arrived on Earth, so not even the primitive fingerprint system could ID them. Their quarters in Coos Bay had been swept Mantis-clean. There could be no DNA or any other identification in the postbang investigation.

Each team member wore a vital-signs pack on his or her belt. Any change in the bearer – such as death – and the pack would detonate. There would not even be a corpse to autopsy.

With the exception of the cylinders, it was all perfectly normal gear for a Mantis mission.

Brigadier Mavis Sims had taken the same oath as Sten. But she chose to interpret it differently.

She could not remember having slept since she returned from the phony kriegsspiel and being recruited for the conspiracy.

There were five generations of Simses who had served the Empire. The family motto, just a touch embarrassing in its blatancy, was 'Faithful unto Death.' None of the Simses had abandoned that faith.

Now, deep in the heart of another sleepless, echoing night, Brigadier Sims decided she would not shirk it, either.

The atmosphere in the communication room of the main lodge had gone from high-pitched excitement to nervous boredom. Military techs had bustled about for hours as the Imperial fleet approached the Honjo system. The members of the council had literal front-row seats as the maneuvering commenced. A dazzling array of impressive commands were fired at the fleet commander. Responses, terse and warriorlike, crackled back. One entire com wall was ablaze with winking red and green lights marking the progress.

It was one helluva good show – to start with. But then the routine absolutely necessary for any large-scale action began to drag. And drag. And drag. There were endless countdowns at each stage. Then the clocks were reset again for another crucial juncture.

By the time the fleet had parked, pulled on its stealth cloak, and started baiting the hook for the Honjo, the privy council was considering canceling the whole thing for lack of interest.

Not for the first time in the past two hours, Kyes compared the action to the few combat livies he had seen. He could understand now why the livie makers steered well clear of any hint of reality. In a livie, all that was needed was a maximum three-minute conference of the warrior brass to set the target. That would be followed by a 'what it all means to us' scene, in which each character mused on his or her lifelong goals and objectives. If he or she was warm and cuddly, the character was usually doomed. If cynical and bitter, that character was sure to see the light in the gore that followed. Then entire legions of fleets would be launched in blaze of fast-cutting action. The formula would require a momentary victory, followed by a setback in which all seemed lost. And finally the bravery and cunning of the heroes would conquer all.

Kyes did not like livies. But he liked this show less.

He stirred slightly as the little tacship crossed the invisible line that marked the beginning of Honjo territory. At any moment there would be a loud protest broadcast by the prey, backed up by a small, heavily armed patrol to warn the tacship away.

The plan was for the tacship to ignore the warning. If that went on long enough, the Honjo patrol would certainly fire. Then the wrath of the Imperial fleet would descend on the helpless Honjo to repay them for their temerity.

For a long time, there was nothing at all.

The Kraas sent out for more food. The big banquet table had already been emptied twice. Most of it had been drunk or devoured by the twins. They ate until even the skin of the fat one was stretched to bursting. Then they excused themselves, so that the obese one could help 'Sis' into a lavatory. Loud sounds of vomiting followed. Then the two exited, the thin one flushed with effort and glowing with saintly joy at her after-the-fact temperance.

At first, Malperin, Kyes, and Lovett had been revolted. But the second time around, they became oddly fascinated. It was certainly more exciting than what was going on up on the big com board.

As the waiters were hauling in more supplies, a voice crackled out. A Honjo voice!

'This is Honjo Center to unknown tacship. Please identify your-self.'

The tacship was silent, and the excitement in the com room came sparking back. Each of the five leaned forward, waiting.

'Honjo Center, to unknown tacship. You are in violation of our borders. Turn back. I repeat, turn back!'

Still no response, just as according to plan. On the big screen, they could see the tacship moving inalterably on. Another flurry of warnings came from the Honjo, with similar negative results. They could see the small patrol now. A tech whispered to Kyes that the monitors showed that they had gone from alert to full armament. Any moment, a missile would be fired.

Then there was a loud, unconscious groan. Against all predictions, the Honjo patrol was retreating!

'Unknown tacship,' came the voice of the Honjo commander. 'Be warned! We are recording this violation of our sovereignty. And it shall be immediately reported to the proper authorities.'

'Wot's bleedin' happening?' one Kraa burst out. 'Why don't the bastards shoot?'

'Clottin' cowards,' the other screamed. 'Fight, you drakhs. Fight!'

Despite that odd cheering section, the Honjo did just the opposite. The patrol sensibly turned tail and ran.

The council members were mortified. Techs ducked their angry glares about the room, looking for someplace to set responsibility.

'What will we do?' Lovett hissed.

'Clot 'em. Let's go anyways!' the fat Kraa said.

'I don't know,' Malperin said. 'Are you sure we ought to? I mean, doesn't this change everything?'

Kyes thought it did – but he was not sure. They were so close. The patrol was tiny, the fleet waiting. All that AM2 just sitting there. Maybe . . .

At the moment, the com screen blanked. Then the startled council members found themselves staring at Poyndex, their chief of Mercury Corps.

The colonel made no excuses or apologies for the interruption. His face was pale. His manner, bloodless. 'I have been notified that an assassination team is at this moment in place and prepared to strike.

'Gentlebeings, you will immediately put yourselves in the hands of your security personnel. There is no cause for extreme alarm. If you follow security procedures, all will be well.'

The council members jolted around as the door burst open and grim-faced security beings pushed into the room. Then the five rulers of all the Eternal Emperor had once surveyed allowed themselves to be hustled away like little children astray in a wilderness.

Somewhere in the far-off Honjo system a fleet awaited orders.

The team closed in on the late Sullamora's estate. At first they had traveled fast. There were still gravsleds overhead that were clearly not Security vehicles.

At daybreak they had sheltered in a river cave that F'lesa had pinpointed. They had eaten a tasteless meal and tried to sleep, only to be awakened by earthquake rumbles. Quick hand signals were exchanged – reflexively, without orders, they had gone nonverbal, even for whispers. The signals gave redundant, obvious information, variations of 'Target on ground,' but they broke the silent isolation.

Now, any overhead had to be considered hostile.

Just at dusk, they moved again. Ten kilometers outside the estate, the first passive sensors were encountered. They were quickly given electronic 'You don't see anything' signals, and the team moved on.

The sensors became closer together, and more sensitive. But again

they were spoofed successfully. Then there was an old road, with
a patrol, its time passage exactly what Dum and Dee had filmed.
Routine and proper security are oxymoronic. Roving five-man
patrols. Mantis, most likely. Again, evaded. A N'Ran crouched to
Sten and signed scornfully: 'I could dance.'

They went on.

A kilometer or so outside the estate, Sten found a hilltop with
a decent line of sight and fair overhead cover. 'Here. Set up,' he
signed.

The cases were opened. Two missiles came out. They looked to
be standard Imperial short-range, self-homing, fire-and-forget,
ground-to-ground weapons. They were not. The propellant had
been replaced by a reduced amount of a slow-burning solid fuel.
The missiles would be fired from very short, closely estimated range.
More explosive went in. The homing mechanisms also went into
the trash. More bang went in their place. Space was left for a
primitive guidance system near the missile's stern. A small pitot
was welded into the base.

Telescoping rods were untelescoped, crossed, and pinned together
into simple, X-shaped launching stands. The Archulers unshoul-
dered their packs. Each pack contained a two-kilometer reel of
chained molecular wire. One end of the wire connected to the
missile, the other to a monopod-mounted passive light-intensifi-
cation sight with a single, small joystick. The N'ran were ready.

The rest of the team stripped off the phototropic uniforms. Under
them, they wore Imperial combat fatigues, exactly the same as those
worn by the guard units inside the estate. Sten motioned them
down the hill.

More sensors. Physical security barriers, including some archaic
razor-wire. Booby traps, passive and active. Guards.

Easy. No problem. A little too easy?

Shut up. A hollow. Signal – flat of hand, going down. Needless.
The team dropped. Just in front of them was the final wire – and
the compound.

Now the bloodbath should begin – preferably on one side only.

Phase One, scheduled to begin when Sten keyed a tone-com,
would be the firing of the first missile. The second would follow
ten seconds later. Sten had felt – correctly – that any modern guidance system would be countermeasured or just blocked. So he went
primitive. The guidance system was via that wire the Archulars had
lugged in.

Wire guidance had been discarded millennia earlier as an

absurdity. Its faults were many: The operator was required to remain in one place and guide the missile to its target. He must have line of sight to the target. The target might also be looking his way and have some objection to being rocketed. Not a problem for Sten – he was back-stabbing, not playing Leonidas.

The wire could snag or break. Not this wire.

But the biggest problem had been the real catch-22. If the missile traveled at any kind of speed, it would take a guidance operator who could also dance on a rolling ball to hit the target rather than over- or under-shoot or, worse, send the missile into out-of-control yawing. They had to slow the missile down. That would give the target time to acquire and destroy the missile and most likely its operator, as well, but that was not a real factor. Luxury estates did not shoot back – Sten hoped.

First the missiles would sequentially impact on the target area, resulting in chaos, flames, and screams. Sten and his team would arrow into that chaos with 'Rescue' in their shouts and murder in their hearts. They would terminate any surviving council members, then withdraw, break contact, and head for the pickup point.

The tone-com would also signal Kilgour to bring the tacship to the surface and low-fly upriver to a present RP.

Then they could all go home and get drunk.

Stop hesitating. Go, lad.

Sten touched the button.

One . . .

The first missile was launched and nap-of-the-earth guided into the estate's main building.

Three seconds . . .

Faye Archuler pitched a sausage charge over the wire and pulled the fuse cord.

Six . . .

The first missile 'crept' forward, at little more than 200 kph.

Eight . . .

The charge exploded, slicing the fence open like a gate.

Ten . . .

The second missile launched.

Eleven . . .

Sten shouted, 'Grenades!' The team thumbed timers and hurled grenades into the compound.

Thirteen . . .

Sten was the first on his feet and charging through the hole in the wire. It may have saved his life.

Fifteen . . .

The grenades exploded, huge flares broadcasting confusion through visible-invisible spectrums.

Eighteen seconds . . .

Imperial Security sprang the trap.

Two armored gravsleds floated into sight, their multiple chainguns yammering. A missile launcher snapped up from its silo, tracking.

Twenty-one . . .

Sten's first missile was just four seconds from impact. The gravsled chainguns' sensors found the incoming missile. Solid collapsed-uranium slugs sheeted through the air – and the missile shattered!

Twenty-four . . .

The missile launcher acquired its target. Twenty counterbattery missiles spat into the night.

Twenty-eight seconds . . .

The missiles impacted on Sten's launch site. The two N'Ran disappeared in a howl of explosions.

The second missile, no longer under command, soared vertically.

Twenty-nine seconds . . .

Akashi's boot heel slammed down on a mine sowed less than an hour before. The charge took his legs off at the groin, and shrapnel scythed through Montoya.

The nearby blast caught Sten, flipping him up and back into the wire. He hung, limply.

Montoya's vital-signs pack blew, purple in the night.

Thirty-one . . .

High overhead, Sten's second missile exploded harmlessly.

Thirty-six . . .

The guns on the gravsleds tracked down . . . ammunition drums clanged as the loads automatically changed and the guns yammered on.

Larry and Faye Archuler were cut nearly in half.

Thirty-nine . . .

A sniper found the running Havell in his sights . . . lost him in a grenade blast . . . then touched the trigger. The AM2 round blew Havell's chest away.

Forty-two . . .

Corum and Valdiva zagging . . . rolling . . . firing . . . The chainguns found and smashed them.

Sten found himself flat. Stunned. Disoriented. He started to his feet – and the Mantis reflexes took over. He rolled, over and over, somehow keeping hold of his broken-stocked scattergun. Explosive rounds stitched centimeters over his head, and he was back in the hollow. Safety. Stay here, his mind said. They won't see you. They won't find you.

His body disobeyed. He ripped out of his combat harness, thumbed the switch on a grenade, and threw the vest back, into the wire.

The first grenade detonated – and the others went off in sympathetic explosions.

Sten was up, stumbling. Away. You're blown. Move! The others! Clot the others – they're dead! Follow the damned orders I'm issuing!

A five-man patrol came out of the smoke. Gun up, trigger held back – and red spray instead of men, AM2 bullets exploding the razor fence behind them and its sensors.

Through, skin ripping.

Water-sound. Run, damn you. It doesn't hurt.

A bank. Flat-dive over – fearing rocks, hoping water. Neither. Smash into the cushion . . . the ripping cushion of rusted high-piled concertina wire.

The knife out of your arm, man.

Slashing.

Nothing to slash. Somehow the knife was in its 'sheath,' and Sten was crashing forward, into the water and through the shallows.

Someone behind him was firing.

Bullet-splashes.

Deeper. Dive. Go under. Hold your clottin' breath. You don't need oxygen.

Now. Surface. One gasp – go under. Swim if you can. Let the current carry you. Away. Down the river.

One hand moved inside his uniform, found a tiny box, slid the cover back on the box, and pressed a stud.

Swim. You can.

Safety.

Downriver. Alex. The pickup.

Sten knew he would never make it.

Kilgour paced the control room of the tacship, waiting. It was not much of a pace – no more than four steps at the maximum before he would slam into something.

The ship was grounded on the river beach chosen for the pickup point. Alex had the hatch open. His orders were clear and exact: remain in place until one hour before daybreak or if discovered. If no one is at the pickup point, return to the ocean. Try to remain near mouth of the river. The team would try, if the pickup was blown, to E&E to the ruins of Reedsport. If no contact was made, he was to head offplanet and report.

In the not-very-distance, Alex could hear the sounds of hell. He hoped it was being given, not gotten. Once more he cursed Sten, then broke off in mid-obscenity as an ululation began from a com speaker.

One screen showed a projection of the target area. Just outside it, a tiny red light blinked – from the river. Midriver, the map told him.

'Clot!' The obscenity was heartfelt. The light – and signal – came from a standard search-and-rescue transmitter. Each member of the team had carried one, with orders to activate it *only* if they missed pickup. Certainly not anywhere close to the target zone.

An SAR light. One.

Kilgour zoomed the projection back, to see if there were others. Nothing.

His fingers found a mike. 'This is pickup. Go.'

Nothing but dead air. The light continued to blink.

Kilgour took about a nanosecond to decide that those clear and exact orders could get stuffed. Seconds later, he lifted the tacship, banged the drive selection into Yukawa power – and be damned who could see the torch – and drove forward, upriver.

A screen flashed at him. Six gravsleds.

Alex took one hand from the controls and slapped a switch. The tacship's chainguns blasted. The tacship yawed, ripping through the top of a redwood grove, and almost went in before Alex had control again. He shot through the falling debris of the gravsleds and a voice from a speaker smashed at him:

'Unidentified tacship! Ground, or we fire!'

Alex was forced to lift out of the gorge. He banked the ship into a tight spiral, took three steps away from the control board, and hit ALL LAUNCH on the long-activated weapons panel. Eight Goblin XIX's salvoed upward. He found time to hope the medium-range anti-ship missiles' brains were awake, and there he was back at the controls, diving down into the gorge; the cliffs dropped away, and Kilgour was almost overflying the blinking light – and into the alerted target zone.

He spun ship, still under power, his stabilizing and nav-gyros screaming, killed power, and went to McLean power.

Far overhead, a nuclear fire blossomed.

Kilgour splashed down and was at the hatch. Just upstream, a body floated down toward him, motionless. Then an arm lifted, trying to swim.

Kilgour stretched . . . almost fell in . . . then had the body by its ripped coveralls. He flipped the man into the ship and was back behind the controls and under full power, hands darting across the controls, barely finding time to cycle the lock closed as the tacship clawed for altitude, straight up, toward and through the nuclear blast that had formerly been an Imperial warship.

It may have been the instant fury of Kilgour's reactions, or just the luck of the Scots. But he cleared planet – and vanished into silence under full AM2 drive.

Behind him Sten lay unconscious. His mind concussed and his body, having done its duty and preserved the organism, shut down until repairs were made.

Chapter Twelve

The librarian and her staff were considering their futures when – or rather if – their boss ever departed. One thought fondly of suicide, another planned a complete breakdown. The librarian herself considered one of two new careers: as a staffer for an orgy livie production company, or, perhaps, as a serial murderer.

Her job had suddenly become a complete, dawn-to-dawn nightmare.

It had not begun like that, nor had it been like that for nearly five years. In fact, she had been enormously envied for getting the post.

Somewhat dissatisfied, certainly overqualified and without time to do her own research and publishing in her prevous job as head librarian at a large university, she had been contacted, out of the blue, by an executive search service. She was offered what she thought was the ultimate job – at triple her present salary. Did she mind relocating to a different system? No. The headhunter seemed unsurprised, as if he knew everything about her. The position was as a private librarian. The woman demurred – she had no intention of burying herself in some recluse's dusty archives and letting the world pass.

Nothing like that at all, the man explained. He suggested she visit the planet of Yongjukl and investigate her new job. She would have a round-trip ticket. He offered to accompany her. She declined. The librarian was quite attractive – and the headhunter seemed disappointed.

The library was nearly mansion-size and was but one building on sprawling grounds. The main house dwarfed the library. It was secluded, with more than a thousand square kilometers of guarded, secure grounds. Her own quarters were lavish. There was a full staff: cooks, cleaners, gardeners.

Not that the librarian was imprisoned. She had her own gravcar, and a large, sophisticated city was no more than an hour or two away. She was allowed to keep her own hours – as long as the system remained current. If she ever needed help, she could hire as many day-workers as necessary.

Computers? Scanners? Filing robots? State of the art – and new models provided regularly.

She asked if she had permission to pursue her own studies and research. Certainly. Could she have visitors? If she chose. However, if she left the grounds, she was required to carry a remote. She must consider herself on call dawn-to-dawn. An unlikely possibility.

It seemed too good to be true. She felt like a character in one of the goth-livies she had supposedly given up when she was twelve but still 'lived,' somewhat guiltily, in her occasional bubblebaths.

Especially since there was no one in the mansion. No one except the staff. And none of them had ever met the mansion's owner.

When she returned to her own world, her first question to the headhunter was: Who would I be working for?

The man explained. The mansion – and its grounds – were part of a family estate. Which one? I cannot tell you that. But the mansion must remain with the family, and be maintained. If not – it is a matter of a rather elaborate and eccentric trust, my dear – an entire commercial empire would be disassembled.

At the head of the family is the young heir, the man continued. You may never meet him. He is extremely busy and prefers living closer to the Empire's center. But he is an unusual man. He might well show up one day. Alone or with an entourage – in which case he will require absolute privacy. The man shrugged. It must be nice to be so wealthy that you can order your life that precisely.

If I take this position, the woman asked – which you can accept on a weekly, monthly, or yearly contract, the headhunter interrupted – I must keep that a secret? No, not necessarily, the man said. It seems to be a favorite topic about once a year by the planet's newsvids. Say what you wish – it is not as if there's anything to hide.

Thinking dark thoughts of windswept castles and disguised, royal lovers, she accepted the position.

For eleven years, it was paradise. Staggering amounts of material churned in daily. It seemed the unknown heir subscribed to every scientific, military, or political journal in the Empire. The material was scanned, summarized, and mostly discarded by a computer/scanner who seemed to have completely elitist tastes. It was, the woman once thought, a machine that seemed programmed to provide an instant update for someone newly risen from the grave. The computer had two sysop stations. One was in a sealed room, the other belonged to the librarian. The sealed unit seemed to contain, she learned when she snooped in boredom, some files that were inaccessible to the rest of the system.

Annually the entire files for that year were deleted. Then the machine began all over, collecting, summarizing, and storing.

Until a little more than six years before.

At that time, the computer had switched modes and begun storing everything. The librarian did not notice until year's end. She panicked – just slightly. Had she done something wrong? She did not want to lose her position. Not only was she perfectly happy on this world, having met and loved a wonderful succession of mates, but she was publishing important analyses in a steady stream, the envy of her far-lesser-paid and, to their minds, overworked colleagues in the field. The man at the other end of the emergency contact number soothed her. Not to worry, he said. Just continue. So continue she did.

Now she was going quite insane. Because, to everyone's astonishment, the heir – a man she thought most likely a legal myth by now – arrived. A small ship set down on the small landing pad. One man got out, and the ship instantly lifted away.

Guards met him. 'Sir, this is a private—'

The man said words – words everyone had been told would be uttered if their boss ever showed up.

No one knew what to do and cowered for their jobs.

The man asked to be taken to his room. He showered, changed, and asked for a simple meal. Then he buzzed and asked to be shown to the library.

In the huge hall he politely told the librarian that he would appreciate it if she remained on standby. He unlocked the door to the second sysop station, and the madness started.

He seemed to scan everything – and want more. She had to hire assistants. He appeared insatiably curious. Again, the librarian thought of someone raised from the dead. No, she corrected herself. Someone who had been in longsleep, like the starships in ancient times before AM2 drive.

It went on, the man ate sparingly, slept little, but soaked up information like a sponge. Once, when the door opened for a moment, she saw that he had five screens scrolling simultaneously and a synth-voice giving a sixth stream of data.

The librarian prayed for sleep.

Then it stopped. The man walked out of the room, leaving the door open.

He said he was sleepy.

The librarian agreed blearily.

He told her he would shut down the system.

Yes. The woman and her equally zombied assistants stumbled for their quarters. The librarian noticed – but it did not register until days later – as she passed the room where the second sysop station was, that the computer seemed to be punching up files and then deleting them en masse.

It did not matter.

All that mattered was sleep.

The man slipped out an ignored side gate to the mansion onto the road. He walked down the road, briskly. He wore nondescript clothes – just another of that world's blue-collar workers.

He stopped once. The walls of the mansion's grounds stretched solidly down the road.

He felt slight regret.

The computer had told him that when he left the staff would be paid off with handsome bonuses and encouraged with larger bonuses to relocate offworld. The mansion, the library, and the outbuildings would be razed within two weeks. Then the bare grounds would be donated to the planetary government for what-ever purposes it saw fit.

A pity. It was beautiful.

The computer told him there were ten others like it scattered around the Empire.

He now knew six years of history. His plans – no. Not yet. But he had been given another destination.

Lights blazed behind him. A creaking gravsled lofted toward him, laden with farm produce for the early markets. The man extended his hand.

The gravsled hissed to a halt. The driver leaned across and opened the door.

The man climbed inside, and the gravsled lifted.

'Dam' early to be hitchin',' the driver offered.

The man smiled, but did not answer.

'You work for th' rich creech owns that palace?'

The man laughed. 'No. Me an' the rich don't speak the same tongue. Just passin' through. Got stranded. Dam' glad for the lift.'

'Where you headed?'

'The spaceport.'

'You're light on luggage. For a travellin' man.'

'I'm seekin' a job.'

Snorted laughter came from the driver. 'Golden luck to you, friend. But there's dam' little traffic comin' in or out. Times ain't good for spacecrew.'

'I'll find something.'

'Dam' confident, ain't you? Like a fellow who thinks like that. Name's Weenchlors.' The driver stuck out a paw. The man touched thumbs with him. 'You?'

'I use the name Raschid,' the man said.

He leaned back against the raggedy plas seats and stared ahead toward the lightening sky – toward the spaceport.

BOOK TWO

IMPERATOR

Chapter Thirteen

An hour after dawn, Security let the five members of the privy council out of their shielded bunkers into the fog-hung compound. They looked at the craters where the assassins had exploded as they died, the two rows where the dead Security beings lay covered, the torn wire, and the shrapnel-ripped buildings. They could not see the hilltop, where smoke trailed up from the N'Ran's launch site, and the warship Alex's blind-launched Goblins had flambéed was a radioactive cloud, drifting and contaminating its way inland.

Four of them shared anger – how could this have happened? The other, Kyes, was trying to label what emotion he did feel. In all his years, no one had ever tried to harm him physically. Destroy his career and life – but that was in bloodless executive chambers.

All of them were outraged. Who and why?

The Kraas, hardly strangers to physical violence, were pure rage, but with something else behind it: the instinct of cunning.

'We want the bosses. This un's a conspiracy, not a buncha wild-cats on a bust-out.'

'I agree,' Kyes put in.

'The *real* bosses c'n wait,' the thin one said. She had understood exactly what her sister was hinting. 'Till Monday, anyway. What we want are th' evil beings who planned this atrocity. Nobody else but th' Honjo.'

'Clot that clottin' tacship,' the fat one said. 'We got us some *real* bodies now.'

Lovett, as always, reached the bottom line. 'Conspiracy. Indeed. Far superior to any violation of territorial limits by a tacship.'

'I will issue the orders to the fleet,' Malperin snapped, and was inside.

'Righto,' one Kraa said. 'First we snag the AM2. Then we kill
– slow – whoever actually come a'ter us.'

'Them,' her sister agreed, 'an' some others. We've been needin'
an excuse for some housecleanin'.'

It was a peculiar curiosity that social entities could take on a
personality of their own – a personality that remained the same
for many years, even though the beings who first established the
entity's policies which had given it that personality were long dead
and forgotten. To psycho-historians, such an organization was an
'Iisner.' The same could be applied, on occasion, to military formations. One of the most famous examples was a tiny unit called the
Seventh Cavalry. The unit, from inception, was fairly poorly led
and suffered enormous casualties in combat, culminating in one
entire element being wiped out to the last man. Over the next
hundred E-years, in three successive wars, even though they had
been modernized with wheeled or in-atmosphere transport, they
were still abysmally generaled and regularly decimated.

A more modern example was the Imperial 23rd Fleet, now
ordered to attack the Honjo worlds and seize their AM2 caches.
When the Tahn wars had begun, the 23rd had been obliterated,
mostly due to the incompetence of its admiral, who had had the
good grace to be killed during that obliteration.

A new fleet was formed. It fought through the rest of the war,
officered indifferently at best and known throughout the Imperial
Services as a good outfit for anyone curious about reincarnation.

For some completely unknown reason, the 23rd was kept on
the rolls when the war ended, when far superior, more famous,
and 'luckier' formations were broken up and their cased colors
returned to depot.

Its admiral – until recently the fleet's vice-admiral – was one
Gregor. He had replaced his CO, Mason, when Mason refused to
follow the privy council's orders and requested relief.

Oddly enough, both the relieved and reliever had crossed Sten's
orbit. Mason had been Sten's brutal nemesis during flight school
and a particularly lethal destroyer commander in the Tahn wars.
He was a man without pity for his own sailors or the enemy, but
he was one of the best leaders the Empire had.

Gregor, on the other hand, had begun his military career as a
failure. He had been in Sten's Imperial Guards' Basic Company
and had been washed out for slavishly ordering, as trainee company
commander, a by-the-book attack that was obvious suicide. He had

returned to the tourist world where his father was a muckety – not as much of one as Gregor bragged, but still one with clout. The old man had sighed, put another tick mark in Gregor's failure list, and put him to work in an area where he could screw nothing up. Gregor's father was an optimist. By the time the Tahn wars began, Gregor wanted out – out of the division he had bankrupted, out of the relationship he had ruined, and away.

The Empire took almost anyone in wartime. They took Gregor – and commissioned him. This time Gregor discovered the path to success: Think about your orders first. If they aren't obvious booby traps, follow them slavishly. Develop a reputation for being hard. No one, during time of war, will be that curious about things like prisoner policy or retaliation. Gregor got promoted.

He decided that Imperial Service – particularly with the political connections he had been careful to make – was his forte. Particularly with the AM2 shortage. Tourist worlds without tourists were not, to him, the pattern of the future.

He had arrived with his reputation in front of him. Mason, a *real* hard man, had taken two weeks to decide that Gregor was not only an incompetent but someone destined to preside over a future version of Cortés's obliteration of the Aztecs.

He was correct. Unfortunately, Mason ran out of time.

The privy council had looked carefully for exactly the right admiral to head the attack on the Honjo system. In a way, they chose correctly. Mason would have followed orders and used just enough surgical force to convince the Honjo they were outgunned and outnumbered.

But they went too far. The Kraa twins had decided that, in addition to their other talents, they had a freshly discovered talent for military tactics. Their concept of 'good tactics' was as subtle as the way they handled labor disputes in the mines.

Mason asked to be relieved. He was. Disgusted, he decided to disappear for a long vacation, helping some retired friends restore old combat spacecraft for a museum. It saved his life.

Seconds after the change in orders from the privy council, Gregor ordered the 23rd Fleet into action. His fleet still looked impressive, even though some of the weapons systems were off-line, waiting for replacement parts that would never arrive; the ships themselves were at seventy percent or less of full complement, and the command 'Full emergency power' from any power-plant engineer would have been regarded as an order for 'Full public sodomy.'

Peace had struck hard at the Imperial Military, especially in personnel. The privy council had offered nothing but encouragement to anyone who wanted to leave the service. Many did. There was still a scattering of the dedicated in the fleet. And hard times on civvy street had provided other qualified sailors. But more than not, the 23rd's personnel were what should be expected: those who fell, dropped, or were pushed out of civilian life.

Still worse, most of them knew themselves to be marginal. Pay was sporadic, punishments arbitrary, and privileges awarded and withdrawn haphazardly. Morale was just a word in the dictionary between mildew and mud.

Ten worlds were chosen for the first attack – as an 'example in frightfulness.' Two were the AM2 'warehouse' worlds. The other eight were system capitals. For both targets, the weapons and their deployment were the same.

Neutron bombs were carpet-sewn across city centers and the warehouse worlds' control areas. Instantly, no life – and the blasts did not set off any of the stored AM2. Neither Gregor nor the privy council had thought warnings or declarations necessary preludes to war.

Gregor then made a broadbeam cast for the Honjo to surrender. First mistake: he had vaporized all the Honjo leaders who had the power to negotiate with the Empire. Second mistake: he had scared the Honjo into, he thought at first, paralysis.

Berserker rage can sometimes, on initiation, be mistaken for terror.

Gregor's fleet took up parking orbits and set patrols around the AM2 worlds. Then they brought in the slaved transports that would make up the 'spacetrain.'

The council had underestimated the supply. The convoy would be at least twenty kilometers from leadship to drag.

And the nightmare began as the Honjo exploded.

There seemed to be no leaders, nor generals. Just – resistance. The workers imported to load the AM2 were as likely to club a guard down and smile in the dying as work. They sabotaged any crane or beltway they got near. Robot systems and computers were crashed.

Gregor tried hostages, reprisals.

None of it seemed to matter to the Honjo.

The Emperor might have been able to tell the privy council that. The Honjo were hardheaded traders, and before they had learned that a contract was sharper than a sword, they had been excessively fond of sharp objects and private settlements of disputes.

The Honjo slave laborers – those who survived – were returned to their home worlds. Fleet sailors were onplaneted and used for the work force.

The situation got worse.

Small strike forces – squads, platoons, companies, irregulars – were landed. A one-sided guerrilla war began. Imperial soldiers and sailors could not open fire in the maze of buildings, each building a monstrous bomb. The Honjo had no such compunctions.

The fleet itself was attacked by such patrolcraft as the Honjo had, those light, boxy transports with three brave men or women at the controls and a bomb in the cargo hold. Kamikaze – the divine wind – worked.

It seemed as if the entire Honjo culture had held its breath for a moment and then heard, whispering from the dim past, a war leader's words: 'You can always take one with you . . .'

It was a siege, but not a siege. The besiegers arrived – and died. A battle, but not a battle. A perpetual series of alley murders. There seemed to be no way of stopping them. Put out destroyer screens to shield the big boys? Fine. The Honjo would attack the destroyers. Even a spaceyacht with a cabin full of explosives was enough to take a destroyer out of combat. Three . . . or six . . . or ten such spitkits . . . and then survivors went on for the battlewagons.

Gregor bleated for reinforcements.

There were none that could be sent.

There *were* ships – and men – standing by on the depot world of Al-Sufi. All they needed was fuel. Once fueled, they could support Gregor. But Gregor had the fuel . . .

Men – and ships – died.

Gregor knew better than to abort. The fleet *must* return with the AM2.

Gregor's officers and long-termers started hearing rumors then. Rumors from the Empire itself. Something was happening. People – leaders – they knew were being relieved and brought to trial. There were whispers of executions. All the deck sailors of the 23rd could do was work in a frenzy and pray that the final cargoes would be loaded before they all died. No one was willing to give odds, either way . . .

Mavis Sims did not expect a reward for betraying her fellow officers as part of her sworn duty to the Empire.

At best, she knew that her career would be over and her friends would send her to Coventry.

It was worse.

She should have known better. Regicide, even attempted regicide, has its own laws from investigation to punishment, laws limited only by whatever humanity the king chose to allow. Robert François Damiens, tortured and torn into four parts by horses, could have shown her that. The Eternal Emperor himself had paid little attention to the statutes in his clean-up after the Hakone plot failed. And the privy councillors were far less saintlike than the Eternal Emperor – or that declining monarch Louis XV either, for that matter.

When Sims had decided she must expose Mahoney's conspiracy she alerted the highest-ranking Intelligence officer she knew and told him of the assassination plan, when and where. No more.

What would happen next . . . she would not think.

What *did* happen was that Sims was arrested and her mind systematically ripped apart on the brainscan. The expert 'interrogators' had no interest in Sims's survival, either as an alert human or as a brainburn.

Yes . . . ten other officers at the table. Record faces. Does Sims know their names? Record them. Next meeting. Yes. Here. The amphitheater. Single-vision for this. Who is speaking?

One of the interrogators knew.

'Clottin' Mahoney! But he's dead!'

Continue scan . . . we'll report as necessary. Now. A party. Dammit . . . that group in the corner never looked at her. Never mind. They're most likely duped elsewhere.

'Dammit-to-hell! There's Mahoney again.'

'Who's that smaller guy in mufti beside him?'

'Dunno. Look. He's talking – and Mahoney's listening.'

'Do we have an audio?'

'Negative. Sims was just passing that room when somebody came out and shut the door behind them.'

'Get a make on the little one. Anybody your Mahoney shuts up and listens to is somebody the council's gonna want bad.'

When it was over, nearly eight hundred of the nearly one thousand conspirators and their aides present for the kriegsspiel had been positively identified. Among them – Mahoney and Sten.

And when it was over, Sims's body was cremated. Her fiche vanished from Imperial records. Five generations of Imperial service ended – in night and fog.

That was the cover name for the round-up operation: Nightfog. Target lists were made and sent out. They were to be implemented not only by Mercury and Mantis operatives, but by the council's private armies as well.

Some of the conspirators were arrested and tried publicly. Some of them, prodded by threats to their families, or more often just drug-programmed, confessed that the Honjo had indeed organized the conspiracy, through an outlaw general named Mahoney. Then they were permitted to die.

Others just vanished.

Innocent or guilty, the Imperial Officer Corps was shattered – shattered in self-image, shattered in fear, shattered in paranoia. All of them knew that Nightfog II . . . or III . . . or? could happen.

There were eight hundred names from Sims's brainscan, and eight hundred names on the original list.

Later estimates varied, but at least seven thousand beings were killed.

People had personal enemies. Each of the privy councillors, except Kyes, cleared up some of their own problems as the list was passed around – and as it grew.

When the death-lists arrived on the desks of the Security people chosen to make the pickups, it was simple for the officer or thug in charge to make an addition. Or two. Or six.

There were, of course, mistakes.

A writer of children's fiche named White, much loved and respected, was unfortunate to live in the same suburb as a retired major general named Whytte. The writer's house was broken into in the middle of the night. The writer was dragged to the center of his living room and shot. The writer's wife tried to stop the killers. She was shot, as well.

When the mistake was revealed, the head of the murder unit, a Mercury Corps operative named Clein, thought the matter an excellent joke.

Chapter Fourteen

Alex saw the beast raise its head from the trencher of meat and fix bloodshot eyes on Sten. The huge brows beetled into a murderous frown. The being wiped the gore from its lips with the long brush-tail beard and grimaced at some foul thought, exposing thick, yellow teeth.

The creature lumbered to its feet, harness creaking under the weight of many weapons. It came forward three steps, knobbed, hairy paws brushing briefly on the floor. It was a meter wide from the neck down and weighed in at a fearful 130 kilograms. Although only 150 centimeters high, it was massive power in a smallish package. Muscle cells were easily as dense as Kilgour's, despite his heavy-worlder's genes. Its spine was curved, and its great trunk was supported on legs like bowed tree trunks.

The being raised itself to its full height, brandishing an enormous stregghorn. His shout filled the big hall like a large explosion in a small cylinder at depth.

'By my mother's beard!' it bellowed at Sten. 'This is unbearable.'

The being waddled to the table and loomed over Sten. Drunken tears welled out of the gaping holes the Bhor called eyes. Blubbering like a hairy infant, Otho collapsed next to Sten, his breath laced with enough stregg to peel the hide off a deep-space freighter.

'I love you like a brother,' Otho wept.

The Bhor chieftain turned to his feasting subjects. He gestured with his stregghorn, spilling a pool that could drown a small human.

'We all love you like a brother!' he roared. 'Tell him, brothers and sisters. Are we not Bhor? Do we hide honest feelings?'

'No!' came the shout from the more than a hundred assembled warriors.

'Swear it, brothers and sisters.' Otho shouted the order. 'By our fathers' frozen buttocks – we love you Sten!'

'By our fathers' frozen buttocks . . .' came the return shout, amplified by a more than a hundred Bhor maws. Otho flung himself on Sten and sobbed.

Alex shuddered. He did not envy his friend's popularity with these beings.

Across the great hall there were a few human warriors sprinkled among the Bhor. Of all the admiring eyes watching Sten – the returning hero – one pair viewed him with special interest. Her name was Cind. She was very, very young and very, very lovely. It was that special kind of beauty that grabbed at the heart through the loins. Cind was also one of the most highly regarded practitioners of that supremely lethal art – sniping.

Her own personal weapon had started life as an already-exotic Imperial-issue sniper weapon. It fired the normal Imperial AM2-charged, Imperium-shielded round, but instead of using a laser as propellant it used a linear accelerator. A variable power automatic-estimate scope gave the range to target. The scope could then be adjusted laterally on its mount – in the event the nominated target was sheltered behind something. It was a weapon that could shoot around corners. The rifle was never offered on the open market, not even to Imperially equipped allies. Cind had acquired hers on the black market and then further modified it for her own tastes – thumbhole stock built for her, increased barrel weight for better balance and less 'recoil' flip, double-set trigger, bipod, and so forth. As issued, the rifle was heavy. Cind's modifications made it still heavier. But despite her slender form, she could lug it hour after hour over the hilliest terrain with little effort. So much for the alleged inability of female humans to possess upper body strength without hormone implants.

The problem with the rifle was that its ammunition, like every other form of AM2, was currently very scarce. So Cind had trained on every other weapon she could find that could reach out and tweep someone long distance, from crossbows to projectile weapons.

Like most of the Bhor warriors she was cross-trained in all fighting skills. On a ship, for instance, she was a boarding specialist and had proved herself on several hairy engagements.

The young woman was a Jann, or perhaps more correctly an ex-Jann. The Jann had been a suicidally dedicated military order, the striking arm for the Talamein theocracy that had once ruled the Lupus Cluster with genocidal hands. The Wolf Worlds, as the systems now controlled by the Bhor were dubbed, had long been a minor thorn in the Eternal Emperor's side. It was minor only because the cluster was on the outskirts of the Empire. It was not so minor in the view of the Bhor. The warrior trading culture was quickly being killed off by the xenophobic Jann. They had become very nearly extinct.

But many years before Cind was born, an important discovery was made well beyond even the Wolf Worlds. It was new deposits of Imperium X, the substance used to shield, and therefore control, AM2. The people of Talamein and the killer Jannissars, however, lay at the crossroads where the shipments of Imperium X had to pass. Flailed on by their homicidal religion – the worship of Talamein – the Jann became a cork in an extremely important bottle.

Sten and Alex had headed a Mantis team sent in to pull the cork. In the bloody sorting out that followed, Sten eventually had taken advantage of a deep gulf in Talameic theo-politics, placing two competing pontiffs in bloody competition with one another. They both died. To Sten's dismay, the immediate result produced a third religious leader, as powerful as he was traitorous. He was also a handsome hero – the proverbial 'Man On A Horse' – that attracted the fanatics even more than his passion for Talamein. But suddenly that final leader decided he was Talamein himself, denounced his own faith as being sinfully misguided, called for peace, and then suicided. It was a lucky turn. Luck, in that case, was provided by a brutal assault on the prophet's stronghold, followed by Sten's carefully thought-out hand-to-hand reasoning with the man and an injection of a hypnotic into his veins, followed by The Programming, The Speech, and The Self-Martyrdom.

With the reluctant blessings of the Eternal Emperor, Otho and his Bhor subjects were raised up as the new rulers of the Wolf Worlds.

Most historians agreed that thus far it had worked out fairly well. The Bhor tended to let other beings think and do as they please, so long as they did not interfere with the operations of the Lupus Cluster, or trigger new quarrels.

Oddly, the Faith of Talamein collapsed along with its power. Despite ancient roots, it had become so repressive that the surviving believers were delighted that their noses were no longer pressed against the rough stone wheel of Talamein. It helped that the sight of the two competing pontiffs had become so ridiculous that even peasants tilling distant soil had become embarrassed.

The Jannisars themselves became crusaders without a cross,

ultimate ronin. They found other, peaceful lives but remained both ashamed and proud of their heritage.

Cind had grown up in such a household. The stories of the past were told to her, privately, around the family hearth with the old weapons hanging above it, or sometimes loudly at family/clan reunions held in very secret places.

Cind had grown up as a throwback – she was one of the former Jann who had the old love of battle. Since childhood she had disdained the ordinary playthings of other young Jann. Toy weapons were her favorite. Vidbooks on great battles and heroic deeds stirred her more than any fairy tales. So it was only natural that when she came of age she volunteered for the Bhor military. Her culture's old enemies – but the only game in town.

Her instinctual ability with the rifle quickly won her favor among the Bhor. Now, whenever there was conflict requiring arms, Cind was among the first to volunteer for action and also among the first to be accepted. Her youth was no handicap at all. In fact, it was most probably a plus, since the Bhor loved a fight almost more than stregg, that powerful and evil potion Sten had first become addicted to and then passed on to the Eternal Emperor. The Bhor encouraged instincts like Cind's in their own young and boasted of them in their huge feasts and drinking bouts.

As Otho drunkenly blubbered and patted his clearly embarrassed friend, Cind gazed with adoring eyes at the great Sten. This was the being whose exploits were boasted of more than any other in the Bhor drinking halls. No Bhor who had been even vaguely involved in those exploits could walk down a public byway without drawing admiring looks and comments. Over and over again the tale was told, and each time Sten and Alex shone in greater and greater glory. Especially Sten. He was younger than she imagined. She had been expecting a hoary graybeard filled with stiff dignity. She also found him most handsome.

Otho had drawn away and was conversing with Alex Kilgour. Cind saw Sten look absently around the room. She thought she had never seen a being so lonely. Her heart went out to all the imagined horrors the great Sten must conceal in his breast. She ached to coax them out, to comfort him. Sten's eyes swept over her . . . then . . . Ohmigod . . . He's looking back! At me! She grew uncomfortably warm, and then his eyes moved on. Oh, dear, oh, me, if only they had lingered. Would he see her worth? Understand her passion for her only true friend – the long-range rifle? Of course he would. A great warrior like Sten would immediately know her feelings about such matters. Cind determined that somehow, some way, they would meet.

She turned back to her meal, unaware of how nasty an affliction youth could be.

Alex drained the horn and let Otho refill it. The Bhor chieftain had pulled him aside and was drunkenly quizzing him. Sten's manner was greatly troubling him, Otho said. His mood was so dark, and Otho was at a loss to dispel it. He told Alex he had only gotten a thin smile when he had reminded Sten of their first meetings, back when the Bhor had been handing out Jann captives to all the ships and bloodily executing them in the ancient, joyful Bhor rite of the blessing.

'Remember that clottin' Jann's face as we stuffed him in the lock?' Otho said. Alex remembered. 'By my mother's gnarly beard, was that a funny sight. He was so scared his face was screwed up like we'd given his nose a dozen twirls.

'It was only two or three – and we'd hardly tortured him at all. Then we fired him out to ice up his guts and drank his soul to hell! Ah, those were the days.'

He clapped Alex on the back with a paw like a half-ton club. Even Kilgour was ruffed a mite by that. 'Aye,' was all he said. But before Otho could think that he shared Sten's glum disease, Alex remembered to roar with laughter at the thought of those gory times.

'What's wrong with our Sten?' Otho asked. 'There's no fire to him. Point out the being who has wronged our brother and I vow we will slay him now!'

Alex would have been delighted if the matter were so simple and Sten's dilemma could be cured with an old-fashioned Bhor Blessing. Right now, the thought of guts in space was far more cheery than any Sten had entertained since they had fled Earth.

Kilgour had run like the gates of hell had been unlocked and all the demons in it were at his heels. This was not much of an exaggeration. If Kilgour had not acted so quickly, not only would they have been pursued, but they would have been caught. Alex threw caution and the laws of physics to the wind. He jinked and jolted and veered the little tacship about until every joint pairing gave a tortured scream of pain. He used every trick he had been taught, and invented a few besides, to elude detection. Once clear, he transmitted a fast 'run like bleedin' drakh' to Mahoney, then shut down and made like a ghost.

Mahoney would have to take care of himself. Th' braw gr't clot's used t' it, Alex thought, although not unfondly. Kilgour *liked* Mahoney. Considered him a Gaelic kin. Alex hoped Ian made it intact. But there was little else he could do about it. If they all survived – and that was certainly an immeasurable 'if' – they had a fallback, emergency rendezvous point. Not Poppajoe's. They had agreed, if the mission went awry, not to test their luck twice there. But all that would be in the very doubtful future.

Kilgour assumed the wrath of the privy council would be so great that they would go to any and all means to bring them to bay. He was correct. So – where to hide? Where could they go to ground? There were two crucial elements the hiding place would require. The first was that no one was likely to look for them there. The second – and far more important – was that if anyone *did* look, he and Sten would not be betrayed.

It took awhile to figure it out. Sten was no help. How could he be? The lad was definitely bad off. Alex had strapped Sten to the medtable in the tacship's tiny treatment center and punched in a trauma program. He could hear the little hisses and tricklings of the medic bots at work. The sounds were far too busy for comfort. Eventually, as he dodged in and out of warp to throw off pursuit, they calmed a bit. He looked into the small cabin and saw Sten lying on the medtable. A little less pale. But still out – puir, wee lad.

The perfect hideout finally dawned on him. It involved calling in a debt, but there were few beings who owed Sten more. He punched in a course for the Lupus Cluster – and the Bhor.

They were a bit more than halfway through the journey when Sten was finally able to get about feebly. As company, he was clottin' awful. Stone face. Absolute silence. He conversed rarely, and then it was confined to a few grunts. At first Alex thought it because he was still on the road to recovery. Then the trauma-center computer informed him that no further treatment was necessary and gave Sten a clean bill of health. At last, Kilgour had to admit that his friend had suffered a far greater wound than the physical ones that had temporarily incapacitated him.

He hadn't the faintest idea how to deal with it, or even how to bring the topic up. So he gritted his teeth and left it alone.

Then one day Sten broached the matter himself. They were eating dinner – in total silence. Sten had lately formed the habit of staring straight into his dish while he ate. Never speaking, never looking to one side or another. And certainly never raising his eyes as he shoveled in food – more as if it were fuel than anything potentially flavorful. Kilgour watched him out of the corner of his eye.

Sten popped in a hunk of something. Chewed. Swallowed. Another hunk. Another mechanical repetition. Suddenly he stopped mid-chew. His face grew dark with inner fury. Then he spat the food out as if it were poison, slammed to his feet, and slammed just as loudly out. That time, Alex decided not to ignore the incident. He waited a few moments and then went to Sten's quarters. The door was open, and Sten was pacing back and forth, working off the angry energy. Alex waited at the door until he was noticed. Sten saw him, stopped, then shook his head.

'I'm sorry, Alex,' he said. Kilgour determined to bite the bullet and shake Sten up if he could.

'Y' aught t'be,' he said, forcing irritation in his tone. 'Y' clottin' aught t'be.'

He went on, reaming Sten's butt. Sten was told that once again, he had spoiled Alex's dinner. And he was such terrible company that he had driven Kilgour to thoughts of murder, or suicide. He had been behaving like an adolescent, Alex said, and it was time he grabbed himself by whatever pride he had left and started thinking about how he was affecting others, such as his longest and dearest friend, one Alex Kilgour.

Alex felt like drakh when he started – hitting the lad while he was down. But as he went on he warmed to the task. Sten *had* been getting to him, dammit! And he needed to be told. Then he saw that Sten was not listening – or was only partly listening. His head was down and his fists were clenched until the knuckles were white.

'I blew it!' Sten hissed. 'I clottin' blew it!'

'Aye,' Alex said. '*We* did thae, lad. I' spades. But y'ken, 'tis nae th' first time. Nae wil't be th' last.'

He had known all along what was haunting Sten. And with the opening he had just achieved, he tried to put it in perspective. He talked about all the other missions that had gone awry, the heaps of corpses left behind. They had suffered far worse things in the past, had witnessed and been partly responsible for far more dead. Alex knew he was pissing in the wind. But he had to try, just the same.

This was not just a sudden case of the guilts. It went back to Sten's reasons for abandoning his career more than six years before. The Tahn conflict certainly had been the costliest in terms of lives, as well as credits, of any war ever. Even on their own infinitely unimportant level, Sten and Alex had been forced to sacrifice so many lives that the foul taste of blood could never be washed out. Sten had grown sick of playing butcher – which was why he had not only resigned but had turned his back on the only family he knew. Living family, at least.

Some of that also had to do with Kilgour's own decision to quit. But he had Edinburgh, with family and ancestral friends.

This time, what made it harder for Sten to pay the butcher's price was his long self-imposed exile. There was no way, no matter how hard he had continued to train, that he would not blame the blow-up of the mission on his own rusty skills. Morally, if he felt that way, he should have turned down Mahoney's urging to lead the mission and helped Ian find someone else – someone fresher, someone not so tired and bitter.

Alex laid all of this out for Sten. He cajoled him. He cursed him. But nothing did any good. How could it? In the same position, Alex knew he would probably feel the same way.

The silence resumed. It lasted the remainder of the trip. And beyond.

Cind faithfully attended every one of the numerous feasts the Bohr had laid on to honor the returning heroes of the Jann war. She couldn't know that one of the key reasons for the banquets was Otho's clumsy attempts to break Sten out of his gloom and self-blame. But she couldn't help but notice how drawn Sten seemed, how oblivious he appeared to his surroundings, as if he were lost in some torment that no normal being could imagine. It seemed terribly tragic to her – and romantic.

She had finally gotten up the nerve to enter Sten's exalted presence. After considering how best to present herself, she had bought a costume so daring that she blushed even to think of it dangling in her locker. When she put it on and looked herself over in the mirror, she had almost pulled a sheet in front of herself so she would not have to look. Cind smoothed her already blemishless features with the most expensive and exotic makeup she could find, then dotted herself with a perfume guaranteed by the salesbeing to make strong human males fall at the feet of the woman wise enough to seek out this particular musk.

Cind dared the mirror again. She thought she looked like a clotting joygirl. If this is what men wanted, they could . . . she couldn't think of what they ought to do, but she was sure that with thought she would come up with something suitably nasty.

That even included Sten. Clot it! He would have to take her as she was.

She showered and scrubbed off all the offending stuff, then threw away the bitty thing that had disgraced her closet. Instead she chose one of her best uniforms. It was made of a fine leatherlike cloth and fit as if the beast who had borne the skin had been genetically bred just for Cind's fine young body. Her face was fresh and glowing from the scouring, her cheeks rosy from the bold thoughts she entertained.

Cind looked herself over in the mirror again. Oh, well. It would have to do.

She could not have picked more wisely. Sten had once had a lover from this part of the Empire. Her name was Sofia. Lady Sofia was a woman who entertained ambitions for the Imperial Court. Sten had helped her achieve them. A long time passed until he and Sofia had met again. It was at a Function, thrown by those greatest of all Imperial hosts, Marr and Senn.

The make-up and perfume Sofia had worn were not much different than Cind's – although vastly more expensive. And as for her dress – Sofia had worn nothing at all except some scattered glitter dust.

Faced with all that pulchritude, Sten had done what Sofia had least expected. He had run like the wind – into the arms of a homicide lieutenant, one Lisa Haines, a woman who was much more Sten's style.

Cind knew that this particular feast was going to be semi-formal – for the Bhor, at least. Preceding the usual gluttony, there would be a receiving line to greet the honored guests. She called in a heavy favor with a Bhor friend and found a place at the end of the line.

Otho paraded Kilgour and Sten into the hall and past the line. After his stint as chief of the Emperor's palace guard, there was little Sten did not know about such polite entries. He shook the hand of each being, looked them in the eye, and smiled. It was not a great smile, but it would have to do. Then he passed on to the next. Still, by the time he reached Cind he was anxious to hie himself to the safety of his table. He gave her a perfunctory handclasp, smiled, and started to move on.

Cind held the hand tight. It was just for a moment, but it was enough to make Sten hesitate, so as not to be rude. Then he found himself looking at an absolutely lovely young woman with a stunning uniformed figure, face as fresh as nature itself, eyes clear and innocent, and the sober serious look that only the young could adopt and still be charming.

Cind spoke in a rush, to get it all out before Sten moved on. 'Admiral Sten, I want you to know this is the greatest honor in my life. I've studied all the details of your actions during the Jann conflict, and I'd like you to know just how much of an inspiration you've been to me.'

Sten couldn't help himself. He had to laugh. But it was not the kind of laughter anyone – especially Cind – would take offense to, or think she was the object of.

'Thank you,' he said. He meant it. He started to move on. But Cind wasn't through.

'If ever you have a free moment,' she continued, 'I would very much appreciate if I could steal a little of it. There are so many questions I'd like to ask. Any warrior would. Although, I'm sure I'd bore you.'

Then she turned on her best smile. It was far from shabby. It was the kind that lit up whole rooms. One did not have to look too closely to realize there were all sorts of other invitations implied.

Sten would have had to be a dead man not to have understood that this young lady thought him very attractive and would be delighted to share his bunk. This time, he didn't laugh. Instead, he gave her his most sincere thanks and asked her name. Receiving it, he promised he would certainly remember her and would be delighted with her company – if he ever had the time. He gave her a sad little smile at this last bit. He meant it to say, of course, that he unfortunately never would. But, ah, well . . .

Only then did he move on. By the time he reached his table he had all but forgotten her – but not entirely. Although she was very young, Sten was not made of ice. He was flattered. His steps were just a bit lighter as he walked.

Cind watched him go. As far as she was concerned the meeting had gone perfectly. She was so pleased that she wanted to hug herself. She thought that close up, Sten was even more handsome. Mission accomplished. Invitation made. Invitation accepted.

Now it was up to her to make sure Sten had the time.

Sten tossed in his sleep, the thin covering knotted around his legs. He was back on Vulcan, a seventeen-year-old Delinq hiding from Baron Thoresen's Sociopatrolmen. Sten had taken refuge with Oron, the brainburned king of the Delinqs. He was weary from running so long and hard. Sten felt a slender body slide onto the soft mattress. It was Bet. Seventeen, as well. Naked and lovely. Eager for him. Lovely. So lovely.

He gasped out of the depths of the dream and found a willing, wriggling form in his arms. What the clot? Gently he pried the lady away. It certainly wasn't Bet! But she *was* lovely. The young lady moaned and grabbed for him again. For a moment, Sten almost went for it. He was still so far gone into the dream – which had proved to be very real – that he had almost no resistance.

Then he thought: who was this woman, anyway? Mmmm. More kissing and stuff. Then he remembered the sincere young lady in the receiving line. What was her . . . Cind. Ooohh boy! Careful, Admiral. This is not a lady one screwed and forgot. Once bedded, she would be his responsibility. Mmmmm. More stuff. More kissing. Yeah, but . . . But me no buts, you clot! This is serious business. How'd you like someone as nice as this on your conscience? Aww . . . Come on. What's a little . . .

Sten plucked Cind away again. She started to protest, but he gently covered her mouth with a hand. He tried to explain to her that this was definitely not a good idea. He was flattered and all, he said, and he was sure she was the most wonderful human-type female in the Empire, but he was in no position to start up any kind of a relationship. So, although he would regret this moment the rest of his life, would Cind please, please, get her clothes on and go?

It took awhile. But Cind did as she was told. When she was gone, Sten punched the drakh out of his pillow. He did not sleep again that night. For once, it had nothing to do with nightmares of a blown mission.

As for Cind, she was hurt, to be sure. She was also more in love than ever. By thinking so much of her that he was willing to forget her attentions, Sten was promoted from hero to godhood.

Cind consoled herself. There would be another time, with a far different result.

S'be't!

Kilgour was not present at the meeting, but he had arranged the entire thing. Otho was primed and almost sober.

The Bhor chieftain had asked Sten to go for a walk with him beside the little lake in a glen not far from his headquarters. It was no accident that the lake he chose was a memorial to the Bhor casualties suffered during the Jann war.

As they strolled around it, Otho pretended to seek Sten's advice on his plans for the Lupus Cluster. It was also no accident that all those plans assumed a future laden with a plenitude of AM2. Otho laid it on thick, just as Alex had coached him to. It was his own idea to mention also – in unsparing detail – the hardships the people of the Wolf Worlds had suffered during the reign of 'those privy council clots.' Not only had extreme deprivation been caused by the shortages of AM2 – which Otho assumed was intentional on the part of the council – but all business involving the mining and export of Imperium X had also ceased. He also did not exaggerate when he said he saw a time, a year or so away but no more, when the Lupus Cluster would cease to exist as an entity. One planetary system at a time would be lost, until all were as alone as they had been in the primitive days, when no being had known for certain that other living things existed beyond the upper atmosphere.

Sten listened and not just politely. All that Otho said was true. Although what he could do about it, he didn't know. At least he could listen. As they strolled around the small lake, he began to notice that its surface shimmered like no other he had seen before. He realized it was because the bottom consisted of an immense black slab, polished to mirror-brightness. There were little imperfections pocking the slab. At first he could not make them out. He thought it might be algae. Then he realized that they were names, the names of the Bhor dead, honored there by their brothers and sisters, mothers and fathers, lovers, and friends.

He found himself near tears when he understood the meaning of the lake. Otho pretended not to notice.

'I must speak to you frankly, my friend,' the Bhor chieftain said. Without waiting for a response, he went on. 'It is no secret that you are suffering. To tell you it is only the affliction of an old soldier will not help. This I understand. To say it is no more than the swollen joints a farmer earns from long years behind a plow is equally as useless.

'Another foolish comparison. This one involves a confession. You understand that not *all* Bhor choose the, ahem, Way of a Warrior.'

Sten raised an eyebrow but kept his thoughts to himself.

'I had an uncle – who was a tailor. Do not laugh! By my father's frozen buttocks, there has never been a living thing who loved to work with cloth like this uncle I am speaking to you about. Many years passed. Pleasurable and rewarding years. And then his hands began to ache. His knuckles grew great knots. So thick and painful he could barely manipulate them. You understand what a tragedy this was to my uncle?'

Sten nodded. He did.

'Did he give up? Did he cease the toil that gave him so much pleasure? Or did he damn the eyes of the streggan ghost that afflicted him and drink until he could feel no more pain? And then – and only then – continue his work?'

Sten said he assumed the latter. He believed stregg, named for the ancient nemesis of the Bhor, to be a powerful reliever of pain.

'Then you would be wrong!' Otho bellowed. 'He did not. He gave up. He died a bitter and broken being. And this is the shame of my family, which I swear to you I have told no other. Except, perhaps, when I was drunk. But, I swear, I have never revealed it sober. Never!'

Sten was beginning to feel a little stupid. His friends were treating him as if he were some helpless child. Well, perhaps they were right. Maybe he did need a swift, hard kick. Poor Otho was trying so hard.

'What is it you want?' Otho shot at him.

'What?'

'What do you want? These . . . things, who rule in the place of the Emperor. You owe them a debt. Are they not your enemy? Do they not deserve your hate? Why do you treat them so shabbily? Make them happy. Kill them!'

'I tried,' Sten said weakly.

'So try again. Don't be my uncle with the cloth.'

Sten wanted to say that killing them would satisfy nothing. At least not in himself. But he didn't know how to explain it to his rude, rough friend.

'You want more than death? Is that it?' his rude, rough friend asked.

Sten thought about it. The deeper his thoughts swam, the angrier he became.

'They are assassins,' he hissed. 'Worse than that. When they killed the Emperor, they might as well have killed us all. Soon we'll all be living like animals. Sitting in front of caves. Knocking rocks together to get a bit of fire.'

'Good. You are mad,' Otho boomed. 'Now think about how to get even.'

'Getting even isn't what I want,' Sten said.

'By my mother's beard. We're back to that again. What do you want? Say it. Then we'll board my ships and see all their souls burning in hell.'

'I want . . . justice,' Sten finally said. 'Dammit. I want every being in the Empire to know the council's crime. Their hands are bloody. Justice, dammit. Justice!'

'I don't believe in justice, myself,' Otho said gently. 'No true Bhor does. It is a fairy story created by other, weaker species who look for higher truths because their own lot is so miserable.

'But I am a tolerant being. If justice is your meat, load up my plate, my friend. We both shall eat.

'Now. Decide. What form do you wish this justice to take? And by my father's frozen buttocks, if you retreat to that pool of emotional muck again, I shall personally remove your limbs. One by one.'

Sten didn't need that kind of coaxing. It suddenly came to him exactly what kind of justice would do.

'Load the ships, my friend,' Sten said.

Otho bellowed with delight. 'By my mother's great, gnarly beard, there's a Blessing upon us. We'll drink all their souls to hell!'

Chapter Fifteen

The computer was a bureaucrat's dream. As a pure storage center, it had few equals on the civilian market. But the key to its beauty was its method of retrieval.

The R&D team leader had come to Kyes with the design proposal ten years before. Kyes had spent four months with the group, firing every thinkable objection and whole flurries of 'supposes' to test the theoretical limits. He had not found one hole that could not be plugged with a few symbols added to the design equation.

He had ordered the project launched. It was so costly that in another era Kyes would have automatically sought financial partners to spread the risk. Certainly he had briefly toyed with the idea. But the computer – if it could be brought online – would reap such enormous profits that he had dismissed the thought.

More important than the profits was the potential influence.

The computer was a one-of-a-kind device, with patents so basic that no other corporate being could even contemplate a copy without risking loss of fortune, family, reputation, and well-being to Kyes's battalions of attorneys. From the moment it was first proposed, he knew it would replace every system used by every government in the Empire. And the terms of its sale would be set by him and him alone.

Once installed, his influence would grow as quickly as the newly created wealth. After all, only one firm – his – would be permitted to perform maintenance and periodic upgrading. In short, mess with Kyes and your bureaucracy would collapse. The state itself would quickly follow.

Almost every action of any social being created a record. The first problem was what to do with that record so that others could view it. If there was only one, no problem. It could be put under a rock, the spot marked, and someone with directions could retrieve it at his leisure. But records bred more quickly than cockroaches. Hunter-gatherers rapidly ran out of space on cave walls; scribes filled libraries with parchment; clerks jammed filing cabinets until the drawers warped; and even at the height of the Empire, it was possible for data to swamp the biggest computers.

But that was no longer so severe a problem. More banks or link-ups could always be added. Modern systems had gone so far beyond light optics that speed was also no encumbrance.

There was one threshold, however, that no one had ever broken through: how to find one small byte of information hidden in such a great mass. The great library of legend at Alexandria reputedly employed several hundred clerks to search the shelves for the scrolls their scholarly clients requested. Days and weeks might pass before a certain scroll was located. That did not please the scholars, who were usually visiting on a beggar's budget. Their many bitter complaints survived the fire that destroyed the library. And that was in the long time past, when there was not much to know.

In Sten's time, the problem had grown to proportions that would stagger a theoretical mathematician contemplating the navel of the Universe.

Consider this small example: A much-maligned commissary sergeant has been ordered to improve the fare at the enlisted being's club. Morale is sadly sagging to the point that the commander herself is under the scrutiny of *her* superiors. Suggestions are made – many, many suggestions – that *will* be carried out. One of the suggestions concerns narcobeer. But not any old narcobeer. The commander recalls one brand – whose name she disremembers

– that she shared with the troops on some long-forgotten battle-ground a century or more ago.

That is the only hint. Nothing more.

The commissary sergeant swings into action. Fires up his trusty computer. And the computer is asked to find that clottin' beer. The list he receives will almost certainly include the brand favored by his commander. But it just as certainly will be buried in a million or more possibilities, with no means of narrowing the search – short of ordering every one and spending several lifetimes letting the commander taste-test each one. Although enjoyable, this solution has obvious flaws.

With Kyes's computer it would be no trouble at all. Because it had been designed to understand that living minds had definite limits. The computer worked in twisted paths and big and little leaps of logic. Any simple explanation of this computer would be in serious error.

However, it was basically taught to think of itself as a chess master, engaged in a game with a talented inferior. The chess master knows she can conceive of many moves, with any number of combinations, well ahead of her opponent. But, in a single game, the amateur is quite likely to win. His limited ability may become a plus under such circumstances. The chess master might as well roll dice, trying to figure out which stupid ploy the dimwit has in mind.

Kyes's brainchild would summon the commander – or at least call up the commander's records. A series of questions would be asked: a short biography, a few details of that long-ago drinking session, for example, and certainly a medical examination to deter-mine the reaction of the being's tastebuds. Voila! The narcobeer would be located and morale boosted. The sergeant and commander would return to good graces. Happy ending through better electronic living.

When Kyes introduced Sr. Lagguth, the chief of the AM2 commis-sion, to his baby, the being instantly fell in love. With such a machine, he could track the path of an errant electron on a flight through a star storm.

The next bit of information, however, made him fall just as quickly out of love.

'Forget the AM2,' Kyes said. 'It's not important.'

Lagguth stuttered that that was the task set for him by the privy council – that the whole future of the Empire rested on locating the Eternal Emperor's golden AM2 fleece. Even when the raid on the Honjo was completed, the resulting AM2 bonus would only stave off the inevitable for another seven months at most – not counting the terrible cost in fuel the Empire was expending to finish the theft.

'Haven't you learned your lesson, yet?' Kyes said. 'The Emperor's secret died with him. We're never going to find it. At least, not the way we've been going about it.'

Then he told Lagguth what he had mind.

Sr. Lagguth violently protested. He did not say he thought Kyes was mad – although that certainly might have been hinted at. But he did say he would immediately have to report the matter to the rest of the council, and he would have to get their permission to abandon his search and to take up the new one.

Kyes did not explode, or threaten, or call the being all kinds of a fool. Instead, he rang for a clerk, and in a moment or two she appeared, wheeling in a great stack of readouts on a cart. The readouts were copies of the report Lagguth had delivered not too long before to the privy council, the one in which he said that the AM2 would be located within thirteen months.

Kyes strolled about the room while Lagguth stared at the report, considering his many sins.

'Would you like to change your conclusions in that report?' Kyes asked finally.

Lagguth remained silent.

'I had a team of my own people go over it. They found it . . . interesting,' Kyes added.

Lagguth's mouth gaped – he wanted to speak – then snapped shut again. What could he say? Every page of the report was fiction. He might as well have said two months, or six months, or – never.

'Shall we try it my way?' Kyes purred.

The logic was impeccable. Sr. Lagguth was convinced.

The old woman was a delight. She wore her gray hair long and tumbling down to her waist. It glowed with health. She had a high-pitched giggle that charmed Kyes, especially since she let it ring out at his weakest jests. Even then, there was no falseness in it. Despite her age, which the investigators estimated at 155, her figure was good and she filled her orange robes in a pleasing manner. From what he knew about such things – if he had been human, Kyes assumed he would have found her still attractive. Her name was Zoran. She was the elected leader of the Cult Of Eternal Emperor, insofar as they had real leadership.

Zoran and her group had been shadowed by his investigators for some time. They were a puzzling lot. Most of them lived ordinary lives and were employed at ordinary jobs. During that time they dressed and mostly behaved like everyone else. The only main difference was their attitude. They were absolutely cheerful beings. There seemed to be no setbacks or disappointments that disturbed them. His chief detective swore that if the immediate demise of Prime World were announced, they would giggle wildly and then go on about their duties. They would probably only add a 'Last chance for the word' when they donned their robes, kicked off their shoes, and wandered the streets preaching their peculiar beliefs.

Zoran explained away some of the misconceptions about their thinking to Kyes, giggling all the while.

'Oh, we *certainly* don't think of the Eternal Emperor as a god.' Giggle. 'Or, at least a god, per se.' More giggling. 'He's more like an emissar— You know—' giggle '—a representative of the Holy Spheres.'

Kyes wanted to know what a Holy Sphere might be.

'Very good question,' she said. 'They're, well, round, I suppose.' Giggle. 'And holy'. Thirty seconds of sustained giggling. 'Actually, it's just concept. One you accept, or don't. If you accept it – you can see it. In your mind. But, if you don't—' Massive giggling. '. . . well, of course you won't see it at all.'

Kyes laughed himself – the first real laughter from him in ages. 'I suppose I'm one of the blind,' he said.

'Oh, no. Not at all. At least, not completely,' Zoran said. 'Otherwise I wouldn't be here talking to you.'

Kyes puzzled at that. How could she be so trusting? His motives were far from pure. In a mad moment – the giggling got to a being after a while – he almost confessed this. But he didn't.

'Of course, there might be some who would say that you were thinking of using us,' the old woman said. This time, when the giggle came, Kyes jumped. 'But how could you? All I have is this poor vessel.' She dramatically drew her hands down her robes, outlining her body. 'And it is filled with the joy of the Holy Spheres.' Small giggle. 'Use us if you wish.' Bigger giggle. 'There's more than enough joy for everyone.'

'But wouldn't the joy be even greater,' Kyes answered, trying to avoid being *too* smooth, 'if more beings believed as you?'

That time, there was no giggle from Zoran. She studied him, her eyes sharp and clear. Kyes could feel himself being measured.

'You were correct in your assumption that my feelings are not far apart from yours,' he continued. 'I know nothing about Holy Spheres. Or gods. Or godly representatives. But I do believe one thing. Very firmly. And that is the Eternal Emperor is still with us.'

Zoran was silent. Then, she said quickly, 'Why is it necessary for you to believe this?'

Kyes did not answer – at least not directly. He was starting to come up to speed with the woman.

'You've stopped laughing,' was all he said.

'What do you have in mind to help others hear our thoughts?' the old woman asked. 'Money?' Kyes said there would be money for her order. 'Temporal support?' Kyes said that as a member of the privy council, his support could hardly be thought of as anything else.

'What do you want in return, then?' she asked.

'Only what you would give me, even without my support,' Kyes said. 'I want information. I'd like to be notified when any of your members – no matter where they reside in the Empire – report a sighting of the Emperor.'

'You're right,' Zoran said. 'None of us would withhold that kind of information. It's what we're trying to convince others of, isn't it?'

It wasn't necessary for Kyes to answer.

'You'll be deluged,' she said after a while. 'Our religion – if it can be called that – tends to attract many individuals with, shall we say, frantic minds.'

'I'm aware of that,' Kyes said.

Zoran stared at him for a long time. Then she let loose with one of her wild, ringing giggles.

The bargain was set.

Kyes continued to extend his net across the dark waters. As he did so, he could not help but keep peering into the murk hoping to catch sight of the great, silver shadow of the Eternal Emperor lurking in the depths. The exercise was pointless and agonizing. He was very much like a starving being who had bought a lottery ticket. The hope the action generated seemed harmless enough. At least there was something to dream about for a while. But the hope was just a thin coating on a tragic pill.

But Kyes was an old master of self-control. He recognized the glooming for what it was and continued apace. As his colleagues scrambled frantically about with their bloodletting at home and in the Honjo worlds, he put all of his marks into secret play.

Now there was only one mark left, one key being to suborn. Potentially, the most difficult and dangerous of all: Colonel Poyndex, the chief of Mercury Corps. But when he finally determined what the cost would be, Kyes did not hesitate for a moment.

The colonel was as chilling in person as he had been on the screen when the assassination plot had been announced. Poyndex listened intently to every word Kyes had to say. He never blinked or smiled or even shifted in his seat once he had settled.

Kyes carefully skated around his own beliefs and merely restated the logic. The Emperor had reportedly disappeared – he didn't say 'died' – before. And he had always returned. Also, the supply of AM2 always followed the same course: diminished during the alleged absence, plentiful when he came back. That part could be charted – and had been by Lagguth's staff and Kyes's computer. The great historical shifts in the AM2 supply appeared to match the times when rumor and myth held that the Emperor was gone.

Finally, Kyes was done. He eased back in his seat, keeping his own expression as blank as the spy master's.

'I wondered why you met with that Zoran woman,' Poyndex said. 'Now it makes sense. It didn't when my operatives first reported it.'

Kyes clawed back his instinct to gape, to be shocked that Poyndex apparently routinely shadowed any member of the ruling council. He had been advised that such comments were one of the colonel's favorite ploys – to win the upper hand with a seemingly casual verbal blow.

'I thought you might be puzzled,' Kyes shot back. 'That's why I thought we should talk.'

He was hinting that the shadowers had shadows of their own, operating at his behest. It was a lie, but a good one. Poyndex allowed an appreciative nod.

'Regretfully . . .' Poyndex deliberately let this trail. 'I don't see how I can help. My department's resources . . .' Again, a deliberate trailing off to indicate lack of same. 'Also, I fear I would be exceeding my authority.'

It was not necessary for Poyndex to detail his agency's awesome responsibilities and the additional burdens it now bore as a result of such things as the disaster in predicting the Honjo as a relatively soft target.

Lovett would have bottom-lined Poyndex's statement immediately. The deal – if there was to be one – would begin with increased resources and more authority. Kyes was no slower. He had come prepared to make one offer and one alone. He believed the price was set so high, that no one – especially a spy master – could resist.

'My colleagues and I have been considering a matter for some time,' Kyes said. 'All of us are concerned that certain views – important views – never come to our attention. In short, we feel a lack of depth on the privy council.'

Poyndex raised an eyebrow. The first show of emotion! Especially since the spy master had no idea where Kyes was going. He saw the eyebrow forced into place – a bit irritably, like a cat angrily coaxing back an unruly tuft of fur. Kyes was pleased. Poyndex could be handled. No trouble at all.

'What would you say,' Kyes said, 'if I proposed that you join us? As the sixth member of the privy council?'

Kyes was absolutely delighted when the spy master gaped like a freshly landed fish!

Chapter Sixteen

Sr. Ecu hovered at the edge of the lake. The sun was warm, and the rising moist air from the Bhor memorial allowed him to float without effort: a tic of a winglet for steadiness; a flick of the tip of the three-meter tail to keep his eyes on the small being walking toward him across the grass.

In most other circumstances, the Manabi would be enjoying this moment. The warm air and sun were pleasurable, the setting perfect. He appreciated – as only the Manabi could – the contrast of his dark body, with its red-tipped wings and pure white sensing whiskers, against the mirroring lake with its small, rocky beach, and the deep blue-green of the healthy lawn.

He had reluctantly agreed to the meeting. To him, further involvement with any of the surviving conspirators was not only pointless – witness Fleet Marshal Mahoney's dismal failure – but extremely dangerous. Ignoring the invitation, however, might create equal, or greater, peril.

One stray word from the conspirators – deliberate, or otherwise – would implicate the Manabi no matter how tentative their previous role. It took no imagination to know what form the privy council's reaction would take. Imagination was one thing the Manabi were more than blessed – or cursed – with.

Sten did his best to appear casual as he approached. He wanted no hint of self-doubt, although he had a clot of a lot of it. He had already invested a week of preliminary discussions with Sr. Ecu. Diplomacy was a maddening art. Still, he threw everything he had been taught and learned into the effort. There were the circlings to begin with, as each being measured, tested, and got to know the other. Then there was a host of initial discussions – never once hitting, or even coming near, the point.

It did not help his confidence to know he was dealing with the most skilled diplomat from a race of ethereal beings who were individual experts before they had left their childhood behind along with their milk sting.

He had consulted heavily with Kilgour and Mahoney well before Sr. Ecu's arrival. Even now, his two friends were ablaze with the effort of launching the main body of his plan. Weapons, ammunition, fuel, and supplies were being gathered. The Bhor were already rehearsing, and Otho's patience was wearing thin. When Sten had said 'load the ships,' he was being symbolic. By the time he explained that to the literal-minded Bhor chieftain, Otho was ready to blast off with a ragged crew aboard an iffy warship. Suicide was *not* painless, Sten kept telling Otho. Eventually, he made his point.

Sten was vastly relieved when he and Kilgour had finally reached Mahoney. After seventy-five years as chief of Mercury Corps, Ian had found little difficulty in staying many steps ahead of his pursuers.

Mahoney had just kept moving. He would go to ground for a few days in a well-chosen hidey-hole, then pop up to see what was going on about him, moving on again before suspicions were aroused. By the time Sten and Alex had contacted him through Jon Wild, their old smuggler friend, he had already hidden in a dozen wildly disparate spots, using an equal number of identities. The faster and more often one moved, Ian always said, the less perfection was required when it came to forged paperwork. The role was the thing, he said. The whole thing. That, and being able to think on one's feet and shed the role like old, itchy skin.

Sten's former commander had instantly seen the value in his plan, and they had put it into motion. The key was the Manabi and their spotless reputations for honesty. Without their agreement, the plan had far less of a chance. However, considering his recent, explosive failure, Mahoney urged Sten to take point in the discussions. He would come in later, if needed. Sten agreed. But he was far from sure. One thing was certain, however: whatever the outcome, Sten was determined to proceed. Still, he wanted Sr. Ecu. He wanted him bad.

Today was the day. It was all or nothing. His goal was simple and did not require total victory. He only had to drive in a big enough wedge to get a glimpse of sunlight.

Sten could only see one way to go about his task. He had to hard-ass the Manabi. But first, as his father used to say, he had to get Sr. Ecu's attention. In this case, however, his father's suggested club would not do.

He waved a greeting when he was a few meters away, then knelt on the grass. He placed a small black cube on the ground, gently pinched the sides, and stepped back. The cube began to unfold. As it did so, Sten sensed a slight flutter in the air and Sr. Ecu floated closer. He could also sense the being's curiosity. Sten did not turn. Instead, he kept his rapt attention on the unfolding cube. It was show time, folks.

The cube became a base for a little holographic display: a moving, almost-living art form that Sten had wiled away the time with most of his life. The one he had picked as a gift for the Manabi diplomat was not all that elaborate. Sten had built replicas of entire ancient mills and factories and towns, all with active workers and residents going about their programmed daily lives. This hologram was an off-the-shelf kit that took him no more than six hours to complete. Of course, by now he was highly skilled at his hobby.

But it was not the difficulty of a display that necessarily attracted him. Sometimes it was just nice to look at, or it was oddly moving, or it had something to say. The gift for Sr. Ecu had a little of all of these.

The cube was gone, and in its place was a meadow converted into some sort of arena surrounded by makeshift wooden bleachers, which were filled with a cheering crowd of humans. Their costumes were early twentieth-century Earth, and if one listened extra closely, so were their comments. Hawkers moved in and out of the crowd, selling all kinds of odd foods and trinkets. Gangs of tiny wild boys ran about, getting into minor mischief.

After all that sank in, the observer started looking at the strange little object in the center.

Suddenly the object shuddered and belched a miniburst of smoke. Followed by a sharp *kaaaklacka*. Sten could feel the Manabi move in even closer. Sensing whiskers brushed his shoulders as Sr. Ecu jockeyed for a better view. At the sound, the gangs of wild boys abandoned mischief and ran for the fence that enclosed the field.

Another *kaaaklacka*, and it became a bit more obvious. What they were both looking at was an ancient flying machine. Twin wings joined by struts. Stubby. A strong little propeller in front. A tiny pilot was in the cockpit. An equally small coveralled ground-crew member was turning the prop. He leapt away as the explosive sound came again. Except this time the prop kept turning, stuttering at first, with small pops of engine smoke – warranted by the model manufacturer to smell like castor oil. Then the engine sounds smoothed out, the crewman was kicking away the blocks at the wheels, and the little plane was moving down the field.

A sudden roar, and it surged forward. There was no way it had enough runway to clear the stadium. Sten could feel the tension in the winged being by his side. The pilot hauled his stick back, and the plane abruptly rose into the air. The crowd gasped. Sten thought he could hear something similar beside him.

Stick around, Sr. Ecu, he thought. You ain't seen nothin' yet.

The biplane pilot opened his act with a daredevil series of turns and flips and barrel rolls.

'That's not possible for such a machine,' Sten heard Sr. Ecu whisper. He said nothing in return.

Then the plane went into a long dive – straight for the ground. The crowd shrieked in terror. Sr. Ecu, who knew all about gravity, could not help but flip a winglet in reaction. It jolted his body upward a few centimeters. Still the biplane came on and on. At the last instant, when Sr. Ecu could no longer stand the suspense, the pilot pulled away – almost brushing the ground and holographic disaster. The crowd shouted in relief, then rose for loud applause.

'Remarkable,' Sten's companion muttered.

The pilot saluted his admirers with another long series of rolls and dives and turns. Then he steadied out, and the engine sound shifted. The plane arced gracefully through the sky. White smoke streamed out behind. Gradually, that trail of smoke made the pattern clear.

Skywriting!

'What's he saying?' Sr. Ecu had become Sten's emotional captive – at least through the end of the show. Again, Sten said nothing.

Finally, the pilot was done. The smoke lettering hung over the field like a high-flying banner. And this is what it said:

Anyone Can Fly
At . . . . . .
THE AIR CIRCUS

Sten stepped quickly forward and pinched the sides of the display; it became a small black cube again. He picked it up and offered it to Sr. Ecu. 'What do you think?'

'Did they really do that?' Sr. Ecu asked. He did not wait for the answer. It was obvious. 'You know, I've never really appreciated before what it was like to be permanently grounded by an accident of genes. My God, how desperately they wanted to fly.'

'Beings will risk a great deal,' Sten said, 'for a little freedom.'

There was a long silence from the Manabi. A flip of a wing took Sr. Ecu into a long, slow glide over the lake. Sten knew he was pondering the names on the slate bottom, the names of the permanently grounded Bhor. Another flip, and he came gliding back.

'Where did you get it?' the Manabi asked.

'I made it,' Sten said. 'Just a kit, really. But it was fun.'

'When?'

'Last night.'

'Then you really did make it for me.' It was a statement of realization, not a question.

'Yes.'

The Manabi remained quite still.

'Ah . . .' he said at last. 'Now we begin . . . A very good opening, Admiral.'

'Thanks. And you're right. Now, we begin. But first, I have a little preamble. I had it all worked out in the best diplomatic form I could imagine, and then I thought, to hell with it! I should just speak my mind. Say how it is.'

'Go on.'

'There's a lot of doublethink between us. After a week I'm still trying to figure out how to put my case to you. And you're still trying to figure the best way to say no and be done with me. In other words, we're both grounded. Neither of us can get any forward motion, much less clear the stadium.'

'Fairly accurate.'

'The thing is,' Sten said, 'you're more earthbound than I.'

The Manabi stirred, surprised.

Sten filled in a few more blanks. 'You see, from my point of view, you're still stuck with a previous action. One you now think was not that wise. Trouble being, you can't take it back. Not completely. You have to wonder if we have blackmail in mind. Are we going to hold the club of betrayal over you to force your continued support?'

'Well? Are you?'

Sten let Sr. Ecu's anxious question hang for a while.

'No. We're not,' he said finally, firmly – a promise.

'You can speak for everyone?'

'Yes.'

'Why are you being so . . . magnanimous? Or is it temporary?'

'If we fail, everyone is in the same drakh. That includes the supporters of the privy council. When this is over, if there are any pieces to pick up it might make me rest easier in my grave to think a few Manabi might be about to help. And, no. The decision isn't temporary. For the same reason.

'But my real reason is loyalty. You once left your neutral corner to support the Emperor. This is why you even spoke to Mahoney when he came to you. Out of that same loyalty. Actually, logic is a better word for it just now. The same logic that once brought you to the Emperor's side – meaning prog zero for any kind of future without him – allowed you to be swayed by Ian. Isn't that so?'

'Again . . . yes.'

'Now you've seen Mahoney's plan fail. Dismally. Meanwhile, all over the Empire beings are being rounded up for the brainscan – and then the slaughterhouse. No wonder you're shy of us. I would be, too.'

'You make a better argument for my case than yours,' Sr. Ecu said. 'In my sphere, this means there's a great deal more to come.'

'You got it,' Sten said. 'To begin with, what happened was my fault. Not Mahoney's. He was in command – but I was there, in person, and I sure as clot didn't pull out in time. I crashed that plane, not Mahoney.'

'Admirable that you should shoulder the blame, but it only underscores my uncertainty – in even meeting with you. Do you have some – what is the phrase your kind favors – ace up your sleeve?'

'Maybe. Maybe not. Right now, what I *do* have is your attention. Let me tell you what is going to happen next. If you return to your fence sitting.

'We'll ignore it. But will the privy council? How long before their paranoia reaches out to the Manabi? Failing that, as this AM2 situation gets worse, they're going to be looking for repeated opportunities. The Honjo are only the first. There'll be others.

'How much AM2 does your cluster have in its storehouses? Enough to tempt them?'

It was not necessary for Sr. Ecu to answer. They both knew the Manabi had more than enough.

'And can you stop them? Do you have the means, much less the spirit? I'm not talking about bravery now. I'm speaking of pure meanness. Digging in like the Honjo. Willing to die for every square centimeter of turf. Can you do that? Are you willing?'

Again, there could be no answer but one. The Manabi were diplomats, not warriors.

'What do you propose?' Sr. Ecu asked. That did not mean he was going for it, only that he was willing to listen. But now that Sten had the Manabi going for the bait, he wanted to dangle it awhile. No way would he let this big flying fish off the hook.

'I only want you to watch and wait,' Sten said. 'I have something I need to accomplish. To show you *we* have the will and means. In return . . .'

'Yes.' Real abrupt. Sr. Ecu was going for it.

'In return . . . I want the opportunity to speak with you again. Or Mahoney, if that's how it ends up working best. Probably I'll be busy. So Ian it will be. If you agree. Will you at least do that?'

How could Sr. Ecu reject him? He did not. Instead he asked to see his gift again. He wanted to visit the air circus – where anyone could fly.

It worked out exactly as Sten had predicted. No sooner had Sr. Ecu returned home than he found a request for him to meet with a member of the privy council. Actually, it was no request at all. It was a summons.

The council members had discussed at length how to handle the Manabi. They as yet had no suspicion of them. But their purge, and especially the long, drawn-out invasion of Honjo sovereign territory, had produced howls all over the Empire. They badly needed to keep things glued together, at least for a while. To do that they needed the support of the Manabi. Badly.

There was some discussion of whom to send. Malperin was mostly favored, because she had the best diplomatic skills, at least as far a businessbeing could go. But even she saw drawbacks in that. If Sr. Ecu sensed the slightest opening, they were lost, she said. They had to act from strength. What they needed was a master of the bottom line.

They sent Lovett.

That meant there was no foreplay.

Lovett deliberately chose a small, shabby park for the meeting. There was little room for the graceful Manabi to maneuver, and he had barely cleared the fence when dirt and dust particles began clogging his delicate sensing whiskers. Lovett waited just long enough for Sr. Ecu to get really uncomfortable. The healthy black sheen of the Manabi's body turned to gray. The lovely red tinge shaded to a sickly orange. Then he let him have it.

'We want a statement from you,' he said. 'I've got a copy of what we have in mind with me. Okay it now. You can read it later. At your leisure.'

'How very thoughtful of you,' Sr. Ecu said. 'But first, perhaps I should know what exactly we're to agree to say. The topic . . . would be especially enlightening.'

'It's about the assassination business,' Lovett snapped. 'You know . . . you say you deplore it – etcetera, etcetera.'

'We certainly do deplore it,' Sr. Ecu agreed. 'It's the etcetera I'm worried about.'

'Oh . . . no big thing. It lists those responsible. Calls for their punishment. That sort of thing. Oh . . . and yeah. The Honjo. We figure any right-thinking being will back us on liberating all that AM2. Can't let wild types like that have all that fuel. Do what they please. When they please.

'I mean . . . it's legal as drakh. Our actions, that is. We license the AM2. Therefore we have the right to see that it's used properly.'

'I see,' the Manabi said. And he certainly meant it.

'So that spells it out. Got a problem with any of it?' Lovett spoke as belligerently as possible. He wanted there to be no mistake about what would happen if Sr. Ecu did object. So he continued just a touch longer. 'See, if you do, we've all got problems. My friends on the council have to be sure whose side everyone is on. Times are tough. Tough actions are required. You're either with us – or the Honjo. Okay?'

Sr. Ecu did not think it was okay. However, there was no way he was fool enough to say so. Instead, he explained that he had rushed to the meeting so quickly that he had failed to get any kind of blanket approval from his own government. This was a terrible oversight on his part, he apologized. But it was a necessary formality.

Otherwise, he could not legally speak for all the Manabi. And was this not what Lovett wanted?

'No. I want it settled. I want no loopholes some sneaky legal types can slip through later. Okay. Get whatever approval you need. Make it good. Make it soon. Do I make myself clear?'

Sr. Ecu said that Lovett spoke with impeccable clarity.

The privy council's ultimatum put Mahoney in what Kilgour called the catbird's seat. Ian only vaguely understood what a catbird might be, but he hadn't the foggiest what kind of a seat the being might prefer. Something lofty, he assumed. Mahoney knew he had assumed correctly when he was spared the long dance Sten had suffered through in the initial negotiations with the Manabi.

Sr. Ecu got directly to the point. Without preamble, he described the spot between the rock and the hard surface in which Lovett had placed him. Both options were intolerable.

Ian didn't say 'We told you so.' Nor did he waste Sr. Ecu's time by making appropriate soothing noises. Instead, he was as direct as the Manabi. He sketched out Sten's main plan.

What the young admiral had in mind, he said, was a murder trial. The trial would be conducted by an independent tribunal, composed of the most prestigious beings in the Empire. The previous loyalty of each representative had to be beyond question. To ensure that the proceedings were impeccable, Sten proposed that Sr. Ecu act as a neutral referee. He alone would be granted the authority to see that all evidence and testimony were handled with complete fairness.

During the tribunal's proceedings, Sten and Mahoney would do their absolute best to guarantee the security and safety of each member.

'How possible can that be?' Sr. Ecu asked.

'It isn't – totally. That's why I said we'd do our best. No more.'

'Quite understandable,' Sr. Ecu said. 'And fair.'

Mahoney was not surprised at the answer. It was a far better pledge than any offered by the privy council. He went on to say that he and Sten would make sure that every moment of the trial would be broadcast as widely as possible. It was Sten's intent that every being – no matter how distant or lowly – would have the opportunity to learn the impartial details of the proceedings. He did not have to point out that the privy council would also do everything possible to prevent such publicity.

'Will you invite them to defend themselves?' Sr. Ecu asked.

'Of course.'

'They will refuse.'

'So?'

Sr. Ecu mused a moment. 'So, indeed.'

It was not necessary to explain that if the tribunal came in with a guilty verdict, it did not mean that the members of the privy council would meekly turn themselves in to their jailers. It was moral weight Sten was after, enough to tip the balance. Handled correctly, the decision would punch so many holes in the privy council's power bucket that all their allies would leak away. What else did they have to offer, besides AM2? And that they had found impossible to deliver.

'Who will choose the members?' Sr. Ecu asked next.

Mahoney said that only a Manabi could be trusted enough to do such a thing. The same went for the mechanics of meeting with potential appointees. Sr. Ecu would have to launch a supersecret effort, shuttling from one system to another, all the while making sure that no tracks of any kind were left behind. He was to have complete freedom in this, not only for reasons of trust and secrecy, but for practical ones, as well. Without the Eternal Emperor, who else had those kinds of skills?

Sr. Ecu had some thoughts of his own about the Emperor, but he did not share them with Mahoney. He would have been surprised that Ian's thoughts ran along similar lines. And Mahoney would have been equally surprised that the being's thinking added a great deal of weight to his decision.

As the Manabi was drifting toward agreement, Mahoney flash-thought about the second part of Sten's plan. He had revealed not one detail of the reasons for Sten's absence. It was not lack of trust that kept him silent, but the old inviolate Mercury Corps rule of 'Need to Know.' Besides, if he had told about the mission, he was not sure which way Sr. Ecu would decide. If Sten failed this time, all bets were off. The independent tribunal would be an empty exercise.

'One final question,' Sr. Ecu said. 'What is the legal basis for this tribunal? What's the point, if we do not have the force of law?'

'There'd be none,' Mahoney said. 'Sten thought you'd ask that, however. And he said to tell you he hadn't a clot of an idea. We don't exactly have regiments of Imperial legal scholars at our command.'

'No, you don't,' Sr. Ecu said. 'My problem is that I can't imagine a circumstance where the Emperor would have ever allowed such a thing. He wouldn't have permitted anybody that kind of power. Not over him. And the problem we have now is that the council is acting in his name. With the same precedents and force of law.'

'Oh, I don't know about that,' Mahoney said. 'As old as this empire is, something like this must have occurred at least once.'

'I think you are right,' Sr. Ecu said. 'And once is all we need . . . Very well. I'll do it.'

Fleet Marshal Ian Mahoney was very relieved. He and the Manabi hammered out a few more details, and then it was time to go. Sr. Ecu had one parting comment that Mahoney puzzled over for some time.

'Oh . . . yes . . . I have a message for our young admiral,' Sr. Ecu said.

'Yes?'

'Tell him whatever the mission he's on now – if it should fail . . .'

'Yes?' There was a bit more tension in Mahoney's voice.

'Tell him I still expect to meet with him again. No matter the outcome. And I only hope it's someplace where *all* beings can fly.'

'He'll understand this?' Mahoney asked.

'Oh, yes . . . he'll understand.'

Chapter Seventeen

The man who called himself Raschid looked at the sign: EXPERIENCED COOK WANTED. LONG HOURS, LOW PAY, FEW BENEFITS, HARD WORK, FREE FOOD. The man smiled slightly. It was honest, at the very least.

Above the ramshackle building a sign blinked in several colors, all of which hurt the eye: LAST BLAST TEA-ROOM AND DINER. Below that: PROP.: DINGISWAYO PATTIPONG.

A knot of three very primed sailors lurched out of the barroom next door and down the cracked plas sidewalk. Raschid smiled politely and stepped out of their way. One of the sailors looked regretful but passed on.

Again, Raschid smiled, his smile broadening as he heard the Yukawa-whine of a ship lifting off from the field just beyond a blastfence. The produce-sled driver had been correct – the spaceport was full of ships that had not lifted for some time and would likely never lift again. But there was traffic.

Raschid entered the diner.

The man who greeted him was very small and very dark. There were about ten tables and a counter in the diner. The small man was the only other person inside.

'Sr. Pattipong?'

'You police?'

'No. I want a job.'

'You cook?'

'Yes.'

'No. Not cook. Maybe cook where people not use knife if order wrong. Too pretty be cook down here.'

Raschid did not answer.

'Where you cook last?'

Raschid muttered something inaudible.

Pattipong nodded once. 'Maybe you cook. Cook never say where last. Too many wives . . . alks . . . children . . . police. Come. We see.'

Pattipong led Raschid through the door into the kitchen, watching his expression closely. Pattipong nodded when that gawp of surprise came.

'Yes. Not good. I build station for gooood cook. Cnidarians. Stay two, almost three years. Then . . . go. Leave me with bathtub for cook station.'

The Cnidarians were intelligent aquatic corallike polyps that grew together as they matured . . . into mutual hatred. They . . . it must have been very, very good. Because Pattipong had specially built the kitchen. It was a now-drained tub, with all the necessary appliances and counters built circularly around it.

'Not good. Take gooood cook know how to use.'

Raschid climbed into the pool.

'Couple eyes. Over easy,' Pattipong ordered.

Raschid turned the heat on and put a pan on the fire. He brushed clarified butter from a nearby bowl on it, picked up – one-handed – two eggs from another bowl, and in a single motion cracked them both into the pan and disposed of the shells. Pattipong nodded involuntarily. Raschid chopped the heat down and waited as the eggs sizzled in the pan. Pattipong was watching his wrist closely. At just the right moment, Raschid flipped the eggs. They slid smoothly onto their blind sides.

Pattipong smiled. 'You cook. No one else do that right.'

'You want anything with your eggs?'

'No. Not want eggs. Hate eggs. Eggs make me . . .' Pattipong waved his hand across his buttocks. 'Everybody else like eggs. I serve eggs. You have job. You cook now.'

Raschid looked around the rather filthy kitchen. 'Cook later. Lunch is an hour away. Clean now.' Pattipong's speech patterns seemed habit-forming.

Pattipong considered, then bobbed his head. 'Clean now. Cook later. I help.'

And so began the Legend of the Eggs of Pattipong.

Pattipong described them on the menu as Imperial Eggs Benedict. For some reason, the name bothered Raschid. He argued – mildly. Pattipong told him to get back to the kitchen. 'Imperial good name. Thailand . . . best elephants Royal Elephants. Or so I hear.'

It started from boredom. The lunch crowd had been nearly nonexistent, and it was hours until dinner. Raschid wasn't sleepy enough to walk back to the tiny room he rented for a nap, didn't feel like drinking, and had no desire for a walk. It started with baking. Raschid felt about baking, mostly at least, the same way Pattipong did about eggs. It was too damned unpredictable, and he never understood exactly what ingredients should be changed to match the temperature, the humidity, the barometer, or whatever made his loaves look suddenly unleavened. But there were exceptions and this was one of them.

He had made sourdough starter a week or so before – warm water, equal amount of flour, a bit of sugar, and yeast. Cover in a nonmetallic dish and leave until it stinks.

He used that as a base for what were still called English muffins. They were equally easy to make. For about eight muffins, he brought a cup of milk to a boil, then took it off the stove and dumped in a little salt, a teaspoon of sugar, and two cupfuls of premixed biscuit flour. After he beat it all up, he let it rise until double size; then he beat in another cup of flour and let the dough rise once more.

The open-ended cylinders were half filled with the dough. Raschid did not mention that the short cylinders had been pet food containers with both ends cut off. Even in this district, somebody might get squeamish.

He brushed butter on his medium-hot grill and put the cylinders down. Once the open end had browned for a few seconds, he flipped the cylinder, browned the other side, and lifted the cylinder away, burning fingers in the process.

He added more butter and let the muffins get nearly black before putting them on a rack to cool. For use – within no more than four hours – he would split them with a fork and toast them.

He next found the best smoked ham he – or rather Pattipong – could afford. It was thin-sliced and browned in a wine-butter-cumin mixture.

'Best, it should be Earth ham. From Virginia. Or Kerry.'

Pattipong goggled. 'I didn't know you had ever been to Earth!'

Raschid looked perplexed. 'I – haven't. I think.' Then it was his turn to goggle. 'Dingiswayo – the way you just talked.'

'Normally, you mean? I slipped. Normal too much trouble. Talk too much trouble. Like eggs. Just hot air. Besides . . . talk short, people think you not understand. They more careful in asking what they want. Not careful in saying what they think you not understand.

'And around here,' Pattipong said, lapsing into a full speech pattern, 'you need all the edge you can get.'

That was true. The spaceport's traffic may have been light, but there were still stevedores, sailors, whores, and everyday villains looking for amusement – which was often defined as laying odds on how long it would take someone to bleed to death in a gutter. Pattipong kept a long, unsheathed knife hidden under the pay counter.

Raschid went back to his recipe. The browned ham was put in a warming oven. He had lemon juice, red pepper, a touch of salt, and three egg yolks waiting in a blender. He melted butter in a small pan. Then his mental timer went on. Muffins toasted . . . eggs went into boiling water to poach . . . the muffins were ready . . . ham went on top of the muffins . . . two and a half minutes exactly, and the eggs were plopped on top of the ham.

He flipped the blender on and poured molten butter into the mixture. After the count of twenty, he turned the blender off and poured the hollandaise sauce over the eggs.

'Voila, Sr. Pattipong.'

Pattipong gingerly sampled.

'Not bad,' he said grudgingly. 'But eggs.'

Raschid tried them on a customer, a sailor drunk enough to be experimental. The man sampled, looked surprised, and inhaled the plate, then ordered a second plate. He swore it sobered him up – now he was ready to start all over again.

'Like sobriety pill? Maybe great invention. Cure diseases. Sell through mail.'

'Clot off,' Raschid snorted.

The sailor came back the next day – with six friends.

The port police started dropping by around lunchtime. For some reason, Raschid felt uncomfortable – with no idea why. They ate, of course, on the cuff. Lunch was no longer slow.

Raschid came up with other dishes: something he called chili, and something he called 'nuked hen.' He convinced Pattipong that the customers wanted something more than the bland, airport/diner standard dishes Pattipong had previously featured on the menu.

'You talk. I listen. I do. Make curry. Curry like mother made. Customers try – I laugh. Get revenge for all yata-yata-yata talk all time.'

Pattipong's curry may not have been quite that lethal – but it was nominated.

'Know why I listen to you?' Pattipong asked.

He waved an arm out of the serving window. Raschid looked out at the dining area. It was packed. Pattipong had even put tables and chairs out on the sidewalk. Raschid knew that they had been getting busier, but he really hadn't realized just how much. The crowd was different. There were still the bruisers and brawlers, but Raschid saw suits and some uniformed port authorities, as well. There were even two orange-robed members of the Cult of the Eternal Emperor. For some reason, they made him just as uncomfortable as the policemen did – also for equally unknown reasons.

'Last Blast now hot place to go. Walk wild side . . . eat good. It last for while. Then they find new place. Happen before. Happen again. Hard thing to remember. Not expand. Not drive old customers away.

'These people like . . . like insect that buzz . . . buzz . . . flower to flower. Then vanish.'

'Butterflies?'

'Butter not fly, Raschid. Work. No more jokes.'

Raschid went back to his stove. Another damned order for

Imperial Damned Eggs. He was starting to share Pattipong's hatred
for eggs.

Raschid was glad Pattipong was making money. But it meant
nothing to him.

He felt . . . as if he were waiting. For someone? For something?
He did not know.

Others noticed prosperity, as well.

It was very late. The Last Blast opened early and closed late –
but this was getting absurd. Around midnight they had a gaggle
of guests, all caped in formal wear. The thea-tah crowd.

Raschid was exhausted. As soon as he finished stoning and oiling
the grill he was for his room, the fresher, one drink, and unconsciousness. They had a new hire – a baker, one of Pattipong's
innumerable relatives – coming in. Raschid was supposed to train
him – a clear case of a double amputee teaching ballet.

He heard the scuffle and argument from the front. Another
damned robbery. Pattipong had a dump near the pay counter –
almost all money went into a sealed, time-locked safe. Since they
would lose only a few dollars in a heist, it was easier just to give
the robbers the till than fight back. Safer, as well. The next morning
Pattipong would tip the port police, who would find the thief and
either have him make restitution or, if he had spent the money, just
break his thumbs for an hour or so.

This sounded different.

Raschid picked up a heavy cleaver and went to the kitchen
doorway. Then he set the cleaver down on a shelf and looked out.
He instantly knew – but did not know how he knew – what was
going on. Four heavysets. Flash expense. False smiles and real
menace. He walked over to Pattipong.

'G'wan back, cookie. This don't pertain,' one of the thugs said.

'Protection?' Raschid asked, ignoring the man.

Pattipong nodded. 'We pay. No stinks. Furniture not busted.
Customers protected.'

'Are they connected?'

'Hey. We told you get out of it.'

'I not see before. New. Not connected. No connections now.
Old boss go hoosegow. Baby new bosses still fighting.'

'Knock off the drakh. We made our offer. Polite folk respond.'

Pattipong looked at Raschid. 'You think we pay?'

Raschid shook his head slowly – and spun the heavy glass match
bowl on the counter into one man's face.

Pattipong snapkicked the second – a man nearly two meters tall – under the chin. The man stumbled back and went flat.

A third man grabbed a chair. The chair came up . . . Raschid went under it, head-butting. The man dropped the chair and sagged. Raschid double-fisted him on the back of the neck, and the man was out.

Pattipong had his long knife about halfway out, and the rules changed. The last man's hand slid toward his belt. A gun.

Raschid, having all the time in the world, spun right . . . two steps back toward the kitchen, hand reaching inside. Whirl . . . the gun was coming up. Finger touching the trigger stud. Raschid overhanded the cleaver. It smacked into the tough's skull with a dull sound not unlike an ax striking rotten wood.

Pattipong hurried to the door. 'No cops.'

He came back inside and shook his head at the carnage and the scatter. 'This not good.'

'Sorry. But he was—'

'You misunderstand. Not bad he dead. Bad he dead not neat. Messy. Take two, maybe three hours to clean up. Long day. I was sleepy.' He started for the com. 'I call cousin. He pick up bodies. Leave maybe in front of police station. Let three explain one, when they wake.'

He touched buttons.

'You not bad fighter. For cook.'

Raschid was looking at the moaning or unconscious human and formerly human debris. Feeling . . . feeling as if there were a curious observer behind him. He felt . . . he felt . . . push it away . . . nothing in particular. A necessary act.

He went to work helping Pattipong.

Two men sat at Pattipong's counter. Both wore what might appear to be – after suitable degreasing, cleaning, pressing, and sewing – uniforms.

Beside one man was a captain's cover, with formerly gold braid on its bill. Raschid had seen braid go green, even black, with age, but this was the first he had ever seen what looked as if it were infested with barnacles. The cap may have suggested the man's position – little else did. It was not merely the grime: he was a tiny little rabbity person, with the twitching mannerisms of that creature, as well.

The other man, a hulk, had the peeling braid of a ship's officer on his sleeve and on his breast a COMMAND-QUALIFIED ribbon.

On the man's shoulder, Raschid could make out a round patch: PEASE SHIPPING.

Both men were drinking caff and arguing. The 'captain' – if that was what he was – looked fondly at the lined bottles of alk behind the counter. The other man – mate? – shook his head. The rabbit sighed and whined on. Raschid could make out bits of what he was saying.

'Undercrewed . . . clottin' agent . . . converter leakin' . . . bonded freight . . . sealed destination . . . client I never heard of neither. Not good, Mister Mate. Not good at all.'

Raschid, pretending to wipe the counter, came closer.

'The contract good?' the mate asked.

'Cashed it this morning,' the rabbit said grudgingly.

'Then what'a you care? Damn few cargoes come wi' a fuel guarantee, Captain. What's to worry what we're carryin'?'

'I'd hate like hell to finish my career gettin' taken off as a smuggler.'

The mate looked the little man up and down. 'Career? Pattipong, more caff.'

Pattipong, unsmiling, refilled the mugs.

'Where's the best place to sign on some casuals?' the mate asked.

'For you? For Pease Lines? Maybe try port jail.'

'Thanks, Patty. I love you, too.'

Raschid spoke. 'What slots you got open?'

The mate evaluated Raschid carefully. 'Greaser. Cook/com. Second engineer. If you got papers.'

'What's your com rig?'

'World's oldest VX-314. Your grampa could'a known it. We call it Stutterin' Susie.'

'What's the pay?'

'Standard. Three hundred a month. Found. Got a sealed destination. You can pay off there, or stay on when we pick up a cargo and transship to a new port.'

'Three hundred's cherry-boy pay.'

'That's the offer.'

Pattipong was signaling from the kitchen.

'Sorry,' Raschid said. For some reason he thought he was supposed to say yes.

The captain was about to bleat something. The mate stopped him.

'How good a cook are you?'

'Order something.'

'What about the com?'

'Bet the check whoever your last idiot was didn't triple-ground the box,' Raschid said. 'That'll give a Vexie hiccups all the time.' He went back into the kitchen.

'You drunk? Drugs? What wrong with job?' Pattipong asked him.

'Nothing, Dingiswayo. It's just . . . time to go.'

'Look. I give you better pay. Give you . . . quarter business. No, eighth. You stay.'

The two merchant officers were arguing inaudibly.

'Those two . . . Jarvis, Moran. Bad. He weak. Drinker. Moran . . . busted down from skipper. Killed men. Ship . . . *Santana*. Boneyard. Recycled. All Pease ships same. Junk. Certificates forged. Out of date. Line pick cargo where can. Not care where go. Not care kill crew, lose ship. Insurance always paid prompt.'

'Sounds like an adventure.'

'You full hop. Adventure someone else, in livie. You watch – adventure. You do – deep, deep drakh.'

'You. Cook,' Moran growled. 'We'll go 450.'

'And slops?' Raschid pressed. 'M'gear got left aboard m'last.'

'Happens when you jump ship. But yeah. We'll go it.'

The wait was over.

Chapter Eighteen

All nightmares end. Eventually the last of the pirated AM2 was loaded onto the transports, and the 23rd Fleet could lift for Al-Sufi and then home base.

But even escaping, men died. A Honjo had positioned a booby trap, fused with a pressure-release device under one freighter. It went off when the freighter lifted, and the blast took out two more cargo ships and one of the destroyers providing overhead cover.

Just out-atmosphere an Imperial corvette was sniped. An offplanet Honjo lighter had mounted a single missile on its cargo deck, managed to infiltrate through the fleet cover, and waited. The missile killed the corvette, and one of Gregor's cruisers blew the lighter and crew into nothingness. But by that time killing Honjo – in greater or lesser quantities – was no longer thought a victory. It was merely a duty that might – but probably would not – stave off one's own death for a few hours.

Admiral Gregor ordered the fleet into a standard convoy formation. It was by-the-book but not tactically bad. It looked like a three-dimensional mushroom with a base. The mushroom's 'stem' was the transport train, with light cover outside the main formation. The mushroom's 'cap' was his heavies, with destroyers and cruisers screening to the front. The base was two heavy-cruiser squadrons with their screens, giving rear security. They should have been unnecessary – but they were potentially vital.

That was just part of the bad news Gregor gloomed over at his battle computer. The only data he had was bad, with one exception: fuel.

His fleet AM2 chambers were at full battle load – probably the only ships in space these days that were, Gregor thought. In theory that should have meant he could have ignored the council's economy dictum and ordered full battle speed toward Al-Sufi. Well, if not full battle, then at least to whatever max drivespeed the transports were capable of.

He could not. His fleet had taken too much damage in the Honjo's guerrilla raids. Damage ranged from hull integrity to warped drive chambers to blown tubes to almost anything the Honjo's ingenuity had come up with to destroy or cripple the Imperials. Two cruisers had even been slaved together and given external emergency drive from one of Gregor's tenders.

His fleet was limping – limping at many multiples of lightspeed, but still limping. Which meant that the 23rd Fleet was vulnerable to a stern attack. Gregor considered abandoning any units that could not hold top transport speed. Then he shuddered and decided against that course. He would face enough flak as it was.

He decided that the only salvation his career had was returning to Al-Sufi with the AM2 – all the AM2. That might keep him his flag. Maybe.

Scowling, he scrolled on. The siege-that-was-not had been incredibly expensive:

Crew casualties, all categories: twenty-seven percent.

Ship casualties, all categories: thirty-five percent.

That, factored into his already-dismal combat-readiness factor before invading . . .

Gregor did not want to run the figures.

A second admiral was no happier with the state of the universe.

Fleet Admiral Fraser sat grounded, along with her command, on three of the Al-Sufi worlds. Her orders were clear: Hold in place until the 23rd Fleet arrives. Fuel from the AM2 transports. Combine forces with the 23rd, yourself to assume command as CINCCON. Continue mission to Prime World sector. Further orders will be given at that time.

She had a fairly good idea of what shape the 23rd was in. Gregor had tried to make his reports sound as favorable as possible. But since complete lies were not permissible, Fraser expected a ragtag collection of limpers.

Fraser, an aggressive leader, believed the Nelsonian dictum that no one can find himself in too much trouble if he steers toward the sound of the guns. She would have cheerfully modified her orders, lifted, and gone to immediate support of Gregor's wounded fleet.

But she could not. Combined AM2 available: not more than one half an E-day cruising range – for *all* her ships.

Fraser was not a happy admiral.

The 23rd was coming home. Gregor's navigational section had suggested a circuitous plot from the Honjo Sector to Al-Sufi. Gregor had rejected it.

He had some good reasons: the status of his ships, the poor skill-levels of too many nav-decks in following the proposed multiple-point plot, and finally his fear of inexperienced deck officers having to maintain convoy position. No, he thought. He did not need the added calumny that would come, for instance, if two of his battleships suddenly set collision courses.

Besides, Gregor was starting to regain some of his customary poise. He called it confidence; his staff preferred 'arrogance.'

Who, in these times, could challenge an Imperial fleet? Even in its present state of combat semi-readiness? Almost no one. Who had the fuel to chance battle? It took power to steal power. The course would be linear – or as 'linear' as navigational trajectories could be under AM2 drive.

Watches passed. Gregor felt himself proven right.

Negative contacts. Except for two.

One was reported as a small squadron of light attack craft. System patrol? Raiders? Gregor neither knew nor cared. The 23rd was far too strong for them to attack.

The second contact was laughable.

A trading ship blundered across the 23rd's path. A destroyer matched orbits with the ship. Nothing to worry about – just a trader, from some unknown culture called the Bhor. The ship's intelligence – also mail, censorship, sports, and recreational fund – officer took the time to check a fiche. Bhor? He whistled to himself. They were a very, very long way from home looking for business.

Sten looked at the projection of the based mushroom. He spun it through a couple of 360s, muttered, then brought the focus in to as tight as his 'trading' spy ship had managed to get. He ignored the immediate breakdown of estimated forces on another screen. He had it memorized already.

A third screen lit: BATTLE ANALYSIS READY.

Sten ignored that screen, too.

He got up and started pacing back and forth. He had an esti-mated four E-days, given the Imperial fleet's current speed, to come up with a Plan, position his troops, and attack.

Kilgour and Otho sat nearby. Alex was busy at his own computer; Otho was stroking his beard and looking at that mushroom.

'Straight in, straight on. They won't expect that,' the Bhor chief-tain said.

'No,' Sten agreed. 'Neither would I. But I'll bet I could figure out a response before we got in range.'

'It was a suggestion.'

'Accepted as such, rejected as such.'

He looked at Kilgour's screen. Kilgour was scrolling the hourly update from Sten's fleet.

Fleet. Eighty-three ships. Most of them warships, but none of them lighter than an equivalent Imperial cruiser-class, and all of them intended for cluster security/interdiction missions. Others were armed traders and armed auxiliaries. Weapons, electronics, and countermeasure suites would be at least one and more likely five full generations behind the Imperial warships. Not good.

Worse: FUEL STATUS. Maximum range, at full drive: eleven E-days. Getting fuel for the raid had stripped the Lupus Cluster nearly dry. At present the fleet was 'parked,' with all non-essential systems off. They were masked from the projected trajectory of the Imperials behind a collapsed star.

The status screen cleared, then added a needless worry: MAXIMUM TIME REQUIRED TO ABORT . . . UNDER PRESENT CONDITIONS . . . Meaning that if they stayed parked, they had the equivalent of two E-centuries. UNDER NORMAL DRIVE . . . eleven ship-hours . . . UNDER BATTLE DRIVE . . .

Sten did not look at that figure. He concentrated on the mushroom. It would not have been his choice for a convoy formation – the heavies were concentrated at the front. Better to carry them outside the formation near the center, for ready response in any direction if an attacker feinted. Feinted. Hmm. Yes, Admiral. With what are you going to pull your ruse? Eighty-three ships, remember? Against . . . against too many.

On-screen, the mushroom's cap started sliding back and forth on the fleet's 'stem,' like a winding-down toy gyro. Kilgour was beaming at him.

'Dammit, Alex! Quit gamin'!'

'Thae gamin', ae y'put it, i' another suggestion, Boss. Or hae Ah noo leave t' suggest?'

Otho rose. 'By my mother's insect-infested beard, we must cure this bickering disease.' He owled a prox screen. 'Nearest contact . . . we have lifetimes. Time for stregg, time even for the hangover. I'll get the horns.' He palmed a bulkhead door and slid out.

'Sorry, Alex,' Sten said.

'Dinnae fash. Y' want t' hear what I was thinkin't? 'Tis jus' a wee thought, Boss. Ah nae hae a scheme.'

The mushroom's gyroing, Alex went on, came as he projected near-simultaneous attacks from various directions at the Imperials. 'Slide aroun', slide aroun', an' sooner come later, thae'll lose comman' cohesion. All Ah need f'r't t' be a plan is, p'raps, anoth'r two, three hundred ships.'

Otho came back with the stregg. Sten had something wandering in his backbrain. He put the horn in its stand untouched.

'My turn,' Sten said. 'First, I know where to hit them.' He touched a point on the fleet's projected overall passage. 'Here.'

'Good. Thae'll be sloppy then.'

'Maybe even how. Clot the ships. Clot the weapons. Clot that they've got all the damned AM2 in the universe. Think about the troopies. Who we going against?'

'Your mind has fled,' Otho said. 'We are fighting the Empire, and you are lacking stregg. Drink, my Sten.'

Sten ignored him and went on. What kind of Imperials were they facing? This was hardtimes and peacetimes. The ships would most likely be officered and crewed by an odd mixture – experienced war veterans/careerists and new, or fairly new, volunteers.

'Thae hae th' facts ae history arguin' wi' you,' Alex agreed slowly.

'Second. Their Admiral Whoever. Rules and regulations. Right way, wrong way, navy way.'

'Frae one formation? Estimate frae insufficient data. Theory only.'

Sten grinned at his stocky friend, who seemed to have found a new avocation as a strange-talking battle computer.

'Formation, yes. Also the response to the trading ship. Destroyer screens shifted . . . like so. Heavies closed toward area of threat . . . so. Reaction – one ship to close with unknown, two detached in front of the screen for backup. Just like the fiche tell you in Staff School.'

'Still theory.'

It was.

'Second. Alex, if I give you . . . four ships, can you rig two spoofs?'

Alex thought. 'Ah kin. But thae'll noo be world-class. No' enow time, no' enow gear f'r a good 'llusion.'

'One more time. Think about the troopies.'

'Ah.'

'Now, won't that get your mushroom slippin' an' slidin'?'

'Might.' Kilgour sank his horn and got up. 'But we'll hae t' hit 'em hard an' fast. Ah hae a sudden date wi' a tech. If y'll excuse me?' And he was gone.

Otho winced. Hard and fast. That meant full power and being marooned in space if they did not capture the freighters.

Sten caught his expression. 'Don't worry. If we lose – and are still alive but out of power – we'll have Kilgour knock out the ports, issue oars, and we'll row home.'

Otho laughed and smacked his lips. The upcoming battle prom- ised to be fast and nasty. He had an addition to the unformulated plan. Would this fleet have a common com-link frequency to the admiral? Very probably. Could it be detected quickly? Almost certainly. Could it be analyzed, pirated into, and blanketed? Given a com with enough power . . . yes.

'Four of my ships, at the least, have links strong enough to shout from here to Hades in a whisper. That is not a factor,' Otho said.

Shout . . . whisper? Sten put aside Otho's idea of analogies and asked what he had in mind. Otho continued. When he was finished, Sten sat down, drank stregg, and ran the idea through. It was brutal. Bloody. Practical. About what one would expect from a Bhor warrior – or a Mantis operative.

'Service soldiers,' Sten thought aloud, 'would want revenge. Conscripts . . . particularly if these people have seen hard times on Honjo, as we've heard. Yes.

'Refill the horn, my friend. My mind is starting to work. One slight modification to your idea, however. We'll need six, maybe eight, of your best and bloodiest . . .'

Cind went ballistic one nanosecond after getting the orders from her section officer. She was detached for special duties and ordered to turn in her weaponry except for her pistol and combat knife. Then she drew her weapon for this battle – a battle that would be led by Admiral Sten himself. A battle that would win glory for all.

Her weapon was a small camera with a transmitter attached. A joke? No. Because she was human, and those clottin' Bhor never really . . . No. She was the only human. The other seven beings in this special detachment were Bhor – all of them just as homicidally angry as Cind.

She refused the order. The officer shrugged and ordered her confined to quarters. She relented but wanted to protest the assignment.

''Twill do you no good, woman.'

'Why not? I've got rights!'

'So file a protest if you like. I was ordered to pick eight of my best shipboard fighters. Eight who were most likely to find themselves in the heart of battle. And eight who might survive the fray. I chose accordingly.'

'Clot the compliments! I want to protest.'

'As I said, protest as you like. The orders came directly from the Great Otho and Admiral Sten himself.'

Cind recovered her chin from where it sat on her collarbone. Sten? Why this shaming?

No. Stop being a child. Sten was Sten.

There must be a reason.

If you can understand Sten's thinking, she told herself, then you may truly be on the Way of the Warrior.

Chapter Nineteen

The 23rd Imperial Fleet was attacked less than one ship's day from safety.

Once contact was made with Al-Sufi and the waiting reinforcements, Gregor relaxed. He ordered stand down from General Quarters. Modified Readiness – one third at combat stations – was the new status. The rest of the Imperial sailors were ordered to clean ship and themselves.

Gregor thought himself a humane commander and knew his troops would not want to port looking like tramps. Also, if there were livie cameras there, a formation of slobs would reflect poorly on Gregor himself.

The first attack came as Gregor was luxuriating in the fresher: '*All Hands . . . Battle Stations . . . Raiders Attacking!*'

Gregor found himself on the bridge wearing the full-dress white mess jacket he had laid out – and briefs. He quickly analyzed the screens.

'Sir, I've already ordered the formation shift toward the enemy's angle of attack as per your standing instructions.'

Gregor swore at the Officer of the Deck and then punched up the ECM officer.

'Screen the attackers.'

The man seemed puzzled, then touched keys slowly, as if he did not have his signal orders memorized as reflexes. Nothing happened. The attackers continued in, coming from the high forward port quadrant. He ran another program . . . the raiders vanished! Only two ships remained on-screen.

Gregor was about to scream at his flag officer and break the ECM officer when another alarm shrilled. Another formation was coming low forward center – the real attack. Gregor took command and ordered the battle formation shifted down toward the foe.

The mushroom cap seemed to spin as the battleships changed formation and their cruiser and destroyer screens followed. There were two collisions – a cruiser physically 'brushed' a destroyer, and two destroyers slammed into one another. The cruiser had some survivors.

In the ECM center, the officer was still following orders and screening the attackers. On his fourth try, just as he was convinced that these were for real, the second set of raiders disappeared. Once more, two ships – the spoofers – remained.

There was a stunned silence on the bridge. Then alarms once more, and a third, larger, near-fleet-size attack began.

'Flag!'

'Sir.'

'I want you in ECM. Make damned sure we aren't being fooled again.'

The officer ran. Gregor determined to wait for a few seconds before he ordered more changes. Meanwhile, his twin set of orders and their countermands continued wiggling the mushroom's cap as ship captains and squadron commanders tried to reformulate the dome of attack.

The third attack was most real.

Sten shut the chatter of battle commands out of his mind and focused on the bridge's main battle screen.

He was attacking in a crescent formation. He would dearly have loved to have several hundred more units – the halfmoon was very thin. Necessarily so – Sten, hoping the Imperials would be stupid enough to think he was planning an envelopment, wanted the tips of the crescent spread beyond the Imperial defense dome's area.

The Imperial mushroom was looking a little ragged. Part of its cap was shifting toward the attackers. But a segment appeared not to have gotten the word and was restabilizing into normal convoy formation.

At the rear of the stem, the cruisers were deploying fairly efficiently, the base swinging up to cover the transports.

'Com! Are we linked?' Sten asked.

'All ships receiving.'

'Sten to all ships. Standby on Longlance launch – as ordered.'

'Waiting . . . waiting . . . all ships ready, sir.'

'Countermeasures,' he said to another officer. 'What're they doing?'

'Their detectors have us . . . two . . . six launches made. Five ineffective . . . one acquired.'

'Kilgour. Talk to me.'

'Range closin't . . . seven seconds . . . three . . . mark!'

'All ships. Launch!'

Missiles spat from the Bhor fleet—but not at the same time. Sten had ordered a ripple fire from the rearmost ships forward. As the missiles cleared the forwardmost Bhor ships, weapons officers armed and aimed the ship-killers. There were not that many missiles launched—at least for a major battle—but all were meant to arrive on target at the same moment.

'Alex. I want that wedge between the heavies exploited. First section . . . individual control . . . acquire and launch when ready.

'Countermeasures! What're they doing?'

''B' Kholoric . . . not much!'

'Report, dammit!'

The Bhor tried his best to assume the role of an efficient, toneless Imperial officer. 'Minor launches . . . most directed at incoming missiles. Correction. I have a mass launch. Central control is on overload.'

On-screen, there were sparkles between the two closing fleets: operator-guided antiship missiles, Kali II's, most likely. They would be taken out – or they would hit. That was not part of what Sten should be thinking about.

He turned off the 'but what if we're one of the unlucky ones' part of his mind and looked beyond the sparkles. He grinned suddenly and made a comment frowned on in Basic Admiral School.

'Kilgour! You owe me a stregg! The bastard's by-the-book!'

Gregor was, indeed. There were many possible responses to an envelopment. The best response would have been for Gregor to break the dome into a spearhead or even line formation and attack the center of Sten's fleet, break through the crescent – which was no more than two ships deep – circle, and destroy Sten's fleet in detail.

But that would have meant leaving his transports unguarded except by the cruiser force. No doubt this Imperial admiral had read of Cannae. But there was a big difference: Sten was not Hannibal, nor did he have any heavy infantry to slam the horns of the crescent shut and trap the attacker.

Instead, the admiral was putting his fleet online. It was

counter-envelopment evidently, such as the Turks should have used at Lepanto. Not bad. It would, in time, destroy the Bhor fleet. In time.

The gap that formed when the Imperial formation was still in its dome remained as ships clouded toward the new formation, ready for Sten to exploit.

'All ships,' Sten ordered. He was broadcasting in clear, having no time for codes or the polyglot spoken on the Bhor bridges. He hoped that the Imperial admiral's response time would continue as laggardly as it had so far.

'Standing by, sir.'

'I want a blink on that hole in the Imperial formation,' he ordered another com officer. 'To all ship screens. Now.'

'Transmitted, sir.'

'Good. All ships . . . maneuver point as indicated . . . X-Ray Yaphet . . . signal when ready.'

'All units ready, sir.'

'Maneuver . . . now!'

The Bhor captains, any of whom could maneuver a single-tube transport sideways up a cobblestone alley, snapped their orders. Sten's crescent folded over on itself and became a wedge. It was just like an acrobatic squadron – but on-screen he could see the big difference. His fleet was taking hits. Lights indicating individual ships changed colors – *Hit . . . Lost Nav . . . Hit . . . Drive Damage* – or just vanished.

He ignored them. He also ignored the low murmur of a low-ranking weapons officer at the ship's own board. 'We are acquired . . . homing . . . impact nine seconds . . . I have counterlaunched . . .'

But he was damned relieved when he heard, 'Hit! Incoming destroyed.'

The Imperial formation was a real shambles, spitting missiles in all directions. Sten would not have liked to be in the center of that kaleidoscope as it changed shapes and then fragmented further.

'Fleet status,' he snapped.

'Fifty-one units still report full—'

'That's enough.' Later – maybe – there would be time to worry about casualties and pickup.

'Otho. Do you have their command frequency?'

'On-screen. Ready to pirate.'

There was a large screen, set away from the main control area. On it was an Imperial admiral, giving orders. Otho had the audio blanked. Sten thought he recognized the admiral . . . no. Impossible.

'Team Sarla . . . go!' he ordered.

'Acknowledged.'

'Team Janchydd . . . go!'

'Janchydd . . . attacking.'

'All fleet units. Individual control. Acquire targets and exploit. Command, out.'

The real battle began. The Bhor swirled into the melee like so many piratical Drakes against an armada. This was the best possible use of their talents. Most of the traders had vast experience at going one-on-three against raiders. Going against – and winning – by always doing the unexpected, lashing out in all directions and with missiles and electronics, every bit as berserk as their ancestors.

Between Gregor's standing orders and battle experience from the Tahn wars, most of the Imperial ships were expecting to fight a conventional battle against conventionally arrayed enemies.

This main battle had all of the symmetry, logic, and clarity of a feeding frenzy. Sten turned his attention away. The Bhor could not win – sooner or later numbers would out – but they were not supposed to.

His two combat teams were: Sarla, two cruisers that had been hurriedly converted to assault transports; Janchydd, eleven light escorts – corvettes and patrol craft. Just as many ships as Sten had calculated to be controlling the slaved transports. He knew how the Empire ran its convoys, so all of the escorts had been given the electronics and sensors of deep-space tugs.

Sten had named his teams after old, barely worshiped Bhor gods for morale reasons. If there could be Victory, these two teams would gain it.

Now he waited – if waiting could be defined as hanging on to an upright on a chaotic ship's bridge while the ship itself was in the middle of a Kilkenny cats' brawl.

Team Sarla: The two assault ships closed on an already-damaged battleship, well inside the BB's minimum safety launch range. A Bhor missile blew most of the ship's stern away, and the assault ships' ports yawned. Lines were jetted across by scouts, and the three ships were linked.

Armored Bhor went across the lines – and they boarded the Imperial warship.

'First wave across,' came the broadcast.

'Otho!'

The Imperial admiral's on-screen image blanked and was replaced by a blinding succession of visuals that would have gagged the biggest splatter-hound director of livies.

The Imperial battleship was already a slaughterhouse from missile hits. More Imperials died when the assault transport's missile dumped the ship's atmosphere. They may have been suited, but many of them had not closed their faceplates or pulled on gauntlets. It was hard to fight a ship wearing armor.

Then the Bhor ravaged through the ship. They had explicit orders: No prisoners. Play to the cameras.

The Imperial officers and crew died to the last being. The deaths were filmed by Cind and the other camera operators, their images selected for maximum effect at a mix panel in Sten's control room and then rebroadcast on the Imperial command link.

It did little for a young sailor's morale when a ship-screen showed a CIC with beings just like himself standing with their hands raised in surrender being butchered like so many hogs. Some ships blanked that frequency – and lost any link to command for many seconds while a secure link was being established. Other ships left the screen on, allowing every slaughter to burn into the minds of their crew members.

Team Janchydd: The control ships for the transports were lightly armed and armored. They could offer little resistance against the weapons of the Bhor escorts. Six of the eleven stopped firing after taking hits. Two plugged on, still fighting with what armament they had. Three more blew into debris. One Bhor ship was lost.

Techs boarded the six control ships and took over the navboards for the AM2 transports. Their escorts closed, slaving to those ships. That was not enough. If more transports – and AM2 – couldn't be 'stolen,' Sten's mission would be very close to a failure. But Team Janchydd's sailors had initiative.

The two still-firing command ships were battered into surrender. They also were boarded and seized. Somehow the Bhor electronics wizards also picked up control frequencies for two of the destroyed Imperial command ships.

Team Janchydd's commander gave the word. Slowly the convoy – the mushroom's stem – broke apart as the Bhor ships diverted the transports, just as a tug would take over a liner's controls while docking.

The heavy cruiser squadrons reacted late to the attack – but reacted. They formed for a counterattack.

Sten saw the counterattack on-screen, put another indicator on the formation, and sent it out.

'All fleet units,' he ordered then. 'Targets indicated. Priority target. Individual control. Go!'

He did not wait for an acknowledgement.

'Otho. Phase Two,' he said.

Otho triggered a switch. A prerecorded disc started broadcasting on the pirated command frequency. It showed a grim, heavily armed Otho looming into the camera, flanked by Sten and another lethal-looking Bhor. It may have been Sten's show, but he knew he did not look nearly as horrid as Otho.

The Bhor chieftain's voice boomed: 'All Imperial units! It is useless to continue the resistance. You are ordered to surrender. Fire yellow-blue-yellow flares to save your lives. Ships surrendering will remain unharmed.'

Sten had not been stupid enough to think that cheap ploy would get him an entire Imperial fleet to white-flag. All he was after was further confusion.

He got it. A few ships obeyed. Some of them were fired on by other Imperial ships. On other ships, panicked sailors mini-mutinied, which gave their officers problems more immediate than what was happening outside.

Thirty-nine Bhor ships slammed into the cruiser formation, and another confusion began. The stolen transports broke away from the battle area. Their controllers put them on full drive.

Now, Sten thought. 'All units. Break contact!'

This is the turning point. I've stolen their clottin' gold. The Imperials have two options. Please – what the hell were the names of those damn Bhor gods – hell, any god paying attention right now . . . let me be lucky. Let that clottin' admiral be consistent.

Gregor was. Finally having patched a second secure com link to his fleet, he should have ordered a general pursuit of the raiders, under individual or squadron control. He didn't. Perhaps he had heard of Hattin, where Saladin had decoyed a crusading army into the desert and then slaughtered them piecemeal. For all he knew there could be an ambush element lurking out there somewhere.

He ordered all fleet elements to regroup – by elements, by squadrons, and then into main fleet formation. Regrouping, at the very least, requires a visible standard for soldiers to head toward. This battleground was a little short of signposts. Ships hunted for their leaders. Com links were a bleat of confusion. None of it was helped by Gregor's own stream of impossible-to-obey commands.

Sten's forces pulled away.

Team Sarla, with no one left to kill, had already pulled back onto their assault ships. Cind stood to one side of the assembly deck, the normal silence/battle of post-combat letdown unheard. She had learned something that day indeed from Sten. From then on, she resolved to dance close attendance on him. To learn, and to . . . She smiled to herself.

Sten's getaway appeared to be working. He chanced a bit of humanity and ordered ten ships to pick up survivors from the crippled Bhor ships. As they could . . . if they could. They were to try to get the ships under power, but abandon any ship not capable of full drive.

It would get ticklish now. At full drive, his units would soon start running out of power.

He gave more orders. Bhor ships closed on the stolen convoy. On each, their best fueling techs were waiting. Only two Bhor craft ran dry – and Sten had full-powered ships ready to slave to them and transfer energy.

'Y' jus' might hae pulled th' biggest heist a' all, Admiral.'

Sten managed a grin, then forced himself to another station. 'Casualties?'

There was not much joy in this victory. He had lost almost half of his force. Otho walked up beside him and looked at the same figures. 'Better than I had expected. Worse than I had hoped. But the gods decide.'

Sten nodded. Perhaps. But why the hell did they have to be so murderous?

'Remember that pool, Sten.'

Sten remembered. And now he had fuel to fight his war.

BOOK THREE

PATER PATRIAE

Chapter Twenty

Five minutes after boarding the *Santana*, Raschid decided that Pattipong could have added several more deep deeps to his description of the drakh he was stepping into. Then he wondered why it had taken him so long to realize it.

It had probably been the mad scurry. Both Captain Jarvis and Mate Moran seemed to go into Overdrive Decision Time as soon as they hit the field. It could have been, Raschid thought, that if they hesitated to consider anything other than immediate lift, unpleasant alternatives would come into play.

The *Santana* was several generations beyond qualifying as a tramp. It must have been marked for salvage several times before its owner decided there was still life and profit in the hulk.

Beauty there had never been. As the port gravsled deposited Jarvis, Moran, and their new cook at the ship's boarding ramp, Raschid had tried to figure what the *Santana* had been designed for. He was blank. The ship consisted of three elongated acorns, X-braced together fore and aft. In the middle, between the acorns, a long cylinder stretched above the main hulls. Engines and drive area, Raschid guessed. But why in front? Could the tub have been originally built for some other drive than AM2? Impossible. No one would have bothered converting such a dinosaur. Nor would they have kept it in commission. Would they?

One acorn contained control rooms and crew quarters, the other two cargo. The crewpod was as puzzling inside as the *Santana*'s exterior. Raschid got lost several times before he found the galley and his quarters. Passageways had been sealed off, then cut open at a new owner's whims. He passed compartments filled with long-abandoned machinery that must have been cheaper to chop from a system than rip out for scrap. Raschid was expecting the worst when he reached his kingdom. He was an optimist. The twin stoves were so old that they were probably wood-fueled. Later for that problem. He found his compartment and was grateful. It was pig-filthy, of course. But at least cook's hours and cook's privileges gave him his own quarters.

The bunk – if the sagging pallet against one wall deserved the title – had safety straps. Raschid seriously, if illogically, considered strapping himself in before lift. That way, if the *Santana* disassembled, as it seemed to have every intention of doing, there might be a recognizable corpse for the pauper's field burial.

Raschid wryly thought that this, indeed, was going to be every bit the adventure Pattipong had promised and waited for the ship to lift off Yongjukl.

Ships did not 'scream' into space, except perhaps in stone-age film documentaries or in embarrassingly amateurish livies. But the *Santana* did just that – or perhaps he was anthropomorphizing. He felt a little like screaming himself. The McLean generators told him that 'down' was half a dozen different directions before the Yukawa drive went on. The bridge held the ship on Yukawa until the *Santana* was out-atmosphere. A gawd-awful waste of energy – but most likely shifting to AM2 drive in-atmosphere with this scow was an invitation to demolition.

A com buzzed.

'Cookie. Stop arsin' about. Officers' mess, one hour. Crew to follow.'

Raschid went back to the galley where he was met by Moran. Raschid noted that the mate was carrying a side arm. Moran took Raschid to a storeroom, unlocked it, and told him to select whatever he needed.

'How many bodies am I cooking for?'

'From these supplies – me, the skipper, first engineer. Crew's supplies are off the galley. You'll be sloppin' twelve of them.'

Raschid was not surprised to find that the supplies in the locked room were not the same as in the crew larder. Officers' rations were standard ship-issue, but the crew's victuals appeared to be long-stored military-type goods – issued to a military that would have mutinied itself into oblivion generations earlier. Yes. Mutiny.

Raschid planned menus with what he had. He was a genius, he felt, at being able to cordon-bleu any drakh given him. Genius, yes, but not a god. Spices? Some sweet syrupy-tasting synthetic. Salt . . . and those old military rations appeared to have been salt-cured. What other condiments were in the larder had long since passed into tastelessness.

He combined foodstuffs into a concoction he hoped would be taken for a stew, put that on the heating range, and made dinner for the officers.

He need not have worked too hard. Jarvis had retired to his quarters to reward his abilities at getting the *Santana* once more outward bound. Moran ate – if a conveyor-belt blur of consumption was eating – whatever was in front of him and made a valiant try at his napkin. The first engineer, a morose woman named D'veen, consumed half of what was in front of her and disappeared into the engine spaces. She, like Moran, was armed.

Then he had to deal with the crew. He was in for it.

He was not – at least not for six watches, while the sailors sobered enough to appear at the table and hold down what he put in front of them.

Raschid spent the time cleaning his galley and thinking. What was he doing there? More importantly, why did he feel he was in the right place? Unanswerable. Clean the galley. Moran turned down Raschid's request that he be allowed to suit up, seal the galley, dump the atmosphere, and let the grease boil into a residue.

'First . . . I don't know if the bleed valve works. Second, I ain't chancin' hull integrity. Third, there ain't no guarantee we can reseal after you get done. Fourth, ain't no pig down there'd appreciate the work. Fifth, I got drakh on my mind. Get your butt off my bridge. Next time you won't walk off.'

Raschid got.

That night, Moran grudged a compliment. The mess in front of him was better than usual. Raschid blandly explained that he had used some new seasonings. Glucose, acetone bodies, minerals, fats, creatine . . . Moran told him to shut up before Raschid reached uric acid.

The crew had sobered enough to concentrate on their new enemy: Raschid. There was nothing that could be done about the ship, except pray it made it to a landing where one could desert. That sealed cargo – it would prove trouble in its own time. Their still-unknown next port? It would be another sinkhole – the *Santana* took only those cargoes that nobody would handle for worlds that no one but the desperate would land on.

The officers? Jarvis was either drunk and invisible, drunk and visible, or a sober, ghostlike image, huddling on his own bridge.

Moran? Bitch to the mate and hope there's still some med supplies left in what was called sick bay. Raschid admired – intellectually – Moran's lethality. The man seemed unable to give a command without a blow, and the blow *always* hurt, just enough for an instant, an hour, or a day's agony, but never badly enough to take a man off watch.

D'veen? Why bother? She kept the *Santana*'s drive working. 'Sides, she's no different 'n any of us. Took any slot offered to get away from dirtside. Times're tough f'r any deep-space sailor. Take it out on the cook. Somehow he's responsible for the slop. Don't matter if he come on on'y an hour b'fore lift.

Raschid ignored the complaints, insults, and then threats for a while. Then the following sequence of events occurred: A tureen went against a bulkhead. The thrower went after it. Someone came out with a knife. The knife became two pieces, and Raschid attempted to duplicate the effect on its wielder. Two other crewmen jumped Raschid and went against the tureen-bulkhead.

This crew was exceptionally thick, Raschid decided, deep in the dogwatches, when he heard the fumbling at his door. After the flurry subsided, he rousted out the off-watch and had them carry the avengers to the sick bay. He bandaged as best he could. He did not have the supplies or knowledge to straighten the second man's nose, but he consoled himself that he was not the first or even, most likely, the tenth to smash it. He set the third man's leg and the next day, when Moran threatened to brig the now-useless sailor, convinced the mate he could use some help in the galley.

Not that there was much to do between planetfalls. On a normal ship there would be maintenance, cargo handling, and so forth. On the *Santana*, why bother? Scrape rust . . . and one could well go right through the hull.

That added to the mutterings – the crew had little to do when they were off watch. Moran was even a lousy bully mate – as long as crewmen stayed out of his sight and showed up for their watch, he didn't care.

Very, very stupid, Raschid thought. Matters were getting tense. The crew had gone beyond complaints into sullenness. They were beginning to talk once more, some of them, two, sometimes three at a time, talking very quietly in corridors or unused compartments. The talk could be of only two things: murder or mutiny. Or both.

Raschid watched closely and listened where he could. There were three sailors he thought would be ringleaders. He used his new potwalloper to background the three.

Then he sought them out. One had been part of the off-watch

ambush party. All T'Orsten wanted was trouble, and promised that part of that trouble would be thin-slicing Raschid at the first possible moment.

The second was a basic bully. Cady. All she was unhappy about was that Moran was a more successful, more dangerous bully.

The third, however, was a bit more complex. Engine Artificer Pitcairn. She tried to sound no different than the others and mostly succeeded. But Raschid heard the echoes of some kind of education in her speech. He paid close attention to the woman – and his attention was noted.

She sought him out in his quarters.

'Wanted to ask you something about dinner,' she began, and pointed to the com.

'It's clean,' Raschid said. 'Moran or somebody had an induction pickup inside. It don't work no more.'

'Pretty sophisticated for a hash slinger.'

'Not sophisticated. Just careful.'

'You SDT?'

Raschid shook his head.

'Didn't think so. Pease Lines don't hire nobody but scabs. Or those who don't claim a union card.'

'Like you?'

'Hard stayin' militant when you been beached for a couple of years. Plus where I boarded, union organizin' was a bit risky.'

Raschid's curiosity about Pitcairn was satisfied. The Ship, Dockside, & Transport Union was on hard times. It was famed as a militant and understandably aggressive organization; the Empire's down economy made it easy for bosses not only to force yellow-dog contracts on any spaceport workers, but to blacklist any union official or organizer.

'Reason I wanted to talk . . . this drakh can't keep on the way it has been,' Pitcairn said. 'If Moran don't beat somebody to death, Jarvis'll get blistered an' navigate us into a collapsar.'

'Mutiny's a hard way to go.'

'Nobody said nothing about that. Yet.'

'What other options do you – do we have? I don't see any griev-ance committees lurkin' out the porthole.'

'You're quick,' Pitcairn said. 'Course th' others ain't figured that out yet.'

'How many are in on it?'

'Ten. You'll make eleven.'

'That's a start. But we don't have enough goin' for us. Run up the black flag – that closes out the options. Especially if an officer gets dead or marooned to death in the process. Bosses get hostile, somethin' like that happens. They'll hunt us all down, however long it takes, and we'll be dancin' Danny Deever.'

'You talk like you've got some experience.'

Raschid started to answer by saying 'Not for a couple of thousand years or so,' then stopped. Where the hell did *that* come from? He wasn't Methuselah.

'I read,' he said instead. 'But let's say nobody feels real logical and the drakh comes down. What then? We got ourselves a ship. Maybe half a fuel load. With a cargo. Which gives us what? This scow ain't suited for smuggling, and the on'y place people go piratin' is in the livies.

'Say we head for whatever Smuggler's Roost we can find. What are we gonna get for what's in the hold?

'Somethin' better. Where we headed? What kinda armpit? Desert with cannibals, or someplace where we klonk Moran over the head, jump ship, and live with what we got?'

'Good questions,' Pitcairn said after thinking. 'We need more skinny. Can't compute with what we got. Problem's gonna be keepin' somebody from gettin' assed, goin' berserk, and we got blood on the bulkheads.'

'You rabble-roused for the union. With only twelve goons to worry about, you oughta have no trouble keepin' 'em under your thumb,' Raschid said.

'For a while,' Pitcairn said, 'I can do it. But they ain't gonna stay in a holdin' pattern forever. We better get more info quick.'

Four ship-days later, they did. Their destination was the Cairenes – specifically, the capital world of Dusable.

'That ain't good,' Pitcairn observed. 'I organized there for about twenty minutes. If there was an honest being in the whole damn system, I never met him, her, or whatever. Plus they got a righteous depression goin'. We jump ship there, we'll be on the beach a long, long time.

'You know anything about Dusable?'

Raschid was about to say no, but didn't. Because he suddenly realized he knew a whole hell of a lot about the system and the way it worked. But he could not remember ever having visited or read anything about the Cairenes.

'A little,' he lied. 'That's one piece. Now, it'd be real nice to know what's the cargo.'

'I asked Moran. Got my chops slapped for doin' it.'

'Hercules helps those who help themselves.'

'You pray to your gods. I'll stick to Jack London. We decide to tippy-toe out th' lock, Moran sees the lock alarm go off, an' you an' me'll be out there till we figure a way to breathe space.'

'The lock alarm's been disconnected for a week. I made sure at least one suit ain't leaky. I'll check another one right now.'

'Well, well. First the bug, now the alarm. For a cook, you'd make a fair spy. All right. First watch. Moran sleeps like a corpse, long as you don't try to go in his compartment.'

They went out the air lock as quietly as they could. Raschid winced at the air-hiss and the whine of the lock mechanism. Both of them pulled themselves out of the open lock, making sure the attractors on their boot soles had no chance to clang against the hull. Pitcairn aimed a line-thrower and fired, and the grapnel at the end of the line snagged through an X-beam.

They hand-over-handed their way across to the cargo hold and inside, then opened their faceplates, found prybars, and went to work.

'Bless m' clottin' sainted mother,' Pitcairn swore after a while. 'There's at least *one* somebody on Dusable ain't in no depression.'

The cargo was entirely luxury goods. Exotic foods. Liquors. Wines. One case held jewelry.

'We been livin' on swill, an' all this was just across the way. I'm tryin' not to lose it, tear Moran's face off and order a hog-out. What next?'

'Interestin',' Raschid observed. 'You note there ain't no customer ID on any of the packing lists. Just: *As Per Instructions To Captain.*'

'Okay. I say again my last. What next?'

'I think . . . maybe a mutiny.'

'That sets real easy. Then what do we do with all these goodies? Smugglers'll pay heavy credits for what's here.'

'Maybe that's the option. Mutiny first, questions later.'

The mutiny came off painlessly, to use the term broadly. Raschid had given explicit orders, so only four of the twelve conspirators were used – those Raschid thought would not go berserk.

Jarvis was easy. Cady, on bridge watch, waited until the captain got tired of wearing his gun-heavy uniform coat and hung it up. The next time Jarvis paced by, a bar of soap in a stocking was applied with some firmness to his medulla oblongata. He was carried to his cabin and, after the cabin was searched for more weapons and the sealed shipping instructions taken, locked in.

Moran took a bit more skill. One sailor, selected for her slenderness, draped herself on an overhead conduit running past Moran's compartment door. Moran was buzzed for his watch. He came out, and the sailor prayed and dropped.

The flurry before Moran pitched her the length of the corridor gave Raschid, Pitcairn, and T'Orsten time enough to rat-pack him. Eventually Moran was hammered into unconsciousness.

They knew he had to have weapons stashed in his compartment, so they locked him in a bare and disused room. The fresher worked, and they could slide meals through a narrow slit cut in the door's base.

Raschid fingered his split lip, then went for the engine spaces and D'veen. He carried Moran's gun as a completely empty threat. D'veen took no threatening whatever. All she asked was that when the mutineers were caught and tried, they would testify that she had put up a magnificent battle.

'We have no intentions of being in front of a court,' Raschid said. 'But if so, we'll save your ticket.'

The mutineers held their council of war in the officers' wardroom – after Raschid and Pitcairn had made a careful selection of goodies for a victory feast. They allowed one half bottle of alk per sailor – and Raschid thought that was too much.

He was right, but Pitcairn had made sure that only she and the cook were the ones with guns. T'Orsten bellowed rage at being informed that he *could not* toss Moran out the lock. He *could not* orgy out on the luxury cargo. And he *could not* revenge himself on D'veen.

Raschid let him bellow, saw that T'Orsten wasn't letting steam but building for a berserker, and blindsided him. They tucked him away next to Moran and went back to the wardroom.

Raschid opened, read the sealed shipping instructions, lifted an eyebrow, and passed the sheets across to Pitcairn.

'I guess that settles what's next,' she said. She was a little pale. 'We look for some smugglers, dump the cargo and the ship, and do our damndest to vanish.'

She quoted from the instructions: "Land bleat-bleah section, transmit blurt-blurt signal. Cargo will be off-loaded by personnel bearing authorization personally signed by Tyrenne Yelad, duplicate signature below.'

'Just the whole goddamned system's MaxMoFo, is all. And we just took his toys away. Nice going.'

There was something moving in the back of Raschid's mind. Yelad . . . Yelad . . .

'Workers of the *Santana*, haul ass! You have everything to lose including your chains,' Pitcairn finished.

'No,' Raschid said. 'No,' he went on. 'I think we make delivery.'

Ignoring the gape, he fielded a bottle and poured himself a celebratory drink. Things were going very well, indeed.

Chapter Twenty-One

The Privy Council reacted in confused fury to the raid on the AM2 convoy. The crime against the Empire – *their* Empire – seemed an even greater felony because they had stolen it themselves. Add to that the tremendous cost in blood and credits, the enormous hopes they had placed on the many extra months the AM2 shipment would have provided, and, finally, the humiliation that a wild gang of pirates had bested Imperial forces.

Plots within plots were hinted at within the fabric of the raid. Were the Honjo themselves involved? No one knew. The Kraas suggested that perhaps they had not been too far off the mark when they made up the accusation of Honjo culpability in the conspiracy to kill them. The make-up of raiders was equally as puzzling. What were the Bhor doing so far from home? Malperin believed they were just mercenaries. Adding weight to her argument was that the human on-screen during the Bhor's terrorcast had been identified: Sten. Kyes's target earlier, who had been identified as that smaller man in civilian clothes at the conspirators' kriegsspiel. Ex-Mantis, and a longtime associate and probable friend of the man they had once believed dead: Fleet Marshal Ian Mahoney, the man who had plotted their assassination on Earth. As soon as Sten and Mahoney had been connected, most of the council members were sure that Mahoney was the man behind all their troubles.

They were careful in not stating their exact reasons – such as the very good possibility that Mahoney suspected them of slaying the Eternal Emperor. So they took a care when maligning him, especially in front of the newest member of their body, Colonel Poyndex.

If Poyndex wondered at the extreme paranoia of his new colleagues, he kept it to himself. He had joined them prepared to expand his influence to the fullest. With that in mind, he made no attempt to soothe their anger.

The privy council wanted heads – and they wanted them now. Poyndex offered up all his skills in helping them to widen the continuing purge. A new and vastly greater list of suspects was devised. Hunters were sent to track them down and bring them to swift justice. Poyndex was careful that his signature rarely appeared on any of those orders, and when it did, it was always following everyone else's.

The purge was not setting well with the council's dwindling allies. Many of the victims had friends or relations in those crucial areas. Poyndex knew that could not be helped. He reasoned that the council would be satisfied long before they drowned in the very blood they were spilling – and he was doing his best to pad the list of suspects with beings of little importance to anyone.

In only one area did he subtly rein them in. When they started looking for new targets from which to steal AM2, he drew the line.

'I think we should delay on this matter awhile,' he said.

'Give us one reason why,' Lovett snapped.

'After the incident with the Honjo,' Poyndex said, 'even a fool would suspect that your real reason for the attack was the AM2. And that they were innocent of any conspiracy.'

'I see your point,' Malperin said.

'Bloody hell!' one of the Kraa twins exploded. 'Wot's an Honjo or twelve to any fella? Bunch a shutfists, that's wot they be. 'N everyone clottin' knows it! They'll get little sympathy.'

'Possibly,' Poyndex said. 'But if we immediately attack another AM2-rich system – no matter what the excuse – then all our allies will feel as if they were potential targets, as well.'

'Too right,' the fat Kraa said. 'Me 'n Sis got some good candidates.'

'I'm sure you do,' Poyndex said. 'And I think all these things should be taken into consideration. But not now. Not just yet. Or else we'll lose too many of our supporters.'

They saw the wisdom in his advice. But just to make sure, Poyndex suggested some particularly bloody actions that could be taken as part of the purge. It helped a great deal to keep them all relatively calm. He also helped them launch a massive effort to bring the beings responsible for the AM2 theft to justice. Poyndex had sniffed the rotten fish the council was attempting to hide: Ian Mahoney, former chief of the same intelligence department Poyndex commanded. How very interesting. Was Mahoney just a rogue? Possibly. Possibly not. Why were his colleagues so afraid of the man?

Poyndex was sure that one way or another, he would soon learn the reasons behind all of it, and that the answer would be useful to him. Meanwhile, as the junior member of the privy council, he would do his best to satisfy.

Besides Poyndex, there was one other relatively pleased member of the council.

Kyes had found it difficult to hide his boredom. He cared not a whit what the outcome was of all this. He did his best to appear interested and to add his opinion to the debate when warranted. But on this particular day of fury, Kyes had received extremely good news.

The data banks of his one-of-a-kind computer were now full to the brim, thanks to the assistance of Lagguth, Poyndex, and a whole host of historical ferrets. The computer had been crunching all the data for weeks, and at last it possessed all of the facts, rumors, and half rumors they could find on the Eternal Emperor.

Kyes had almost dreaded asking the question. It was all very well for him to believe as he did, but believing did not make a thing so. As a scientist/inventor, Kyes knew that better than anyone. Was he mad to think the Eternal Emperor was not dead? Despite all the evidence? The witnesses? The filmed assassination itself?

Only the computer could answer that. It had been fed every detail of previous reported attempts on the Emperor. But what if he asked and the prog was unacceptably low? Kyes was certain that if he were not already mad, such an answer would drive him over that final brink. But if he did not ask, he would never know. Kyes was literally in the position of a being who has been told that whether he would live or die was a known quantity. All he had to do was look in the crystal ball to find out. It was just as hard to look as it was to ignore it.

Finally, he looked.

The prog was ninety percent plus that the Eternal Emperor was alive.

With that news, Kyes was ready to move.

Far away from that debate, there was another extremely happy being.

Sr. Ecu had labored hard since his meeting with Mahoney. As his assistants pored over legal tracts, ancient and modern, he had put out careful feelers on Sten's proposal that an impartial tribunal be formed to try the privy council for the assassination of the Eternal Emperor.

Of course, such a question had not been asked outright. But, working from a narrow list of systems that were guaranteed not to leak even a hint of his disloyalty, much less run shouting panic-stricken from his presence, he had felt his way around the edges of his goal.

He knew now that if such a tribunal were proposed, there were beings he could convince to join the panel. It would be very difficult, but far from impossible. Before he could ask, however, the Manabi needed a legal basis for such a body. Else, the whole exercise was pointless.

Sr. Ecu found his precedent.

As he suspected it might, the answer came from the early days of the Empire. It was during the time – well over two thousand years before – that most of what was now the Empire did not exist. In fact, places that were currently heavily populated and considered the very heart of the Empire had then been wild frontier regions, where there was little law and equally little order. It was a time when six years or more could pass before an Imperial circuit judge visited any of those regions to settle local disputes.

The Eternal Emperor had been well aware that many things could go very wrong if left to fester. So he encouraged the creation of local magisterial panels, empowered to settle nearly all civil claims. Their decisions could be appealed to the region's Imperial governor, but the length of time to get a hearing, much less a presence, was so formidable that few took advantage of that option.

In the matter of major, life-threatening felonies, the Emperor had been far more cautious. Sr. Ecu could read his concerns between the lines. Jailings and executions could easily become a tool of vengeance. It was unlikely that the Eternal Emperor was concerned as much about the morality of such actions as he was that unsettled crimes would create further instability, blood feuds, and spreading wars.

So in those cases, the magisterial panels were slightly limited in their authority. If a suspected violent felon were hailed before them, the panels were only to determine if there was a great likelihood that a crime had actually taken place, what manner of crime it might have been, and whether the being(s) before them was probably responsible. To determine the evidence, they were empowered to subpoena witnesses – bringing them to the bench by force, if necessary – to arrest all suspects, and to hold in contempt of court any being who opposed them.

If the evidence pointed to the suspect before the bench, they could indict him for the crime. If he were considered extremely dangerous, they could back up the indictment by imprisoning him until an Imperial judge arrived to try the case.

The system worked so well that the Emperor had kept it alive for many hundreds of years. So Sr. Ecu had not one case to back his claims, but millions upon millions of them.

He had found the means of justice. Now, all he needed were the judges.

Chapter Twenty-Two

The big cop was in a surly mood as she paced the dock. The gnarly *Santana* sat silent at its berth. The ports remained firmly closed despite repeated efforts to get someone – *anyone* – to respond.

Lieutenant Skinner muttered obscenities under her breath, casting dark looks at the idle workers who were grinning at her difficulties. Her scab crew remained silent. If the crowd's humor turned to violence they were too far from their home ward to expect any assistance. There would be no reprisals. The SDT Union was too strong and its pockets too deep, even in this time of awful unemployment.

Skinner could not figure out what had gone wrong. Her ward captain had said this was a plum job. A little favor for Tyrenne Yelad that'd go into Skinner's merit book.

All she had to do was retrieve the *Santana*'s cargo. A few personal and *private* things for the Tyrenne. It was a job to be handled with Skinner's usual discretion.

Skinner's use of scabs was hardly unusual, or even provoking. In such cases one approached the appropriate union steward who would estimate the number of beings required for the job. The mordida would be set at double their prospective wages – then scabs would be allowed to unload the cargo, while the steward spread the money around to those who normally would have toted those bales. Keeping a nice taste for himself, of course. That was only right. Skinner had picked up more than a few earners of that type herself as a Dusable officer of the law.

Okay, so what had gone clottin' wrong? They had trundled up to the freighter, but no one had come out. Impatient, Skinner had gotten on the horn to see what was the hang up. No response. She tried again. Still no answer. What kind of game was this? She had sufficient mordida in her pocket to pay off anyone, from the captain of the *Santana* down, if necessary.

The steward exited his office. From his look deep drakh was about. 'Get your butt outta here,' he snarled.

'What the clot for? We got a deal. *Remember?*'

'The deal's off. Only reason I'm tellin' you, 'stead of sendin' a couple of guys to thump you first, is we done business afore. So I owe you a warnin'. Now, get!'

Skinner blew herself out to her most coplike proportions – which were considerable. But before she could deliver her full wrath at this scrote, she heard cheering. She whirled to confront the new threat – and gaped.

It was Solon Kenna! Advancing with a phalanx of aides, a big crowd of SDT workers, and a livie news crew. Ohmigod. Skinner knew it was time to make herself scarce. She should have known. This was an election year. In fact, the election was only two weeks away, which made things even stickier. Especially since Tyrenne Yelad's challenger was Kenna himself. Clot the ward captain! She was gettin' out.

Solon Kenna took position in front of the ship. He was an immense, elderly man who bore his girth like the seasoned pol he was. His nose was bulbous from many hours and many bottles, but his eyes and instincts were sharp. And he had a smile that would swallow a swamp beast. He turned the full force of that smile on his pet newscaster.

'I will speak no further on the perfidy of my opponent,' Solon Kenna said. 'Instead, I will let the facts speak for themselves. They will soon reveal themselves when I assure the poor mistreated and honest laborers inside that they are among friends – and they exit with the awful evidence of Tyrenne Kenna's greed.'

'Hang on a sec, boss,' the newscaster said. 'You sure you wanna say perfidy? I mean, callin' the butt-wipe a lyin' sack might be going too far. But – I don't know. The word's kinda thick. Might make folks think you're stuck up.'

'No problem,' Kenna answered. 'Fix it any way you like. I trust your professional judgment.'

'Second question, what do we call these guys?' the newscaster asked. 'We don't wanna say they're mutineers, right? I mean, that's not the drift of this bit, is it?'

'Absolutely not,' Solon Kenna said. 'What we have here is an injustice of enormous proportions.'

Before he could continue, there was a cheer from the dockworkers as the main cargo port of the freighter creaked open and the ragged crew members stepped out.

Raschid kept to the sidelines, watching with oddly professional interest as the events unfolded. Pitcairn proved to be a great inter-view subject. The other mutineers took their hints from her and Raschid thought they all did a credible job. But the illicit cargo would have won the day, regardless. Kenna handled it like a seasoned pro. His expression shifted from sadness, to anger, to outrage at the greed of Tyrenne Yelad, expending dwindling AM2 credits for luxury items while his own people starved.

Not bad, Raschid thought. Although the guy had an unfortunate habit of tossing off fancy words when they weren't called for. It didn't matter that he misused them. The people he was aiming them at wouldn't know. They would possibly take offense only because he might be coming across too pompous. Still, he was mostly getting in all his shots.

Once again he puzzled at why he knew so much about this sort of thing. But he pressed the question away, along with that odd feeling he had of being watched by something or someone just out of view.

He saw Pitcairn pointing in his direction. Kenna looked over and smiled a big wolfish grin. Raschid did not know what that meant, but he would soon find out. Solon Kenna was motioning the livie crew to keep back and was coming his way. Raschid decided to stay put and play the cards as they were dealt.

Kenna planted himself in front of Raschid, lighting half the dock with his grin.

'How you doing, friend?' he said. 'I'm Solon Kenna. The humble representative of these poor working beings.'

Then as Raschid took his hand to shake, Kenna leaned closer and whispered. 'I got word you were coming,' he said. 'We need to talk – later.'

Raschid hesitated, then nodded. 'You're right,' he said. 'We need to talk.'

The Cairene System was a dozen or so lightly populated agro-worlds and the big, dense port planet of Dusable. This is where the late Tanz Sullamora had made his second fortune – in shipbuilding. The factories, which had groaned under triple shifts during the war, were now desolate. The AM2 crisis had struck nearly every part of Dusable.

That would be bad for any planet. But on Dusable, it was disaster. Because the Cairene System was a political throwback. On Dusable there was really only one industry: politics. There was barely a being on the planet who did not owe his or her existence to patronage, from pot scourer, to sewer worker, to cop, to business owner, to joygirl, to ward boss, to the Tyrenne Yelad himself.

It was an unwieldy system, and corrupt to the core, but it had worked for centuries, and worked very well, For thirty years Tyrenne Yelad had ruled. His patronage was so vast there was little hope he would ever be defeated. Still, just because he won with case every four years did not mean that his opponents were in any way helpless.

There were checks and balances in this system. No matter that they were equally as corrupt. Under the Tyrenne was the Council of Solons. Each member ran a group of wards, whose voters he rewarded with jobs, advice, and influence. A perfect Solon made sure no one went without. If one had trouble with the grocery money, one went to the ward captain. Same for a spouse with a brutal or drunken other. Paid hospital stays were assured. Fines were leavened, or even dismissed.

Bribe money flowed in and out of all this. Joygirls paid their pimps, who paid the cops. The cops themselves paid for prized beats such as vice, or traffic in the rich resort areas. They also paid for rank, which placed them higher on the mordida ladder. Mob bosses paid both ways: cops on one end, pols on the other. And all those people paid the ward captains – who, in turn, poured all the credits into the coffers of the Solon controlling their district.

The Solons, in turn, shared the mordida with the key leaders who actually ran the whole thing. Tyrenne Yelad was a good example of one such leader. He had come to power as a reformer, as had the Tyrenne before him. This election, the new hopeful reformer was Solon Kenna, president of the Council of Solons and Yelad's worst enemy. Kenna's power came from the unions, particularly the SDT, which was why, after three tries and three defeats, Kenna was convinced that this year was his best chance. The hordes of unemployed beings had put big brass knuckles on his fists. He had been slugging it out with Yelad for more than six months. But now, two weeks before the election, he had not been able to deliver a knockout. If he couldn't, Kenna's long run was over – unless there was a miracle. He was hoping that Raschid was that miracle. The more they talked, the surer he became.

At one point Raschid had quizzed him about the credit situation. How full were Kenna's campaign coffers? Kenna said he had sufficient. Raschid shook his head and advised him to get more, much more. Kenna asked why.

'Unruh's First Law,' Raschid said. 'Money is the mother's milk of politics.'

The answer spoke volumes. This man was no dry political-science scholar. Kenna had seen too many elections lost with that type. Raschid was obviously an expert street politician who knew how to play the game from the top right down to the gutter.

Kenna found it easy to be candid with Raschid, because . . . he *knew*, dammit. The guy *knew*! The next question, however, threw him into temporary orbit.

'Why are you telling me all this?' Raschid asked. 'What do you expect me to do about it? I'm just a ship's cook. A mutinous one in some lights.'

'Come on,' Kenna sputtered. 'You can drop that. You're among friends, here. Besides, I've already been filled in. I knew you were on your way.'

'Who told you?' Raschid asked.

Kenna figured it was a try on – so he bit. 'It wasn't anyone I could name right out,' he said. 'You know that as well as I do. I got it from . . . back channels. We were advised the *Santana* was inbound. With a cargo I'd be a fool not to inspect. More importantly, I was told there would be a man on board posing as the ship's cook. And that he was the absolute best there was in political strategy.

'I can't tell you how we all reacted here. To know that some very important outsiders were with us. And that rescue was on its way.'

Raschid considered. For some reason, it all made sense to him. Although he wondered why those outsiders had not informed him as well. He buried that. It was another test, maybe the final one.

'Okay,' Raschid said. 'You got your boy. I'm on board.'

Kenna breathed a heavy sigh of relief.

'Who else is in the race?' Raschid asked.

'Only one other,' Kenna said. 'Solon Walsh. And he doesn't have a chance. Although the guy's as handsome a pol as has come along for three forevers. But he's young. And he's stupid.'

'What's his bit?'

'Reform,' Kenna said dryly. 'He's trying to steal the march from me, I guess. Because that's my main platform. Walsh can't seem to get any ideas of his own.'

'He's probably got Yelad behind him,' Raschid said. 'But real quiet. Walsh is intended to bleed off support from you.'

Kenna was startled, then comforted again. It was just the way he had seen it.

'All right . . . here's how we go,' Raschid said. 'We need three things.

'First, we need a Dummy. Second, an Issue.'

He took a long swallow from the brandy glass Kenna had been constantly filling since the meeting began.

'What's the third?' Kenna asked.

'Easy,' Raschid said. 'Then we steal the election.'

Chapter Twenty-Three

The tiny and the meek may never inherit the earth – but they can sometimes rock it worse than the most catastrophic earthquake.

Napoleon's hemorrhoids. He'd slept poorly the night before a battle, and napped the next day. Twenty-five thousand of his soldiers died, and he was no longer an Emperor.

Three woman cipher clerks conspired. The secrets of Earth's Third Reich were revealed. At least ten million Germans died.

And Zoran mentioned, with giggles, what one of her 'frantic minds' had reported. There was a new shrine, she said, shaking her head at the credulity of some of her followers. Not a mountaintop where the Eternal Emperor had appeared to the faithful, nor a large pile of crutches, abandoned after he had worked miracles.

'Loaves and fishes' – giggle – 'might be the comparison,' she said. Kyes was blank. 'Oh. My apologies,' she said. 'There was an ancient cult on Earth. Called Christers. That was one of their miracles.

'My frantic mind has less than that.

'Eggs' – large giggle – 'for pity's sakes. Not millions of them, and not used to feed the starving. But sold.'

There was a small spaceport restaurant, on a world called Yongjukl. 'I could not find it in my atlas, but I suppose it is out there somewhere.' According to Zoran's acolyte, it served food exactly like that the Eternal Emperor favored. Using his exact recipes; 'Or at least,' Zoran added, 'those that were reported before the Eternal One chose to absent himself for a period.

'A minor . . . fetish' – giggle – 'of ours? I have cooked and enjoyed some of those recipes myself.'

Kyes interest was sparked – the Eternal Emperor, indeed, fancied himself a gourmet chef. But if Zoran had cooked some of his recipes . . . that did not compute. Had to be a restaurateur with a new gimmick.

Ah, but no, Zoran continued. These recipes had been taught to the owner by a mysterious chef who had appeared, worked for a few periods, then disappeared.

'My frantic one takes this as a precursor. Of course, he swears the descriptions of this mysterious man in the white apron are exactly what you would expect a man seeking miracles to say. Oh, well. When the Emperor does choose to return from his time with the Holy Spheres, I question whether it would be in a greasy spoon.'

Kyes was in contact with Yongjukl. He ordered its most skilled and subtle psychologists to talk to the cult member – and to any other customers of that restaurant who might have seen the cook.

The descriptions varied, of course, but overall they fit the Eternal Emperor exactly. Kyes had the restaurant's owner questioned.

The owner refused to cooperate. Instead, he threw the investigators out of his dive – named, Kyes noted, the Last Blast.

Kyes ordered the owner, a human male named Pattipong, followed. He could not be. He changed clothes and washed before shutting down, so electronic tracers did not work. Surveillance experts, singly and teamed, tried to track him. Pattipong lost them all, every time, and reappeared the next morning to reopen the Last Blast, smiling as if nothing had happened and he was completely oblivious to the attentions.

Kyes started to order Pattipong's arrest but stopped himself. You are on to something. Finally: Do not panic. Do not rush to judgment.

He told Lagguth and the computer team to load and analyze *all* events occurring on that world within the last six years, concentrating on the last few months. If the mysterious cook was the Emperor, he would not have used Yongjukl as a base for very long. Or so Kyes thought – with no logic behind him.

The computer found a mansion, or the remains of a mansion. It had been, for some generations, among the holdings of a very rich, very mysterious offworld family who never visited their estate. Recently, however, a ship had landed on the grounds and one man had gotten off. The ship had immediately lifted. The man was the family's heir apparent. He had stayed in seclusion for a brief period of time and then disappeared. The mansion's staff had been paid off, the mansion torn down, and the grounds donated to the government. The mansion – and who owned it – had already been a favorite mystery story for the local media. Its destruction created a one-day wonder. But there was no more information, and the story disappeared.

A mansion, Kyes thought excitedly. Equipped with the most elaborate library and computer. That was enough. He ordered Pattipong's arrest. Two of Yongjukl's most skilled operatives went out to seize the tiny man. Dingiswayo Pattipong killed both of them and vanished once more, this time for good.

Kyes held in red, red rage. He forced himself to rethink. No. This was not a disaster. Analyze it. HUMINT has failed – not surprisingly. But artificial intelligence . . .

He ran Yongjukl, the worlds around it, and the galactic cluster it was in through every analysis possible. He found what he was looking for.

Kyes's quest was almost over.

Chapter Twenty-Four

He started with the Dummy.

Raschid stayed in the background for an hour or so while Kenna laid the groundwork with Solon Walsh. Even Walsh's keen-eyed aide, Avri, started ignoring him after a while as her boss played the political mating game with Kenna.

It was Raschid's professional opinion Walsh had most of the makings of an ideal candidate. He was young and sleekly handsome. He spoke without stuttering. He had a steady, clear gaze. There were no food spots on his clothing, and his carefully arranged coif had a charming habit of going slightly out of kilter after a few minutes of conversation. It made him seem more relaxed and genuine. In some areas Walsh had received some expert advice.

The man exuded honesty. That had everything to do with lack of IQ. That open, wide-eyed look was there because there was nothing behind the optic system. But stupidity could be a candidate's greatest asset – as long as he listened to the right people. Raschid figured the right people in this case was Avri.

'I'm surprised to learn there's so much common ground between us,' Walsh said as the political dance wound down. 'I mean, I had no idea you felt that way about taxes, for instance. Wow! After all this time our whole argument with one another disappeared, just like that.' He snapped his fingers by way of illustration.

Solon Kenna made with a gentle, fatherly smile. 'A misunderstanding, that's all,' he said. 'See what happens when two honest beings speak frankly?'

'That's real good drakh, and all,' Avri interrupted. Walsh shot his aide a nervous look, ready to fold if Avri gave the word. Good.

He could be handled. 'But where are we at? What's the deal? There's gotta be a deal, else you wouldn't be blowin' all this smoke.

'Now, if you think Solon Walsh is gonna take a little earner and fold his tent . . . I don't know . . . Whatcha got in mind?'

Kenna handled it without a blink. More points for him. Raschid was feeling better and better about his plan.

'Right on the mark as always, young Avri,' Kenna smoothed. 'I'll let Sr. Raschid help me with this. I really can't stress too hard that this being's credentials go far deeper than I can say. Far deeper.'

Avri's eyes narrowed as Raschid joined the game.

'Solon Kenna and I have run through this every which way we can,' Raschid said. 'Thing is, everybody agrees we have to have a change. Tyrenne Yelad just isn't making it anymore. Trouble is, any way you cut the deck, Yelad keeps coming up on top. Because Walsh and Kenna cancel each other out. Am I right?'

Avri nodded firmly. She had a hint of a smile at her lips, which Raschid knew meant he had to beat Yelad's mordida, plus the after-election promises.

'So. What Solon Kenna proposes to do is pull out. And throw his support to you.' He nodded in the direction of the stunned Walsh.

There was much surprised babbling. But Raschid got the meeting back on track and spelled out the details. Kenna would slip a hefty wad of credits to Walsh, who would put his campaign into high gear, splashing his name all over and hitting the stump hard. That would be just the outward display, however. The real money would be aimed at those few mighty wards with a big number of independent voters, folks who held out to the last so they could get the biggest pay-offs.

Meanwhile, Kenna would run a lackluster campaign, letting some of his support bleed off.

'Two nights before the election,' Raschid said, 'Kenna pulls out. Says he's seen the light, and all. Credits it to the persuasive words of his worthy opponent – one Solon Walsh. Then throws his support to you.'

They did not go for it right off. Nobody ever does. There had to be bullet-proof assurances that there would be no last-minute betrayal. These were made. And the rest of the terms were set. Walsh would be Tyrenne. In return, Kenna would wield even more clout than before. Avri did not give a clot about the giveaways. She was more interested in being the power behind a Tyrenne's throne.

'It still ain't enough,' Avri said. 'Even if we join forces, Yelad's still got the vote edge. Too many independents. Maybe we can squeak through on that.

'But he's the man with the pad. He can always top whatever we got by voting the graves.'

What Avri was referring to was that delightfully old-fashioned system still in play on Dusable. There was a joke that no one ever really died. The death certificate got dumped into Yelad's computer banks and that person's name remained on the voting rolls. When Yelad's people saw the count going against them, they voted the dead. Or the living, in the case of people who had emigrated from the Cairenes but were still there on the voting rolls.

Of course, Yelad could not be too blatant about it. Millions and millions of nonexistent voters would be too much even for the corrupt people of Dusable. Appearances were important. So Yelad's staff kept careful watch on the real voting, an easy task because of the deliberately out-of-date method of vote-casting. First off, every adult being was required by law to vote. The ward/mordida system could not work unless everybody was in the game, physically and psychologically. Second, each person registered with the solon of his or her choice. An ID card was presented at the polls, and the vote cast was registered upon it for a ward captain to examine later. So much for the secret ballot. Finally voters were physically required to go to the polls, rather than voting by computer at home, unlike most citizens of the Empire. This gave a master thief like Yelad all kinds of interesting ways to cheat.

'How do we get away from *that*?' Avri asked.

'We got it covered,' Raschid said. 'It'll be tricky, but that's what makes the game fun. But we'd like to keep all that to ourselves awhile. If you don't mind.'

No one did. Kenna was taking all the risks. Avri knew nobody would be mad at Walsh. He was just the Dummy.

The deal was done. Then Raschid tackled the next part: the Issue. Yelad represented the status quo. Kenna, labor. But Walsh had nothing but empty words. He needed a target. Raschid had the gringo ploy in mind. Nobody in the room knew the term's origins except Raschid, and he wasn't saying, but they knew what it meant. Attack the outsider, somebody big and far off you could blame all troubles on.

So Walsh's issue was the privy council. It was their fault things had been bungled since the death of the Emperor. It was their fault there was no AM2, creating such bleak times. Yelad would be forced to defend them. If he did not, he was doomed with the all-powerful Imperial council.

When Raschid had brought it up prior to this meeting, Kenna had been so excited he contemplated forgetting the whole deal with Walsh and keeping his own campaign running. Raschid doused that idea. He pointed out since Kenna was already President of the Council of Solons, the privy council would be highly annoyed at this attack. Kenna did not want or need that kind of attention, Raschid strongly advised. The thought also made him feel personally uncomfortable, although once again, he did not know why.

'Let the Dummy do it,' Raschid said. 'They'll figure he's just grabbing for straws because there's no way he can win. They won't care one way or another what a Dummy says, and they'll ignore the whole thing.'

It was not necessary to spell that out to Walsh. Avri knew what it meant, which was more than enough.

Kenna was in high spirits as they exited the bar. Everything was on track. Raschid wanted him to stay happy, so he praised his performance.

'The trick you just pulled was invented by a master,' Raschid said. 'It's called a rossthomas.'

'Which means?' Kenna asked with lifted eyebrows.

'It means that now the fools in this town are on our side,' Raschid said.

Kenna laughed all the way back to headquarters.

There were other meetings with key beings who had to be bribed, clued in, brought into line, or a combination of the three. The results were happily similar.

One meeting, however, Raschid thought best to handle alone.

The mob boss's name was Pavy. She was known as the hardest, canniest, and most unforgiving of all Dusable's crime royalty. Her turf was a dozen of the biggest independent wards. Not one coin came through any of them that did not have its edges well skinned. She ran all vice – from joygirls and joyboys to the most addictive narcotics. Her loan sharks were the toughest and most knowledge-able. Her thieves the wiliest. Pavy was also stone gorgeous.

She was of average height, but in the clinging body suit she wore when she greeted Raschid her legs climbed into the upper atmosphere. Her hair was a dark, close-cropped skullcap, and her eyes were as black as any he had ever seen – with hard, gleaming, diamond points of crafty intelligence. They met in a cozy little room deep inside the one-square-kilometer warren of vice she called The Club.

Pavy ordered her thug assistants out of the room after the preliminaries. Raschid had already been fine-toothed for weapons in the bombproof room just inside the entrance. Not that Raschid could not have snapped that long slender neck with one hand – which Pavy knew as well as he. Still, she had dismissed her bodyguards. From the look in her eyes, Raschid knew that the woman had already taken his measure. He was there for a deal, not to kill.

After they left, she refilled their glasses with the aromatic liquor she favored, dropped the jeweled slippers from her feet, and settled back on the soft settee, her legs tucked up under her. She gave Raschid a silent toast with her glass and sipped. He followed her lead.

'Now tell me what you have in mind,' she purred. Raschid did not make the mistake of thinking the purr was anything other than that of a very deadly tiger.

He spelled out the program. The fix was in, he said, although he couldn't tell her exactly how it was going to come off. Pavy nodded. That groundwork had been more than satisfactorily settled by Kenna's people. Then he told her what he wanted her to do, just sketching the main points; the little details could be spelled out later. Pavy's smile grew as he talked. She liked this. It was going to be very expensive for someone. She laughed a couple of times, then told him what she wanted in return, a sum that would keep a small planet happy for a year. Raschid shaded the price by one fourth, but only because he sensed she would distrust him if he didn't try. Then Pavy surprised him.

'What's your end?' she asked. 'What did you tell Kenna you wanted?'

'I didn't say,' Raschid answered.

'That's wise,' Pavy said, nodding. 'If you win you can probably get at least as much as he's giving me.'

Raschid figured she was right. In fact, Kenna had asked him the same question. What did Raschid want in return? He knew it disturbed Kenna to be told he would find out when it was over. Why had he done that? Raschid was not sure. All he knew was that the price would come at the proper time.

Pavy asked him about other political battles he had been involved in, as one criminal to another, giving him the out of dodging anything that might be incriminating. But that was no problem. As far as Raschid could figure, this was the first election he had ever worked, so he lied. Political events came tumbling out of him, complete with victories and desperate setbacks and stunning reversals. Oddly enough, as he told the stories and she kept their glasses full, he realized that he was not lying at all.

Finally, it was getting late. Time to go. Pavy's hand hovered over the button to call for her thugs to escort him out. Then she flashed him a most peculiar smile. It was glowing, and her lips were soft, her eyes wide and wanting.

'You could stay longer if you liked,' she whispered very softly. Long nails brushing the microthin body suit. The rasping sound gave Raschid the shivers.

He considered her request – because that was what it was. Why was this woman so suddenly attracted to him? He saw the reason. It was from being so close to power – real power. But he was just Raschid. Wasn't he? Where was the power? Then he knew it was there. Inside him. But not why. Nor who. Yet.

Raschid stayed the night.

The 45th Ward was one of Tyrenne Yelad's lesser bailiwicks. It had not always been so. The chief occupation of the sprawling neighborhood involved the plasfill contracts for the Tyrenne's massive public-works programs. Before the AM2 crunch, all of Dusable had been busy one way or another in these projects. Bridges were built duplicating perfectly good arcs a few klicks away. As were unnecessary roads. Or tall, gleaming public offices that were always in short supply. The reason for this was that each time the public payroll was padded, new offices were required for patronage. Departments continuously warred with other departments for more employees, thus increasing their power, and posh offices to house them in, thus increasing their prestige.

So there was always a tremendous need for plasfill. The 45th had always prided itself on supplying the thinnest gruel at the highest price possible. These big profits made the world go around.

Then came hard times. Yelad had to throw one of his wards off the plasfill sleigh – the 45th. Now people were beginning to hurt in the 45th. Long lines lined up daily before the ward captain's door. By day's end, the captain had barely whittled into the line.

So when the official gravcar hummed into the neighborhood, it was greeted with quiet but keen interest. The windows were shut and darkened, but it was no mystery who was inside. The car flew the tiny flag of Tyrenne Yelad.

It cruised slowly through the neighborhoods, as if inspecting the shuttered shops and 'For Sale' signs on the businesses. The people of the 45th who were about that day – and there were many, since jobs were scarce – wondered about its purpose. Was the great Tyrenne Yelad there with some great surprise? A bonus contract for plasfill? A few shabby vehicles chose to follow at a discreet distance.

The Tyrenne's car made the turn that led to the ward captain's house. Aha! Good news.

Suddenly, the gravcar sped up. As if harsh orders had been given and the driver was heading back.

At that moment, a small, tubby, darling child of a boy darted into the street after an errant ball. The gravcar sped on. The child looked up with wide, innocent, and oh, so frightened eyes, frozen. But there was still plenty of time for the car to stop. On it came. People screamed warnings. Mothers wailed in empathy. The child turned and half stumbled toward escape. Then the gravcar accelerated. Almost as if it had been done on *purpose*. The car clipped the child, and, to loud shrieks of horror, the boy was hurled into the air. He crashed to the ground, blood spurting. The gravcar came to a fast stop. A uniformed driver leapt out. People ran toward the accident. The driver drew a pistol and shouted for them to stay back. They did.

Then he marched to the corpse of the boy and stood over it. He looked back at the gravcar. A window hissed open, and people thought they could see someone motioning an order. The driver scooped up the body and dumped it in the gravcar as if it were trash. Someone shouted a protest. The driver snarled an oath and waved the gun. But the crowd was furious. Beings started running for the gravcar. The driver leapt inside and sped away, leaving angry voters behind. Voters who now cursed the very name of Tyrenne Yelad – a being who scorned them so much that he killed their children.

Inside the car Raschid flung the driver's cap into the back. Beside him, the corpse stirred, then sat up.

'Gimme a clottin' rag,' the boy's corpse said.

'Pretty good first act,' Raschid said as he handed a cloth to the boy, who began wiping away the fake blood.

One close look at the 'boy' would reveal the lines in his face and the cynical twist around his eyes. He lit up a giant tabac, inhaled deeply, and blew out, filling the car with the cloud. This was a boy who had been in the acting business for fifty years or more.

'Think you can do it again?' Raschid asked.

'No problem,' the boy said. 'I could do it three, maybe four more times before I get too tired. And careless, if you know what I mean.' Raschid said he did.

'How about a little drink break?' the boy asked.

'Nope. The thirty-sixth first. Then you get that drink.'

The boy cursed, but Raschid did not mind. Raschid could tell the actor was very happy with the work.

Lieutenant Skinner was one pissed-off cop. It was collection day, and the first stop had put her in a foul mood. She always started her rounds with a tidy little joyshop. It was a private deal, so she didn't have to share the earner. She also had a cute little joyboy she had been diddling every collection day for the past few months. That morning, however, there was no earner – and no joyboy.

The frightened and confused manager burbled out that the earner had already been picked up. He said a couple of real scary cop thugs had dropped by an hour before. They were there for the juice – said from now on Skinner was out. It had not taken much in the way of heavy leaning – the manager's face was bruised, and he walked with a limp – to make the message stick. They had also picked up the joyboy and said he would be working at another house.

Skinner was damn sure the toady manager was not lying, especially after she administered a professional beating of her own. Afterward, she stormed out of the joyshop, vowing revenge. Then it sank in. It would not be that easy. Her captain didn't know about this little caper. Frustrated, pissed, and confused about who the cop interlopers might have been, Skinner continued her rounds. Each place she went, the story was the same. Skinner began to realize that the beat she had spent so much money in payoffs to acquire had been turned upside down.

Steaming through her big beak like an ancient engine, Skinner headed for the cop shop to clue her captain in. An interdepartmental turf fight had just been launched.

Skinner had one more large jolt awaiting her. It was no mere fight, nor was it over a single piece of turf. Somehow or other, outright war had been declared. But by whom, no one would know until it was too late.

Kym was young and blond with innocent eyes and a not-so-innocent body. She was also a wicked little number who haunted pickup spots outside her home ward. A Lolita lick of her lips, a hip thrown just so, a jut of milky breasts, and the mark was soon in her clutches

– thanks to the knockout gas and sharp knife she kept tucked away in her skimpy costume.

Kym was also the apple of her daddy's eye and a minor hero in her neighborhood. Well-raised child that she was, Kym always brought all her loot home to Poppa. Since he was a sewer superintendent on Yelad's pad, that equalled large local clout.

But there had been a wee misunderstanding one night. Kym got picked up by cops who were too stoned out on narcobeer to check her out, so they hauled her to the slammer and booked her. To everyone's dismay, there was no choice but for Kym to go on trial. Nobody liked that, even Tyrenne Yelad's enemies. After all, juice on Dusable had to stay universally sweet, or the whole jug would go sour.

But such slips had been made before. The procedure was to have a little trial. The cops would get a minor scolding for busting somebody so obviously innocent, and Kym would be home again in her daddy's loving care and back out on the streets pursuing marks.

That was not what happened. The judge convicted the child of all charges – and threw the book at her.

In the howl of outrage that followed – picked up and played for all it was worth by Kenna's pet livie casters – the judge slipped out of town to retire to a life of newly wealthy ease, leaving Tyrenne Yelad holding the bag.

Avri praised Raschid to the heavens for the inspired dirty work. 'Stick around,' Raschid said. 'I got a new twist on that new twist.'

The juice went so sour in a score of key wards that it consisted almost entirely of solid matter.

Cops went after cops. The mobs went after everybody. Shops were bombed out, joyhouses raided, and gambling dens ripped off. Muscle banged muscle, and the innocent got in between – assuming that anyone on Dusable fit that description. The capper was the Mother's March for Kym.

Two thousand angry women from her ward hit the streets. Huge banners bore the innocent profile of the dear child. There was wailing and weeping and much colorful tearing of hair. Kenna's livie crews were out in force to cover it for the home folks, running down the dreaded incident for the thousandth time for their viewers. There were lots of close shots of her stunned daddy, who wobbled along at the head of the parade. Pop looked great, blasted on narcobeer, with eyes red-rimmed from cavorting on the cuff at a joyshop Raschid's people had steered him to. He was the portrait of stunned sorrow.

Screaming oaths, the women converged on the Tyrenne's headquarters, where a phalanx of cops waited. The lawbeings were in full riot drag – helmets and shields and clubs and gas and blister guns.

The women drew up before the line of cops. There was more shouting and screaming. Livie crews recorded the stand-off.

Suddenly a big gravtruck burst out of a side street. Cops identically clad to the Tyrenne's guards boiled off, kicking and punching and flailing about with clubs. The women howled in agony as the stunned *real* cops gaped on. Who were those guys? The phony cops ducked out of sight as the women recovered and went for blood. The battle would go down in Dusable history. Hundreds of mothers were injured in a scene witnessed by the entire planet.

Yelad's good name was quickly being reduced to a synonym for drakh.

The Dummy performed like a champ.

The best researchers and speech writers mordida could buy spilled out a tsunami of attacks on the privy council. Ad spots that would stop an overheated ox in its tracks were created. Raschid was all motion, ripping and tearing and putting the whole back together.

Solon Walsh delivered. In spades.

He started with a rather sad talk on the hardships of the beings of Dusable, leaving open the question of who was to blame for the troubles. But at his next appearance, he struck the pose of an outraged and betrayed citizen. He was aboil with facts that had just come to his attention. AM2 was being deliberately withheld from the Cairenes. Prize contracts had been wrested away. Solon Walsh bellowed for justice in speech after fiery speech. Dusable needed a strong hand now, he preached. One who owed nothing to those devil rulers on the privy council.

Tyrenne Yelad reacted mildly at first. He was surprised at the slickness of Walsh's campaign. But Avri assured Yelad that it was all part of the plan to leech off reform support from Kenna. Since Yelad was personally handing over mordida for Walsh's campaign kitty, he was reassured. As for the attacks on the privy council, what did he care? Those exalted beings certainly didn't, since the attacks came from a noncandidate like Solon Walsh.

Just to keep things square, however, he had his own speech writers make some minor course corrections. He delivered a few mild speeches defending the privy council.

Raschid made sure that each and every one of them was exploded out of proportion. He turned Yelad's mild defense into gigantic ad spots in the skies, complete with thundering volume, which warped every word Yelad spoke.

Then the other drakh started hitting the fan: The curdled juice. The internecine cop warfare. The mob attacks. Et cetera, et cetera. Yelad was so busy rushing about trying to plug the spurting leaks that he did not notice that Solon Kenna – his archenemy – was barely running a campaign at all.

Three nights before the election, the Tyrenne called an emergency meeting. His confidence was shaken.

Yelad looked like a ball top – skinny bottom and skinnier uppers, with a big round bulge in the middle. He chose his tailors so that those defects were emphasized rather than lessened. The clothes themselves were of materials just above middle class. Yelad lived in the same small ward home he had grown up in. He was nice to his mother, spoke well of his wife, and was understanding about the mishaps his brat children got themselves into. All of those artifices he had developed over many decades of campaigning. The message was: As a man of the people, Yelad possessed many of the people's flaws – but also many homespun strengths. It was one of the many reasons he had won term after term.

Not counting his vast patronage, of course, or his giant, smooth machine. On that night, however, nothing was smooth. Yelad was half drunk, one of many bad habits he had slipped into after years of easy victories.

'Whaddya mean, ya don't know what's behind it? What am I payin' ya clots for? Clottin' lazy bastards, that's what ya all clottin' are. Drakh under my feet.'

He stormed and raged, and his aides cowered, waiting for the awful storm to break. It didn't.

'I'll tell ya what's goin' on. It's that clottin' Kenna. Pullin' a sly one. Yeah, well . . . we'll see what's what, we will. I'm pullin' out all stops. Ya hear! Dumb clottin' low-down piece of drakh bastards . . . s'what I got.'

Many, many yessirs later, he was soothed enough to grit out orders. With times so tight, he needed a mandate. A mandate of historic proportions.

Teams of thugs and poll riders were doubled, the hired phony voters nearly tripled. Waiting in the wings were those grave vaults to be voted when the final count came in.

Tyrenne Yelad had plenty of funds. What he lacked was

organization. After so many years of constant victories, he required a far smaller team to administer the elections. Now he ordered heavies hired by the hundreds. They all hit the ground running – and instantly stumbled into each other and crashed to the ground. But the worst blow came before all that, on the night following the meeting. Less than forty-eight E-hours before the election.

Raschid watched calmly from the sidelines as Kenna oiled onto the big outdoor platform. His eyes swept the audience, making sure his shills were at work, pricking up the vast crowd. Every news livie crew on Dusable was accounted for. Even Yelad's pets had come running when word was leaked a few hours before Kenna's regularly scheduled speech. The talk was that a stunner of a development was about to unfold. The news crews forgot their loyalties, overwhelmed by that headiest of all scents: political bloodshed.

Kenna took up position. The ovation aroused by the shills was deafening. Solon Kenna bowed humbly and raised a weak hand, grinning and begging them to stop . . . 'Stop . . . I really don't deserve all this outpouring of love.'

The shills hit the button again just as the crowd was starting to believe that they really ought to stop as urged. The ovation was louder than before. Raschid let it go for half an hour, then motioned to let it gradually subside.

Kenna laughed and thanked everyone for such a spontaneous show of support. Then composed his face into a portrait of somber wisdom. He briefly sketched his long career of public service, reminding one and all of the hard fights in their behalf. Then Kenna confessed that he had been overwhelmed by doubts in the course of this campaign. He was getting on in years, he said, and he realized that he might not be able to carry on the banner as Tyrenne.

The crowd was hushed. Beings were beginning to get the drift. A few shouts of 'No . . . no . . .' could be heard. Raschid's magic was such that they were truly spontaneous, not the work of shills. Finally, Solon Kenna reached the end. There was a dramatic pause.

'I have been listening most carefully to the views of my opponents,' he said at last. 'And I have come to the conclusion that only one true voice speaks for us all. I therefore announce . . . I am withdrawing from the race . . . and—'

The crowd erupted in fury, but Kenna commanded them to silence with his august presence.

'And I throw my support to that most worthy of all beings on Dusable . . .'

On cue, the Dummy walked out on stage to the amazement of the entire planet.

Solon Walsh approached his colleague, tears streaming from his eyes – it had been Raschid who suggested to Avri the astringent in the kerchief.

'I give you . . . our new Tyrenne . . . a being for the new ages . . . Solon Walsh!'

People went mad. Fights erupted. Livie crews smashed into each other trying to get tighter shots, or sprinting off for their standups.

But in the middle of all the madness, the perfect picture was on the stage. As soon as the news crews realized it, they were back to work shooting the image, breaking heads and standing on fellow beings to get it.

It made a grand, instant campaign poster. Solon Kenna and Solon Walsh, weeping in joy, their arms flung about one another in loving unity.

Raschid thought the whole performance had gone well enough. He had done far better in the past, but all in all, he had to admit . . . Then his mind did a small, dizzy slip. When had he done better? With what? Then the roar of the crowd took him, and he banished the doubts.

The hard part was next. There was still an election to steal.

Election day dawned to the thunder of Tyrenne Yelad's shouts of outrage. His eyes were two blood holes from railing all night at the Judas Solon Walsh. Finally, his aides got him calmed enough to order the counterattack.

Yelad slammed down at his desk and began poring over his illegal options. Confidence quickly returned. He believed his political arsenal would have made even the late Eternal Emperor weep.

The steam hissed to a stop. Yelad composed himself and ordered up a jug of his headiest brew to steady the nerve for the long day and night ahead.

At that moment a badly frightened aide burst in. Bad news in the 22nd Ward – one of Yelad's greatest strongholds, with one million honest votes in pocket and two hundred thousand from the grave vaults.

In his fear, the aide told it badly – which meant from the beginning, each detail drop by drop. Yelad shouted at him to bottom line it at once. But the being stumbled so badly that Yelad gritted his teeth and told him to start anew.

The 22nd Ward was an island, surrounded by factory-polluted seas. For the working class, which meant all of the voters, there were only two convenient routes in and out of the ward, great bridge spans built with a vast hurrah and a flurry of mordida twenty years before.

'Yes! Yes! I clottin' know that. Spit it out, you little drakh butt!'

'Well . . .' the aide wailed. 'One of them just collapsed.'

'Clot!' was all Yelad could gobble. The voter traffic would soon make the other bridge impassable. And although there had been no injuries, people might fear to even chance that one.

Yelad sucked in half his jug of spirits in one go.

The day was not beginning well.

As Yelad tried to gather his wits, Raschid was being let into the deep, gloomy underground heart of the big building that housed Dusable's computer balloting system.

The toady ushered him and his three-being team of techs to a steel vault. The heavy door hung open. Inside was a snakes' nest of boards and old-fashioned optic wiring.

It was almost too easy. But Raschid knew that in politics, one took it any way it came.

Where earlier there had been two thousand women marching for Kym, election day saw fifteen thousand mothers march out from two wards. Whole gravtrucks of police fled before them.

For three hours they paraded from one ward to the next, gathering beings of all sexes behind banners bearing the likeness of the martyred girl mugger.

Then they all went to vote, sixty thousand of them. Some particularly irate women voted 130 times or more before the polls closed.

Solon Kenna hit the docks and SDT Union hiring halls at dawn. He spread the bribe money so thick and wide the grease could have easily launched a fleet of destroyers, and as he shook each hand and filled each pocket with credits, he looked each being straight in the eye and issued the order for the day.

'Go vote. Go cause trouble.'

The masses of workers swarmed out the gate. The voting and fighting raged deep into the night.

Solon Walsh addressed the livie crowds armored in solemn, youthful honesty. But his wrath was so great that even his steely hands shook. The bit of paper with the latest awfulness fluttering in his anger as he shook it before the cameras.

'Yet another betrayal, my fellow citizens. The privy council in its wisdom has just ordered our credits devalued by one half! What does my cowardly opponent, Tyrenne Yelad, have to say to that?'

If any one had looked closely, they would have seen only a few handscrawled words written on it. They were from Raschid, a heavily underlined reminder:

'Don't tell this lie with a smile.'

Walsh's stormy brow was a work of art.

At midday, Yelad's emergency press conference to refute Walsh's charges was canceled. There was more grim news from the 22nd: Huge cracks had been found in the remaining bridge.

No more than seven hundred people from the 22nd voted – which meant that Yelad would also not be able to cast the votes of the dead.

The first of several hundred gravtruck loads of phony voters lumbered into Dusable's capital just after dark. All over the planet Yelad was bringing in similar reinforcements. The beings would be escorted from poll to poll to vote for the Tyrenne, receiving a chit for each vote. The chits were redeemable in cash. There were some seasoned pros on board each of the trucks, beings capable of hitting two to three hundred polling spots before the midnight shutoff. For them, it was very lucrative piecework.

Raschid's force waited in the alley until the first truck passed. They swarmed out, swinging clubs and hurling bottles filled with fiery liquid. The beings on the first truck were dragged off and beaten. The truck was dumped off its gravlifts onto its side. Then it was set on fire – blocking the way with its flaming wreckage.

Not that a barricade was really needed. The other trucks were either quickly overwhelmed, or turned tail to run. There was no pursuit. Raschid had drummed it into every thick skull: stick to detail, no matter what. Somebody smashed in the strongbox aboard the truck and started handing out the counterfeit voting cards – just one more detail in Raschid's list.

Gillia was a hardened twenty-year veteran of campaign strong-arming and dirty tricks. But he had found himself getting weary of late, and was thinking of retirement. Out of loyalty to Yelad he had decided to stick through one last campaign. Adding weight to that decision was the notion of the experts that this would be the easiest election of them all. Kenna did not stand a chance, so all kinds of opportunities were left for Gillia to do far more skimming than usual. If he used his wits, he would retire almost as rich as a Tyrenne himself.

When Gillia ordered the lead vehicle to turn into the 103rd Ward, he already knew he had been a rosy-butted fool for thinking that way. The word on the street was that all over Dusable, Yelad was taking a tremendous licking. Punishment squads out to do a little lightweight thumping were on the receiving end of their own beatings. Some fights had erupted into full-scale riots. Gillia himself had seen a Yelad ward office in flames – and that was in the first hour of the night's work. Burning barricades and screaming mobs had blocked his entrance into eight wards.

Meanwhile, Yelad's top operators were doing a great deal of screaming on their own. Gillia had never been greeted by such hysteria from the election brass. His pollriding teams were under tremendous pressure to produce. Snap poll after snap poll showed that the Walsh vote was big and getting bigger. It had to be subverted, and clottin' fast.

Gillia's specialty was seeing that committed voters – committed to the other side – never reached the polls.

As in most places, the elderly and infirm on Dusable tended to vote the ticket. First, after years of backing one party, they were unlikely to change at this stage of the game. Second, they tended to owe their present existence, enfeebled though it might be, to that same ticket. All social welfare, obviously, was under the direct supervision of the local ward captain.

However, it was hard for such beings even to get to the polls. That problem was dealt with using traditional tools. The names of these prized voters were gathered up by the ward captain, who handed out the list to transport teams. On election night vehicles marked with the name of the proper candidate toured the wards, picked up the elderly and the crippled, delivered them to the polls to cast their vote, and then returned them home.

Gillia, and other beings like him, made sure that never happened.

Tonight he had twenty gravcars at his command, all repainted and bearing the name and likeness of Solon Walsh. The game plan was always the same. Spies in the enemy's camp would leak the schedule and names. Gillia would hustle his people out into the appropriate wards. They would go street to street, door-to-door, if necessary, and con the old beings into the gravcars. Then they would dump them fifty or sixty klicks away, stranding them far from their home polling places.

When Gillia's people hit the business center of the 103rd Ward, he issued instructions. The convoy split up and headed for their assigned neighborhoods. Gillia and his two goons continued on alone.

The old being at the first row home he approached greeted him at the door with a confused smile. 'Why . . . what are you doing here, young man? I've already done my duty.'

Gillia figured she was having him on. He sighed. There were always a few citizens who used any excuse to get out of voting. Oh, well. He would have to bruise her some, just like a legitimate poll rider, or she would be suspicious. He raised a weary arm to strike.

The old being scampered back, remarkably swift for her age. What a lot of drakh. He would have to chase her down.

'Wait,' the old woman wailed. 'There's been a mistake . . .'

'Right, lady,' Gillia growled as he cornered her and got into position to smack. Then he became the startled one as she clawed out a voting card. It was stamped with Walsh's name, and time and date of voting. Aw, clot! The old bugger *had* already cast her ballot.

Gillia hit her anyway. He was too worried to make it his best shot – just enough to get her on the ground so he could give her a kick in the ribs.

Then, as his boot swung forward, a heavy hand grabbed his collar and he felt himself flailing back. He slammed onto the floor. He tried to roll to avoid the next blow, but he was past it and the roll came out more like a flop. The club caught him in the belly, and air whooshed out.

Gillia fought for breath. A red haze blurred his view. But through it, he could see a grinning young woman standing over him. She had sloping shoulders, a muscular neck, and shapely arms bulging with muscle. Nearby, he heard the old woman's gloating cackle. Above him, the young woman shifted her grip on the club and brought it down.

Just before it hit and pain and blackness descended, he heard his goons outside screaming in terror.

An hour later, Gillia's unconscious body was dumped in a far-off woods, as was every member of his poll-riding team.

Meanwhile, all the gravcars were seized and repainted with Yelad's name and likeness. Raschid's own dirty tricksters spread out through the Tyrenne's own wards.

'Can't let a good move like that go to waste,' Raschid had told Avri.

Pavy had been more than happy to supply some of her best mob muscle to the game.

Tyrenne Yelad attacked one hour before the polls closed. Three hundred handpicked goons raided Walsh's headquarters, under orders to break every head, wreck every office, and carry off every document they could find.

The small force outside the building put up a token fight. It was quickly overwhelmed and put to flight. The bonfire team got busy outside stoking up a blaze into which furniture, documents, and anything else flammable would be hurled. A squad hastily assembled a steel ram and smashed through the double doors. A moment later Yelad's goons poured inside.

Raschid laughed as the goons rushed up the stairs. Just before the first wave hit him, he gave the signal. His shock troops leapt out of their hiding places and counterattacked. There were five hundred of them, all just as big, mean, and willing to hurt as Yelad's forces.

Raschid caught the first goon by the club arm. There was a dry snap as he broke it; then he spun to the side and grabbed the next goon by the ear, which he used as a lever to hurl his attacker to the floor. The ear came away in his hand and the being's head gave a bounce on a jutting stair. Raschid hurled the torn-off ear into the startled face of a third brute. As he booted the goon in the crotch and reached for a fourth victim, he saw Yelad's forces buried under the wave of counterattackers.

This was going well. There was nothing Raschid liked better than hands-on electioneering.

Lieutenant Skinner reached the last Walsh polling spot a few minutes before the doors closed. Despite the lateness of the hour, she was in no hurry.

Election night was usually one of Skinner's favorite times. There was always plenty of pleasant hitting to do and heaps of spare mordida about.

This time, however, she was one unmotivated cop. All over, the juice had stopped. She was starting to feel poverty-stricken, and her captain whined that he was no better off. Well, clot him! She was sure he was just looking out for himself. In other wards, her colleagues were moaning over the same misfortune.

So she had hit the streets with no hopes and little oomph. It did not improve her mood any to learn that she was right. Not only was there no mordida, but every citizen was as likely to attack her as to spit in her eye.

Her main job was to greet Yelad's phony voters when they arrived at the polls. She and her six-being team were supposed to hustle them off the gravtrucks, make sure they voted fast and correctly, then load them back on the vehicle to be rushed to the next spot.

Almost no one showed. Skinner got on the horn right away. The first time the shrieking voice on the other side shouted that it was just a mess up, some kind of delay. Skinner said sure and got off. She was not calmed by the hysteria in that voice. The second time, same thing. But, from then on out, all lines were jammed. Skinner realized with a shock that all over Dusable the same thing was happening. Cops like her were making the same panic calls.

Oh, well. She would just duck her head, do her job, and go home and get drunk when the election was over.

During the whole night only a few gravtrucks arrived. But even that was no solace. Because there was a surprise awaiting them at each poll. Joygirls and joyboys were out in force, guarded by so many mob pimps Skinner would have had to have been afflicted with a death wish to interfere. The pleasure sellers would mince up to the mark, throw a little seduction into the air, and the deal would be made. Instead of Yelad, the phony vote would go to Walsh. The payoff, a few sweet minutes in a handy dark place.

There was nothing Skinner could do about it. She didn't have the muscle. After a while, she started getting horny herself. By the time she reached the last stop, she didn't know whether she was too pissed to be horny, or too horny to be pissed.

Her jaw dropped when she saw one of the joyboys working the line of voters. It was her own little lad! Ah, how she had missed him. When she saw his curly locks and soft mouth, all thoughts of anger disappeared.

Lieutenant Skinner fished out her voting card and joined the line.

Clot it! Her vote was going to Walsh.

In the Cairenes – especially on Dusable – there was a puzzling mechanical law that struck every election period. No sooner were the polls closed than the main computer would jam up and crash.

There it would sit for half the night while teams of expensive techs were rushed in to tinker at its works and shake their heads over bitter caff.

At the appropriate time, there would be huzzahs of victory from the techs, and the computer would kick in, counting the votes and spitting out the results.

There was never any suspense in this final act. Yelad always won.

The Tyrenne huddled in his yawning office with his top aides. Despite the nightmare that had stalked him all day and night, Yelad's mood was fairly light. It helped that he was drunk. It helped still more that the mechanical law of Dusable elections had cut in right on time. Saved by a crashing computer! He chortled, took a slug from the bottle, and growled for his chief registrar to get to it. The screen lit up on Yelad's desk. *Now* he would see what he would see.

The way it was supposed to work – clot, the way it *always* worked – was that now the real count would begin. The broken-down computer would hum into action. Its first task was to tally the enemy wards. That would let Yelad know his opponent's strength. Then he would have his own vote counted, and the margin of victory adjusted by the millions of grave votes he had at his command.

He had to be careful. If he cheated too blatantly, the shrill questioning could wreck the first year of his new term. This time, however, Yelad was throwing caution off the roof. Walsh's tactics had him aching for revenge. He would bury the little clot in a landslide of historic proportions.

Yelad jumped when he heard his registrar groan. What the clot? Walsh's vote was coming in. 'Flooding in' was a better description. In ward after ward he was sweeping to victory!

A half hour later Yelad was suddenly sober. He was in deep drakh. Walsh's margin was so great that Yelad would have to vote every dead being in his files. He steeled himself and chugged down half the bottle. Fine! He'd do what was necessary. Hang what happened next. He would still be Tyrenne.

Impatiently he ordered his registrar to start the tally of wards. He settled back for a long night of counting.

The night proved short. One hour later the awful truth began to sink in.

Yelad's vote was nearly nonexistent.

Later, he would figure it out. Somebody had mickied the computer. All across Dusable, every time a committed voter hit the button, it would be recorded instead for Walsh. The official total gave him less than half-a-million votes.

Dusable's dead rested easy in their grave vaults that night.

Yelad had lost.

From that time forward he would be mocked as 'Landslide Yelad.'

Raschid did not attend Walsh and Kenna's victory party. Instead, he had a very private meeting with Solon Kenna in his offices. It was time to set his price.

The thought came to him as he was watching the election feed on the livie box. It was followed by an overwhelming feeling of urgency. He had to act. Fast.

As he rushed to his hastily arranged meeting with Kenna, the dense clouds that had boiled in his brain for all this time began to thin out, then lift away.

He had passed the Final Test.

Kenna was relieved when Raschid told him what he required: a fast ship, loaded with all the AM2 it could hold, ready for lift within six hours. Kenna thought that no price at all. He figured Raschid would beggar the mordida coffers. Not that it wasn't well worth it. In fact, from his viewpoint, Raschid's payment was so little that even Kenna's crooked soul stung a bit.

'Are you sure,' Solon Kenna pressed, 'that we can't do anything more?'

'Maybe you can,' came the answer. 'I'm not sure. But right now, why don't you just stick tight. Enjoy yourself. I'll get back to you.'

The Eternal Emperor shook the hand of one singularly happy politician.

Chapter Twenty-Five

The Key to the Kingdom looked unimpressive – deliberately so. It was a small moonlet, one of dozens larger and smaller, orbiting around a Jovian planet. The system was notable for only two reasons: it was completely without commercial value, and it was two steps beyond nowhere.

The moonlet had been constructed several centuries before. An asteroid was chosen for its size and worthlessness. Deep space crews were paid to excavate patterns across the asteroid and to install cables in those patterns. The excavations were filled in. The first crew was paid off and informed that their work had been part of a classified Imperial project. Then a second crew was brought in to construct a small underground shelter and, a few klicks away, an underground dock, hidden from line-of-sight to the shelter by a high ridge. Into the shelter went generators, supplies, and several elaborate and undescribed coms. The second crew was paid off. Somehow, as time passed, the beings who had worked on either crew got the idea that the classified project had been a failure, just another unspectacular research pan-out.

Drone tugs moved the asteroid to its chosen location around the gaseous giant and nudged it into orbit. Later Mantis teams, who were not told of the asteroid's existence, were sent in to provide security monitors in the system.

There were four other 'keys' scattered around the universe, their location known only to the Eternal Emperor. They all had the same purpose.

The coms were set to accept only the Eternal Emperor and contained every screening device conceivable, from DNA pattern to pore prints, even to include the specious Bertillon classification. If anyone else entered the shelter, the coms would melt down into incomprehensible slag.

The coms were linked to a ship, somewhere in . . . another space . . . and to the roboticized mining/factory ships around it. On signal, the recommendation from the ship would be changed. Transshipment of AM2 would begin.

The long trains of robot 'tankers' could also be controlled from the moonlet. Under 'normal' circumstances, such as The Eternal Emperor having died accidentally, they might be routed to the conventional depot worlds. Or, under differing circumstances, else-where. To reward the faithful and punish the heathens – or vice versa, depending on what the Emperor decided was the quickest, most expeditious way to regain control.

The Eternal Emperor crept into the system. He was in no hurry whatsoever. He repeatedly consulted the elaborate pickups he had requested be installed in the ship donated by the grateful Kenna.

If any of the sensors showed *any* intrusion into the system – a lost mining ship, a drone, or even a wandering yacht – there was only one choice. Instantly abort and move to whichever moonlet was convenient for a secondary command site.

There was nothing reported by any of the out-system sensors. The Emperor chanced an arcing sweep over the system itself. Nothing. Emboldened, he re-entered the system and closed on the gaseous giant. All pickups were clean.

He came in on the moonlet on the hemisphere opposite the shelter and nap-of-the-earthed to the dock. Its ports yawned – again, pickups clean – and he landed.

The Emperor suited up, made sure the suit's support mechanisms were loaded, and started for the shelter.

Halfway up that ridge, he muttered under his breath about being too paranoid. It was not easy staying low on a nearly zero-gee world. He had no desire to 'pop up' into range if anyone was waiting at the dome, or to punt himself into orbit. Not only would jetting back be embarrassing, but he would be too easy to pick up if he was walking into a trap.

A few hundred meters from the shelter's entrance – just another slide-blocked cave – he stopped. He waited a full six E-hours, watching. Nothing. The way was clear.

The suit's environment system whined, trying to stabilize the temperature and recycle the sweat pouring from the Emperor's body. His fingers unconsciously touched his chest. Under suit, skin, and muscle the bomb waited.

He unsealed his pistol's holster and took a tiny com from his belt. He slid a wand-like probe out. In a rush, he went across the open space to the slide area. The probe was inserted into a nearly invisible hole, and the Emperor touched a button. After a moment, the slide opened. The Emperor could feel the vibration under his boot heels.

He walked into the cavern. The door slid closed behind him. Lights glowed on. He checked a panel. Again, no intrusion. The heaters were on full blast, and atmosphere was being dumped into the shelter. Very good.

He walked to a door, palmed it, and the door slid away. Inside, there was a small bedroom/kitchen/living suite. He closed the door behind him and glanced at another panel. Atmosphere . . . ninety-five percent E-normal. Temperature . . . acceptable. He unsealed his faceplate.

He felt hungry. The Emperor hoped that he had provided

adequate rations. He would eat, then activate the com. He walked to the com room entrance – and the world shattered! He was greeted not by gleaming, waiting readouts and signal gear, but by cooled masses of molten metal.

Instantly the signal began, in his brain:

Exposure . . . Trap . . . Discovered . . . Self-destruct! Self-destruct!

Another part of his brain:

No. Wait. Trap not confirmed. Too much time. Cannot recommence program without terminal damage to goal! Return to standby! Program override!

The bomb did not go off. Not even when the storeroom door opened and a voice said, 'My security operatives were not as sophisticated as they believed.'

The Emperor saw a space-suited figure, tall and gaunt. An arm reached up and opened the suit's faceplate. It was Kyes.

Again, the order . . . and again, somehow, the command was overridden.

'I am the only being in this system – besides yourself,' Kyes said.

The Emperor found he could think once more. He said nothing, very sure that his voice would crack if he spoke. Kyes waited, then continued.

'Your progression here – and to return to your throne – is clever. It reminds me a bit of an Earth-legend I read. About a human named, I recall, Theseus.'

'It could not have been that clever,' the Emperor managed.

'Not true. For anyone to look for you, let alone find you, requires beginning with an insane belief: that you did not die. And then incredible resources.'

Kyes indicated the destroyed com sets.

'My apologies for the ineptitude of my personnel. Although I am sure other stations besides this one exist. The resumption of the AM2 shipments can still begin – although that is meaningless to me.'

The Emperor considered that. The situation was becoming . . . not familiar, but it appeared to be within understanding and possible control. First assumption: Kyes was planning to cut a deal and betray his fellow conspirators. No. He had said that AM2 was meaningless. Kyes wanted something else.

'You said you and I are the only beings in this system. To ask the obvious question: What is to prevent me from simply shooting you and escaping?'

'Why would you do something such as that?' Kyes asked in astonishment. 'Revenge? Hardly a sensible motive, let alone Imperial. Especially considering that our attempt to . . . alter the chains of power . . . failed.'

Failed? Instant analysis: Kyes's previous statement that 'you did not die,' and now this. The situation was improving – Kyes had not understood everything.

'Even if you desired to indulge your whim . . .' Kyes lifted a transmitter from his belt. 'Standard vital-signs transmitter. If it ceases broadcasting, my support team will move in. I do not think that you could escape their net.'

'You are making some large assumptions, Sr. Kyes. I *have* been known to indulge myself on occasion. Privilege of the purple and all that.'

'True. At first, when I established where you were headed, I thought of an ambush – while I remained safely in the wings. Tranquilizer guns . . . gas . . . whatever. Instantly immobilize you, hold you in a drugged state until mind control could be accomplished. But I did not think any plan I conceived would work. You've slipped through too many nets in the past.

'Besides . . . if I offered you violence, you would be almost certain to reject my offer.'

'I am listening.'

'First, I offer you my complete, personal loyalty and support. I will do anything – either from within or without – to remove the privy council.

'I am not trying to convince you that my assistance would in any way decisively ensure the outcome which I see as inevitable. But I could make their downfall happen much more rapidly, and probably decrease the amount of havoc they can wreak as they are destroyed.

'Once your Empire is restored, I offer you my continuing loyalty and support.'

'Turning one's coat,' the Emperor said, 'tends to be habit-forming.'

'It will not happen. Not if you fulfill your part of the bargain.

'But that is as may be. You might choose not to be reminded of . . . what has happened by my presence. In which case I accept exile, which in no way will lessen my offer to assist in any way conceivable.

'However, I can offer something still more important. My entire species as your freely consenting – "slaves" is not a correct word.

But that is, in essence, what we would be if you can conceive of any slave leaping into chains.

'This, too, is easily achieved.'

'Your people,' the Emperor observed, 'certainly would be welcomed if they chose to become total supporters of my Empire. Not, unless I am missing something . . . easily achieved, as you just said.'

'You are wrong.'

'Very well then. What, specifically, am I to deliver?' the Emperor asked, although he was suddenly, sickeningly aware of what the answer had to be.

'Life,' Kyes said hoarsely, almost stammering. 'Immortality. You perhaps understand the tragedy of death. But what if it occurs at a preset, biologically determined time, a time when a being is at the full height of his powers and awareness? The tragedy of our species.

'I want – and I want for my people – eternal life. The same immortality you have.

'I offered to make a bargain. I will better it. I will now guarantee everything I said. As your subject, I ask for this gift.'

And Kyes awkwardly knelt.

There was silence – a silence that lasted for years.

'You poor, sad bastard,' the Emperor finally said.

Kyes rose. 'How can you reject this? How can you ignore my logic? My promises?'

The Emperor chose his words carefully. 'Logic . . . promises . . . have nothing to do with it. Listen to what I am saying. *I* am immortal. But—' He tapped his chest. 'This body is not. You are asking a gift I *cannot* give. Not to you, not to any other being of any other race or species.'

Kyes's eyes were burning lances. 'This is the truth?'

'Yes.'

And Kyes believed. But his stare continued. Uncomfortable, the Emperor turned away. Again, there was the long silence. The Eternal Emperor reached deep into his bag of tricks.

'Perhaps . . . perhaps there is a compromise. I am willing to make a counter-offer. You help me destroy the privy council, and I will find the resources to commit to a research program, funded and supported as a Manhattan Project.

'It might take generations. Such a program – if a solution can be found – will not help you or your generation. But that is the best offer I can make.'

He turned back. Kyes had not moved.

'It is unsatisfactory,' the Emperor started, 'compared to what—' He stopped.

There was no response whatever from the Grb'chev. The Emperor moved out of Kyes's line of sight. Neither Kyes's head nor eyes shifted. The Emperor went to him and moved his hand across Kyes's field of vision. No response.

Perhaps it was the shock, realizing that there was no Holy Grail for Kyes or his species. Perhaps it was less dramatic – he *was* far beyond his time.

Kyes's mouth fell open. Digestive fluids dribbled from it.

The Emperor quickly checked the vital-signs indicator on Kyes's belt. All physical indicators . . . normal.

He snapped his faceplate closed and hurried toward the exit, then turned back.

The idiot that had been Kyes still stood as it had, held erect by the weight of his suit.

'Poor, sad bastard,' the Emperor said again.

It was the best epitaph he could manage – and the only one he had time for.

BOOK FOUR

'MORITURI TE SALUTAMUS'

Chapter Twenty-Six

The scholars of Newton wore a perpetual puzzled expression that an agro-world student once compared to a cow who had just had an inseminator's burly fist jammed up its behind. As the Tribunal neared its opening, Sten saw the puzzled look jump to open, smiling surprise. Kilgour said it was as if the fist had been replaced by the real thing.

Never in its dusty, academic history had the thousands of professors who toiled on the university world been paid so much attention.

When word was purposefully leaked of the event about to unfold, livie crews from all over the Empire raced to Newton to beat the expected privy-council crackdown. Newton's administration was nearly buried by requests for permission to attend, not just from news teams, but from political experts, legal scholars, historians, and the merely curious.

Sten, Alex, and Mahoney scrambled like mad beings to set up a security system to sift through the millions of requests. The task was especially difficult, because the whole idea was to give maximum exposure to the Tribunal's proceedings. They managed to get it all in hand – plus hundreds of other details – before the public opening.

Meanwhile, Dean Blythe, his faculty, and the millions of students who attended the many colleges that made up the university system, were besieged for interviews. No dull fact, boring reaction, or drab bit of color was too lowly for the news-hungry media. For a short time every resident of Newton was a livie star.

The information hunger was particularly intense, because although Sr. Ecu had revealed the general purposes of the Tribunal – sitting in judgment of the privy council – he had kept the nature of the charges secret to all but the judges. Everyone believed the bill of indictment involved the AM2. In other words, conspiracy to defraud. Sr. Ecu could only imagine the surprise when the real charges were announced: Conspiracy to murder.

Sr. Ecu had chosen Newton because of its long history and reputation for impartiality. He had expected, however, tremendous difficulty in getting Dean Blythe to agree to host the Tribunal. Instead, once the security precautions had been detailed, the agreement was quickly reached. It helped that Dean Blythe had been an Imperial general before he had taken up the life of a scholastic. More importantly, one of the first places the privy council had chosen for its budget cuts was Newton. Those cuts had been followed by a host of others as the Imperials trimmed and trimmed to keep the economic ship afloat.

A hefty donation of the AM2 Sten had stolen smoothed the rest of the way.

A huge auditorium was quickly prepared. A long court bench was installed on the stage for the members of the Tribunal. The backstage area was converted into offices for the legal support group. Outside and inside, potential security danger areas were plugged. Teams of guards were assigned to the livie-crew techs responsible for installing communication lines.

Meanwhile the Bhor fighting ships spread out around the Jura System and its capital world of Newton, or began patrolling areas believed most likely for attack routes.

In the midst of all that, the members of the Tribunal and their retinue arrived. Sten and Alex personally greeted each being and assigned the bodyguards who would shadow them from that moment on.

Sr. Ecu had chosen three beings to sit as judges over the privy council. Despite the great danger involved, he had no shortage of volunteer candidates. The depression triggered by the privy council's actions had become so deep that many systems feared for their own survival far more than they did Imperial reprisal.

The three systems he eventually drew from were among the most respected in the Empire – as were the beings who would form the Tribunal.

The first to arrive was Warin, from the great agricultural worlds of Ryania. He was a big, ponderous thinking being whose heavily bone-plated skull hid a three-brain mental system capable of sifting through mountains of conflicting information. Warin was slow and to the point, but he always arrived with plenty of thinking ammunition. He was also completely open-minded as far as the crimes alleged against the privy council.

The second was Rivas, from the distant frontier territory of Jono. Rivas was a slender, quick-witted human, noted for his ability to find middle ground where little existed – an important, much honored skill in the wilds of Jono, where there sometimes seemed more opposing viewpoints than people. He had warned Sr. Ecu that, although he despised the current actions of the privy council, he did not necessarily believe that they were all acting out of selfish motives. His opinion of Kyes, for example, was quite good. His previous dealings with the being had all gone well and had shown Kyes to be honorable.

The final member was perhaps the most respected. Her name was Apus, and she was the Queen Mother of Fernomia. She was very old and cared not a bit that her title carried no royal authority. Her many daughters and granddaughters oversaw the billions of females and few million males who made up the populations of the Fernomia Cluster. Despite her age, her health was excellent, her six spindly legs sturdy, and her mandibles as fluid and flexible as when she had been young. She confessed to Sr. Ecu that she despised the members of the privy council – especially the Kraa twins, who some years earlier had cheated her people out of a fortune in mineral rights – but Sr. Ecu knew that would not affect the Queen Mother's impartial consideration of the evidence.

The three beings were installed in comfortable, well-guarded quarters. Just before the Tribunal was convened, Ecu huddled with the three judges to lay out the rules they would operate under.

It was agreed that he would be the Tribunal referee. It would be his responsibility to see that all evidence was fairly presented and weighed. Any rulings he made could not be overturned. He would also be the public spokesbeing for the Tribunal. All queries would be addressed to him, and he alone would be permitted to answer – after consulting with the three judges. It was also agreed that Sr. Ecu would be responsible for gathering evidence and presenting witnesses. The three voted to invest him with authority to swear in court officers to accomplish these things.

Afterward, Sr. Ecu rushed about, dotting the 'i's and crossing the 't's on the final details.

When Sten was summoned to Sr. Ecu's garden quarters, he noted how tired the old diplomat seemed. His sensing tendrils twittered with nervous exhaustion; his color was gray and poor. But Sten had no time to sympathize or comment – Sr. Ecu ordered him to raise his right hand.

Sten did as he was told.

'Do you swear to uphold the integrity of these proceedings and the ancient laws of the Empire under whose sanctity we act?'

Sten swore he did.

'Then, by the authority invested in me I appoint you chief officer of this Tribunal,' Sr. Ecu intoned.

Although he had known exactly what was to happen, Sten felt a little intimidated by Sr. Ecu's stern speech. It was also a little comforting that the old diplomat meant every word he was saying. This Tribunal would be no sham.

As he left the garden, Alex and Mahoney were waiting to enter. A few minutes later, they returned, as quiet and humble as he.

In silence, the three started back for their quarters. But as they did so, a small group of guards broke away from the ones posted outside. Sten gaped at them as they took up position around him.

One of them was Cind. Her eyes shone with excitement as she hustled her charges into proper order. Then she drew up before Sten and snapped him a sharp salute.

'Is everything to your satisfaction? Sir!'

'What in the world are you talking about, woman?' Sten grated out.

'Why, this is your bodyguard, sir,' Cind said, barely suppressing a grin. 'If there are any complaints, please address them to me – the commander of *your* guard.'

Sten sputtered he wasn't having any of this. He didn't want a bodyguard, or need a bodyguard. And furthermore . . .

'Sr. Ecu's orders. Sir!' came Cind's response.

Before Sten could argue any further, his two friends burst into laughter.

'Better do as you're told, young Sten,' Mahoney admonished.

'Aye, lad,' that clot Kilgour said. 'Ye're a braw an' noble person, noo. Cannae be riskin't th' life ae th' chief ossifer ae th' court, noo can we?'

As a very happy Cind escorted him back to his rooms, Sten had murder in his heart – and two likely victims chortling nearby.

The opening of the Tribunal was delayed half the morning as thousands of beings converged on the hall. Assigned seats were quickly filled, and the inside temperature soared past the ability of the climate machines to keep control. Outside, thousands of the curious fought to get within seeing and hearing distance of the vid screens and big speakers set up to display the proceedings.

Troops forced wide avenues through the crowds to admit the news livie crews. Their warrior tempers were sorely tested as they pushed and prodded, rather than breaking heads, or simply opening fire. Eventually, order was restored.

A great silence fell as every being craned to get a view of the still-empty stage. It was not just the threat of violence that kept the peace, or anticipation of a one-of-a-kind event in Imperial history.

Above the stage was an immense portrait of the Eternal Emperor. It was a romantic likeness, grandly heroic, of the style favored by the late Tanz Sullamora. Except for the eyes. Sten shivered when he looked at them. They bored straight out, stabbing into the soul of every being.

Sten knew the look. 'Well, you puny little being,' they seemed to ask. 'What have you got to say for yourself?'

The icy grip of that painted glare was broken when Sr. Ecu gave a flip of his tail and skimmed out over the stage. The only sound from the crowd was an unconscious drawing in of breath. Then the three Tribunal judges followed. They took positions at the bench.

There were a few hushed whispers as legal clerks wheeled in carts of documents. Dean Blythe took up his post to the far right. He was to oversee the sanctity of the computer that would serve as the official recorder.

Livie crews dollied in for a series of symbolic tight shots, starting first with Warin, then Rivas, then Queen Mother Apus – and finally Sr. Ecu. The old diplomat waited a few dramatic moments, then spoke.

'The proceedings of this Tribunal are now officially open.'

Such a simple sentence, but it brought a gasp from the crowd. Everyone knew that from that moment on, every word uttered was a direct challenge to the privy council's authority.

'We are present to hear evidence concerning grave charges brought against the governing body of this Empire. The fact that these proceedings are being held under armed supervision to protect us from this same body is to have no influence on any member of the Tribunal. All three judges have agreed and sworn to this.

'My first official act of these hearings is to invite the presence of any and all members of the privy council to answer or refute any evidence brought against them.

'This is no empty act on my part. I personally plead with each and every one of them to respond . . .

'Now, for the reading of the bill of indictment:

'Members of the privy council, you have been charged with conspiracy to murder the Eternal Emperor.

'In your absence, a not-guilty plea will automatically—'

The rest was buried in the screaming, shouting reactions from the crowd. It took three more hours to regain control.

By then, there was not much time left before the Tribunal recessed for the day. The only action of real note was that the three judges drew straws to determine who would speak for the privy council, and who for the prosecution.

Queen Mother Apus – who despised the Kraas – ended up their fervent official supporter. Sten was amazed how quickly and ably she took up the task, despite her hatred for the twins, as well as their colleagues. Rivas, who was partial to Sr. Kyes, became the privy council's prosecutor. His voice became instantly tinged with bitter irony whenever a speck of evidence was brought forth against the council.

Sten would have loved nothing more than to become one of the crowd, to witness the events and see justice fairly done, just like any normal being who was fortunate enough to be in this place.

But that, as the Bhor might have said, was not to be his fate. 'At the forges of the gods,' Otho had once said when deep in his stregghorn, 'it is our curse to always be the hammer when they strike.'

Chapter Twenty-Seven

Poyndex was not a being of temperament. Long before, he had put away anger with his childhood toys. He left elation behind with adolescence. In fact, there was not one emotion he did not have under control. Ambition was the only fruit he nourished in this garden of the middle ground. Achieving power was his only pleasure.

So as his colleagues on the privy council raged at the 'shocking and spurious allegations' of Sr. Ecu's Tribunal, he knew fear for the first time in his life. He saw the power slipping away.

The instant he saw the liviecast of Sr. Ecu's announcement of the murder charges, he believed it was true. The reaction came from the gut. As he rushed to the hastily called meeting of the council, the surer he became. It became clearer to him as he entered the enormous building the council had constructed as its headquarters. The odd, towering tree that grew up through the central courtyard seemed withered and ailing. For Poyndex, who was not a being taken to symbolic thought, the condition of the rubiginosa still seemed to bode ill.

It just made more sense that the assassination of the Emperor was not the act of a lone madman. A conspiracy was far more likely. And who had the most to gain from such a plot? The answer became all too obvious as he entered the meeting room.

Everyone was in a bellowing rage. The Kraa twins were purple with fury. Lovett kept pounding on the polished meeting table, screaming for bloody action. Malperin was letting loose an odd stream of obscenities at the awful lies being told.

When he saw the violent reaction, Poyndex knew his instincts had been on the mark. He was looking at the beings who killed the Eternal Emperor.

Why else all that outrage? If the charges were false, then it was merely a ploy by their enemies. The council members were all experienced businessbeings who had dealt with such mudslinging all their professional lives.

He also noted their faces when they were in between bellows, gasping for breath. He did not imagine the guilty looks of fear they exchanged. The capper was the Kraa twins. In their anxiety, they immediately switched roles. As they consumed the usual huge quantities of food, the skeletal one stopped her endless trips to the fresher. Instead, the obese one became the twin who was constantly heading off to vomit.

That's when the fear struck him. He had only just achieved his lifelong ambition. As a member of the privy council, Poyndex had reached his dream of great power. He knew he could swiftly consolidate and strengthen it even more as he learned which buttons of manipulation to punch. Poyndex had never had any thoughts of being a great tyrant, a single ruler. He liked staying in the shadows, where it was safer. Also, like Kyes, he had no love of the trappings of office and was content to let his fellow members shine in whatever sun pleased them. Poyndex knew he could get what he wanted far more easily as the being who gave favors, rather than took them.

Before the Tribunal's charges were announced, Poyndex had only just begun to recover from the blow of the loss of his mentor. When Kyes – or the gibbering thing that had been Kyes – was brought back from his mysterious journey, he knew he had lost his main supporter in any contest of wills with the rest of the council.

But, if anything, his colleagues became more dependent on him. They listened closely to his cool advice on all matters, not just those involving the military or intelligence, but on Imperial policy as well. There was no talk of filling Kyes's post with a new council member.

Now that he thought of it, their reaction to what had happened to Kyes was also very odd. They took it quietly – mildly, almost. They asked no real questions and hastily arranged for the poor creature to be cared for in a top-secret military hospital for the insane. Actually, they seemed relieved. Poyndex thought it was because there was one less guilty party who could tell the tale.

As the privy council struggled to come up with a counterattack, Poyndex knew the first thing he had to do was cover his ass. It was apparent, no matter what the outcome, that these beings were doomed. It was not important if they destroyed the Tribunal and its allies. The charges would eventually bring them down.

Poyndex was determined that he would not go down with them. So, as his colleagues debated, he started rummaging through his bag of survival tricks.

The Kraas wanted to fire fleets out in all directions. Every system vaguely involved with the Tribunal would be crushed and garrisoned with Imperial troops. Lovett and Malperin shouted approval. Poyndex waited until some of the steam went out before he spoke.

'I share your outrage,' he said. 'Although I am not listed by name in these awful lies, I consider an attack on any single member an attack on us all. But we still have to face reality. There simply isn't enough AM2 to accomplish a tenth of what you are saying.'

His words were greeted with sober silence. What he said was true. They began narrowing the scope of the operation, bit by bit, Poyndex subtly coaxing them on. Finally it was decided there would only be one target: Newton. A crack fleet would be sent, and all surviving parties – if any – would be hauled back to Prime World for punishment. Malperin cautioned that the troops might not be all that loyal, considering the recent military purges. Poyndex knew that she also was worried that the assassination charge itself would spark a revolt. It was a very guilty statement, one that the others quickly took up. As much as possible, only intensely loyal beings would man the fleet.

Before agreement was reached and the fleet sent, Poyndex raised a purposeful warning flag – for the official record.

'I'm sure, of course, this is what must be done,' Poyndex said. 'You've argued so persuasively. However, it would be remiss of me not to point out the dangers in this action.

'Some might argue that it would be better to ignore the whole thing. You've already ordered an Empirewide blackout of the proceedings. Continue it. Make no response. Then let them slink away. We could arrest them at our leisure. Also, the attack itself might backblast. Our own allies may become fearful. But I'm sure all of you know these things. I'm only pointing them out so that no little detail might be overlooked.'

'Bloody hell on th' allies,' one Kraa snarled.

'If we *don't* act, some fools might think those outrageous charges are true,' Malperin said.

'Send the fleet,' Lovett said.

Poyndex sent the fleet. However, as he was issuing orders all around, he called in his most trusted aides. There was a great deal of ass covering to be done.

Poyndex had to get ahead of events before they ran him down.

Chapter Twenty-Eight

Imperial captain of the Guard (Retired) Hosford topped the hill, rested on his staff, and gave himself five solid minutes of wheezing before starting downslope, across the next valley, and up the next ridge. Foothills, he thought. Foothills of the clottin' Himalayas, you ought to add.

Not only did he feel himself too fat and too old for this assignment, but it was a perfectly empty and thankless one.

There had been two things eternal about the Empire. A pistol and a bomb had proven one to be mortal. The other was the Gurkhas.

The Gurkhas were the best soldiers any world had ever produced, human or otherwise. Most people hoped that a species of still-more lethal killers would not appear – or that if they did, they would be as firmly on the side of the Empire as the Gurkhas. The Gurkhas and the Empire were one and the same to the many, many people who had seen them on the livies.

The privy council wanted them back. Both because they wanted absolutely faithful, absolutely incorruptible beings for their bodyguards, and to legitimize their own rule.

Hence Captain Hosford's mission.

Hosford had been – years, lifetime, lifetimes ago, he thought – commander of the Gurkha bodyguard at the Emperor's palace of Arundel. He had been a very promising officer, guaranteed for high rank – as, indeed, was anyone picked for Captain of the Guard.

The assignment was glamorous – and gave its holder no time for a personal life, as Sten had discovered when he had replaced Hosford in the position.

All went well – until Hosford fell in love. Completely, absolutely. So much so that he had covered the walls of his quarters with paintings of Maeve. Maeve never said anything, but Hosford realized the choice was clear. The assignment – or her.

He called in every favor he could to get out. The military powers did not like one of their chosen ones changing the plans they had for him. So the only assignment offered was an exile post on a frontier world. Hosford took it, and Maeve went with him.

Obviously there was no more career for him in the Guard. He resigned his commission, chose not to reenlist when the Tahn wars started, and wandered with Maeve. He had thought that wandering aimless, but he had once plotted his travels and realized that they led, in a perfectly logical pattern, to Earth.

And the Gurkhas.

The Gurkhas who had survived Imperial duty may have been rich, but Nepal was still a very primitive province. It was kept that way by its king, who claimed that his succession ran back to when the mountain gods were born. He must protect Nepal and his people. The country was a sacred place, from the peaks of Dhaulagiri, Annapurna, and Chomolungma to the Gautama Buddha's birthplace in the Lumbini Valley. In practice that meant the Nepalese were actively discouraged from becoming too 'civilized.' They no longer died of the same diseases, nor was tuberculosis endemic, and lifespan was extended – if not by 'civilized' Imperial standards – but it was still a hard, primitive tribal existence. Hosford wanted to help.

He was not permitted to settle in Nepal – no foreigners were allowed in the country except in limited numbers for brief visits. But he and Maeve found a home in Darjeeling, in the nearby province of Gurkhali, once part of a long-fragmented nation called India.

From there, he did what he could. He encouraged education and teachers inside Nepal, assisted any old soldier he could, and helped and found work for the depressed, near-suicidal young men who were rejected from the military.

He and other ex-Gurkha officers were allowed into Nepal twice a year to distribute pension monies, to offer any technical education they could, and to recruit – until six years earlier, when the Emperor had been murdered and the Gurkhas returned home. Every year, Hosford was commissioned by a representative of the privy council to try recruiting once more. Every year he was greeted with smiles and whiskey and told: 'We serve the Emperor. Only.'

The first two years he tried arguing: The Emperor was dead. Were they planning to abandon their military tradition? Their answer was: 'No, Captain. We are not foolish. When the Emperor returns, so shall we. But serve this privy council? Never. They are worth less than one yak pubic hair.'

Why did he keep returning? The commission was part of it – he left the monies with village heads for their own purposes. But just being in the mountains, being in Nepal, being with the Nepalese was reason enough.

One more year, he groaned. One more trip. One more rejection. This must be the last one. Otherwise his body would be found, years later, dead on some unknown hillside when his heart gave out. This . . . well, no. Perhaps next year. But that would definitely be the last.

Ahead lay the Gurkha Center in the hamlet of Pokhara. Hosford shifted the heavy pack of credits and marched on. He knew what he would see from the next hilltop. The center, and some of his old comrades waiting. Somehow they always knew when he would be there. They would be drawn to as rigid attention as their age permitted. At their head would be ex-Havildar Major Mankajiri Gurung, who, unless he was actually his son, Imperial records said was over 250 years old. Them . . . but that would be all.

Pokhara, in fact, was a confusion of noise, music, and youth. Almost, Hosford estimated, a thousand of them, drawn up in what screaming old men were telling them was a military formation, and if they shamed their clan or Captain Hosford they would be tied up in barrels and rolled into the headwaters of the Sacred Ganges to disappear into the sea.

In front of the assembly stood Mankajiri. He saluted. Hosford returned the salute. He should have waited to ask, but could not.

'These are . . . recruits?' he wondered aloud.

'Such as they are. Mountain wildflowers compared to men of our wars, Captain. But recruits, if they pass your careful eye. Their medical records wait for your examination.'

'Why the change?'

'Change? There has been no change.'

'But you said you would never serve the privy council.'

'Again, no change. These men will serve the Emperor. He is returning. He will need us.'

Captain Hosford felt a cold chill down his spine – a chill that had nothing to do with the icy winds blowing down from the nearby mountain tops.

''Ow lang wi' the' squawkin't an' squeakin't frae th' Tribunal gae on?' Kilgour wondered.

Mahoney shrugged. 'Until every lawyer has his day in the sun, and until every challenge the privy council can come up with now or later is answered.'

'Ah hae no plans,' Kilgour said grimly, 'frae much of a later f'r th' clots. Thae drove me off Edinburgh. Thae'll be ae accountin' f'r that. Wi' me. Nae wi' a court ae law.'

'Alex. We aren't vigilantes,' Sten said.

'Ye're intendin't to force us inta th' path ae righteousness frae somebody's namesake? Nae. Nae. I' this all collapses, an' Ah'm morally cert it shall, thae'll nae gie us a wee home back in Mantis. Morally corrupted, we are, we are.

'Ah'll nae adjust t' ae world where y' need more on ae villain than enow t' authorize the usual.' Alex drew a thumb across his throat.

'If you're through, Laird Kilgour. We are now sworn officers of a legitimate court,' Sten said, grinning. 'While the lawyers are dicin' and slicin', we have to go out and get some concrete evidence for them to chew over when they get tired of talking about whether the Magna Carta's bridge-building ban might pertain.'

'Ah'm noo through. But Ah'll shut m' trap.'

The three of them studied the screen projections.

'I've been fine-combing,' Sten started. 'Trying to read – or at least read a summary of – everything that's appeared on the privy council, from its establishment to the assassination. I've got another team doing the same thing to the present, looking for possible ancillary crimes.

'But let's start with two specific crimes of blood,' he said. 'First is the murder of Volmer. Why was he iced? We know a pro hit him on an open contract. The contract was let by a crime boss, now dead. The assassin is gone, too. Right?'

'So Chief Haines told me.'

'Do you think she was holding out on you?'

'No.' All three men were relaxing. This was very familiar to them – the standard plotting session any Mantis Team went through before they opened a mission. The fact that it concerned regicide and high treason was another issue entirely.

'Is she worth talking to again?'

'Probably.'

'So somebody's going to Prime,' Sten said. 'Volmer, one of the privy council, gets killed. Why? Was he passing on the conspiracy against the Emperor? Was he trying a power grab on his own?'

'W' nae hae that enow t' guess.'

'No. Input: Just before his murder, the privy council met – on Earth. It's the only time that I can find them meeting away from Prime. At least from the public fiche.'

'We need to verify that.'

'A visit to Prime, once more,' Sten agreed. 'I'm not sure we'll find any dirt looking at Volmer's death. But it's worth checking.

'Now. The biggie. The Emperor is taken out by one crazed assassin. Chapelle. A nut-case. Is there any chance that he was a lone lunatic? And that the privy council, already conspiring toward takeover someday, seized the opportunity?'

'Negative,' Mahoney said flatly. 'They moved too quick. And they're not that bright. Except for maybe Kyes.'

'Agreed. I ran through your notes, Ian. You had Chapelle's life day by day – and then he disappeared a month or so before he showed up with a gun. Error on your part? Did you have to get out of town before you found those pieces?'

'Negative again. He vanished. All I had is that he'd been seen in company – twice – with that guy who looked rich and way out of . . . oh for the love of God!' Mahoney exclaimed in sudden exasperation, realizing something.

'It nae hurts,' Kilgour said, looking interested, 't' rechew the evidence. Continue on, frae love ae God, Fleet Marshal.'

'Rich guy. Control, of course. Which I already thought, not being a total dummy. But I never ran the MO. Crooks use the same modus operandi. So do I, so do you, so does the thug there who isn't pouring. I think it's acceptable to add alk to the equation. My mind's starting to work.'

'Ah.' Sten got it, and went to pour Mahoney his requested drink.

'Exactly. Ignore the preliminary drakh for the moment, which would have been: Sullamora ran the wet work end of the conspiracy. Died in the blast. Burble, burble, who cares about whether it was an accident or not. The interesting fact is that Tanz Sullamora was too good to ever meet with somebody who's going to pull the trigger. So there had to be a cut-out.

'Control. Projected profile. Please record this.'

Sten snapped on a recorder.

'Intelligence professional. Established – clean, classic operation. To find or create a psychopath, steer him in the correct direction, and put him in the right place with the right weapon. Chapelle would have had no connection to the organization itself, nor to any high-level person in that conspiracy.'

'Ah'll gie thae,' Alex said. Both Sten and Kilgour had their Professional Skeptic hats on. Nothing was true, everything was false – the only way to penetrate any kind of apparat.

'I knew that way back when. Control was always who I wanted. Didn't think things through enough. Problem with having spent the last few years runnin' so'jers instead of spooks like you two clowns.

'Anyway. Professional. First I looked at the Empire. Mercury, Mantis, and ex-both. Nothing.'

'Verified . . . or are you being sentimental and protecting the Old Boy's Network?'

'The Emperor,' Mahoney said harshly, 'was a friend of mine. Erase that from the recording. I didn't fudge on that one.'

'Thae's many espionage pros out there hae naught t'do with th' Empire, an' ne'er hae,' Kilgour said.

'Exactly. Now. Back to the MO. Little trick of the trade. You want to run a safehouse, run a drop, have a team on standby – or anything else nefarious. You don't find a warehouse in the slum, unless you're an amateur or a criminal. Find yourself a nice, rich, bohemian, if possible, neighborhood, where nobody knows or cares who's coming or going, and pride themselves on minding their own business.'

'Ah. Rich man – Control – shows up in the slum. Blows in Chapelle's ear, who always thought he was meant for greatness. Disappears him – still on Prime, of course,' Sten reasoned. 'Control built him, taught him, armed him . . . in a nice, safe, rich mansion in a nice, safe, rich suburb. Prime again.'

'Clot Prime,' Mahoney said. 'Read my lips and listen to what I just said. MO, MO, MO. We all reuse something that works. Rich . . . rich . . . rich. How many pros use that as a working tool? Can't be that many, can there?'

'It's a big clottin' universe,' Sten said. 'But no. We're in a little tiny subculture here.'

'I already thought of some names.'

'Fine. You got it, Ian. You're in motion. Question – curiosity – how will you get him to sing? If you find him?'

Mahoney sneered.

'Sorry,' Sten said. 'I'm telling my grandmother how to suck eggs. Shut the recorder off. Back to my line of reasoning, such as it is:

'If I were running the conspiracy, I'd want to have the fewest number of meetings possible. I've got one probably established now – the conference on Earth before Volmer was killed. Was there a second or third meeting? More? It seems to me that Sullamora would have informed everyone when he had his ducks – Chapelle, Control, possible opportunity, et cetera – in a row.

'The meeting would not be in an official place. Fear of bugs, of course. Now, I'm making a big jump. None of the privy council-types trust each other.'

'Nae a jump. Thae'd be even greater clots than thae be if they did.'

'So this meeting, if it occurred, might be on neutral but very clean turf. Question: Did the privy council have any meetings like that?'

'Some lad's headed twa Prime,' Alex said. 'Suggestion. Amateur plotters clean a'ter themselves. But ne'er think ae then puttin' in ae false trail. Meetin' ae Earth? How wae it arranged? Nae spontaneity, a' course. So Ah'll – pardon, whoe'er goes t' Prime – look for paperwork. I' there's naught, thae was a conspiracy meetin', aye?

'Same wi' any other meetin' a'fore th' Emp' gies slaughtered, pardon, sir.'

'Good,' Sten agreed. 'That's a way in. Anyone else have any sudden flashes? We can leave the backup team in place looking for Sins After the Bang.'

'Ah'll pack,' Alex said, finishing his drink.

'You will,' Sten agreed. 'But not for Prime. I'm the one.'

'Y're known an' a desir'd target, lad. Dinnae be playin't hero.'

'I'm not. Everything on Prime leads through Haines – or could, anyway. Who's she most likely to cooperate with?'

'Ah'll gie y' th' loan ae a mattress manual, Burns' love poems, an' a crook champagne distributor Ah know. But where am Ah headin't twa?'

'Like I said before. We're officers of the court now. But we're understaffed. I'd feel real comfortable with more. Say . . . ten thousand?'

Kilgour considered. 'Hae much ae th' AM2 we stole kin Ah use?'

'Beyond what we had to give back to the Bhor . . . what we need for power here and for the Bhor cover fleets . . . whatever it takes. But bargain hard.'

'Grannies' wi' eggs once more, lad. I'll gie Otho f'r transp'rtation. Ah hae an idea where I'll look.'

'Don't bother Otho. He's busy. I already lined up your ride.'

'Ye're smilin' lad. Ah dinnae like thae smile.'

'Trust me, Laird Kilgour. You're gonna love it.'

Ships flickered into existence, so many minnows swarming to bait around the Jura System. Then, again like minnows, they formed into two fleets and went into parking orbits. Unlike minnows they were not silver, were not uniform, and mostly were not very sleek.

The first fleet landed one ship on Newton. Sten was waiting. Jon Wild, king of the smugglers – or at least their spokesman for this moment – stepped out. Again Sten marveled at his appearance. Not a pirate, not a brawler, Wild looked more like a clerklet or an archivist.

The meeting was very brief – merely a declaration of confederacy. It had taken awhile for Sten's emissary to find Wild, but only moments for the message to be conveyed and understood.

Smugglers needed four things to succeed: Trade laws, transport, cunning, and client prosperity. The privy council had destroyed one and nearly another of those preconditions. No matter how clever a smuggler is, Wild told Sten, if he can't fuel his ship he might as well stay home and farm potatoes. And what boots it if he can find fuel, but his customer has no way of paying for the smuggler's goods?

'So what can you promise me, Sten? Beyond access to the AM2 you seem to have . . . acquired?'

'Not the good old days. The AM2 flow stopped with the Emperor. But with the privy council condemned, they will eventually fall. I find it hard to conceive that *anything* short of complete chaos could be worse than what we have now.'

'Smugglers, as a last resort, can live with chaos,' Wild mused. '*Somebody* must carry the cargoes. Very well. For intelligence . . . scouting . . . transportation . . . troopships as a last resort . . . you can depend on us. For a time. Until boredom sets in, or those happy anarchists of mine decide to listen to someone else.'

Sten requested Alex's presence when he boarded the 'flagship' of the second fleet – revenge for Kilgour having stuck him with not only a bodyguard, but an acolyte as well.

He had hoped to surprise Alex.

It did not work very well. Kilgour looked at the projection of the motley throng their ship was closing on and called up the *Jane's* fiche. After glancing at a few entries, he glowered at Sten.

'Y' bastard.'

Alex knew.

'Y'd stick me . . . y'r mate. Y'r wee lifesaver. Th' charmin' an' sophisticated lad whae taught y's all y' ken noo. Y're bent, lad. Y'r proper surname's Campbell!'

'Probably. But do you know a better pilot? Or a group of people better able to keep your potential – and I quote, officers of the court, end quote – under control?'

'M'tongue'd blacken i' Ah agreed wi' y'. An' dinnae be restatin' th' obvious when tha' wee airlock opens.'

Ida was waiting for them. If anything, she had gotten even fatter. She still wore a loose, flowing Gypsy dress, probably with nothing under it, but it was a dress made of the finest fabrics. Tailored – if it was possible to tailor for a blimp. Also, her slangy language had improved – at least a little.

She whooped happily seeing her long-ago Mantis commander and started to buss Kilgour before she remembered their continuing, reason-lost, half-jesting feud. 'You hadda bring him.'

'He gets in trouble without a minder,' Sten agreed.

'Noo, *thae*'s th' question ae th' hour,' Alex said. 'Who's th' keeper an' who's th' bairn? I' fact, Ah mean.'

Ida led them to her quarters. A bridge suite on a prehistoric ocean ship might have been more luxurious – but that was unlikely. Tapestries. Couches. Tables barely visible under a galaxy of delicacies.

'And it all clears for action in ten seconds,' Ida said proudly. 'Action stations, and this is a countermissile battery over there – launchers are under the floorboards right now. Over here's an emergency CIC. And the bath becomes a med clearing station.

'We've got Scotch from Earth. Real Scotch. What they call a single-malt. Not that clottin' imitation I read our late and lamented Emperor poured.

'My own lager for you, Kilgour. Not that you'll appreciate it.'

Ida Kalderash was a Romany – a Gypsy. The race/culture still existed, and still thrived, living as they did outside conventional society and its rules with a very keen eye for the credit – acquired as an individualistic Rom might see fit. Instead of caravans they used spaceships – for trading, smuggling, or just traveling for adventure and profit. Their customary laws – kris – required them to respect fidelity, their family, and returning favor for favor. Within the Rom. And even then, the customs were hardly commandments.

It was unheard of for a Rom to serve in the military, let alone the supersecret Mantis Teams. How and why Ida ended up on Mantis Section 13, under the command of Lieutenant Sten, was an even bigger and even less answerable puzzler. She had been carried on the rolls as pilot and electronics specialist. She was also their unofficial banker, gambler, and 'investment' specialist. At the end of a mission the 'investments' would be liquidated, and the team members would be flush enough for truly exotic leaves.

When Mantis 13 had been broken up and Sten transferred to the Imperial Guard, Ida had refused re-enlistment and vanished back to her culture.

She had surfaced – in absentia on a fiche – after Sten and Alex had escaped from the Tahn prison at Koldyeze and returned to Prime. The surfacing had been the announcement that she had accessed their pay that had been held while the two were POWs and invested. And invested. She had not explained – but both men became fabulously wealthy. They had been . . . and might be again if the privy council were destroyed and they were no longer fugitives.

Ida had found a unique finale for the announcement: she had turned and hoisted her skirts at them.

As Alex had observed, 'Th' lass still dinnae wear knickers . . .'

'My family will join us for the feast,' Ida said. 'They're curious to see how much I lied about you two gadje. Don't clot it up, Alex.' She led them to a sideboard and poured three drinks into crystal goblets. 'To the dead past . . . and a prayer this clottin' present will soon join it.'

Ida had turned somber.

'Your message was welcome, Sten,' she said.

'I didn't think it would have as large an effect.'

'You expected just me – or me and my vita – my family?'

'That was the best I had hoped for.'

'Times've changed for all of us. You're an admiral. I am now Voivode, chieftain of my band. Other voivodes have been known to listen to me, even if I am a woman.'

'There's more to this many of your people showing up than just you being a heavyweight, Ida. Gypsies, from what I know, what you taught me, don't get together on anything,' Sten said skeptically.

'No. That is what we are – and there've been terrible tragedies because of this in our past. And another tragedy is on the wind.'

Ida explained. The gypsies may have been outsiders, but they maintained careful intelligence contacts beyond their culture.

'That clottin' council that killed the Emperor's decided that we're lice on the body politic. Mainly 'cause we still have enough AM2 to hold together. They think we've got more'n we actually do – they don't know when a gypsy can't wander, he dies.

'So there'll be an open order on us. Seize our ships. Seize our cargoes. Seize the fuel. What happens to the people on board . . . not mentioned.'

'Th' Guard'll nae honor *that*.'

'The Guard's changed. Some of them won't. But some of them will. And how many systems think the universe'd be better without us stealin' their chickens, gold, and daughters? Too clottin' many.

'We are not going to wait this time. We are not going to try to turn invisible or hide.

'Your Tribunal's a damn slender reed, Sten. But it's the only one we can see in this clottin' swamp that's risin' up on us.

'So there'll be feasts an' speeches an' debates an' prob'ly a clottin' knifin' or two. Don't mean drakh. You'll end with us swearin' eternal fealty. Or anyway until the privy council's dead meat or you happen to leave the barn unguarded.

'Enough of that.' Ida forced herself into cheerfulness. 'So I'm takin' this clottin' tub on a recruitin' drive, eh? You housebroke yet?'

'Nae, lass. 'Tis nae healthy. Drink i' one end, piddle oot th' stern. Keeps th' system on-line.'

'You'll fit right in,' she said. 'Fill the glasses, Admiral. Damn, but I like that! Clottin' gadje Admiral for a barkeep!'

Sten poured. 'Don't mind bartending at all, Ida. By the way, two sets of thanks. First for taking care of our money . . . now this.'

Ida and Alex drained their glasses. Sten just sipped at his. Ida frowned.

'I can't stay long,' he explained. 'I've got my own little trip to take.'

'And where, Admiral, does it say in the clottin' regs you can't travel with a crawlin' hangover?'

Sten considered. No, it didn't.

And so, yes, he did.

Chapter Twenty-Nine

Sten landed on Prime World with two covers: a livid scar and an Impossible Quest.

The scar was a benign parasite, surgically transplanted onto his face. Nearly two centimeters wide, zigzagging artistically from his scalp line to the corner of his eye and down to his chin, it was part of the 'Great Lorenzo' dicta: The best disguise is the simplest, and one that won't blow off in a strong wind. Anyone looking at Sten would see only the horrible scar, no matter how carefully he instructed his mind to be polite. Sten had used versions of the gimmick before, from an alk-ridden nose to partial baldness to a simple, completely shaven head. It worked – almost all the time, at least.

Sten's main concern was that when he extracted from Prime, the parasite might have decided it had found a home everlasting. Kilgour reassured him.

'Dinna fash, lad. I' thae happens, we'll score y' a wee eyepatch an' y' kin join th' pirates.'

The Impossible Quest was equally simple. Truth: At the close of the Tahn wars one D'vid Rosemont had appeared on Prime. A flashy, loud-talking, loud-living entrepreneur, he announced his newest business – converting Imperial spacecraft, particularly the tiny, evil tacships, into luxury yachts. Regardless of the inherent absurdity of the premise, Rosemont prospered. For a minute and a half.

Prime's Fraud Squad had taken an interest in Rosemont – his company, yet to produce a single yacht that anyone could find, looked very much like a con game. And then Rosemont vanished, leaving bare bank accounts and a warehouse with three tacships inside. All of that was true.

The harried but friendly – and badly scarred – man appeared on Prime.

False: His name was Elijah Braun. Sten/Braun was credentialed as a private investigator, working for a law firm located on a faraway world between Lost and Nowhere. Rosemont had an heir, who wanted whatever estate existed. Braun knew that the man had not been declared legally dead yet, but the heir was convinced that Rosemont was a victim of foul play, rather than a con who had skated with the swag. Braun was convinced that the heir, already rich, was drug-addled. But a case was a case. Besides, he prattled to the official issuing him his sixty-day visa, it would give him a chance to see Prime, the center of everything and the universe's Most Glamorous World.

'You've seen too many livies, Sr. Braun. Or else you're a history buff. Prime ain't what it was, and it's getting less like it every day.'

The official glanced hastily over his shoulder to make sure that his innocent statement had gone unheard. But Sten filed that glance. Unsurprisingly, the privy council's internal security was in full.

Sten noted them everywhere: street cleaners who ignored litter but noted passersby; inept waiters with big ears; clerks who never clerked but listened; block wardens; concierges who asked questions far beyond what was normal. All precautions by the privy council against a largely nonexistent threat. And they were expensive precautions – the council was spending money for all those informers, money it simply did not have.

Sten marveled once again at the odd tendency all too many beings had to want to spy on their neighbor for any reason whatsoever.

None of them thought beyond the moment of what would surely happen when – not if – the privy council fell. Sten remembered the riots on Heath near the end of the Tahn wars. Not only had the mob ripped anyone in uniform apart, but they had revenged themselves on the Tahn's amateur gestapo in the process.

Not that Sten felt sorry for them. He just wanted his cover to stay intact long enough for him to get in, find what he was looking for, and go home.

He did, however, take a precaution. The current powers did not know everything. Mahoney had told him of a few, very secure, disused safe houses on Prime that might still exist. One at least did. Sten armed himself with a secondary set of false documents that were stashed there.

He then proceeded in his role as Braun. He found an inexpensive hotel, found the landlord of that warehouse, and taped the three hulks inside. He interviewed investors and acquaintances of the vanished Rosemont. He went to the Fraud Squad. They gave him access to their files, and a Visitor's ID.

Braun, over a period of days, professed first bewilderment and then suspicion. He was starting to believe that the heir might be right. Rosemont had not vanished. *Something* had happened to the man. He did have some less-than-palatable acquaintances on the back-alley side of town. Murder, maybe. Suicide? Rosemont, Braun said, had appeared very depressed before he vanished, then turned suddenly cheerful. 'He found his back door,' suggested a bunco expert, but he gave Braun the names of some friends in Homicide.

Then, timidly, he asked permission to speak to the chief of Homicide. 'Y're crackers, an' you're wastin' your – an' her – time. But she's got a policy. Talks to anybody, no matter how loony.'

Braun said he was aware that Chief Haines was very busy, especially in these troubled times. So he had prepared a summary of his investigation, complete with a list of questions he would like to ask. He clipped a copy of his Visitor's ID to the fiche, and it went forward.

Sten felt like drakh. He was preparing to use – and possibly jeopardize – a friend and former lover.

He had often wondered about their affair. In one way, it had been the only 'normal' relationship Sten had experienced. But in another, they had been lovers by circumstance, co-investigating a conspiracy. And their affair had never really ended – Sten had gone off to fight a war, been captured, escaped, and returned to combat. Haines had been drafted into Military Intelligence, and somehow they had never reconnected. He had thought, sometimes, before the privy council made him outlaw, of dropping a line to her, just to see . . . see what, Sten? If there's still a there there?

Probably, he thought, Kilgour was right. Both of them were getting 'morally corrupted' – and getting too moral to soldier successfully in the dirty midnight wars they had grown up in.

Don't get too moral, he prodded himself. Honest spies get trusting and dead. Join the Purity League when this is over if you wish.

He had sent the fiche in to Haines hoping to avoid heart attack city. He hoped she would figure out his intent.

It took two days before he was summoned to her office.

The temperature could have frozen a nova.

'Sr. Braun,' Haines said. 'I've gone through your fiche, and your questions. Reviewed our own files. Everything my department has suggests you are on a dead end.'

'I might well be,' Sten said. 'May I record?'

Without waiting for an answer, he put a battered taper – at least its exterior was battered – on her desk and turned it on. Then motioned to her to keep talking.

Haines frowned but continued telling Braun why thinking Rosemont's disappearance was anything other than what it appeared was a blind alley.

Sten had enough. He touched another button on the taper. 'Your bug is suppressed. It's getting fed synthesized chatter.'

Haines came around the desk, almost into an embrace, then stopped herself. 'I'm married now,' she said very softly. 'Happily.' That was softer still.

Another world of might-have-been vanished.

'I'm . . . glad for you,' Sten said.

Haines managed a smile. 'I'm sorry. I must say I've thought about . . . things. As they were. And . . . sorry. At least I can try to lie as well as you do, and let's say that I think of our time together as a lovely moment in the past. Emphasis past.'

'Yeah. That's best. I guess, anyway. But who wrote that dialogue? Sounds like a livie.'

'Best I could manage. Right off the top. Now,' Haines said, trying to be businesslike. 'I'd like to be flattered and think you're here to – more livie dialogue – relight the flame. In spite of your being one of the Ten Most Wanted in the Empire. But I think I know better. Dammit.'

She turned away for a moment. 'That scar?' she asked without turning back.

'Make-up.'

'Thank God.' She turned back. 'Now I'll get angry. I'm getting used.'

'Yes.'

'First I wondered if I was getting set up. Then I changed my mind.'

'Thanks for that much, anyway. But I need help. You were the best contact.'

'Sure. Good old Haines. We were pretty good in the sack, so let's see if she'll roll again, just for old times' sake? Let me ask you . . . If I wasn't involved, and you were, would you have gone so far as to pull moonlight on the mattress?'

'I know you're pissed, Lisa. But that's a little—' He broke off, letting it go.

Haines took several deep breaths. 'Oh, hell. You're right. But I'm not going to make a career of apology.'

And she was in his arms. For a long moment.

'It *was* pretty good, wasn't it?' she asked.

Sten said yes and kissed her. Finally, she broke away.

'But I wasn't lying. Sam'l is a wonderful man. Probably, to be honest, a little bit more the kind of person I should be with. Not some rogue with a dagger in his arm and murder in his heart. So . . . let's try it as friends. Never tried to be friends with somebody I was in – involved with before. So maybe I can learn something.'

Part of Sten wanted to cry. 'Sure, Lisa. Friends.'

Haines started acting like a cop again. 'First, how clean are you?'

'Clean. For at least a few more weeks.'

'I gathered,' Haines said, tapping the fiche, 'that you're running a mission. Your ex-boss have anything to do with it? I thought so. Against the council?'

Sten nodded once more.

'One question – and you'd best not be lying to me. Last time around, after we policed up everyone involved with the late Kai Hakone, there were some bodies in alleys. By Imperial Order. What I'd done is collaborate in a murder conspiracy. I didn't like it then, and I don't like it any better now.

'So if there's what I've heard you call "wet work," or "personal contact" at the end of this . . . don't even ask me.'

'No. This is for the Tribunal.'

Haines goggled. 'Son of a bitch,' she said slowly. Of course, in spite of the privy council's blackout, she had heard the Tribunal's announcement of its intent to sit in judgment on the council. 'I'm thinking. Yeah. The whole thing – your idea?'

'It was.'

'Son of a bitch once more,' she said. 'I said I wouldn't apologize. But I do. For the last time.'

She grinned. 'You know . . . maybe in another hundred, hundred and fifty years, if you spend some time in a seminary, you might actually be permitted to join the human race.

'Okay. What do you need?'

Another misunderstanding had been corrected by Alex Kilgour before he left on his recruiting drive. Oddly enough it had minor echoes of what Sten was realizing and saying to Lisa Haines.

Kilgour had informed Sten's bodyguard that for the moment they were no longer needed on their special assignment. They were reassigned to general court security.

Cind had requested an interview with her temporary commanding officer. The first question she had asked Alex was why the change? Had they done something wrong?

'First strike, on y', soldier. Security is security. Y' dinnae need t'know. Sten's got bi'ness ae his own.'

'Request reassignment, sir.'

'Ae what? Pers'nal backup f'r him?'

'Something like that.'

Kilgour growled. 'Th' firs' an' only time Ah got involv'd wi' a task, m' Mantis topkick took m' back ae th' barracks. She wailed upon m' melon an' informed me Ah'd best learn t'be a professional ae m' task or go back t' sheep-shaggin'.

'She wae right.

'An' shoud do th' same t' you.

'But Ah'm sophisticated, noo. I c'd gie th' order – "So'jer, soldier!" – 'n hae done wi' it.

'But Ah'll gie reasons. So gie your head oot ae y'r gonads or where e'er it's lurkin't, an' listen close.

'One, y'r bosses know whae they're doin't. Second, y're complete wrong f'r whae th' boss is doin't. An' dinnae yammer ae me aboot th' longarm an' how y'been studyin't intell'gence. Ah knoo all ae thae already.

'You're wrong f'r th' run because y're too . . . strikin'. You dinnae e'er, e'er, e'er want to be notable i' y'r task is snoopin't ae poopin't. An' y're a so'jer. So'jerin' is a diff'rent discipline thae spookin't.

'But thae's as may be. Last – an' best – reason, y're too clottin' young. Y'believe in things. Y'dinnae ken th' depths ae depravity i' th' spirit. Unless y' grew up bein' nattered ae by Calvinists, ae Ah did. A spook must hae one thing runnin' throo his mind ae all times: Trust nae soul, an' always, always think th' worst ae most selfish ae any an' all.

'A hard an' evil lesson. One y', t'be honest, w'd be best not learnin't.

'Gie y'self back t' th' duties assigned, noo. Ah'll wager thae'll be more'n enow blood t' come. Y'll hae chances t' distinguish y'self ae th' eyes ae y'r superiors or e'en the boss, i' thae's your fancy.

'Dismissed.'

Kilgour sighed when she had left. Christ on a pogo stick, he thought. He was starting to sound like a fatherly command sergeant major. Gettin' old, Kilgour. Gettin' old . . .

At first Sten thought going to Prime was nothing more than an ego-damaging, high-hazard bust. He was looking for three things: any more information on the murder-for-hire of the press lord Volmer than Haines had been able to give Mahoney; a paper trail for that first – question mark – meeting of the conspirators on Earth; and whether or not there had been another meeting before Chapelle was put in motion. Plus, as a secondary goal, whether there was anything more on the Chapelle/Control/Sullamora link than was known, in spite of Mahoney's proclamation that it was relatively unimportant.

Thus far, he had done a very good job of getting zeroes. No, Haines had nothing more on Volmer or the 'suicide' of the assassin. She frankly admitted that she had not worked the case any further – it was clearly political. These days people had been known to vanish when they started asking uncomfortable questions about politics. She added, however, that she did not think there was anything to collect, at least not until the privy council was deposed and, it was to be hoped, indicted.

Zero One.

As for anything about that meeting on Earth, Sten found a complete vacuum. As far as he could tell, there had been *no* contact between members of the council before they somehow, telepathically, sensed it was time to gather at Sullamora's lodge. At least that was all that was in the open archives and what governmental archives Haines had been able to gingerly pry at. Kilgour had been right – the privy council had been smart enough to destroy or classify whatever memoranda had passed between them but not smart enough to make substitutes. Interesting. Ordinarily that would have been enough for Sten, as an intelligence professional, to take action on. But as an officer of the law, he was trying hard to stay somewhere close to its limits and requirements.

Zero Two.

As for his side quest – he found a mansion that had been rented shortly before Chapelle vanished by a retired colonel general named Suvorov. From some kind of Pioneer Division or Battalion or whatever they called those military things, the estate agent told him. Suvorov was right – the estate agent remembered his dress and credit rating clearly. Solidly built, he thought. Oh yes. A scar on his neck. Don't remember which side. Might I inquire why you're asking, Sr. Braun? Proof that the father my client is looking for is not this man. Thank you for your time.

Big clottin' deal. A smooth operator who used the haunts of the rich to launch his operation. They knew that already. Name – false. Build? Who knew? The scar? Probably as phony as the one Sten was wearing.

Slightly More Than Zero Three. But not much.

The second meeting? He could find no trace of any final parley among the privy council before the assassination other than in their official chambers. He did not think they were dumb enough to plan the death of the Emperor in what they must think to be certainly bugged offices. And were they so skilled that they could set up a conspiracy that ran of itself? Nobody, including Sten, was that good. But where was the evidence?

Zero Four. So far.

Sten wanted Haines to be single, the sky-floating houseboat over the forest to still be there, two bottles of champagne, and the vid disconnected. Oh, yeah. A little general peace without paranoia or goons would go nicely.

He contented himself with one solitary short beer and an equally solitary brood.

He glimmered an idea. But it would, he thought, be in plain view. If the privy council were as paranoid as he thought them to be, he could be strolling into a trap. One set not specifically for Sten, but for anyone with the curiosity of a not particularly bright cat.

It seemed, however, the only and last option.

*

From first appearances, Hawkthorne had changed very little since Sten and Alex had gone there under deep cover to hire mercenaries for what they called 'The Great Talamein Beatup.' It still was fairly anarchic – any planet that specialized as a hiring hall for soldiers-for-hire had to have a fairly lax government where the ultimate law was laid down by whoever had the heaviest weapons.

But the mercenaries on Hawkthorne looking for a contract were different from the psychopaths, crooks, opportunists, and would-be kingmakers before.

The Tahn War had changed everything.

Any war produced, in its aftermath, mercenaries. They came from the losing armies, from suddenly stateless soldiers, from the ranks of war criminals, from the bored who wanted to continue experiencing that one insane moment of pure life that was combat, and from those who just could not go back to the farm. Generally they were highly professional. But as peace went on, there was a deterioration in quality. Some got killed, some found their kingdom beyond the clouds, some grew up and realized that that moment of life was surrounded by death, and others drifted on to more stable situations that required only the occasional use of violence.

That had been Hawkthorne before.

The Tahn wars created a new horde of professionals. And the necessary economic cutbacks of peacetime, plus the hamwitted policies of the privy council, had made them potential mercenaries.

Admirals would sign on as ship executive officers. Guard generals would cheerfully command a battalion or even a company. Sergeant majors would wear the blank sleeve of a private without complaining – at least for the moment.

Alex could pick and choose. He did.

Sten dreamed of ten thousand 'officers of the court' and hoped for five thousand. Alex could have gotten one hundred thousand. He could afford to be generous.

Money? Nae problem. If the Tribunal failed to start the fall of the privy council, how much was left in the coffers would be completely unimportant once everyone involved bought a fast ticket out of town.

Fuel for combat ships? Kilgour had a 'train' full.

He could have enlisted some with a full meal and the promise of regular rations to come.

For some, there was even a more subtle offer, made quietly and in person: If the privy council were toppled, the Imperial military would need restructuring. The corrupt, the incompetent, or those who had bloodied their hands in the purge would be removed. *Some* kind of military would be – had to be – retained. Alex said that frankly he had no idea what it would be. He let the thought dangle.

He stood at the ramp of Ida's flagship and looked down at his army.

From up there, one could see the threadbare uniforms or the shabby termination-of-service civvies some others wore. One could not see the gaunt, hungry faces.

From there, the lines of soldiery and their ships behind them were as rigidly in formation as any Guards unit on formal inspection.

Put 'em in propit dress, he said to himself. Gie 'em a banner to follow, an' lead 'em to a war wi' paper bullets. Thae's happiness.

Kilgour's . . . Killers? Cheap. Kubs? Stupid. Klique? Clack. Kilgour's Keeks? Nae. Jus' a few of 'em were ex-intelligence. Ah. Kilgour's Kilted Kvetchers.

He gave the orders and watched proudly as 'his' army, who would never know it, boarded ship for lift-off.

Frae a mo', Ah wae a gen'ral.

An' did y'a like it?

He suddenly had a vision of those soldiers at their fate. Dead slowly or quickly. Bodies shredded beyond reconstruction. Blinded. Crippled. Insane.

Then another vision: He saw all those soldiers wearing a motley of civvies. Bankers, farmers, wives, workmen, tourists in the streets, factories, homes, and pubs of the vast estates Laird Kilgour owned but somehow never got around to asserting his total authority over, back on Edinburgh.

Better. Far better.

Answers y'r wee question, doesn't it, now, he thought. And he ordered the officer of the watch to seal ship and prepare for lift.

No one in the Cult of the Eternal Emperor knew exactly *how* they heard. But suddenly, in a thousand thousand meeting halls on an equal number of worlds, everyone *knew*.

They had been given a great honor.

One of the privy council had become a fertile ground for the True Belief. Not only a ruler, but the being most reputed to be the most intelligent.

Now he had vanished. No explanation was given by anyone. It was not as if Kyes had regularly appeared in vids of the council – but now it was if he had never existed.

The explanation was simple.

The Mighty Kyes had seen the light. As a reward, he had been taken, *in corpore*, to commune with the Holy Spheres, just as the Emperor had.

Kyes, they knew, would not return, any more than the handful of saints who had achieved equal reward. None of them were, after all, the Emperor himself.

This was an event. Kyes would be numbered among the Blessed.

But more importantly, the believers could sense something else:

The time was coming. The Emperor would return soon.

They readied themselves. For what, they did not know. They did not even know if their services would be called for.

But – and let it be so, let us each have a chance to serve, they prayed – they were ready.

'Your pardon.'

It was not an apology for intrusion, but a command. Sten looked up at the librarian.

A less likely one he had never seen. Not that librarians fell into physical archetypes. But it was the uncommon one who had a flushed tan from a life mostly spent outside, on foot patrol. Nor did many of them have scarred and callused knuckles. And none wore hard-toed, cushion-soled boots, let alone that telltale sag and wear on the belt that came from a holstered gun.

'Yah?' Sten said.

'You're readin' about the council, right?'

'So? It 'gin th' law? Some kinda new law passed since I got up this morn?' Sten slurred.

The man did not answer. 'Please could I see your ID?' Again, a command.

Sten took the ID from his pocket and passed it to the man looming over his terminal. It was not Braun's ID, but the standard, generic phony he had scored from Mahoney's safehouse. According to the card, Sten was a caretaker, hired to mind the closed consulate of a frontier world.

'Janitor, eh?' The security goon passed the card back. 'Jus' readin' about th' Lords outa curiosity?'

The Lords. New term.

'Nawp,' Sten said. 'M'kid wanted to know how th' world worked. Shamed m'self not knowin'. Thought I'd better read up some. Got, well, laid off las' week. So got some time while I'm lookin' f'r a new slot. T'rble, lookin' stupid front a y'r own son.'

The man grunted and walked back to the front of the library.

Sten swore bitterly. Very nice indeed when a being could end up in the slammer for going to a library and going through public records. Just a hell of a good government. Be glad you're non-existent, son of mine, he thought.

Sten had figured the council just might be paranoid enough to put a trace in the libraries. He had found a shop specializing in actor's supplies and purchased the best pancake makeup available. The clerk had glanced at Sten's scar, winced, and not asked any questions. Sten pretended to be embarrassed by having to buy the makeup and also said he was an amateur actor, and he could use a fake mustache in the production he was in. The pitying clerk went along with the pretense and sold him one.

Scar covered, mustache in place – Sten tried to keep from whuffling it as if he were Rykor, or touching it to see if it had come unglued yet – he entered the library.

He was glad he had taken precautions – he had spotted the phony librarian immediately.

Staying with the cheap cover, he had started the search at PRIVY COUNCIL – FUNCTIONS AND DUTIES, beginning when they ascended to total power and staying clear, for the moment, of the time frame he was interested in. Scrolling through the flackery and propaganda wasted a full morning. Then he chanced PRIVY COUNCIL – HISTORY (FROM FORMATION TO PRESENT).

That, evidently, was where the security indicator alarm had been hidden.

He scrolled on, glancing every now and then at the front desk. The goon seemed satisfied.

HISTORY . . . hmm. NG.

Okay. What next?

PRIVY COUNCIL, PICS. ANY PERIOD.

Endless head and shoulders for thumbnails. Group photos at ceremonies. All very official. Very few, Sten noted, of the Kraas. Maybe they knew what they looked like. Almost nothing on Kyes.

Got any other – whoops!

Sten back-scrolled, hoping he had seen what he thought he had.

I have you, he thought fiercely staring at the screen, which showed all five of the councilors hurrying into the entrance of some kind of hall. They were surrounded by security. The pic was rather poorly framed, and Sten saw, in the corner, a cop headed for the camera, an angry look on his face.

So somebody had shot a picture – looked as if he was either a freelancer or a citizen – of the bastards. The cop was headed for him to try to grab the pic. Good thing the photog was wearing' track shoes or was bigger'n the cop, Sten thought.

Now. What was it?

He read the caption.

Some kind of sporting event. Gravball? Whatever that was. Sten had about as much interest in athletics as he did in watching rocks grow. He had suffered through the obligatory games in the service, rationalizing them as part of the necessary physical conditioning. This was the Rangers against something called the Blues. Teams. The Blues were offworld, the Rangers from Prime. Big match – a hundred thousand people, including privy council to watch . . .

Game played at Lovett Arena.

Oh clottin' really.

Sten did not know how many of the privy council were sports freaks. Not that it mattered. This was the *only* occasion he had been able to find, both in the library and in Haines's records, where the council had assembled on more or less neutral ground to 'enjoy' a non-work-related event.

He noted the date and shut down.

'Clottin' impossible to understand, this politics,' he confided to the librarian. 'Grab a bite, an' spend the rest of the day readin' sports. Pick up a few coins bettin' at th' bar.'

The thug grunted. He didn't care.

Sten could have found a secure com and checked with Haines. He thought it better not to. He probably should have just pulled out and let Haines's police fingers do the rest of the walking. But he was finally on to something. Damned if he was going to let somebody else find the gold from his lead.

He did not eat a midday meal, however. He kept the library's entrance under watch, just in case the goon was *really* looking for brownie points. Nothing.

He came back, deliberately belched in the goon's direction, and went to his terminal.

SPORTS. RANGERS, HISTORY.

Nothing. He jumped ahead to the date of that big match. Blues undefeated three years . . . Rangers won . . . big riots as usual. Nothing. At least nothing he could see that tied the event to any councilman.

He was getting closer.

Lovett Arena.

He was sweaty-palmed. Another tracer, and that goon might not listen to any explanations. How do you winkle in? Try . . . and his fingers touched the keyboard. AMPHITHEATERS. CURRENT. ENTER.

He was not watching the screen; he kept his eye on the security man across the huge chamber. The man did not move.

No . . . no . . . damn, but these people on Prime have got a lot of sports palaces. Lovett Arena.

History?

Try it. Built by Lovett's grandsire . . . equipped for every kind of sport conceivable, land, water, or aerial. Lions vs. Christians, Sten wondered. PICS.

He looked at picture after picture, ignoring whatever was in the foreground and what was happening. He was looking at the arena itself.

Clot. If those bastards were going to conspire . . . no. Everything was too open. But wait a minute – that was interesting. ENTIRE ENTRY:

BEHIND THE CHEERS:
How a Stadium Keeps You Fed,
Warm, Safe, and Entertained.

Clottin' poor title.

Parking . . . underground . . . security offices . . . my.

So Lovett's grandfather built himself a private suite, did he? Clottin' awful-looking. Why would anybody hang the heads of dead animals on a wall? Let alone those paintings. But what a wonderful place for a conspiracy to meet. The big game as cover . . . bigwigs like sports, especially if they get private seats . . . privacy.

Sten had proof – enough for him – that there *had* been a final meeting before Chapelle was put into play. How could he get backup, enough to take to the Tribunal? Mucketies needed servants when they played. Were there bartenders who had been around that night? Joygirls? Boys? Maybe barkeeps. But not sex toys – not even the Kraas would be that careless.

What else? He punched out of SPORTS, and took a chance on WHO'S WHO. He entered LOVETT.

His attention was fixed on the screen. Usual plaudits. Educational . . . interests . . . entered family banking empire on death of mother . . . Hmm. No entry . . . even in this jerk-off log of him being a sports loon.

Sten's concentration was broken as the library's door banged closed. Damn!

Three uniformed cops entered.

Sten crouched away from the terminal and down an aisle with stacked fiche on either side to a door.

It was locked. His fingers went into a fob pocket and came out with a small tool. Seconds later, the door was unlocked.

He went through the door and relocked it behind him. He heard a shout from the reading room.

Sten, even as he looked for an exit, blinked. This was one hell of a library. Huge vaulted ceiling. Row after row after row of stored fiche, vids, and even books.

He heard fumbling at the door and shouts to get the key. A body thudded against the door.

Sten's fingers curled, and his knife dropped from its sheath inside his forearm into his hand. He ran down into the stacks, loping easily like a tiger looking for an ambush site.

The cops, the security tech in front, got the door open and came into the chamber.

They saw nothing except a couple of robots filing material. They heard nothing. The security man whispered orders: Spread out. Search the whole room.

The cops started to obey perfunctorily. Clot, there they were, wasting time because some clottin' piece of drakh counterspook sees shadows on the wall and wanted them to bust the cops of some private puke. Then the reaction hit them. Maybe a private puke – but one who could somehow go through a locked door.

'We'll stay together.'

Two of them took out their guns. The third had a truncheon ready.

'You first, hero.'

A tiny, lethal-looking projectile gun appeared in the secret policeman's hand.

They went into the tiger's jungle.

Suddenly a tall case teetered and crashed sideways. The teeter gave one cop and the security thug time to flat-dive out of the way. The other two were caught by the heavy case and its cascading contents. The first case brought a second one across from it slamming down. They floundered and shouted. Somebody fired a round that whined up into the library's ceiling and ricocheted wildly.

There was a scuffle as the 'tiger's' pads moved him away, deeper into the stacks.

The two went on, leaving their trapped partners to work their own way free.

One of the trapped cops was wedging his way through a snow-storm of papers, his leg still caught under the case, when he heard a quiet thunk . . . and the whiny scratch of somebody trying to take his last breath through a crushed windpipe.

Then there was a sliver of death at his throat. 'Scream,' Sten ordered. 'Real loud.'

The cop followed orders.

The scream was still echoing as Sten slit the man's throat, came up, and darted into another row.

The security goon and the surviving policeman ran up. They had a second for a shocked gape at the two corpses and the gouts of blood before shock turned into horror and a metal-bound folio discused in from nowhere, smashing into the cop's forehead. He collapsed bonelessly.

The security man went for the door, backing . . . whirling . . . trying to keep from screeching in horror and running into what he knew would be the tiger's final trap.

A fiche clattered on the floor. He spun – nothing. Then he whirled back, gun hand out. Sten stepped in behind him. The goon went limp as Sten severed his spinal cord. He let the body fall. Two flops and it was a corpse.

Now Sten had all the time in the world.

He found an exit and, nearby, an employee's washroom. He swabbed solvent, and the mustache came off into the disposal; and the makeup was scrubbed clean.

Then he went out the door.

Police gravsleds were howling toward the library. Sten trotted down an alley, then slowed. He strolled onward, glancing curiously as the official units whined past.

Just another citizen of Prime.

Chapter Thirty

'*John Stuart Mill*, this is New River Central Control. We have you on-screen. Do you wish landing instructions?'

Mahoney's pilot keyed a mike. 'New River Control, this is the *Mill*. Negative on that. Landing permission established at Private Port November Alpha Uniform. Will switch frequencies. Over.'

'This is New River. I have your fiche on-screen. Switch to UHF 223.7 for contact with November Alpha Uniform. November Alpha will provide locator only, no control personnel at port. New River Control, clear.'

The pilot swiveled his chair. 'Five minutes, sir.'

Mahoney nodded and keyed the intercom mike to the crew compartment. His ship was a barely camouflaged covert insert craft, renamed for the moment after an old Earth economist. Mahoney thought it a nice addition to the cover he was using.

The screen lit and showed ten beings, armed and wearing Mantis Team tropo-camouflage uniforms. All of them were not only ex-Mantis but soldiers Mahoney had used for missions back when he commanded Mercury Corps.

'We'll be down in about five, Ellen,' he told the burly ex-noncom in the compartment.

'We heard, boss. Sure you want us to just stand by? We could have him out by his boot heels in a couple minutes.'

'Just stay in a holding pattern. Either he's who I want, in which case he might have more firepower'n we do, or he's not. Do me a favor? You hear shootin', scamper right on in. I'm getting too old for another body reconstruct.'

'Yessir. We're ready.'

Mahoney reached over the pilot's shoulder and picked up the

com mike. 'November Alpha Uniform, November Alpha Uniform. This is the *John Stuart Mill*, inbound for landing.'

A voice answered. '*Mill*, this is November Alpha. Landing beacon triple-cast, apex two kilometers over field. No winds on field. Land as arranged. Potential client plus two others only. Any other crew remain in ship. Please observe these minimum safety precautions. I will meet you at the main house. Out.'

Mahoney clicked the mike twice to indicate that he understood. He grinned at the pilot. 'Please, eh? Perhaps he is my boy.'

The ship set down in the center of the small, paved field. The port opened, and Mahoney climbed out.

It was hot, dry, and dusty. To one side of the field stretched scrub desert and then low mountains. On the other were vast stretches of white-fenced, very green pastures. The air was very still. Mahoney heard a bird chirp from a nearby orchard, and, from the pastures, the hiss of irrigation equipment.

He walked up the winding road toward the scatter of buildings. Pasture . . . white fences . . . barns there. Chutes. A breeding establishment? He saw a very old quadruped – an Earth horse, he identified – grazing in a field. No other animals.

He walked past metal-sided sheds, their doors closed and bolted. Stables. Empty. There was a low wall, and a gate standing open.

He entered and walked through an elaborate garden that looked as if it had gone too long without enough maintenance. There were three robot gardeners at work, and a human near them. The man paid him no attention.

Hard times, Mahoney mused. It takes credit to keep a horse ranch going.

He was, however, impressed. He had seen no sign whatever of security devices, guards, or weaponry. But unless he was completely lost, they were there.

A man stood in front of the main entrance, waiting. He was a bit younger than Mahoney. Not as tall. Stocky. He looked as if he worked out on a fairly regular basis. Not an ugly man, not a handsome man. He wore an open-neck shirt, expensively casual pants, and sandals.

'Sr. Gideon,' he greeted. 'I am Schaemel. Please come in. I have refreshments.'

The sprawling house – not quite a mansion – was decorated with heavy furniture made of real wood and leather. The paintings on the walls were old and all of realistic subjects.

'Each year,' Schaemel observed, 'I manage to forget how hot

and dry New River is in late summer. And each year I am reminded. That is a wine-fruit concoction. It is refreshing.' He indicated a punch bowl containing ice and a milky liquid. Mahoney made no response.

Schaemel half smiled. He ladled punch into a tumbler and drained it. Mahoney then got a drink for himself.

'So your corporation's getting whipsawed, Sr. Gideon. A hostile takeover on one side, a union organizing on the other, and you think the union's a setup. Everyone's playing dirty and you need an expert. Excellent presentation, by the way.'

'Thank you.'

'One thing I particularly admire,' Schaemel continued, 'is your attention to trivia. John Stuart Mill as the name for your yacht, indeed. Perhaps a bit too capitalistic – but nice, regardless.'

Mahoney's hand brushed his pants pocket, and, back in the ship, the ALERT light went on.

'I'm very, very glad,' Schaemel said, 'that it was you who showed up. I have been waiting for some time for something like this – or something else.

'I certainly never believed the stories of your suicide, Fleet Marshal Mahoney . . . I believe that was your rank when you "retired." Spies suicide – not spy masters.'

'You are quick,' Mahoney said. 'So can we drop the "Schaemel" drakh, Venloe?'

'I thought that identity was safely buried. But then, I thought *I* was, too.'

Mahoney explained: how few real professionals there were; how fewer were not involved with a government, megacorporation, or military; and lastly Venloe's characteristic MO.

Venloe looked chagrined. 'And all these years you think you never leave a trail. Tsk. I am ashamed. So how am I to make amends for having engineered the assassination of the Emperor?'

'You assume I'm not here to nail your guts to a tree and chase you around it half a dozen times. The Emperor was also my friend.'

'So I have been told. And I have heard stories about you . . . preferring field work on occasion. But if you just wanted me dead, you would not have bothered to introduce yourself before the bangs began. Direct confrontations can produce contusions on both sides – and you are hardly a young hero any more.'

'Not correct,' Mahoney said, and the easy casualness vanished for a moment. 'If I weren't after bigger bastards I well might've shown up and personally cut your heart out.'

'Careful, Mahoney. You corrected me on one of my errors, I return the compliment. We do not take things personally in our trade. It can be suicidal.

'But since that is not on the agenda, may we change the subject? You may tell whatever troops you have for backup they can relax.'

He walked to a desk and put his hand flat on what appeared to be a blotter. 'My own people are standing down.'

He seated himself and indicated that Mahoney do likewise. 'I could probably guess what you want. But tell me, anyway. I assume it has something to do with this ludicrous Tribunal I've heard bruited.'

'It is. We want you to testify as to the conspiracy. Publicly.'

'Me? On the stand? That would be a new experience. Hardly good for my future employability.'

'Times don't appear to have been that good, anyway,' Mahoney said, looking pointedly out the window at the empty stables.

'The circumstances of my last assignment have forced me to be most careful as to who my employer is. I have turned down some very lush deals because of my supreme egotism in trying for the biggest target of them all.'

'Poor lad.'

Venloe ignored Mahoney's sarcasm. 'Say I agree, however. I stand up in a courtroom and say – say exactly what? That I was hired by one Tanz Sullamora after having performed tasks satisfactorily for him previously? That I located and developed the asset Chapelle and positioned him? And all the details around that? Perhaps. But is that all?'

'Of course not. Sullamora's dead. Nobody gives a clot about him. We want the others. Kyes. Malperin. The Kraas. Lovett.'

'Tsk. You want what I cannot give.'

'But you will.'

'You misunderstand. I *cannot* provide such details. I could testify that it is my moral belief that the rest of the privy council was part of the conspiracy, certainly. But proof? Sullamora never mentioned their names to me. I never met with them, nor with anyone I thought to be their direct representatives. Don't glower, Mahoney.

'I can offer evidence. My presence here. I fled Prime, of course. But I returned to my home of over twenty years rather than vanish into a new identity and a new part of the universe where I was a complete unknown. Obviously I did not collect my payoff; obviously. I have not gone to anyone looking for it. Now, if those bloody-handed idiots on the privy council had any idea that I was Control for that touch, don't you think they would have arranged my disappearance or co-option? More likely the former?'

Mahoney held his poker face. But he did not like what he was hearing.

'So, Mahoney, as I said, I am not your smoking gun, nor do I know where it might be. I will reluctantly offer you a deposition as to my knowledge – but that is all.'

Venloe got himself another tumbler of punch and waved the ladle in Mahoney's direction. Mahoney shook his head, no. Venloe went back to his chair.

'Impasse, is it not? You can kill me . . . try to kill me. But you certainly cannot get out alive. You said you were after bigger bastards – I assume you want to see them gotten.'

'Not quite an impasse,' Mahoney said. 'You are going to pack, and you are going to return with me to Newton. You may be telling the truth, you may be lying. We will find out, for certain.'

'Brainscan? Never. People have been known to die – or to be scrambled – under the cap. If that's the choice, I'd rather fight and conceivably die here.'

'You won't get dead. Or brainburnt. The scan will be done by Rykor. She is—'

'I know of her. The best. But, I confess, somebody wading through my soul gives me shudders.'

'The poor clot who'll do the wading through what you call a soul is the one who'll get the collywobbles.'

'Let me consider,' Venloe mused. 'If I say no, and somehow both of us survive the ensuing . . . discussion, what will happen next? Certainly you will somehow leak the word of my existence to the privy council, expecting them to clean up tracks that are not even there.

'Exactly what they would do. Imbeciles. I do not like this option.

'On the other hand, I go with you. Accept brainscan. Testify. Perhaps your Tribunal will succeed and somehow the forces of' – Venloe's voice oozed sarcasm – 'truth, justice, and the Imperial Way magically triumph, and the council falls. Or, what is more likely, their own ineptitude will destroy them.

'In either event, I am quite safe. Protected, in fact. I might not be able to follow my own trade, but I would certainly be kept in the style to which, off and on, I have become accustomed.'

Venloe was telling the truth. A political assassin, unless he was killed in the first moments after the assassination or was proven absolutely to be a lone maniac, would be coddled until his death by the state. Whether he talked or not – the hope was that sooner or later he would choose to tell all, even if at that point in time the only beings interested were historians.

Venloe thought, in the hot dry silence. 'Very well. I shall assemble my security beings and disarm them. Call for your escort to come in now. They can help carry my luggage to your ship. We have a bargain.'

He held out his hand, palm forward.

Mahoney just stared at it. After a moment, Venloe got up and left the room.

Solon Kenna had been in an observatory exactly once before in his life, and that time he had been young, drunk, and lost. Now he found them fascinating – or at least this particular one, on this particular night, looking at this particular projection.

He looked once more at the screen, reassuring himself that delirium tremens had not finally set in.

They were still there, hanging in a parking orbit around Dusable.

Alarms had cacophonied when the fleet was reported. Kenna turned pale and Tyrenne-elect Walsh even paler when told what it probably was and meant. Ships. Many, many ships. Somehow the privy council must have decided that the defeat of Tyrenne Yelad was injurious, and sent the guard.

Dusable's handful of customs patrol ships launched and swept toward the waiting fleet, loudly proclaiming peaceful intent on every band com-able. In the lead ship was Walsh, representing his system.

Kenna had immediately scuttled for shelter. Deep, deep shelter that would rapidly involve plastic surgery and departure.

There was no response.

And no one had ever seen ships like them – although they were clearly of Imperial design.

A ship was boarded.

And then the celebration began.

The ships were robots – robot freighters. Each of them – and the fleet reached out to forever – held enough Anti-Matter Two for one world's full consumption for one year, at maximum peacetime use.

Dusable, in ten years, or fifteen, had never seen that much AM2. And where the clot had it come from?

Kenna crept out of hiding and went to the observatory to verify that Walsh and his crews had not suddenly discovered hallucinogens – and then he realized.

Christ, Christ, Christ, he thought.

That Raschid was connected, he certainly knew. That he was – somewhere – a being of clout was also a given. But that he was – no.

Kenna stood and turned around. He looked up at an old portrait on the wall, part of the dedication plaque of Imperial Observatory Ryan/Berlow/T'lak. The picture was a standard royalty pose of The Eternal Emperor.

It was also, of course, a perfect image of Raschid.

Kenna had heard and even used the old political phrase: 'Who was with me before Chicago?'

'I was,' he muttered. 'I was. We all were.'

Times were going to be very, very good for Dusable and Solon Kenna. He guessed that the son of a bitch *was* immortal.

He considered the suddenly changing future and what it might portend, especially for the recently elected Walsh. Next election . . . the hell with it. For now. The next election was not for some years.

He then considered finding a church and praying to any god in particular for giving him, Kenna, the brains to realize what was going on before it went on.

But he brought himself back to reality – and treated himself to a bottle.

Mahoney knew he was in serious trouble.

Rykor came to him in her gravchair, rather than wanting to see him in her chambers or, if matters were very cheery, around the huge, deep saltwater tub that stood in for the frigid arctic waters, crashing storms, and looming icebergs of her home world.

Rykor, from her whiskers to her vast blubber to her flippers, resembled, at least to Mahoney who had so dubbed her, a walrus.

When Sten had come up with the idea of the Tribunal, Mahoney had immediately started finding the tools. One of them was Rykor, formerly one of the Empire's chief psychologists. He found her in bored semi-retirement. Liking Sten, having vast if a minority appreciation for Kilgour's sense of humor, liking Mahoney, and – not to be admitted – something beyond the boring sanity of her own race, she had agreed to join in the hunt.

'Well?' Mahoney asked without preliminaries after Rykor's huge gravchair hove into his quarters.

'Quite interesting, this Venloe,' Rykor began. 'Quite beyond the

pale. A *truly* amoral being. I have read of such but never experienced one. My empathy glands remained inactive throughout the
entire scan.'

Rykor's empathy glands, located near where humans have tear
ducts, automatically responded to the plight or pain of any being
under her care. So she seemed to weep while possibly suggesting
the most dire fate for a patient.

'What do we have?'

'First, Venloe's health—'

'Hopin' he's dying in convulsions and realizing he'd best stay
healthy as a horse, I don't want to hear about his health. I assume
excellent. GA.'

'I think we – that is, you and I – should prepare an "Eyes Only"
fiche from this scan. His profile is a textbook one and, properly
censored and edited, is a valuable contribution to psychology. For
you . . . some of the operations he was involved with in the past,
you might find interesting and instructive.' She whuffled through
her whiskers thoughtfully.

'What about the big one?'

'Oh, he is guilty, just as he says. Interesting how precisely he
analyzed, with no formal training, Chapelle, and was able to pull
his strings without ever an error.

'And Sullamora was Venloe's employer and paymaster. But that
is all.'

'Nothing? Not one goddamned memo he happened to see over
Sullamora's shoulder from the others? Come on, Rykor. Just one
thing. The council all got drunk and sang "We'll be glad when
you're dead, you rascal, you." Anything.'

'Nothing. Of course, Ian, realize that this is a Tribunal. His
testimony might not be allowed in an exact trial. But I suspect it
will be admissible for the Tribunal at least.'

Mahoney tried to look cheerful. 'Well, it's not what I was hoping,
but it'll help. I guess. Have you drained him?'

'Pretty much.'

'Hell.'

'Don't give up, Ian. You might, indeed, find your smoking gun.
Venloe said he gave Sullamora a piece of advice. Not because he
cared, you understand, but because he wanted to make sure he got
his final payment. He told Sullamore – it was part of a warning
for Tanz not to attempt a double cross – that he himself should be
careful. Sullamora said something about that not being a factor.
He had taken out insurance.'

'Which we shall never find. If he did cover himself, the privy council would have shaken down his estates, his banks, his offices, and his friends looking for it. They would have found it. We won't – if it was there at all.'

'Ian. Cheer up. Perhaps I should tell you a gem of a jest. Alex Kilgour told it to me just after he returned.'

'No. Not only no, but obscenity no. I have heard Kilgour's jokes, thank you. Telling one would only make me feel worse. And if you tell it anyway, I'll – hell.

'Worst thing about being an ex-Fleet Marshal is you can't threaten anybody with court martial!'

Trying to find out what happened the night the privy council got sports-happy and decided to attend the Ranger-Blues gravball match was, if not simple, fairly safe. Sten held to his vow that, if possible, he would run the rest of his investigation through Haines.

The first question was to find a suitable secondary cover for asking any questions about anything involving the privy council.

Haines and Sten invented one.

Murder, thankfully, has no statute of limitations. So on the night in question, it seemed that a certain woman had been murdered. The suspect was her mate, who had vanished. He had recently been picked up on another charge, halfway across Prime, and alert police work had found that he was the primary suspect in his mate's murder.

Unfortunately, so the concocted story went on, he had an alibi. He had been working as a temporary barkeep on the night in question – working Lovett's private party.

Haines made the correct calls. Once again, Sten was grateful that she was a hands-on cop – the fact that the chief was working an investigation did not raise eyebrows.

Lovett evidently not only viewed the arena and the decorating of the private suite as an eternal legacy, but its employees as well. The maitre d' for the suite had worked for Lovett for more than thirty years. He was happy to cooperate with the investigation – especially since, being a law-abiding being, he started by exploding the mythical suspect's alibi. Leave it to an amateur, he snorted. He probably could have claimed to have worked any of the prole beerbars in the stadium itself, but not the suite. Long-term-only employees up there, especially on the night in question.

'Are you sure?'

'How could I not be?' the man retorted. 'Biggest game in decades, and the privy council itself attends. But I didn't need the usual staff – it was just the six of them. Not even aides or security. So just four people worked the suite that night – me, Mart'nez and Eby behind the bar, Vance runnin' if they'd wanted anything from the kitchen. They weren't eating that night. Not even the Kraas. Excuse me, but that last thing I said – it won't be in the record, will it?'

Haines reassured him. The man said he would be happy to call that murderer a liar in court. Haines said she doubted that would be necessary – there was already enough evidence. She was merely checking any loose ends.

Then she asked, quite casually, 'Must have been quite a thrill, being around that much power.'

'I didn't think it would be,' the maitre d' said. 'After all, Lovett's had some parties with important people before. Not one tenth as many as his father, but a few. Even less, now that he's so busy ruling everything. No more'n one or two since – since the Emperor was killed.

'As I said, I thought I was over being impressed. Not true. I wish I weren't so honest, though.'

'Why?'

'Oh, if I didn't object to stretchers, I wager I could come up with some snappers about what happened that night, and how maybe one of them asked my advice, or anyway thought I ran the smoothest operation ever.

'But I do – and it didn't. Guess they had something important to talk about. Didn't watch the game much, I saw. And any time any of them wanted a drink, they went over to the serving station themselves.

'At least I got to watch the game on a back-room screen, which surprised me. Usually, big events like this, when Sr. Lovett shows up, I'm so busy running back and forth I have to get it from the vid the next day.'

Haines smiled and walked the man out of her office, then went down a few floors to where the poor, harried Sr. Braun had managed to borrow a tiny office, where he was buried in archives, on another empty attempt to prove that Rosemont was no longer among the living.

Sten mused over the information for a moment. 'Business. Bloody business. No aides, keep the help in the kitchen. That was the meeting I want.'

'Documentation, Sten. No witnesses.'

'I'm not sure that's correct. Emphasis – *business* meeting. They leave . . . and probably take their security with them. No cleanup – no *ElInt* cleanup. And the suite's not been used much since then.

'Lisa, friend of mine youth. Do you have four beefy men who'll do you a favor – no violence, only minor law-breaking – and never ever talk about it? It's got to be clean – I don't want any backblast on you. If there's a problem, I'll find my own heavy movers.'

Haines smiled. 'You aren't a cop who gets promoted if you don't have mentors. Rabbis, we call them. Hell if I know why. And when you get rank, you become a rabbi. I could probably get you half a precinct.'

'Good. Four men. I'll get some coveralls made up. Lovett Arena needs help. And good, reliable old APEX Company is coming to the rescue. I'll need a medium gravlighter. Also clean.'

'Again, easy. I'll get something from the impound yard.'

Sten pulled down and consulted a map. 'Okay,' he said. 'Here's the drill. Two days from now, eight hundred hours, I'll want them – here, at the corner of Imperial and Seventh Avenue. I'll drop them off when we're loaded.'

'Two days? Why not now?'

'Because a very dejected Sr. Braun has finished with his investigation and now feels that the Imperial Police were correct. He is returning to his home world to report failure.

'I had two extraction routes. One was if I came out clean, the other if the drakh came down. I'll use the second, since I'll have a bit of a cargo.'

'I think I know what you're going after. Why can't the analysis be done here? My techs don't ask questions.'

'Lisa, remember what kind of murder we're talking about? Don't trust your people too much. I can't – and won't. And like I said, I'm not willing to leave you holding the bag. Anyway, I'm gone. I've got to look up an old friend.'

He gathered his papers quickly.

'Thank you, Lisa.'

'Sure. Although I didn't do very much.'

'No. You did . . . a great deal. Next time around . . . I'll buy you and Sam'l, it was, your anniversary dinner.'

He kissed her briefly, still wanting more, and was gone.

His schedule would be tight: make sure Braun appeared to board the next liner off Prime, contact the liaison with Wild's smugglers, and get a ship down for its cargo. Assuming the cargo would be there.

*

The manager of Lovett Arena was quite impressed with the polite technician and his crew, especially since there had been – as best he knew – no complaints about the business machines provided in Sr. Lovett's suite.

'I would hope not,' the technician said. 'This is strictly routine. Our records show APEX installed the equipment more than five years ago. In a room where people spill drinks, possibly smoke tabac, and food is present? How would we look – what would be left of our reputation – if Sr. Lovett himself tried to use one of our computers and it crashed on him? We are proud of what we represent.'

The manager was impressed. A service company actually servicing, without ten or twelve outraged screams and threats of legal action? Especially since he himself had been unable to find the original contract with APEX.

They stripped the suite bare of anything that went beep or buzz. Sten almost missed the conference table, then realized that it contained a simple computer/viewer suitable for reading, reviewing, or revising documents. But that, and everything else, went onto gravlifts, down into the bowels of Lovett Arena, onto the gravlighter, and then vanished.

It was more than a month before the arena's manager realized that he had been victimized by an exceptionally clever gang of high-tech thieves.

The machines were carefully loaded onto one of Wild's ships, sealed against any stray electromagnetic impulse, and transported to Newton.

Technicians went to work. Sten and Alex hovered in the background. They may have been somewhat sophisticated technologically, Kilgour especially, but this was far beyond their level of expertise.

It was almost impossible to erase anything from a computer. If a file were deleted, its backup would still exist. If the backup were deleted, the 'imprint' would still be there, at least until something was recorded over it. Even then, restoration could sometimes succeed.

The computers were first. From them came an astonishing confused burble of various contracts indicating that Lovett and his friends were hardly straight-arrow businessmen. That information was recorded for possible later release to civil courts, after and if the council was toppled. There were no computer phone records.

But that table was it.

Around it, years before, Sullamora had laid down the law to the other conspirators. At that time, he was the only one who had hung himself out to dry – contracting for the murder of the press lord, contracting for Venloe's services. He put it flatly – all of them were to sign a 'confession.' It was a card made of indestructible plas. On it was a formal admission of guilt, a preamble to assassination. Kyes had been the first to insert the card into the table's viewer and sign, and the others followed. Each member of the conspiracy received one card, signed by all members.

And a technician found it.

The retrieval was spotty, broken by intermittent images of a smiling older couple – someone's parents, possibly, interminably walking past some nondescript scenery. A homevid?

But it was still there:

WE, THE . . . PRIVY COUNCIL, AFTER DUE CONSIDER . . . COME TO
THE . . . CONCLUSION . . . ETERNAL EMPEROR . . . INCREASINGLY
AND DANGEROUSLY UNSTABLE. . . DETERMINED TO . . . FOLLOWING
. . . TRADITION . . . STANDING . . . AGAINST TYRANTS . . .
HISTORICAL RIGHT . . . REMOVAL . . . AND HEREBY AUTHORIZE
. . . MOST EXTREME MEASURES . . . DESTRUCTION . . . TYRANNICIDE
. . . TO ENSURE FREEDOM . . .

The document may have been broken, but it was quite obvious. And absolutely untouched at the bottom were the personal marks, the 'signatures': Kyes. The Kraas. Tanz Sullamora. Lovett. Malperin.

'I'll probably be able to restore more, sir. There's still some ghosts I haven't ID'd and pulled off the hardware.'

Sten was quite happy.

It may have been missing some nonvital screws and springs, but Mahoney – and the Tribunal – had the smoking gun.

Chapter Thirty-One

Sten wanted a little R&R. Badly. He knew he had reason enough to feel brain-, body- and nerve-damaged, but guilt kept whispering in his ear. He ought to be sitting in the back of the courtroom, listening to the careful work of the Tribunal as it moved toward its conclusion.

This was a moment in history. What would he tell his grandchildren? 'Yeah, I was around. But was off gettin' drunk and tryin' to get laid, so I can't tell you a whole lot.'

Kilgour seized the logical high ground. 'Clot th' granbabes y' nae hae, an' likely ne'er sire. Gie y'self off. Thae'll be bloody work t'come. Gore aye up t' our stockin' tops.'

Mahoney backed him, telling Sten that he did not think there was any likelihood that the Tribunal would want any evidence submitted of the blown murder run on Earth. 'Still, Admiral. I'd prefer you were out of town if they start callin' witnesses. Get going. Enjoy yourself. I'll send if I need you.

'Which will be soon. Not surprisingly, the privy council is planning a response. With moils and toils, they've put together a fleet of their bullyboys. Most loyal, most dedicated, and all that drakh. Translation – those who got their fingers the dirtiest proving their loyalty during the purge.

'When they arrive, we should have a proper welcome. Otho's shaking out a strike element from his ships. He thinks nothing could be finer than to put you on the bridge.' Mahoney laughed. 'See how fascinatin' a career in the military is? One day a police spy, the next an admiral again.'

Sten kept to himself his feelings about the military in any configuration, retired to his quarters, and thought about his vacation.

Go to some tourist town and troll for company? No, he thought not. Not that he was suffering the pangs of lost love – at least he didn't think so. But no, it didn't feel right.

Cities? Not that, either. He had heard the yammer of the ugly throngs on Prime, and right now *any* city reminded him of that.

Stop brooding. Hit the fiche. You'll find something that jumps out at you.

He did.

Rock climbing – the hard way.

It was possible to climb anything using artificial aids – climbing thread, piton guns, chocks, jumars. So, of course, the 'pure' climbers revolted and climbed with no aids whatsoever.

Sten thought that could be mildly suicidal. He was not *that* depressed. But there was a bit of appealing madness there.

He picked a climb – a vertical needle deep in one of Newton's wilderness areas – and equipped himself with a minor climbing outfit that included enough artificial aids to be able to belay himself as he climbed. He bought a tent and supplies and cursed when he realized he would have to carry a com and a miniwillygun. Most Wanted, remember, boy.

He found Alex and told him he was off. Kilgour, far, far too busy minding security on the Tribunal, barely had time for a farewell grunt and an arm around the shoulders.

Sten found his rented gravcar – and something else. He had forgotten that the word 'solitary' was banned, at least until the present emergency was over and the council safely in their graves or prison cells. Waiting was his seven-Bhor-strong bodyguard and Cind, equipped similarly to Sten. He thought of protesting, but realized he would lose. If not to them then to Kilgour or Mahoney. It was not worth the battle.

But he issued strict orders.

They were to pitch camp separately from his, at least a quarter klick away. He didn't want their company – sorry to be rude – and he certainly did not want them on the rock with him.

'I don't think the council's assassins – if they have any tailing me, which I don't believe – will go boulder-swarming to make the touch.'

The Bhor agreed. Cind just nodded.

'Easy order to follow, Admiral,' one Bhor rumbled. 'The only record my race has of climbing is when we were chased by streggan.'

So Sten's R&R began on a somewhat less than idyllic note. That slightly off-key note continued to sound. The pinnacle was everything it had looked on the vid, punching straight up for almost a thousand meters through the low clouds. It was at the end of a small, rising alpine meadow with its own spring and bone-breakingly cold pond. The meadow was surrounded by the pinnacle's sky-touching big brothers. No one lived in the meadow, except for some small tree-dwelling marsupials, some long-wild bovines, and, Sten thought, a small night-loving predator he never saw.

He pitched his tent, and his bodyguard followed orders, pitching their camp one quarter kilometer, to the exact pace, away, semi-hidden behind brush on the other side of the pond.

Sten cooked, ate, and went to bed just after dusk. He slept dreamlessly, then rose, collected his climbing pack, and headed for the rock.

For a few hours he lost himself in the rhythm of the climb, the feel of the rock under his palms, and the attention to balance. He wedged a nut into a crack, tied himself off, and dug into his day pack for a snack. He looked up. Not bad. He was almost 250 meters up. Maybe he could spot a bivvy site farther up, do a one-man siege later on, and actually get to the summit before his vacation ended. He had already spotted at least six other fascinating routes he wanted to try.

Then he looked down.

Eight faces looked up at him. His bodyguards were sitting in a semicircle near the base of the pillar, doing their job. Hell. Climbing was not a spectator sport.

He thought of throwing a piton or shouting something. Come on, Sten, he told himself. Aren't you being a little childish? However, he found himself climbing down a couple of hours before he had planned, and the descent was not nearly as mind-absorbing as going up had been.

The next day, he tried another route, this one chosen not just for its interest, but because he did not think there was an observation point for his damnably faithful bodyguards.

They found one anyway. He forced himself to ignore them and climbed on. But his concentration, his ability to lose himself, was . . . not shattered. He still reveled in what he was doing. But he was . . . aware of other things.

That night, after he had cooked a rather unimaginative, under-spiced curry and eaten solo, he found himself sleepless. Across the pond, he could see the low flicker from the Bhor's campsite. They must have found some dry wood and built a tiny fire. He could almost, but not quite, hear voices. Almost, but not quite, hear the crystal chime of a laugh.

Sten swore to himself again. He hunted through his expedition pack and found a bottle. Then he put his boots back on and found his way around the pond to the firelight. There were only four bodyguards around the fire. He tapped the bottle against a tree and stepped forward. Cind and a Bhor came out of the blackness and lowered their weapons.

'What's wrong?' she snapped, eyes sweeping the night.

'Uh . . . nothing. I . . . just had trouble getting to sleep. I thought . . . if I wasn't intruding . . .'

They welcomed him to their campfire and politely sipped from the bottle of Imperially synthesized 'Scotch' Sten had brought along until they could find an excuse to dig out their own supply. Stregg. The Eternal Emperor had once said that stregg was to triple-run moonshine – whatever that meant – as moonshine was to mother's milk.

Regardless, Sten and his bodyguard got royally potted. The quiet alpine meadow was broken by occasional shouts of 'by my father's frozen buttocks' and other Bhor toasts. The evening was culminated when three Bhor threw Sten into the pond.

A very juvenile evening, Sten thought confusedly when he woke the next day. Then he hurt too badly to assess the adultness of his situation. He was still in the Bhor camp. His head was pillowed on one Bhor's calf, and another Bhor was using his stomach for a pillow. Sten realized that he was being attacked by lethal air molecules, smashing into his body everywhere.

Cind and a Bhor walked – lopsidedly – into the camp.

'Wake up, you scrots,' she snarled. 'It's your shift. Oh, Christ, I hurt.'

'Hurt quietly then,' Sten whimpered. He found the bottle of Scotch that was still unfinished and chanced a swallow. No. No. His stomach tried to climb the distant pillar. He got to his feet. His soles hurt. 'I am going to die.'

'Do it quietly, then. Sir. Admiral.' Turnabout was fair and all that.

By rights, Sten should have proven his ability at command and taken everyone for a five-klick run or something equally Admirally-Heroic. He managed to strip off his coveralls and – clot decency – wade into the pond until the freeze told him that the molecules were not attacking. Then he pulled his coveralls back on and decided to eat something.

There was no climbing done that day.

But from that point, the R&R became something very different from Sten's original plans.

One of the Bhor asked about climbing. Sten showed him some of the tricks on a nearby boulder. Cind had already taken a basic climbing course, although the course had specialized in going up the sides of buildings.

And so it went. Climb during the day. Twice he just went for hill-scrambling around the mountain bases nearby. At night, they ate communally. Sten moved his tent into the Bhor campsite.

He spent a lot of time with Cind.

She was easy to talk to. Sten supposed this was some kind of breach of discipline. What discipline? he asked himself. You aren't even an admiral any more – technically. Even if you are, do you want to be? He managed to get Cind to stop calling him by his rank, and even to drop most of the 'sir's' with which she salted her speech.

He told her about the factory hellworld he had grown on. He mentioned – briefly – his family. He told her about Alex Kilgour, and the many, many years they had adventured together.

He did not tell war stories.

Cind, at first, was disappointed. Here was a chance to learn from the greatest warrior of them all. But she found herself listening to other tales – of the strange beings he had encountered, some human, some otherwise, some friendly, some less than that. Again, there was no gore to those stories.

The alpine meadow heard, many times, the chime of crystal.

Cind talked about how strange it had been, growing up as the daughter of the warrior sect of a jihad-prone religion, a religion not only shattered by war but one whose gods had been proven frauds and degenerates. It had seemed natural to her to gravitate toward the Bhor. 'Although now I wonder sometimes. Was I just going from wanting one kind of belief-shelter' – she used the Talameic word – 'to another?'

Sten raised an eyebrow. True or not, it was a sophisticated observation from someone as young as Cind.

He told her about the worlds he had seen. Tropic, arctic, vacuum. The redwoods of Earth. His own world of Smallbridge.

'Perhaps . . . I could show it to you. One day.'

'Perhaps,' Cind said, smiling very slightly, 'I would like to see it. One day.'

They did not sleep together. Cind might have gone to Sten's tent, if he had asked. He did not.

A very odd R&R, Sten mused, as his self-alloted vacation time expired and they loaded the gravcar. Not what I expected . . .

But maybe what I needed.

Chapter Thirty-Two

The Tribunal was nearly ready to announce its decision. After the last witness had been called and the final bit of evidence presented, the judges withdrew to their chamber. Several weeks of back-breaking clerical work followed as they pored over the mounds of testimony.

At first, Sten felt it was a great privilege to be allowed to watch. He, Alex, and Mahoney huddled in the far corner as Sr. Ecu and the three judges debated the relative worth of every detail. As recorder, Dean Blythe oversaw the efforts to officially document the private proceedings for legal history. Sr. Ecu was particularly wary that whatever the outcome, there would be no oversight anyone could use against them.

The judges assumed their roles with a fury. Warin remained totally impartial. Apus, despite her hatred for the Council, was an ardent defender. Sometimes Sten had to shake himself to remember what her true feelings were. One side of him grew angry when she relentlessly hammered away in the privy council's defense. The other side of him admired her for taking her duties so seriously.

Still, it was hard not to get pissed when things like the information he had retrieved from Lovett Arena were dismissed as nothing but rubbish, a trick of science or possibly even planted evidence.

Rivas, on the other hand – who only disagreed with the council for philosophical, not personal, reasons – became their angry tormentor. In public, and even in the privacy of chambers, he shouted down any attempt to weaken the case against the council. Sten did not bother the reasonable side of himself when Rivas went at it. He purely enjoyed the being's constant attacks. It was Rivas who kept pointing things back, talking about how circumstance after circumstance could not be ignored. And he mightily defended the council's secret agreement as proof of opportunity to conspire, if nothing else.

Then, as the weeks lumbered on, Sten's eyes glazed over. Alex and Mahoney were no better. They slipped away whenever possible. Unfortunately, dodging the waiting livie newscasters was worse than boredom. So mostly they stayed and dozed.

But finally it was nearly over. The Tribunal was getting down to the vote. Rivas and Apus had shed their roles as advocates and had joined Warin in impartial consideration. The suspense had Sten's interest stirring again. He leaned forward so that he would not miss a word.

'I don't think we can delay any longer, gentlebeings,' Sr. Ecu was saying. 'Are you ready for your decision?'

Sten did not hear the answer. Alex had planted an urgent elbow in his ribs. Mahoney was at the door making frantic motions for them to join him outside chambers.

Mahoney wasted no time. As soon as the chamber doors closed behind them he collared Sten and Alex.

'It's Otho,' he said. 'There's some very strange business at the spaceport. We're wanted. Now, lads.'

As they hurried for the spaceport, Mahoney filled them in with what little he knew.

It seemed that they were being blessed with a high-level visit – from Dusable.

'What do those clots want?' was Sten's first reaction.

'Thae's all snakier villains ae any Campbell,' was Kilgour's.

'That's all too true,' Mahoney said. 'But we can't be judging too harshly. We need all the help we can get, no matter how slimy the source.'

By help, Mahoney said, he meant that no matter how crooked, Dusable was a recognized governmental body in the Empire – an important body. Not only that, but no mere representatives had been sent. Accordingly to Otho, the newly elected Tyrenne Walsh was on board, as was the president of the Council of Solons, that master of all political thieves, Solon Kenna.

'They are here to officially recognize the Tribunal's proceedings,' Mahoney said. 'Also, any bill of indictment they may hand down. So they're ready to jump in front of the cameras and announce their stand against the privy council.'

Sten did not need a refresher course in politics to know what that meant. When slimy pols like Kenna and Walsh climbed on board, the political winds were definitely blowing in the Tribunal's favor. And when the council's other allies saw that, there was a good chance of many more shifts in the balance.

Only Otho and some of his Bhor troops were at the ship to greet them. The ship had just landed and the ramp run out. He hastily advised Sten that livie crews had been alerted and would soon come crushing in.

'By my mother's long and flowing beard,' he growled, 'luck is sticking with us. I knew you were lucky the first I met you, my friend.' He gave Sten a heavy slap on the back.

Sten noticed that crude as Otho may appear, he was too wise a ruler not to figure out for himself what the sudden support from the Dusable fence sitters would mean for him. No political explanations were needed.

The ship's doors hissed open, but it was long moments before anyone stepped outside. Then Walsh and Kenna emerged, their aides following in an odd straggle. Sten was confused. He expected a typical display of pomp. Maybe it was because the livie crews had not arrived yet. Still, the two pols made a rather drab appearance.

Walsh and Kenna approached – a bit nervously, Sten thought. They almost jumped when Otho growled orders for his troops to draw up to smart attention – at least, as smart as any bowlegged Bhor could be. What was bothering the two? This should be an expected, if a bit puny, honor.

Mahoney stepped forward to greet them. Sten and Alex moved with him. There was a muffled sound inside the ship. Sten was sure it was someone cracking out a command – and he swore he recognized that command. Personally, knew it. He barely noticed as Walsh, Kenna, and their entourage hastily ducked to the sidelines. Sten was too busy gaping.

Squat little men with dark features and proud eyes exited in a precise spear formation. Their royal uniforms glowed with the records of their deeds. Their kukris were held high at a forty-five-degree port arms, light dazzling off the burnished facets of the blades.

Sten knew those men. He had once commanded them.

The Gurkhas! What in hell's name were they doing here? On a ship from Dusable?

Then he saw the answer. He saw it. But he didn't believe it. At first.

The most familiar figure in Sten's, or any other being's life, marched at the apex of the spear line. He towered over the Gurkhas. He looked neither left nor right, but kept those fierce eyes fixed royally ahead.

Sten could not move, speak, or salute. Beside him, he felt the frozen shock of his own companions.

'By my father's frozen buttocks,' Otho muttered. 'It's Him!'

As it reached them the spears parted and then reformed. Sten found himself staring into those oddly ancient/young eyes. He saw the recognition, and heard his name uttered. Alex jerked as his own name was mentioned after a momentary furrow of those regal brows.

The man turned to Mahoney and gave him a wide, bright grin.

'I'm glad you stuck around, Ian,' the Eternal Emperor said.

Mahoney fainted.

Chapter Thirty-Three

Not all of the privy council's vengeance fleet was composed of bloody-handed loyalists to the New Regime. Blind obedience cannot make up all of a resumé – particularly when the assigned task *must* be accomplished.

Fleet Admiral Fraser, not happy with her orders but as always obedient, commanded the attacking force from the bridge of the Imperial Battleship *Chou Kung* – such as it was. The privy council had stripped AM2 depots bare of their remaining fuel for the fleet. There was enough to get them to Newton, engage . . . and then that stolen AM2 convoy had best have been parked in the Jura System if any of them planned a return journey.

One problem Fraser did not have: her ships were not as under-manned as customary. Would that they were, she thought. The council had ordered all ships brought to full strength. So just as the fuel depots were stripped, so were noncombatant ships and ground stations.

Of course none of the commanders sent their best if they could avoid it. Fraser dreamed of having six months – no, a full E-year before she could beat the new fleet into command unity. Even that long would be a miracle, and Fraser thought wistfully of what she had read about draconian disciplinary methods used on water navies.

And of course there were volunteers. Some eager for action, more because they had chosen to back the council in the purge. If the council fell, these officers could expect no mercy whatsoever from the inevitable courts-martial that would be ordered, courts-martial that, almost certainly, would be empowered to order the ultimate verdicts.

Fraser did what she could as the fleet bored on through nothing, running constant drills and even going to the extreme of ordering some ships' navplots slaved to their division leaders.

She was not pleased – but she felt quietly confident, without underestimating her probable foe. She had carefully analyzed the slaughter of Gregor's 23rd Fleet. It had been skillfully handled, but the tactics were more those of raiders than conventional combat forces. Plus the defenders of the Jura System had a fixed area that must be defended. Fraser planned to bring them to battle well clear of the system. She would divert half her reserves to hit the Jura worlds, Newton being the primary target. She would have to split her forces, but certainly the defenders would have to do the same. Once the rebel units were defeated, Fraser's fleet would land on Newton. At that point, her responsibilities would end – which she was very grateful for.

The orders the grim-faced men in the accompanying troopships had were sealed, but Fraser, if she allowed herself to think about them, knew what they were.

A com officer interrupted the silence on the flag bridge. 'Admiral . . . we have an all-freqs broadcast. Source of transmission . . . Newton.'

'*All* frequencies?'

'That's affirmative. Including our own TBS and Command nets. Also it's going out on all the commercial lengths we're monitoring.'

'Jam it. Except for the Command Net. Ship commanders' eyes only. I have no interest in my sailors seeing any propaganda.' An all-frequency cast could only mean that the self-styled Tribunal had reached its verdict.

'We . . . can't.'

'*Can't?*' Fraser did not need to say anything more. That was a word that did not exist.

The com officer wilted, then recovered. 'No. Broadcast strength's got too much power behind it. Only way to block the transmission is to cut the entire fleet out of external communication.'

That was a chance Fraser could not take. 'Very well. Scramble as best you can. Patch a clear signal through to my set.'

'Yes, ma'am.'

Fraser and the other ship COs and division commanders saw what happened clearly. Other screens on other ships showed murky, partial images and speech. But the specific details of what happened were not necessary and, in any event, were quickly word-of-mouthed by any sailor standing duty on a command deck.

The vid showed the inside of the huge auditorium chosen for the Tribunal's hearing. The three solemn-faced judges sat, waiting.

A door behind them slid open, and a Manabi floated out. On either side of the door stood two stocky small humans, wearing combat fatigues and slouch hats, chin straps in place below their lower lips. Both of them were armed with willyguns and long, sheathed knives.

An off-screen voice commented, 'All beings witnessing this cast are recommended to record it, as said before.'

There was silence. Then the Manabi, Sr. Ecu, spoke.

'This is the final hearing of the Tribunal. However, circumstances have altered intent.'

Fraser lifted an eyebrow. That kangaroo court was actually going to find no charges against the privy council? Not that it would matter.

'This is not to say that a verdict has not been reached. It is the finding of this Tribunal that the beings – Srs. Kyes, the Kraas, Lovett, and Malperin – who style themselves as the privy council are indictable.

'This Tribunal finds that a conspiracy for murder was planned and executed by these named beings, as individuals and as a group. We further have found, in accordance with one of the so-called Nuremburg statutes, and so declare their council is a criminal organization.

'Other charges which have been brought up before this Tribunal, up to and including high treason, will not be found on.

'We therefore charge all courts and officers of the law, both Imperial and individual, with the task of bringing the aforenamed

members of the privy council to a criminal court, to defend themselves against the charges found.

'However, this finding is not the only or the most important
purpose of this cast.'

Ecu floated to the side and turned to face that door.

It opened.

The Eternal Emperor entered the courtroom.

There may have been pandemonium, or the sound might have
been muted. Fraser did not know. Certainly there was a boil of
chaos on her own bridge. Eventually she forced order on her own
mind, ignoring the shock that all she believed and served was no
longer true, and shouted for silence.

And silence there was. Sailors may have stared at their dials and
controls – but all that existed was the words that came from that
screen.

'I commend the members of this tribunal. The investigators, the
clerks, the officials, and the judges. They have proven themselves
my Faithful and True Servants, in a time when such loyalty has
become a warrant of death.

'They – and others – shall be rewarded.

'Now, we face a common task. To return the Empire to its
greatness. It will not be easy.

'But it can – and will – be done.

'The work in front of us must be accomplished. There will not
be peace, there will not be order until the Empire stretches as it
did before, giving peace, prosperity, and the rule of law throughout
the universe.

'I thank those of you who remained loyal, who knew the privy
council spoke out of fear, greed, and hatred, not in my name. But
there are others.

'Others who for whatever reason chose to march under the bloody
banner of the council. I order you now to stop. Obey no orders
from the traitors. Listen to no lies or instructions. If you bear arms
– lay them down. You must – and will – follow my orders. You will
follow them immediately. There has been enough crime, enough evil.

'I specifically address myself to the misguided beings who are
manning Imperial warships, on their way to attack this world and
myself.

'You have two hours to obey. All ships of this criminal fleet are
ordered to leave star drive and assume parking orbits in the system.
No weapons are to be manned. At the end of this time, you are
directed to surrender to my designated units.

'You are Imperial soldiers and sailors. You serve me – and you serve the Empire.

'Two hours.

'Any men, units, or ships failing to obey will be declared turn-coats and outlaws and hunted down. The penalties for treason are very clear and will be meted with great severity.

'Surrender. Save your lives. Save your honor. Save your Empire.'

The screen blanked. An audio came on, saying something about all physical attributes of the man who just spoke – the Eternal Emperor – being cast on a separate channel. Skeptics were invited to compare them with easily available public documents.

Fraser paid no attention. She served the Empire – and now, once more, with a vast relief, the Emperor himself.

'Flag! I want an all-ships link! Captain! On my command, stand by for secondary drive.'

'We are going to—' someone on the bridge said.

'Serve the Emperor,' Fraser interrupted.

The com officer shot her.

He himself died two seconds later, as Fraser's aide slashed Fraser's weighted baton across the officer's neck.

There were other guns and ceremonial knives out. A blast went wild and disabled the main drive controls. The flag bridge was a melee of mutiny – if that was what it was.

Secondary command centers never went on line – they too were in chaos.

The *Chou Kung* drove on, still under drive.

In miniature, that hysteria and devastation was the entire Imperial fleet as it Kilkennied itself.

Some ships obeyed – and were attacked by others still loyal to the council. Other ships tried to continue the mission toward the Jura System. Still others managed to 'disappear' into normal space and Yukawa drive. Division commanders snarled com channels, looking for orders, guidance, or agreement.

Then Sten attacked.

The Eternal Emperor had lied about the two hours of grace.

The late Admiral Fraser had correctly analyzed Sten's tactics in the raid on the AM2 convoy. The Bhor, the Rom, and the mer-cenaries were, indeed, more comfortable in single-ship or small-squadron attacks. She was also correct that the Tribunal's fleet would not be capable of a conventional defense against a conven-tional attack.

Sten found a third option. He deployed his entire fleet as a slashing cutting-out expedition, coming down on the Imperial units. His orders had been very simple: Attack any ship that is showing signs of fight. Hit them once – hard – and hold full speed. Regroup and reattack. If they go into normal space, go with them. Make sure they're either broadcasting a surrender signal or their main drive is disabled.

'Do not board. Do not close with and destroy. Ignore any ship obeying the Imperial orders.

'This is not a battle to the finish. Otho, I don't want any of your people playing berserker.'

'What happens after they're broken?' a mercenary captain had asked.

'Sorry, Captain. There's no time for looting. I say again – no boarding. This whole damn mess is almost over. Let's not get anyone killed unnecessarily.'

'What about Imperial survivors?'

'There'll be SAR ships put out. Eventually.'

And that was how the battle was fought. Slice through . . . form up . . . hit them again.

Sten fought his ship – a cruiser – and three others. Time blurred. Each combat was different, each combat was the same. He gave his orders through a cold, clear anger.

The Emperor had returned.

Very well. So let's end it.

Eventually there was no one left still firing that was worthwhile shooting back at. Sten came back to himself, staggered with fatigue.

He looked at a chronometer.

The ship-day was nearly ended. He checked the main battle-screen. The scatter of indicators gave no sign that just hours before there had been a fleet to attack. It was, indeed, over.

So much for the nits.

Now for the vermin they had bred from.

Chapter Thirty-Four

Poyndex noticed the tree had lost half its leaves. Like the privy council members who awaited him on the top floor, the rubiginosa seemed to be cowering at the news: The Eternal Emperor was back!

When he saw them huddled in their chairs, he realized that 'cowering' was a poor description. Each of them had heard the executioner's song and was dying inside. Malperin looked half a century older. Lovett was a shrunken, pouch-faced little being.

The Kraa twins were the most changed of all. The one who had once waddled about in thick wads of fat had become a baggy, anorexic thing. Her skin drooped disgustingly. The once-thin Kraa had turned herself into a bulging pink ball, skin stretched tight around the new fat.

There was no question on any of their faces that the being who called himself the Eternal Emperor was exactly that.

All four beings leaped on Poyndex as if he were the last lifeboat leaving a hulled ship. He could barely make out the questions in the frightened confusion. 'The Eternal Emperor . . .' '. . . What shall we do . . .' '. . . Where can we run . . .' '. . . Should we fight . . .' '. . . Can we fight . . .' On and on. They were working themselves into a suicidal frenzy. They were so hysterically afraid of the Emperor that they were ready to board ships and fling themselves onto his guns with all the troops they could command.

That was not what Poyndex wanted.

He soothed them and sat them down. He put on his saddest, most understanding face. 'I think I know how to save you,' he said.

They looked up at him, sudden hope in their eyes. Anything would do now. But Poyndex was not after just anything. He believed he had found his way back to power.

'I have not been charged with any crime,' he said. 'In whatever actions that were taken before I joined you, I had no part. Therefore, it should be no trouble at all for me to personally approach the Emperor.'

No one protested, or warned him that it might be certain death, that no matter how blameless he might be, the Emperor was quite capable of killing any being vaguely involved with the privy council. Poyndex smiled to himself at that great showing of concern from his colleagues and friends.

'If you do not object, I'll offer the Emperor a deal.'

Poyndex's proposal was simple. The privy council had lost, but they could still cause an enormous amount of damage and shed a great deal of blood. He urged them to retire to the emergency bunker that had been constructed deep under the rubiginosa tree. It was an ideal command center, plugged into every military channel. The bunker itself was constructed to withstand anything up to a direct nuclear explosion. From there they could fight to the death if the Emperor refused the deal.

Poyndex would point all that out to the Emperor. Then he would say that the privy council had no wish to cause so much harm if it could be avoided. In the interest of all the innocent beings of Prime World, they would agree to lay down their arms if granted their lives.

'No prison,' the once-fat Kraa snarled. 'Me sis couldn't bear the filthy thing.'

'I'm not suggesting prison,' Poyndex said. 'I'm suggesting exile. Under the terms I plan to negotiate, you would be permitted to freely board your private ships and flee to the farthest reaches of the Empire. Beyond the frontiers, if the Emperor wishes it. And you would be forbidden ever to return.'

'Do you think he'll go for it?' Lovett whined.

Oh, yes, Poyndex assured. Yes, indeed he will. The Emperor, like Poyndex, was a practical man. Then he told them they ought to proceed instantly to the bunker. There should be no delay – in case the Emperor struck unexpectedly.

Poyndex watched the privy council members hurry off to the fates he had planned for them, like beasts to the butcher.

Chapter Thirty-Five

The Kraas, always aware of that area of the human back between the third and fourth ribs, were the first to correctly analyze the subtext of the Emperor's transmission: 'Clottin' Poyndex! Clottin' bassid set us up an' sold us out.'

Why not? They would have done the same, had they the chance.

'Shoulda knowed,' the now-fat one growled. 'Sit here in this clottin' bunker, waitin' an' waitin' an' waitin'. We got no forces in space, th' air, or holdin' the ports.'

Their screams of outrage were the loudest it had gotten in the privy council's underground retreat in days. The Kraas had spent the time since Poyndex had left on his 'negotiating mission' gorging and purging. Malperin and Lovett found themselves together frequently – but with nothing to say. They might have been a pair of silent ghosts, haunting the cellars below the castle they once ruled from.

The guards and servants learned the art of swiftly and silently following whatever orders they were given and then disappearing into their own quarters.

Then came the announcement, on the special wavelength set aside:

'This is the Eternal Emperor.

'I have been approached by an emissary of the traitorous privy council. They wanted conditional terms for their surrender.

'I reject these, in the name of civilization and the Empire itself. There can be no negotiation with murderers.

'I demand immediate, complete, and unconditional surrender.

'Citizens of Prime World—'

At that point the Kraas had began screaming. No one in the

com room heard the details of what else the Emperor ordered. It was nothing surprising: Prime was declared under martial law. All military personnel were to report to their barracks and remain there. Officers and noncommissioned officers were to maintain discipline, but no more. All ships to ground and remain grounded or be fired upon. Police were instructed to keep public order – without violence, if possible. Rioters and looters would be punished . . .

Nothing surprising.

Until the end:

'Imperial forces will be landing on Prime within the hour.'

Impossibly, the Kraas' howls became louder.

Trapped . . . clot that . . . out of here.

One of them was on a com to the capital city of Fowler's main port, giving hurried orders to the commander of their 'yacht' – a heavily armed ex-cruiser – and its two escorts, ordering preparation for immediate takeoff.

'Why?' Malperin wondered in a monotone. 'There is nowhere to run to.'

'Clot there ain't! There's allus a back door!'

The other Kraa broke in. 'Even if there ain't, damned sure rather go down fightin' than just waitin' f'r th' butcher's hammer!'

And they were gone.

Lovett started to pour a drink. He put the glass down, unfilled, and sat. He stared at Malperin. The silence returned.

A flotilla of tacships were the first to scream down and across Soward's launch grounds. Other flotillas provided Tac Air over the rest of Prime's ports.

The lead tacship's exec/weapons officer reported three ships, drives active.

'All elements . . . Fairmile Flight . . . Targets as indicated and illuminated . . . Goblin launch . . . *Fire!*'

Non-nuclear medium-range missiles spat out of the tacships' tubes, homing on the Kraas' three ships. Three blasts became a single fireball belching up thousands of feet.

And Mahoney ordered in the fleets.

Sten, as per orders, was the first to bring his in. Destroyers and cruisers hung over Soward and Fowler. He brought his own battleship and its two fellows down onto Prime – flashthought: A bit different than when I skulked out of here last – and behind them the assault transports landed, and armor and troops spilled out.

Kilgour tossed Sten his combat harness, and Sten buckled on the webbing that held the heavy Gurkha kukris and a miniwillygun.

He would command the assault on the council's bunker himself. The Eternal Emperor had given him explicit orders: he wanted the Kraas, Malperin, and Lovett – alive if at all possible. He did not want to see, he added, the work of Sten's Tribunal wasted.

'Admiral.' A screen was indicated.

Five armored gravsleds pulled onto the field about three kilometers away. Four were standard squad combat types; the fifth was a command unit.

'Ah think w' flushed some ae them,' Kilgour said, mentally plotting their intended destination, that fireball that had been the ready-to-lift ships.

Before Sten could issue orders, a tacship bulleted across the field, scattering area-denial cratering bomblets. The blast flipped two of the sleds out of control, and a third lost power and slammed, nose first, into the smoking, newly dug ditch.

Two were left. Their pilots spun them through 180 degrees, back the way they had come.

But Sten saw that their exit had been sealed, not by Imperial forces or bombing, but by a screaming, boiling mob. Armed and unarmed. Human and alien.

The gravsleds fired into the mob. Beings fell and were shattered. More replaced them.

The squad gravsled was disabled and grounded. Someone, somewhere, had found, stolen, or seized an anti-armor weapon and fired. The blast disintegrated the gravsled – and sent its attackers spinning.

The command sled changed course once more, this time toward the grounded Imperial ships.

It never made it.

Sten saw the flash as a homemade incendiary landed on its top deck and fire poured down into the McLean intakes. The sled shuddered to a halt. Sten saw the rear ramp drop and then—

He *thought* he saw two beings come out: one enormously fat, the other looking like a skeleton wearing a tent. Their hands were upraised, and they were shouting something.

And then the mob poured over them.

Sten turned away from the screen.

'Ah hae i' recorded,' Kilgour said. 'We'll need ae frame-b'-frame f'r an' ID an' confirm't thae wa' th' Kraas. Thae'll be nae enow lef' f'r th' autopsy.'

Sten nodded, still not looking at the screen. 'Let's go, Mr. Kilgour. I want the courts to have *somebody* to bring to trial.'

The assigned Imperial troops were no better or worse than the rest of the Empire's units Sten had faced lately. It did not matter – Sten had already assumed inexperience and formed his spearhead from the mercenaries.

He assumed they would have to fight their way through the streets of Fowler to the privy council's headquarters – but they did not. The riots and the revenge had already swept through the streets they took: overturned gravcars and -sleds, some burnt-out; improvised barricades; bodies, some uniformed, some not.

Burning and burnt businesses and buildings.

Three times bodies dangling from street lamps.

But nothing they had to stand against.

Surprisingly, there was order, of sorts. Civilians directed traffic as best they could – what little traffic there was. More civilians patrolled the walkways.

The sergeant commanding the combat squad in Sten's assault gravsled stuck his head out of the hatch, shouted a question to one of the civilians, and received an answer.

'Cult a' the Emp, sir. Helpin' pave the way, sir.'

Sten thought the cult practiced nonviolence. Perhaps the bruised man he saw being frog-marched by three large women had tripped and fallen downstairs. Or maybe there would be a confession to make later.

He heard the sound of firing as his assault force closed on the council's headquarters.

There were bodies in the mottled brown of the Imperial Guard and riddled gravsleds in front of it. Sten dismounted and was greeted by a sick- and worried-looking captain, a young woman who could not decide whether to cry or swear. It had been the first time she had led a unit into combat – and the first time the unit she had so carefully knitted together took casualties.

She neither cried nor swore – but professionally made a sitrep. The council had guards inside the building – there. Four anti-track launchers sandbagged there and over there. Snipers and rapid-fire weapons upstairs in the building itself. All orders to surrender had been ignored.

Sten thanked her and issued orders. She was to pull her company back. Make sure the area was sealed – nobody out but, more importantly, nobody in. Especially not another lynch mob.

The captain watched in awe as Sten and Kilgour issued a string of orders to their mercenaries and Bhor troops. You get good, Sten thought, when you're doing it for the fortieth or four hundredth time around and you're armored against seeing your people get killed.

He brought up a company of heavy tracks and used them to bulldoze barricades and smash through the buildings around the headquarters to provide firing positions. Heavy weapons were readied, and fire was opened against the snipers and crew-served guns.

'Th' wee anti-track launchers,' Kilgour said. 'Ah hae their medicine ready.'

He did.

Kilgour had ordered snipers – the best an' y' ken who y'be, dinnae be tryin't t' smoke me – into flanking positions.

As Sten ordered a gravsled to move forward, he sensed Cind moving in close to him. Out of the corner of his eye, he saw her scanning the confusion for hidden danger – danger against him.

The antitrack crews aimed – and were sniped down. More of the council's – soldiers? secret cops? private goons? – ran to replace them.

Willyguns cracked, and the new gunners never made it. A third try . . . and volunteers suddenly got scarce.

'Mister Kilgour?'

Alex shouted orders, and Sten's hand-picked squad doubled into the lowered troop ramp of a heavy track.

'Y' dinnae hae t' be knockin't,' Alex ordered the track commander. 'An' gie y'self a bit ae coverin't fire. Go!'

The track ground forward, turrets flaming. Its tracks clawed over one of the abandoned antitrack launchers, and then the multiton monster exploded through the entrance of the council's building, into the huge atrium.

The ramp banged down, and Sten and his 'arresting officers' came out. He noticed the green-encrusted fountains and what must have been some kind of tall dead tree in the atrium's center. The tank had felled the tree as it slid to a halt before the troops dismounted.

Sten glanced at the small map case he held. 'Bunker entrance is . . . over there. Move slow, dammit! Don't end up makin' history by bein' the last one dead.'

Good advice, Sten thought. Listen to it. A dead admiral being the last casualty of this . . . war? Revolt? Insurrection? Whatever might rate more than a footnote.

*

They went down and down, into the bowels below what had been the privy council's proudest construction. Cind and Alex kept close to Sten as they moved from cover to cover like cautious snakes.

There was no need to be careful.

There was no resistance.

Malperin and Lovett were found sitting in a room. They did not seem to hear Sten's orders.

Cind stared at the two beings, at the husks who had once been her rulers. Sten thought he saw pity in her eyes.

Kilgour repeated Sten's orders.

They finally responded to his growls. They stood when Alex told them to, were strip-searched for weapons and suicide devices without protest, then followed the arresting squad back up and out.

It almost seemed, Sten thought, as if they were secretly glad it was all over.

He wondered if their apathy would continue past the moment when the trial began.

Chapter Thirty-Six

'Sit down, Sten,' the Eternal Emperor said. 'But pour us both a drink first.'

From long habit as former commander of the Emperor's personal guard, Sten knew he was at ease when drink was mentioned. But being 'At Ease,' and being 'at ease' were difficult under the circumstances. It had been many years since he had a shot of stregg with the boss. And in those times, Sten had thought that the word 'Eternal' was merely a symbolic title, if he thought of it at all.

He noticed, however, that when the Emperor took his drink, he only gave it an absent-minded sip. Sten did the same.

'I won't thank you for all you've done,' the Emperor said. 'The words would seem silly. At least to me.'

Sten wondered what was up. The Emperor, despite his pose of informality, was being damned formal. That usually meant he had a surprise up his sleeve. Sten hoped it did not involve him. He saw the Emperor frown at him slightly, then look at the barely touched stregg in his own hand. The frown vanished, and the Eternal Emperor tossed it back in one swallow. He slid the glass across the table for more. Sten drank his own down and redid the honors. He felt the stregg light its way down and spread out its warmth, but he still felt no more at ease.

He wished like clot he could ask the Emperor how he did it. Where had he been for all those years? What had he done? And why in clot wasn't he dead? No, best not ask. The Emperor was jealous of his secrets.

'The last time we talked together,' the Emperor said, 'I was doing my damndest to give you a promotion. You turned me down. I hope you aren't planning on making that a habit.'

Oh, clot, here it comes. Sten braced himself.

'How does head of Mercury Corps sound?' the Emperor said. 'I'll raise its command grade and give you a second star. How does that sound, Admiral?'

'Retired admiral, sir,' Sten said, gulping. He had to get it out fast. 'And I hate to seem ungrateful and all, but no thanks. Please.'

Sten saw the cold look knot the Emperor's brow. Then it eased slightly.

'Why?' It was a one-word command.

'It's like this. I've spent my whole life soldiering. In public service, if you will. I've been rewarded far more than I could have ever dreamed. I was nothing. A Vulcan Delinq. Now, I'm an admiral. And you want to make it with two stars. Thank you, sir. But no thanks.

'I have to start making my own life. Find a place for myself in the civilian world. I was confused before. Maybe I still am. But only a little. Because I'm looking forward to it. It's time for me to start doing the usual, dull human business.'

Sten thought of Lisa Haines, and how undull his life might have been if events had not intervened. The whole time he had spoken, he had kept his eyes down. Now he looked up to see the Emperor glaring at him, eyes white steel.

'I'm not doing a good job of this, sir,' Sten said. 'I'm not explaining very well. It's not something that comes out easy for someone like me.'

He said no more. The Emperor would let him know if more was welcome. The glare shut off. The Emperor chugged half his drink, then lifted his legs up on his desk and eased back in his chair.

'I understand,' he said. 'I'm asking you to make a big sacrifice. Actually, another big sacrifice. But I don't think you realize the situation.'

He finished his drink, leaned over, and hooked the bottle with a finger, poured, and shoved the stregg back to Sten. They both drank – and refilled.

'But look at the mess we're in,' the Emperor continued as if there had not been a halt. 'Beings are starving. Millions have no work. Just about any government you look at is near collapse. Just getting the AM2 to the right places and fast is going to be a nightmare. Much less all the other troubles I see ahead. Now what am I going to do about all this – without any help?'

Sten shook his head. He had no answer.

'So why is it a big surprise when I ask someone like you – with all those years of public service, as you said – to stay with me now? Where else can I get that kind of experience?'

'Yessir,' Sten said. 'I see your point. But—'

'But me no buts, young Sten,' the Eternal Emperor said. 'Look. I'm not asking for me. I'm asking for your Empire. How can you refuse? Tell me that. How can you look me in the eye and refuse to help?

'But don't answer yet. Forget Mercury Corps. I have a better idea. I'm making you my chief troubleshooter – with some kind of fancy plenipotentiary sort of title. Help me out with heads of state, tricky negotiations, and any kind of major crisis situation.

'And for your first job, I want you to help me out with the Bhor. I want to do something special for them. They've been my most loyal subjects. They were your idea way back, if I recall.'

'Yessir,' Sten said.

'So. They're going to have a big celebration in the Lupus Cluster. Honoring my return and all and the victory over those clots who wanted to be my enemy. I want you to go there for me. To the Wolf Worlds. Be my representative at the ceremonies. I can't think of a being they would appreciate more. Can you?'

'Nossir,' Sten said. And as he said it, he knew he was doomed.

The Eternal Emperor was right. There was no way he could refuse him this – or the rest that would follow.

*

The victory celebrations aboard the Bhor fleet lasted all the way back to the Lupus Cluster.

Cind kept a close watch on Sten. He joined in all the toasts and the parties and kept up with his hard-drinking friends, Otho and Kilgour. But in repose, his face became a mask, revealing nothing. She knew him better now. She could sense the thoughts churning through his mind – but what those thoughts were, she had no notion.

Cind saw him jolt up once in the middle of a toast to the Eternal Emperor and look up at the portrait on the ship's banquet compartment wall. He stared at it for a long time, then shook his head and downed his drink. A moment later he was laughing and talking with his friends again.

But Cind would remember that look for a long time – and wonder what was on Sten's mind.

Chapter Thirty-Seven

Malperin and Lovett sat in a cell aboard the Emperor's personal yacht, the *Normandie*. It might have appeared a rather comfortable suite, but the doors were locked and guarded, any conceivable or potential weapons had been removed, and there were sensors monitoring their every breath.

The fog they had been in when Sten captured them had begun to lift.

They had been told they were to be tried. The trial would take place on Newton. They would be offered the finest defense counsels in the Empire, and an adequate time to prepare whatever defense they chose.

Cautiously, mindful of the monitors, the two had begun discussing what they should do, what defense might be offered. They had begun to use circumlocutions as they planned, and, against logic, to whisper.

There had been six of them once – determined to reach for the highest power of all. And, for a moment, they had held it.

Now . . . forget the deaths and forget the cell. Life is to be lived, Malperin said. Lovett managed a small smile.

There was a tap outside, and the compartment door opened.

A man entered. Neither tall nor stocky, he looked to be in good physical shape. He was wearing expensive civilian clothes. He was not an ugly man, not a handsome man.

'Gentlebeings,' he said softly. 'I have been assigned as your escort and aide for the trial.

'My name is Venloe.'

Mahoney stormed into the Eternal Emperor's private office, spewing obscenities. He held a fiche in his shaking hand.

'Lord, Ian. What happened?'

'Some clottin' drakh-head on the *Normandie*! Playing God! "Prisoners managed to escape cell. Found way to lifecraft. Attempted to enter. Security officer tried to apprehend, but was forced to . . ."

'"Shot while attemptin' escape!" Christ! Clottin' bastard can't even find an original excuse.

'All that work. Sten'll kill that clottin' moron – but I'll have beaten him to it! Jesus Mary Mother on a gravsled! I'll crucify the clot! Have his guts for a winding sheet.' He broke off. 'I do not believe this. Clot!'

The Emperor picked up the fiche, put it in a viewer, and scanned the decoded message that had been transmitted in the Empire's personal command code.

He scanned it again, then grunted. 'Not good, Ian. Not good at all.'

'Not good . . . okay.' Mahoney brought himself under control. 'You're the boss. How high do we hang this – whoever did this? Not that it matters. What's the spin for damage control?'

The Emperor thought a moment. 'None. What happened is what happened. And I'll arrange the proper way to deal with our ambitious gunman. But that's all. No investigation, Mahoney. That's an order.' He paused. 'So we've lost our war crimes trial. I don't think it matters. There's too much of the privy council's drakh left around for anybody to be much interested in what happened to Malperin and Lovett.'

'That's it,' Mahoney said incredulously. 'Those two just . . . vanished?'

'Something like that. As I said, what happened is what happened.

Pour me a drink, Ian. We'll drink their souls to hell, like Sten's hairy friends say.'

Ian stared at the Emperor, then got up and went to a table, where he found the decanter of stregg.

The Eternal Emperor turned his chair and looked out the window at the once-blasted site of his palace, Arundel. Reconstruction had already begun.

Mahoney could not see his face.

The Eternal Emperor smiled.

About the authors

Chris Bunch is the author of the Sten series, the Dragonmaster series, the Seer King series and many other acclaimed SF and fantasy novels. A notable journalist and bestselling writer for many years, he died in 2001.

Allan Cole is a bestselling author, screenwriter and former prize-winning newsman. The son of a CIA operative, Cole was raised in the Middle East, Europe and the Far East. He currently lives in Boca Raton, Fl. with his wife, Kathryn. For details see Allan's website at www.acole.com

Find out more about Chris Bunch and Allan Cole and other Orbit authors by registering for the free monthly newsletter at www.orbitbooks.net